The Ambassador's Wife

A Novel

Kristina Stangl

In dedication to my loving family. Thank you for always supporting me through it all.

To my beloved pets, Jeremy and Jewel, may you both rest in peace and forever walk, play, wander and leap through the pages of my novels.

Lastly, in loving memories to my late aunt, Barbara Ann, and to my late grandmother, Shakire, in which the characters of Barbara Barrett and Grandmother Shakire are loosely based upon.

Also by Kristina Stangl

The Enchanted Forest Saga:

The Curse of the Dark Horseman

The Sleeping Knight

The Emerald Prince

Silverheart:

Cupid's Serenade

Sex, Lies & Politics:

The Ambassador's Wife

Wake Up, Darling

My Life is a Soap Opera

Kill Me, Kiss Me

www.kristinastangl.com

THE AMBASSADOR'S WIFE

CONTENTS

Chapter 1

On a cold December afternoon, Kate stared outside of her grandmother's window to eagerly watch the snow fall upon her family's garden. Precisely one week ago, their garden was covered in bright sunshine, along with blooming white daisies and tall evergreens that flourished throughout their vast open acres. At that time, the crystal blue sky was adorned with pink and emerald green hummingbirds flying high above in the air, all chirping the sweet and joyful melodies of nature. Amazingly, this again, was only but a mere week ago. Come today, all had vanished. The once sunny and cheerful garden was now replaced by a dark and gloomy scene; consisting of a bleak and heavy blanket of thick white snow, accompanied by icy frost and the howling winds of winter.

Unfortunately, due to the stormy weather, Kate and her family were advised to shelter in from the piling snow. Determined to find joy even in the most mundane of circumstances, Kate found enjoyment in gazing outside of her frosty window; all in the hopes of catching a rare glimpse of a fallen snowflake. A snowflake, she thought, was so incredibly beautiful and rare, that only a person patient and willing enough to wait for it, could eventually, see it, one day.

"Kate, come away from that window," cried Shakire, her grandmother. "I need you and Jennifer to help me in the kitchen."

Taking one final glance, Kate hoped for the best. But alas, her hopes were premature; for the winter snow was still progressively falling and there was still no sign of a single snowflake, in near sight.

"We better hurry Kate, I think that she might have a nice surprise for us," said Jennifer, with a twinkle in her eye.

Jennifer was Kate's sister— her twin sister to be precise. Both sisters were identical twins, with the same facial structures, blue eyes, fair complexions, petite body structures and tall in height. However, the only exception between them were their hair colorings, in which Jennifer's hair was naturally blonde, while Kate's was brown. Other than this singular difference, both girls were identical; even down to the very same freckle located right underneath their chins.

However, it wasn't very difficult to distinguish the twin sisters apart; for once they spoke, it became abundantly clear, as to which sister was whom. Jennifer, the lively, romantic and passionate twin, often spoke carefree to whatever and whichever came directly to her mind; whereas, Kate, the practical, shy and reserved twin, analyzed her thoughts and calculated her words more carefully before sharing them publicly with others. While Kate preferred to spend her Saturday nights at home reading a Jane Austen book, along with a warm cup of Earl of Grey tea; Jennifer, in contrast, was more interested on attending parties and finding her modern-day Prince Charming. Due to their opposing natures, Shakire often referred to them as the sun and the moon; in which Jennifer, along with her bright yellow hair, was the sun and Kate, with her shiny and dark hair, the moon. Ironically, this reference was entirely appropriate for them too, since their own given middle names meant exactly that in the Turkish language. Just like the sun, Jennifer was named Jennifer Guneş; and just like the moon, Kate was named Kate Aylin.

At seventeen years old, the twin sisters came to visit Shakire's home for their winter holidays. Located on the northwestern coast of Türkiye, bordering the Marmara and Aegean Seas, Shakire lived in a small but modest city called Balikesir. Their mother, a native of the land, had married their father, an American soldier, who was previously stationed there in their small town. As a result, the twin sisters were born and raised in New York City. While they primarily resided in New York for their schooling, their winter and summer breaks were spent almost entirely and exclusively in Türkiye with Shakire.

Following their grandmother's directions, the twin sisters walked into their kitchen and saw Shakire already seated at the table. To their surprise, right next to their grandmother, were three separate small cups of coffee. Without their prior knowledge, the warm beverage had already been carefully brewed and poured right into the golden ceramic expresso cups, along with their matching saucers.

"I thought that you needed help?" asked Kate, surprised by the sight before her eyes.

"Actually, I still do," admitted Shakire, with a huge and bright smile, as she took her first sip of coffee. "Although I might have already taken the liberty to prepare us some nice Turkish coffee; now, I'm in need of your help to drink them."

"Wonderful!" exclaimed Jennifer, happily. "Does this mean, what I think it means?"

"Yes, it does," replied Shakire. "Once we finish drinking our coffee, we'll do a little round of fortune telling with the coffee grounds. A nice unexpected treat to a cold and dreary winter's afternoon, don't you think?"

Excitingly, both sisters were happily in agreement. Drinking Turkish coffee was one of their most favorite pastimes at Shakire's home. Coffee time was also their bonding time together. In addition to fortune telling, Shakire also used this opportunity to share tall tales and exotic stories about their history and culture with them; and in return, the sisters also confided about their own secret dreams and life pursuits to their grandmother. Even though their coffee readings were entirely for fun, it was also often claimed by several other family members and nearby neighbors, that Shakire's predictions did actually come true, from time to time. Although Shakire tried her best to teach and share this natural gift to her granddaughters, the art of coffee reading, or tasseography, was something that just came naturally to oneself and wasn't a trait that could really be learned, nor taught. Therefore, rather than attempting to decipher the meaning for themselves, the twin sisters simply quietly sat back and enjoyed themselves, as they listened to Shakire's reading, instead.

"There, I'm done!" shouted Jennifer, as she quickly gulped her last sip of coffee, and then, hastily flipped the empty cup upside down and back onto her saucer. Upon closing the cup, Jennifer promptly spun the object around her in a circle, and then at long last, she made a wish.

"That was fast," observed Kate; who, in contrast, preferred to savor each and every last bit and morsel of her coffee.

"Alright, my dear Jennifer. Let's have a look at it," Shakire instructed.

Following her grandmother's instructions, Jennifer quickly handed her cup and saucer over to Shakire. Upon receiving it, Shakire proceeded to flip the cup right side up; after which, she slowly began to inspect the dried coffee grounds.

"Hmm," began Shakire. "I see several lines in your cup. My dear, I believe that you shall travel the world."

Happy with her grandmother's prediction, Jennifer privately smiled to herself. Unbeknownst to most, Jennifer had secretly dreamed of traveling the world.

"I also see a large diamond ring, with lots of coins," Shakire continued, "You will marry wealthy and also be a very famous woman, at the same time."

Bringing Jennifer's cup even closer towards her, Shakire slowly pulled down her eyeglasses to carefully examine the remaining coffee grounds directly with her naked eye. After a few extra silent minutes of concentration, Shakire finally spoke and said "But…"

"But? Is something wrong?" asked Jennifer, suddenly concerned with the possibility of something being potentially troubling and an exception to perfection.

"Nothing to worry about, my dear," replied Shakire, as she attempted to console her granddaughter. "But," she continued, "I do see two rings. I'm afraid that you will marry twice, after all."

"Twice?" asked Kate, this time, who was equally surprised by this particular revelation.

"Yes, two marriages," Shakire confirmed. "Although you'll marry your first husband at a young age, your second marriage will occur much later on. Unlike your first, your second marriage will be a happier, prosperous and longer union, with wealth and children. He will also be a far better and more ideal match for you, too."

"I suppose that as long as my second husband is far wealthier than the first, then I'm perfectly fine and content with that," laughed Jennifer, not at all bothered by the prospect of marrying twice.

"Either way, I shall record this information into my diary, and in twenty years' time, we'll know as to whether or not you were right," added Jennifer, boldly.

"Jennifer, must you write and record about everything inside of your diary? Our coffee times are meant to be for fun only!" exclaimed Kate.

"Kate, if I'm to become a famous celebrity one day, then I might as well start recording this information now, in time for my future biography. But enough about me, it's time to look at Kate's now," said Jennifer, as she was now determined to shift the focus away from herself and onto her sister.

"Alright my dear Kate, please finish up your cup, and then, let's go ahead and take a look," Shakire instructed.

Under any normal of circumstances, Kate would have much better preferred to have taken her sweet time to savor each and every last sip of her coffee, while eating either a sweet pastry or a chocolate bar on the side. For Kate, preparing, serving and drinking Turkish coffee was an art, in which there was a famous Turkish proverb: a cup of coffee amongst strangers can spark a new lifetime of friendship. And indeed, Kate was a true believer of this very wise, yet true proverb.

Following her grandmother's request, Kate drank the remainder of her coffee. Unlike Jennifer's coffee, which was bubbly and sweet with sugar; Kate drank her coffee plain, strong, dark and bitter. In contrast to Jennifer's sugary coffee style, Kate's coffee's aroma was bold and masculine, and the color of her drink was as dark as charcoal. To top it all off, the rim of her cup was covered by a thick layer of foam; similar to the same sea foam found throughout the Mediterranean Sea.

After taking her final sip, Kate turned her cup upside down onto the saucer to allow her coffee grounds to fall and settle along its surface. Since the shapes and symbols formed by the coffee grounds were meant serve as a helpful guide to her grandmother's fortune telling, Kate took extra care to give a good and thorough spin around. After a few brief moments to allow the coffee grounds to dry, Kate slowly handed her coffee cup and saucer over to her grandmother.

"Thank you, my dear," said Shakire, as she graciously took the cup and saucer from Kate's hands.

While Shakire focused on the coffee cup, Kate sat nervously awaiting her grandmother's predictions. Although Shakire had previously read her coffee grounds a hundred times over; most of the times they were rushed, light-hearted and purely for fun, without much thought or effort. However, today, Shakire appeared to be in a more serious mood. Unlike before, she seemed to be in full concentration and so, Kate wondered if this time, her predictions today were meant to come true.

Lifting the cup up from its saucer, Shakire stared deep into the pits of her coffee grounds. Carefully, she examined each image and symbol with extra care, as she traced each image with her index finger. For a long while, Shakire remained silent, in full concentration. As the clock ticked away, Kate began to wonder and worry as to what was taking her grandmother so long to reveal her predictions.

"Grandmother, are you not finding anything in my cup?" asked Kate, finally, breaking their silence.

"No, I definitely do see something; but Kate, you have a very interesting cup," revealed Shakire, at long last.

"I do see books, a large university, podium, and an audience…you will be a teacher, one day, Kate," Shakire predicted.

"Well, that's to be expected," huffed Jennifer, sarcastically. "We all know as to just how much Kate loves her books and school. But what about marriage?"

Apparently, Jennifer was far more eager to inquire about Kate's future, than Kate was to ask about herself.

"I do see marriage, too," replied Shakire. "But Kate's marriage will come about under very peculiar circumstances; but I dare say, in the end, hers will be a tremendously happy and romantic marriage, indeed."

"Peculiar, in which way?" asked Kate, most curiously.

"Yes, peculiar, in which way?" echoed Jennifer.

"I cannot say for certain," answered Shakire. "But Kate, circumstances beyond your control will bring you to him. Fate, it seems, will cross your paths together, in the most unexpected way. Furthermore, you'll know that it's him, when he first kisses you…in the snow."

"The snow?" exclaimed both Kate and Jennifer, excited by that revelation.

"Yes, the snow," Shakire confirmed. "And Kate, I do see a little snowflake in your cup, too."

"A snowflake?" asked Kate, stunned by this new prediction. How amazing that only but a few minutes ago, Kate sat ever-so patiently staring away at her window, and waiting and hoping to see a snowflake. How strange that her one wish would somehow magically appear inside of her cup?

"Yes," replied Shakire. "There's a snowflake and a very beautiful one at that, I dare say. The edges are rough, but the design is almost as beautiful as a winter rose. And right next to the snowflake, is a lovely white pearl."

"Oh, that's Kate's favorite gem, the pearl," interrupted Jennifer.

"Yes, I know. And next to the snowflake and pearl, is the man," added Shakire.

"Kate is going to marry a snowman," Jennifer playfully teased.

"No, that isn't it," replied Shakire. "Kate, one day, this man is going to fall madly in love you. But first, you have to overcome some obstacles. Like all important tasks, you'll have to climb your mountain, before you acquire your treasure. But in the end, it will be all worth it; for he's your soul mate."

"How romantic!" cried Jennifer. "A kiss in the snow, snowflakes, roses, pearls and all! It must be true love, Kate!"

Kate blushed. Only time would tell.

Chapter 2

Five Years Later…

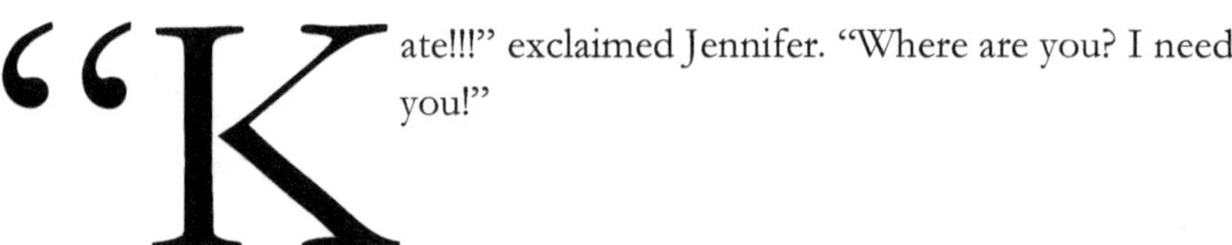

"**K**ate!!!" exclaimed Jennifer. "Where are you? I need you!"

Alas, Kate was nervous and absolutely dreading this phone call. Gazing straight across at her vanity mirror inside of her bathroom, Kate's untidy appearance certainly caught her attention. Sadly, her brown hair was not yet combed and appeared rather messy. Meanwhile, her pink cotton robe was dreadfully wrinkled all throughout and was stained with various brown patches of coffee, all scattered about. Unfortunately, even Kate had to reluctantly admit to herself, that her own eyebrows were long overdue for a good tweeze.

"Ah," Kate sighed to herself, in frustration.

Sadly, she let herself go. Prior to today, Kate desperately tried her best to delay this very conversation. How was she going to explain to her sister, that she wasn't going to attend her wedding? That, she was far too preoccupied to board a plane and fly over to California from New York? That, she was going to sadly, miss her own twin sister's upcoming wedding?

Her own flesh and blood? To a groom, whom she didn't yet have the liberty to meet, prior? How was she ever going to confess to her sister, that she needed to stay behind in New York City, in order to finish her graduate school application?

For several weeks now, Kate avoided Jennifer, at all costs. As of recently, her sister got engaged and the wedding was soon approaching…and fast, too. Luckily, for Kate, her sister lived on the opposite side of the country, so surprisingly, the physical distance between them actually worked in her favor. However, as Kate continued to stare across into the mirror; this time, the image that she saw reflected back to her wasn't of herself, but of her sister, instead. Alas, her sister's face was staring back at her in the mirror. Mocking her. Haunting her. Their styles might have been vastly differed, but they still shared the same face. Her face. Her sister's face. Suddenly, Kate was overcome by guilt.

Attempting to put on a brave front, Kate exited her bathroom and entered into her living room. As she sat down onto her trusty old but comfy blue velvet sofa, that was located inside of her small Manhattan apartment studio, Kate quickly muted her phone line. After all, Kate still needed time to carefully ponder, as to how she was going to have to tackle this important, yet extremely delicate conversation with her twin sister.

"Any ideas, Tabitha?" Kate asked her orange and yellow tabby cat, who was walking nearby.

Situated in close proximately to her university, Kate lived alone in a one-bedroom studio apartment, along with her beloved cat, Tabitha. Overall, her small apartment was simple, cozy, humble and modest: there was a small kitchen with a tiny stove and two cupboards, along with a combined open concept living and bedroom; a bathroom with a walk-in shower and lastly, but most importantly, a tiny balcony with a spectacular view that overlooked Central Park. By far, the balcony was Kate's favorite spot in her entire apartment. Often, during her free-time, Kate made a daily effort to drink her tea, right outside of her balcony to watch the city dwellers pass on-by.

As a student, her tiny apartment was surrounded by various history books and plants, that could be found throughout her small but humble space. Although she didn't possess much furniture, clothes or personal items, Kate used the extra available space to store spare books and additional fern plants, in their place. Apart from these items, Tabitha's many cat beds were also all scattered about, throughout the apartment. But of course, Tabitha much better preferred to lay near Kate's side, either on the sofa or inside of Kate's bed. Naturally, like all cats, Tabitha was a fan of her daily dose of petting.

"Meow…" purred Tabitha, as she walked by Kate and rubbed her furry body against her master, hoping for a pet.

Immediately, taking notice of Tabitha's cue, Kate began stroking the cat's yellow and orange fur. Surprisingly, it was rather comforting and therapeutic to pet Tabitha, for it helped Kate to briefly relax and forget about her impending problems. Well, briefly… after all, her phone was still out and laying down above her coffee table…

"Kate!!" yelled Jennifer again. "Are you even listening to me?"

The screeching sounds of Jennifer's angry and screaming voice caught Kate's and Tabitha's attention. Upon hearing Jennifer's high-pitched scream, Tabitha fearfully leaped out from her owner's lap and inadvertently, managed to bump into Kate's favorite fern plant, in the process. As the plant and its accompanied terracotta pot came crashing down, it smashed into a hundred pieces, as it fell across her living room floor. The loud smashing noise scared Tabitha so much, that the poor cat ran as fast as lightning and straight into the kitchen, along with her tail tucked safely in-between her shaking hind legs. Unfortunately, Kate's living room was now a complete mess that was covered in soil and dirt, along with broken pieces to a once beloved terracotta pot and a disembodied plant.

"I guess that even animals can get scared, too," Kate whispered to herself.

Ironically, just like the mess laying before her, Kate's life felt much of the same. Her problems all began two weeks ago, when she first received an unexpected wedding invitation in the mail. The invitation not only announced Jennifer's upcoming wedding, but of her soon-to-be engagement party, as well. Although Kate couldn't have been more thrilled and excited for her twin sister's happy event; the timing also couldn't have been more wrong. Unfortunately, Kate was already in the process of working on her graduate application, which just so happened to also coincide with Jennifer's upcoming engagement party and wedding nuptials—both of which, were only mere days apart from each other.

Originally, Kate planned to apply for an extension to submit her graduate application to a later date, so that she'd have additional time to fly back and forth between New York and California, without the risk of not completing her thesis proposal before her assigned deadline. Sadly, Kate's proposed extension didn't sit too well with Professor Zaman, Kate's mentor and the Chair of New York University's history department. As the department chair, Professor Zaman made all of the final decisions, as to which students were (and were not) admitted into the doctoral program. Tragically, for Kate, Professor Zaman personally requested that she remain in New York for the entire duration of the upcoming month. Furthermore, Professor Zaman also denied her extension request, on the mere basis that an extension wouldn't be fair to the other applicants, as he had a duty to remain impartial.

Although Kate was greatly disappointed by his decision, she also knew that her future career solely rested upon his favor; therefore, she ultimately chose to stay behind to remain under his good graces. It was a sacrifice that she knew that she had to make; but at the same time, she still felt so incredibly guilty about the entire situation. However, Kate still remained hopeful that eventually one day, Jennifer would come to understand and forgive her. Therefore, due to these reasons, Kate avoided her sister like the plague.

"Jennifer," began Kate, nervously, "I have some news…"

Ten Minutes Earlier...

As Jennifer sat down inside of her bridal dressing room, wearing her newly customed designed Coco Chanel wedding dress, that was made from pure silk all the way from China, she looked straight across into the mirror and smiled. After all, she looked ravishingly beautiful. Much to her delight, her hair and makeup looked exquisite. Just like she had requested right before, her blonde hair was neatly pulled aside and gently tucked away into a secured bun, held by a sparkling diamond pin. Furthermore, her makeup was also impeccable: a smokey brown shade of shadow and matching dark eyeliner carefully applied and smudged across her eyelids, along with a glowing shade of peach reflecting across her cheeks. Furthermore, she was wearing an antiquate pair of white studded diamond earrings, which had been lent to her by her new mother-in-law. Happily, Jennifer stared right across at her image and smilingly approved.

Alas, today was going to be the happiest day in her entire life. After all, she was about to marry the ultra-wealthy and handsomely dashing Mr. John Barrett and start her brand-new glamorous life abroad. Although Jennifer never imagined getting married so-soon right after college; somehow, her groom-to-be unexpectedly swept her off her feet and now, she was most eager to quickly marry him and become the new Mrs. John Barrett, the ambassador's wife.

Surprisingly, they had only known each other for a mere matter of a few weeks, but that was enough for her. John was charming, handsome, wealthy and he, to top it all off, was about to start an exciting career abroad. Given that Jennifer was a born romantic, the very thought of embarking on a new and adventurous life abroad was simply too good of an opportunity to pass. This was going to be the life that she always envisioned. This was going to make her happy. She could just feel it. Although a recent college graduate herself, Jennifer already knew that she didn't want the traditional life of either a stay-at-home suburban housewife, like her mother; nor a workaholic career woman, like her own twin sister aspired to be. To Jennifer, both life-styles required a woman to dedicate themselves most entirely to either a household or to a career; neither of which, Jennifer was remotely interested on having. Instead, she wanted a carefree life that was dedicated to herself and to herself alone— along with the financial freedom to do so, too.

Marrying for money and prestige, was that such a terrible thing? After all, lots of other people did far worse. In truth, Jennifer didn't consider herself as a terrible person; but rather, she was just a woman, who had other ambitions and desires that differed from most. Ultimately, Jennifer yearned for love, fame, wealth, adventure and freedom. The freedom to live her life on her own terms and to make her own decisions. As luck would have it, she happened to meet John by chance and now, by marrying him, he was going to provide her with the access to all of the above and more. Therefore, when he unexpectedly asked her to marry him and to join him overseas, she immediately agreed. Why, any woman in her position would have, wouldn't they?

But did she love him? That was the million-dollar question. She, herself, wasn't entirely too sure; but in truth, it didn't matter. John was handsome, wealthy and agreeable. But most importantly, as the future ambassador's wife, she was going to live very comfortably, from here on out. She was going to have access to high scale fashion, live in exclusive state mansions, mingle with celebrities and world leaders, travel the world in style and have a full-time staff of her very own. A new and glamorous world that was very different from her own unglamorous and normal middle-class upbringing. It was a real-life fairy tale. She had finally met her real-life Prince Charming. At this point, all that she needed to do was to simply say the word 'yes.' It really was just that simple. Thus far, everything came to her at ease; literally, handed over to her on a silver platter. So easy, that in fact, the only real challenge that she faced these past few weeks, was planning her upcoming wedding on such a short notice.

Luckily, for Jennifer, she hired an entire wedding entourage team to take over that important task. Since John came from a wealthy family from San Francisco, Jennifer had access to some of the best VIP wedding planners in the entire country. Although her entourage team successfully planned her wedding to the utmost perfection thus far; for some odd reason, no one in her team was able to locate her twin sister. Not a single staffer. Much to her disappointment, Jennifer suspected that her own twin's lack of appearance was a clear indication that Kate was more likely going to skip out on her big day. For once, Jennifer hated the prospect of being right.

As Jennifer continued to stare directly into the mirror, her smile slowly faded and soon transitioned into a frown. Ever slowly, the more she gazed deeper into the mirror, she started to see the face of her own twin staring right back at her. Suddenly, at that precise moment, Jennifer began to wonder as to where exactly was that very twin of hers right now. Had Kate been here, then she would have known that her wedding had been rescheduled earlier to today, in order to accommodate John's new assignment. As the clock continued to tick away, Jennifer grew more frustrated by her sister's lack of appearance. Therefore, Jennifer, filled with emotion, forcefully pulled out her mobile phone from out of her purse and directly dialed Kate's number.

"Kate!!!" exclaimed Jennifer. "Where are you? I need you!"

Much to her disappointment, there was a long pause on the other side of her phone call. Curious, Jennifer wondered if anyone was even on the line to begin with; but then, she suddenly heard background noises, including a very distinctive "meow," which clearly was Tabitha, Kate's ever-annoying cat. Jennifer very well knew that Kate was indeed, on the other line, but hadn't yet answered her; and so, this time, she yelled even louder:

"Kate!! Are you even listening to me?" she violently screamed.

Once again, there was another period of silence. Suddenly, Jennifer took a deep breath. She didn't want to scare, nor intimate her sister. Jennifer was already well aware that Kate was busy with her own schoolwork; and at the same time, she was also very proud of her accomplishments. If circumstances had been different, Jennifer would have gladly delayed her wedding ceremony to a later date, in order to accommodate for her sister. But alas, time also wasn't on Jennifer's side, either. Recently, her groom had been accepted into the State Department and now, he was going to be appointed as the new U.S. Ambassador to Egypt. As soon as they were wed, the newlyweds planned on boarding a plane directly headed to Cairo, Egypt, so that John could start his new post.

For these reasons, Jennifer sympathized with Kate; therefore, she didn't hold her absence against her. Truly, Jennifer understood that her sister was only working towards her dreams; just as she was about to marry into hers. Although Jennifer wasn't upset, nor angered by Kate's decision, she continued to hold the hope that maybe, by some odd miracle, Kate would still miraculously make it to her wedding.

"Jennifer," began Kate, nervously, "I have some news…"

"Kate," Jennifer interrupted this time, as she took another deep breath and finally said, "I understand, if you can't make it."

"You do?" replied Kate, who was taken aback by this surprising admission.

"My wedding is too short-notice, and I'm sure that you're probably still busy with school," answered Jennifer, determined to get straight to the point.

"Yes, actually, I am," replied Kate, in all honesty. At this moment, she was truly stunned by her sister's unexpected and positive reaction.

"Kate, it's okay. I do understand, but I'm still disappointed, just so you know…" admitted Jennifer.

"Jennifer, I really did try. It's just that my professor won't grant my extension. But I promise, one day, I will make it up to you," Kate vowed.

"It's okay, Kate. I just wish that you could have at least met John, before our wedding. You would have liked him. He actually kind of reminds me of you," said Jennifer.

"Really?" asked Kate. This was yet another surprise. I suppose today was just one of those days meant for surprises, Kate thought to herself.

"John's also a big history buff. He seems to know a lot of random facts, also like you," Jennifer explained.

"How funny, too bad that I won't be able to meet him, until after your wedding," remarked Kate.

"Yeah, I know," responded a disappointed Jennifer. "But at least everyone else will be able to attend, with the exception of grandmother."

"Jennifer, do you remember grandmother's predictions, all those years ago? On that cold winter's day back in Balikesir, when we drank our Turkish coffee in her kitchen? I remember that she predicted that you would marry twice," Kate recalled.

"Ah, yes," said Jennifer, recalling a far and distant memory that she had since long forgotten, but was now, reminded of. "That's true, she did predict that. But you know, John isn't my first fiancé, he's actually my second. Remember Alex from high school?"

"That's right! You were first engaged to your high school sweetheart!" exclaimed Kate.

"Grandma must have seen the 'marriages' as engagements, and my first engagement did come at an early age. Therefore, according to her calculations, my engagement to John is technically my second engagement, so I should be good in the clear," Jennifer concluded.

"Ah, that makes perfect sense. You must be right." Kate agreed; and then, suddenly, she wondered as to how soon after the wedding, would she be able to see her sister, once again.

"Do you plan on having a long honeymoon?" Kate asked, curiously.

"Not a long honeymoon, but right after the wedding, we're going to fly directly to Egypt, so that John can start his new post, immediately," replied Jennifer.

"Oh my gosh! You'll be leaving this soon? For how long?" asked Kate, now concerned at the possibility of not seeing her sister in-person, in the immediate future.

"I'm not entirely sure, but this is one of the reasons as to why I wanted to see you at the wedding. To say goodbye…" Jennifer sadly revealed.

For a long moment, the sisters remained silent, as they each comprehended this news and new adjustment. Although they came into the world together, with Kate the elder by five minutes, and now, as young adults, they were each growing apart and moving on with their own separate lives.

 "I'm going to miss you," Kate finally admitted, after a long and delayed pause.

"I'm going to miss you, too," Jennifer agreed, as she wiped her tears away from her watery eyes.

"Jennifer, I promise you that as soon as I'm done with this graduate program, I'm coming to visit," Kate promised.

"I'll be waiting," added Jennifer.

Finally, both sisters closed their phones, as they went about their separate ways on their own paths. Jennifer, now fully dressed in her entire wedding attire, including her veil, grabbed her wedding bouquet, forcefully pushed through the doors of her bridal room and marched directly towards the church to meet with her groom. Meanwhile, Kate, cleaned up the mess in her apartment, fed Tabitha a bowl of tuna, threw on a black pants suit, grabbed her black tote and gently pushed through the doors of her apartment, as she walked over towards the university to meet with her professor.

Chapter 3

The wedding was grand, beautiful and extravagant. All five hundred guests were in attendance, including the couple's respective families and friends. The church was decorated and adorned with various bouquets of red roses, pink tulips, white daffodils and marigolds. The weather was beautifully sunny and warm. While Jennifer walked down the church's aisle, the sun shined and sparkled against her white wedding grown through the rose-colored glass windows, which also miraculously projected a soft blush colored aura that encircled around her.

Overall, the ceremony lasted no longer than an hour. Afterwards, the crowd exited the church and gathered outside into the garden to attend the afterparty. It was there in that very garden, that Jennifer was soon approached by her new mother-in-law, Mrs. Barbara Barrett. An elegant, fashionable woman in her late sixties, with a curvy figure and short brown hair styled in a pixie cut, Barbara arrived on the scene wearing her famous shade of purple and signature Miss Dior perfume scent. Barbara, a wealthy widow from California, spent most of her retired days either traveling, decorating her many properties around the world, or attending various social luncheons with other retired socialites, like herself. Since John was Barbara's only child, she was thrilled that her son had finally married and was insistent upon connecting her new daughter-in-law with the very best wedding planners in the country.

"Congratulations, my darling!" exclaimed Barbara happily, as she kissed Jennifer's cheek and gave her a big hug.

"Thank you so much, Barbara. I don't think that this wedding was even possible, without your recommendations," Jennifer admitted.

"Oh, nonsense," huffed Barbara, as she waved her hands carefree up into the air.

"I'm sure that you would have found a perfectly good wedding planner on your own, if I hadn't recommended Celeste and her team," she continued, "I'm just so glad and relieved that John's finally settled down. After all, he's going to be an ambassador now, so naturally, it's only proper that he should also take a wife, as well."

Jennifer shook her head in agreement. She then looked straight ahead and saw John walking towards them. But he wasn't alone. He was accompanied by an older gentleman and another young woman; both of whom, Jennifer had not yet met before.

"Hello, Mother," said John, upon his arrival.

Slowly, John proceeded to bend down to kiss Barbara's cheeks. Afterwards, he reverted his attention over to his new wife, gave her a kiss and said with a smile, "And hello to my new wife."

Jennifer was tickled. She was now a wife. A wife to the new ambassador. Just standing over six feet tall, her new husband had dark black hair, bluish-green eyes, with a fair completion. But apart from being physically attractive and handsome, he was also charming and polite. Ah, yes, her new husband was dashing, handsome and wealthy— all the ingredients to her perfect match on paper. He was everything that Jennifer had dreamt of and more. He, as she concluded, was perfect.

"Oh, my darling John!" exclaimed his mother, Barbara.

Immediately, recognizing the couple standing right next to John, Barbara said, "And a hello to you too, David and Amy."

"Jennifer," interrupted John. "I'd like to introduce you to retired Ambassador David Lawrence and his daughter, Amy. David's my coach and mentor. Last year, he even helped me with my State Department application. But most importantly, he's also like a real father figure to me."

For a moment, Jennifer looked on and studied John's mentor. Although David was similar in age to Barbara, but rather than sporting a full set of colored hair, his hair, in contrast, was salty white and black peppered. Furthermore, unlike Barbara's smooth face, David had a few wrinkles, especially around his eyes. Overall, he was impressionably well dressed, sporting a black Armani suit, with a silk blue tie adorned around his neck. Staring closer at him, Jennifer noted that David resembled that of a strong, charismatic, confident and mature man, who embodied that of a true professional. Due to his retired profession, Jennifer presumed that David, over the years, must have possessed an abundant amount of wealth through his various life experiences acquired in his given field of expertise. Having now met him in real-life, Jennifer wasn't at all surprised, in the very least, that David was John's mentor. In fact, upon closer inspection, David even resembled an older version of John.

After establishing her own observations on David, Jennifer soon turned her attention over towards his daughter. Amy, a young woman in her late teens, had a very sweet and fair face, along with an innocent smile. Closely resembling her father's similar physical features, Amy had black hair, green eyes, a fair complexion, and she was dressed almost entirely in the color blue.

"It's very nice to meet you both, Mr. Lawrence and Miss Lawrence," said Jennifer, as she extended her hands over to greet them.

"Same to you, Mrs. Barrett," replied David, joyfully.

"And a many congratulations to you and John on your new marriage," added an excited Amy.

"Mrs. Barrett, I have a special wedding gift for you and John. Amy, hand me the envelope," David commanded, as he quickly snapped his fingers at his daughter.

Following her father's instructions, Amy opened her purse, reached in and then handed him the envelope. Promptly, David took the envelope and swiftly gave it directly over to John.

"John, I'm so very proud of you," said David, beamingly. "I, along with Amy, are beyond the moon that you'll be following in my footsteps and joining the agency. But most importantly, I'm extremely delighted and overjoyed about your new marriage to this lovely bride of yours."

"Let's have a toast!" Barbara cheered, as she also motioned and signaled to the waiters to come and deliver some champagne to their private gathering.

"Yes!" jumped Amy, excited about Barbara's suggested toast.

"Yes, let's have a toast," John agreed, but with a caveat. "All of us, except Amy, of course…"

Leaning over into Jennifer's ear, John whispered, "She's still only nineteen."

"Oh, just let her try some," cried Barbara. "It's a wedding, after all."

Within moments, the waiter arrived and brought over four separate glasses of champagne, along with one single glass of sparkling water, reserved for Amy. As they raised their glasses up into the air, David continued on with his speech.

"As I was saying before," David continued, "John, I'm so very proud of you. You're like the son that I always wished I had."

Briefly, David paused momentarily to wipe away a tear from the corner of his eye, before continuing on.

"And because of this," he continued, "I want to present you and your new wife, with a copy to my latest will. One day, should anything happen to me, John and Amy will together, inherit all of my vast properties and estates."

"David!!! You're simply too kind!" exclaimed Barbara, who was just as stunned and surprised, as everyone else. Well, everyone except Amy. It seemed that Amy was already well aware of her father's new will and wasn't at all in the very least, surprised.

"I cannot accept this," said John firmly. "David, you're too kind, but what about—"

But David soon interrupted him and said, "John, I'll be very offended, if you object to this; so please just say thank you, make me happy and accept my wishes."

For a long moment, John stood quietly still. Sporting the absolute professional poker face, he exhibited no emotions, nor facial expressions. As a result, Jennifer found it rather difficult to detect his inner thoughts. After much silence, John finally gave his answer.

"David, thank you," said John, at long last, as he moved to hug David.

"Aww, how lovely," remarked Barbara. "David, you're simply the best."

"Coming from you Barbara, that's a real complement," David laughingly replied. "In any case, it's now getting late, and Amy and I should be on our way back to the hotel."

"Do you have an early flight tomorrow morning?" asked Barbara.

"Yes," answered David. "On Monday morning, Amy resumes her college classes, so we want to be sure that we're packed and ready to go first thing, tomorrow."

"In that case, have a safe trip my darlings. Remember, please do come and visit me sometime in Napa," said Barbara.

"David and Amy, please let me escort you all over to the exit," said John, as he immediately, took the liberty to lead them from out of the garden and back into the church.

After their departure, Jennifer soon found herself alone, with Barbara.

"It's such a tragedy about what happened with his real son," Barbara whispered over to Jennifer.

Taken by surprise by this news, Jennifer inquired, "Really? He has a son?"

"Ah," sighed Barbara. "David's eldest son, Owen. David hasn't spoken to him in years. They're estranged, you know."

Without anyone looking, Barbara, slowly leaned in closer and whispered into Jennifer's ear, "Owen Lawrence was in the military and was a rising star. He had such good prospects; so promising. But he was also a drunk, and sadly, his alcohol got him kicked out of the military. It was a dishonorable discharge! Plus, coming from the son of an ambassador, it was such a disgrace and an embarrassment to David and his entire family, too. A real scandal!"

"Oh my!" exclaimed Jennifer, in astonishment.

"Oh, my indeed," agreed Barbara. "This is why I tell you now, my darling Jennifer, that when you become a part of an ambassador's immediate family, there can be no scandals. You must be straight forward and clean. No skeletons in the closet."

Leaning another inch closer into Jennifer's ear, Barbara further emphasized, "But if there should be any skeletons, well…then…it must remain hidden and buried away into that closet, so that the darkness covers it completely. You do know what I mean, right, Jennifer?"

Suddenly, Jennifer clearly understood that Barbara's story was meant to serve as both an insight into David's family, while at the same time, also acting as a forewarning about her own impending future. For all of her worth, Jennifer was rather fond of Barbara; and so, she wanted to ensure that her new mother-in-law had absolutely nothing to worry about. Therefore, she simply nodded in agreement with her and further added, "I do understand, Barbara. May I ask, what became of Owen?"

Comforted by Jennifer's reassurance, Barbara continued on with her story.

"Well, no one really knows. It's a bit of a mystery. In fact, no one has ever seen Owen, ever since he abruptly left the military. After that, he just disappeared. Sadly, it's been rumored that David's late wife, Elizabeth, was so heartbroken by the entire situation, that she actually died from a broken heart soon afterwards! Imagine that! Terrible, just terrible!" exclaimed Barbara, sympathetically.

"Now," Barbara continued, "Poor David is a widower and living all alone with young Amy. It's a good thing that David met John at college, and that he's has become some-what of a surrogate father figure to him. I, myself, was so sadden by the untimely passing of my late husband, Richard, just a few years ago, too. Luckily, David's been such a good influence on my son, and now, John is to be an ambassador and…"

Suddenly, Barbara quickly grabbed hold of Jennifer's hand and said, "And now he has you, and I don't have to worry as much about him anymore. I simply couldn't be more delighted."

Happily, Jennifer smiled and gave Barbara a small pat on her shoulders. After all, it was comforting to know that she was accepted into her new family by her new mother-in-law.

Soon afterwards, John returned back to the garden. Upon seeing him, Jennifer politely excused herself from Barbara's company and quickly joined her new husband's side. As the day grew into night, and the party grew tiresome, the newlyweds were more than ready to retire for their first evening together, as husband and wife. And so, they bid farewell to their guests and together, they walked over to their getaway car. As Jennifer waved her final farewell to all of her many guests with her left hand, her right hand reached over for the car door.

Once seated comfortably inside of their car, Jennifer sat down and waited for John— who had briefly stepped away to gather the remainder of their belongings back at the party. As she waited for his return, Jennifer stared at her new wedding ring to admire its' beauty and smiled. The ring was beautiful. It was a gold band, with a large, yet peculiar shaped white pearl, located right in the center of the ring. It was encircled by several other smaller blue diamonds that orbited it. Although it wasn't the sort of jewelry that she'd have chosen for herself, for she preferred diamonds over pearls; it was nevertheless, a lovely and enchanting ring. A perfect ring, for the perfect wife, she reflected.

However, the longer that Jennifer stared at her new ring, she eventually, noticed a blemish. Upon closer inspection, she soon realized that it was a spec of dirt, located right above the pearl's top surface. Hoping to remove it, Jennifer quickly began rubbing the ring against her dress.

"There, it's gone," said a relieved Jennifer to herself.

But as soon as the blemish was gone, Jennifer then saw a crack on one of the surrounding blue diamonds. This wasn't something that she couldn't easily fix, like before. Naturally, Jennifer was disappointed, for she was going to need a new ring. Maybe, even a replacement?

Suddenly, her wedding finger began to itch. Determined to stop the itching, Jennifer abruptly removed the ring from off her finger. Having done so, she immediately felt a huge sense of relief and freedom. Looking down at her bare finger, Jennifer noticed that it was now slightly swollen and red. Her ring was far too small, she thought. Why, her ring was so small, that it nearly suffocated her finger, by limiting her own blood circulation. A blemish. A crack. A swollen finger. Jennifer worried that this perfect ring was perhaps, not perfect at all for her. Although a lovely ring, she concluded, it just didn't seem to work for her.

"This ring isn't right for me," she reluctantly admitted to herself.

After arriving to this conclusion, Jennifer knew that she needed to devise a quick scheme to dispose of this unwanted item, while acquiring a replacement, at the same time. Although she didn't want to offend her new husband by rejecting his ring, especially, since it was, after all, a family heirloom; however, at the same time, if she was going to bear the burden of wearing it, then it needed to be a ring that was more suitable for her. A ring, specifically designed for herself, that reflected her own unique personality.

The reality was that Jennifer needed a ring that was bold, flashy and glamorous. In contrast, her current ring reflected none of these essential qualities. Rather, it was traditional, safe and predictable. No, she didn't want a new ring, she concluded; nay, she needed a new ring! However, now that she realized this, how was she going to deliver this upsetting news to her new husband?

"I'll just say I lost it," she decided. "Then, he'll be forced to buy me a new one. He'll have no other choice. But this time, I'll pick the right one, for myself. Afterwards, I'll mail this pearl ring over to Kate, and then, tell her that it's a gift. Since Kate loves pearls so much, I'm certain that she'll appreciate this unique piece of jewelry as art. Yes, this will all work out!"

At that very moment, John entered the car and was right about to give her another kiss, when Jennifer stopped him midway and told him her very first lie; of which, would grow to become many throughout their marriage.

"John," Jennifer began, "I seem to have lost my ring…"

Chapter 4

The morning sun shined across Jennifer's face, as she lay down on the beach. Her legs stretched across her beach blanket, while she squeezed her toes to play with the seashells on the golden sand. The gentle ocean breeze blew against her soft porcelain face, while the sound of the crashing waves brought a gentle ease to her heart. All in all, she was blissfully happy and romantically in love. Taking a sip of her raspberry cocktail, Jennifer suddenly stood up to adjust her straw hat and black cat eyed sunglasses. As she stared across towards the sea, she noticed John swimming upwards and towards the shore. Amazingly, he looked happy, too. Equally, they were each enjoying their honeymoon, together. Taking another sip of her drink, Jennifer happily watched on, as she enjoyed her breathtaking and beautiful view.

Meanwhile, John arose out from the sea and made his way over to his new bride, who was currently, lying down on a nearby chair and sunbathing in her black bikini. Barefoot in the sand, he excitingly ran towards her, while wearing only his red swimming trunks, with his black hair soaking wet. As he glided across the hot sand, he continued to run until finally, at long last, he reached her side. Once near to her, John swiftly pulled Jennifer up from her chair and brought her body close to his. As he embraced her within his caring arms, he leaned down, lifted her face to meet his, and then sealed her lips with a kiss. He then reached for her right hand, brought it towards his lips and finally, kissed her hand.

"Mrs. Barrett, do you approve?" asked John, while never once, having let go of her hand.

"I do," replied Jennifer, happily.

Of course, John was naturally referring to the new wedding ring, which he recently acquired for her, as of yesterday. Rather than sporting another pearl ring, Jennifer now, wore a brand new sparkling pink diamond ring, which was held together by a gold band, made out of twenty-four karats of gold. It was most certainly an extravagant and exquisite piece of jewelry; a ring that she had personally chosen for herself, the day following their wedding.

When she first told John about the missing ring, he was, as expected, initially disappointed, since the ring had been a family heirloom. However, he quickly got over his disappointment; and then, soon afterwards, he promised her another replacement ring, but this time, one of her own choosing. Delighted by his offer, Jennifer quickly jumped at the nearest opportunity to shop for her new replacement ring.

After they boarded their plane to embark upon John's first diplomatic assignment in Egypt, he surprised her with an unexpected honeymoon vacation in Nice, France. It was there in Nice, that John took her to Tiffany & Co., so that Jennifer could personally select her new ring. As John pushed opened the entrance doors into Tiffany & Co., Jennifer joyfully skipped over to the counter to gaze upon the various shiny jewels that lay before her. Much to her delight, John also promised her that she could select any ring of her choice, without any budgetary constraints. This prospect thrilled her so much, that she tried an endless supply of rings; as many as she possibly could. However, after trying on several rings, in the end, she narrowed down her choices to three finalists.

The first ring was John's recommendation. It was another pearl ring, similar to her first wedding ring; however, the pearl was perfectly round in shape this time, without any imperfection and was surrounded by even smaller shaped emerald stones. Overall, it was a lovely ring; however, it was yet another pearl ring and Jennifer still wanted diamonds. Meanwhile, the second ring was the jeweler's suggestion and it was a square-shaped purple diamond, that also just happened to be one of the most popular designs of the season. Although it was another nice option, Jennifer still didn't want a ring that everyone else in town had. The truth was that Jennifer was fearful of appearing rather too "common." Alas, the third ring, which was Jennifer's personal choice and favorite, was an extremely large, yet expensive sparkling pink diamond. Out of the three selections, this ring was unique, pink and romantic; traits that reflected Jennifer's own personality and favorite color. Although Jennifer had taken all three rings into careful consideration, in the end, she followed her own heart and chose her favorite as her new ring.

While in Nice, the couple spent their honeymoon at the world famous Le Negresco Hotel, along the French Rivera. The hotel, built in 1912, was located on the Promenade des Anglais on the Baie des Anges in downtown Nice. The hotel sat upon pristine real estate and location, and directly overlooked the Mediterranean Sea from across the street. Since the sea and the board walk were only mere steps away, the newlyweds opted to spend their days at the beach and their nights back at the hotel.

As John gave Jennifer another kiss, he grabbed her hand and led her towards the sea. When they finally reached the shore, John lifted her up and carried her away into the water. Surprised by his sudden move, Jennifer giggled out of excitement. As they moved deeper into the water, Jennifer continued to hold onto him, as they began floating above the sea. By now, it was already late in the afternoon, and the sea was calm and gentle. The air was clear, crisp and clean. Most of the tourists and staff had already left the beach for dinner, so the area was now, quiet and empty.

While still holding onto to John tightly, Jennifer threw her straw hat back towards land and then, she lay her head to rest along his bare chest. As the sun began to set, the turquoise blue waters reflected an orange pink glow, right along the horizon. Furthermore, the sky was also clear and amazingly, there wasn't a single cloud or bird in sight. Looking down at the sea floor, Jennifer saw tiny orange fishes, swimming near her legs. Somehow, they managed to tickle her feet, and so, she began to laugh. While still holding onto John, Jennifer lifted up her head up to meet his eyes, and to her sheer surprise, she saw that his sparkling blue eyes actually matched the same exact coloring, as the sea below!

"Oh, John, this is so romantic!" exclaimed Jennifer, happily.

"You find this romantic, eh?" asked John, deviously.

"Yes, I do. The fresh air, blue water and just simply being in the French

Rivera. It can't get more romantic than this!" Jennifer concluded.

"Oh, but it can," added John.

Suddenly, the distant sound of a violin playing a classical tune, could be heard from afar. At first, the sound was faint, and Jennifer wondered if someone had actually left a radio playing outside. However, the sound of the music came closer, and then closer and closer. Strangely, she wondered as to why this was. Finally, out of curiosity, Jennifer pulled herself away from John, and then, she turned her head to look back towards the shore. It was from there, that she saw a real-life musician, standing right there on the beach and playing the violin. Surprised by the sight before her, Jennifer's eyes widened, as she began pinching herself to determine, as to whether or not, this was actually a dream. Finally, she turned back to face John again, and she asked him if what she just saw was actually real or a figment of her imagination.

Amused by her question, John beamingly smiled and replied, "It's very real, my darling, and he's here for us…and so are they…"

Peeking beyond the violinist, Jennifer noticed that right behind him, there was a small picnic table, decorated with silver plates, dinner glasses, along with a bucket of ice and champagne. The table was covered by a white embroidered cloth, and decorated with a crystal vase that included a large bouquet of red roses in the center of it, along with two white candles that were already lit with a fire. Furthermore, on each separate ends of the table, there were two small red velvet chairs. At the end of those chairs, stood two French waiters, formally dressed in their traditional uniforms. It had seemed that while the newlyweds enjoyed their day at sea, John was secretly busy planning a romantic dinner for them back on land, as well.

Together, John led them out of the sea and back onto dry land. After they dried themselves off with a beach towel, the couple walked over to the dinner table. Once they reached the table, John pulled a chair out for Jennifer to sit in. As she took her seat at the table, John moved across to sit in his own chair, opposite from her.

"John, this is truly lovely. Thank you for doing this," said Jennifer, as she graciously thanked him.

"Anything for my bride," admitted John, happily.

"Madame," interrupted the waiter. "Would you care for some champagne?"

"Yes, please," replied Jennifer, as she lifted up her champagne glass, in the direction of the waiter.

"I'll take some, too," John instructed, as he motioned to the waiter to pour him a drink, as well.

"May I ask, what type of champagne is this?" asked Jennifer, who was most curious, as which type of bubbly drink they were about to consume.

"It's from my family's vineyard. Another wedding gift from my mother," replied John. "It's the rose version, 2006. It has a sweet taste and a lasting aroma. It's light and has notes of fruit, mainly peach and pear flavorings."

"Oh, how lovely!" exclaimed Jennifer.

As the waiter finished pouring the champagne into John's glass, John signaled for both the waiters to leave.

"Are they leaving already?" Jennifer inquired, who was surprised that the waiters were already going to leave them, so early in the evening.

"Not the musician, just the waiters. I prefer to serve you dinner, by myself," replied John, as he gave her a charming wink.

"Ah, then what's on the menu?"

However, as she uttered those very words, she also noticed that on the table, there were five silver platters, which had been covered by accompanying silver domes. Just what sort of meal did John prepare for them? Jennifer wondered, to herself. Suddenly, John abruptly rose up from his seat and walked over towards her side of the table. Once he arrived by her side, he removed the first silver dome to reveal their dinner's entree.

"For the main course, it's Duck a-l'orange, with rosemary roasted potatoes and grilled asparagus. It's a famous delicacy from this region. I hope you enjoy it," he said.

"John, this looks absolutely delicious," Jennifer happily complemented, while feeling rather hungry.

Delighted by her approval, John happily smiled and moved onto their second plate. As he removed the dome, the next item on the menu was revealed.

"For dessert, it's a French chocolate lava cake. Another famous delicacy from this region and my personal favorite," he excitingly announced.

Thrilled by his choice of dessert, the chocolate cake was like no other cake that she had ever seen before. It was dark, covered with rose petals and powdered sugar, and to top it all off, it was in the shape of a heart.

"What a stunning cake!" she exclaimed.

But alas, there was one final plate still remaining on the table, which hadn't yet been revealed. Just what were the contents of the last plate? Ever-so-curious, Jennifer inquired about the mysterious fifth plate.

"This one is a surprise. I'll reveal it, towards the end of our evening. In the meantime, bon appetite, Mrs. Barrett," he announced, as he returned back to his seat.

Meanwhile, as the couple were busy away eating, the musician continued to play sweet and soft melodies for their entertainment.

"What a lovely tune. Which song is he playing?" asked Jennifer.

"It's called romance no. 2 in F major, by Beethoven," replied John. "But he can play something else, if you'd like. Francois is very talented. He can play anything. Please just ask."

"Oh, no, I didn't mean to suggest that he play another song. I rather like the tune that he's currently playing, that's all," Jennifer quickly replied.

"Jennifer, please don't ever feel obligated to simply agree with me, or anyone else for that matter. You're my wife now, so I hope that we can remain honest with one another. I might be the new ambassador, but as my first lady, you also have an equally important role to serve in my administration, as my partner. And as partners, I do hope that we can grow to become better friends and allies," he said, in the most serious of tones.

Friends and allies? What an interesting concept. Not once, did Jennifer ever consider him to be a friend, nor an ally. He was always just her boyfriend, then her fiancée and now, her husband. Just why did she need another friend? Friends were so…what's the word…ah…yes…trivial! Plus, she already had plenty of friends…which was more than enough for her…perhaps…even…too…much. So why, in the world, did she ever need another one?

As for her new role as his first lady, Jennifer was still a bit in the dark, as to what exactly her new daily duties were supposed to entail. However, now wasn't the proper time to dwell on such dry matters, during their lovely dinner. Therefore, she simply smiled at him and without uttering another word, she proceeded to eat the remainder of her delicious meal in peace.

After taking his last bite of dinner, John slowly rose up from his chair and walked over to her side of the table. At long last, he was now ready to reveal the contents of the last dish. As he gently lifted the dome up from the plate, to Jennifer's surprise, there was a red velvet box laying right on top of the empty plate.

"What's this?" she asked, in sheer astonishment.

"Please, open it," John instructed her calmly.

Upon his command, Jennifer reached over and grabbed the box. The box was square-shaped, medium sized and made from a thick red, almost burgundy colored box. In the front of it was a golden latch. Quickly, Jennifer pushed up the latch and proceeded to pop open the box. When she finally opened it, a shiny shimmering glare flashed before her eyes. The light was so incredibly powerful, that it nearly blinded her. When her senses eventually returned, she saw a sparkly necklace laying right in front of her. The necklace was covered with diamonds, and in the center was a pink diamond pendant. It was the same exact shade of pink, that just so happened to match her new wedding ring, too.

"I wanted to give you this necklace to accompany your new ring. I hope you like it," John sincerely admitted.

"John, this is simply beautiful," said Jennifer, tearfully.

Swiftly walking over to her side, John gently placed the necklace around her neck. Immediately, Jennifer was tickled by his generosity and kindness. Up until now, everything had gone in her good favor. She graduated from college, married a wealthy ambassador, acquired a vast collection of fine jewelry, and at this very moment, she was already embarking upon a new trip around the world. Truly, Jennifer was enjoying the finest riches in her young life and as far as she was concerned, she was living in a fairy tale. Everything, it seemed, was perfect. But perhaps, dear reader, this was a bit too premature for her to presume, for in life, can anything really be that perfect?

Later on, that evening, the couple stood outside of their hotel balcony to watch the night sky. As the moon rose up and its bright stars shimmered across the infinite dark sky above, Jennifer took a private moment to admire not only the moon, but of her new husband, as well. And just like the dark sky, his dark hair shined against the moonlight. His blue eyes, which normally appeared turquoise during the daylight, now resembled a more violet shade of blue.

"John, do you think that we'll always be this happy?" asked Jennifer, as she leaned down against his warm chest.

"I certainly hope so," he replied, as he pulled her closer to him, and wrapped his arms around her. Once she was tightly bonded within his embrace, he slowly bent down and gave her another kiss.

Being the romantic as she was, Jennifer looked at him and said, "Let's leave it all to fate. Tonight, if we see a shooting star, then we'll know that this happiness will last forever."

Happily, John agreed and the couple remained together, held within their embrace, as they jointly watched the stars shine and glimmer from up above. However, a few minutes later, a cold draft of sea breeze suddenly blew across into their direction. Unfortunately, Jennifer, who was wearing a light and thin sheer dress, grew chilly. After a long day at the beach, she decided that it was best to return back into their bedroom and retire for the remainder of their evening.

However, John wasn't bothered by the chill, at all; for he was, in contrast, warmly dressed for the occasion, wearing a blue knitted sweater. Therefore, he, unlike his new wife, chose to remain outside on the balcony. As he stood there and admired the moon, he realized that tonight's sky, in particular, was truly a spectacular sight to behold. The moon was bright and full, with all of its surrounding stars shining and illuminating the dark sky above.

Meanwhile, as John's attention was focused on the celestial orbit above, suddenly, out from nowhere, a thick and dark cloud floated across the open sky. It was a dark grey and puffy storm cloud that was so large and thick, that within moments, it swiftly came and swallowed up the bright moon, and consumed the entire night sky with a dominating and aggressive force. This was very unexpected. The forecast didn't predict any rain to occur during their trip. On the contrary, the weather was expected to be sunny, clear, blue skies, with the absence of rain. Quickly, John rushed back inside into his room and closed the door shut behind him. And, dear reader, it was a good thing that he did, for as soon as he closed the door, it began to rain…heavily.

Chapter 5

Due to the unforeseeable storm, which no one had predicted, the newlywed's flight to Egypt was delayed by several days. The rain, which began on late Wednesday evening, poured into the night and gradually grew into a thunder and lightning storm by Thursday morning. For the next three days, the rain continued to pour and pour, until all the streets of Nice were completely flooded, and the local shops and restaurants were all forced to close down until better weather. All of the residents and guests were required to shelter-in-place and wait for the storm to pass.

As such, the couple remained at their hotel, as they waited for the storm to pass. While Jennifer spent most of her time at the spa and gym, John stayed behind in their room to catch up on his reading. As he sat in his reading chair, he briefly put down his book to take a break. Slowly, he got up from his chair, walked over to the window nearby, and watched as the rain fell across the city. Surprisingly, the endless rain made him feel a bit uneasy about his upcoming journey. If his original plans had stayed on course, then he was already supposed to be in Egypt, by now. Come Monday, John's predecessor, the soon-to-be retired U.S. Ambassador to Egypt, Terrance Phillips, was officially retiring from his post on Monday morning, at precisely 11:59:59 am. Effective 12:00:00 pm, Monday afternoon, John was going to be sworn in to take his oath, as Phillips' replacement.

John's dreams of joining the agency and becoming a U.S. Ambassador were only days away from coming into fruition. As a young man, John was a prodigy who excelled at almost anything and everything that he set his mind to. In fact, John spent most of his youth preparing for this very moment. Growing up, John traveled the world with his parents. Both sides of his family were descended from wealthy clans originating from San Francisco; all of whom, made their vast fortunes during the gold rush era many generations ago. Apart from their respective families' inherited royalties, his parents owned a private vineyard in Napa Valley and made additional ongoing profits through their wine company, Barrett & Son. With the money earned from their company, it allowed his family to tour all of Europe, Africa, Asia, South America and the continental United States. It was during one of these trips, that John discovered (at a rather young age too) what his true purpose in life was meant to be.

His life altering moment happened one day in India. John, who was fifteen years old at the time, briefly drifted away from his parents' tour group to explore the streets of Mumbai on his own. As he walked down the dirt roads, he wandered into an open bazaar, located on the main market center. The bazaar was certainly a sight to behold. It was loud, noisy and engulfed by a sea of people, all ranging in various age groups. The vast array of colors displayed across the bazaar was truly a breath-taking vision. There, every possible design, texture and color were all flashing and sparkling all around, similar to that of a rainbow, right after a storm. The bazaar extended for miles on end, and from the glimpses of it, it seemed to contain every buyer's personal shopping wish. As he passed by the various tea, spices, silk, gold, clothing, furniture and artifact shops, John was absolutely amazed by all that he saw. In fact, John was so mesmerized by the stunning sights before him, that he wanted to capture and commemorate it with a timeless photograph. Without thinking any further, he suddenly stopped in the middle of the street and reached into his backpack to pull out his camera.

But as John prepared to take his photograph, he was unexpectedly interrupted by a young Indian woman. The woman, who was in her mid-twenties and dressed in a traditional Indian blue sari, with her hands stained with red dye, asked him if he wanted to buy one of her straw baskets. At first, John kindly rejected her offer. However, the more John objected, the more persistent the woman became. As John declined for a third time, the woman still pleaded with her offerings. Surprisingly, she even went as so far, as to showcase him all of her inventory, ranging in various sizes and colors. John, who was still a teenager at the time, had no interest in acquiring baskets, regardless of their designs or functions. However, young John was thoroughly impressed by the woman's eagerness and determination. In the end, his curiosity got the better hold of him, and so, John directly inquired as to why she wanted to sell him these baskets so badly.

It was there, that the young woman told him that her name was Aasha. At the ripe age of merely twenty-four years old, she was already a widow with three young children; all of whom, were under the age of eight years old. Two years ago, her husband and youngest child, an infant, died from malnutrition. After their deaths, Aasha, who, herself was an orphan raised by her late grandmother, had no other family to turn to for assistance. Since her late husband was the sole provider for their household and their only source of income, upon his death, she could no longer afford the rent to their apartment. As a result, Aasha and her children were evicted from their home and forced to live outside on the streets of Mumbai. For several weeks, the family sought shelter in abandoned slums, as they eagerly searched for the scraps of food left behind in waste cans— all the while, they desperately sought to hide from other dangerous criminals and policemen in the neighborhood.

However, one day, a miracle happened: Aasha and her children were discovered and rescued by a group of traveling American missionaries. The Americans, who, themselves, had gotten lost in the great big city of Mumbai, wandered off into their neighborhood, where they managed to stumble upon her eldest son, Sanjay. The young boy, who was six years old at the time, was playing soccer with his friends out on the street. Having learned a bit of English from grammar school, Sanjay was able to effectively communicate with the Americans. Through the use of his limited English, Sanjay was able to provide them with the directions to their local church. The Americans were so incredibly impressed by Sanjay's assistance, that they further inquired about himself and his family. The young boy was certainly not a shy child and without any hesitation, he quickly confessed to them all about the tragedies that unfortunately befell his family. Moved by his heartfelt confession, the Americans acted upon their hearts and enduring faith, and they requested to meet Sanjay's mother immediately. The boy did what he was told and once the Americans saw their living conditions firsthand, they offered them sanctuary at their local church, along with a small room for shelter, food to eat, and water to bath and drink from. Aasha and her children gladly accepted their offer, and then thereafter, they immediately moved into the church on that very same day.

During their stay at the church, Aasha and her family were provided with daily English lessons. Wanting to provide them with more improved future economic opportunities, the church leaders believed that it was imperative for the family to become proficient in the English language, especially for the young children. After studying rigorously for several months, Aasha, along with her children, all became fluent in the English language.

A year later, Aasha was introduced to a local banker, who specialized in micro-loans. For no less than $0.25, but no more than $10.00 U.S. dollars per week, the banker lent money, interest free, to the locals—provided that they could convince him that they were worthy of his investment. At the time, the most common borrowers in their region were farmers. A farmer, who specialized in corn, for example, was required to provide the banker with an itemized list of their expenses and estimated profits. Since the average expense consisted of $1 for seeds and $2 for soil, the farmer stood a chance to earn a profit of corn for $3 per batch, within the span of a given month. Using this projected forecast, the farmer was ultimately expected to make a profit, and in return, they were also expected to return the borrowed $3 loan back to the banker, as a form of repayment for their original loan.

As for Aasha, her trade was in baskets. Basket weaving was a specialized skill that went back several generations within her family, and it was a skill that she knew very well. When she explained her trade specialization to the banker, he offered her a loan for $5; $2 to purchase the straw to weave the baskets and another $3 for the color dye to stain them. For the past month or so, Aasha worked tirelessly to weave all of her baskets. Once they were made, she was absolutely determined to sell out all of her inventory at the market that same month, in order to pay off the banker, once and for all. Ultimately, her goal was to save up enough money to purchase a small home in the city for her family.

Aasha further expressed to John, as to just how grateful she really was to the Americans, the banker and her local government, whose new micro-lending policies in her region helped people like her to overcome poverty. Without such policies, she explained, then Aasha would never have been able to receive such a loan in a more traditional banking system. Under the leadership of their new mayor, her city fought a long and hard battle to implement these new micro-lending policies, in order to help more lower-class families to rise out of poverty and seek entrepreneurships. Lastly, Aasha also revealed to John that her own name in her language, Hindi, meant hope, and it was a name most fitting for her. After her husband's and infant child's death, Aasha was finally hopeful that a better life was now possible for her and her family.

John was incredibly touched by Aasha's tale. As the first and only born son of the Barrett family, John never before truly understood what it meant to experience hardship and to live in poverty. He had certainly read about economic woes from various publications and journals, but he never actually met a real-life person, who lived and experienced it firsthand. Prior to his encounter with Aasha, John lived a rather sheltered life, and he rarely interacted with anyone outside of his own immediate inner circle (which, also happened to be, within the same economic and social class, as he). Aasha was his first acquittance with someone, who came directly from poverty and lived to tell their tale. Her struggles and experiences certainly left a permanent impression and imprint within. Through her honest and heartfelt account, his own heart had been pierced and his eyes opened to the harsh reality of the world.

Compelled by his emotion, John bought all of Aasha's inventory, on the spot. Surprised by his genuine act of generosity, Aasha suddenly began to cry hysterically. In an effort to comfort her, John reached over to pat her shoulders. However, Aasha, instead, threw her arms around and embraced him with a warm hug. She was so incredibly grateful for his kindness, that she reached deep into her pocket, opened his right hand and gave him a special gift. Afterwards, John stared back down at his palm and saw a single white pearl. It was a large white sea pearl, that was also strangely shaped. At first glance, it didn't resemble any jewelry that he had ever seen before. Especially, nothing at all like his own mother's vast jewelry collection.

Joyfully, she praised and complemented him for his sincere kindness. According to Aasha, John, at age fifteen, already had more compassion in his heart than most men, doubled in his age, had or even had the capacity to have. For several weeks, Aasha stood outside in the sun and dry heat, desperately trying to sell her baskets; and in that time, she had only sold a mere total of three out of her nearly thirty baskets. The kindness of John's actions not only provided her with the economic means to now buy a small house for her family, but she also now had the financial funds to repay her loan to the banker.

As Aasha happily smiled at John, she made only one special request: to save the pearl and to bestow it upon his future bride on their wedding day. Although John was touched by her sentimental gesture, he was also a bit hesitant, too. Even though Aasha meant well, John still didn't want to take the pearl away from Aasha, who might later on, change her mind and seek to sell it as income, one day in the near foreseeable future.

"Are you sure?" asked a young John to Aasha.

"I am. This is my desire. The pearl chooses its owner and now its chosen you. It's rightfully yours. When you look at this pearl, please remember the kindness that you bestowed upon me here today. And one day, when the time is right, another person will do the same for you, in return."

"Aasha, thank you. I promise that I will," said John. "But are you certain that you don't want to keep this for your children or to sell it one day later on, for yourself?"

"Not at all. Even in my most destitute of days, I'd never sell this. I simply cannot. For you see, if you sell this, then you lose its blessing. You can only give this pearl away as a gift, with good intentions and a pure heart," she replied.

The shine from the white pearl caught John's eye, and he brought the pearl closer to his eyes for inspection.

"This pearl is very beautiful. How did you come in possession of this? Do you know why this pearl is so strangely and oddly shaped?" asked a curious John.

"It was given to me by my grandmother, right before she died. The pearl is oddly shaped for a reason. My grandmother told me that it's to remind us, that true beauty is found within life's imperfection," Aasha sighed, as she wiped a tear from the corner of her eye.

"When I was living out in the streets," she began, "I was so devastated by my overall situation, that I asked all of heaven as to why fate allowed all of these terrible things to happen to us? I angrily asked, why my husband and baby had to die so unfairly young, while I was left to stay behind to continue to live and suffer in this ongoing misery, here on earth? But, then, when I thought about these things, I also saw the faces of my other children. While looking at them, I saw their smiles; their eyes widened by their excitement to play and their overall, passions for their tiny little lives. Poverty is all that we have ever known; but yet my children are still happy. Finally, it dawned on me, that it was through the imperfection of our life circumstances, that I saw the true beauty of my children. My children smile and laugh every day; yet there is no promise of tomorrow for them. There's no guarantee that they'll have food tomorrow or that we won't die from starvation before this week's end. But yet, they still cherish the sunshine and continue to play outside in the fields with their friends. They play as if tomorrow does not matter, for they are already happy and content with today, living in this very moment. Eventually, when I came to realize this, I finally understood the true message of the pearl. Without suffering, there can be no relief; without sadness, there can be no joy; without darkness, there can be no light. It is through the imperfections, the flaws, the challenges, where the beauty and the light of this world still finds a way to shine. Even if it's limited to only the happy faces of my children, reflected on the pearl's outer surface. And now, I say this, with all of my heart, that through the eyes of my dear children, I also came to discover that my own purpose is to live my life, for however long or short it maybe, in dedication to them. This is what gives me the daily strength to carry on and to move forward. It's the sole reason as to why I continue to make these baskets and to sell them at this market. I do this not for myself, but for my children. Once you discover what or whom you love most in this world, John please dedicate yourself to them or the cause, and never let it or them go."

Throughout his life, John cherished Aasha's wise words and kept the pearl nearby him, at all times. Years later, upon his engagement to Jennifer, he finally took the pearl to a jeweler to have it custom altered to attach to a gold wedding band, along with blue sapphire diamonds that were part of an heirloom, through his late father's ancestral private collection. Taking Aasha's advice to heart, John saved the pearl for his future bride. Furthermore, he even chose the blue sapphire diamonds to accompany the pearl, in remembrance of Aasha's blue sari that she wore on that memorable day. Unfortunately, after Jennifer confessed that she lost the ring; initially, he was greatly saddened by the news. However, he then recalled Aasha's wise message to him, all those years before, that the "pearl chooses its owner." Therefore, if the ring was truly meant for John, then one day, it would find its way back to him, again. If not, then it was meant to bless someone else. The universe in action, as he thought to himself. In the end, this hopeful belief brought much solace and comfort to him.

As John began to gather the baskets, Aasha called for her son, Sanjay, to come and help assist him. Sanjay, who was now eight years old, came quickly running down the street. Upon his arrival, he joined John, as they stacked all of the remaining baskets together, one by one. Having placed a few baskets into his backpack, John carried away the rest within his arms. Meanwhile, Sanjay, placed the remainder of the baskets above his head, and the rest under his arms. Although they were able to gather all of the baskets, John still feared about their transport. Since the hotel was rather far away, he feared that eventually, they would lose their balance, along the way. However, before John could dwell on this matter any further, Aasha quickly bid farewell to them and before he knew it, they were already off on their journey and heading back to his hotel.

However, they didn't travel too far. Midway up the street, Sanjay managed to trip over a small pebble, that was laying along the road. As he fell down onto the dirty street, Sanjoy dropped all of his baskets down onto the dusty floor. Immediately, John swiftly came running to his aid. After pulling the boy back up, John stared at the road ahead and suddenly, he felt a sense of hopelessness. Given the great distance, it was nearly impossible for them to continue on with their long journey, while still carrying all of these baskets. But, as fate would have it, a white cow, wearing a large golden bell, along with a garland made of marigold flowers around its neck and dragging an empty wooden wagon, magically came trotting down the street.

"Look!" exclaimed Sanjay, in pure excitement, as he pointed with his finger straight ahead at the white cow.

Following Sanjay's suggestion, John stared ahead and was amazed to see the glorious white sight standing before him. Never before in his entire life, had he ever seen a white cow. And yet, here it was… a white cow, of all things, conveniently walking itself, right in the middle of a busy Indian street.

"Does he have an owner?" asked John, in bewilderment.

"No, these cows don't owners, they're free. They roam the city, all by themselves. Look, he's trying to help us!" Sanjay shouted, as he began to joyfully jump, up and down, in the street.

To John's surprise, the young boy was right. It was, as if this white cow had been plucked straight out of a fairy tale and magically transported here, to come to their rescue. And somehow, this white cow not only managed to trot on by, but it also parked itself, right in front of them. As impossible as it seemed, John swore that the white cow even signaled to them, by the tilting of its head, to come and jump onto its wagon and follow her lead.

"Is this really happening?" asked John, in amazement.

"Yes!" Sanjay excitingly yelled. "Come on, John. Let's throw these baskets into the wagon and go!"

Within seconds, they each threw all of their baskets into the wagon, hopped on board and then took off. After riding sometime up the street, they eventually arrived to the front entrance to the hotel, where upon, the white cow came to a final and complete stop. Quickly, John and Sanjay hopped off and gathered all of their baskets, as they waved farewell to the white cow. Although John was stunned by what had all just occurred right before his very own eyes, Sanjay was not; for the young boy trusted in his belief that fate, in her purest of forms as a white cow, found her way to help them, in their desperate time of need. Since there really was no other logical explanation, John reluctantly accepted the boy's theory that the mysterious white cow was none other than fate, herself.

Afterwards, John arranged for a taxi to escort Sanjay back to the bazaar. Later on, that same evening, John bestowed the baskets, as gifts to his fellow travelers from his tour group. From that day forward, John decided to pursue a career in the government. Inspired by Aasha's difficult experiences, he too, wanted to help others to live better lives. Since John was clever, smart, charismatic, persuasive and already a world traveler, he decided, on that memorable night, to become a diplomat and to strive to promote universal policies designed to assist and aid people in their greatest need of service, on a global scale.

Upon returning back to the United States after his trip to India, John dedicated himself, wholeheartedly, to his academic studies by learning as many foreign languages as he possibly could, including French, German, Arabic and Turkish, to start. Since he was a natural academic prodigy, he excelled in each and every one of the various subjects that he was enrolled in. By the time John was ready for college, he was already fluent in all four languages, and even started learning a fifth language, Spanish. At college, John studied in the international relations department, where he eventually came to meet retired Ambassador David Lawrence. The two soon became fast friends and due to their mutual bond over traveling, David quickly became his mentor and college advisor. The close relationship forged between them couldn't have come at a better time too; for it was during John's sophomore year in college, that his own father, unexpectedly passed away from a sudden stroke. Although John and his mother, Barbara, were left devastated by their loss, David slowly came to fill in as that missing void of an absent father, and he, the absent son, in both of their lives. In time, David grew to become the surrogate father that John needed in his transition into adulthood. Plus, with David by his side, John had the adequate resources needed to successfully prepare and study for the State Department's rigorous examinations.

By his twenty fifth birthday, John graduated from college with joint Master's degrees in international relations and history. During this time, he also passed the State Department's written and oral examinations, with exceptionally high ranking. As a result, John was not only accepted into the program, but he was also immediately promoted from an incoming freshman diplomat to a high-ranking ambassador, who was going to manage an entire American embassy, along with its staff, all under his wings. Since John was fluent in Arabic, he was also going to replace the outgoing and soon-to-be retired U.S. Ambassador to Egypt. Although the vacancy to this position lasted for several long months, the agency just didn't have enough qualified candidates to fulfill this crucial and critical role by recruiting an Arabic speaker, who specialized in the region. However, once John passed his examinations with flying colors and his background checks cleared, the agency quickly moved to secure him by offering John the position, with his scheduled deployment to the Egypt post to take place, as soon as possible.

At long last, John was more than ready to start his dream career. His checklist was just about done. He got his degrees. Checked. He studied five languages and was fluent in at least four of them. Check. He studied for his exams and passed. Check. He even took etiquette and dancing lessons to better help prepare him for official state dinners and other public events. Check. At this point, the only thing that was outstanding was that of a wife. Realistically, John understood that a young and unmarried ambassador might be perceived by the public to appear as rather immature and weak, especially, by other foreign diplomats. Therefore, to prevent such a negative impression, John was determined to ensure that he was securely married off, before he departed for Egypt to begin his new career. Furthermore, a wife, he thought, could also help serve as both his partner and as a supporter to his new role and mission; while, also at the same time, befriend and interact with the other wives of his fellow diplomats.

Luckily, for John, by this time, he already met Jennifer. They briefly courted for a matter of weeks, before he decided that she was agreeable and suitable enough, for the role of his new wife. Overall, Jennifer was lovely, social, and beautiful. But most importantly, above all else, she came from a normal middle-class and decent family, free from any scandals or drama. Besides, they were amiable with each other, too. He had cared for her, but did he love her? He still didn't have an answer to that. It was still too soon. But in truth, John didn't really understand what love meant, in the first place.

As a man, who dedicated most of his adult life in academic pursuits, he didn't truly comprehend the concept of romantic love. For all the Lord Byron poems and Shakespearean tragedies that sat along the dusty shelves of his home library, they all spoke romantic words that his heart failed to cling onto, for he simply didn't recognize it, nor could he comprehend it. Truly, his heart remained unmoved and untouched by their romantic words. But in contrast, John was a rather serious, logical and practical man, and he knew, at the very least, that he was amiable in his new bride's company and that within itself, was good enough for him. Eventually, with time, he calculated and predicted that their relationship would come to evolve into friendship and from there on, he was certain that it would one day transition into love, or whatever love was meant to be.

However, he, himself, wasn't entirely convinced that his new bride really loved him, either. As a couple, they never once experienced that special spark between them; instead, it was more of a mutual attachment. Secretly, he self-acknowledged that perhaps, Jennifer cared for him, just as he did for her. However, when they first met, Jennifer made it clear to him that she wanted to marry a wealthy suitor, whose elevated economic and social status would help to enshrine her to obtain a more independent and financial free life, in contrast to her own middle-class upbringing. For this condition, John didn't judge her, nor did it bother him, in the very least.

Based upon his own academic studies, marriage, historically, was generally regarded as a business transaction; a union between two families for the further acquisition of wealth, property and kingship. Recalling his own early memory of Aasha's struggles, John knew very well as to just how important economic freedom really was, especially for young women. Since John was able to provide Jennifer with the financial means that she so desperately sought; she in return, promised to remain by his side to support him in his new career. Therefore, for these reasons, John made his formal offer of marriage to her, and she gladly accepted. Since John was already wealthy on his own right, he didn't have the pressure to marry another wealthy suitor. Furthermore, time, was also, ticking away and he needed to marry soon. Therefore, their union was more or less, a marriage of convenience; with Jennifer being at the right place, at the right time. However, in the meantime, he was content with their new relationship and was more than ready to start his new career abroad.

Friday came and went, and so did Saturday, and by Sunday morning, the couple still remained in France. Unfortunately, the storm evolved into an obstacle, that John could no longer wait to self-resolve. No matter the circumstances, he had to be in Egypt come Monday morning, that much he knew. By Sunday afternoon, the storm finally withered down and the sun began to creep out from underneath the clouds. After much wait, John finally decided that now was his ideal chance to leave; and so, he and Jennifer quickly packed their belongings, called for a taxi and headed down to the airport.

But once they arrived to the Nice Airport, a bolt of lightning managed to unexpectedly strike a large palm tree rooted nearby, causing its branch to come crashing down, thereby, destroying a local powerline. Unfortunately, the fallen powerline resulted in a black out, in which the entire Nice airport remained in complete darkness. As a result, all flights, both incoming and outgoing, were postponed and rescheduled to early Monday morning. Furthermore, to limit the excess crowd size, the remaining passengers were asked to leave the airport. This troubled John greatly, for if he waited until tomorrow morning, then he risked the chance of not making it on-time to the Cairo embassy to start his new post.

As a result of his difficult situation, John pondered about their traveling options. Due to his limited time frame, he didn't have many other alternative options. Unfortunately, he didn't have enough time to contact his mother to arrange for a private jet from California, because by the time the private jet would eventually get cleared for departure, his post would have already long begun. Furthermore, he also couldn't rely on the agency sending him a government plane, because his trip to France was due to personal matters (albeit his honeymoon) and not for business. Lastly, he also couldn't opt for a train or ferry boat, because the storm inadvertently ceased all land and marine operations, until Monday morning. Alas, the only feasible alternative remaining was to simply stay close by to the airport and gamble on the next available flight.

Hoping to improve his circumstances, John walked over to the concierge and explained his urgent circumstances to the airport staff. Although all of Sunday's flights were cancelled, there miraculously, was a scheduled midnight flight to Cairo, still available. If they caught the red eye flight, then they were guaranteed to arrive in Cairo by eight o'clock on Monday morning; allowing John a four-hour travel window to commute from between the airport to the embassy. Relieved, John hastily agreed and booked the flight almost immediately.

After securing the tickets, the couple waited at their hotel and then, eventually, they returned back to the airport later on that evening. By midnight, they boarded the plane and lifted off for Egypt. For the next four hours, they flew mid-air at ease, until around four o'clock in the morning precisely, to their surprise, their plane suddenly landed in Istanbul.

"Istanbul? What's the meaning of this?" cried John, confused by this unexpected landing.

According to his previous discussion with the airport staff in Nice, the plane was supposed to be a direct flight from Nice to Cairo. Determined to find answers, John swiftly rang for service. Moments later, a flight attendant arrived to John's cabin; thereupon, he inquired as to why the plane landed in Istanbul and not Cairo. Unfortunately, John was informed that a last-minute change had been made by the airline. Due to the flight being practically empty, the pilot decided to make a stop-over in Istanbul, to serve as a transfer point to pick up more passengers. However, the flight attendant reassured John that he didn't need to change planes, as the plane wasn't expected take off for another two hours.

Disappointed, John sighed out of frustration. Slowly, he was beginning to lose his patience. An extra two hours would push his arrival later onto ten o'clock. Although he'd still have plenty of time to make it to the embassy by noon, he would be cutting it rather close. But since there wasn't anything else that he could do, John decided to sleep it off. If he had to wait, then he might as well get some rest, in the meantime. Hopefully, by the time he awoke again, he'd already be in Cairo. And so, John fluffed up his pillow, pulled up his travel blanket, closed his eyes and fell fast asleep.

Six hours later, John awoke to the sound of Jennifer's voice. At long last, they had finally landed in Egypt. Stretching his arms wide, John stood up and swiftly made his ways out of the plane. Minutes later, after they finished passing through customs, they arrived at the baggage claims for their luggage. Staring at his watch, it was now 10:35 am. They had a little more than an hour to collect all of their belongings and catch a taxi to the embassy. Originally, John requested for an embassy driver to pick them up at the airport; but since this was a last-minute flight, he was unable to coordinate the pick-up. In addition, since most of the staff were already busy preparing for Ambassador Phillips' retirement ceremony, John knew that he was still better off going with a taxi.

Fifteen minutes later, at 10:55 am, the couple continued to wait at the baggage claim, as they watched all of the other passengers from their same flight collect their luggage and leave…except for them. One by one, John watched as all of the various bags and suitcases slid down the carousel. Patiently, he waited for his and Jennifer's brown Louis Vuitton luggage set to arrive, as he watched the other red, blue, green, black and orange colored suitcases circle around the carousel. Sadly, every possible luggage arrived on that darn carousel… except for theirs. Finally, when John was about to lose all hope, their luggage finally came sliding down the carousel. As John reached over to retrieve them, he was relieved. However, once he looked at the conditions of the bags up-close, he noticed that the entire luggage set was now tattered, dirty and even the famous LV monograms were now faded and peeling.

"Our luggage!!" cried Jennifer, in horror. "Oh John, they absolutely ruined our designer bags!!"

Sadly, John agreed with her, for it was true, their luggage was completely destroyed due to the airline's negligence. However, they had no additional time to waste and crying over damaged goods wasn't going to solve anything. Glancing over at his watch, John saw that it was now 11:10 am. Suddenly, he began to panic. He had less than an hour to make it to the embassy. Although he understood Jennifer's justified concerns, at this point, he was willing to buy her the entire Louis Vuitton store the next time she visited, if that guaranteed that he would make it to the embassy on time.

"Come on Jennifer, we need to go now," John pleaded, as he began pulling their damage luggage behind him.

"But John, it's a Louis Vuitton! The airline needs to compensate us for damaging our belongings!" Jennifer angrily demanded.

"Jennifer," began John, as he was starting to grow rather impatient with her.

However, after taking a deep breath, he calmly said, "I understand your concerns, but we really need to leave. But I promise to take you to the nearest Louis Vuitton shop tomorrow, and you can buy whatever you like, as a replacement."

"Really?" replied Jennifer, who was happily surprised by his generous offer. "You, promise?"

"Yes, yes," he said, trying his best to wrap up their conversation, as quickly as possible. "But right now, at this very moment, we really need to run for it!"

With great urgency, they promptly rolled their luggage down the hallway and exited the airport. Soon afterwards, they caught a taxicab, right outside on the curb. While the driver proceeded to load their luggage into the car, John sat down and stared at his watch again. It was now 11:15 am. Finally, he was relieved, for he still had enough time to make it to embassy before noon.

As they entered into the road, John instructed the driver to take them to the nearest U.S. embassy at Tahrir Square. For the next twenty minutes or so, they drove down the streets of Cairo, smoothly. Luckily, the traffic was at a bare minimal and to their advantage, all of the traffic lights were green. After dealing with all of the chaos from this morning, everything was starting to run seamlessly, according to plan. Soon enough, John was going to arrive to the embassy. However, at 11:35 am, the taxi suddenly and unexpectedly, came to a complete and total stop.

"Why are we stopping?" asked John, confused by this new detour.

But within moments, the answer to his very question literally came rolling out. Suddenly, the sound of a loud horn was played. Looking straight ahead, John saw that the taxi stopped right in front of a train track. And right there, in front of him was a huge train headed straight their way!

"It's a train," said the driver, in a calm tone. "We must wait for the train to pass, first."

"How long will this take?" asked John, nervously.

"It depends," replied the driver, not at all concerned about the wait time.

"John—" interrupted Jennifer, "Look at all its carts. This is a long train. It might take a while."

"Sir," asked John, "How long do these types of trains, normally take to pass?"

"I've seen some of these trains carrying well over a hundred carts. Sometimes more. If this train has that many, then it can easily take maybe another thirty to forty minutes to pass, or so," replied the driver.

"Thirty to forty minutes!" exclaimed John. Now, he was officially panicking.

"Yes, especially, if this train is bound for Ethiopia or South Africa. Due to the delays caused by our most recent storm, they might be playing catch up. Why, just a few days ago, our streets were all flooded from the rain. Luckily, it's since cleared up. We've only now reopened all of our local businesses today, in time for today's festival," the driver explained.

"Today's festival?" asked John, who was now, completely surprised and worried about this new revelation.

"Yes, it's Eid al-Fitr," replied the driver.

Overwhelmed by the planning of his trip, John forgot and overlooked that today marked the beginning of the annual Eid al-Fitr holiday. The holiday, known as the Festival of Breaking the Fast, marks the end of the holy month of Ramadan in Islam. For one month, Muslims across the world fast each day during Ramadan, from sunrise to sunset, as commemoration for their prophet Muhammad's first revelation of the Holy Qur'an, the Islamic religious holy book. During this holy month, Muslims worldwide participate in fasting, reflection and prayer. At the end of

Ramadan, Muslims throughout the Islamic world, celebrate Eid al-Fitr at their local communities, often by engaging and participating in very extravagant and lavish gatherings, such as festivals, parties and other street celebrations. And today, of all days, was *the day*.

Looking outside the car window, John saw hundreds of people gather right outside of the streets, preparing to celebrate. With the conclusion of the morning prayers at the mosques, the people were ready to celebrate. Immediately, John glanced down at his watch. It was now 11:40 am. He had twenty minutes left to make it to the embassy.

"Are there any other alternative routes, that we can take to get to the embassy?" asked John, anxiously.

"By car, no. We must wait for the train to pass. But by foot, yes," replied the driver.

"John," spoke Jennifer, "I'm sure the embassy will understand, if we're late."

But John wasn't ready nor willing to accept this as a failure. Today, was his first day in office, and no matter what, he intended to keep his oath. Come hell or high water, he was going to arrive to the embassy by noon, even if it killed him!

Determined to overcome this new challenge, John asked the driver what the distance from the train tracks to the embassy was. Surprisingly, he was told that it was only a few more blocks away, if he continued down the street by foot. Taking a deep breath, John began collecting his thoughts. He needed to strategize. And fast. Given their current dire situation, he knew that he couldn't depend on the taxi any longer. Ultimately, John needed to travel by foot. However, the streets were too crowded and there was absolutely no way, that he was going to be able to walk fast enough to push through that sea of people.

After much thought, John concluded that he needed something that allowed him to travel by street, yet quick enough to move faster than his own two feet. Quickly, John scanned the streets, searching for either a bike, or a vespa, or a scooter, or a skateboard or even roller skates. Anything that had wheels; but alas, he saw neither. Sadly, John was right about to lose hope, when suddenly, right before his eyes, he saw the solution to his dilemma: A white camel.

Standing at the corner of the street, was a white camel. The tall, hairy beast stood under the bright, burning sun, while it was busy chewing dried grass within its hungry mouth. Carefully, John observed the animal from afar. The camel was tied to a wooden fence and standing nearby, was its' owner, a shepherd. Curious enough, a picture booth was adjacent to the camel, making it appear that this particular camel was a popular tourist attraction. But today, the streets were filled with locals, not tourists. Determined to seize this rare but amazing opportunity, John swiftly acted upon his impulse and swiftly, he jumped right out of the car and ran as fast as he could directly over to the shepherd.

When John finally reached the shepherd's side, he asked him if he could temporarily borrow his camel. At first, the shepherd didn't appear to understand much English, so John quickly reverted to Arabic to communicate with him. Once again, John asked if he could borrow the camel to reach his destination, which was only a few blocks away; however, the shepherd was reluctant to accept his offer. Hoping to persuade him otherwise, John reached into his shirt pocket and pulled out a $100 U.S. dollar bill. Afterwards, he waved the currency to the shepherd and much to his relief, the shepherd finally accepted his bribe. Thereafter, the shepherd moved to untie the camel from the wooden fence and then, he handed the rope over to John.

Now, holding the camel and rope tightly within his hands, John returned back to the taxi and called for Jennifer to join him. Meanwhile, Jennifer, who was still seated inside of the taxi, looked straight ahead at the camel from outside her window, and immediately, she was left appalled and disgusted by the hideous sight before her. Why, the mere sight of the camel, who was covered in dirt, along with mud all over its feet, made her cringe. Truly, the beastly animal was filthy and smelled of pure musk! Although Jennifer greatly sympathized with John's desperation; but at the same time, this really was too much for her!

Currently, as it stood, her honeymoon was already a disaster. Due to the storm, she spent most of her trip stuck in-doors, rather than enjoying the beautiful sunshine at the beach, as she had originally intended to do.

Furthermore, to add more insult to injury, the power outage was yet another irritating matter. Not to mention, her new Louis Vuitton luggage was absolutely destroyed by the incompetent airport staff! However, Jennifer was willing overlook all of these misfortunates; but alas, the camel was truly the last straw! While John was more than welcomed to travel by camel, for that was his own prerogative; Jennifer, however, had no intention of joining him, under any circumstances!

"John, if you don't mind, I rather not," she replied harshly and coldly.

"Ride the camel, if you like, but I'm staying here in the taxi. Once the traffic clears, I can just meet you at the embassy."

"Absolutely not," John remarked. "You're a foreigner in a new country, and you don't even speak a word of the local language. As a gentleman and for your own safety, I can't leave you here, alone and unattended, with a good conscience. Please leave the bags in the car, and the taxi driver can drop them off at the embassy. But you, out now!"

Although Jennifer dreaded the very thought of touching that dirty and disguising animal; sadly, she had to agree that he was unfortunately right. It was true, she was a foreigner in a new country, and she didn't understand the local language, at all. Not a single word. Even though she hated the prospect of riding this camel, but given her limited options, she was going to have to suck it up and make John pay for it later.

"Alright, alright already, I'm coming," said Jennifer, as she reluctantly climbed out of the car.

But as she began walking towards him, her black Christian Louboutin's began to experience some difficulty gripping onto the uneven street pavements. Without taking no more than three steps, she suddenly lost all of her balance. Within seconds, her left shoe's heel snapped and completely detached itself from its sole.

"Oh my God!" exclaimed Jennifer, as she quickly fell, slamming down hard onto the ground.

Immediately, John ran towards her, while dragging the camel right behind him.

"Are you alright?" he asked, as he offered to help her back up and searched to see if she had any injuries.

However, Jennifer quickly got up on her own and dusted herself off. Fortunately, she had only a few minor scratches, here and there; but it was nothing that she couldn't handle. But then, once she saw the condition of her beloved shoe, she suddenly began to cry hysterically.

"Are you hurt?" asked John, now gravely concerned that she might be indeed injured, after all.

"My shoe!!!!" shouted Jennifer, loudly.

Looking down, John saw that she was indeed, referring to the broken heel of her beloved shoe. Realizing that her cries were not of pain, but of vain; John glanced back down at his watch. It was now 11:49 am. He now had exactly eleven minutes to make it to the embassy.

"Jennifer," spoke John softly, "You have a choice. Either, I break the second heel to the other shoe, so that you can continue to walk in these as flats; or, you can take both shoes off yourself and walk barefoot. It's your choice."

"What?" gasped Jennifer, in bloody horror. "John, do you realize that these are Christian Louboutin shoes? As in, the Christian Louboutin! Why, it would be a crime against humanity to mutilate such a beloved pair of shoes!"

Now, John was growing impatient and was almost at his wits ends. Sadly, they could no longer afford to waste any more time. One way or another, John needed to motivate Jennifer to carry on and fast. Realizing as to just how valuable and important her shoes were to her, he promised that if she agreed to continue on this path with him, then he would buy her a dozen more pairs of Christian Louboutin shoes. Miraculously, his bribe worked and she immediately stopped crying. And then, to his delight, she quickly removed her shoes and together, they both hopped onto the one humped camel.

"Do you even know how to ride a camel?" asked Jennifer, with a raised brow.

"Sure, I do. Why, they're just like horses," replied John, perhaps, a bit too confidently.

Back in California, John was an excellent equestrian, with several years of practice riding prestigious and well breed horses. Much to John's credit, he naturally, presumed that riding horses and camels were one in the same. But sadly, dear reader, he couldn't have been more wrong!

Finally, as John grabbed hold of the camel's strap, he gently tapped the camel to signal their departure. But unfortunately, the camel made no such attempt to move. Determined to try again, John tapped for a second time and again, no movement. Staring at his watch, it was now 11:52 am. He still had eight minutes to go.

Meanwhile, as John was busy persuading the camel to depart upfront, Jennifer, sat behind at the camel's back rear and was feeling rather uncomfortable and miserable, for she greatly dreaded this upcoming ride. Firstly, the camel smelled absolutely terrible. Secondly, the animal's odd shape, felt so incredibly harsh against her soft and delicate body. Thirdly and lastly, since she was seated on the camel's behind, she could also feel the camel's tail, as it swung back and forth. However, the only glimmer of hope that she held onto was the prospect of buying her new pairs of Christian Louboutin shoes. And so, Jennifer closed her eyes, as she wrapped both of her arms around John's chest and hung on for dear life!

By 11:53 am, John was still determined to make the camel move. After his second attempt failed, he then put more force as he whipped the camel's strap for a third time, and as luck would have it, this time it worked! Almost immediately, the camel quickly jolted down the street and pushed through the busy crowd. In less than a minute, the camel managed to travel in full lightning speed across, and was only a few buildings away from the embassy. As the camel continued traveling down, crowds soon gathered and watched on in amazement, as John led the animal to the gates of the American embassy.

At 11:58 am, Ambassador Terrance Phillips had already given his farewell speech at his retirement party. By now, he finished cutting and serving his cake, and was just about to take his first bite of his German chocolate cake, when suddenly and unexpectedly, he was interrupted by a loud roar of cheers and applauds coming from both within the embassy's compounds and outside of the embassy's gate. Looking straight ahead, Ambassador Phillips saw a young man and woman on a camel, and standing right in front of the embassy gate, waiting to be let inside. Both were professionally dressed, with the man wearing a suit and the woman a dress. Suddenly, it then occurred to Terrance that his successor, Mr. John Barrett, hadn't yet arrived to his party.

"My God!" exclaimed Terrance. "Is this him?"

At precisely 11:58 am, not a minute before nor a minute after, John arrived to the embassy by camel…and on time. Alas, he did it! As he jumped off the camel and helped Jennifer down, another crowd from the festival formed, right across the street, and began cheering, whistling and clapping at them. Soon afterwards, the embassy gates opened and the staff also came rushing out towards him, all cheering and clapping along the way. Suddenly, John realized that his desperate attempts to make it to the embassy on-time, was somehow and miraculously, perceived to be part of an entertainment performance; albeit, his grand entrance into the embassy. Not wanting to disappoint, John decided to humor the crowd, and so, he smiled and gave a bow. But Jennifer, on the other hand, did not smile, nor wait for him, either. Instead, she quickly walked right pass him and escorted herself through the embassy gate, while murmuring under her breath "…a camel is definitely NOT the same as a horse…"

Somehow, John managed to overhear her, but rather than confronting her, he simply released a large laugh from deep within his belly. It was comical after all! Not everyone arrives to their first day on the job by camel, and he had waited all these years to get here, too. It felt like a dream. Blissfully, John pinched himself, to see if this was real. It was. As John prepared to walk through the embassy's gate, he looked up into the sky and saw a faint rainbow shining down on him from up above a white cloud. At long last, he thought, the long storm had finally passed. And he was right too… but only with regards to the weather.

Chapter 6

While John toured his new office and building, Jennifer sat in the waiting room and was assisted by two young female interns. Upon her arrival, the interns gave her a spare pair of slippers, along with an empty bag to keep her damaged Christian Louboutin's in. Once Jennifer was settled in, they offered her a glass of water, which she gladly accepted. After her first sip, she placed her glass on the table. Afterwards, Jennifer pulled a compact mirror out from her Chanel purse, to tidy up her appearance. The camel ride had been rough. She still had specs and traces of dust, all scattered about throughout her clothes. There were even strands of her precious hair that had fallen right out from her bun. Sadly, her face had a bit of sunburn, and her lipstick was smeared across her lips.

Attempting to make herself more presentable, Jennifer quickly powdered her face to cover up the sunburn, tucked her loose strands of hair back into her bun, and wiped away her old lipstick and reapplied a fresh new coat. Then, she reached back into her purse, pulled out one of her spare pair of gold earrings and then, put them on. Finally, she took a sniff of herself. Yuck! She actually smelled like that horrid camel! This was unacceptable! Hoping to kill that dreadful camel scent, Jennifer reached back into her purse, pulled out her small traveling Chanel number 5 perfume bottle and sprayed a few sprints across her neck and body. Meanwhile, the two young interns just stared at her, with awe and amazement. However, Jennifer, on the other hand, simply didn't appreciate, nor cared for this unwanted attention. Having spent the past ten hours traveling by air, car and camel, Jennifer was extremely tired, and she certainly, wasn't in the mood on entertaining anyone, other than herself.

"Is there a reason, as to why you two are staring at me?" asked Jennifer, as she slammed shut her compact.

The compact closed so abruptly, that it actually startled the two young interns, as they awoke from their daydreaming and blushed from embarrassment.

"We're sorry," replied the first intern. "We didn't mean to stare. We're just so amazed, as to how you and the new ambassador arrived to our embassy."

"Yes," replied the second intern. "We've never seen such a grand entrance!"

"It was just so… so… romantic!" exclaimed both interns.

Remarkably, Jennifer found this hard to believe. It was ironic that these two young ladies found their camel ride so romantic, when she, the ultimate romantic seeker herself, didn't find it romantic, at all. In fact, it was far from it. Rather, Jennifer found it to be silly, irritable, embarrassing, a nuisance and if it hadn't been for the prospect of acquiring her new Christian Louboutin shoes, then she would be still waiting comfortably inside of that taxi.

"You and your husband must be madly in love," sighed the second intern.

Dissatisfied by their unwanted attention, Jennifer quickly put her black sunglasses on, grabbed her belongings and then, rose up from her chair. After all, it was a long and tiring day, and she was simply too exhausted to entertain their lingering host of questions.

"Yes, my husband and I are madly in love," she replied coldly.

"Now, if you don't mind," she said, as she pushed the ladies aside and walked past them. "Do tell my husband that I'll be waiting for him in the limo. Now, direct me to the driver."

Upon her command, the two ladies immediately escorted Jennifer outside and over to her limo. While Jennifer waited for John, she pondered about her decision to marry. Did she make a mistake? Even though she was married for only but a few days thus far; but somehow, her married life was already moving along in a different direction, than what she originally had imagined. Although her honeymoon started out promising, with her acquiring a new ring and enjoying a romantic getaway trip to the French Rivera, the remainder of their time together was dreadful! Sadly, the storm forced her to confront and acknowledge that once all of the romantic dinners and parties were over, things weren't as she hoped it to be. To her surprise, when left alone in his private company, Jennifer noted that they really had very little to nothing to say to each other. Tragically, Jennifer failed to foresee this quality, prior to her marriage. However, with the aftermath of the storm, she was forced to unfortunately recognize her own incompatibility with her new husband.

This revelation came to her during the storm, while they were forced to shelter-in-place. When they weren't making love, Jennifer realized that they just didn't have much to talk about, afterwards. While their lovemaking was decent; afterwards, it was just followed by a long period of silence. In an effort to break the quiet and awkward mood, they mutually agreed to watch television; however, they couldn't even agree as to which programs to watch. While John opted for biographies, documentaries and the news, Jennifer wanted to watch the fashion channel, celebrity gossip shows and soap operas. Since neither party could decide on which program to watch together, they opted to revert their attention over to their streaming accounts. However, this too, proved problematic. While Jennifer's queue was filled with romantic comedies, John's queue was all foreign cinemas. Since neither of them were willing to compromise on the evening feature, they decided to turn to their tablets, instead. Unfortunately, this also served as yet another roadblock for their evening, because their tablets didn't sync either: Jennifer's tablet was mainly retail shopping apps, while John's were all e-books and the news. In the end, the couple chose to each do their own activities, independently. While John stayed inside of their hotel room to read his history books about antiquity, Jennifer visited the hotel spa and gym, all by herself.

Out of frustration, Jennifer sighed. It was still too early to evaluate her marriage. After all, she had only just arrived to Cairo, after a long journey and now, she was tired. For now, she thought, all that mattered was the fact, that she married well and as a result, she was about to start her new glamorous and privileged life. Just like her favorite movie star icons, she too, was going to wear all of her favorite designer clothing, including Chanel, Versace, Gucci and Louis Vuitton. Also, she was the new ambassador's wife, the first lady to this embassy. In a few weeks' time, she was going to start hosting official state dinners, attend exclusive parties, mingle with important people, and most importantly, she wasn't going to work for another day, for the rest of her life. Indeed, her future was bright; but yet, at the same time, it was also sealed. Finite. Predictable.

Contemplating about her unknown future, her heart, suddenly, felt empty. For some reason, there was a missing void starting to grow in there. Sadly, Jennifer didn't seem to understand as to why this was. Oh, why didn't she feel this way, before her marriage?

Looking back, Jennifer came to the realization that courtship and marriage, were really two different realities. At the time, when she first dated John, their lives primarily revolved around their romantic escapades. But now, with the honeymoon over, her new reality was slowly settling in; and because of this, she wondered as to how the rest of her life, from here on out, was going to pan out. And this very thought, made her dreadfully nervous.

A few minutes later, John arrived and joined her in the limo. Since the mansion was only down the street from the embassy, the ride was rather short. Curious, Jennifer inquired as to why that was and to his credit, John explained that the agency had a policy that required diplomats and their families, along with their staff, to live in close proximity to the embassy, in the event of an evacuation, disaster relief, war or any other local or international emergencies. Furthermore, he also explained that the mansion was a further extension of the embassy and was considered as part of government property, owned, operated and maintained by the U.S. federal government and was tax-payer funded.

"Think of it, as our version of the white house," he said, with a wink and a smile.

As soon as the limo pulled up to the front gates to the estate, Jennifer was left memorized by the stunning sight before her eyes. With white columns standing tall, the estate, along with its mansion appeared to be an old Victorian building, which sat above on a tiny green hill. In the front of the mansion, were hundreds of newly blossomed and brightly colored crimson red roses. The roses were so incredibly dark and vivid, that they appeared more violet, than red; and amazingly enough, the roses managed to cover the entire property, from all four corners of the compound.

"It's so beautiful," Jennifer remarked, in amazement.

"Why don't you go ahead and take a look," said John, as they pulled up to the driveway and he stepped out of their limo.

"Do you mind, if I join you later on, for dinner?" asked Jennifer, who was by now, already outside in the front garden, and busy smelling one of the crimson red roses, nearby.

"Not at all. Take your time. In the meantime, I'll take care of these bags and see you later this evening. But Jennifer, whenever you decide to enter the mansion, please have one of the staff give you a formal tour of the estate," he said.

Soon afterwards, John left with their belongings, while Jennifer remained behind in the garden to smell and admire the roses in peace and solitude. As she sniffed the red rose, she immediately recognized as to just how truly wonderous its scent really was. Surprisingly, there was a rather unique and unusual aroma, that was unlike any scent that she had ever encountered before. The scent was innocent yet mature; sweet yet bitter; and desirable yet naughty. It was, by far, the most exotic and rarest of scents. Sadly, it failed to match any other similar fragrance from her own personal perfume collection. No, she thought, a decoy perfume wasn't possible. It was truly one of a kind.

After smelling its delightful scent, she then moved on to admire its overall beauty. The color was so vivid, bright and intense, that the petals were closer to silk or velvet, than it was to a flower. Closing her eyes, Jennifer peacefully listened to her surrounding environment. Located on private land, the mansion sat in a quiet part of town and was otherwise, exclusively secluded. Wonderfully, it was calm, serene and peaceful.

Having admired the rose for far too long, Jennifer quickly reopened her eyes. Admiration, she thought, meant nothing if she couldn't physically touch it for herself. And so, without a second opposing thought, Jennifer extended her hands outwards and towards the rose bush and then, she sought to take possession of it. Miraculously, she was almost nearly successful on plucking the rose from right out of its bush, too; when alas, she unfortunately managed to prick her right index finger against a large but sharp thorn, located on the outer rid of rose's stem.

"Ouch," screamed Jennifer, as the thorn sharply pierced into her delicate and soft skin.

Quickly releasing her tight grip on the rose, Jennifer promptly placed her hand down to her chest. As she looked to see the sore, she noticed the thick red blood streaming down from her index finger and flowing downwards onto her hand.

"Madame Barrett!" exclaimed a woman from afar.

Immediately, Jennifer turned behind and saw an elderly woman in her early sixties, soon approaching her. She was elegantly dressed in a seafoam green suit, with her short blonde hair neatly arranged and wearing a full set of makeup. To Jennifer's amazement, the woman looked like an older version of herself.

"Madame Barrett," said the woman, again.

But as she spoke, she immediately noticed the blood streaming down Jennifer's hand. "Madame, are you hurt?" she inquired, concerningly.

"I seem to have pricked my finger, right on this rose bush," replied Jennifer. "I was just admiring these roses, and so, naturally, I wanted to pick one for myself."

"Ah, I see," replied the woman. "They are indeed very beautiful roses. Perhaps, one of the most beautiful flowers that we have around here at the estate. Let me have a look at your hand."

Following her command, Jennifer extended her hand forward. Swiftly, the woman quickly grabbed hold of it and began inspecting her wound.

"Aww, that's a nasty prick," said the woman, in a heavy French accent. "Not to worry, I do have a handkerchief in my pocket, that should take care of this matter."

Pulling the handkerchief out from her pocket, the woman promptly wrapped it around Jennifer's finger. Upon doing so, it immediately stopped the bleeding; however, the dry blood left a lingering stain across Jennifer's palm. Noticing the dry blood, the woman reached into her other pocket and then, she pulled out a second handkerchief to wipe away the remaining stain.

"Thank you," said Jennifer, who was most gracious for the woman's assistance.

"You're welcome, Madame Barrett," said the woman. "By the way, my name's Gloria Renaud. I work here at the embassy. From now on, we'll be working closely together."

"It's very nice to meet you, Mrs. Renaud," replied Jennifer.

"Please, call me Gloria," she said.

"Alright, Gloria," Jennifer corrected.

For a long somber moment, the women peacefully and quietly admired the roses. Finally, after much silence, Gloria said, "I don't blame you for trying to capture it. You know, they grow them here, in order to provide the estate with some extra privacy and security. But I, too, must admit, that I'm also guilty of admiring these roses, too, in my own special way. Every time I pass by this garden, I always wonder how they always seem to remain ever-so lovely and beautiful, all year round. I, too, have been tempted to pick one for myself. However, once I get close enough to capture it, I also catch a glimpse of their thorns, and then, I'm reminded that sometimes, in life, things are better meant to be admired from afar. Wouldn't you agree, Madame Barrett?"

"I suppose you're right," Jennifer agreed, as she now felt almost regretful for having tried to do so herself, only just a short while ago.

"But, with that said," Gloria continued, "Over the years, I also have learned that if one wants a rose…"

And then, ever-so slowly, Gloria walked over and stood right in front of the very same rose that Jennifer had previously attempted to pick. While staring directly into Jennifer's eyes, she said, "then one must learn how to pick it *correctly*."

Intrigued by her unusual prolonged enunciation of the word "correctly," Jennifer asked, "And how does one do that?"

"Do you really care to know?" asked Gloria, in return, with a distinctive smile.

"Yes, I think I do," replied Jennifer, boldly and confidently.

"Alright, I shall tell you. But first, do you know how to play chess?"

"No, I do not," replied Jennifer, in all honestly. "I must admit, I've never really been interested in playing 'games,' for I personally feel that they're a total waste of time."

"Oh, that's such a shame Madame Barrett," replied Gloria, disappointed by her admission. "Perhaps, once we become more acquainted, then I can persuade you, otherwise."

"Perhaps," Jennifer retorted. But, she, of course, was only merely being polite. Jennifer knew who she was and no matter the circumstances, her opinion wasn't going to change. Not even for games.

"In either case, to pick the rose properly, then one needs to understand three rules," explained Gloria. "Rule number one, understand your limitation. In order for me to acquire this rose…this very same rose, that you, yourself, tried to pick, right before I arrived here out in the garden, then one must first acknowledge that they will never obtain this rose directly, because it is protected by several layers. Now, I do realize that you aren't familiar with the game of chess, but if you were, then you could say that our rose is equivalent to the queen. And just as the queen is protected by several pawns, so is our rose. Furthermore, our rose is protected not only by all the thorns that encircles it, but also by the other neighboring roses, as well; such as the surrounding leaves, shrubs, insects and even the very rosebush itself, on which, this rose lives, grows and thrives upon."

"You do have a point," interrupted Jennifer.

"Rule number two," continued Gloria, "One must always locate the rose's thorn or thorns, ahead of time. In other words, you must uncover the rose's defense mechanism. I, must ask myself, that apart from the obvious thorns seen from the outer surface, are there any other hidden obstacles behind the petals? Are there any new tiny sprouted pricks of thorns emerging and ready to bloom? Madame Barrett, once you know where these thorns lie, then you will be privy to the advanced knowledge on knowing how to stay away from them."

"How interesting," Jennifer acknowledged.

"Finally, the third and final rule, and perhaps, the most important rule of all: once you discover the rose's weakness, you must attack. As you can see, your rose cannot be plucked from its front, for there is a very large and sharp thorn blocking its path. I, presume, that this must have been the very same thorn that pricked your finger from earlier. Furthermore, the rose also cannot be plucked from its behind, for there, most likely, is yet another hidden thorn," explained Gloria, as she simultaneously, pulled a pencil out from her pocket.

Then, within the blink of an eye, Gloria, while using her pencil to press down against the back petals, quickly exposed a hidden thorn, located directly beneath it.

"How did you know that was going to be there?" gasped Jennifer, upon seeing the hidden thorn.

"From experience, Madame Barrett," replied Gloria, with a confident smile. Pointing to the bottom stem, she said, "You can only pick it here, at the bottom, in which, I prefer to call it the rose's Achilles' heel."

Suddenly, Gloria quickly snapped the rose off from the bush with her bare hands, and gave the flower directly over to Jennifer. Needless to say, Gloria's fingers and hands were free from any harm nor injury.

"Gloria, that was amazing! I must admit, that was rather clever of you!" exclaimed Jennifer, in admiration.

At long last, Jennifer took possession of the rose. As she stared and admired the rose's beauty, now safely tucked away in her hand, she was overjoyed; as if she had finally won her first victory in battle. However, her joy was short lived; for she soon acknowledged, that out of the hundreds of other roses, which also grew in the garden, she had only but one. Eventually, with time, this single rose would wither away and perish. Alas, Jennifer realized that what she needed, instead, was an army of roses. A rose bouquet of her very own. Although she, herself, was never a fan of board games, Jennifer understood that maybe…just maybe…learning how to play the game of chess wouldn't be such a bad idea, after all. After all, she didn't need to be an expert chess player, she just needed to, at the very least, learn how to protect the queen; aka, herself.

Gloria, having trained many government representatives and their families over the years, so many that even Gloria, herself, lost count, understood Jennifer's reaction. As she smiled at Jennifer, she said, "Follow me into the mansion Madame Barrett, there's much for you to learn."

Chapter 7

Once Jennifer entered into the mansion, she was immediately transfixed by the stunning beauty surrounding her new home. For as beautiful as the mansion's exteriors were from the outside, the interior was far more exquisite in comparison— almost palace like. While standing in the grand foyer, she carefully observed the freshly painted white walls, with matching marbled floors. In the center of the room, was a set of two identical spiral staircases. The property had two separate floors, along with plenty of French styled windows strategically placed all throughout the mansion; which in return, managed to capture all of the natural light from the garden.

Much to her surprise, when Jennifer spun around, she quickly noticed that her new home was already pre-furnished. Throughout the mansion, there were complete sets of furniture, including sofas, chairs, tables and artwork. Carefully, they were all meticulously prearranged, starting from the first floor to right above the staircase, and leading up into the second floor. Furthermore, directly across from where she stood, there was a statue of Cleopatra and a portrait of King Tut.

"Is this house already furnished and decorated?" asked Jennifer, in surprise.

"But of course, Madame Barrett. We've been expecting you and the new ambassador for weeks now, so we've been busy preparing," replied Gloria, as a matter of fact.

Out of disappointment, Jennifer sighed to herself. As a new wife, she was looking forward to decorating her new home. In fact, Jennifer was so excited about this very task, that she even asked her wedding planner, Celeste, to serve as her new interior decorator for this property. However, it seemed that Jennifer's plans were premature, for Gloria had already completed the task without her.

Glancing across the room, Jennifer saw more Egyptian artifacts. Apart from the Cleopatra statue and King Tut portrait, there were also scarab figurines and hanging scrolls, all written in the Arabic script. The décor was, needless to say, an acquired taste. Sadly, it was a style that she, herself, would never have chosen for her guest house, let alone, her own primary residence.

"Is there a reason, as to why there's so many…Egyptian artifacts, in here?" Jennifer inquired, as she was secretly annoyed by all of the unorthodox and distasteful home décor.

"Madame Barrett, we're in Egypt," replied Gloria, in a very stern and strict matter, as if her one sentence response perfectly summed it up best.

"Most importantly," she emphasized, "It's part of the agency's protocol. As you will come to learn, all embassies are expected to reflect the cultural and historical décor of our local host country. It's what we, in the embassy, refer to as 'promoting friendly relations amongst nations.'"

"I see. Well, that's rather unfortunate," replied Jennifer, in all earnest. "I must admit, I was previously looking forward to decorating this mansion, myself."

"Oh, not to worry Madame Barrett," interrupted Gloria, cautiously. "You will have many other opportunities to do lots of other things. Many, many other opportunities, I dare say. In fact, we're having an upcoming state dinner soon. Perhaps, you should coordinate your own outfits by establishing a new wardrobe for yourself. We have some of the best designers in the world, who work for us."

"I would very much like that!" exclaimed Jennifer, excitingly.

Although Jennifer might have lost her opportunity to decorate the mansion, creating a brand-new wardrobe removed any other reservations that she previously might have had.

"Splendid!" exclaimed Gloria, with much relief. "In that case, let me give you a brief tour of the mansion and then, show you to your room."

Having agreed to her offer, Gloria proceeded to give Jennifer a tour of the first floor, including the parlor, the kitchen, the dining room and a few of the offices. After viewing the first-floor interior, Gloria briefly showed Jennifer the backyard. Finally, she escorted her upstairs onto the second floor, to tour the remaining bedrooms.

"The second floor is primarily reserved solely for the bedrooms," Gloria began. "Naturally, you'll be assigned your own private chamber and wing. However, given that you and the ambassador are newlyweds, we took the liberty to deliver your belongings into his bedroom. But if you prefer, we can later relocate them into your own private quarters, instead."

"Let's keep my belongings there for now, but on a temporary basis. However, moving forward, I prefer to keep my belongings inside of my bedroom, as I do enjoy maintaining my own personal space," replied Jennifer, directly.

"But of course, a lady is entitled to do as she wishes, based upon her own discretion. However, if, for whatever reason, you decide that your assigned room is not of your liking, then you're most welcomed to take another bedroom, of your own choice," Gloria added.

"Gloria, exactly how many rooms are there?" asked Jennifer, who was now, most curious about the precise sizing of the mansion.

"On the first floor alone, there are twenty bedrooms," replied Gloria. "And another additional twenty used primarily for offices and staffing rooms, excluding the kitchen, dining room and parlors. But on the second floor, we have about forty."

"My God, this is a hotel!" exclaimed Jennifer, in amazement.

"Yes, it rather is," laughed Gloria. "In any case, Madame Barrett, your room is down the hall and on the right. But before, I bid you farewell, the chef conveys that dinner begins promptly at five o'clock this evening. Lastly, we are scheduled for a meeting tomorrow morning, at precisely ten o'clock. In that time, I will formally introduce you to the rest of the staff and provide you with further instructions."

After settling into her new bedroom, Jennifer returned back downstairs to meet John for dinner. As she entered the dining room, she was met by the butler, Eton, who was a tall, balding man, and in his late seventies. Promptly, Eton escorted her over to the main table and seated her accordingly to tradition; with John at the head of the table and Jennifer by his right side. The dining room was an extravagantly large and spacious space, with white walls and matching marbled floors. Similar to the rest of the mansion, the room was also covered with local Egyptian décor. According to Eton, the room has mostly been used to serve as the primary location for the embassy's official state dinners. And in the center of the room, was a tall and ancient looking, white colored grandfather clock. Based on its appearance, the clock seemed to have been made from solid oak wood, adorned with golden dials and a matching golden pendulum, which continuously swung back and forth.

Once the clock stroke precisely at five o'clock, Eton formally announced their dinner menu. In celebration of the Egyptian culture, the menu's primary entrée was a local Egyptian dish consisting of chicken kebab, served with sides of wild rice pilaf, tomato and cucumber salad, lentil soup and red wine. As Eton poured the wine into Jennifer's glass, she managed to take a peek at the bottle and noticed the Barrett & Son label listed right there.

"It's a complementary gift from my mother," spoke John, who just so happened to catch Jennifer's spying eye from the corner of his.

"Your mother ceases to run out of inventory for her endless collection of fine wines," replied Jennifer, sarcastically. "Perhaps, next time, she can send us a bottle of Dom Perignon, for a change?"

"Wine from a competitor? Come now, Jennifer, we both very well know that my mother would never do that. Why, she takes a lot of pride in our family's business. After all, it's part of heritage," replied John, laughing.

Although Jennifer wasn't amused by his answer, she kept her silence. After their recent long journey and travels, she decided that ultimately, she would much rather sit peacefully and enjoy her wine, than to instead, further discuss about Barbara and her ever-annoying and growing wine collection.

"Cheer up, Jennifer. We're in Cairo, after all. Let's toast to our new beginnings, here in Egypt!" exclaimed John, happily, as he took his very first sip of wine.

However, Jennifer, who wasn't as equally joyfully as he, tried her best to fake a smile, as she reluctantly joined him in and took a sip of her wine.

"How was your afternoon?" asked John, attempting to sooth the current gloomy mood at the table.

"Well, Gloria gave me a brief tour of the mansion and garden. It is a lovely estate, but…" she began.

"But what?" asked John, who was, at that moment, now concerned that something was troubling her.

"John, I can't help but be distracted by all of this Egyptian décor. I mean, I do understand that the mansion's décor should reflect the cultural values of the host country, but at the same time, are we archeologists? Honestly, I find all of this a bit too much! While I can understand the acquisition of a few minor native art pieces, but some of these items truly belongs to a museum. They are, without a doubt, simply too graphic and vulgar, even for my taste. For example," began Jennifer, as she reached over for her steak knife and then pointed in the direction of a statue, located right at the front entrance of the room. "Is this necessary? Must we really stare at this, as we eat?"

Following the pointed direction of her steak knife, John looked ahead and saw that standing across from them, were clay statues of a very naked Cleopatra and Mark Antony. The famous lovers were lumped together and engaged in a rather enticing embrace.

Humored by her innocent annoyance, John laughed aloud and said, "It's only art Jennifer, don't take it too seriously. They're just cultural icons, that's all."

"But naked? Seriously, this isn't something that I want to stare at, while I eat," replied Jennifer, who, unlike John, wasn't at all humored or entertained by such a dreadful sight.

"If it bothers you that much, then why don't you discuss this matter with Gloria. Perhaps, she can help you," John suggested, as he took another sip of his wine.

"Actually, I might just do that," Jennifer agreed. "Anyways, I have a meeting with her tomorrow, so I'll bring it up then."

"Good, so now that this matter is settled, let's move on and discuss about my day..." began John, as his entire face beamed with pure excitement and delight.

While John enthusiastically shared about his day, starting with his tour of his office and building, to meeting with his new staff and learning about his upcoming and exciting new missions, Jennifer was not an equally excited listener. Sadly, within mere seconds of his discussion, she soon found herself disengaged with the entire conversation. As John continued on with his story, Jennifer's mind began to wander off. As he spoke, she thought about her own to do list, including what she was going to wear to tomorrow's meeting and how she was going to redecorate the mansion. And tragically, the more he spoke, the more she stared straight ahead at the grandfather clock right across from her and watched as the clock's busy dial swung back and forth, in an endless cycle…that was sadly, far more entertaining than her own current engagement.

Unfortunately, for Jennifer, it was only half past five o'clock. Thus far, they had only been recently served their first appetizer, consisting of warm soup. Sadly, there was still their main entrée and dessert left to go.

As she pretended to actively listen, Jennifer forced a smile. Although John was the perfect gentleman in public, in private, she found his conversations a bit dull, unexciting and dare she admit it, rather…well…boring. Sadly, she failed to find any of his stories interesting or compelling, at all. After a long while of forcing her fakest of smiles, Jennifer accidentally, released an unexpected honest yawn.

But rather than being offended, John simply said, "Jennifer, you must be tired. Why don't we call it a night and retire to upstairs?"

"That's an excellent idea," Jennifer quickly agreed, as she accidentally yawned, once more. And with that cue, the couple excused themselves from dinner and went upstairs to retire for their evening.

The next morning, Jennifer awoke and found herself alone in their bedroom. By now, John, the early bird, was already long gone and away busy at work. Since Jennifer was going to have a busy day of her own, she decided to take a shower and get dressed. As a milestone to her first day on duty, Jennifer wanted to make a positive and powerful first impression. As the new wife to a wealthy and powerful man, Jennifer intended to show the rest of the world that she was an equally attractive, beautiful, well-dressed, ravishing, sexy, confident and strong partner.

After curling her hair, Jennifer skillfully applied her red Mac lipstick and threw on her Chanel white dress suit. As stared straight into the mirror, she approved of her overall appearance. After all, she was now Mrs. John Barrett, the ambassador's beautiful new wife, and she was about to conquer the world. As the mansion's new mistress, she was ready to begin her new life, starting with her new expensive wardrobe. Chanel or Gucci? Louis Vuitton or Coach? Diamonds or Pearls? Jennifer laughed at the thought of diamonds or pearls. Diamonds of course. Taking one final glimpse in the mirror, she knew that she was ready. Spraying on her last sprit of her perfume, Jennifer quickly grabbed her handbag and then, she walked out of the door.

At the stroke of ten o'clock, not a minute earlier nor a minute later, Jennifer was greeted by Gloria in the hallway. Upon her arrival, Gloria quickly escorted her down the hall and into the executive conference room for their upcoming meeting. As Jennifer entered the room, she saw four other members inside, already seated along a round table. Behind them, was a large symbol of the agency's emblem that was mounted right above them and hanging on the wall. The symbolism of the emblem was bold and powerful, for Jennifer immediately interpreted it as a tool to serve a constant reminder, that they were all a part of the government, that they each had a specific role to play, and that their functions, duties and allegiance belonged solely united to the nation state.

"Madame Barrett, let us begin," Gloria announced. "But first, we'll start with introductions. Please, do have a seat."

Following Gloria's command, Jennifer walked over to an empty chair, located at the far end of the table. Once she was comfortably seated, she signaled to Gloria to proceed with the meeting. Gloria approvingly smiled, and then she asked for the first attendee to rise. Within an instant, the young woman, who was in her early twenties and of Chinese descent, rose up from her chair.

"This is Carol Wu," Gloria introduced. "She's from Los Angeles, California and is a graduate from the University of California, Los Angeles, with a degree in broadcasting and communications. Carol is fluent in English, Mandarin, Cantonese, German and French. Currently, she serves as our communications and social media specialist, having joined our agency just a little over two years ago. Carol will be responsible for your official social media accounts and will function as your primary liaison with the general public."

"Wait, am I no longer permitted to use my own personal social media accounts?" asked Jennifer, who was by now, rather surprised and concerned by this startling new revelation.

With over a million followers and growing on her Instagram account alone, she often used her social media accounts to post various pictures regarding her latest fashion trends and travel adventures. The very thought of losing such access, was difficult to imagine…let alone, bear.

"Although you're legally permitted to have personal accounts, it's still *highly* advisable and recommended that you *cease* using them immediately, while your husband is in office," replied Gloria, firmly.

"Given the fact, that you're the spouse of an active civil servant, you too, also represent the agency, both publicly and privately," she continued, "From this moment onwards, anything that you say and do, both professionally and personally, is a direct reflection of the agency. Furthermore, your actions or inactions, for that matter, can also be potentially used against you, by the public, media and foreign countries—both allied and enemy nations. Given these delicate matters, we highly advise that you discontinue and terminate your personal accounts, effective immediately. In return, you will maintain only a professional account, that we can safely monitor and contain, at all times."

"Monitor and contain?" asked Jennifer, with a raised brow. Although this meeting had only recently just begun; but already, not even five minutes into it, she was losing her free speech. Sadly, this felt overwhelming.

"Not to worry, Mrs. Barrett," interrupted Carol. "My specialization is in PR. I promise, I will do you justice with the press."

"Madame Barrett," interjected Gloria. "Rest assured, you're in capable and good hands, with our team. These are simply standard protocols. Very soon, you'll grow accustomed to this lifestyle."

Looking directly at Carol, Gloria said, "Thank you, you may be seated."

"Ladies, I appreciate your assurance, but I'm not sure if I'm ready to agree to any such deal, at this time," replied Jennifer. "I'm very active on all of my social media accounts, so I'm not really certain that I want to give it all up, yet."

"But you will still have social media accounts," Carol jumped in. "You won't be eliminated from any online platform. Technically, you're just getting an online makeover."

"An online makeover? What do you mean exactly?" asked an intrigued Jennifer.

"You will still have an online presence. That doesn't just all go away," replied Carol.

"While you won't have direct access to your own personal accounts anymore, as an alternative, I will, instead, create and manage a new professional account, on your behalf. Plus, in return, I can help build any image that you want the world to see you as: a fashion mogul, the beautiful model wife, the famous humanitarian— anything that you wish. Like I said before Mrs. Barrett, I promise to do you justice."

"So long as it in compliance with our standard protocols, of course," Gloria reminded them.

For a long moment, Jennifer remained silent, as she took a deep breath to absorb all of this new information. On the one hand, she was no longer going to have her freedom to directly manage and control her own social media accounts; but on the other hand, she now had a designated team to oversee them. Plus, they promised to carve out and create a better image of her on a global scale, too. Perhaps, her million followers would grow to another million? Or, better yet, a billion? Or maybe, some of her favorite celebrities were about to experience some healthy competition with her, as the upcoming political socialite? After all, what did she really have to lose? Either way, Jennifer was slowly learning that by her decision to marry John, in the end, she didn't only agree to marry the man alone; but rather, she had also married all of his responsibilities, as well. Unfortunately, these were sacrifices that she knew that she needed to make. Whether or not, Jennifer was ready to admit the obvious truth to herself, deep down within her soul, she already well knew, that in the end, whatever Gloria directed her to do, that was going to happen. It truly was just as simple as that.

"Alright Carol, we have a deal," said Jennifer, as she reluctantly agreed to her offer.

"Fantastic!" exclaimed Carol happily, as she joyfully clapped her hands.

"Madame Barrett, I'm very glad to hear that, too," added Gloria. "In that case, Carol, please begin working on Madame Barrett's new accounts. You are excused from the remainder of this meeting."

Following on cue, Carol immediately excused herself from the room and shut the door behind her.

"Doesn't she need my account information first, in order to begin?" asked Jennifer, who was now concerned about the lack of information that was provided to Carol.

"We've already completed your background check. We've got all of your accounts on file," replied Gloria, confidently.

"Oh," replied a surprised Jennifer.

"Let us continue. Bes, please rise," Gloria directed.

Upon Gloria's command, a short, chubby, bald man, in his late fifties, with a large belly and tanned completion, took the spotlight. Dressed in a dark blue suit, that appeared to be rather ill fitted, Bes took a few extra moments to fully stand; for sadly, his legs were a bit short, and his belly too large for his small and tiny stature. After much struggle, he eventually stood up. Feeling exhausted by the whole ordeal, Bes reached over for his glass of water and took a much-needed sip. Meanwhile, Jennifer noticed that his face coloring was a bit flushed and red, and there even was a peculiar drip of sweat, falling right across his forehead. Wiping the sweat across from his forehead with a handkerchief, he introduced himself as Bes Medina, a native New Yorker, of Spanish and Egyptian descent. However, as soon as he announced his own name, Gloria swiftly interrupted.

"Thank you, Bes. I'll take it from here," said Gloria. She continued, "Bes is our accountant and serves as our budget and financial manager. He's been with our agency for these past twenty-five years and counting. He's fluent in English, Spanish, Portuguese and Arabic. As our accountant, he oversees our annual budget and works closely with me, regarding the purchase and disposal of our agency's properties. While I purchase the property, Bes is in charge of disposing them. He also works with our auditors during the annual audits. To further simplify, Bes deals with all financial matters, including our monthly spending budgets. Additionally, Madame Barrett, this too, includes your monthly clothing allowances."

"My monthly clothing allowances?" asked Jennifer, inquisitively. This certainly caught her attention. "Just how much will that be?"

"That all depends," answered Bes. "Ambassador Phillips' wife was granted an allotment of about $100,000 per month; so, assuming that your husband doesn't object, nor makes any alterations to his current budget proposal for this upcoming fiscal year, then I estimate that it will probably be the same."

"$100,000 U.S. dollars per month!" exclaimed Jennifer, in shock. If this was true, then she was ready to schedule fitting appointments at her nearest Chanel boutique!

"Yes, in U.S. dollars," Bes confirmed.

Happily, Jennifer was beaming with joy. This was the best of news! But, alas, her newfound joy came to a sudden end; for soon after announcing this information, Gloria interrupted to further clarify this particular matter.

"Before we continue on with this conversation, I must address a few pressing matters, with regards to this subject," interrupted Gloria.

"Although I preferred to have reserved this discussion for a later time; however, since it's now on the table, it's best that we tackle it, right now. While, what Bes says is true, that the standard monthly budget for the ambassador's spouse is generally around $100,000 per month— which, thus, amounts to about $1.2 million per fiscal year— there are however, certain guidelines and conditions, that I must first, bring to your attention."

"Well, whatever it is, I'm sure it's no cause for alarm. I mean, a $1.2 million dollar budget is plenty. That should buy me a few of my favorite Chanel and Gucci pieces, from their upcoming spring and fall collections," Jennifer reflected.

"Well, Madame Barrett, that's just it," said Gloria. "Although you're most likely to receive an annual $1.2 million dollar budget for your wardrobe, these funds must be used to purchase clothing and accessories from American designers, only."

"Only American designers? Whatever do you mean?" asked Jennifer, who was confused by her remark.

"In translation, this means that you can only purchase garments made exclusively by American designers, and not any foreigners. Since these are government funds, you are expected to promote our own American culture, traditions and values abroad, while accompanying your husband on official state business. Furthermore, it's considered part of a promotional campaign to support American businesses on a global scale, through the expression of your choice of attire. That's why it's important that you work with your fellow American designers," answered Gloria, directly.

"This is the primary reason, as to why the agency generally rubber stamps the approval for these types of large allocations on our annual budget proposals," added Bes.

"Wait," spoke a distressed Jennifer. "You're telling me that I can only use these funds to purchase American designers? If that's the case, then keep your stupid funds! Besides, my husband is filthy rich, and he can afford to privately purchase my wardrobe on his own funds!"

"Madame Barrett, you're failing to see the point," replied Gloria, while remaining strong and assertive. "Regardless of your family's personal wealth, you are now the wife of an active civil servant. Due to this reason alone, you're required to follow this protocol, just like everyone else. There are no exceptions. Now, I do realize that this may come as a bit of a surprise and shock to you, but I can assure you, Madame Barrett, that there are plenty of wonderful American designers, for whom, you can choose to collaborate with. Trust me, Madame Barrett, every American designer will simply die to dress you, believe me."

"But who exactly is on that list? Is it Chanel, Gucci or Louis Vuitton? All three have stores in the U.S." said Jennifer, as she quickly made the means to point this fact out.

"French, Italian and French, neither of whom, are American. They may have shops in our country, but they're all headquartered in Europe. Besides, they're all owned by Europeans. Sadly, I'm afraid that they don't qualify to be on the list," replied Gloria.

"I can't believe I'm actually hearing this!" exclaimed a distraught Jennifer. "Why, this is absurd! I mean, how can I possibly look my best representing this country, if I'm not wearing Chanel or Gucci, the epitome of high fashion? You do realize, that all of the other wives will be wearing Chanel and Gucci to our state dinners! Why, I'll be the only wife resorted to second class fashion! I'll be the laughingstock for the entire country!"

"Madame Barrett, please calm down," cried Gloria. "The other wives are not of any of our concern. You, on the other hand, are. I beg of you, please do not worry yourself. There are still many wonderful and lovely American designers, who will do you justice. I promise. For example, there's Ralph Lauren and Tommy Hilfiger. Why there's even Calvin Klein. Even Madame Phillips use to dress in Calvin Klein all the time."

"Calvin Klein or Tommy Hilfiger? Are you serious Gloria?" laughed Jennifer, in a sarcastic manner. "Gloria, must I remind you that I am not a suburban middle-aged and middle-class housewife! Why, how can anyone with a sense of decency and class be caught wearing such 'common' designers? I mean, how on earth can one spend $1.2 million dollars, per year, wearing only white T-shirts and jeans? And, I, Madame, am certainly NOT Mrs. Phillips! I am Jennifer Barrett and I, Gloria, have style!!!" exclaimed Jennifer loudly, while stomping her feet to the ground.

Suddenly, Jennifer began to hysterically weep. In fact, her insoluble cries were such a powerful force on its own, that the entire room began to shake and vibrate, as a direct result. Furthermore, upon hearing her cries, the birds, seated along the edge of the office windows, rapidly flew away. While she continued to stomp her feet against the hard wood floor to coincide with her streaming tears, the office walls rapidly trembled. Shockingly, the entire room felt as if Zeus, himself, had thrown down a bolt of thunder from beneath them. Had they not been in attendance, then they would have sworn an earthquake, with a magnitude of 6.0 had recently stuck the Cairo embassy.

Having never experienced such an emotional political figure before, the staff were simply left speechless. In response to the chaos, Bes began to nervously perspire profusely. As his sweat dripped across his face and neck, he reached over into his pocket and retrieved his handkerchief, then proceeded to pat himself dry. Other than drying himself, he didn't know what else to do. He, too, was simply lost for words. But Gloria, in contrast, was calm and collective. She knew exactly how to calm this weeping maiden. With the snap of her finger, she instantly switched gears from her serious and stern composure, to that of a compassionate and understanding motherly figure.

"Now, now," began Gloria, as she reached over to Jennifer and slowly began stroking her hair. "Madame Barrett, please don't cry. I understand that these are big changes for you. But we are all here to support you, and we will help you to transition into your new role. Furthermore, to help aid you on this journey, I've arranged for you to meet with your personal stylist. They will help to curate a new wardrobe for you; while, at the same time, they will also work to elevate and polish your style into a more refined and elegant manner. Please, just promise me that you will keep an open mind, okay?"

Surprisingly, Jennifer was comforted by Gloria's soothing words, and soon enough, she abruptly stopped crying. Wiping away her tears, she quickly agreed to give the new stylist a chance. Honestly, she really had no other choice. At least for now.

Once Jennifer was calm and more stable, Gloria asked Bes to return to his seat, and then, she called for attorney, Tyler Conrad, to take the spotlight.

A young man, in his early thirties, Tyler was African American, tall, slim and handsome. He was well groomed, with finely trimmed hair, and dressed in an ironed pressed black suit, along with a gold silk tie and matching cufflinks. His complexion was dark, and his piercing eyes were a unique mix of hazel green and light brown, almost coffee like. While his predecessor exhibited a rather sloppy demeanor, Tyler, on the other hand, was the complete opposite. Jennifer, herself, couldn't help but notice and admire, as to just how attractive and dashing he was.

"This is Tyler Conrad, our staff attorney," began Gloria. "Tyler is a graduate from American University, in Washington, D.C. Having joined our agency five years ago, he holds a joint juris doctorate and an MBA. Prior to working for our agency, he previously served at the white house, as a legal intern. Tyler is an expert here, regarding all legal matters. Madame Barrett, if you have any legal questions, then I highly advise and recommend that you seek Tyler's counsel. As I always say, it's far better to run the matter by

Tyler, than to risk not doing so. Furthermore, we often run our announcements, press releases and public comments through Tyler first, before formally publishing them."

"Mrs. Barrett, it's a sincere pleasure to meet you," said Tyler politely, as he shook hands with Jennifer.

"Thank you, Tyler, same here," replied Jennifer smilingly, as she reciprocated with his handshake.

"Do you have any questions or concerns that you would like to ask me, at this time?" asked Tyler.

"I'm not sure that I do right now," replied Jennifer.

In all honestly, she had only recently arrived to the mansion as of yesterday. In fact, she was still learning the locations to the various rooms within this house. Legal questions weren't exactly a subject matter that she prioritized, at this given moment.

"Since Madame Barrett doesn't have any legal questions of her own; I, myself, would like to bring up one or two legal matters at this time," Gloria quickly interrupted. "As a general reminder, we are not permitted to attend any political gatherings or functions, such as a protest or demonstration. Now, this is important, so please do try to remember this. If the media should catch us at such a location, whether it be voluntary or involuntary, or just as a matter of being at the wrong place at the wrong time as an innocent bystander, then please be aware that it can be twisted and manipulated against us via the press by anyone of our enemy nations. That's why we must always remain cautious and careful about our surroundings, at all times."

"Gloria, I have never, nor do I ever intend on mingling on any political protests," retorted Jennifer, coldly. "Besides, even in my most destitute of hours, I can't ever imagine myself, engaged with such a crowd. Why, just the very thought of voluntarily standing under the hot burning Egyptian sun is too difficult to even contemplate! Imagine, that much direct sun exposure, alone! Why, that would certainly destroy my youthful face and devastate my pores, forever! Never in a million years, would I allow such a thing! Why, there isn't enough sun block creams in the world to persuade me otherwise!"

"Madame Barrett, I'm very glad to hear," replied Gloria. "Lastly, we cannot accept any gifts, unless otherwise approved by the agency."

"Not accept any gifts?" asked a surprised Jennifer. "Whatever does that mean exactly? I'm I not to accept any gifts from my family? What about birthdays and Christmas gifts?"

"Personal gifts are always an exception," laughed Gloria. "No, what I mean are gifts received from the public, including private firms and other foreign nations. These pertains to gifts granted to us, while your husband remains in office."

"Accepting the wrong gift can be a big deal, especially if the item is caught during an audit," added Bes.

"Now, I'm completely confused," sighed Jennifer.

"Madame Barrett, these are gifts given primarily from foreign nations. If they are allies, then normally, it is acceptable; provided that we run it by the agency, first. However, we cannot accept any gifts from any enemy nations, under no circumstances and without any exceptions. For if we accidentally do, then it might display the false image that we are on 'friendly' terms with the opposing nation or nations, and this mistake, can potentially have an adverse effect and a conflict of interest, within our own American foreign policy."

"I see," replied Jennifer. "But how would I be able to even keep track of all these gifts and who sent them? I mean, I, alone, can barely keep track of my own luggage."

"Not to worry, Madame Barrett, we've already taken care of this. To help facilitate and guide you on this important matter, you'll have a new personal assistant. In fact, she starts this Friday. Her name is Sally Timmons, and she's a transferee from Rome. You can meet with her, once she arrives."

"Where will her office be?" asked Jennifer.

"She'll be station in the mansion, near your office," answered Gloria.

"I have an office?' asked a surprised Jennifer.

"Yes, you do. After our meeting, I'll escort you there to take a tour," Gloria promised.

"Gloria, I appreciate your efforts, but why do I have an office? I mean, my husband is the ambassador, not I," Jennifer remarked.

"All first ladies have their own offices. It's standard protocol," replied Gloria, sternly and as a matter of fact. However, at the same time, Gloria sensed Jennifer's uneasiness towards the administrative duties and responsibilities associated with her new role, so she politely and tactically added, "But, should you choose to find yourself unavailable to attend to the office personally, then your assistant can function, on your behalf. And if there are no more questions, I shall move on and introduce you to Chef Kojin Homura."

Jennifer agreed, and so, Gloria promptly excused Tyler and summoned Chef Homura to stand. As Chef Homura rose up from his seat, Jennifer observed that the chef was very tall, of Japanese descent, and his built and stature resembled that of a sumo wrestler. But for some odd reason, he seemed familiar. Strangely, Jennifer couldn't understand as to why this was, given that this was her first time meeting him.

"This is Chef Homura and he's from Toyoko, Japan. You might already recognize him, as our chef is a bit of a celebrity. Apart from being a retired Olympic world champion sumo wrestler, Chef Homura is also a former judge on the international cooking television show, *Flame*. As such, he's a beloved member of our embassy team," Gloria beamingly said.

Immediately, Jennifer's eyes widen, and she exclaimed, "That's why you look so familiar! I'm a huge fan of your show!"

Tickled by her reaction, both Gloria and Chef Homura laughed.

"Yes, Chef Homura is often recognized for his contribution on the show. Our chef is very talented, and he can cook anything that your heart desires. Anything at all. Whatever you want. At all hours, night or day," Gloria gushed.

"Gloria," interrupted Jennifer, "I hope that I don't sound too rude by asking this, but since Chef Homura is an international famous celebrity chef, why is he working here?"

Once again, both Gloria and Chef Homura laughed at Jennifer's question.

"Care to answer this one, Chef Homura?" asked Gloria to the chef.

Clearing his throat, and with a heavy accent, Chef Homura replied, "Thank you, Ms. Gloria. Mrs. Barrett, the reason I serve as head chef at the agency, is because I want to personally, protect and serve my country."

"Madame Barrett, Chef Homura is certainly an admiral hero, here at the agency," added Gloria, with much delight.

"But Gloria, didn't you just tell us that we are not to mingle with the media, nor have social media accounts? If that's the case, then how's it possible for Chef Homura to be both a chef at the agency and a judge on a tv show? I mean, he was just on the most recent season of *Flame*?" asked Jennifer.

"Well, Madame Barrett," replied Gloria, "Since you are now one of us, I will let you in on a bit of a secret. Our very own Chef Homura is not only a world-famous chef, but he's also one of our best international spies. Why, you'd be surprised, as to just how much intelligence a celebrity chef can secretly gather from the world community, especially, if he's on a highly rated international cooking television show."

"Wow, that is amazing," Jennifer gasped, in disbelief.

"Wow, indeed," Gloria agreed. "Chef Homura has cooked for several world leaders, including both our allied and enemy nations. Furthermore, he's personally thwarted several terrorist and assassination plots to save our own ambassadors, politicians and their families. In addition to Chef Homura's culinary and Olympian skills, he also holds a black belt in martial arts. Overall, he's an invaluable employee at our agency, and we are very lucky to have him on our team. Also, whenever we have new ambassadors and their respective families join the agency, we often rotate Chef Homura in to come and work at that particular embassy, in order to have an extra bit layer of security for all of us. Furthermore, apart from Chef Homura's five stars meals, for security reasons, we do recommend that you always opt to dine in and to avoid eating out at all times."

"Gloria, this is truly wonderful," said Jennifer. "But what do you mean by dining in at all times? How's this a security concern?"

"Food is always a danger for any government employee, for it is the easiest way to depose of any important person, without much detection, through the use of poison," replied Gloria sternly.

Shocked by this revelation, Jennifer clasped her hands together and exclaimed, "Poison! Is someone trying to really poison us?"

"It's always a possibility," replied Gloria., "Unfortunately, we always stand the risk of this. Madame Barrett, are you aware that the number one cause of death for an ambassador, politician or government employee, both domestically and overseas, is by poison? Not by war, or swords, or guns, but by poison."

"I had no idea," gasped Jennifer. This certainly, was news to her.

"Yes, indeed," said Gloria. "This is why, we always recommend eating meals only served at the mansion, for your own safety. But if you happen to be out and about at a restaurant or at an event, and they serve a meal, then please ever-so politely and diplomatically decline to eat it. This includes both food and drinks."

"What about coffee or tea at a café? Surely, those are safe, with such a large gathering?" asked Jennifer.

"Absolutely, not," Gloria quickly answered, while shaking her head in disapproval. "Café, restaurants, weddings, parties—none are safe."

"But what if I'm out, and I'm hungry or thirsty?" Jennifer further inquired.

"If you absolutely, must," began a frustrated Gloria, "Only in dire situations. And if you truly cannot decline a meal for any reason, then please just drink bottled water only."

"Bottled water?" exclaimed a very surprised Jennifer.

"Yes, bottled water," replied Gloria.

"But why?" asked Jennifer.

"Because bottled water is your safest bet," said Gloria.

"I understand it being sealed," began Jennifer, "But surely, this should include any sealed liquids, such as juice, soda or even liquor?"

"Water only," replied Gloria. "And there is a specific reason for this. Colored liquids, such as juice, soda, liquor, even milk, cannot easily detect, as to whether or not a poisonous substance has been added or diluted into the liquid. Often times, the poison will dissolve into the liquid and blend in to match the liquid's color. However, this is not the case with water. Most of the time, not always, but mostly, the poison will alter the clear transparent color of water. This is why bottled water is your safest option."

"Ah, I see," replied an enlightened Jennifer.

"Do you have any other questions for Chef Homura?" asked Gloria.

"No," replied Jennifer.

"In that case, Chef Homura, you may take your seat," Gloria instructed.

As the meeting was drawing near to its conclusion, Gloria began to shuffle through her papers. Using her pen, she proceeded to check off various items on her list.

"Now," she continued, "All of the other remaining staff, including the housekeepers, gardeners and repair men, are all considered as government contractors. While your husband will have his own personal staff at the embassy, we, here at the estate, are technically, your own official staff, with the exception of Tyler, who's our shared on-site staff attorney, since all of the other staff attorneys are stationed back in Washington, D.C. For official business purposes, we maintain offices in both the embassy and at the estate. With regards to security, that department is directly overseen by your husband and their offices are located inside of the embassy; although, they still do maintain a physical presence here, as well. And lastly, a brief introduction to myself. As you are already well aware, my name is Gloria Renaud and I'm the embassy coordinator. I'm originally from France, but I relocated to the United States, upon my marriage. After the untimely passing of my late husband, I joined the agency and have been working here for the past thirty years. In my current role, I serve as the facilitator to our meetings, prepare the agendas and document the minutes to all of our sessions. In addition, I also oversee the purchase of the embassy's property and help assist with our annual audits. I'm also in charge of new orientations, human resources and training other newly appointed embassy staff. I also manage our government contractors and serve as Carol's mentor. Now, Madame Barrett, I do realize that we have covered quite a bit today, but do you have any other questions?"

"No, thank you, Gloria. You've been most informative," replied Jennifer and then afterwards, she then turned her attention over to the remaining staff and thanked them for their participation, as well.

"Splendid!" exclaimed Gloria, happily. "Now, Madame Barrett, before I conclude this meeting, I have a memorandum to give you, regarding the list of official rules that you may want to reference, during your stay here. Please do take a moment to review."

Pulling from the stack of her papers on the desk, Gloria handed over the document directly to Jennifer. As Jennifer received the document in her hands, she glanced to read its contents. It read as the following:

Subject:	Memorandum Concerning the Appointment and Conduct of the New Ambassador, Spouse and Accompanying Family Members on Official and Active Duty
To:	Mrs. Jennifer Barrett, First Lady to the U.S. Ambassador, Mr. John Barrett, Cairo, Egypt Embassy
From:	Gloria Renaud, Embassy Coordinator, U.S. State Department, Cairo, Egypt Embassy

1. Cease using all personal social media accounts. An official social media account will be created, maintained and operated by government staff, on behalf of the ambassador and his family.

2. Do not engage, appear or participate in any public gatherings or political events, other than preapproved events and venues determined by the agency in advance, unless otherwise, directed. If a participant seeks to attend any gathering outside embassy grounds, then security will be provided for.

3. Do not accept nor provide gifts to the public or other foreign head of state (HOS), unless otherwise approved by the agency.

4. Official lodging residence will be provided for and arranged by the agency.

5. Building property items and décor will be purchased and overseen by agency staff, in conjunction with other respective intra and inter-agencies, involved with the acquisition of property. The acquisition and disposition of property will be overseen by the local agency staff, and the appointed staff members will be in charge of the embassy's décor, which should reflect the local customs and traditions of the host nation.

6. Food will be provided on-site at the residence. Funds for meals will be included on the annual budget.

7. An annual budget will be created and approved by the Budget Committee Chair. The approved annual budget shall include yearly funds for the purchase of mansion property and goods; as well as funds for the clothing for the ambassador and spouse. In an effort to promote American values overseas, it is required that participating parties wear only American designers. Travel expenses will be further included on the annual budget. All travel must be approved in advance by the agency, prior to travel.

8. Credit cards will be issued and used for official government business, including both travel and property purchases for the embassy.

9. For legal matters, please consult with the on-site localized staff attorney. If the on-site attorney is not available, then contact the agency's main headquarters in Washington, D.C.

10. Promote a positive and dignified image of our country, while on tour and active duty at the host country.

Upon reading the memorandum, Jennifer remained quiet. Alas, she finally felt overwhelmed. Although Gloria had touched upon several key items already listed on this memorandum, Jennifer still wasn't certain as to what exactly she had gotten herself into. Having expected to live a storybook happily ever after life, she blinded married John. But as the reality of her circumstances slowly took hold, she asked herself, what if the life that she imagined, was nothing more than fiction? Better, yet, a fantasy? What if, everything that she dreamed and hoped for, was truly that, of a nightmare?

"Do I need to sign anything?" she finally asked, while feeling, as if she had already surrendered herself over to the enemy in defeat to an unfought battle that was already long lost.

 "Nothing at all, Madame Barrett," laughed Gloria. "You're here. You're already committed. This is for informational purposes, only."

Thus, with Gloria's last and final laugh, she concluded the meeting and dismissed the remaining participants back to their respective offices. As promised, Gloria gave Jennifer a tour of her office and then, she took her over to meet with her new stylist.

By the end of the afternoon, Jennifer acquired a newly customized wardrobe, consisting of various new dresses, gowns, pants suits, casual wear and accessories. Her previous Chanel and Gucci pieces were now replaced by the likes of Ralph Lauren and Tommy Hilfiger collections. But apart from switching her clothing labels from European to American designers, her clothing style had also changed and evolved within the process. Her standard sleeveless and above the knee mini skirt silhouettes, were now replaced with long sleeved and below the knee dresses. Meanwhile, her favorite colors of pink and pastels, had now transitions into shades of brown, black and beige— all neutral tones. Even her colorful and sequin handbags were switched for black leather totes for the daytime, and small silver clutches for evening wear. In the end, the unique girly and preppy image that Jennifer had spent years developing and cultivating for herself in college, abruptly dissipated overnight by the snap of Gloria's fingers. And just like that, everything was now replaced by a new conservative style; a style that all but failed to reflect Jennifer's true and inner character.

Although Jennifer reluctantly accepted these new changes, it was the last and final change that affected her the most. After selecting her new wardrobe, she met with the mansion's beautician. It was there at the salon, that her signature long and flowing blonde hair, which stretched from across her body and had taken most of her teenaged years to grow, was hastily chopped off and transformed into a very short French Bob, leaving Jennifer in a puddle of tears. Sadly, this was not the end. Her bright red lipstick and eyewear were quickly smeared away, and replaced with a more natural and modest makeup style coverage.

Later on, that evening, as Jennifer prepared for her evening meal with John, she sat at her vanity stool and looked into the mirror. Sadly, she had barely recognized the image staring right back at her. Just a few hours ago, Jennifer sat at this very same vanity and had been an entirely different woman. Suddenly, a tear dropped from the corner of her eye. Although it was still too early to determine her fate in this new world, she still felt uneasy. Unexpectedly, she felt a sudden sharp pain in her chest. Jennifer quickly placed her hands across her chest, took a deep breath and wiped away her remaining tears. After all, it was getting late and she needed to hurry downstairs to meet John in time for dinner.

At promptly five o'clock, Jennifer arrived to the dining room, where she was greeted by Eton at the door. She quickly took a seat at the table and waited for John to arrive. As she watched the white grandfather clock in the dining room tick away, the dials slowly graduated from five to a quarter past five o'clock. Time was passing by, and sadly, John was still nowhere in sight.

"Shall we begin dinner, Mrs. Barrett?" Eton asked her, while hoping to obtain permission to, at the very least, serve the first appetizer course.

"No, not yet Eton. Perhaps, Mr. Barrett is still behind at a meeting. Let's just wait a little while longer," replied Jennifer.

"Very well, Mrs. Barrett. I shall inform Chef Homura of your decision," said Eton, as he promptly walked over into the kitchen to inform him about the ambassador's late arrival.

While Jennifer waited for John, she pondered about his whereabouts, as she tapped her fingers against the wooden table, in defiance. Where was he? Why was he taking so long? This wasn't fair. Didn't he realize that she too, had a long day of her own?

Finally, at half past five o'clock, John entered the room.

"Please forgive me for my late arrival, my dear. I fell behind at the embassy. Stacks of visa applications arrived in the mail today," he replied, as he joined her at the table and took a seat.

"I see," replied Jennifer, coldly, as she waved her hands over to Eton, signaling to him to begin their dinner service.

While they sat waiting for their first course, John happily gushed about his day at work. As he discussed about his introduction into his new role, he blissfully glowed from head to toe, and his smile was from ear to ear. This was certainly in contrast to Jennifer's own experience. While John might have had the most thrilling and exciting of orientations, Jennifer couldn't say the same for herself. Her meeting and the events that followed soon afterwards, simply weren't her cup of tea. And while John was certain to become the perfect ambassador, Jennifer questioned, as to whether or not, she was going to be an equal counterpart for the role as his first lady.

But as John carried on with his story, Jennifer wasn't an equal listener. Rather than focusing on his storytelling, like the night before, she simply stared at the grandfather clock across from her, and watched its dial tick back and forth as they ate their meal. Time was passing slowly, and as

Eton poured yet another round of wine into her glass, Jennifer sipped away, as John continued to boast about his day. Although Jennifer was happy for him, truly, she was…she had also hoped, that in between his solo conversation, that he would also, at the very least, grant her a single complement. Just one. After all, she too, like him, had experienced much change today. But, unlike him, she had also undergone physical change, as well. After years of sporting her long hair— a trait that had been her own signature look of her beauty—she was now sitting in front of him, with the shortest hair that she'd ever adorn in her entire life and somehow, he didn't seem to take notice, nor care. As the clock's dials continued to swing back and forth, Jennifer eventually realized that John not only failed to notice the change in her hair, but he also remained ignorant of her new choice of attire and makeup, too. Sadden by his lack of attention, Jennifer took another sip of her wine.

Later on, that evening after dinner, as John slept comfortably and tucked away within the layer of blankets inside of their bed, Jennifer stared down at her husband and began to cry. She was disappointed. Heartbroken. Not once did he ever mention anything about her physical transformation, and that surprisingly, bothered her, immensely. Even though Jennifer was always a confident woman, throughout the years, she had grown accustomed to receiving various complements from the opposite sex, on a regular basis. Whether those complements were regarding her new dress or lipstick color, she was always acknowledged by her suitors, no matter how minor or major the change had been. But for the first time in her life, during one of the, if not, the biggest transformation of her life, the one man, who was supposed to be her husband, failed to acknowledge her. Although the change in her physical transformation might have been overlooked by others, John was her husband and should have taken notice of her recent metamorphosis. After all, this change was important to her. It was her own sacrifice to him to become the wife he expected; and yet, he failed to notice her small, but important sacrifice for him. Was this telling of how their marriage was going to be, in the future? Her, always craving and starving, for his attention? Was his career going to be more important than she? Was she always going to come secondary to him? As Jennifer wiped away her tears, she curled herself beside him, closed her eyes and hoped that tomorrow, things would be different. After all, tomorrow was a new day. A day for new beginnings.

The next morning, Jennifer skipped breakfast and wandered outside in the garden to catch a breath of fresh air. As she sat down on a wooden bench, located in the middle of the garden, she quietly admired the beautiful scenery around her. The day was bright, warm and sunny. The air was clean and fresh, and there was a misty cool spring breeze that flew across through the open air. She was surrounded by millions upon millions of red roses, growing along the green grass, with orange monarch butterflies fluttering about in the open field. Carefully, she tilted her head towards the sun to catch a glimpse of the blue sky and white clouds passing by, and then, she closed her eyes and took a fresh breath of air. It was the first time since her wedding, that she finally felt a sense of peace within her heart.

As Jennifer opened her eyes, she saw a single red rose growing outside of the fence's borders. While the other roses grew along the fence's limited border, this one single rose grew much taller, than all of the rest and even outstretched the boundaries of its respective fence. Unlike the other roses, this particular rose was a much darker shade, than all of the others, too. Curious, she wondered as to why that was. Perhaps, it was because this rebel rose was closest to the sun? Quietly, Jennifer silently stared at the rose, while admiring its strong and rebellious nature, as it stretched higher above all the rest. Somehow, it was as if, this rose was moving away as far it possibly could towards the sun, aiming towards freedom. Happily, Jennifer smiled to herself, for she secretly admired it. Perhaps, if this rose grew taller, then one day, it might even reach above the fence's restrictive boundaries and over into the street, where no one else from the mansion could touch it, or alter its endearing beauty.

However, as soon as this very thought came to her mind, the gardener soon arrived. Passing right by her, he directly walked straight across and over to the fence, while carrying a large pair of scissors with him. As he began trimming and clipping away at the rose bush, Jennifer anxiously sat on watching him from afar; all the while, hoping and praying that he would ignore and miss her favorite rose, and leave it to be, alone and safe. But sadly, this wasn't to be. Rather, the gardener continued to slice and chop the bushes, with the tips of his sharp blade…until finally, he encountered her rose. With one swift swoosh, he quickly snapped off the rose bud from its stem, and its petals came tumbling down, landing on top of the dirty sidewalks, located right outside of their fence.

Immediately, Jennifer rushed over to the scene and peered over the fence. It was from there, that she saw that the once lovely rose, had dwindled away into nothing more than crushed petals, which were torn apart and scattered across the dark shadows of the pavement. Heartbroken, she was left standing speechless. But sadly, the worst was not yet over. Suddenly, a bystander appeared and within seconds, they managed to trample all over the remaining petals, crushing it further into dust. Shocked by this gruesome sight, Jennifer shivered from horror. The once beautiful rose, whose only fault was growing beyond the constraints of mansion's confinement, now ceased to exist. Sadly, it died a tragic death and was violently crushed into a thousand pieces, in the process. Now, that promising rose was nothing more, than a speck of dust, and a forgotten memory of what could have been.

Suddenly, she began to cry. Although Jennifer was well aware that this flower was nothing more than a mere rose, whose fate she couldn't help; at the same time, she bore witness, firsthand, as to the consequences to those, who dare to stretch beyond the restrictive confinements of the mansion… and that outcome was of death and total destruction.

In that fateful moment, Jennifer swore to herself, that she was going to do everything in her power to ensure that she had a different fate, than the tragedy she just bore witness to, only moments ago. No matter what, she was going to conform to the mansion's rules, as she had already previously done. However, this time, she vowed to never reveal her secret intentions to live a separate live, outside of the mansion. No, she was going to keep these secrets, all to herself. Wiping away her tears, Jennifer returned back into the mansion. Once she was back in bed, she lay down and pondered about her afternoon, as she closed her eyes and fell fast asleep.

Later on, that afternoon, Jennifer awoke from her nap by the ticking of her clock. As her eyes peeked at the time, she saw that it was well past six o'clock in the evening. She was an hour late for dinner! Fearful that she upset John and Chef Homura, Jennifer frantically rushed down the stairs. When she finally reached and entered into the dining room, to her surprise, she didn't see John there. Instead, she saw Eton standing alone in the room.

"I'm far too late!" Jennifer cried, "John must have already finished eating. I apologize in advance, for being so tardy."

"Mrs. Barrett," began Eton, "Mr. Barrett hasn't yet arrived."

"Not yet arrived?" asked Jennifer, who was very much surprised by this revelation. "Surely, he must have come down here, already. Why, I'm an hour late to dinner!"

"No, he has not," replied Eton, sternly. "But the dinner is ready, whenever you are."

Surprisingly, Jennifer hadn't expected John's tardiness. In all of her time spent with him, he had never been tardy to any appointment, before. Never. Not once. This was so unlike his character. But, then, Jennifer suddenly recalled, that the night before, John had actually been late, as well.

"Eton," Jennifer began, "Have you heard any news, as to why Mr. Barrett is so late this evening?"

"No, Mrs. Barrett, I have not," replied Eton.

"I see," said Jennifer. "Let's go ahead and wait another ten minutes, or so. Perhaps, Mr. Barrett is attending an unexpected late-night meeting at the embassy."

As they eagerly waited for John's return, Jennifer again stared across at the white grandfather clock that stood before her. When she reached over to grab her glass of water, she unexpectedly managed to catch a glimpse of her reflection on a silver spoon that was located right next to an empty dinner plate. As she stared down at her own reflection, she couldn't help but also notice the empty table…which at the heart of it… was the white elephant in the room. Sadly, this wasn't the life that she had originally signed up for. An empty table without John. A husband, who failed to keep his promise of spending quality time together. A wardrobe that wasn't of her choosing. A stylist, who didn't reflect her own personal desires. No, none of this was her. She didn't fit into this new world. And even though, earlier in the garden, she promised herself, to simply go along with this charade, Jennifer also recognized that she couldn't lose herself completely, in the process, as well. After all, she was still Jennifer.

Therefore, if she was going to survive the next decade in this marriage, then she needed to retain some core essence of herself; in which, she conformed with the rules, but yet, still maintained a touch of her core self, in the making.

Using her silver spoon as a mirror, Jennifer wiped away her nude-colored lipstick off from her lips, and then she reached over the table to grab a small raspberry that laid across from her, as part of a decorative centerpiece fruit basket. Ever-so slowly, she squeezed a bit of juice from the raspberry, then used the juice to apply it across her dry lips, allowing her lips to display her famous signature red color. Afterwards, she proceeded to unbutton the first three buttons of her blouse, exposing her decolletage and bust. Finally, Jennifer fluffed her short hair and pinched her cheeks, turning them from a pale yellow into her natural red hue.

"There," she said happily to herself, "Now, that's more like it."

Distracted by own actions, Jennifer had almost forgotten that Eton was still in the room. However, when she finally caught sight of him, she said, "Eton, there's no need to wait for Mr. Barrett, any longer. I've waited long enough. Whether or not Mr. Barrett eats tonight, is no longer of my concern. Please begin tonight's service now."

"Certainly, Mrs. Barrett," replied Eton, as he quickly walked back into the kitchen to notify Chef Homura that dinner was now ready for service.

As Eton brought out the evening meal, which consisted of roasted fish and vegetables, he poured red wine into Jennifer's glass. Peacefully seated at the table, Jennifer sat back and reached for her glass of red wine. Once again, she stared straight across at the white grandfather clock and saw that it was now half past six o'clock, with still no John in sight. But this time, she smiled to herself, because it no longer mattered. Whether or not John was here, it was irrelevant, because she had already decided, right there and then, that she wouldn't wait for him for anything, anymore. Moving forward, she planned to act upon her own self-interests, from here on out. And tonight, that began with dinner. And tomorrow…well, that was yet to be determined. But either way, the outcome was certain: whatever activities she chose to partake upon in the near future, it was going to work in her favor, no matter what. As she raised her glass solo up high into the air and facing towards the grandfather clock, she gave an empty cheer and laugh, then took a long and glorious sip of her wine, relishing each and every single sip and ounce of her drink.

However, unbeknownst to Jennifer, on that evening, John was unexpectedly called at last minute to visit a neighboring embassy in Croatia, for training. As a result, he was expected to be gone for several days, leaving Jennifer behind in Cairo, with the staff. Unfortunately, John's secretary, Margaret Winthrop, failed to convey the message about his whereabouts over to Jennifer, and it wasn't until he called from his hotel room, in Dubrovnik several nights later, that she finally became aware of his location through Gloria. But by then, Jennifer no longer cared about his affairs, for she already determined that, if he truly cared about her feelings, then he would have found another way to contact her, much earlier. Although Jennifer was a romantic by heart, she was also, very much, stubborn and unforgiving. She might have cared for John, but in the end, she loved herself, far more. Therefore, she decided to set forth to manage her own affairs, without worrying about his. And so, Jennifer came to the conclusion, that if she was going to remain in this marriage, then she needed to continue to portray the dutiful and caring wife in public; but in private, that was another story all together, yet to be determined.

The next morning, Jennifer confidently walked straight into her new executive office, carrying a bouquet of freshly cut red roses in her hand. As she walked down the halls and turned into her office, she was met by a young redhaired woman, whose hair was straight and shoulder length. The young woman was in her early twenties, dressed in black pencil shirt, and was seated at a reception desk, located right in front of her office. As soon as the woman saw Jennifer, she quickly stood, extended her arms to greet Jennifer.

"Mrs. Barrett, it's a pleasure to meet you. I'm Sally Timmons, your new assistant. I just arrived here last night from Rome. Please, allow me to take those bouquet of roses from your hands."

"Thank you," replied Jennifer, as she handed the roses over to Sally.

"Mrs. Barrett, these are such lovely roses. Where would you like me to place them?" she asked.

"Anywhere on my desk will be fine," replied Jennifer.

"Will certainly do," said Sally.

Immediately, Sally took possession of the bouquet of red roses and soon after, she walked down into the kitchen to keep them. While Jennifer waited for Sally's return, she walked over to her empty desk and sat down. Much to her surprise, her office, ironically, was the one room in the entire mansion that Gloria neglected to decorate. Did Gloria not think that Jennifer planned on using her own office? She wondered. But, in truth, it didn't matter as to what Gloria thought. Starting today, things were going to change.

"Is there anything else that I can help you with, Mrs. Barrett?" asked Sally, as she gently placed the vase of roses in front of Jennifer, on her desk.

"Actually, yes, there are," began Jennifer, "First, I need this room to be decorated. Unfortunately, my decorator, Celeste, doesn't do business in this part of the world, so I need you to find me the next best interior decorator in Cairo."

Retrieving her pen and notepad, Sally began recording all of Jennifer's numerous requests.

"Second," continued Jennifer, "I need you to buy me a diary."

"Any preferences?" asked Sally, as she continued to jot down Jennifer's instructions with her pen.

"Nothing in particular, just something pretty," replied Jennifer, in all honesty.

"Okay, something pretty…will do," Sally said to herself, while in full concentration.

"Lastly," said Jennifer boldly, "I want you to mail this ring to my sister, Kate, along with this note."

As Jennifer passed the note over to Sally, the young assistant briefly reviewed it. It read as the following:

Dearest Kate,

Congratulations on your acceptance into your doctorate program! I'm so proud of you! I just know that you're going to be a very successful professor one day, in the near future. And since I also know just how much you love and adore pearls, here's little gift from me to you.

Your loving sister,

Jennifer

Upon reviewing the note, Jennifer pulled out the pearl ring from inside her pocket and just like the roses before, she transferred it over to Sally's custody. And dear reader, that pearl ring was none other, than the very same ring that John had previously bestowed upon her, on their wedding day.

"Wow, what a beautiful ring!" exclaimed Sally, as she held the pearl ring in her hand.

As Sally inspected the ring for herself, she noted the odd shape of the ring; however, this flaw had not once lessened the beauty of the ring in her eyes.

"Mrs. Barrett, this ring is so incredibly beautiful. Why on earth, would you ever want to give this lovely ring away? Even as a present?" asked Sally.

"It's for my twin sister. As lovely as this ring is, it's just not for me. I, personally, prefer diamonds. Always have and always will. But Kate, on the other hand, she's loved pearls, ever since I can remember. She will appreciate it and take care of this ring more than I, that much I'm certain of," replied Jennifer.

"Very well then," replied Sally. "I'll have this ring mailed out today."

"Thank you, Sally," said Jennifer.

As Jennifer sat down comfortably in her chair, she lifted her feet up and placed them over her desk. Staring at both, the bouquet of roses on desk and her pink diamond wedding ring on her finger, she smiled to herself. Mission accomplished. When she first married John, she wanted a diamond ring, as a replacement to the pearl ring. Done. Then, when she initially arrived to the mansion, she wanted not just a single red rose, but a bouquet, and now, she finally had it. She won.

As she held her hand high above in the air and towards the light, allowing her diamond ring to sparkle against the sunlight, Jennifer beamed with delight. After everything that transpired, she was finally content with the outcome of her circumstances. While she acknowledged that she might have made some mistakes along the way, she was now on the right track. Starting today, she was going to start making the right decisions for herself, and herself alone, from here on out.

Chapter 8

Excerpts from Mrs. Jennifer Barrett's Diary

February 10, 2013

Dear Diary,

I honestly haven't written in a diary since my teenage years, but now, I think it's good time to start. Ever since I read in a magazine that all famous celebrities have some sort of private journal or diary of their own, I decided that I should have one too. In the event, that I one day later publish a biography of my own in the future, then I will already have some written material, ready and available-on-hand to publish. As this is my first entry, I probably should introduce myself to you. My name is Jennifer Barrett, twin sister to Ms. Kate Stanley, a doctoral candidate from New York, and the wife to Mr. John Barrett, the U.S. Ambassador to Cairo, Egypt. Most people closest and dearest to me simply refer to me by my given name, Jennifer. However, to the rest of the world, I'm known formally as the ambassador's wife; a title that I've adorned since my marriage.

My husband and I have been married for almost a month now, and we live full-time in Cairo. Between my husband's busy schedule and my duties at the mansion, we seldom see one another. He's often busy away traveling on duty for official business. As a result, I only see him for a limited times sporadically at the mansion, either during our occasional private dinners or at our formal state dinners. As such, we've already moved into our own separate and private bedroom and living chambers; with his chambers on the east wing, and mine located on the west wing. Since relocating to Cairo, I've had only two intimate evenings alone with my husband and that occurred during our first week in Cairo. Ever since then, I haven't had a romantic evening alone with my new husband.

To say that I'm disappointed is only partially true. Was I madly in love with my husband when we first married? Yes and no. In hindsight, I think I was more in love with the idea of marrying him, he, a handsome, wealthy and up-and-coming ambassador, than I was of marrying John, as the man, himself. It was only after our wedding that I soon came to the realization that we had almost nothing in common and if given a second chance, I'm not certain that I would have made the same decision to marry him.

As of now, I don't think John realizes that I feel this way, because he's too preoccupied with his career, right now. I think the harsh reality of my unique situation is that John wanted more of a trophy wife, than he did of just me. But I cannot fault him for that; for I, too, am guilty of much of the same. Our marriage was a union of convenience; but yet, I still patiently await romance and my happy ending. In the meantime, I continue to play the part of his adorning wife and I must say, I think I've done a pretty good job portraying this image, too. Additionally, if I'm being perfectly honest, I do also privately enjoy all of my new privileges, including the parties, the travel, the personal assistant, the wealth and the exclusivity; but at the same time, I also feel a bit numb and empty inside, too. Honestly, I am lonely and with John away for extended periods of time, I wonder as to how much longer I can continue to live this way, before I begin wishing and craving for the arms of another man. My assistant, Sally Timmons, suggests that I take a hobby to clear my mind and I think that she's right. In fact, I just might take her up on that offer.

February 12, 2013,

Dear Diary,

Today, was my first chess lesson with my instructor, Badi. Since writing my first diary entry last week, I decided to take Sally's offer and took up chess, as my new hobby. But since I'm not familiar with the game of chess, I told Sally and Gloria Renaud, the embassy coordinator, that I needed someone, who had the patience and ability to teach an amateur learner, such as myself. Both Gloria and Sally reassured me that that wouldn't be a problem, and Badi was highly recommended by Bes Medina, our budget manager. Apparently, Badi is a well experience chess instructor, who also previously trained the former ambassador during his tenure.

To say that Badi is a good instructor is an understatement! He's absolutely perfect in every possible way. Not only is he attentive, patient, caring and understanding, he's also extremely attractive and handsome! Truly, he's a dream! His dark eyes, skin and black hair simply makes me want to melt! He's like an Egyptian God! I know, I know, I know…I shouldn't be talking like this, as I'm still, technically, a married woman. Although I realize that I shouldn't feel this way, but I also can't help, myself. Plus, with John away at the embassy working late nights, I feel more isolated and alone. I'm just so lonely here at the mansion! But for now, I think it's best that I stop writing. Goodnight diary.

February 13, 2013

Dear Diary,

Tonight, John and I had our first argument. It happened at dinner. Since tomorrow is Valentine's Day, I, naturally, like all normal wives, presumed that John was going to surprise me with a special gift or getaway trip in celebration of our first holiday together, as a married couple. But to my grave disappointment, he instead, formally announced at dinner, that starting tomorrow, he'll be embarking on a business trip to Croatia that's expected to last for several weeks, if not, months. To make matters worse, he actually asked that I stay behind and remain in Cairo alone, while he travels solo. Furthermore, due to confidential matters and security reasons, he will not disclose the specific reasons for this trip to me.

Upon delivering this sad and disappointing news, he carried on as usual and proceeded to calmly eat his meal in silence, without a single care about my feelings. After a long period of silence, when it finally became abundantly clear to me that he had absolutely no intention of giving me an early gift, nor the promise of a postponed celebration for this momentous holiday to a later date due to his absence…sadly, my anger got the best of me. Unfortunately, and I'll be the first to admit this too, but I may have uttered a few curse words that I might live to later on regret…but regardless, in the end, at least, I told him exactly how I felt, which is that I don't want to spend the next several weeks alone in this godforsaken country! Honestly, diary, this desert heat and blazing sun really disagrees with my fair complexion and moody temperament!

But tragically, my words hold no merit with regards to my husband; for he's simply determined to do as he pleases. However, truth be told, even when he's here at the mansion, it's as if, he's already a million miles away from me. His days are spent at the embassy and his nights alone in his chambers. I hardly see him. Often times, he skips dinner with me, and instead, he prefers a cold sandwich, along with a warm pot of tea, in the library. Imagine that! Truly, he rather stay in the company of dusty old books, than an evening alone with me, his own wife!

My marriage no longer feels like a real marriage anymore. John is too preoccupied and dedicated to his career, and nothing else apart from this seems to matter to him anymore, including me. But I promise you this, diary, if John still doesn't surprise me with a Valentine's gift before he leaves tomorrow, then I will never forgive him!

February 18, 2013,

Dear Diary,

Five days ago, John left for Croatia, and I haven't heard from him ever since. Not one word. Not a single message, phone call, email, letter…nothing. Worst of all, I received no gift, nor an acknowledge of a happy holiday wish. Nothing. Sadly, this is exactly what I feared would happen, too. To say that he left on good terms is to tell a lie. But let me explain. The day he left, I finally confronted him about his neglectful behavior and about him spending too much time at work. Initially, he denied it. But afterwards, after much reflection on his part, he came to understand my sentiments. Wanting to make amends with me, John promised that after his trip, he would strive to do better. But sadly, I'm not entirely certain, as to whether or not to believe him. Even though I vowed that I no longer cared about his general affairs; but regardless, I'm still his wife, and I have needs, too, both emotional and physical.

With John away, my focus has been redirected over to the affairs of the mansion. After much thinking, I've come to the conclusion that, if I must wear American designer clothing, then it must cater it to my own personal style, no matter the objections. For example, those dreadful high buttoned blouses are simply annoying and a no go! Sadly, I find that they completely drown my neck and are generally, so difficult to breathe in! To avoid this unfortunate wardrobe disaster, I've decided, that from now on, I'm going to style them by unbuttoning the first three buttons on each of my blouses. In addition, I've also decided that if I'm required to wear a plain black or neutral dress or suit, then I'll accessorize it with a bright colored scarf, handbag or jewelry.

Currently, I'm already clashing heads with Gloria. She's already objected to my "enhancements" and burgundy lip colored choice; but with John away, there's not much she can do. Although I'm still technically adhering to the rules, I'm also making my life bearable to live here, too. But the truth is that I don't want to lose nor forget myself along the way. Therefore, with these little adjustments, it helps me to remember as to just who I am. But most importantly, I'm still a young woman in my twenties, and I simply refuse to dress older, than my actual own age!

But apart from this, I also secretly suspect that Gloria is in fact a spy; or at the very least, an ally, to John's secretary, Margaret. I suspect this, because whatever I say or do in this house, somehow, the message still gets directly delivered over to John, one way or another. At first, I originally suspected Sally, but now, I don't think so. Sally is simply too busy, as it is. I suppose this might be due to my own fault. After all, I've been overwhelming the poor girl with so many tasks. But I what can I say, I need them done!

February 23, 2013,

Dear Diary,

I might have done something that I may later come to regret. I didn't plan on this, but it just happened. With John away, I decided that I needed something to distract my thoughts with…and so…I called Badi for another chess lesson. Upon my phone call, Badi promptly arrived to my office and all seemed well. As planned, we discussed the rules of the game, along with various strategies, as to how a player can protect their queen, etc. However, suddenly and unexpectedly, as I was trying to reach over to grab the knight, our hands ever-so gently collided. At first, we both blushed from embarrassment, and we awkwardly laughed at the accidental collision and carried on as normal with our game. But then, it happened once more for a second time. Unsuspectingly, our hands lightly pressed against each other, where it remained for a prolonged minute. But unlike before, this time we no longer felt ashamed nor embarrassed. This time we both felt perfectly comfortable with this happy accident.

And so, as our hands embraced…so did our arms…then our bodies and…before I knew it…Badi was kissing me directly on my mouth. Passionately. Forcefully. Endlessly. Throwing all the chess pieces and board onto the floor, Badi swiftly scoop me up from my chair, carried me off and threw me down onto the table, where he continued to kiss me with such fire and intensity, that the heat and flames from his body penetrated straight into my own skin. After kissing me for what felt like an eternity, he leaned forward and before I knew it, his entire body was pressing down upon me. Slowly, he grabbed and pulled my breast out from my dress, and from there, he began caressing and massaging them with his bare hands. As he was about to rip open the remainder of my dress, Sally unfortunately walked in on us. Having heard the commotion of the fallen chess board and pieces in the next room, she came rushing into my office and caught us in a rather compromising position. Sadly, diary, I'm sorry to say, that had Sally not walked in on us, then I'm fairly certain that we would have gone all the way with our lovemaking.

Determined to keep her silence, Sally swore to me that she won't say anything to anyone. But, should she even attempt or consider doing so, and betray me in the process, then I think that I also made it perfectly clear to her that I'm not afraid to ruin her career and even go so far, as to fire her without a reference, should I ever have to resort to that extreme length. Therefore, I think it's safe to say that I have her silence, at least for now.

March 1, 2013,

Dear Diary,

Right now, I'm writing from inside of my hotel room at the Ritz Carlton Cairo. Yesterday, I spent the entire night with Badi, alone. As it was our first night together, I suggested that we spend it as far away as possible from the prying eyes of the mansion. But shockingly, it almost didn't happen. Sadly, with security constantly hovering around, I was afraid that I wasn't going to be able to even sneak out of the house, without an agent following me. However, I surprisingly learned something new from this risky experience; which ironically, actually works to my benefit. With John out of town in Croatia, there's less of security's overall presence at the mansion. Furthermore, I've also discovered that at certain peak hours, security will even go so far, as to shift and relocate the majority of their operations, from the mansion and over to the embassy. Luckily, for me, it was during one of those peak hours, that I was able to secretly escape and meet Badi alone, at the hotel. As for my alibi, I lied and told Sally that I was leaving to visit a dear friend of mine, who was briefly staying in Cairo for the weekend. Honestly, I doubt that she truly believes me, but it really doesn't matter. But moving forward, my romantic rendezvous' really must happen, when John is away.

Overall, Badi's wonderful. He's everything that I've missed in a lover. He's tender, passionate, caring and warm. Truly, I haven't felt this way in a very long time. But sadly, I'm not entirely sure as to how long our relationship will last, because beginning next week, I'm going to start my etiquette and dancing lessons.

Starting next month, the mansion will be hosting a conference and state dinner. The invited attendees will include both John and myself, along with the ambassadors from Italy, France, Tunisia and Morocco. The scheduled event is intended to further expand and strengthen our U.S.

alliances with other selective Mediterranean nations, including Southern European and North African countries. As the first lady and the hostess for this upcoming event, I'm expected to manage and oversee the state dinner, entertainment and décor. As such, I'll be meeting with Gloria, Sally, Chef Homura, Bes, Carol and Tyler to go over the formal planning. Since this will be my first-time hosting a state dinner, Carol suggested that I partake in an etiquette course, as a form of good PR, which I agreed. In response, Gloria, of course, God bless her annoying soul, recommended that I also take dancing lessons to accompany my training, to which I immediately, refused. However, my opinion soon changed, once Sally advised me that dancing might actually work in my favor. According to Sally, if I learned how to properly dance, then I could also incorporate my new dancing skills into my event. As per Sally, more dancing, equals less table talk and dull conversations; as to which, I was immediately sold to her brilliant idea. As such, starting next week, I'll be immensely busy with coordinating everything. And so, in the meantime, I plan to enjoy as much time as I possibly can with Badi. Although I realize that this romance won't last forever; but at least for now, I'm going to have a bit of fun with him, while I still can.

March 8, 2013

Dear Diary,

Today, was my first lesson on etiquettes and to my surprise (and let's be clear, it certainly wasn't a pleasure), the one and only Gloria was my instructor! Apparently, as the embassy coordinator, she's not only limited to training employee staff, but as it turns out, her training also extends over to include the ambassador's family, as well. Unfortunately, this certainly caught me off guard, and I'm sorry to say, but I honestly hated and detested the entire experience with her!

First, of all, Gloria makes such a big deal about every tiny little thing! For example, in today's lesson, she helped to demonstrate to me as to the proper way to greet a guest, including how to effectively say hello; partake in an effective handshake; engage in a thoughtful smile; and to wave, curtesy, hug, stand, walk, sit and rise…and etc.…the list just goes on…and on…and on! But to my shockingly disappointment, apparently, I've been performing these commonly everyday routines, all wrong my entire life! Imagine that! To make matters worse, Gloria even carried a wooden metric ruler with her, during the entire session! In fact, she constantly used that damn stick of hers, as an actual weapon to ensure that I stood straight, tall, and with my stomach sucked in all the way, with my chin held high! And, if God forbid, I accidentally slouched…well…then to my disadvantage, she was right there to smack me from my behind, using that annoying ruler of hers!

And then, after we finished rehearsing my greeting techniques, she moved on and had me practice walking up and down the hallway, while carrying a large and heavy book above my head, as a "balancing" lesson! First, she initially asked that I carry a small copy of the book, Pygmalion; but when I refused, she punished me by having me carry and balance a much heavier encyclopedia, instead! To say that my head is still sore from that poor decision is an understatement. Now, I'm tired and I have a pounding headache! Perhaps, I'll take a dose of Tylenol and call it a night.

March 9, 2013

Dear Diary,

Today, I continued on with my training, but this time, I spent the majority of my day in Gloria's and Chef Homura's company. Together, we studied the proper protocols, relating to the correct use of table wear, including the effective and elegant usage of utensils, plates and drinkware. Furthermore, they discussed in great length and detail, as to which items should be used for which types of plates and meals, and where to place the used utensils back onto the plate, after each use. Amazingly, we even tackled the art of folding napkins, too. To his credit, Chef Homura tried his best to teach me origami, by folding a paper napkin into a swan. But truthfully, I think that my version of the "swan," actually looks more like a handbag, than anything else (but I personally, don't think that's such a bad thing, either; as I do love purses!).

All was going well, until we approached the topic concerning the dinner menu. While Chef Homura and I both agreed to serve fish as our main course; Gloria, as annoying as ever, objected and instead, she suggested that we strike out fish and replace it with beef, along with an alternative vegetarian dish. According to her, seafood is considered to be a highly sensitive and risky choice to serve as a main dish, because, as I later came to learn, many of our invited guests have either special dietary constraints or food allergies to shellfish. Therefore, because of these reasons, it's considered as more ideal to provide our honored special guests with an alternative to fish. Furthermore, Gloria explained that in the past, poultry and beef have always been a state dinner favorite, as well as the safest dish to serve, in terms of food allergies. Lastly, Gloria also highlighted the unofficial fact that since several of our guests are vegan, it's always a good idea to have at least one vegetarian dish on hand for every event.

After much discussion, in the end, I reluctantly agreed to her suggestions. Afterwards, we then moved onto the discussion concerning desserts and beverages. While Chef Homura and I both agreed to incorporate white wine and crème brulèe onto the menu; Gloria, once again, voiced her objections, ever-so delicately. Displeased by our decision, she, instead, highly advised that we replace our choice of white wine with a version of red wine, since she believes that red is more palatable with beef; whereas, white is best served alongside with fish. And if that wasn't enough, she also suggested that we select an alternative to crème brulèe, as several of our guests also have egg allergies. Needless to say, in the end, we all decided to go with the red wine and the dessert was completely changed and replaced by raspberry and lemon sherbet. Once again, sadly, Gloria won.

Last, but certainly not least, once the meeting was over, the matter concerning the décor came into our discussion. Since the color gold has always been a favorite of mine, I suggested that we incorporate my preferred color into the dinnerware and tablecloths. But surprise… surprise… surprise…this time, I was actually met not by one, but by two opposing forces: Gloria and Chef Homura! Immediately, they both cried out in horror, yelling aloud that my choice in the color gold was far too vulgar, distasteful and flashy. Furthermore, if I actually moved forward and still used it, then I would have greatly offended my invited guests by inadvertently sending them the negative impression that we, as the host country, are far wealthier and more superior, than the rest of the other guest countries in attendance—some of whom, are still part of the developing world classification. But please, come on! Really, this is absolutely ridiculous! I just don't agree! After all, it's only a color!

However, in an effort to move this annoying matter along, I bite my tongue and reluctantly agreed to their concerned requests. In the end, we just settled upon using good old plain and boring white for almost everything. Sad and depressing choice of color, yes, I know; but as I'm learning along the way, politics is also about sacrificing the little things, in order to trade off and gain what you really want, in the very end. Thus, while I was willing to forgo the general décor; later on, I eventually, won my preferred choice in the final selection of our centerpiece. Although I might have lost our first battle; in the end, my bouquet of red roses, along with a bright yellow bow, will be part of the official centerpiece for all of the tables. And, while I had originally desired gold for the bow; as an alternative, I happily settled for yellow, which is still within the same family wheel of color.

As much as I dislike Gloria's constant suggestions— which often feels more like nagging than anything else— I do suppose that at certain occasions and rare moments, she's sadly, right. Personally, I honestly had no idea, as to just how much politics really goes into planning a simple dinner! But next time, I'll be wiser and work to ensure that I avoid this matter altogether! Perhaps, I'll delegate Sally to deal with this all, from now on!

March 11, 2013

Dear Diary,

I can't even believe that I'm writing to say this, but today, was my first dancing lessons…and guess who was my assigned dance instructor and partner? Any tries?? No… it wasn't Gloria…whom, by the way, turns out that she's also a classically trained ballet dancer too…imagine, Gloria, a former prima ballerina! Hard to imagine, right? Anyways, did you guess…or have you given up, by now? Alright, let me just tell you. My dance partner is none other than…Bes Medina, our budget manager!

Bes, who's short, chubby, bald and with a terrible habit of constantly sweating due to his nerves, is my new dance partner! Yes, this is laughable! Luckily, I'm not new to dancing, having trained in gymnastics and some occasional ballet in my youth. Although Bes has the least-likely figure for dancing; he surprisingly, has some rather good moves and decent chorography.

For today's lesson, we practiced dancing the salsa, the tango and the waltz, together. Like I said before, since I do have a background in dancing, learning the steps to these dances wasn't too difficult for me. However, I did have to control my laughter, as Bes was constantly drying his sweat glands with his handkerchief. Honestly, I can't even image someone else, like my own twin sister, Kate, on ever having to learn these dances from the likes of Bes! My sister, who's never danced a single day in her entire life, is so lucky to be halfway around the world, right now. But one day, I'll have to personally invite her to one of these events, so she can watch my dancing in-person!

March 13, 2013

Dear Diary,

By being busy with all of these various event planning, I've unfortunately, neglected my relationship with Badi. As soon as this upcoming state dinner is over and done with, I'm resuming my romance with Badi, again. Although I tried to schedule another chess class in-between my free time (wink, wink), Gloria highly advised that I retain my focus on the party, first; and then resume my lessons, afterwards. Honestly, I don't want to draw any suspicions; and so, for now, I'll just have to wait. Meanwhile, I've also already written to Badi, and fortunately, he seems sympathetic to my situation, so we'll see how it goes.

March 15, 2013

Dear Diary,

Today, I met with Carol and Tyler to go over the invitations. Luckily, Gloria miraculously managed to catch a cold, and so, she stayed back at home…thank God! As a standing-in, I brought Sally, as a happy replacement. Like I previously wrote in my last entry, in the near future, Sally will take over the coordination of all state dinners, on my behalf. As such, I thought it most appropriate that she shadow me at these meetings, as she will soon take over.

Unlike my previous meetings from before, today's meeting was so simple, relaxed, straight forward and efficient. Having done their homework and preparation, well in-advance; Carol and Tyler gave me three sample invitation templates to choose from. While Carol designed the cover and logo, Tyler drafted the invitation's script and introduction, as well as cross referenced the written language to help ensure that it was legally appropriate and culturally sensitive to my invited foreign guests. When I opted for the second version, which was a royal blue background, with silver font colored design, I wonderfully received no opposing objections or difficult attitudes, from either party. Just a simple: yes, Mrs. Barrett. Honestly, diary, that was certainly a most welcomed breeze of fresh air!

After selecting the invitations, we then moved on to discuss about the hired photographers and my social media accounts. With regards to our official press release, Carol recommended that I schedule another follow-up meeting with them, post-state dinner to further discuss and confer, as to which photographs, I should nominate and select as my finalists for print publication. All in all, Carol and Sally agreed to post my approved photographs onto my official social media accounts to document the event, while Tyler will focus on writing the content for each post and review it, at the same time, to ensure that it also meets our legal standards. Upon the conclusion of our meeting, I followed Carol's advice and rescheduled a second follow-up meeting for after the upcoming event.

Surprisingly, I also came to discover that Carol is expected to one day replace Gloria's role, after she retires. Hopefully, that day comes soon. Fingers crossed! In my opinion, Carol will make a fantastic embassy coordinator. I can see it already!

March 17, 2013

Dear Diary,

I know that I should have waited to see Badi, but after this morning's dancing lesson with Bes, I secretly snuck out of the mansion and met Badi at the hotel. Since Gloria's still sick in bed and everyone else here is busy away planning the party, I decided to take my chances. Luckily, it paid off and my afternoon with Badi was pure heaven! As soon as I arrived, Badi carried me away into the bedroom, tore off all of my clothing, and then, he kissed and devoured every inch of my body! And I enjoyed every last minute of it!

But sadly, what will become of us? That, I don't yet know. The truth is that I don't actually see my relationship with Badi lasting forever, because today, he told me that very soon, he'll be traveling to Dubai for a chess championship tournament. But, of course, we shall wait and see.

March 20, 2013

Dear Diary,

With five more days to go until the party, I just received news today that John will be returning back home soon. Unfortunately, I haven't spoken to him ever since he left; and quite frankly, I couldn't care any less. However, I also can't help but wonder, as to how our relationship will be, from here on out? Will John change his neglectful ways? Will he still want a romantic relationship with me? I honestly, don't know.

March 23, 2013

Dear Diary,

Last night, John returned back home and instead of a happy reunion, we had another fight. With all honesty, I'm still upset about his abrupt departure and lack of communication. But most importantly, I still don't forgive him for forgetting about Valentine's Day. If John thinks that I'm going to welcome him back with open arms, after hearing nothing from him for weeks, then he's certainly the crazy one and not I!

But perhaps, he's really crazy, too; because after he arrived, John, honestly, expected me…of all people…to be happy to see him! In fact, he even so much as expected a kiss! That's certainly laughable! As if I'd kiss him, after everything that's since transpired.

Naturally, I rejected him; but to my surprise, he actually had the audacity to accuse me of being impatient and unsupportive of his official duties abroad! Can you believe that? I, the one who continues to maintain the public image of the ever-compassionate and dutiful wife, was the one who failed? I think not! Well, diary, I just rolled my eyes, when I heard that pathetic line. As for my response, you ask…well…it was more reactionary. Rather than yelling back at him, I simply grabbed one of his mother's annoying wine bottles in his office and threw it directly at him. Hard, too. And directly aimed right at his head. But sadly, I'm sorry to say, my aim was a bit off, on account of my new manicure. Meanwhile, as the wine bottle just nearly missed his precious head, it still managed to somehow hit and smash against the wall, where the glass broke into hundreds of tiny pieces all throughout his office floor, along with the red colored wine splashing about and staining all of his office's white walls and matching furniture.

Afterwards, John took off and I haven't seen him, ever since. I suppose my wine throwing incident will spark some gossip and nasty rumors amongst the staff; but truly, I don't care. At this point, the only thing I'm dreading is having to see him again tomorrow for our dinner rehearsal. But I'll let you in on a little secret: a long time ago, I studied drama in college. So now, I'm going to have to just start channeling my inner acting skills, in order to get through these next couple of days.

March 24, 2013

Dear Diary,

I had my first dress fitting today and I must say, I think that it went rather unexpectedly well. After much debate, I've decided to wear a Calvin Klein dress. Although I wasn't looking forward to wearing a non-Chanel outfit, to my surprise, my new dress turned out to look surprisingly decent…almost even…nice. The dress design, itself, is fairly simple. It's a modest black dress, that's form fitted and provides a low neckline, so that, I can still reveal a bit of skin that's not too much, but also not overly matronly. In summary, it's not ultra conservative; but yet, it's still classy. At last, with this item finally checked off my list, I still need to select my hair, makeup, and accessories too; but perhaps, I'll just have Sally sort that all out for me tomorrow, too.

As for John, I heard from Sally that he also had his own suit fitting today, as well. Currently, we're still not on talking terms. Although our relationship is sour at the moment, he was still ever-so polite, professional and cordial during our dinner rehearsal last night. At one point in the evening, I, hoping to get a reaction from him, while we danced, might have "accidentally" stepped and crushed one of his toes. Even though he really did try his very best to ignore it, his face said otherwise and as a direct result, he turned bright red. I know…I know… I'll admit that I was wrong to have done so, as it was such a terrible and bad deed. However, at least, this way, I proved to myself, that he's still human and capable of feelings, after all. Honestly, sometimes, John just acts way too serious, that I, myself, ponder as to whether or not, his heart isn't made of stone and is even capable of love. Either way, his reaction was priceless! Ah, happy wife, happy life!

March 25, 2013

Dear Diary,

Our dinner was tonight and what a spectacular event it was! The ambassadors from Italy, France, Tunisia and Morocco all arrived, along with their wives and staff; and I, for the first time, served as the hostess and the lady of the house. All in all, I think that everything went rather well! And to top it all off, the evening ended with a grand scale display of fireworks! It was a surprise gift from the French Ambassador. Imagine that!

Our evening began by first welcoming and greeting our new guests into the mansion, upon their arrival at the grand foyer. Even though John and I are still privately dealing with our own personal marital woes, we still managed to put on a brave face and together, we put aside our differences and publicly smiled, as we portrayed the ever-so happy, united and loving couple to our invited guests. Ah, diary, if only people knew the real truth!

As I previously wrote in my last entry, I wore my new black Calvin Klein dress, along with a pair of diamond studded earrings and a matching diamond necklace. Since my hair is still relatively short, Sally curled it and then styled my curly locks with freshly cut rose petals. Although my makeup was soft and natural looking, I also took a bold risk and wore a bright red colored lipstick on my lips. Yes, I understand that this might sound a bit scandalous, but what can I say, I simply couldn't help myself! With all of these darkly dimmed candle-lighting found throughout the ballroom, I just knew that bright lips were necessary, in order to make a grand and glamorous statement. Plus, given that this is my introduction into high society, I knew that it was imperative that I made a first good impression.

Apart from yours truly, John was also elegantly dressed and was quite the dashing gentleman. To be honest, he was, by far, the single most handsome and attractive man in the entire room. In fact, I even heard whispers and chatter from the other wives, who also thought the same, just as I. Ever sophisticated, he wore a black silk suit, with a white blouse and a navy-blue tie. Although his attire was rather simple, John, somehow, continues to carry himself with so much suave, ease, charm and charisma, that, personally, I really believe that he can even charm the birds right from out of the trees, if he really wanted to. But at the same time, I also can't help but wonder that with all of these charming qualities, then why doesn't he use any of it on me, his wife? Oh well, I'll just have to tackle that matter later on.

As for our other remaining guests and their fashion choices…well…that was certainly entertaining! First off, let me start by saying, that almost if not, all of the male ambassadors wore a standard black suit, similar to John's, which many might regard, as an unofficial state affair's uniform. However, their wives were an entirely different story and they most certainly, weren't limited to any standard uniform. As a result, they were truly the gems of the evening!

My favorite outfit was worn by the Tunisian Ambassador's wife. She wore a stunning turquoise ballroom typed gown, with heavy gold jewelry. Truly, she resembled a-real-life Princess Jasmine, straight from Aladdin! Meanwhile, the Moroccan Ambassador's wife, wore a tangerine-orange colored chiffon gown that highlighted her golden caramel skin, and from afar, she looked just like a shining star. But the one who stood out to me the most, was the Italian Ambassador's wife. She was absolutely gorgeous, and she appeared similar to a runway model, straight from the walkways of Milan. Dressed similar to a Roman Goddess, she arrived wearing a long white and flowing gown. Lastly, and sadly to admit, I can't complement the French Ambassador's wife, at all; for tragically, as she was the most ill-fitted and awkwardly dressed woman at the entire event!

Surprisingly, you'd have thought, that her coming from Paris, the fashion capital of the entire world, that she'd been the most glamorous of all; but no, that wasn't the case, at all. Instead, the black sequin dress that she wore, was sadly, two sizes too large for her own small and petite figure. Meanwhile, her dress straps kept constantly falling off from her broad shoulders. Obviously, she failed to have a proper fitting and, in my opinion, her tailor should be fired. To make matters even worse, she wore absolutely no makeup at all; plus, her hair looked absolutely messy and untidy in appearance. Although her long hair was pulled away from her face and tucked away into a bun, tiny strands of her remaining loose hair kept falling out. Honestly, if I was her, I'd fire not only the tailor, but the entire styling team, all put together!

After our meet and greet with everyone, we moved onto dinner. From there, everything mostly all went straight according to plan. While the wives positively complemented about the center pieces and the overall décor to me, their husbands raved and gushed about their delicious meals over to John. Furthermore, all of my prior training paid off too; for I was able to successfully demonstrate my elegant new table etiquettes properly, as well as having a chance to showcase my polished dancing skills, too!

By the end of the dessert course, we all took to the dancefloor. From there, on stage, I danced my first waltz with John. I'll admit, it was a bit uncomfortable; for he uttered not a single word to me. I suppose that he's still upset and angry with me about the whole wine bottle throwing fiasco from the other day. I can't say that I don't blame him, I guess. Had it been the other way around, then, I, too, might have been upset as well. But apart from that, somehow, I still wonder if maybe he also suspects or knows anything about my affair with Badi? Even though I've tried my very best to conceal our affair; however, with Gloria always lurking around, you just never know if her suspicions might have reached the prying ears of Margaret. In any case, we danced only one dance, and then, we parted our own separate ways. In the end, I unexpectedly spent the remainder of the evening dancing away with the French Ambassador!

Since the French Ambassador's wife's gown was so badly ill-fitted and uncomfortably faulty, she decided to remain seated and skipped dancing. I, personally, thought that was a smart idea, too; for if she'd even have tried to bother to dance, then I'm absolutely convinced that her dress would have fallen off completely, leaving her left standing bare naked and feeling embarrassed, with her reputation in tatters. Imagine, what a scandal that could have been! Good God, I can just image Gloria dying from such a horrendous sight! Honestly, she really does make such a big deal over everything, too!

Like I wrote before, tonight was a lovely, and I happily enjoyed it. Also, to my sheer surprise, the French Ambassador was rather flirty! But, I suppose, with such a plain looking wife, it's only naturally. Why, dancing with me was probably the highlight of his entire year! Now, I'm officially tired, and I'm going to wash up and get ready for bed. I have an early meeting tomorrow morning, so I'll write back later on, to fill you in!

March 26, 2013

Dear Diary,

Sadly, I don't even know where to begin. There are no words. All I can say, is that I was so incredibly upset this morning. But let me explain. Earlier this morning, as I was walking down the hallway to attend my meeting, I was unexpectedly stopped by Gloria, midway down. It was there, right in the center of the hallway, where she inappropriately accused me of flirting with the French Ambassador; and thereby, embarrassing not only John and myself, but the entire embassy, too, last night! Shocked by these cruel and untrue accusations, I was absolutely taken aback and appalled by such a notion!

For the record, it was the French Ambassador flirting *with me* and not the other way around! According to Gloria, the French Ambassador's wife contacted John's office to complain about me. This morning, John's secretary, Margaret, answered the phone call and reassured her that this wasn't the case; but rather, a grave misunderstanding. However, Gloria warned me that the French Ambassador's wife is notorious for having the reputation of being a jealous woman; and unfortunately, if we don't take immediate action, then she might even go as so far, as to spread negative rumors about us, as a form of retaliation.

Upon learning about this unfortunate truth, Gloria then accompanied me to my meeting. From there, the original topic of my meeting immediately shifted gears and instead, we reverted our discussion with the other staff members, as which methods we should opt to utilize, in order to mitigate and deescalate this crisis and prevent the outbreak of a scandal. Ultimately, our shared goal was to construct a new narrative, to challenge any potential opposition. But to be perfectly honest, everything happened so quickly, that I hardly understood as to which final decisions were eventually decided upon, on my behalf. Before I knew it, Gloria quickly took command of the entire situation, and within the blink of an eye, she was already swiftly debriefing and directing the others, as to what our next steps were going to be.

To my surprise, I seemed to be the only person nervous; for everyone else looked calm and unmoved by the entire situation. Sensing my uneasiness, Carol approached me and explained that although these misunderstandings do happen from time to time, that the embassy staff are professionals and are well trained, so no matter what happens next, I'm in good hands. Furthermore, the staff did not delay not a single moment; for as soon as the meeting concluded, they quickly went to work.

Immediately, Sally and Gloria contacted a local French florist to reserve a bouquet of yellow roses to be deliver to the French Ambassador's wife's office. According to Gloria, yellow roses are symbolic and represents friendship and forgiveness; therefore, an exchange of yellow roses was meant to serve as our unofficial declaration of peace. Meanwhile, Carol and Tyler reviewed all of last night's photographs, and after much searching, they miraculously managed to locate a "friendly" photo of the two of us ladies, together in a pose, along with our husbands by our sides. In the photograph, we had just met and greeted each other in the grand foyer, with a handshake, as we both were pictured smiling, face to face, with one another. Right next to us, were our respective husbands, also shaking their hands with one another, while also smiling. This single handily was the million-dollar shot that showed all four us, happily together, as we publicly displayed our friendly relations out into the world.

After we all agreed to use this particular photograph for my social media accounts and press releases, Carol began drafting an announcement and Tyler assisted her with the specific language. It's funny, that even with a simple online publication, it still requires a lawyer's input. By the end of the day, the flowers were delivered, along with a personalized note, that included a poem written by Robert Frost about friendship. Soon afterwards, an announcement was released to the public and Bes contacted the associated press to release the official photographs over to the media.

After everything that's happened, I think that it's all going to be okay. Thanks to our fast response, I truly believe that I avoided a messy scandal; of which, I was completely ignorant of being an unwanted party to, just the night before.

June 8, 2013

Dear Diary,

It's been a few weeks since I've last written, but my mind and heart have been preoccupied with Badi. Last week, Badi returned Cairo from his trip to Dubai, along with a trophy! I'm happy to share that he recently won the chess championship tournament!

While John is away in London, I've had the mansion all to myself; and so, last night, I snuck out of the mansion to secretly meet with Badi. My plan is to spend this entire week alone, in his company. Previously, I told Sally that I'll be traveling to New York to visit my sister. Hopefully, she'll share this news with Gloria and the rest of the staff, if they ask and this can serve as my alibi. Alright, Badi is pulling me away from you as I write this, my dear diary, so now I must dedicate the remainder of my afternoon to him!

June 17, 2013

Dear Diary,

A lot has transpired since I've last written. It appears that my love affair with Badi has now come to an abrupt end. Yesterday, he shared the news with me, that after winning the chess championship, he's been offered a full-time position teaching chess professionally to the elites of Dubai. He's already accepted the position, and now, he's asked that I join him. Sadly, I declined his offer. The truth is, I'm just not ready to leave John. Even though we've been married for only a few months, I'm just not ready to leave this life of luxury entirely behind, right now. Perhaps, when John returns back from London, then I'll ask that we seek marriage counseling.

However, our marriage might not be the only problem for us right now. There's a rumor of a revolution brewing here, in Egypt. There's been widespread protests across the country, seeking to overthrow the political regime of the Egyptian Prime Minister Mubarak, after running the country these past thirty years as a dictator. As we speak, John is attending a conference in London, joined by other ambassadors, all discussing as to what shall become of their respective embassies in Cairo, should a revolution break out. Right now, for the first time, even with John away, the mansion is surrounded by extra security agents, at all possible corners. They arrived early this morning and already set up camp. It's a good thing that I met with Badi privately last night, because as of right now, there's no possible way for me to escape from here anymore.

August 2, 2013,

Dear Diary,

I'm writing from my new temporary apartment in London, located right outside of the Paddington train station. Since my last entry, an Egyptian revolution broke out and it was rather ugly. The embassy was attacked. All the windows were smashed into pieces; the doors broken into and the locks ripped open apart. The offices were left in a complete mess, with all of the filing cabinets flipped over upside down and thousands of documents all scattered about and thrown across the floor. Additionally, most of the furniture and art décor were either destroyed or stolen from out of their premises. In summary, the embassy resembled that of a bomb exposition; in which all that remained was nothing more than ruble, garbage rubbish and the footprints left behind by ugly thefts and thugs.

Luckily, all staff were evacuated ahead of time and none were inside of the building, when the invasion took place. In response to the advanced intelligence John received back in London, he promptly closed down the embassy and returned all nonessential staff back to the United States, just days before the revolution took place, on June 30, 2013.

As for myself and the staff at the mansion, John classified us as essential employees and to continue our operations, he relocated us over to London, to await until further notice and instructions. And, so, as of now, Gloria, Carol, Tyler, Bes, and Eton are all residing at the Marriott London. As for myself, I rented a small private London flat for myself, Sally and Chef Homura. It's a small three-bedroom apartment, located within a nice, quiet and residential neighborhood. What can I say, Sally is my personal assistant and my right arm, while Chef Homura is my world class chef and is equally, my left arm. Besides, without Sally, who else is there to attend to my affairs, while we're away from the office? Plus, how can I eat a proper and decent meal in London, the plain food capital, without my favorite chef?

Meanwhile, John's away and currently in Washington, D.C., staying at the agency's headquarters. Right now, he's meeting with his superiors to decide the fate of our Cairo embassy, and to discuss as to whether or not, he'll be transferred to a new location. Although John successfully evacuated all of the embassy employees ahead of time and safely returned them back home; the revolution, however, still managed to expose some detrimental pitfalls from within the agency's internal operations. Although the mansion remains standing and intact; sadly, it too, suffered some external damages. The rioters managed to break through the iron gates and trespassed past the front doors and entered the grand foyer. Several priceless artworks, including many Egyptian sculptures and trinkets were stolen or vandalized in the lobby, as well as the destruction of a select few guest vehicles parked outside in the garage. Even though John stationed several U.S. Marshals to remain at the premise, they still failed to prevent and stop the rioters from breaking in and entering into our territory.

Since the majority of U.S. Marshals stationed here are career retired police officers and former military officers, most of them are primary deployed to deal with nonaggressive civilians visiting the embassy and mansion. Generally, many lack any sophisticated training to prepare for a full-scale war-like invasion, such as what we experienced last week. Due to their lack of preparation and planning, our embassy was destroyed and the mansion was left in such a poor condition. Upset by their failures, John swore that he will seek to terminate their services and contract another security firm to serve in their place.

As of now, I'm rather enjoying my time here in London, while I await to hear further news from John. If he should transfer to a new embassy, then I'm hoping that Gloria will either stay behind in Cairo, be reassigned to another embassy, or at the very least, retire. Even in London, she's still criticizing my outfits. Why, even last night, after I spent the evening visiting the theater to watch the Phantom of the Opera with Sally, I received a late-night telephone call from Gloria, scolding me for wearing a pink Chanel satin dress! Imagine, the nerve of that woman! Now, I do realize that Chanel is not an American designer; however, this was my first evening out as a civilian. Plus, I'm in England, not Egypt! Apparently, Margaret was also a guest at the very same show, and unfortunately, she spotted us at the balcony from her seat down below. Needless to say, she directly informed Gloria about our whereabouts, as well as a detailed account of my questionable fashion choice. Honestly, diary, I'm really at my whit ends with these two ever prying women! They're worse than the paparazzi!

October 5, 2013

Dear Diary,

I'm now writing from Dubrovnik, Croatia, which will serve as John's temporary post, until the beginning of next year. As I last wrote, John was in Washington, D.C., discussing about the aftermath of the Egyptian revolution and the fate of our embassy.

At the meeting, it was decided that the agency was going to temporarily close the Cairo embassy down, until further notice; and in the meantime, John will be reassigned to a new post. Given that the U.S. Ambassador to Croatia is on temporary leave and John was personally trained directly under him, the agency determined that John was the best fit to serve as his temporary replacement, until January 2014. Afterwards, John will then be eventually transferred to a new and undisclosed post. Furthermore, it was also determined that effective January 2014, all of the Cairo embassy and mansion staff will also be transferred to new offices and locations, as well. In the interim, all nonessential staff are currently on extended leave, with the exception to the essential staff, who are all here with me in Croatia…including Gloria and Margaret, most unfortunately.

Yes, believe me diary, I really did go so far, as to ask John to fire them; but sadly, he refused. Instead, he told me that regardless of my personal feelings, it was just simply not practical to do. Given their combined thirty plus years of service, their termination without adequate due cause, was virtually impossible, without creating internal conflict. Sadly,

I suppose he's right. But either way, I'm still greatly disappointed.

Although we're still unaware of John's next post, his request to outsource security to a private firm was granted. Effective January 2014, John will no longer use the service of the U.S. Marshals and will instead, hire a new private security firm of his choosing. In fact, John's been working with Bes to finalize this year's upcoming new fiscal budget to incorporate this new expenditure.

As for myself, so far, I'm enjoying my time in Croatia. It's truly a beautiful and remarkable country. The city of Dubrovnik is a medieval and fairy-tale like town, consisting of old castles, romantic historical architectures and traditional cobbled stone roads, all spread across this ancient city. Plus, the beaches here, alone, are just simply gorgeous. The Adriatic Sea is absolutely breathtaking. The water is turquoise in color, that it's almost like living and swimming in a postcard. In the mornings, I usually walk down the cobbled stone roads, while I explore the old castles and ancient ruins, along my path. And when I'm not exploring the city, I'm often sunbathing at the local beach or swimming in the sea.

With regards to my relationship with John, that's still to be determined. I recently brought up the matter concerning marriage counseling to his attention, but as of right now, he's just too busy and asked that we postpone this discussion to a later time. Currently, we're still sleeping apart and in separate bedrooms, and I hardly see him, except for our occasional dinners together. But even during dinner, he's still silent and distant from me. Why, we hardly speak at the table, if not to ask one another to pass the salt or pepper. Honestly, diary, I can't help but wonder, if he suspects or knows anything about my affair with Badi. However, if by any chance he does know something, then he continues to remain ever silent about this subject.

Do I feel remorseful about my affair? No, I don't. Truthfully, I enjoyed my time with Badi, and I don't regret not a single moment of it. Badi brought me company and joy, when I was otherwise, alone and miserable. Furthermore, if John truly loved me for me, then he wouldn't have gone several weeks away without contacting me. Without thinking about me. Without missing me. If he can survive extended periods of time and not wonder about my whereabouts, then why should I miss him, in return? Pray tell, why should I remain faithful? As far as I'm concerned, I'm legally married to him, in name only.

February 15, 2014

Dear Diary,

I know, it's been a while since I've last written, but not to worry, I'm here to update you with all that has transpired. We are now in Athens and John has been appointed as the new U.S. Ambassador to Greece. The embassy is located at the capital and similar to Cairo, the mansion is only a few blocks away. All of our Cairo staff transferred with us to Greece, with the exception of our butler, Eton, who decided to retire, instead. Now, we've got George, as his replacement, who was highly recommended by Chef Homura. Apparently, George once worked with Chef Homura on the tv series *Flame*. But, sadly and unfortunately, Gloria is still with us…and I couldn't be more displeased…

Since moving to Greece, we've all pretty much had a smooth transition here. The new mansion is very similar to the former Cairo estate, with an almost identical architectural exterior structure and interior layout. In addition, the garden and landscape resemble our previous residence, along with roses growing and thriving about. The furniture is somewhat similar; however, instead of Egyptian cultural art, we now have ancient Greek statues everywhere…and I mean, literally, everywhere. From the lobby to the bathroom, to the kitchen to the dining rooms, to the offices to the bedrooms, there's at least one ancient Greek God and Goddess statue in each room, at a bare minimum. Why, Athena's in the dining room, Hercules' in the lobby, Cupid and Psyche in the grand foyer, and Hades and Persephone in the salon! But, sadly, the worst of all, the ultimate crown victor is our guest washroom located on the first-floor. In that room, apart from the golden replicas of the twins, Apollo and Diana, sprouting water from a bright yellow and bronze washing well, sitting right above the toilet, is a massive portrait of Zeus, stark naked, in all of his glory, and standing tall and proud right above Mountain Olympus, along with the rest of his fellow Titans; each of whom, are equally standing proud and tall, in their own natural and nude states! I mean, honestly, this is way too vulgar and over the top! But, of course, as you might have already guessed by now, this was all Gloria's doing. By the time I finally saw the portrait delivered and hung up, I had long admitted defeat. At this point in time, I have other more pressing and important battles to fight, rather than arguing with Gloria about the mansion's décor. No, diary, I've got far more urgent matters to attend to; and one of them, being the matter concerning John.

Since arriving to Greece, my relationship with him has very much been up in the air, and there are many issues still left unresolved. For the past several weeks, he's been busy recruiting a new security firm for both the embassy and the mansion. After much review, he eventually settled upon the Orion Securities firm, which is an American private security company from New York that specializes on protecting and safeguarding former politicians, celebrities, and other wealthy Americans and their families. The firm was highly recommended by his own mother, Barbara, who herself, was introduced to the firm by its Chief Executive Officer, Lucas Oliver.

While attending a charity event in New York, Barbara stumbled upon Lucas in the most heroic way. The Orion firm was contracted to serve as the security for the event, and it was on there after dinner, as Barbara exited the ballroom, a theft suddenly jolted from out of the shadows and attacked her. Hastily running towards her, the theft managed to slam Barbara down onto the ground. As she fell down to the floor, the thief quickly grabbed her purse in the process and then, he ran off.

However, in a twist of fate, Lucas, who was also serving as a security officer that night, saw what transpired from down the hall, as he was patrolling the scene on duty. Within moments, Lucas swiftly ran after the theft and miraculously caught him before he got the chance to get away. Before Barbara even had a chance to react, Lucas was soon by her side and helping her back up. By the time Barbara returned standing, her stolen purse was safely returned and tucked away within her arms, while the thief placed in handcuffs and thrown into jail. Amazed by his swift and effective actions, Barbara requested his business card and before the night's end, she called John immediately to not only praise her new hero, but to also provide him with Lucas' contacts directly.

Although John isn't the sort of a man, who can be easily persuaded, even by his own mother, he was regardless, still grateful to Lucas for helping his mother, during an unfortunate event. In the end, John ultimately decided to include Orion as one of his candidates for his list of potential government security contractors. However, after much research, John was thoroughly impressed by Orion's highly sought-after reputation and cliental list. Furthermore, since time was running short, with the added headache of our relocation from Croatia to Greece, John finally agreed to hire Lucas Oliver as the new head of security, along with his company, Orion Securities, to serve as his new and official government security contractor.

Since recruiting a new security team was his top priority at the time, I allowed and permitted for some distance and space to continue between John and myself, so that he could concentrate on this important task. But, having said this, I also presumed that once this task was over, then we'd revisit the subject concerning my request for marriage counseling. Sadly, my hopes for a session turned out to be a failure. As of now, John simply refuses to attend marriage counseling, and I blame Gloria and Margaret for this. For whatever reason, they are both convinced that if we went through with this, then, one way or another, it would have been leaked to the press; and thereby, somehow ruin or tarnish our image as a happy and credible couple. After installing this fear into him, John actually agrees with them and now, sadly, marriage counseling is forever out of the question.

However, if I'm being honest, the main problem is that apart from sleeping in separate rooms each night, which really isn't an issue for me anymore, as I much prefer my own bedroom and private space; but rather, it's that we haven't been intimate with one another in months. The truth is that I, as a young woman, crave intimate moments and nights alone, with my husband. Otherwise, without intimacy, then how can this even be a real marriage? A marriage without it, is just a friendship at best; and as far as I'm concerned, I don't even consider us much of friends, as we have very little in common to begin with.

When I finally cornered John about our lack of martial relations, he blamed his long nights at the office for the sole reason for this; however, I don't agree or believe him. Instead, deep within my heart, I think he knows about my affair with Badi, and he just can't find the means to admit it, nor forgive me. But, at the same time, I also wonder, if he has another lover of his own, too? After all, he's always away, so anything is possible.

Finally, to top it all off, last night was Valentine's Day. You'd think that it would have been a happy occasion for us; but no, instead, it was another year of disappointment. After making John feel incredibly guilty for ignoring and missing the holiday last year, I forced him to take us out on a romantic dinner together, which surprisingly, he agreed to do. Although I made sure that John drank several glasses of wine, by the time we finally arrived home, and I finished escorting him upstairs and into my bedroom, he unexpectedly fell fast asleep on the sofa and actually stayed asleep, until the next morning…so much for trying to have at least one romantic evening alone with my husband!

March 15, 2014

Dear Diary,

Alright, you have my permission to call me a fool, but I'm in love again! Of course, just like most romantic adventures, I wasn't looking for love, it just found me. After moving to Athens two weeks ago, John was busy setting up and reorganizing the new embassy. Meanwhile, I, once again, found myself all alone in the huge mansion, and slowly, I began to feel extremely lonely, bored and practically forgotten.

Given that Sally generally oversees and takes care of almost all, if not, most of my business and personal affairs, there isn't really much left for me to do. As a result, I find myself with an unlimited supply of free time, on an ongoing and daily basis. Once more, Sally suggested that I take up another new hobby; but to Gloria's rare credit, she suggested that I, instead, do some sightseeing here, at the capital. According to Gloria, with all of Greece's historical sites, ruins and museums, it's impossible for me to remain bored. And so, I took Gloria's offer, and she hired a private tour guide to show me around the country. Enter Demitri…

Demitri, my new tour guide, is the personification of a modern-day Greek God. He's handsome, strong, courageous and beyond attractive for an earthly being. He's an angel. He's Zeus on earth. Similar to my affair with Badi, this too, wasn't planned, at all. From the first moment we met, there was an instant spark of attraction between us, and almost immediately, I felt the lightning bolt of electricity shoot and penetrate right between us. Honestly, I've never felt this before; not even with John or Badi. And, for some odd reason, I just knew that he felt the same way, too.

At first, we just remained cordial and on friendly terms. While we toured across the city, I just smiled on and kept my feelings hidden to myself. Even as we walked up the hill to reach the top of the Acropolis, I kept a safe distance behind him. Why, I even rejected his helping hand to climb up those steep steps! Ultimately, I rejected him, for I knew, that if my hands touched his, then surely, it was going to be the end of me.

However, as much as I tried my very best to resist any urge to touch him, fate intervened. As we drove along the coastline of the Aegean Sea, we decided to take a brief rest stop by the cliffs, so that I could take a moment to breathe in the cool sea air breeze, while admiring the sea from high above, with a bird's eye view. Looking back at, it was the best decision too, for the view was absolutely breathtaking and there's really no words that I can write to describe, as to just how incredibly beautiful it was to see and experience it, in-person. Honestly, diary, the water was so transparent and clear, that you could actually see the emerald green fish swimming from right underneath the sea. Meanwhile, the sunshine was so bright and sunny, that even my pink diamond ring sparkled a new variation of pink reflected against the sunlight, that I, myself, have never once seen before.

Suddenly, at that precise moment, that same pink sparkle shining from my ring, caught hold of my eyes and in that split second, I was completely blinded. With my sudden loss of vision, I soon lost my balance, tripped over a pebble and was about to tumble off the cliffs. Luckily, Demitri, who was right behind me, came to my rescue and quickly ran up towards me. Within moments, he safely caught me up in mid-air and scooped me up into his caring arms, as we, together, landed backwards safely onto land.

It was there, as I lay within his strong and muscular arms, that my eyes finally met his, for the very first time. To my surprise, his eyes were kind, gentle and understanding. Having been so close to death, I suddenly realized that nothing else in this world mattered. At this very moment, I was alive, safe and in his protective arms. And then, before I knew it, he leaned down and gave me a kiss on my lips. At first, he was hesitant, but once I returned his kiss, the repressed fire and passion finally exploded between us, like a pair of matchsticks finally lite, at long last.

Thereafter, he swiftly whisked me away into a nearby cave; all the while, still carrying me within his strong arms. Upon entering the cave, he quickly tore off all of my clothes like a demanding beast, and then he entered me with such force, which stemmed from his own intense longing and desire. For a brief second, I was startled by his sudden invasion. However, diary, please don't be too alarmed, for I thoroughly enjoyed every last minute of it! Our lovemaking in the cave continued on throughout that afternoon, and by the time it was finally over, we were both so incredibly exhausted, but nevertheless, equally pleased and satisfied with the overall experience.

Flash forward to now, it's been two weeks, since that first romantic encounter, and the romance hasn't stopped ever since. I still meet with Demitri every afternoon, for our daily tours across Greece. Unlike Badi, it's a bit easier to carry on with this affair. As my tour guide, I'm justified to travel alone with him, without any questions. But that's where I must end this entry, for now. I'll be leaving soon to meet with him again, and I really must get ready. Today, we're off to the botanical gardens. Wish me luck!

December 1, 2014

Dear Diary,

It's been several months since I've last written, and it's time that I fill you in on all that's transpired. These past few months were truly wonderful, and I've been so blissfully happy. With Demitri, I'm no longer sad or lonely. Although my affair with him was unplanned, I honestly haven't felt this excited and thrilled about anything else, in a very long time. The passion that I feel for him is unparallel to another. Whenever I'm with him, there's simply a fire that burns deep within my heart; and when he's away, he's all that I think about, both night and day. Yes, these are dangerous emotions, especially for a married woman, such as myself. But diary, I just can't help but feel this way. Ever since my relationship with Demitri began, I haven't missed Badi, nor have I thought twice about John, at all. In fact, this is also one of the main reasons as to why I've stopped writing in this diary, altogether. Lately, I've been so preoccupied with him, that I've stopped doing a lot of other things, too. Honestly, it's a good thing that I've got Sally to handle all of my affairs; otherwise, I would have neglected them all, just as I have done to you too, diary. But sadly, I fear, that my romance with Demitri, is on its last breath and will soon come to an abrupt and tragic end.

Just as I had feared, today, after breakfast, I was confronted by Gloria about my affair. As I was about to leave the mansion in the early morning to meet with Demitri, Gloria managed to stop me in the lobby. Attempting to avoid conflict with her, I told her that I was late for a prior engagement; however, that still didn't deter nor stop her from requesting a private meeting with me in my office. Given the seriousness in her tone and the genuine look of concern in her face, I decided that it was best to meet with her once and for all, and to get it over as quickly as possible. But, I'm afraid, that decision is something that I've since come to regret.

As soon as the doors to my office closed, Gloria confessed to me that she's known about my romantic relationship with Demitri this entire time, just as she knew about my affair with Badi, as well. When I asked her how she was privy to this information, she refused to answer me. Instead, she warned me that the reason as to why she didn't mention anything about Badi before, was because she knew that it was a fickle affair that wouldn't last beyond a season. Therefore, there wasn't any need to alert anyone. Recognizing that in some marriages, extramarital relations do happen, Gloria told me that in her many years of working at the embassy, I'm not the first wife that's she's ever witnessed carrying on with an affair before, while their husbands are in office, nor, am I expected to be the last. However, unlike the others before, my relationship with Demitri became too serious, and Gloria felt that my own heart grew too attached to a man, who wasn't even my own husband. According to her, I'm in dangerous territory, and if I fail to change my ways, then she predicts that everything will end badly for me.

Attempting to instill fear within me, she said that if my relationship leaked to the press, then it was going to be a scandal of infinite proportion. It certainly would have tarnish not only my honor as a lady, but in the process, also damage the reputations of both John and the embassy. After warning me about the consequences of my affair, she finally gave me an ultimatum: end my relationship with Demitri, in exchange for her silence; or have her tell John the truth, herself directly, if I continue on with my romantic relationship. In the end, I gave into her demands and promised to end it. As it currently stands, she's accepted my promise and in return, she's vowed to remain silent on this matter, forever.

Now, I'm here to reflect to you, diary, my feelings about all of this. Looking back at it, I really had no other choice but to accept her ultimatum. I don't want to be the center of a scandal, especially, since the mansion will be hosting an upcoming state dinner for NATO members. The NATO members are expected to arrive in Athens next month, in time for their annual conference. It's certain to be a spectacular event, to be sure. All of the world's most famous politicians and tech elites will be attending, not to also mention John's family, too. Why, he's already invited Barbara, David and Amy to the event; however, I suspect that perhaps only Barbara will attend, as Amy is still away at college.

Diary, I must confess, I'm a bit nervous seeing Barbara again. I haven't seen her since our wedding. I'm simply afraid that she'll recognize and sense the distance between John and I. Honestly, I'm not yet prepared to answer any of her lurking questions, should she grow suspicious about us. However, I've decided that if John's family are allowed to attend, then I shall invite my sister, Kate, too. Although I haven't revealed any of my plans yet to anyone, I generally believe that a change of scenery and a break from her studies might be beneficial for my twin sister. But, diary, I'll admit one las thing, and that is that I also have an ulterior motive: my twin sister is also meant to serve as a distraction to Barbara. With Kate around, I'm certain that she'll be able to keep Barbara preoccupied with plenty of conversations and away from me! I suppose, one could say that this is my attempt at killing two birds with one stone!

January 3, 2015

Dear Diary,

Tonight, was the NATO state dinner and considering how stressful this week was for me, everything turned out to be better than I expected. The evening began with our official portraits taken with the photographer. Each ambassador and their families are required to have at least one official photograph taken at the event, so John and I met in the gallery, where we proceeded to walk hand-in-hand, as a couple, and over to the photograph room. Sadly, that was the most awkward walk that I've ever taken in my entire life!

As he escorted me down the hall, he uttered not one word to me, not a single word. Complete and utter silence. His body was tense, his face was stern, and he looked angered and a bit red. He's still upset with me, this much I know. In the past, he often ignored my presence and exerted no emotion; however, this time, he was mad and it showed. Although I do believe that Gloria's kept her vow of silence, I think that John must have discovered about my affair from someone else. But who else could have known? Diary, this remains a mystery to me.

As we walked down the hallway, I felt so incredibly uncomfortable around him. It wasn't until we reached the foot of the staircase that his demeanor finally changed. Within an instant, his tense body released his stiff hold, and he became calm and collective. Meanwhile, his red face returned back to his original pale coloring, and his tightly gripped jaw released from its stern posture and quickly transitioned into a smile. The man I walked with from one end of the hallway to the other end, was an entirely different person. It was if I had been in the presence of two very different people. The version of John, whom I met at the gallery, was completed transformed. He was a real-life Doctor Jekyll and Mr. Hyde, in the flesh.

When we finally reached the public domain, he smiled and waved to our guests. As we descended down the staircase, out of sheer routine, he grabbed hold of my hand, as we walked over to the photographer. And if I had somehow assumed that all was forgiven now that we were in public, then, sadly, I was gravely mistaken. Although John smiled and gave the impression that we were a happy couple, his grip on my hand told me, personally, otherwise. He's still very much angry with me. In fact, his tight grip on my hand was so strong and intense, that I nearly lost my balance and was about to trip over the hems of my dress, and fall right then and there on the red carpet. But before I tumbled down, John caught me in mid-air, brought me back up, leaned in and then whispered into my ear.

"Whatever you do, wherever you go, and whomever you see, I no longer care," he whispered angrily. "But tonight, for the sake of our guests, I'm asking you to please remain professional and to join me with a smile."

His request completely caught me off guard. Up until this moment, he's never once spoken to me in this way before. He's always been the calm and collective one. The ever endearing and forgiving gentleman. However, this time, he was very serious, demanding and assertive. A first for his character. I, on the other hand, will confess that I'm usually the emotional one and at times, the troublemaker. I'm not ashamed to admit this, for I know it's true. However, his reaction was the first time I saw another side to him. A vulnerable side. A wounded side. A hurt side. And then, I just knew. He felt betrayed. It was as if, a sharpened knife was plunged straight through his heart by a trusted ally and companion. All the while, learning the truth about their betrayal on the precipitous of their own impending death, just as Julius Caesar had felt when dying within the arms of his dear friend, Brutus.

From his eyes, I finally saw the truth for myself: he knew about my affair. There was no longer a shadow of doubt, in my mind. He knew. Whether or not, he was aware of Demitri or Badi, or both, it really didn't matter. Regardless, he just knew that I was unfaithful, and that I had betrayed him. And now, he was hurt and probably even, hated me. Despised me. Resented me. And for the first time in our marriage, I actually felt… guilty.

Yes, there's a first for everything. Although John was mostly an absent partner, who might have driven me into the arms of other men, he still didn't deserve to learn about my affairs from anyone else, other than myself. For at least, if I had told him directly, then maybe, he would have understood, as to why I did what I did, from my perspective. And why, might you ask, was the real reasons as to why I did what I did? Well, diary, if I'm being perfectly honest…and this, diary, is a bit hard for me to admit it, but here it goes… I don't love John. Never have, and I don't think I ever will.

Do I find him attract? Yes, I still do, as he's a handsome man; but at the same time, I don't feel that same attraction that I felt for him before our marriage. But if I'm being perfectly honest right now, I don't think I even felt that same passion for John, ever, and Demitri helped me to recognize this. When I'm with Demitri, I feel such passion and intensity. My heart is constantly racing around him. I've never felt this way with John before. Personally, I think John feels this same way too, which might be why he never seems to miss me, while he's buried away in his work. Ultimately, it's because I'm not a priority for him, and I probably never was. I do not blame him; he, like myself, probably wasn't even aware of it either. But alas, here we are, in a world that expects us to be the example of the ideal happily married American couple, when in reality, it couldn't be any further from the actual truth. While truth might be a rare commodity, it still isn't as equally valuable as propaganda. With all honesty, I haven't yet seen our photograph taken together; but if I did, then I'm sure I'd laugh by the sheer mockery of it all. If only they had known!

After taking our photograph, John escorted me over to the banquet hall and from there, we eventually entered into the ballroom to attend the state dinner. Near the front of the room, we were seated at the same table as the Canadian and Brazilian prime ministers and their ambassadors, along with their families. Although a non-NATO member, Brazil is a long-time strategic partner and major ally to the United States; therefore, they were one of the few non-NATO member countries to receive an exclusive VIP invitation from us, to attend our state dinner. As John and I welcomed our guests at the table, Barbara soon arrived and sat right next to me. However, just as I had feared, Kate was absent; so much for my plans.

After engaging upon a few polite conversations with the other wives at the table, our appetizers arrived. However, Barbara, of course, wasn't one to be avoided. Assuming that she would be too preoccupied with the newly served appetizers, I proceeded to grab my butter knife and began spreading the caviar onto my cracker. Hoping to bite and relish my caviar and cracker in peace, I saw, from the corner of my eye, Barbara waiting eagerly to speak to me. Unfortunately, as soon as John and our guests exited the table to mingle with the other visiting ambassadors and their wives in the room, she cornered me. With only just the two of us left at the dinner table, she boldly asked if everything between John and I was alright. Naturally, I lied and told her that everything was perfectly fine. Nevertheless, she still looked at me with suspicion. Although John and I might have our differences, we still publicly put on a good show, so I'm not sure as to why she should be suspicious or skeptical about anything about us, at this point. Unless, he told her something? I can't help but wonder. But, at the same time, I find this unlikely, as John is too private of a person. In general, he never shares his deepest feelings nor emotions to anyone, not even me, let alone Barbara.

To avoid any further interrogation from Barbara, I kindly excused myself from the table and took a walk around the room. After a few minutes of touring about, a male voice, from behind me, began to speak:

"Mrs. Barrett," he said, "Would you care to dance?"

As I turned around to face him, to my surprise, the Brazilian Ambassador was standing right there, in front of me. He was in his early fifties, tall, dark, chubby, balding and overall, a rather unattractive man, with a large nose. Although I wasn't interested in dancing with him, I reluctantly agreed, as I felt it would have been rude to have declined, especially, as I was this evening's hostess. However, as soon as I grabbed hold of his hand and was about to walk over to the dancefloor, John arrived and interrupted us. Having thanked him for entertaining me, John informed him that his wife was urgently searching for him back at his table. After excusing himself to return back to his wife, John, out of obligation, took it upon himself to take the Brazilian Ambassador's place, and escorted me over to the stage.

Diary, this is where it gets a bit uncomfortable. Although John is generally, social and well-manner, he uttered not one word to me while we danced. Furthermore, as we smiled and waltzed across the ballroom, he remained distant and cold towards me. Finally, as he twirled me around, he broke his silence, leaned in and warned me to stay as far away as I could from the Brazilian Ambassador, for he's notorious for seducing married women. Immediately, my heart sunk down to my knees, upon hearing such news. Even though I've been unfaithful to John; I, too, have my own standards. I don't just sleep with anyone. But in that moment, my ego plummeted as far down as to hell, for I realized, with much clarity, that John, having learned about my past affairs, now presumed that I was a dishonorable woman, who could just as easily sleep with the Brazilian Ambassador, as the next man who smiled and flirted with me, regardless of their backgrounds. And that, diary, was a painful revelation, indeed!

At long last, we finally finished the dance. As soon as the music ended, John left to meet with the Turkish Ambassador, while I hurried back to take my seat at the dinner table. Having previously sought to avoid Barbara, at all costs; I, now, welcomed her with open arms. In truth, she was my happy distraction to an otherwise, miserable evening. But to my surprise, once I arrived, I noticed that my table was actually empty. Instead, everyone else were either busy dancing, or walking about in the room and socializing with one another over a cocktail. As I pulled out my chair to take a seat, a noticed a small white envelope placed directly above my chair, along with my name written on the front of the envelope. It was a letter addressed to me. Curious as to what this letter was regarding, I gently pealed open the envelope's seal, pulled the sheet of paper out, and began to read its contents. To my sheer surprise, it read as the following:

To the most beautiful woman in this party,

I'm sorry that we weren't able to have that dance, but if you'd like to try again and more, then meet me at the Hilton Hotel in Athens, room 502. I'll be waiting.

Sincerely,

Your Brazilian Admirer

Shocked and horrified by having received such a nasty letter, I stuck my hands back into the envelope and there, hidden on the far back pocket, was a key to his hotel room! Imagine, the nerve of that dirty old man! As if someone, as highly respectable such as myself, would ever sleep with the likes of a low and filthy man, such as he! Angrily, I quickly grabbed the letter and key, and hid them in my pocket. Feeling the urgent need to destroy it, I decided to walk over to the nearest restroom, with the determined mission to rip the entire letter apart, and then flush its remains right down the toilet! But, as my hands were about to reach for the handle to the restroom door, I heard a female voice call for me from afar.

As I quickly turned around, I saw that the woman calling for me was none other than the French Ambassador's wife. Apparently, she was seated across from me at the ballroom, and she had followed me over to the restroom. Having received my bouquet of yellow roses, along with my lovely note, she personally, wanted to apologize to me for any misunderstandings that may have arisen between us, since our last state dinner about a year ago.

Ah, I thought to myself. Here was *the* woman, who not only accused me of flirting with her extremely unattractive husband, but she also had the nerve to call John's office directly, to complain about me! She even went as so far, as to threaten to shame and bad mouth my good name to the press. Honestly, diary, if it wasn't for my staff, who rigorously and strategically worked to mitigate and divert her evil and sinister plans, then my reputation would have been ruined. Yet, after all of this, now, here she was standing right in front of me and asking for truce.

Since I promised John earlier tonight that I was going to be on my best behavior, I reassured her, with the fakest of smiles in my utmost convincing way, that all was well and forgotten. Honestly, diary, what else could I say? Then, all of a sudden, she unexpectedly hugged me. As I stood there, cringing in the fact that I was physically locked in an unwanted embrace with an enemy, it then occurred to me, that in my back pocket was that letter. Now, diary, I've never claimed nor pretended to be a saint, but a good idea is a good idea and revenge is best served to those who start the fire. As my grandmother always use to say, 'If you can't handle to fire, then don't light up the match!' While the French Ambassador's wife remained in my embrace, I slowly reached for the letter from out my pocket and ever so carefully, dropped the letter into an open pouch on the side of her purse. Once she pulled away from me, we bid our farewells. With her gone, I decided to go to the restroom, anyways, to freshen-up and reapply my lipstick for the remainder of the evening.

Once in the restroom, I stared straight into the restroom mirror and smiled. As I stood there, admiring myself for enacting my well-deserved revenge for the evening, let alone the entire year, I saw Barbara strolling out from one of the restroom stalls.

"My darling, Jennifer," said Barbara, as she walked over the vacant facet, right next to me. "It's a good thing you stayed away from that Brazilian Ambassador tonight! His wife is an incredibly jealous woman! Why, she spent the entire evening at the table, complaining to me just how much she has to constantly chase him around town to beat up all of his many mistresses! Imagine that! This woman has absolutely no class at all to confide and tell me about such things! I, a total stranger! My goodness, dare you have even bothered to have danced with him, then she would have certainly taken it the wrong way, believe me! It's a good thing that I sent John over to stop you two from dancing! You certainly dodged a bullet with that one!"

Diary, you know, the irony of it all, was that prior to all of the events leading up to tonight, I was most afraid of how my evening with Barbara was going to turn out. However, in the end, she was actually, the one who gave me the best of ideas. Upon hearing Barbara's revelation, I quickly exited the restroom and hurried back to the dinner table, just in time, to catch the Brazilian Ambassador's wife alone. Once I came face to face with her, I, personally, thanked her for her hospitality with chatting and entertaining Barbara this evening. Then, I reached into my pocket, pulled out the hotel key and placed it on the table. Surprised and astonished by my actions, she stared at the key and asked me what the meaning behind this was.

Continuing with my revenge, I told her that while I was walking back into the ballroom, I saw her husband publicly kiss the French Ambassador's wife on the lips, in the hallway. Then, I saw him pass a note over to her, along with this key. However, as soon as the couple left, it appeared that the French Ambassador's wife accidentally dropped the key onto the floor, right outside of the restroom. Given that she, the Brazilian Ambassador's wife, had been so kind to Barbara tonight, I thought that it was only fair and justified that she learned the truth from me, and that she, of all people, should take the rightful possession and ownership of her husband's hotel room key. Now, diary, as hostess, I'm well aware that, out of privacy, there's a policy of not placing cameras near the restrooms; so, if I were to claim that I saw the couple kissing there, and given that everyone else was in the ballroom, apart from myself, then who's to say that I'm the one lying, and not they? Fool proof, I am! Nevertheless, the Brazilian Ambassador's wife was so incredibly grateful for this news, that she promised to treat me to high tea, the next time she's in town, which in return, I graciously accepted. Raged with anger, she quickly grabbed her belongings, along with my used butter knife from the table, which I found odd and peculiar, and then she took the first available taxicab straight over to the Hilton Hotel in Athens.

Afterwards, I too, bid farewell to my remaining guests and retired upstairs to my bedroom. Since writing this entry, I can already hear Gloria and Sally in the hallway gossiping about some "scandalous fight" that abrupted between the French and Brazilian Ambassadors' wives this evening. Somehow, one way or another, the fight escalated and resulted in the Brazilian Ambassador's wife giving the French Ambassador's wife a case of the black eye! And to make matters worse, apparently the Brazilian Ambassador was seen by the hotel staff running down the lobby stark naked, with his wife chasing after him, with a butter knife from behind! The same butter knife that still has traces of my dried caviar from dinner, on its blade! Imagine that! In the end, I suppose that the French Ambassador's wife was lonely enough to accept my invitation from the Brazilian Ambassador, and the Brazilian Ambassador's wife was crazy enough to catch them in the act. Ah, karma is a bitch indeed and revenge is so incredibly sweet! In the meantime, I think I'll avoid traveling to France and Brazil in the near future, at least for a good while.

January 5, 2018

Dear Diary,

I can't believe that it's been four years, since I last wrote an entry in this diary! Believe me, I didn't forget you; but I'm afraid, I thought I lost you! Luckily, I recently found you again, hidden away in one of my traveling suitcases that I, somehow, forgot to unpack! But, not to fear, I'm here to sum up what's transpired these past four years.

When I last wrote, we had recently held our annual NATO state dinner in Athens, while John was still the U.S. Ambassador to Greece. As you may recall, there was also a scandalous fight between the French and Brazilian Ambassadors' wives that evening, in which, yours truly, played a minor role in that fiasco. After that unfortunate event, the relationship between France and Brazil soon soured and deteriorated. As a result of that argument, the French government began boycotting Brazilian goods, and even went so far, as to place an embargo against the importation of Brazilian nuts into France.

Offended by such foreign policy, the Brazilian government did likewise, and retaliated by banning the importation of French macaroons into Brazil. The back-and-forth disputes between the two nations continued throughout that year, until finally, as I, myself, recently came to learn from Gloria, the dispute came to a conclusion, once the French Ambassador's wife wrote a hand-written apology letter directly to the attention of the Brazilian Ambassador's wife, along with the delivery of a certain bouquet of yellow roses. As you may recall, I, too, had done the same. It appears that the French Ambassador's wife took a direct page from my rule book, karma indeed! After that display of truce, all was forgotten and life returned back to normal. Eventually, both countries removed their embargos, reopened their ports, and the world community took a deep sigh of relief. Alas, France and Brazil were, once again, good friends and allies.

However, what the world might not realize, is that sometimes, disputes and wars amongst countries and nations often arise as a result of petty, behind the scenes, disputes. This has been true throughout the ages, even spanning all the way back to the time of the Trojan war, when beautiful Helen left her husband, the King of Sparta, for her lover, Paris. Whether you view Helen's decision as an act of love for her lover, or as an act of betrayal to her King; the truth is, Helen's decision alone, sparked a full-scale war, which costs the lives of thousands of people, as well as the eventual fall of a once great kingdom. And ever since then, not much has changed. The world and humanity are still the same. Only the passage of time, separates us, from ourselves and our ancestors. We, as humans, are all people made from the same cloth, consisting of power, lust and greed. And if you think about it, even World War I, was a bit of a family dispute. Apart from the assassination of the Archduke Franz Ferdinand of Austria-Hungry that served as the catalyst for the war, the war was primarily fought by George V of Great Britain, Tsar Nicholas II of Russia and Kaiser Wilhelm II of Germany; all of whom, might I add, were the grandchildren of Queen Victoria of Great Britain and were thus, all first-cousins. Can you image just how different the outcome of the war might have been, had these stubborn cousins simply held their prides for the better sake of humanity, had met, conferred and resolved their disputes over a nice family dinner? A vastly different outcome, I, personally, do believe!

And that evening proved just as memorable, not only to the French and Brazilian Ambassadors, but to John, as well. As it turned out, John had gotten along so well with the Turkish Ambassador, that he was invited to help serve as an advisor for an upcoming pipeline project. Under this multibillion-dollar project, the goal is to link the natural gas line running from Russia into Türkiye, through the Black Sea. This, in return, will allow Türkiye to provide natural gas to both Europe and Asia, and provide other European countries with an alternative to the high cost of natural gas, which is currently monopolized by the Belarusian government. Furthermore, since John is very charismatic and already has positive relations with the other neighboring European countries, the Turkish Ambassador gladly offered him a chair at their negotiating table. When the agency back in Washington D.C. got word of this offer, they quickly pulled John out of Athens and swapped him with the then-ambassador in Istanbul, so that John could take over the Istanbul post and become the new U.S. Ambassador to Türkiye, permanently.

With John stationed in Istanbul, he will have direct access to oversee this project in-person, while also promoting American interests in the region. Also, since the pipeline currently passes directly through both the American embassy and air force base, the agency also has vested interests on the development of this ongoing project. Ultimately, if this project proves successful, then the lower cost of natural gas will create new economic and business ventures in the area.

Upon acceptance of this new position, John, myself and the rest of the embassy staff, all packed our bags and belonging and moved across the

Aegean Sea, from Athens to Istanbul. And so, somehow during this move, I must have forgotten to unpack you from one of my many travel suitcases. Luckily, I recently decided to do some overdue spring cleaning, and happily, I finally you, my diary, once and for all!

As an ambassador's wife, I've already learned not to get accustomed or comfortable living in one specific geographical location; for in a moment's notice, we can all be transferred and relocated, once again. Since marrying John, I've moved at least five times to five different countries, all within the span of five years. However, for these past three years and counting, we've been living in Istanbul, and I, personally, think we'll continue to live here for a while longer. The Istanbul mansion is almost identical to our previous Cairo and Athens mansions: all are white, with similar exterior and interior structures, architectural designs and landscape. Just like before, the new mansion is also down the street from the embassy. However, the only difference between them all, are that the red roses in the garden have been replaced with pink roses, instead. Additionally, they're all different varieties and shades of pink, too. Some range from the palest of pink to almost white, to bright hot pink, almost close to the shade of purple. Personally, I must admit, I rather like the roses here a lot more. In fact, in the garden, some of the roses even matches my wedding ring, too!

As for John and I, a year after our move to Istanbul, we mutually agreed to live our own separate lives. While we're still legally married, we agreed to continue our public charade as the happily married couple, for the sake of John's career and my own economic lifestyle. Our marriage is no longer based on romantic love, but instead, economic and political reasons. And so, because of these reasons, he lives on one end of the estate, while I on the other. As a result, we seldom see each other, with the exception of certain public engagements and social events. Furthermore, we even dine apart now; but in truth, this is because John is always so busy these days, and mainly eats and sleeps in his office or at the library. Whether or not he has another mistress or lover, I honestly don't know. However, I highly suspect not, because I know that John's one true and only love is his job, and no wife or mistress can ever compete, nor come in-between him and his honor to his civic duties.

As for myself, well diary, you already know that I'm a romantic; so naturally, I've continued to have my healthy share of lovers, over these past few years. But eventually, these romances do grow old, and now, I find myself, lonely and in search of a real partner. Although, from the outside, the life of an ambassador's wife can appear exciting and glamorous, overtime, if one lacks love or a sense of self-purpose from within, then, I can't help but ponder: is this world really worth being a part of, anymore?

I've pondered this question, over and over, in my head, since arriving here. Istanbul is one of the most romantic cities in the entire world; and yet, I feel so incredibly lonely. And with time passing by, I'm not as young, as I use to be, when I first married John. I'm aging, as we all are; but eventually, I know that in the long term, I'm going to need someone by my side, as my one true love and partner. And surprise, surprise, diary, I want a child of my own, too. I've never imagined myself wanting to be a mother before, but this sudden urge and feeling towards motherhood suddenly came to me one day, as I was walking down the streets of Istanbul.

After finishing my afternoon shopping and buying a new set of jewelry for another upcoming state dinner, I, somehow, accidentally turned at the wrong corner of the street and ended up standing, right in front of a school. To my surprise, it was a preschool filled with very young children, ranging from the ages of three to five years old. Having unexpectedly arrived, I noticed that I happened to be there at the same time as their recess.

Curious, I watched on as I saw the children all happily smiling, laughing, frolicking and playing outside in the sunshine. As I stared across at them, I, for the first time, in a rather long time too, joined them in a smile. And, diary, this wasn't one of my usual fake or pretend smiles for the public; but instead, a real, honest and genuine smile. A smile that miraculously stemmed directly from my heart. Why, I had almost forgotten what a real smile felt like, too.

Suddenly, when I least expected it, a beautiful young girl walked over to me and handed me a daisy. Lovely as she was, she had blue eyes and golden blonde hair, with a bright pink bow headband, all dressed in purple. While playing, the girl managed to gather a bunch of daises and held them tightly bound, within her delicate and tiny hands. And then, those same tiny hands found me, as she gently placed one of her white daises into the palm of my hand. Me, a complete stranger. Afterwards, she soon ran off and joined the rest of the other children to play outside on the playground.

But, diary, something happened to me, the moment she gave me that flower on that afternoon. While I held that daisy, that beautiful, sweet, pure, soft, white and innocent flower that's the complete opposite of a rose, within my hands, and as I watched that same adorable little girl dance and skip right across the playground from afar, I suddenly imagined that she was my own daughter. It was ironic too, for she even resembled me, as a child. And then, with much clarity, I realized, that I not only wanted a child, but that, I wanted a little girl of my very own. In that very moment, I just knew that I wanted to be a mother to a daughter, and that everything else in my life, up until this point, was artificial and meaningless.

For years, there was always a missing void, that sat deep and locked away within the chambers of my own heart. And for all the men I chased, and for all the romances that I engaged upon over these years, none of those relationships ever brought complete satisfaction nor peace to my heart. There was always something missing. Not even Demitri, completely filled that empty void. For on that playground, I knew that for all the gowns, jewels, diamonds, mansions, cars and parties, I was ready to trade all of these in instantly, if it meant that I could be a mother to this little girl. Because being a mother and loving a child is the one true love in this world that can never be faked, no matter how hard one tries. And after years of acting and pretending, having something real and authentic, suddenly began to mean so much more to me, than I had ever wanted to previously admit to anyone, let alone, myself.

Although I've never once considered being a mother before; somehow, over the years, my opinion changed, as I grew and evolved, as a person. After searching for so long, I finally found a real and genuine purpose, in my life: motherhood. But, since coming aware of this revelation, I've also had to acknowledge, that if I'm to go through with this and become a mother in the near future, then John can never be the father to my child, for I simply refuse to raise my future child, in the world that I'm currently a part of. Alas, my marriage of convenience was no longer a convenience, and my sham of a marriage to John needed to finally come to an end. Unlike before, this time, I need to remarry someone else for stability, family, love and most importantly, to live my own life as a private citizen, away from the spotlight.

As I said before, John isn't a terrible man, we're just not compatible and I don't think we really ever were, even from the very beginning. I, personally, need someone who's willing to dedicate themselves to a family, and not solely their occupation alone; just as John, himself, probably needs a wife who's more patient and adaptable to his lifestyle, than I am. Or perhaps, I, too, am wrong. Maybe, what John needs is the complete opposite. Maybe, he needs a woman who's willing to push him, to move beyond his own comfort zone, and to learn how to experience love and life, beyond the confinement of the walls of the embassy and the mansion?

But alas, that isn't for me to decide nor dwell upon, any longer. He needs to discover that one, for himself; not I. And so, diary, I've recently gone ahead and done the impossible. In fact, I'm sure you'd be pleased, even proud to know. A few days ago, I finally asked John for a divorce. Even more surprising, he agreed, without any hesitation. However, given our past history, his reaction shouldn't have come as much of a surprise to me, as we've both been unhappy for a long time in our union. To be fair, I'm sure he's also tired of our constant bickering behind the scenes, and my occasional vase throwing at him, from time to time. Perhaps, he too wants another wife? A more compassionate one, at best? For I know, that if the roles were reversed, that's what I would have wanted. But of course, divorce never comes easy, for people like us.

While John and I, both agreed to divorce, our advisors, naturally, advised otherwise. Gloria, Sally, Bes, Carol, Tyler and Margaret immediately held an emergency meeting, to try to convince us to cancel our divorce and to seek marriage counseling, instead. Now, imagine if they all had been on my side the first time, when I originally suggested marriage counseling, all the way from the very beginning, several years ago? The hypocrisy of it all! Of course, John and I disagreed with them all, as we both knew that the expiration date to our marriage had long passed. One by one, they each tried their best to persuade us to remain married; but alas, we finally made it perfectly clear to them that our decision was final, and that there wasn't anything else that they could do or say, to convince us, otherwise. Our minds were made up and everyone else needed to accept this new reality. Once the news finally sunk in, Gloria and Tyler asked to speak to both of us, privately. Since most likely, our divorce will draw negative publicity, Gloria and Tyler asked that we wait to announce our separation, until after the upcoming presidential election. Since the current American President is the one who appointed John to the Istanbul post, John remains a direct representation and extension of his administration. Therefore, any negative press about John will also be a reflection on the current President and his administration, and given that this is an election year and the race is rather close, Tyler and Gloria advised that we wait a few more months, before releasing our announcement.

Meanwhile, as I happily wait for these next few months to pass before my soon-to-be-divorce, I'm looking for new hobbies to keep myself busy and entertained. Sally suggested that I take up tennis as a new sport, and I think I might do that. I've heard that the tennis instructors here are very handsome, and you know, diary, I'm also in search of a new prospective husband and father to my future child, so perhaps I'll give tennis a try, after all. Until next time diary, hopefully, it won't be another four years until my next entry!

Chapter 9

Jennifer entered the bedroom and closed the door, right behind her. Now, at long last, she was alone with her new Belarusian lover and tennis instructor, Ivan Koval, inside of their private hotel room, at the Four Seasons Sultanahmet in Istanbul. After they finished drinking their bottle of champagne, Jennifer slowly began undressing her clothing, until she was left wearing nothing but her satin black lingerie. Ivan shivered with excitement. After all, she was wearing the black lace lingerie that he specifically requested she wear, during their last game, on Tuesday afternoon. It was there, at the tennis court, where Jennifer made her intentions known to him. He, in return, gladly accepted her proposal. What started as a standard lesson on how to properly swing one's racket, soon turned into a passionate kiss, igniting the birth of a new and steamy love affair.

With one tug, her lingerie straps fell down across her chest, revealing her plump and perky breasts. Slowly, she removed her hair pin, which had previously secured her medium long blonde hair into a neat and tight bun. As she released her hair, her silky and shiny strands gently fell across her soft, delicate and radiant body. Ready to seduce her new lover, Jennifer proceeded to remove her remaining garments. As she pulled off her black and lacy thong, she kicked it across the room and stared directly in the eyes of her lover, Ivan, who was at the foot of bed, seated near the edge. Now stark naked, she smiled at him from afar, as she made her way towards him.

Ever since their first kiss at the tennis court, Jennifer longed for this particular "private" session to be intimately and exclusively alone with him. Being completely naked and exposed, she slowly walked over to him. After weeks of innocent and harmless flirting, their romance was finally about to graduate onto the next level. As her leg gently collided against his knee, the mere touch of her body, made him shivered with excitement. After fantasizing about her for so long, he was dying from the anticipation. When she finally reached his side, he swiftly pulled her towards him. With one rough tumble, they both fell onto the bed, with Jennifer landing right on top of him. As they came face to face, Ivan leaned forward and together, they began to passionately kiss.

At first, he kissed her on her neck, with such longing and desire; and eventually, he slowly moved his way up to her chin, then her cheeks, and finally her lips. When Ivan's mouth pressed down against hers, Jennifer could also feel his tongue, caressing the outer corners of her lips, as he slowly pushed his way into the opening of her mouth. Welcomed by his entry, she lunged forward to follow his lead. As their tongues united and their kisses grew more and more passionate, Ivan suddenly pulled away from her lips and instead, began kissing the remainder of her body. From her legs to her inner thighs, and then to her most private of areas. This certainly, caught Jennifer off guard, and she blissfully moaned with desire.

Slowly, Ivan began caressing the rest of Jennifer's soft and delicate body, with his strong and muscular hands. Eventually, his hands soon found their way up towards her large pair of breasts, which as of now, were voluptuous, full, round, tender and pink. Most eager to make their acquittance with her female treasures, Ivan's hands cupped her breasts with his bare hands. With both pairs of breasts sitting within the company of his demanding palms, he gently squeezed them and immediately, she let out a squeal of desire. As he squeezed once more, she pushed her head back, swinging her long blonde hair back and forth, while releasing yet another moan of pleasure. Her moans excited him, and so, he squeezed once again; but this time, much harder, than before. Eventually, his desire for her overcame him, and the mere touch of her body, could no longer suffice. He needed to taste her, all for himself. And so, Ivan brought his mouth over to her breast, and slowly, he began sucking on her nipple, with his entire mouth, including his tongue.

Repeating the same process on Jennifer's other breast, she once again, moaned from the intense pleasure she felt by his contact. Slowly, Ivan positioned himself close to her inner thighs, and from there, he began kissing and caressing her, from down below. As Ivan touched and kissed her most private of parts, he could feel and see that she was now, wet and ready to surrender to him, once and for all. Understanding her growing desires, he also acknowledged, that he, too, was ready. More than ready. Alas, the time had finally come, for him to enter and become one, with her.

Eagerly, he ripped off all of his clothing, until he was left with nothing, but his bare skin. Afterwards, he moved and soon covered his entire naked body over hers. At long last, his sweet lover was now underneath him. They were ready. As her warm smile met his, she slowly lifted up her legs, parted them, and then, she quickly wrapped them around his buttock, as she welcomed him right into her. Aroused by her invitation, Ivan quickly positioned himself and once he felt confident and at balance, with one swift thrush, he entered her with full force. As he invaded her body, she moaned from happiness and pure pleasure. Furthermore, the more she moaned, the harder he thrusted himself forward and far deeper into her. As her body moved along with his, the rhythm of his penetration grew progressively faster and stronger. Eventually, his movements were so forceful, that together, they managed to shake their bed and nearby furniture, along the way, as the two lovers became one.

As Ivan continued to build up speed, he eventually lost all of his self-control and as such, he had no other choice but to surrender over to his own carnal desires. Determined to make her his, once and for all, he pushed harder and entered her with full force. Jennifer, in return, enjoyed every last minute of their lovemaking; and so, to further increase their mutual ecstasy, she reached over to grab his buttock with her hands, and slowly, she pulled him even closer to her, so that he could enter her, even deeper. As she did that, Ivan immediately screamed from joy and happiness, while she let out a seductive smile of her own.

After they both reached their climax, Ivan rolled off of her. However, Jennifer wasn't yet ready for their lovemaking session to come to a complete end. No, she certainly wasn't. And so, she quickly decided to take matters into her own hands. With one swift move, she quickly changed her position and crawled back up, seated directly on top of him.

Slowly, Jennifer reached over to his chest and tenderly, she began twirling his chest hair with her fingers. As Ivan closed his eyes, Jennifer gently squeezed along his nipples, leaving Ivan in a pure state of bliss. At long last, she was the Goddess that he had long been waiting for and she, alone, found a way to turn his entire body alive. Thoroughly enjoying her ability to make him feel so incredibly good, Jennifer reached over to his side and carefully, she began kissing his neck passionately, while sucking the life force right out of him. Eventually, she made her way up and came face to face with him; and then, she forced her lips onto his. As she pushed her tongue through his mouth, their tongues soon met and intertwined, with one another. Slowly, they began to passionately kiss…and then…the more they kissed…it rapidly increased, as if tomorrow didn't exist!

A few minutes later, Jennifer's face was flushed and her body was red, sweaty and ready to invade Ivan. Determined to claim him, Jennifer soon climbed on top of Ivan again, and carefully, she aligned and positioned herself with him. Once seated directly above him, she slowly spread her legs as far and as wide apart as she could; and once, she found her opening and his package, she slid her body right inside of him. As she moved deeper and further into his body, Ivan screamed from ecstasy and pleasure. Having discovered his most sensitive part of his body, Jennifer knew exactly as to how to make him feel like the most important man in the world.

Seated right on top of him, Jennifer continued rocking back and forth, as she slowly and gradually built up her own rhythm. With each swing, their bodies grew more accustomed to one another. Given that this was her first night with Ivan, Jennifer wanted them to enjoy this experience together. As she continued to rock slowly, her thighs continued to spread further and wider apart. The more Jennifer swung, the more she could feel his large maleness inside of her, pricking all her sensitive nerves from within her. As she plunged further inside of him, she released a large sigh of pleasure.

Her moans of pleasure excited him so much, that he, too, screamed from joy and excitement. Inspired by his cries of love, Jennifer decided to rock even faster and harder, until finally, she was swinging so fast, that she was practically flying across the room and riding him all the way to the finish line. And the faster she rode him, the more her breast, which were now fuller and firmer than ever before, were bouncing up and down, and flying back and forth, up in the air. Mesmerized by the glorious sight before him, Ivan reached up and squeezed her breasts as hard as he possibly could, and with all of his inner strength.

Upon releasing his firm grip on her breasts, Jennifer immediately released a loud and forceful scream, due to the high degree of her excitement, along with the intensity of her pleasure. Overall, this entire lovemaking experience with Ivan was not only delightful, but it also gave her a new sense of freedom. At long last, she was in control at the driver's seat. Sex was the one thing in her life, where she was in complete and utter control. She controlled whom she had sex with, where and when. She had the power to choose her own lovers, and the power to dismiss them. She had to power to choose her own location for the lovemaking. And when. It was the one power that she had that didn't involve anyone else's discretion; where she had complete freedom, without limitation. And she loved it. No, more than that. She enjoyed it. She savored it and took her time to fully embrace it. Sex was impowering and liberating. But most importantly, it was also her escape from life at the mansion, from being the ambassador's wife.

Rocking her body up and down above him, Jennifer tossed her hair from side to side, while squeezing his chest, as she bounced above him. Ivan released another moan of pleasure, as Jennifer continued to thrust harder, pushing her body deeper into his. Following her instincts, she continued to move faster and faster, until finally, she reached her climax and screamed so loud that the birds seated along the balcony terrace, flew away. But this wasn't quite the end. For after their climax, Ivan scooped her up from up their bed and brought her out onto the balcony terrace to give her one final passionate kiss to seal their lovemaking. It was a risky move, given that the balcony was out in public view; but then again, they were located high above, on the tenth floor, so who could see them?

After their lovemaking, Jennifer waited for Ivan to dose off to sleep. Luckily, she didn't have to wait too long either; for Ivan was so exhausted from their afternoon adventure, that he soon fell fast asleep, shortly afterwards. As he peaceful slept next to her in their bed, she stared down at him and pondered to herself. Should she continue on with their romantic relationship? Or just end it, right there and then? But wasn't Ivan a good lover? Yes, he was and more; and she had thoroughly enjoyed their lovemaking session together, too.

But apart from their lovemaking, did Ivan really have anything else, more substantial to offer? Was he a good candidate to be her next husband, or even, the father to her future child or children? Although Ivan was handsome and friendly, Jennifer still didn't see him worthy enough to be as a potential new husband, nor as fatherly material. If anything, Ivan was a good time and sadly, that's as far as it went.

"No, he will not do," she whispered to herself, underneath her breath.

After that truthful admission, Jennifer slowly leaned over to Ivan and kissed him goodbye, but this time, it was for good. A few minutes later, Jennifer, now, fully dressed in her clothes, grabbed the rest of her belongings and exited their hotel room. It was now four o'clock in the afternoon, and she wanted to eagerly return back home, before anyone else in the mansion grew suspicious about her mysterious whereabouts. As she entered into the elevator, her private mobile phone suddenly began to vibrate, to alert her of an incoming new text message. This was certainly a surprise and rather odd too, since no one else knew about her private mobile phone number, not even the staff or John. In fact, she specifically went out of her way to purchase this private mobile phone, in secret all by herself; in order to communicate directly with her lovers. Additionally, to ensure that none of her former lovers had access to her secret number, she constantly changed it regularly, right after each and every breakup and separation. Oddly enough, with this latest number, Ivan was the only person who knew it; and yet, he was currently still fast asleep, back inside their hotel room.

"Maybe, it's just a telemarketer," Jennifer said to herself.

As the elevator's doors slid opened, Jennifer walked out and entered into the hotel's lobby. For the sake of time, she decided to simply ignore the message and to review it later, once she arrived back home to the mansion. However, fate, it seemed, had other plans in store for her that afternoon. As Jennifer was about to exit out of the hotel, her pink diamond earring suddenly got lose from her ear and fell down onto the floor, nearby the front entrance.

"My earring!" exclaimed Jennifer, as she frantically dropped down onto the floor to search for her missing pair.

The fallen earring was part of a set, gifted by John to match her pink diamond wedding ring. Given that she didn't want anyone to discover her secret affair, Jennifer didn't want to leave any evidence behind at the hotel that could be later traced back to her, including her jewelry.

"Do you need any help?" asked the man.

"I've lost a pair of my earring," replied Jennifer, not once bothering to look back up to acknowledge him.

Crawling down on her hands and knees, Jennifer desperately tried to search and relocate her lost item. Unfortunately, at that precise moment, because Jennifer was simply too preoccupied to remove her sight from the floor, she failed to see what was right in front of her. However, this lack of attention, only amused the man.

"It wouldn't happen to be this particular pair, now, would it?" asked the smiling man, as he held and waved the missing and sparkling pink diamond earring up in the air.

"You've found it!" she exclaimed, happily.

Finally, lifting her head back up to see and confirm that the earring was indeed hers, Jennifer managed to also catch sight of the unknown man, who had unexpectedly come to her rescue. To her surprise, he was rather attractive and middle-aged. Elegantly dressed in a khaki suit, he had fair complexion, blonde curly hair and brown eyes.

Out of embarrassment, Jennifer immediately blushed. After kneeling and searching on the floor, her dress, along with her hands, were now all covered in dust. Suddenly, in the presence of a handsome stranger, Jennifer felt a bit embarrassed by her untidy appearance, which in general, was so unlike her. As she struggled to rise, the man quickly came to her aid and helped to lift her back up.

"I'm such a mess," admitted Jennifer, innocently, as she began to brush off the dust and dirt from off her dress.

"Nonsense," said the man, laughingly. "You've just had a bit of an adventure, that's all."

"Adventure? That's an interesting way of putting it," she said.

Slowly, he reached over, grabbed her hand, and then, he gently placed the missing earring back into her possession, safe and sound.

"My lady, here you are. Returned to its rightful owner," he said.

"I really don't know what to say," she admitted.

"A simple thank you will suffice," he replied, with a smile.

"Thank you…" began Jennifer, when suddenly, she realized that she didn't even know his name, in the first place.

However, right on cue, the man sensed her confusion and so he quickly added, "Selim. My name's Selim, by the way."

"Selim," Jennifer repeated. "That's a rather unusual name."

"It's Turkish," replied Selim. "It means one's whose safe, true, strong and sincere."

"Safe, true, strong and sincere," Jennifer repeated. "Those are fine qualities in a man."

Surprised by her honest admission, Selim immediately laughed, and then, he smiled, from ear to ear. For some odd reason, even in the presence of a perfect stranger, Jennifer felt strangely comfortable around him. Having never met him before, she already felt immediate ease and peace with him. For some odd reason, he felt like a soft and fluffy cloud that she had just happened to land upon, on her way back down from falling; both literally and figuratively.

"Well," she began, as she cleared her throat, "Since we're at introductions, I should tell you that I'm Jennifer and…"

However, at that exact moment, she managed to catch sight of her own reflection in the mirror, located nearby. Much to her fear, she looked far worse than what she had originally expected! Apart from a dirty dress, her leggings were torn to shreds, with a large rip running from her hips and all the way down to her ankles!

"My leggings!" exclaimed Jennifer, in horror.

Although initially surprised by her sudden outburst, Selim soon saw the defect, and almost immediately, he promptly understood the origins and reason to her negative reaction.

"Jennifer, please don't be alarmed," replied Selim, calmly. "There's a restroom right across from us. Perhaps, you can freshen up inside. If you wish, I can gladly escort you over to there."

Grateful for his suggestion, Jennifer gladly accepted his offer and assistance. As they walked across the room, she tightly held onto his arms. Surprisingly, Selim was the perfect gentleman. And a handsome one, at that, too. Although they had only just met, Jennifer could already sense and feel that Selim at his core was a rather good guy.

Once they arrived to the restroom, Jennifer quickly rushed in and removed her leggings, almost immediately. Afterwards, she dusted the dirt off from her dress and then, she washed her face with cold water from the faucet. As she looked in the bathroom mirror, Jennifer briefly fixed her hair and reached into her purse to grab her lipstick. However, she accidentally reached for her phone, instead. Although it wasn't her intention to grab her phone; but since it was now already in her hands, Jennifer decided to quickly open her phone to check on the time. Given that this was a last-minute split decision, Jennifer was also forced to read the unread message, which she received only a few minutes ago back at her hotel room.

To her horror, Jennifer saw the most terrifying message! It was a text message that included several explicit and intimate photographs of Ivan and herself, together alone at their hotel room! Without a shadow of a doubt, Jennifer came to the realization that someone followed them into the hotel this afternoon. Not only did they spy on them in private, but they also managed to take compromising photographs of them together, during their lovemaking. Horrified by the photographs, Jennifer continued to scroll further down the text message. Eventually, once she reached near the bottom of the message, she read the following:

> If you don't want these photographs leaked to the world, then meet me in one hour the Istanbul grand bazaar's main entrance. I'll be there waiting, wearing a green coat and black scarf. Don't be late.
>
> Signed,
>
> Anonymous

After reading the last sentence, Jennifer nearly dropped her phone onto the floor. Someone captured extremely personal, intimate and embarrassing photographs of her with her lover! Someone knew about their affair! But worst of all, these photographs were also evidence that she had been unfaithful to John! But who was the mystery sender? Who was Anonymous? Who followed her and why? What were their intentions and motives? Were these photos intended to destroy her and John's reputation, or just her own? And if these photos were leaked, then how would it affect her impending divorce? Would she be shunned by society? Would John be forced to resign? And was the sender someone she knew? An enemy or an acquaintance? A friend or a former lover? Or even, a complete stranger?

Determined to find answers, Jennifer scrolled back to the top of the text message to locate the sender's telephone number. However, much to her dismay, the sender didn't have a normal telephone number. Instead, the sender's telephone number was listed as a four-digit number that read: 1111. Was this a foreign entity or a private corporate number? Did this message originate from a landline or a mobile device? Unfortunately, it simply was just impossible to tell.

"What should I do?" asked Jennifer to herself, aloud.

Closing the text message, she looked at her phone's clock. It was now 4:10 pm, and she was supposed to be back home at the mansion before 5:00 pm, in time for dinner. However, until this new threat was resolved, the mansion would have to wait. No matter what, Jennifer knew that in the end, she was going to have to visit the grand bazaar to meet with her anonymous blackmailer and deal with his ransom. Regardless of her feelings, Jennifer couldn't risk not going. She had to go. For she feared, that if she didn't, then who knew as to what other damages could arise from her lack of appearance? No, she was determined to go and confront her blackmailer and deal with the consequences, once and for all. However, unfortunately, Jennifer also knew that she had to go alone. Since no one else knew about her affair with Ivan, she couldn't risk telling or bringing anyone from the mansion to serve as an escort for her. No, she needed to be brave. She was going to have to face this person, alone and by herself.

What did her mystery blackmailer want, in exchange for their silence? Money, most likely, thought Jennifer. That wouldn't be a problem. She was already well prepared to pay them off, with as much money as they wanted. This wouldn't be an issue. Whatever it took to get rid of them. Yes, Jennifer told herself, this will work out. I will overcome this. I will be okay.

Once more, Jennifer reviewed the text message again to see the original time sent. It was 4:00 pm, on the dot. Closing the text message, she looked at the current time. It was now 4:15 pm. In less than an hour, Jennifer was going to come face to face with her mysterious blackmailer. If she was going to arrive on time, then she needed to leave now. Luckily, for Jennifer, the grand bazaar was only a few blocks away from the hotel, so she had enough time to travel by foot. Walking was ideal, she thought, for no one else would see her, amongst the crowd. Plus, taking a taxi was too risky, because someone could recognize her. Having decided her form of transportation, Jennifer quickly threw her phone back into her purse and walked out of the restroom. However, she had completely forgotten about Selim, who was still waiting for her outside.

"I'm so sorry Selim, but I really need to go," said Jennifer quickly, as she began to speed walk towards the main lobby.

"Can I call you a taxi?" said Selim, as he tried to catch up to her speed.

"Not necessary, my destination is nearby. I'll just walk," she replied.

"By yourself, during this late hour? Jennifer, Istanbul is a big city. It can be extremely dangerous after dark, especially for a young woman, such as yourself, traveling alone. Do you want me to come with you?" asked a concerned Selim.

Touched by his sincere kindness, she graciously declined his offer. If circumstances had been different, then she would have gladly accepted. But as it was, she couldn't risk Selim, or anyone else for that matter, from discovering her blackmailer and all of her secrets. Secrets, that she intended to keep buried alive, at all costs.

"No, that won't be necessary, but thank you, Selim, for your concern. I do appreciate your offer," she said.

Disappointed, Selim was a bit lost for words. Although he was well aware that they had only just met and that he, as a perfect stranger, had no right to pry any further; he still, didn't want their conversation to abruptly end, in this way, either.

"Well, if you ever change your mind, or if you return back to the hotel, then please just give me a call," said Selim, as he handed over to Jennifer his business card. "Or," he continued, "if you happen to be in the neighborhood, or want a cup of coffee, I'm available."

"Selim Yildiz, Hotel Owner of the Four Seasons Sultanahmet, Istanbul, Türkiye," Jennifer read aloud. She was impressed.

"You own this luxury hotel?" she asked, most curiously.

"Yes, and a few others properties across Europe," replied Selim. "But give me a call sometime, and I'll treat you to a VIP dinner at one of our exclusive restaurants here, complementary, of course."

Tickled by his offer, Jennifer already liked Selim. Perhaps, he was the type of man that she needed in her post-divorced life, after all. But, before she began daydreaming about Selim, she stopped herself short. Time was ticking away and her blackmailer was waiting. She really needed to go and now. However, once she dealt with this blackmailer once and for all, she planned on resuming her pursuit of Selim, afterwards, in the near future.

"I promise to take you up on that offer, Selim," said Jennifer. "But for now, I really need to go."

After bidding him farewell, Jennifer quickly exited the hotel and began speed walking her way down to the grand bazaar. By 4:50 pm, she finally arrived to the front entrance. Since it was towards the end of the business day, most businesses and shops started closing down for the evening. As a result, the bazaar, along with its surrounded streets, were completed flooded with a sea of hundreds of people, all walking about. But even within this large crowd, Jennifer still tried her best to scan through them, as she desperately attempted to search for the person, who was wearing a green coat and a black scarf.

"Well, at least, I'm not alone. There's still plenty of people outside," she murmured to herself.

Continuing to scan through the crowd, Jennifer's eyes frantically moved from left to right, front to back, searching for anything with the color green. Practically, anything remotely resembling green, even in the shade of blue. Then finally, when she least expected it, a voice from behind her suddenly spoke.

"Hello, Jennifer," said Anonymous.

Immediately, Jennifer froze. Alas, she knew this was *the* person, her blackmailer. Although she mentally prepared herself for this moment and promised herself, that no matter what, she was going to be brave, while remaining calm, collective and rationale, and that she was simply going to just pay this person off and be done with it; it was much easier said than done. Instead, the reality was that the mere sound of their voice, sent a shiver down her spine, and instantly, her body completely froze, out of fear. Even her own heart managed to skip a beat! Dear God, she thought, whatever happens, please let me survive this! I'm not ready to die! Not before I become a mother! Suddenly, her life flashed before her eyes.

After overcoming her initial shock, Jennifer forced herself to regain her muscles and face what stood before her. As Jennifer slowly turned around, she saw that before her was indeed, her blackmailer. As promised, the person was wearing a green coat and a black scarf. But the person was still standing in the shadows and Jennifer couldn't see their face as clearly, from afar. Right there and then, she decided to announce herself.

"Yes, I'm Jennifer," she began. "Now, let's get this over and done with. Tell me how much money you want for these photographs."

"Not so fast," said Anonymous. "I do have other motives and interests, beyond just the money."

Slowly, the figure emerged from out of the shadows. As Jennifer stared straight ahead, she finally caught sight of their face. It was a familiar face too, and not that of a stranger.

"You?" she said, in complete and utter shock. "But why?"

But before the blackmailer could reply, Jennifer saw that their left hand was holding a gun and it was directly pointed at her! Dear God, she thought, now wasn't the time to negotiate with them! Instead, she needed to run now and fast!

Dashing like a bolt of lightning, Jennifer jolted past her blackmailer and pushed her way through the crowd of people at the bazaar. She ran as fast as she possibly could, while simultaneously shoving her way through the mass of people. Jennifer tried to pace herself, as best as she could, in order to control her heartbeat, which was beating so fast that she was afraid that she would soon pass out. As she continued to run, she had absolutely no idea, as to where she was going to go. But wherever her end destination was, it didn't matter. She just had to keep running.

For a brief moment, she turned around to try to spot her blackmailer, but she could no longer see them. As she ran, she passed by several coffee shops, jewelry, clothing and spice shops along the way, that eventually, she, herself, no longer recognized her location, anymore. She was now completely lost. Lost in the grand bazaar.

Jennifer was so stressed that she began to feel hot, sweaty and dizzy. Her eyesight also grew blurry, and she couldn't see through all the bright flashing lights from the bazaar, anymore. As she ran further and further down the hall, she turned around and squinted her eyes, and she faintly saw the color green, from afar. It was a greenish figure. It had to be them! And they were catching up to her, too! Out of fear and desperation, she continued to run; but her strength was beginning to deteriorate, and her vision continued to decline. Finally, she reached the far remote corners of the bazaar, where the jewelry quarters and spice markets intersected. She needed to turn right to continue down the straight path; but, out of panic, confusion, exhaustion and a blurred vision, she accidentally turned left. As a result, she ended up at the edge of a very large and steep staircase, where she immediately, lost all sense of her balance and sight. Suddenly, she fell forward down the staircase, and she began tumbling and tumbling and tumbling…

Chapter 10

One Week Later in New York City...

Dr. Kate Stanley stood at her classroom podium at New York University, tapping away with her fingers against the wooden stand. She looked across the classroom and watched her freshman class eagerly flip through their textbooks and notepads, searching for answers. Some looked shy and nervous. Others, simply unprepared. A few, sadly, just not interested, as evident by their gum chewing, phone scrolling and yawning. And one, tucked away in the far corner of the classroom, fast asleep and...snoring? Well, that certainly was surprising! Did anyone of her student study and prepare for today's lecture? As the classroom remained silent, Kate decided to pose her question, once more.

"To repeat," she said, "Can anyone identify the primary reasons and root causes for the decline, and the ultimate collapse, of the Ottoman Empire?"

Kate waited for a few minutes to pass, and still, no one spoke out. She scanned the classroom once more, hoping for any response. At this point, Kate was willing accept any answer, even if it was the wrong one. At least with a wrong answer, it meant that her students were awake, participating and willing to take a gamble. When that ultimately failed, she then moved her attention towards the classroom's front row.

There seated right at the front row was Jason, her favorite student. Sure enough, his hand was already raised straight and high above in the air, most eager to respond to her pending question. Whether or not, it's common knowledge, the truth is that every professor, sometimes intentionally and mostly unintentionally, will have a favorite student, from time to time; and for Kate, that was Jason. While most professors don't plan, nor seek out for a favorite student, it unfortunately, comes with the territory. Everyone simply needs a hero in their time of need, even in a classroom. And since no one else made any attempts to answer her question, Jason was once again, going to have to be that lucky student, to step in and save the day.

"Yes, Jason," replied Kate, acknowledging the young man and nodding him permission to proceed with his answer.

"It was due to the sultans' short comings and the viziers rise to power," replied Jason, ever so confidently.

"Excellent, Jason!" exclaimed Kate, "That's true. Now, can you tell me the name of that system in place, which allowed for such short comings to flourish?"

"That would be the Kafes, or in English, the cage system," replied Jason, beamingly.

"Very good!" exclaimed Kate, jovially. "Now that Jason has introduced us to this subject, let's touch upon the cage system today and discuss it further."

Kate then walked over to the chalkboard, picked up a piece of a think white chalk and began writing the words "the cage system" on the chalkboard.

"Now," she continued, "Think of the cage system like a bird cage, or better yet, a gilded cage, in which the sultan's palace was exactly just that, one enormous golden gilded cage. And within that golden cage, behind the palace's walls, the sultans were raised with wealth beyond measure. They were surrounded by the most luxurious amenities and goods, including beautiful silk clothing, an endless supply of national gold, jewels, coins and treasures; a vast array of exotic foods and desserts; countless servants to dote upon their every need, as well as a large pool of administrative professionals to tend to their public affairs, both domestic and international. Additionally, they maintained ownership of the most rare and prestigious animals found throughout the empire, including Arabian horses, camels, lions; and a haram filled with beautiful women to serve as their wives and concubines. Now, class, my question to you all is this: what exactly happens to one, who is safely tucked away in such an environment, particularly, during the turn of the twentieth century?"

Kate waited for a few minutes for her question to resonate with her students. Finally, another student, Sarah, who sat across the room, opposite from Jason, raised her hand. Kate cracked a slight smile, along the corner of her mouth. At long last, she was delighted that one of her other students was willing to participate, and join in the conversation.

"Yes, Sarah, please," said Kate.

"Well," began Sarah, with a bit hesitation, "A sultan living in a gilded cage, would also experience isolation."

"Fantastic answer," replied Kate, proudly.

She was always proud when her students gave it a try and was spot on.

"Now, Sarah, can you please further expand upon that statement. How and why would the sultan have been isolated? And from what or whom?"

"Umm…well…I suppose that the sultan living in the palace would have been isolated from the rest of the world. While he might have been distracted by the allure, magic and wonders of the palace; at the same time, he would have also grown ignorant about other worldly affairs, right outside of his palace walls," replied Sarah, after much reflection.

"Well done, Sarah!" exclaimed Kate. "You are absolutely correct. Now, this brings us to the next area of our discussion. What or whom would have caused, or have allowed the sultan to grow so ignorant?"

Kate waited for Sarah to respond, but this time, another student, Becky, decided to chime in and raised her hand. Kate was thrilled. This discussion was growing more and more interesting for her students, by the minute.

"Yes, Becky," replied Kate, happily.

"The sultans' lack of knowledge about their worldly affairs at the time, was a direct result of both their mothers and their viziers. They each had their own agendas, and they actively and ambitiously sought to grab political power, for themselves. As long as the sultans retained them as their primary confidents and political advisors, they maintained the ability to manipulate the sultans, into getting their ways and thus, run the empire based upon their own wants and desires. Furthermore, since the advisors controlled the sultans' education and daily affairs, they kept them isolated from the rest of the world; thereby, creating a co-dependency between them and the sultan. Although the sultan was the legitimate ruler of the empire, behind the scenes, it was their mothers and viziers, who effectively controlled the administration of the empire. Overtime, this vicious cycle continued, and the future generations continued to grow up within this toxic environment. Eventually, the sultans grew more and more out of touch with the rest of society, and the world, at large. Slowly, this caused the empire to fracture and eventually, this led to the empire's ultimate decline, due to the sultans' lack of education and bad decision making."

"Becky, you certainly did your homework!" replied Kate, admiringly, "You are absolutely correct. Now, for those who are unaware of the term 'vizier,' this essentially translates to a political advisor."

As Kate was about to pose her next question, the school bell suddenly rang. Class was officially over.

"Ah wait," said Kate, "One last item, on the agenda. For homework, please start brainstorming as to what could have happened, had the sultans dismissed their advisors and rejected the cage system, altogether? How would the empire have looked then? Would the outcome have been much different, or the same? And was the sultan even capable to have done so, in the first place?"

Not a minute later, Kate's students packed all of their belongings and exited the classroom. Then, she walked over to the chalkboard, picked up an eraser and began erasing all of the texts that she had previously written, only just a few minutes ago. After she finished erasing all of the chalk residue from the chalkboard, she turned around and walked back over to her podium. Once she arrived to the podium, she began gathering up all of her lecture documents, and she placed them back into her purse. However, while she was in the middle of doing this, she suddenly heard a cough. Was someone still in the classroom with her?

Immediately, Kate looked up and to her surprise, she saw a man sitting right in the middle aisle of her classroom. Seated and leaning against the wooden chair, with his legs up and hanging over the seat in front of him, the man looked comfortable. Kate didn't recognize him. In fact, she had never seen him before. But most importantly, he was certainly, not one of her students.

"May I help you?" asked Kate.

"Dr. Stanley, that was a very nice lecture. I thoroughly enjoyed," answered the man.

Kate squinted her eyes to take a closer look at him. He appeared to be tall and husky, but not quite chubby. Rather, he looked more muscular, than anything else. His hair was dark brown, his complexion was light, and his eyes were a deep shade of emerald green. He was rather handsome, she thought. And, he looked to be about in his mid to late thirties. Much older than anyone of her students.

"Aren't you a little too old to be one of my students?" asked Kate. "This is a freshman class, and I don't think you are a freshman."

The man simply chuckled by Kate's question. Obviously, tickled by her statement. Then, he stood up from his seat, and Kate realized that he was much taller, than what she had first perceived. In fact, he was so incredibly tall, that he almost resembled that of an oak tree. No wonder he had his legs stretched over the second chair. Otherwise, he couldn't have fit!

Within seconds, the man quickly walked over to Kate, and he handed her his business card. Upon receival, Kate promptly read it.

"Detective Lucas Oliver, CEO and Chief Officer at Orion Securities," Kate read aloud.

It took her a moment for that to sink that in.

"Wait," she said, almost alarmingly, "You're a detective?"

"Yup, just like the card says," he said, as he tapped the corner of his business card, still held within her hand, with his finger.

"Detective Oliver," began Kate, "I believe the university already employs our own security here. I'm not certain we need your services."

"That's not why I'm here," he swiftly interjected.

Suddenly, Kate grew concerned. If the Detective wasn't a part of the university's security team, then why was he here? Was something amiss? For some odd reason, Kate didn't have a good feeling about this.

"Detective, is everything alright? Or is something wrong? Why are you here, exactly?" asked Kate, rather hesitantly.

"I think it's best we speak in private," admitted Lucas.

Kate looked around the room, and she realized that they were already alone.

"But we are already alone, aren't we?" she asked.

"Trust me, Dr. Stanley, it's best we speak somewhere else; alone and with you, safely seated down," he said.

"Very well," replied Kate, "Let's meet at my office. It's down the hall and to the right. But first, I'll just need a few minutes to tidy up my classroom. Can we meet there, say, in about ten minutes of so?"

"Okay, fair enough," agreed Lucas.

Then, he walked over to the door and just before he exited the classroom, he said, "See you exactly in ten." And then he was gone.

Afterwards, Kate proceeded to pack the remainder of her belongings. However, this time, she now had an eerie feeling, that cloaked around her heart. Something just wasn't right. She could just sense and feel it. But what exactly was wrong? Kate shivered with fear.

Ten minutes later, Kate arrived to her office. As promised, Lucas was there, and standing in front of it. Well, at least, he stood in front of what he thought was her office.

"My office is actually, the one next over," she shyly admitted, trying her best, not to offend him.

"Then, whose office does this one belongs to?" he asked, while staring at the closed door before him.

"It's a vacant office," replied Kate, "The history department is looking to recruit another professor. Once they hire them, that will be their office."

"Any candidates?" he asked.

"It's still too early to determine. We're only at the recruitment stage," she replied.

"Must be difficult to get a position here then?" asked Lucas.

"The university does have standards," replied Kate.

"Including the history department?" he asked, curiously.

"*Especially*, the history department," she emphasized, boldly.

"Well, best of luck to them all," said Lucas, sarcastically.

"I'm sorry, Detective," she interrupted, "But are you here to investigate, as to whom our next history professor will be?"

Once again, he chuckled and laughed at her question.

"Absolutely not. Although, I'll admit, that would have been surprisingly, much more interesting, than what I'm doing now. Maybe, later down the line, I should change my career paths from security to human resources."

Kate laughed too. She hadn't expected him to say that.

"Well, I suppose that would be a rather drastic career change too. But, it's never too late."

"Sadly, in my case, I believe it is too late; as I, myself, would like to retire soon," he admitted.

"Retire? Aren't you a bit too young?" asked a surprised Kate.

"Why Dr. Stanley, not only are you an excellent professor and lecturer, but you are also rather observational. First, I'm too old to be one of your students and now, I'm too young to retire. Are you sure you're not the detective?" said Lucas, with a dry smile.

Kate blushed. Was this detective actually flirting with her? She was starting to red, and she needed to quickly compose herself.

"Here's my office," she began, hoping to change the subject. "Shall we enter?"

Lucas took her queue and motioned himself to open the door. As he held open the door, he gestured for her to pass through, as he announced, "Ladies first."

Once they entered her office, Lucas waited for Kate to sit down. As he waited, he scanned the room and noticed just how very simple her office was. There was the standard desk, chairs, computer, telephone, bookshelf, coffee machine, plants, books and paper. Lots of paper. Stacks of paper. However, that was to be expected, as she was a teacher, after all. But apart from that, her office was rather plain. It didn't have any special decorations, pictures, artwork or anything else personal, that would have otherwise, prevented her from easily relocating to another venue, had the duty called for such action. For it became abundantly clear to him, that everything in her office was easily replaceable and transferrable. Ultimately, she had no attachments. This was certainly good to know. Lucas, as a detective, already knew that a person's office was a fairly good reflection of one's inner personality and character. And as it currently stood, Kate already passed his first test.

"Would you care for some tea, Detective Oliver?" asked Kate, as she prepared a cup for herself.

"Not necessary," he said, "Never been much of a tea drinker."

"Then, coffee perhaps?" she asked, politely.

However, Lucas laughed at such a notion.

"Not unless, you have some whisky there, because if you do, then I'll take an Irish coffee."

"Oh," Kate said blushingly. "I don't believe the university allows us to carry alcohol in our offices."

Lucas laughed again.

"I'm joking Dr. Stanley."

"Oh, I see, that is funny," said Kate, with a wry smile.

Kate then placed her tea down on her desk and sat down in her chair. Sitting directly across from Lucas, she quickly took a sip of her tea. Upon finishing her sip, she placed her mug back down on the table, and then she looked directly into Lucas' deep green eyes. Finally, she was ready to listen to him.

"Detective Oliver, what brings you here?" she asked.

Suddenly, Lucas cleared his throat, sat straight back up within his seat, and his humorous expression grew much more serious.

"Dr. Stanley, I know that we may have gotten off on a more lighthearted start, but," he began, "I'm actually here to see you. I've got to discuss about some serious matters, concerning your sister, Jennifer Barrett."

"My sister?" asked a very shocked Kate. Her heart nearly sunk, by the mere mention of her sister's name.

"Yes, your sister. Your twin, as I do believe," he said.

"Yes, she's my twin," said Kate, most ardently.

"Now, this might come as a bit of a shock," began Lucas slowly, "But your sister has recently gone missing."

"Gone missing? Gone missing? What...what...exactly does that mean, precisely?" she asked, with a half-cracked voice.

Out of fear, she immediately rose up from her chair, and she simply stared back at him. His words pierced her heart, and she wasn't quite certain, as to whether or not, she was ready to hear the rest of his news. Good or bad. This certainly was a shock.

"It's been over a week now, since we've last seen, or heard from her," he revealed.

"A week?" she repeated.

"Yes, a week," he confirmed.

"And?" she asked.

"And nothing. We've not been able to locate her as of yet, but I assure you, Dr. Stanley, we are working on that."

"Has she been kidnapped?" she fearfully asked, almost wishing that she hadn't even asked that very question, in the first place.

"That hasn't yet been ruled out," replied Lucas, "But neither has her simply running away, either."

"Running away?" repeated a shocked Kate. "Why would she have run away? Why, she had a wonderful life! She lived like a real-life princess at that mansion!"

"Dr. Stanley, I don't want to upset you, but these are all, just possible scenarios," replied Lucas, "As we're still investigating this matter, we must evaluate all angles."

"What if it's a kidnapper?" asked Kate, abruptly.

"Then, sooner or later, her kidnapper is going to ask for a ransom, and then we'll catch them. But if I'm being honest, I'm not certain that this is a kidnapping case."

"Why do you say that?" asked Kate, concerningly.

"Because it's already been a week and there's been no ransom note. In my experience, in most kidnapping cases, it takes a day or two, three at the most, for a ransom note to circulate. Furthermore, anyone who kidnaps the ambassador's wife, will most certainly ask for a ransom. Believe me, Dr. Stanley, people who are brave enough to do so, will most likely, seek the maximum profit, too," replied Lucas.

"What do you think happened to her?" she asked.

"Like I said before, I can't say for certain, because we're still investigating this matter. But most likely, I, personally, think she ran away. But hopefully, if we can buy enough time, we can relocate her and then bring her back home," he said.

"Do you think she's still alive?" she asked, feeling horrified that she, herself, had even uttered those very words.

"I don't see why she wouldn't be, as there are no other indications, suggesting this as a homicide case."

"If she did runaway, then why do you think she did that? I was always under the impression that she was happy," Kate whispered.

"Your sister lived a rather complex and complicated life. Being the wife of a civil servant and political appointee is never easy. I don't care who you are, it just isn't. Imagine living your life in a fishbowl…or as you, yourself so elegantly stated this afternoon, and I quote 'a gilded cage'," replied Lucas, with his green eyes, directly staring into her own startled blue eyes.

Kate was stunned and appalled by his reference to her 'gilded cage' discussion. My God, she thought, was he mocking her? If so, now, certainly wasn't the appropriate time to do so.

"Are you honestly equating my classroom lecture about the Ottoman Empire, to that of my own sister's circumstance? How utterly appalling of you!" she exclaimed.

"Calm down Dr. Stanley, that was never my intent. I just thought, that you of all people, would have understood her motives best of all. Especially, if she truly had run away," he said.

"Why would I know her motive? Is it because I'm a history professor? Detective Oliver, that hardly makes me a profiler. I study the past, not the present," replied Kate, rather coldly.

"I assure you; it's got nothing to do with your profession. But you are her twin, are you not? Don't twins' sense what the other is feeling, or better yet, doing? At least, that's what I've heard."

"Jennifer and I have never been those sorts of twins. We've always maintained our own individual personalities. Apart from resembling each other, we're very much the opposite," Kate admitted.

"Yes, you two certainly do resemble each other, rather more than I had initially imagined too. Although your hair color is a bit different and your style as well…"

He began to throttle off, as his eyes concentrated on her, scanning her up and down, measuring her body, within his mind. After much review, he concluded, that Kate had just successfully passed his second test, as well.

"I beg your pardon?" replied Kate. She wasn't certain as to what exactly he meant by 'style,' but she certainly didn't like it.

"It's just that your hair is a shade darker and you dress more conservative…"

"Excuse me?" Kate, shot back. She also didn't like how he used the term "conservative" to describe her.

Lucas understood his mistake, and quickly sought to remedy it.

"Perhaps, conservative is not the appropriate word. Sophisticated is more like it. You are simply more sophisticated than your sister, but I suppose that's to be expected, as you are a professor," he said, finally making direct eye contact with her once again.

Kate did not appreciate Lucas's attention, so she once again shot back and said, "And your point is?"

"Dr. Stanley, it is truly not my intention to offend you. But I'm a detective and I'm simply making observations, as I go," he said, laughingly.

Kate was ready to counterattack and retort against his statements about her appearance, but she stopped herself short. Arguing with the detective about petty matters was obsolete. There were bigger issues, at hand. As Kate sat there listening to the detective, she slowly began to comprehend the seriousness of her sister's disappearance. Never once, did she ever imagine a world, in which Jennifer wasn't a part of. Although they were separated, Kate always strived to, at the very least, write correspondences to her sister, in order to maintain some form of a communication bridge between them. Although they were impersonal, Kate knew, deep down inside her heart, that she could have done more. Much more. She knew that she could have made more of an effort to visit her sister in-person. In fact, she hadn't seen her sister, in well over five years and counting. She hadn't even attended her wedding. She missed that too. Heck, she never even met the ambassador, let alone, know how he looked like. Why, the only wedding photographs she received from Jennifer were limited to just pictures of the bride.

In truth, she missed every single major event and milestone with her sister, these past five years. While her sister always tried to make an effort, by sending her various invitations to her state dinners, Kate always declined them. It wasn't that Kate wasn't interested on attending, it's just that she never had the time. There were always too many papers to grade, too many lectures to draft, and too many seminars to attend. The reality was that Kate simply buried herself, with her work and in her career. But these were all just excuses, excuses and more excuses. In the end, Kate neglected spending any quality time with her twin sister, and now, she thought to herself, what if it was too late? What if, Jennifer was really gone and never coming back? What then? How would her life be, if Jennifer was no longer a part of it? And suddenly, Kate was overcome by tremendous guilt.

"Is there anything I can do to help?" Kate asked, as she wiped away the tears, streaming down her face.

Lucas wasn't so inhumane nor cruel, not to acknowledge that Kate was grieving. Although he was a detective in the security industry field for many years, he wasn't immune to feel compassion, or even pity for his clients and those directly involved with any of his cases. Seeking to comfort her, he reached into his pocket and handed her a tissue.

"Thank you," she said, as she graciously accepted his kind gesture.

"Dr. Stanley, I assure you, I will find your sister, one way or another. I promise you this," he said confidently.

"Thank you, Detective Oliver. I truly appreciate it. As I said before, if you need any help, then please let me know," said Kate.

"Actually, yes," began Lucas, "And I have to admit, I'm rather relieved that you've said that too, because this comes down to the very reason, as to why I'm here, in the first place."

"I beg your pardon?" she asked, now rather confused by such admission.

"I'm here, because I need your help. Well, rather, we need your help," he said.

"Wait, you being here has nothing to do with delivering the news about Jennifer's disappearance to me?" asked Kate, shockingly.

"No, I did come here to serve as the news bearer, but I'm also tasked on asking for your corroboration in this case, which I might add, is most urgently needed at this time," he replied.

"Whatever could it be?" asked Kate, rather alarmingly.

Lucas realized that what he was about to ask her would come as a shock, but he knew he had to ask it, nonetheless. And so, he slowly began, "We need…"

"Yes," she interrupted.

"We need you to…" he continued.

"You need me to…" she repeated his words.

"We need you to pose as your sister," he said finally.

"What??!!" Kate exclaimed, as she almost fell off from her chair, by the shock.

"Are you alright?" asked Lucas, as he came rushing from behind and caught her mid-air, just in time, before she completely fell down.

"I'm sorry," said Kate as she stood up and then, sat back down in her seat. "I thought I heard you ask me to pose as my sister."

"No, you heard correctly," said Lucas, affirmingly.

Kate was utterly shocked.

"But why?" she asked.

"Why don't take a moment to take another sip your tea. Once you've calmed down a bit, I promise to explain everything to you, when you're ready."

Sadly, Kate no longer had control of her voice; but somehow, she managed to nod her head, in agreement. After Lucas left the room to take a brief recess, Kate collected her nerves and forced herself to sip her tea. This entire afternoon had been rather shocking to her. Kate had already experienced a variety of emotions, stemming from fear to distress, to worry to grief, and now shock. This was all too much for a simple history professor, whose only previous stress the night before was figuring out what to feed her cat, Tabitha, for dinner! But before Kate could ponder any further, Lucas returned back into the room. He appeared most eager to get back to business.

"Are you well rested now?" he asked.

"Yes, I think so. I apologize for my reaction earlier," she said, as she took another sip of her tea.

"I understand," he said, "It happens. But if you don't mind, I'd like to get down to business and cut straight to the point."

"Err, yes, the point. And this somehow has something to do with me posing as Jennifer? Can you please further elaborate?" asked Kate, nervously.

"Your sister is married to a very important and powerful man," Lucas began, "The ambassador manages a major American embassy overseas, and he's involved with several critical projects that are key to our country's national interests abroad. Given the nature of his profession, he's also very much in the public eye. And as his wife, Jennifer is equally an essential public figure, as well."

"I see," replied Kate, as she took another sip of her tea.

"The ambassador cannot afford any scandals right now, especially, while he's in the middle of a very important project. As you may already be aware, there's an election this year. Given that the ambassador was appointed by our current president to his current post, we cannot allow any negative publicity to circulate, which might adversely affect both the president and the ambassador, and potentially impact and comprise the upcoming election. Including any negative press."

"Wait, you need my help, in order to divert a possible scandal, regarding the disappearance of my sister?" asked Kate.

"Precisely," replied Lucas, "Now, as I promised, I will find your sister, I give my word. But in the meantime, we don't want it discovered by the public that she's gone missing. As it stands, she's already been gone for over a week now, and we've been trying our best to hide it. But we cannot hide her forever. Soon, people will start asking questions. And by people, I mean the media, the public, staffers and other foreign representatives. And we cannot allow this to happen. We just need to buy some time, until we find her."

"Now, I understand," said Kate quietly. She then asked, "So you need me to serve as a decoy, until she is found?"

"Exactly," replied Lucas, with a devious smile. Then, he added, "I understand why the university employs you, Dr. Stanley, you catch on to matters quickly."

Kate once again blushed. Flattery made her nervous. However, she promptly composed herself and asked, "If I agree," and she emphasized on the word *if*, she continued, "Then, what would I need to do?"

"Does this mean you're agreeing to my proposal?" asked Lucas.

"Perhaps, but first, what exactly do I need to do? Just show up and pretend to be her? I don't even know how to do that! I've got no idea, as to how to even begin to act like her. I never have. Not even when we were children," said Kate, with a wry expression on her face.

Lucas detected Kate's distress and sought to comfort her.

"Not to worry," he began, "You will be trained. You'll have a full-time staff, dedicated to help you on all of this and more," he concluded, as he waved his hand into the air, ever so casually. Then, Lucas leaned across the table and met Kate, eye to eye and said, "All you need to say is the magic words, yes."

Posing as Jennifer was a once in a lifetime challenge, that she never thought she'd ever have to take. Even as children, they never once played the twins switch game, even though they could have many times very easily. But circumstances were now different, and Jennifer needed her help. After years of neglect, Kate felt that she owed it to her sister. As Kate looked down at the table, she suddenly caught sight of the pearl ring that she wore on her finger. It was a gift from her sister. The pearl was large and oddly shaped, but it was still a beautiful and unique ring, that served as a constant daily reminder to her about her twin. Although they'd been apart, Kate always felt her sister presence, every time she wore the ring. As she stared down at the pearl ring wrapped around her finger, she realized that she had to do this for Jennifer. Her sister needed her help and this time, Kate wasn't going to let her down.

"When do we leave?" asked Kate, now looking directly into Lucas' deep green eyes.

He lifted a brow and replied, "So I take it that you are agreeing to my proposal?"

"Yes," said Kate, as she nodded to serve as a secondary confirmation.

"Excellent," he quickly rose from his chair, "We leave tomorrow morning. Meet me at the international terminal at JFK airport by 8 am. We have an early flight to catch."

"But that's not enough time for me to pack or to inform the university about my departure or…," exclaimed Kate, worryingly.

"Not to worry Dr. Stanley, everything has been taken care of. The embassy already contacted your department chair, Professor Zaman, regarding your sabbatical, and your landlord has also been notified. We've already paid for your apartment for a full year, so your landlord will have no objections with your time away. And packing isn't necessary, as you will be provided with a brand-new wardrobe, upon your arrival."

"Oh my God, this has all already been prearranged?" asked a surprised Kate. "But I should also tell you, Detective Oliver, my passport is expired. I haven't traveled in years and never had the opportunity to renew it."

Lucas chuckled at Kate's concerns about her passport. Slowly, he reached into his jacket pocket and pulled out a blue American passport. He then handed it over to her.

"What's this?" asked Kate.

"Why don't you open it and take a look?" he replied, with a smile.

Following his instructions, Kate proceeded to open up the passport. To her surprise, the passport already had her picture in it, along with her name. Furthermore, the expiration date was a future date, valid until 2028! My God, Kate realized, this passport was really hers!

"Wait, how's this even possible?" asked a rather shocked Kate.

"We retrieved a copy of your photo id from the university, and then used the same photograph to issue your new passport. As you may recall, the ambassador does work for the state department, the same department who also oversees the issuance of passports," replied Lucas, as a matter of fact.

Kate was utterly stunned. It appeared that Lucas and his team did do their homework, after all. But there was still one matter that remained unresolved. And this, in Kate's opinion, was perhaps the most important matter of all. The ultimate deal breaker.

"Well, what about my cat, Tabitha? I have to bring her with me," she said, "Don't I need some sort of special animal pet traveling license to do so?"

"One step ahead of you, we've already got the license," replied Lucas. "As I said before, Dr. Stanley, we've taken care of everything. Please, just show up tomorrow at the airport…," then he emphasized the words, "on time."

"Yes, I will, I promise. I won't be late," said Kate, reassuringly.

Finally, Lucas got up from his chair and headed towards the door, signaling the end of their conversation. But before he left, Kate cried out to him. She had one last question.

"Wait, Detective Oliver," she cried, "Where exactly will we be traveling to?"

"Why to Istanbul, of course," replied Lucas, with a smile and a wink.

Then, he walked towards her door and as he was about to exit out of her office, he turned back around and said, "And please, call me Lucas." Then, he smiled once more and shut the door behind him.

And for Kate, the history professor, who had spent much of her afternoon teaching her students about the history of the Ottoman Empire through the pages of their textbooks, was now about to embark upon her own journey to the empire's former capital, Istanbul, to experience it all now, firsthand, for herself.

Chapter 11

By late Wednesday afternoon, Kate arrived to Istanbul. It was a lengthy and tiring journey, but at long last, she finally made it. Even her beloved pet cat, Tabitha, who traveled in the plane's special cargo section, was here with her, too. Kate sighed with relief. It had been several years since she last traveled to Türkiye, not since her own childhood. Now, after all these years, she was finally here, but for very different reasons. Rather than visiting dear old Grandmother Shakire in a remote village by the sea, Kate was here, in the one of the largest, busiest and most populated metropolitan cities in the world. Istanbul, the ancient city located within Europe and Asia, was now Kate's new home base, for the indefinite future. But how long exactly, would she be here? Kate honestly had no idea.

Within three days, her entire life drastically changed. On Monday morning, she was an average history professor at NYU; but, by that very same afternoon, she met Lucas and her average life was no more. After agreeing to serve as her sister's temporary decoy for the time being, she quickly abandoned her simple, yet modest life back in New York, and she boarded a plane headed straight to Istanbul, to blindly venture into unknown territory. For Kate, whose simple life previously revolved around the same daily habitual routine, stepping away from the comfort of that routine and walking into the unknown, was something that didn't come so easily for her.

However, Kate knew that in order to help Jennifer, she needed to cast aside her own selfish fears. To overcome them, Kate told herself, that just like the advice she previously told her own students, one mustn't ever be fearful to ask questions or take risks, even if it's the wrong one. In life, we all must take a gamble, even if it's the wrong one, all for the sake of individual growth and learning. But unlike before, this time, Kate knew that she, herself, needed to follow her own philosophy and to ultimately, practice what she preached. Therefore, she agreed to step out of her own comfort zone and to take her own gamble, all for the sake of rescuing her sister. And as promised, come early Tuesday morning, she arrived to the airport to meet Lucas. To her surprise, they didn't need to check-in. Instead, they proceeded straight ahead to the gateway, with no tickets, nor security screening, necessary.

Upon arriving to the gateway, their flight crew were ready to receive them, including Tabitha, who was safely secured inside of her traveling crate. While Kate and Lucas boarded the plane, the flight crew promptly took ownership of Tabitha. Assuming that they were assigned to the economy class, Kate proceeded to walk further down the aisle, past the first restroom stalls, upon boarding. However, midway, Lucas promptly grabbed hold of her arm and redirected her back to first class. To her surprise, since Kate agreed to pose as her sister, unbeknownst to her, she became, by default, an official temporary government contractor with the agency. In fact, Lucas, himself, summed it up best: Kate was essentially, an "undercover agent." As such, her first official mission as a newly appointed government contractor, was to travel in style via first class, with Lucas, serving as Kate's own official escort and bodyguard.

Once she sat down in the oversized brown leather seat, she turned her attention over to Lucas, who sat directly across from her, on the opposite side of the aisle. After stretching his long legs across the aisle, as he reclined his chair back, he gave her a devious smile. Then, he reached over and opened his jacket, to flash her a peek to his large silver gun, which he hid on the side of his belt.

"Don't worry Kate, you're in good hands," he said, with a wink.

When the plane finally lifted up into the sky, Lucas closed his eyes and fell fast asleep. Meanwhile, Kate took a deep breath. After spending the past few years primarily focused on just her studies and teaching career, this was her first time traveling by plane, in a very long time. She was nervous, too. Curiously, Kate looked over and saw Lucas comfortably asleep nearby. Having ensured her that she was in 'good hands,' Kate decided to join him. After all, it was going to be a long flight anyways, so she decided that she might as well try her best to sleep it off. Much to her success, she did, indeed, sleep for entire duration of that flight, too.

Once they landed into Istanbul, Lucas prearranged for a limousine to pick them up at the airport. Following his directions, Kate only packed a small sized suitcase, containing just her own personal essentials, including her laptop, tablet and mobile phone. However, once Lucas became aware of Kate's devices, he warned her not to use them during the duration of her trip. When she asked as to why that was, he simply stated that as a newly appointed government contractor, her private devices were at risk. He further explained that by using her personal devices abroad, they could potentially be compromised by other foreign actors and governments, and eventually, she could become the victim to various cybersecurity threats.

To compromise, Lucas offered to provide her with newly government sponsored and approved devices instead, which included special government security software by his office. He further explained to her, that as the head of security, his firm also oversaw the embassy's emerging technology and cybersecurity security infrastructures. Kate sighed to herself. The only reason as to why she even brought her laptop in the first place, was so she could retain ongoing contact with her students and university during her sabbatical. But sadly, this no longer appeared to be a feasible option anymore. In the end, Kate truly had to leave everything behind and immerse herself completely into her new, yet temporary role, as her sister.

By four o'clock in the afternoon, they finally arrived to the mansion. Lucas promptly took all of their belongings from out of the limousine, and he brought them inside into the mansion, leaving Kate the opportunity to venture outside to explore the estate, along with Tabitha, by her side. And what a sight it was to behold! It truly was spectacular and magnificent! Well, beyond Kate's own imagination and expectations. Like a shiny, bright and white pearl that shined against the sunlight, while standing firmly on top of a little hill, the mansion was surrounded by a rose garden, that bloomed all around, and closed in by a tall iron gate. From afar, the estate resembled that of a story book fairytale, with the mansion appearing as a replica of a miniature white house.

After strolling past the front gate, Kate opened Tabitha's crate to allow the cat to venture outside, and together, they walked into the garden. Once in the garden, Tabitha quickly jumped up into the air, and she began chasing an orange monarch butterfly, that floated nearby, between the tall grass and the rose bushes. Seeing just how Tabitha looked, as she innocently played and frolicked across the lawn, ever-so curiously, as she played with the busy butterfly with her paws, Kate smiled to herself. In that moment, she realized that this trip not only brought about new changes for her, but even for her own little pesty tabby cat, too. Tabitha, once confined within a small, stuffy and tiny New York apartment, now had the complete freedom to safely run outside, through a gated European garden. Observing just how quickly Tabitha transitioned positively into her new environment, Kate acknowledged that her own cat had already long forgotten about her old home back in New York. Instead, Tabitha was busy and solely engaged with nature, and Kate, had to admit, that she never saw her cat look any happier before. But, although Tabitha already grew accustomed and comfortable at the estate, Kate couldn't help but wonder, if she too would experience the same such luck?

Moving her attention away from Tabitha, Kate began to review the garden, to help herself to grow more familiarized with her new environment. After all, this unknown estate was going to become her new home for the time being, and Kate was nervous with the prospect. The reality of being so far removed from her home, was slowly beginning to dawn upon her more and more. As Kate stared across at the mansion, she thought to herself, that only just a week and a half ago, her sister, Jennifer, was here. Her sister, whom she neglected to visit for years, lived here, in this very mansion. Had Jennifer been living here happily ever after, just as Kate had always presumed? Or was she wrong about happily ever after? Or was this a world a forgotten nightmare that she was about to walk into? Kate shivered at the prospect.

Whether or not, this place was heaven or hell, it remained to be seen. Kate needed to collect her thoughts and remain positive. After all, it was only a matter of time, before Jennifer was eventually found. In the meantime, Kate needed to do everything in her power to help.

Suddenly, the sunlight caught Kate's eyes, and as she looked away, she saw before her, stood a rose bush, located on the opposite side of the lawn. Although the garden was covered by roses on all corners, Kate neglected to pay any attention to them, as she had been distracted by Tabitha. However, once Kate finally took notice, she was absolutely breath taken by their exquisite and rare beauty. In full bloom, the roses were various textures and shades. Walking across the lawn, with her feet moving across the green foliage of the newly cut grass, she approached the rose bush and brought her face as close as she possibly could, in order to study them up close.

Ranging in various shades of pink, stemming from the lightest color of baby pink to almost an off tint of white, to a medium pinkish tone, resembling that of a watermelon to finally, a darker pink tone, almost of a purple hue, similar to that of fuchsia, the roses were a staple to the mansion's allure. Either way, it appeared that all the roses that grew in the garden had some form of pink, one way or another. Suddenly, Kate smiled to herself, as she recalled that Jennifer's favorite color was pink. Somehow, Kate wondered if these roses were colored pink, because of her sister's influence. And if anyone of these flowers were anything like her sister, then perhaps, that explained the origins to the diversity in the roses' color. For, as Kate noted, they were all complexly colored and designed, much like her own sister.

As Kate continued to admire the roses, she unexpectedly, caught sight of one specific rose that grew right in the middle of the bush. Being far larger than all of the rest, this rose was in full bloom and a multicolored ombre, with a lighter pink hue in the middle, similar to that of ballet slippers. In the outer middle, the rose transitioned from a bubblegum tint to that of a velvet lilac tone, on its outer corners. Surrounded by emerald green leaves, Kate was captivated by its beauty and so, she decided to smell the flower for herself. As she bent down, she took a sniff and the rose's aroma, certainly did not disappoint. The smell was sweet, floral and fresh. It honestly, smelt just like heaven, she thought. But suddenly, as Kate was about to take a second sniff, she heard footsteps from behind her.

"You must be Dr. Stanley," said the female voice.

Immediately, Kate turned around, and she saw an elderly woman standing in front of her. The woman was in her late sixties and elegantly dressed, wearing a white chiffon dress, with her hair-colored blonde and pulled back into a secured bun. She wore a full set of makeup, and she appeared to be very well groomed and quite attractive for her age.

"Yes, I'm Dr. Stanley. May I ask who you are?" replied Kate, with a raised brow.

"My name is Gloria Renaud, and I'm the embassy coordinator," replied Gloria.

Taking a few minutes to thoroughly observe Kate, Gloria scanned her up and down, from the top of her head to the bottom of her toes. After quietly studying her, Kate began to grow uncomfortable due to the awkward and prolonged silence. Sensing her anxiety, Gloria, once again, began to speak.

"I must say, you really do look just like her," replied Gloria, as her eyes zoomed closer to further inspect Kate. "I dare say, Dr. Stanley, please humor me and take a spin around."

"I beg your pardon?" replied Kate, who was rather confused by such an unusual request.

"Just a spin, so that I can have a better look of you," replied Gloria, as a matter of fact.

"Alright," spoke Kate, as she slowly gave a twirl and said, "Is that enough?"

"For now, yes," answered Gloria, "And thank you for obliging to me. I must say that your hair is a bit too dark, and your clothes not what I expected. However, not to worry, we'll take care of that soon enough."

"We are twins, by the way," Kate admitted, hoping to clarify the reason as to their similarity.

"Yes, I know, and aren't we all lucky that you two are," she said, as she happily clasped her hands together in excitement.

"Well, Mrs. Renaud, it certainly is a pleasure to meet you," said Kate, with a wry smile.

"Please, call me Gloria," interrupted Gloria.

"Very well, Gloria, it's a pleasure to meet you. And since we're on a first name basis, you can also call me Kate."

"But I simply cannot do that, Dr. Stanley. That's against protocols. You are the ambassador's new wife now, and my superior; therefore, you are Dr. Stanley to me."

"But I'm not really his new wife…" Kate began.

"Real or pretend, it's all irrelevant," replied Gloria, as she waved her hands carefree in the air.

"To us, it's all the same," Gloria further clarified. "As long as you are posing as your sister, *you are already the* ambassador's wife, one way or another, in all our eyes."

"Oh, I hadn't realized that was so," replied Kate, surprised by such revelation.

"You're new here, Dr. Stanley," began Gloria, "There's many things that you'll soon come to learn, as I'm already sure that you know."

"Yes, I'm very eager to learn. Anything that will help aid with my sister's case," Kate added.

"That's very comforting to hear that," said Gloria, with a smile.

"Dr. Stanley," she began, changing the subject, "Have you yet taken a moment to admire our lovely roses, here in the garden?"

"As a matter of fact, yes, I have. I recently just smelled that pink rose over there, right before you arrived," Kate answered, as she pointed towards the flower with her index finger.

"The bright pink one in the middle?" Gloria asked.

"Yes, that very one," Kate replied.

"Ah, I see," said Gloria, "You know, the roses here are very famous. Tourist and locals alike, often come here to visit them. But from outside the gates, of course."

"Is that so?" asked Kate.

"Yes; in fact, even our staff admires them too, even though we work here and see them every day," said Gloria.

"Well, I can't say that I'm surprised," began Kate. "With all the ranges of color, no two roses are quite alike. They're truly breathtaking and a beauty to behold."

Gloria stared directly at Kate and asked, "That rose that you smelled, did you care for its fragrance?"

"Why, yes I did," replied Kate, "It was quiet a beautiful and refreshing scent. Nothing similar to anything else that I've previously ever smelt before.

"Interesting. If that's the case, then why don't you pick and keep that rose personally, for yourself?" asked Gloria.

"You mean, to pluck it, directly from that rose bush?" asked Kate.

"Precisely. You're now the lady of this estate, and a valuable member of this household. You're more than entitled to take any flower you so choose from this garden. Your garden."

"I'm not sure that's necessary," replied Kate, in all honesty.

"Are you afraid of the thorns?" asked Gloria, suspiciously, "Dr. Stanley, I assure you, that won't be an issue. Why, if you'd like, I can teach you how to take from this garden, without ever being harmed."

"It's not the fear of the thorns that prevents me from taking the rose," admitted Kate.

"Really? Then, pray tell, what prevents you? It's a lovely flower. Why, you, yourself, admitted that you enjoyed its smell and aroma. Why not take and enjoy it?"

"Because to take from the garden is selfish. Besides, doing so, would only provide me with a temporary relief," said Kate, boldly.

"Selfish?!" exclaimed Gloria, "Dr. Stanley, whatever do you mean?"

"I realize that this might come as a bit of a shock, but I've never been a fan of bouquets," said Kate.

"Not a fan of bouquets?" asked Gloria, in confusion. For once, Gloria was rather stumped and speechless.

"Well, I should clarify that I love flowers and gardens, but not bouquets," said Kate. "Take that rose, for example. While it's certainly beautiful and lovely, the truth is, part of what makes it so incredibly beautiful and lovely is directly due to its environment. Now, if I were selfish and I plucked and remove that rose from its natural habitat, then I would have essentially, stolen and torn it away from the environment in which it thrives in. Now, if I were to transplant that same flower and kept it hidden away in my bedroom, so that I may selfishly admire it all for myself, then I ask you, what would become of that very rose?"

Although Gloria remained speechless, she managed to give Kate a nod, signaling her permission to continue onwards with her story.

"Very well, then, I shall tell you. Its beauty would soon fade. Its fragrance will eventually, turn against itself, just like a foreign enemy. Soon enough, the sweet and alluring aroma that existed on Monday, will transition into a bitter and sour scent by Thursday. And come Sunday, all it's petals will have fallen and withered away, with nothing left to remain. Nothing, but a dried bud, which once served as the rose's core. Therefore, on the contrary, Gloria, I rather not pick this flower. For if you truly love and admire something, whether it be a rose or even a person, then you leave it alone, as is and in its natural element, unchanged, thorns and all. Besides, by leaving the rose back here and unharmed, then I know that it will survive beyond Sunday. Furthermore, it will also give me an excuse to return back here to the garden to visit it again, in the near future. Additionally, whether or not, I delay my next visit to a week or even the week after, I have the reassurance and knowledge that this rose will still continue to live and thrive here, come rain or shine. Lastly, as I might add, others, not just I, can also have an opportunity to equally admire and love this rose for its beauty, just like you and I currently do today."

"My word, I wasn't expecting that response at all!" exclaimed Gloria, with her hands clasped.

"Not expecting my general distaste for bouquets?" asked Kate, with a raised brow.

Gloria took a few minutes for Kate's answer to sink it and when it finally did, she beamingly smiled.

"You know, Dr. Stanley, in all of my years," began Gloria, "And I have worked at this agency for the past thirty years and counting. I have never, not once, ever met anyone, not a single person, in all of my acquaintances, to have ever given me such an answer, like you just did right now. My word, Dr. Stanley, you're truly a rare one, indeed. Perhaps, both you and I have much to learn from one another. Shall we walk into the mansion, together?"

"Yes, that would be lovely," said Kate. "But I should mention that my cat, Tabitha, is still playing with that butterfly over there in the corner."

Kate then pointed in the direction of Tabitha, who was currently, rolling back and forth, on the lawn. Evidently, Tabitha was still busy and focused on catching that fluttering butterfly with her paws. Once Gloria caught sight of the cat, she suddenly began to laugh.

"Not to worry Dr. Stanley, your cat is in good hands," replied Gloria, laughingly, "The gardener will bring her back into the mansion soon."

"Tabitha really does look rather happy there, doesn't she? Perhaps, the gardener can bring her back in, after an hour or so?" asked Kate.

"Of course," said Gloria, reassuringly.

"Thank you, Gloria," said Kate.

Soon after, the two ladies walked together, side by side, into the mansion. Meanwhile, Tabitha, the lucky cat, got an extra two hours of additional playtime in the garden. Although Kate's and Tabitha's arrival was already off to a good start, the same, could not be equally said, for the butterfly. After all, the butterfly, had one very curious orange tabby cat on its trail, eagerly chasing it, for the remainder of that sunny afternoon.

Chapter 12

The next morning, Kate awoke inside a large white linen bed, with Tabitha curled up into a ball, nearby. As the sunlight pierced through the cracks of her window and shined against her face, Kate remained in bed, as she stretched her body, in preparation for today. After all, yesterday was a busy day and today was expected to be even busier. Having arrived to Istanbul yesterday afternoon after a long flight, she was soon whisked away by Gloria, to tour the vast estate. Much to her surprise, the mansion was beyond all of her expectations. The property consisted of two primary floors, in which, the first floor, had a foyer, salon, ballroom, formal dining room, kitchen, terrace and offices; while the second floor were strictly allocated for the bedrooms. Furthermore, each floor had approximately twenty or so additional rooms to accommodate for visiting diplomats, their staff, and other foreign visitors and guests.

As for the mansion's interiors, the décor was rather surprisingly historical, which Kate, as a history professor, found absolutely delightful. While the estate was modern, reflected by the building's architectural and structural design, as well as the acquisition of contemporary furniture; the décor, itself, was entirely the opposite. With the exception of the bedrooms, the rest of the house appeared like a history book. The estate's interiors were essentially, a real-life museum; in which, the decoration played homage to various Turkish historical and cultural art within each room, including paintings and ceramics from the Ottoman and Islamic empires, as well as, earlier Anatolian Bronze Age artifacts, stemming from the Hittite civilization. Judging from the exterior alone, Kate would never have imaged that the interior was as beautiful as it truly was. A real hidden treasure and gem. Curious about the design choice, Kate inquired about it and Gloria, in return, informed her that it was simply the tradition for the estate to incorporate the local traditions and customs of the host country into the home's design, as a form and expression of good will, acceptance and the promotion of friendly relations amongst the guest and host nations.

After the formal estate tour, Gloria escorted Kate into her sister's chambers, located on the second floor, in the east wing. The wing consisted of a grand master bedroom; a bathroom suite; a private salon; with a tearoom; a walk-in closet, that was honestly, another room within itself; a secondary extra room, that was used as a private beauty station; and lastly, a large balcony, which was accessible from the primary master bedroom. Since Kate was still jet lagged from her long flight the day before, as soon as she arrived into Jennifer's chambers, she fell fast asleep, before having a chance to thoroughly inspect the room, for herself.

When Kate finally rose out of the bed, it suddenly dawned upon her, that the bed that she had just slept in, was indeed, her sister's. The same white linens, blankets, pillows and silken sheets— these were all hers. In fact, Kate noticed that on the opposite side of the bed, it still remained unslept and untouched. Still perfectly made. Ever-so-curious, Kate pulled the tucket blanket out and sniffed the empty pillow. As she expected, Kate could still smell distinct traces of Jennifer's signature Chanel number 5 perfume on that very same pillow. It appeared that Jennifer's bed was never remade, not since her disappearance. Although Jennifer was physically gone, her essence was still present, even within this very bed.

With an upcoming meeting scheduled right after breakfast, Kate realized that now wasn't the time to rest. Instead, she needed to get downstairs, as soon as possible. With no clothing of her own, she realized that she was going to have to borrow a dress from her sister's closet. How strange and eerie it felt to borrow something that wasn't hers, she thought to herself. Never had she ever worn her twin sister's clothes before. Not even when they were children.

Turning on the light switch, Kate walked straight into Jennifer's closet. To her surprise, the closet was as large as her entire New York studio apartment combined! Kate's mouth immediately dropped from shock, and she almost tripped and lost her balance along the way; but luckily, she managed to catch the door's handle to pull herself back up. Once Kate collected herself, she walked over towards the middle of the room, in order to get a better view. The room was circular, with rows of clothing hanging from all sides. In addition, there were two rows of clothing racks, one on the top and one on the bottom. Above the first row of clothing racks, were rows of cubbies that stored a collection of high-end designer purses and handbags. Underneath the second bottom row of the clothing rack, were additional cubbies that stored shoes.

Shocked by the sight before her, Kate realized that there must have been at least, a thousand individual pieces of clothing and accessories. Inspecting them for herself, Kate was astonished to learn that most of these outfits were still brand-new, and in their original packaging, with tags. Kate randomly pulled one of the dresses from off the rack and looked at the tag. It was a Calvin Klein. Kate pulled another and this time, it was a Vera Wang. Curious, she pulled a third dress and it was a Jimmy Chiu. To her amazement, Jennifer's closet wasn't just filled with any ordinary articles of clothing, but instead, they were all famous and expensive American designers!

For the first time, Kate started to feel a bit embarrassed for having arrived to the mansion, wearing only her rather plain and ordinary, off-the rack discounted retail clothes. Even as teenagers, Kate always dressed simple and modest, while Jennifer aimed for high-end and glamorous outfits. Eventually, as Kate grew into adulthood, she transitioned into wearing her standard office pants suits, which was most appropriate for her profession. However, her style, relatively, remained the same, throughout the years. Apart from her mascara and lip balm, Kate seldom ever wore makeup. And her hair was usually thrown up into a simple, no fuss ponytail. However, those days were long gone and times were now different. By the looks of this closet alone, Kate realized that by assuming Jennifer's identity, she wasn't going to be able to play the part, in name alone. Rather, she was going to have to actually start dressing like her, as well. And for some odd reason, the very thought made her knees shake out of nervousness.

But, as Kate reviewed the racks of clothing, a sudden stroke of guilt struck her heart. Although Jennifer was gone, Kate still felt guilty about sorting through her things, without her permission. In truth, it felt, as if, all of this was somehow an invasion to her own personal privacy. Ever since they were children, Kate always respected her sister's boundaries; but for the first time, she was about to cross over them. Although her intentions were true and good, she still wished that the circumstances were different. In a perfect world, Jennifer would have been here with her, and the two of them, should have been searching through these endless rows of clothes, together. But sadly, this was an imperfect world; and now, Kate was all alone and desperately missing her better half. Somehow, in the midst of all of this, Kate couldn't help but feel that Jennifer's disappearance was partly her fault, too.

"I should have visited you much sooner," Kate admitted to herself. "If only I came last year, then maybe you'd still be here…"

Slowly, tears began to run down Kate's face. Taking a deep breath, she closed her eyes and told herself that today wasn't the time to cry. Perhaps, tomorrow, but not today. Today, she needed to be strong. Her sister was somewhere, out there in the world, and she needed her help. Kate needed to fight for her. To help bring her back home. She owed it to her sister.

As Kate wiped away her tears, she decided to wear the newly packaged black dress. After she changed into the dress, she pulled a pair of black leather flats from one of the cubbies and quickly put them on. Once changed, all that was left was her hair.

Walking over into the next room, Kate pushed open the door, leading into the beauty room. As she entered the room, to her surprise, the room was yet another sight to behold! Her eyes immediately opened wide, as she saw hundreds upon hundreds of perfume bottles, all neatly stacked upon an endless supply of shelves, surrounding the room. Kate quickly scanned the perfume bottles, and she saw numerous collections of Chanel, Gucci, Dior, and Versace fragrances, to just name a select few. While the clothing was strictly American, the perfumes, on the other hand, were not.

Kate sniffed the air and to her surprise, the room didn't smell. This was certainly, unexpected. How could a room filled with so many perfume bottles, not smell? Out of curiosity, Kate walked over to the back shelf to inspect, and there, she noticed that the perfume bottles were all sealed. Then, she looked across at the other neighboring shelves, and she saw that they were sealed, too. How odd, she thought. To own all of these perfumes, yet never use them? How could that be and why? However, before Kate could further contemplate, she suddenly saw another shelf above and this time, these perfume bottles were opened. Immediately, Kate walked over and picked up one of the opened perfume bottles. It was the Chanel number 5 perfume, Jennifer's favorite. Kate noted, that out of all of the hundreds of priceless perfumes in this room, in the end, her sister preferred just this specific brand.

Opening the perfume's bottle cap, Kate smelled the sweet fragrance and smiled. It was bittersweet. As she closed her eyes, the perfume's fragrance brought back memories of her sister. Kate imagined her sister being here, in this same room, getting ready for an evening out and using this very perfume, to spritz around her neck. However, once she reopened her eyes, she was confronted with the reality that her sister was really gone, and that she was truly alone.

Like the gowns before, Kate, once again, felt guilty about sorting through her sister's belongings, without her permission. Out of respect for her sister, Kate decided not to use Jennifer's signature perfume. Instead, Kate randomly grabbed one of her unopened perfume bottles and took a spritz. To her joy, the scent was light and refreshing. Simple and fresh. Lovely, but not overpowering.

"This will do," she whispered to herself.

By now, Kate was almost ready, but she still needed to tidy up her hair and put on a bit of makeup. Walking over towards the vanity, Kate took a seat on Jennifer's pink velvet puff stool. As she sat down, she noticed that above the vanity was a large portrait of the French Queen, Marie Antoinette. Elegantly dressed in a royal blue gown, Marie Antoinette was surrounded by various sweet treats and pastries, highlighted by pastel and jewel-colored tones. Somehow, after visiting Jennifer's chambers today, Kate couldn't help but to draw parallels, between her sister and the late queen.

"They both lived like queens," said Kate. And then, bringing her hand to her heart, she added, "But I do pray that Jennifer has a much happier ending than Marie."

Returning her eyesight back towards the vanity mirror, Kate stared at her reflection. Her brown hair was a mess, her eyes were still red and puffy, due to her excess amounts of tears, and her complexion was white and pale. Hoping to improve her appearances, Kate grabbed a hairbrush, nearby. As she was about to brush her hair with it, she noticed a few loose strands of blonde hair, still lingering about inside the teeth of the brush. Suddenly, Kate sighed and took a deep breath. Everything around her reminded her of her sister, even down to the tiniest of details, including this hairbrush. Although Kate knew that her mission here was to play the part of her sister, but every time she saw pieces that reminded her of her missing twin, the memory felt like a constant knife pricking away at her heart. Taking another deep breath, Kate attempted to pick up the hairbrush, but to her dismay, her hands began to shake and tremble. Suddenly, the hairbrush slipped from her hands, and slammed down against the vanity table's marbled counter.

"Get ahold of yourself!" Kate yelled aloud, to herself.

Determined to calm her jittering nerves, Kate, once again, attempted to grab the hairbrush with her two hands. After a second attempt, which proved successful, Kate firmed held onto the hairbrush. Recalling the lingering strands of blonde hair still caught within the teeth of the hairbrush, Kate proceeded to pull them out. Once they were all removed, she rolled the blonde hairs into a ball and threw them away.

"There, that's more like it," she said, as she grabbed the empty brush and quickly brushed her hair.

Pulling her hair back into a simple ponytail, Kate noted, that although her hair now looked decent, she was still pale and in desperate need of color. Scanning the vanity table's counter, she spotted a golden lipstick tube. Reaching for the lipstick, Kate gently removed the cover and opened it. The lipstick was a bright shade of red and appeared used and dull— a clear indication that this particular lipstick was regularly used by Jennifer. Not wanting to overpower her appearance, Kate lightly dabbed the lipstick onto her lips; leaving a faint trace of the reddish color on her lips. Alas, now all that was left were her eyes; however, they were a bit puffy from crying.

Reaching for a tissue box nearby, she quickly wiped away her eyes. As she returned the tissue box to its proper place, she noticed a golden compact laying right next to it. Curious, she grabbed it and noticed that the golden packaging matched the lipstick that she had just used. They were a set. As she opened the compact, Kate observed that in the middle of the palette was a tiny brown hole, exposing the bottom of the compact. Another clear indication that this was another item regularly used by her sister. Using her index finger, Kate lightly tapped from the upper corner of the palette, then gently pressed the power onto her eyelids. Once finished, Kate returned the compact back to its proper place, and then, she looked at her reflection in the mirror.

Much to her surprise, her appearance was much improved. Her hair was more tamed, her face was full of color and her lips were now rosy. But, after a minute or two, Kate still saw her own face. It wasn't her sisters. The reflection staring back at her was her, and her alone. The same dark hair, same fair complexion and same light eyes. Even her expression was still her own.

"How am I going to pull this off? Who's going to believe that I'm her?" she whispered to herself, in desperation.

Although they were identical twins, Kate still wondered if people would truly buy into their charade. Reflecting on their past, Kate recalled as to how much easier it was for them to parade as each other, when they were much younger. This was in part, due to the fact, that they were around each other much more frequently. Therefore, it was so much simpler for them to mimic one another's behaviors, patterns and likeness, because they were a part of each other's worlds. But now, their worlds couldn't be more different or foreign. Year later, their lives no longer aligned. Having lived two very distinct and separate lives for so long, Kate feared that she hardly knew her sister that well, anymore. The fact that her sister left so many of her belongings behind, she wondered if Jennifer really did run away, on her own free will. And if so, then why on earth, would anyone choose to leave this world of luxury behind? The very thought stomped her. Somehow, the same twin sister that she entered into this world with, was now a complete stranger. But regardless of her own feelings, Kate knew that she was just going to have to learn and grow accustomed this new world, because ultimately, she was going to have to plunge forward into it and actually become her sister.

However, before Kate could ponder about this subject any further, she suddenly felt a furry creature rub against her leg, followed by a very distinct purring and meow.

"You, must be hungry," she said, while looking down at her cat, Tabitha. "Come on, Tabitha, let's go into the kitchen and find you something to eat…"

But before Kate could finish her own sentence, her stomach released a large growl, which had caught both Tabitha and herself, by surprise. Having not eaten the night before, Kate's last meal was from the plane. Like her starving cat, Kate was indeed hungry.

"Well Tabitha," said Kate. "It seems that we both might need breakfast after all."

Scooping Tabitha up into her arms, Kate exited her sister's chambers and headed towards downstairs. Having recalled from last night's tour that the kitchen was at the back of the mansion, Kate walked in that direction. She hurried down the hallway, and once she arrived to the kitchen's front door, she pushed it open and entered the room.

To her astonishment, the kitchen was larger than she had ever expected! Although the tour briefly passed by the front door, Kate didn't actually enter the kitchen, not until this very moment. Much to her surprise, the room was enormous and was a mansion, within itself. Stretching over a mile, the kitchen was stocked with shelves upon shelves of food.

"My God! How can anyone go hungry, here? Tabitha, we're in for a treat!" she exclaimed.

But, as soon as she uttered those very words, a tall and round man suddenly appeared at the counter. He was dressed in a white apron and wore a tall white hat. Clearly, he must be the chef, she thought.

"What sort of treats, are you looking for?" he asked.

"Well, I'm in need of some food for my cat here..." she began.

"A cat!" he exclaimed, most excitingly. "I just adore pets! Say, where's the kitty?"

Although Kate was holding Tabitha within her arms when they first entered the kitchen, once the chef appeared, the cat quickly jumped out of her arms and ran onto the floor.

"She's somewhere here..." said Kate, as she tried to scan the room to locate Tabitha.

"Is this her?" asked the chef, who was now holding the cat, tenderly in his arms.

"Yes, that's her," Kate confirmed.

Astonished by Tabitha's immediate warm response to the unknown Chef, Kate stared on and smiled. Now, comfortably wrapped around the tender embrace of the chef's arms, Tabitha began to purr. Given that the cat seldom cared for the company of strangers, Kate looked on, in fascination.

"She likes you," Kate concluded, with a smile.

"It's probably the smell of fish from my uniform," said the chef, as he laughed. "Don't worry, I'll feed her. I have some cat food and milk in the carboard. By the way, what's the kitty's name?"

"Tabitha," replied Kate.

"Tabitha, what a lovely name for such a curious little kitty!" exclaimed the chef, as he stared fondly at the cat. Afterwards, he turned his attention over towards Kate and said, "Dr. Stanley, I'm Chef Kojin Homura. It's a pleasure to meet both you and Ms. Tabitha."

"Same here. May I ask, do you prefer that I call you Chef or Chef Kojin, or even Chef Homura?" she kindly asked.

"Chef Homura will be fine. That's what everyone calls me," he said. "Now, if you would be so kind as to permit me, I'd like to be excused, in order to prepare a nice meal for your kitty."

"Yes, of course. Thank you, Chef Homura," said Kate.

"It's my pleasure," admitted Chef Homura, as he still held onto Tabitha within his arms. But before he left, he turned around and said, "And while I'm preparing Ms. Tabitha's meal, please think about what you'd like to eat for breakfast."

"Oh," replied Kate, as her stomach suddenly growled at that exact moment. Somehow, she'd almost forgotten that she too was hungry and in need of a meal.

"Nothing too lavish," she added, "Just a simple oatmeal will be fine. You do have oatmeal, don't you?"

"Yes, we always serve oatmeal for breakfast. It's a favorite of the ambassador's," answered Chef Homura, with a smile.

The ambassador, why, Kate had long forgotten about him. She'd been so consumed about her sister, that she'd overlooked him. In her mind, his very name was merely a far-off title to an unfamiliar face that she'd always heard about throughout the years, but never saw. Yet, at the same time, she also knew that he was alive and a real person. In fact, having newly arrived to the mansion, Kate could already attest that his presence could be felt everywhere, all throughout the estate. From his name and title plastered across the front gate, in large gold font lettering, to his business cards carefully placed on each vacant table, in every room. Yes, his name was all around her and yet, she knew nothing about him.

Why, she'd never seen a picture of him, let alone, heard the sound of his voice! As it was, there were no personalized pictures, nor portraits of the mansion's occupants. Instead, there were an unlimited supply of various decorative ceramics, statues, artifacts, and historical paintings, scattered across the estate. Although they were beautiful items, Kate couldn't help but notice, they were also very impersonal. Given that this estate was owned by the state, Kate assumed that this might have been the reason for the lack of personalized portraits of her sister and the ambassador. In addition, apart from all of this, Kate hadn't seen Jennifer in over five years. As a result, she never got the chance to meet the ambassador. In fact, she never even saw Jennifer's wedding photographs. Between her acceptance into university and Jennifer's move to Egypt, somehow, her sister neglected to share them with her. As a result, Kate never knew how the ambassador looked like. And as it was, he remained a mystery to her.

While Chef Homura tended to Tabitha's meal, Kate took a moment to ponder about the ambassador. Who was he, exactly? Was he kind and gentle? Or was he the complete opposite, cruel and mean? How did even look like? Would they get along with one another? Did he even know who she was? That she, Kate, was going to pose as his wife? For the first time since her arrival, Kate began to wonder about the ambassador, who at this moment in time, still remained much of a mystery to her.

A few minutes later, Chef Homura returned back to the kitchen, ready to prepare a bowl of oatmeal for Kate.

"Does the ambassador prefer oatmeal, too?" asked Kate, ever so curiously.

"Yes, he does," replied Chef Homura, "And he prefers to add fruit and honey into the dish. Would you care for some fruit, as well?"

"Why yes, I rather like fruit and honey too," said Kate, "But I prefer s—"

"Strawberries," finished Chef Homura.

"Exactly," replied Kate, rather surprised that the chef was able to guess her choice of fruit, so quickly.

"It's my job to know what people want to eat, even before they ask. It's one of my special talents as a world-renowned chef," replied Chef Homura.

"Really? How do you do that?" asked Kate, most intrigued.

"Well," began Chef Homura, as he cleared his throat and continued, "Food and people are very much alike. Both serve a unique purpose: they help satisfy some form of desire or need for a person. Similar to people, some food just tastes better than others, and vice versa. Meanwhile, each has their own unique flavors, aromas, strengths and weaknesses. Based on my own years of experience, some ingredients just complement the dish better than others. For example, tea is best served with honey, not with vinegar. Or that fish is best served with white wine, and not milk. The same goes for people. But if you ask me, I prefer the company of food over people."

"Well, truth be told, I'm in the same school of thought," replied Kate laughingly, "I, too, prefer food over people as well! They're certainly easier to digest!"

"And why do you say that, Dr. Stanley?" asked Chef Homura, who was most curious.

"I suppose it's because people are more difficult to understand. At least, with food, you know what you're getting; if you order chicken soup, you know that you're getting chicken, broth, vegetable, etc. Whereas, with people, you just never know. Sometimes, we make the mistake of placing our trusts within the wrong hands."

"Yes, that is true," agreed Chef Homura. "But," he added, "That's why it's important that we connect with the right sort of people. Like peanut butter and jam, or bread and butter. We just need to align ourselves with people who complements us."

"I suppose you are right," said Kate, "But, for now, I'll take the comfort of food any day. As for people, you just never know. Why, you might ask for a doctor one day, and the next day, out comes a magician, impersonating a doctor! You just never know!"

Suddenly, both Chef Homura and Kate began to hysterically laugh.

"You're a very honest and straight forward lady, Dr. Stanley!" exclaimed Chef Homura, "I respect that. That's pleasant, for a change."

"Thank you, I guess," replied Kate, curious as to why her appearance was a pleasant change.

"And no need to worry about our supply of strawberries, we have plenty for your oatmeal. It's also a favorite of the ambassador too."

"Do you know much about the ambassador, Chef Homura? I haven't yet had the chance to meet him yet," asked Kate, now feeling more comfortable in his presence.

"You haven't met the ambassador yet?" asked Chef Homura, who was surprised and astonished by her admission.

"No, I actually haven't yet. But I'm hoping I can meet him soon," she said.

"I see," said Chef Homura, "Then wait for Ms. Gloria, I'm certain she will arrange a meeting with you and him, soon."

"Oh yes, Gloria," said Kate, "I almost forgot, but I have a meeting with her soon, in about an hour or so."

"Well, then you best hurry up, eat your breakfast and be ready. If you're meeting with Ms. Gloria, then I can promise you that you're going to be very busy," said Chef Homura, as he placed a blue ceramic bowl onto a small table at the back of the kitchen.

"Come Dr. Stanley, why don't you take a seat and eat your oatmeal here?" he asked.

Accepting his offer, Kate walked over to the table and took a seat. As she grabbed her spoon and was about to take her first bite, she suddenly looked down at the bowl, and she noticed that Chef Homura had decorated the strawberries in the shape of a heart.

"How sweet and lovely!" exclaimed Kate, as she smiled at Chef Homura. "Chef Homura, you really didn't have to go through all this effort!"

"Dr. Stanley, it's my pleasure. You're a pleasant surprise and I dare say, I think we are all going to enjoy your company here at the mansion," replied Chef Homura, happily.

"Thank you, Chef Homura. That's very kind of you to say," replied Kate, graciously.

Meanwhile, as Kate began to eat the heart that laid before her, Tabitha was lying down on the little blue carpet beneath her, sound asleep. Chef Homura happily watched on, smiling to himself. After years of preparing single servings of oatmeal for one party, he was glad to finally someone now, who was a worthy recipient to serve the second bowl to. Although Kate still hadn't met the ambassador yet, Chef Homura suspected that out of the two, the ambassador was really the one who was due for an even greater surprise, than the lady, who quietly sat on at the table before him, quietly eating her morning oatmeal away, with her spoon in hand.

Chapter 13

After breakfast, Kate returned back to the grand foyer to wait for Gloria, leaving Tabitha in the care of Chef Homura. As Kate sat down on an empty chair, she took a deep breath, as she attempted to remain calm. Although she felt nervous about her upcoming meeting, she was determined to remain positive and optimistic. Out of the two twins, Kate was always the levelheaded one. While Jennifer was often extreme with her emotions, Kate always remained calm, even during the most challenging of circumstances. Furthermore, during their childhood, as Jennifer's heart constantly raced from excitement and passion, Kate's heart stood calm, steady and predictable, never once skipping a beat for anything.

As promised, at the stroke of ten o'clock, not a second less nor a second more, Gloria arrived. She quickly escorted Kate down into the hallway, turning to the right wing and into the executive conference room. Upon entering the room, Kate noticed a large round mahogany wooden conference table, located at the far end of the room. Already seated at the table, were four unknown individuals, whom Kate hadn't yet met prior. Hanging right above them, was an enormous silver American eagle emblem, along with two American flags, hanging on both sides of the wall, surrounding the emblem.

Noticing an empty seat at the front of the table, Kate quickly walked over and sat down. Once seated, Gloria immediately snapped her fingers, signaling to the rest of the staff, that the meeting now began. Upon her command, the first staffer, a young woman, promptly rose up from her chair.

"Dr. Stanley, I'd like to introduce you to Carol Wu, our communications and social media specialist," Gloria began, "For the past five years, she's been in charge of Madame Barrett's social media accounts, and now, she'll be in charge of yours, moving forward."

"It is a pleasure to finally meet you, Dr. Stanley," said Carol, enthusiastically. "We've been eagerly waiting for your arrival, and I must say, you really do resemble your sister quite a bit—"

"Carol, that will be enough," interrupted Gloria, with an icy tone.

Looking sternly across the room, Gloria's facial expressions remained fierce and assertive.

"As I have mentioned before prior to this meeting," reminded Gloria, "We're here strictly to introduce ourselves and our roles only to Dr. Stanley, and nothing more. Is that understood?"

Silence immediately fell across the room, and even Kate, felt a chill go down her spine. It was quite clear that Gloria ran the mansion and the staff with an iron fist, and everyone was expected to follow. While Jennifer may have been the head mistress of the estate, it was in name only, for it became abundantly clear to Kate, that the true ruler behind the scenes was Gloria. Not wanting to make any new enemies, Kate silently watched on, as the rest of the staff shook their heads in agreement to Gloria's command. To help clear the air, Kate decided to finally speak, but she chose to remain polite and diplomatic. Whatever the icy circumstances might have been between Gloria and her staff, Kate wasn't going to get involved. Her one and only priority remained unchanged. Finding her sister was her mission and her true motivation, and if she needed to hold her pride and bite her tongue, then so, let it be.

"Thank you, Carol, it's a pleasure to meet you too," said Kate.

"Dr. Stanley," interrupted Gloria. "Before we continue any further, I should mention to you now, that everyone in this room is well aware of your true identity. Therefore, will continue to address you by your proper name. However, once we interact together in front of the public, then we will revert to addressing you as your sister. Is that understood?"

"Yes, I understand and thank you, for the detailed explanation," replied Kate.

"Excellent!" replied Gloria, delighted by Kate's agreement. "In that case, Carol, please continue."

"Yes," replied Carol, nervously. "As Gloria mentioned, my name is Carol Wu and I'm the communications and social media specialist here at the embassy. I previously worked with your sister, Mrs. Barrett, to brand and build her social media presence on various online platforms. As you may already know, with today's growing technology, social media now serves as the modern gossip column; the new page six, as many do say. And so, because of this, I try to manage it from within, so that we can control and contain the public image of you, the new first lady, in a more positive, refined and dignified manner."

"How very interesting," said Kate. "It never occurred to me before, that social media was the new page six, but I suppose that's very much possible nowadays."

"It is," agreed Carol. "Which is why it's important for us to work together, in order to help ensure that the pictures, messages and contents that we publish are both appropriate and legal."

"Legal?" asked Kate, who was surprised that the law had a role to play in all of this.

"I suppose that's my department," interjected Tyler, who was seated right next to Carol. "Gloria, may I?" he asked, with his brow raised.

Remaining ever serious and unemotional, Gloria simply nodded with her head, giving Tyler the permission to continue.

"Dr. Stanley, I'm Tyler Conrad, the staff attorney," he began. "I work closely with Carol and your sister. Since the international community has access to view all of your social media posts publicly, I help to ensure that the language and content compiles with all the laws and regulations, both domestically and internationally. Generally speaking, whenever we host or attend an event, Carol will select a photograph and draft a publication, which I, in return, will review for legal compliance, before we formally publish it online."

"How very fascinating," Kate declared. "I had no idea as to how much work went into just publishing an online post…"

"Or tweet," interrupted Carol.

"A tweet, what's that?" asked Kate, most confused by such a term.

"A tweet, you know from Twitter," added Carol.

"I'm afraid, I don't really use social media, so I'm rather unfamiliar with these types of acronyms," Kate confessed.

"Do you have any person social media accounts?" asked Carol.

"Apart from my personal and university emails and mobile phone, I don't use anything else," Kate revealed.

"Really?!" exclaimed Carol, "You don't have any existing social media accounts? What about Instagram or TikTok? Do you at least have those?"

"None," replied Kate. "By the way, what's a TikTok? Is it some sort of clock or a timer? If so, that might be useful for me to use, the next time I have class at the university."

Surprised and astonished by her admission, Carol stared at Kate in bewilderment. Meanwhile, Gloria, on the other hand, simply smiled in approval.

"Dr. Stanley is a well-respected professor in her field, and she has no time to waste on these trivial social media matters," said Gloria, "But I dare say, Dr. Stanley, this does work to our advantage."

"It does? How so?" asked Kate, surprised by Gloria's remark.

"When your sister initially joined our agency, there were…several key elements for her adaptation into public life. One of them, being her private social media accounts. Since she is the wife of an active civil servant, upon her onboarding, she was required to terminate all of her social media accounts. Ever since then, your sister maintains only professional accounts, which Carol directly oversees. Given that you don't have any personal accounts of your own, why, there's absolutely nothing for you to close. This in return, will help to give you an even faster and easier transition into your new role."

"Are you are suggesting that my lack of social media presence is a good thing?" asked Kate.

"Better than good, it's excellent," said Gloria, with a smile. "This is another good quality. You are perfect for this role. Furthermore, without separate accounts of your own, your original identity is less traceable by the public. People will be more likely to believe that you and Madame Barrett are one in the same. Shall we continue?"

Kate simply nodded in agreement.

"Very well, we will proceed forward, as status quo," said Gloria, as she turned her attention over to Carol and Tyler, and asked them to sit down.

Once Carol and Tyler sat down, Gloria brought her focus onto the third member of the staff. He was a short chubby man, who was wearing a white blouse, a red tie and a black pair of trousers. His belly was a bit too large and the belt tied around his waist appeared to be a bit too tight. For a brief second, it appeared that he had struggled to get up from his chair. Eventually, he got up and once he did, his throat was a bit dry, so he drank some water to clear his throat. Then, he reached into his front pocket and retrieved a small blue comb. Using the comb, he began to comb over his hair, which Kate observed, was only a few strands of hair that remained on the top of his balding head. Meanwhile, Gloria was growing impatient.

"Bes, time is of the essence!" exclaimed Gloria, as she snapped her fingers, to get his attention. Her patience, or lack of, was growing thin.

"Ah, sorry for that Gloria," admitted Bes. Turning his attention over to Kate, he proceeded to formally introduce himself.

"Dr. Stanley, my name is Bes Medina. I'm the budget and financial manager, here at the embassy. I oversee the annual budget, the purchase and procurement of new and existing property here at the mansion, and I also work with Gloria to coordinate and oversee our annual audits."

"Mr. Medina, it's a pleasure," replied Kate, as she reached her arm over in Bes' direction to shake his hand.

"The pleasure is all mine," said Bes, as he equally extended his arm and shook Kate's hand. "Please, call me Bes."

"Very well, Bes, thank you," replied Kate.

"And I must say," began Bes, "You do look so much like your sister, although your hair does look a bit different…"

"Bes, please stay on topic," Gloria interrupted and reminded him. Using her pen, she pointed to the direction of the wall clock, hanging right across from them, located on the far end of the room.

"Sorry Gloria," replied a bashful Bes, who now turned bright red. "As I was saying, Dr. Stanley, I'm the financial guru here, so if you have any questions regarding financial matters, please ask away."

"Bes, thank you," said Kate, "This is helpful to know. Although I must admit, since I'm still new here, I'm not exactly sure as to which types of financial matters that I should ask right now."

"The budget," blurted Bes.

"I beg your pardon?" asked Kate.

"Your monthly budget and allowance, to be precise," answered Bes. "Your sister was most inclined about that too. Particularly, hers… yours… I mean… now, your monthly allowance for your clothing and accessory spending."

Stunned by such a notion, Kate couldn't fathom nor conceptualize that anyone could have such a large allowance. It seemed a bit too extravagant. Reaching for her glass of water, she grabbed it and took a sip.

"Does such an allowance system really exist here? Even for clothes?" asked Kate, as she placed the glass of water back down onto the table.

"Yes," replied Bes, "Plus, the agency recently approved for an increasement too. The new allowance rate is $150,000 per month."

"What???!!!" exclaimed Kate, as she knocked down her glass of water and fell forward from her chair.

"Dr. Stanley, are you alright?" asked Carol and an unnamed woman at the far end of the table. Meanwhile, Tyler rushed over and helped Kate back up from the floor.

"I am so sorry," replied Kate, as she rose back up and began dusting herself of. "I just didn't expect that. Is this really true? Was Jennifer's or my, monthly allowance really that much? Isn't that a bit excessive?"

"Well, that's what the agency says, so we must follow," remarked Bob.

"But what if I can't spend all of that money in one month?" asked Kate, still shaking her head in astonishment.

"You just have to spend it; otherwise, the agency will simply cut it out, from future budgets and we certainly don't want to lose any more money from our budget. It's a spend it or lose it, type of scenario," replied Bob.

"Basically, you really must spend it," added Carol.

"Dr. Stanley," replied Gloria, this time, "You're here not only for your sister. You are also representing the United States abroad. Therefore, while you are here on official duty, you are also expected to reflect America's finest and brightest; and sometimes, that begins with our choice of clothing."

"Is that why my sister has so many clothes upstairs?" asked Kate.

"Yes," replied both Gloria and Bes, simultaneously.

"But a bit of caution," began Bes, "There are some rules and regulations to this."

"Of course, I understand," replied Kate. "May I ask what exactly are those rules?"

"Well, first," said Bes, as he cleared his throat once more. He also began to sweat and Kate notice a large tear drop of sweat streaming down his forehead. Bes reached into his pants pocket, pulled out a handkerchief and began patting and drying his wet forehead. It was clear, Bes was nervous.

"Go on, Bes," said Gloria, sensing his hesitation.

"Yes," replied Bes, as he continued, "While you may have this monthly allowance, in return, you must only purchase articles of clothing and accessories directly from American designers. Foreign designers are not included. The reason is the expectation that while you are abroad promoting American interest, you should also strive to equally promote American fashion, style, culture and values through your wardrobe selection; therefore, this rule must strictly remain in place, at all times."

"I see," replied Kate. Given Kate's shock about the allowance allocation, Bes' rules seemed trivial, in comparison. However, as she looked directly at Bes' face, she realized that he was still nervous and that his sweating did not yet stop.

"Now," he continued once more, "Will this be a problem?"

"A problem?" uttered Kate to herself, under her breath. Why on earth would this be a problem, she thought to herself? Suddenly, she noticed that room quickly grew silent, and all eyes were staring at her, waiting for her reaction. How very odd this was, she thought.

"No, Bes, that won't be a problem," replied Kate, confidently. "Thank you for your generous allowance, and I promise to wear clothing from whichever American designers you so choose. Furthermore, I vow to wear it proudly, as an American."

"Splendid!" exclaimed Gloria, as the rest of the attendees in the room released a large breath of relief. Walking over to Kate, Gloria gave her a pat on her back.

"Ah, Dr. Stanley, you truly are a breath of fresh air! I'm so happy you are here," sighed Gloria, happily.

Confused by her admission and their overall reaction, Kate simply smiled back.

"Bes, you may be seated. Sally, please take the floor," Gloria announced.

Suddenly, a young woman with bright red hair at shoulder's length, arose from her chair. Seated at the far end of the table, she had been quiet for most of the meeting. Wearing a simple white dress, she was young and elegantly dressed. She appeared prepared too, for she was holding a pad of paper and a pen in her hands.

"Good morning, Dr. Stanley," began the young woman, "My name is Sally Timmons and I'm your new assistant. I've been working with your sister these past five years, and now I'll be working with you. Whatever assistance that you may need, I'm here to offer my help."

"Thank you, Sally. It's a pleasure to meet you. I look forward to working with you, as well," replied Kate.

"Out of all of us, Sally and your sister worked the closest," interjected Gloria, "As your sister's assistant, Sally remains her primary helper and confidant. Should you have any particular questions about life here at the mansion or about your new role, then I highly recommend that you speak to Sally. Ultimately, she's here to help you transition into your sister's vacant role. In fact, her room is located right next door to yours."

"Is that so?" replied Kate.

"Yes," said Gloria, "Therefore, if you need anything, at any hour, Sally's here for your rescue."

"Thank you, Sally, for your service. I know my sister isn't here to say this, but I'm sure she, and now me, are very appreciative of your hard work," said Kate, who was rather impressed by her strong work ethics.

"Sally, you may take a seat," directed Gloria. Turning her attention over to Kate, Gloria said, "We did have one more member to introduce; however, he seems to be currently preoccupied with your cat, Tabitha."

"Chef Homura?" asked Kate, surprised that her cat somehow managed to enter the conversation.

"Yes, the very one. And as I've already been informed, I do believe that you two have already made your introductions with each other already, this morning," said Gloria.

"Yes, we have, actually," replied Kate, "He was so kind as to serve us breakfast this morning."

"Us?" asked Gloria, with a raised brow.

"Tabitha and myself," replied Kate.

"Ah, yes, you and the cat. Lovely," said Gloria, "Everything's following into order now. However, Dr. Stanley, as a warning, please do keep caution when dining. For your own safety, please only eat the meals and beverages provided by this house. As long as you eat from the meals provided by Chef Homura and his staff, then you shall be fine."

"That's fine. But may I ask, does this policy relate to any secure measures?" asked Kate, concerned about the risks associated with dining out.

"Actually, yes. It is a security measure," answered Gloria.

"It's to prevent poison," added Bes.

"I thought so," said Kate, glad that she received confirmation to her suspicion.

"Excellent, now that that's settled," remarked Gloria, "Before I adjourn this meeting, let's get down to some additional housekeeping, shall we? But before we do, do you have any other questions for me?"

Recalling the state of the unchanged beddings in Jennifer's room, Kate asked, "Gloria, is there a reason as to why my beddings in Jennifer's room still has her smell? It seems as if her beddings were never changed, prior to my arrival."

"Ah," said Gloria, as if a bright light had just flashed before her eyes.

"Excellent observation, Dr. Stanley! While the five of us in this room, along with Chef Homura and security are well aware of your identity, the remaining staff are not. This includes our government contractors, mainly comprised of the gardeners, the housekeepers, butler and transportation. They are all completely unaware, and as far as they are concerned, you are your sister, having just returned back from a vacation abroad, wearing borrowed clothes, along with splash of brown hair."

"I see," replied Kate. She was glad to at least know the truth about the bedding situation.

"But not to worry, Dr. Stanley, I'll request for fresh and newly cleaned beddings and sheets for your bedroom," said Gloria, as she grabbed hold of her pen and then wrote herself a note, on top of her stack of paper, as a reminder to herself.

"But if the contractors are unaware of my identity, then is it safe that you continue to still address me as Dr. Stanley?" asked Kate.

"Actually, for security reasons, your sister often went by numerous aliases, here at the mansion. The housekeepers and gardeners are already accustomed to your sister's various names and titles. But of course, as I mentioned earlier, whenever you are in the public eye, we will all address you formally as Madame Barrett."

"Thank you, Gloria. I appreciate your clarification on this matter," replied Kate.

"And if you have no further questions, I would like to address your remaining timeline for the day," said Gloria.

"Yes, no further questions," replied Kate, reassuringly.

"Excellent," began Gloria, "Now, let's get down to business. In one hour, you have a meeting with Aslan at the salon. Then, you'll have a brief lunch, before you meet with your contract dress maker at three o'clock for your fitting."

"I have an appointment with a salon today?" asked a surprised Kate. At some point, she knew that she was going to have to undergo a physical transformation, but it never occurred to her that it was going to happen so soon.

"Yes, and you're fitting as well. Although I understand that the previous Madame Barrett had a rather large collection of clothes for you to choose from, but at the same time, you still need proper clothes of your own that's tailored specifically to fit your figure," added Gloria.

"Thank you, Gloria. I appreciate your thoughtfulness in this matter," replied Kate, graciously.

"Continuing on," said Gloria, with a smile, "You should be back at the mansion by four o'clock, by which time, the ambassador should also be returning here from his latest trip abroad. You are scheduled to have dinner with him at five o'clock in the dining room."

"Dinner with the ambassador?" asked Kate, surprise that she was going to finally meet the ambassador, face to face, this very evening.

"Yes, the ambassador returns this evening, after touring Germany this past month. Naturally, dining will provide you with the opportunity to acquaint yourself with him. You have met him before, have you not?" asked Gloria, with a raised brow.

"Actually, no, I haven't," replied Kate.

"Really?" replied both a surprised Carol and Sally.

"Well, I haven't seen my sister in years, and the last time I saw her, she hadn't yet married John…ur…the ambassador, I mean," admitted Kate.

"I see," replied Gloria, "Well, then, this shall be a most eventful evening, indeed. In that case, I shall inform Chef Homura to prepare his finest meal, in this honor."

"Oh, you really don't have to, Gloria; any meal will do just fine," interjected Kate, eagerly not wanting to burden Chef Homura with any more additional responsibilities, since he was already busy watching over Tabitha.

"Dr. Stanley, as I may remind you, you're not the only attendee at tonight's dinner, because we also have the ambassador to consider as well. As this will be his first time meeting you, we'll want him to remain in a good mood," Gloria concluded.

"A good mood?" asked Kate. Those words certainly caught her ears and suddenly, her stomach began to turn. Was it possible that the ambassador could even be, in such a bad mood? Kate began to feel nervous.

"Yes, we'll want him to be in a good mood," Gloria repeated.

Suddenly, Gloria spun around to face the staff, clapped her hands, and then, she announced that the meeting was now adjourned.

"The meeting minutes will be available next week via e-mail," added Gloria.

After the staff exited the room, only Kate and Gloria remained behind. As Gloria was busy organizing her documents, Kate decided to pour herself another glass of water. Once again, Kate wondered about the ambassador. But rather than guessing, she decided that now was the time to further inquire about him.

"Gloria," began Kate, as she took a sip of her water, "May I ask you a question?"

Pausing her paper shuffling, Gloria made direct eye contact with Kate, and she said, "Of course, Dr. Stanley, ask any question that comes to mind."

"Thank you, Gloria," began Kate, "I was just wondering, since this will be my very first-time meeting with the ambassador, what kind of person is he?"

Upon inquiring about the ambassador, Kate watched on, as Gloria silently stood still. Kate wasn't entirely certain as to whether or not, her question was negatively met by Gloria. However, Gloria, who remained calm and collective, simply posed another question to her direction.

"What exactly have you heard about him?" asked Gloria, with a raised brow.

"Nothing really, apart from his title. But as a person, I don't really know anything about him, at all," admitted Kate.

"Well," huffed Gloria, "You will meet him tonight, that's for certain. Perhaps then, you can form your own opinion about him, for yourself."

"You're probably right, I'm sorry I asked," replied Kate, feeling a bit embarrassed and ashamed for having asked, in the first place.

"However," Gloria added, "What I can and will say, based solely upon my own personal observations, is that the ambassador can be a bit of a complex character."

"Complex, really? In what way?" asked Kate, most curiously. With her nerves increasing, Kate began to play with her peal ring, which she wore around her left index finger.

Catching sight of the ring, Gloria remarked, "Why, Dr. Stanley, that's a lovely ring, you have there. May I take a look?"

Surprised by Gloria's interest, Kate agreed and handed her ring over to Gloria, for inspection.

Holding the ring within her grasp, Gloria said, "My, my, I dare say, what a lovely ring! The blue diamonds are lovely and the pearl, in the middle, is such a precious gem. Wherever did you acquire such a ring?"

"It was a gift from my sister many years ago," replied Kate, as she too, gazed upon the ring and admired it.

"How kind of her," remarked Gloria, "And to gift you with such a unique ring, as well. Why, the shape of the pearl alone is so unorthodox. It's not perfectly round, but rather oval, with a few bumps around its edges. But I suppose, in the end, that's probably what makes it so extraordinary and special."

"It's true; I know the pearl is a bit skewed and distorted, but it's actually, one of the reasons why I admire it so much to begin with. Even though this ring might be an acquired taste, I'd never trade it in for another piece of jewelry. Not even if they were the royal crown jewels from the Queen, herself!" Kate exclaimed.

"This sentimental attachment, is this because it was a gift from your sister?"

asked Gloria.

"Yes, in part; the other, because I just genuinely like it. To me, it's flaws are what makes it such an exquisite and beautiful piece," Kate confessed.

"Is it fair to say, that you, Dr. Stanley, prefer uniquely flawed pieces?" asked Gloria, now looking at Kate directly in the eye.

"Actually, yes, I think do," Kate confirmed.

"Very good," replied Gloria, smilingly, "In that case, I think you and the ambassador will get along rather well."

"Really?" asked Kate, who was surprised by her remark.

"Yes, I actually do. He's like that pearl, you know. And I dare say, you might even find him to be a rather, *interesting* acquaintance," Gloria concluded.

Taking a moment to reflect upon Gloria's wise words, Kate presumed that the ambassador must have lived a challenging life. Curious as to why that was, she finally asked, "Gloria," she began, "How did the ambassador become this way?"

"Life," sighed Gloria. "When you live and work in this world; this new world that you're now a part of, whether you chose it or not, it changes us. All of us, really. Some of us for the better, some of us for the worse. But, in the end, we ultimately become who we are, based upon our own life experiences."

"How very true. Wise words, indeed," agreed Kate.

Looking at the clock, Kate realized that she was running late to her next appointment.

"But remember one thing, Dr. Stanley," added Gloria.

"What's that?" asked Kate.

"People can always change. Nothing is permanent. We all have the ability to grow and evolve, just like the roses in our garden. It just takes a little bit of sunshine to do the trick," said Gloria, with a smile.

Kate smiled back at Gloria, in return. Although Kate wasn't quite sure as to what awaited her future here; but somehow, Gloria wise words brought solace and peace to her heart. Changing the subject, Kate asked, "My appointment with the salon, where shall I meet them?"

"You won't have to go anywhere, they will come to you," Gloria revealed, "Once Aslan arrives, Sally will inform you."

"Thank you, Gloria. I appreciate it," said Kate.

"Dr. Stanley, you are most welcome. But before I escort you back to the foyer, I just wanted to mention a couple more things."

"Yes, I'm all ears," said Kate.

"First," began Gloria. "As you'll be assuming your sister's role here, you will need a bit of training."

"Training? What sort of training?" asked Kate.

"No need to trouble yourself about it right now, we'll discuss it further tomorrow morning," said Gloria.

"Okay," said Kate. "And what's the second item?"

"Ah yes, that," replied Gloria, as she took a brief moment to compose herself. "The last thing that I wanted to mention to you is this."

Taking a few steps forward, Gloria came face to face directly with Kate.

"As I mentioned before," she began. "As I'm certain that you and the ambassador will get along rather well, I still do have a bit of advice."

"And what sort of advice might that be?" asked Kate, with a raised brow.

"Please strive to make a good impression on him tonight. Since you will be posing as his wife, it's imperative that you two maintain a good relationship, so that your marriage will be convincing," Gloria boldly forewarned her.

"Convincing to whom?" asked Kate, who was most intrigued by her statement.

"Why to the everyone," huffed Gloria, as she waved her arms in the air.

"Part of playing the role of Madame Barrett," she continued, "Is that you must try to convince everyone, from the staff to the visiting diplomats, to even the general public at hand, that you are the ever dutiful, respectful, dignified and loving wife. That you're one half of a super golden power couple. Is that understood?"

"Yes, I see. But what happens if I fail?" asked Kate, now concerned by the prospect.

"Well, if that unfortunate event should ever occur, why then, no one will believe that you're the real Madame Barrett. And believe me, Dr. Stanley, if anyone should think that, well then, I say that the odds of ever finding your sister safely, will be *greatly reduced*," she hissed.

"I won't ever let that happen! I will do whatever it takes, to make this work," Kate vowed.

"I know you do, it's why you're here. In fact, I'm fully confident that you, Dr. Stanley, will not only be convincing, but that you will actually thrive and succeed in this!" exclaimed Gloria.

"Gloria, while I promise to cooperate in every which way that I can," Kate continued, "But I just want you to also be aware, that I'm doing this only for my sister and for my sister alone, and not for any other reason or motive for personal gain."

"I'm very glad you said that," she replied, with a devious smile, "Which is why it's so imperative, that we begin your training, effective tomorrow morning at ten o'clock sharp."

"Alright, until then," Kate agreed.

"But for now," spoke Gloria, "I think it's best that we return back to the foyer."

Exiting the conference room together, Gloria and Kate walked to the foyer. After which, Kate returned back to her bedroom, to wait for

Sally's announcement for her next appointment. One alone in the privacy of her new bedroom, Kate walked over to her balcony and stood outside to get some fresh air. The bird's eye view from the balcony was spectacular. The rose garden was in full view, and from this height, Kate could see the bright sun from afar, peeking right over the fence, past the street and along the horizon. Staring straight ahead, she saw several orange monarch butterflies encircling the pink roses. Closing her eyes, she listened to the sweet melodies to the hummingbirds floating across the open blue sky. It was peaceful and blissful.

However, the longer she kept her eyes closed, she slowly began to see a black and shadowy image. It was a black silhouette that resembled a dark phantom, standing before her. Although Kate couldn't see their face, she could tell that the unknown phantom was that of a tall man. Startled by those images, Kate quickly opened her eyes. Once she saw the bright sun shining before her again, she soon realized that the shadowy figure was only a pigment of her imagination. However, the more she thought about it, she eventually, came to the conclusion that her phantom was none other than the ambassador. While now, he remained much of a mystery to her, she also knew that by nightfall, she was going to finally meet him at long last and place a face to the mystery man, whom she spent most of her day, pondering about.

Chapter 14

Ten Years Ago in New York City...

"**K**ate! They're finally here!" exclaimed Jennifer.

"So soon?" asked Kate. "I'm not even ready."

"Yes," said Jennifer, happily. Peeking through their bedroom window, Jennifer watched as their prom dates, Alex and Tom, parked their rental limousine, right in front of their parents' driveway.

"Oh my gosh, Alex is here and his car looks so glamorous!" squealed Jennifer, as she joyfully skipped around their bedroom.

"Jennifer, they're twenty minutes early. Besides, I still need to finish applying my makeup," said Kate, who was annoyed and getting frustrated by their early arrival.

"Goodness Kate," huffed an impatient Jennifer, "I told you yesterday to get ready early. In fact, I also told you to pluck those bushy eyebrows of yours too!"

Seated on her vanity stool, Kate looked straight across into her mirror. Staring right back at her, was a pair of two bushy and overgrown eyebrows, located right above her eyes. It was true. Sadly, her sister was correct. Kate's eyebrows were indeed, overgrown, bushy and in desperate need of a good tweeze. But unfortunately for Kate, time wasn't on her side. As it currently stood, Kate needed to stop tweezing and quickly transition on applying the rest of her makeup.

"Kate, please try to hurry up! We really need to go soon!" shouted Jennifer.

"Technically," began Kate, "They are too early, and we are on time. Honestly, Jennifer, we should just make them wait."

"But aren't you excited? I know that I'm simply dying from all this anticipation!" exclaimed Jennifer, as she blissfully took another twirl across the room.

"Do you really like Alex that much?" asked Kate, as she turned around.

"Of course, I do!" cried Jennifer, "If I didn't, then I wouldn't have agreed to be his prom date."

"I suppose," remarked Kate, as she applied blush to her cheeks.

"All I know," began Jennifer, "Is whenever I see Alex, my eyes light up, my stomach twirls, and my heart skips a beat…"

"Wait, your heart actually skips a beat?" asked a skeptical Kate, with a raised brow.

"Yes," retorted Jennifer, right back, "It actually skips a beat."

"Hmm…I find that rather hard to believe," said Kate.

"Don't you feel that same way about Tom?" asked Jennifer, who was surprised that her twin sister didn't equally feel the same passion, as she did for Alex.

"Actually, no, I don't," replied Kate, confidently.

"Really? Then why did you agree to be his prom date?" asked Jennifer.

"For practical reasons. Tom is a good friend, and we both needed dates for tonight. That's all," Kate admitted.

"That's all? That's why you accepted his invitation?" asked Jennifer, who was gravely disappointed with her sister's very unromantic reasoning.

"Yes," answered Kate, as she finally finished applying her makeup.

As Kate stood up, she looked at her sister and smiled.

"You look beautiful Jennifer. That pink colored dress, suits you well," said Kate, admiring her sister's outfit for the evening.

"However," added Kate, "I can't say the same about myself. Honestly, I don't think my dress quite fits me that well. Plus, my hair is still messy from that perm."

"Nonsense Kate, you look beautiful too," said Jennifer. "You just need to practice on your confidence, that's all. Besides, I rather like that shade of blue on you."

"You know, sometimes, I feel like that between the two of us, I'm sort of the ugly duckling," revealed Kate, now looking down on the floor, and feeling a bit vulnerable for having admitted such a thing.

"Kate!" exclaimed Jennifer, as she turned her attention away from the window and focused on her sister. Putting her arms around her shoulders, Jennifer looked straight into her eyes and said, "Why would you ever say such a thing like that? You're not an ugly duckling, you're absolutely beautiful!"

"I don't know Jennifer," Kate whispered aloud. She was beginning to grow pale and a tear fell down from the corner of her eyes.

"Kate, you are a silly girl!" cried Jennifer, "We're both beautiful! We're twins, after all, aren't we?"

"Yes," replied Kate, as she wiped away her tears.

Grabbing a hold of Kate's chin, Jennifer began tenderly caressing her face.

"Listen to me," said Jennifer. "If I'm beautiful, then so are you. We've got the same exact face."

"I know," admitted Kate, who shyly looked down, "But you've got that beautiful blonde hair and my hair isn't…"

"Then change it," interrupted Jennifer, "Next time, let's go to the salon and have it colored and styled, professionally."

"I don't know," replied Kate, as her fair complexation slowly returned back to her normal self.

"Kate," began Jennifer, "Your problem is your lack of confidence. If you want to be like me in the future, then you need to learn how to be confident, within your own skin, no matter the condition of your hair…"

"I know, I know," admitted Kate, now regretting this discussion altogether.

"And next time, please listen to my advice. Tweeze those eyebrows regularly, buy properly fitted clothing and whatever you do, never perm that hair again!" she cried.

Suddenly, the girls began laughing and even Kate had to admit, that Jennifer was right. Two days prior, Kate made the bold decision to perm her hair, to replicate a model she saw on the cover of a magazine. Unfortunately, her frugal attempts to save money and opt for a home perm, proven unsuccessful. In the end, Kate's hair was fried, burnt and the curls were almost identical to a poodle. To conceal the damage, Kate pulled her hair back into a bun, and she prayed to God that it wasn't that noticeable.

Walking over to their bedroom window, Kate and Jennifer spied on their respective dates. By now, Alex and Tom were outside, standing in their driveway and waiting for them.

"We could make them wait longer," advised Kate.

"Kate, you are too cruel!" replied Jennifer, laughingly.

"Well, I guess tonight you'll have something to write about in that diary of yours," said Kate.

"Yes, and it will be my best entry yet!" exclaimed Jennifer.

"You're really that excited about our prom tonight?" asked Kate, not at all feeling as equally excited about the matter.

"Yes, but more than anything, I'm excited to be with Alex," sighed Jennifer.

Kate, who had much rather have skipped out on the event altogether and to have remained comfortably hidden away within their bedroom, finally gave into her sister's demands. Having agreed to leave their home earlier to meet with their prom dates, the sisters were about to walk out of their bedroom, when suddenly, Jennifer turned around and gave Kate a warm hug.

"Don't worry Kate," Jennifer said, as she embraced her, "You just haven't met the right person yet."

"I beg your pardon?" replied Kate, who slowly pulled away from her sister's tight grip.

"Kate, one day, you're going to meet the right person, and I swear to you, that stone heart of yours is going to skip a beat, too. Mark my words," vowed Jennifer.

"I guess you better add that into your diary too, because truth be told, dear Jennifer, I, too, believe in love. However, the difference between us, is that I don't believe in hearts skipping beats and what not. It's just not practical," Kate asserted.

"But love isn't meant to be practical at all!" scolded Jennifer.

"Then what is love meant to be?" asked Kate, most intrigued.

"Love is just love!" shouted Jennifer, as she once again, twirled around the room, and falling backwards onto her bed, with her hands held over her chest.

"What exactly does that mean? Surely, there must be a better explanation?" asked a rather confused Kate, who desperately wanted to better understand her sister.

"Kate, there are no words," answered Jennifer. "You just *feel* it."

"Feel it??" Kate repeated aloud. Somehow, that very concept felt so foreign and strange to her. She decided to further inquire about that particular emotion.

"But how do you feel it? And when do you feel it?" she asked.

"There's no timeline. It just happens when it happens. It's like when cupid shoots that arrow into the sky, and it just lands straight into your heart," sighed Jennifer.

Looking directly into Kate's eyes, Jennifer placed her hands around her shoulders and said, "And when it happens, which I know for certain it will, whether it's a year from now or ten, your heart will skip a beat, and then you'll finally know."

"But how will I know that my heart actually skipped a beat? What if I mistake it for something else entirely?" asked Kate.

"Oh, you'll know," smiled Jennifer, "Just you wait."

"But what causes your heart to skip a beat? Is it because of an attraction or a spiritual connection? Why does it happen?" Kate further inquired.

"Kate, this is where all reason ends and love begins," replied Jennifer, "With love, there's no logic, nor justification. When the stars align, they just align. Its madness really!"

"But how do you explain that? There must be some sort of scientific explanation to all of this?" she asked.

"Kate, you couldn't be more wrong. With love, there's no equation, no specific formula, no scientific calculation. Gradually, the heart simply takes over," Jennifer admitted.

"But Jennifer, if the heart gradually takes over, then how does this happen?" asked Kate, who was most persistent.

"It's different for everyone," shrugged Jennifer, "Just as no two types of love are equal."

"I understand that," said Kate, "But how was it for you and Alex?"

"Well, I can only speak from my own experience," began Jennifer, "When I first saw Alex, my heart skipped a beat. I think this was due to my initial attraction to him. Then, afterwards, as my curiosity about him grew, a spark ignited around my heart, and I began to feel these strange and sentimental feelings about him. Slowly, with each passing day, as I grew to learn more about him, that very spark evolved into a flicker of a flame. Eventually, that flicker grew into wildfire, that swallowed up and consumed my entire heart. After which, I felt this constant burning sensation within my chest, that I myself couldn't understand. I was bewildered. My chest burned with so much passion and desire, that my mind and body grew paralyzed; and I, became entirely consumed with only Alex. Even now, he's still in my every passing thought. Constantly within my mind. When I first wake up and open my eyes in the morning, he's the first person I recall. Whenever I eat or drink, I always wonder about him. Even when I go to sleep, he's the last person I think about, and the only person, whom I dream about. Whenever we're apart, I long and yearn for our reunion. As far as I'm concerned, Alex is my first and one true love. And because of this, I know, firsthand, that with love, eventually, logic ceases to exist. In the end, even the most intellectual of minds submits to the will of the heart. To me, love is similar to a supernova, bursting stardust out into the vast reaches of the universe. And, after discovering love, there's no turning back. It's here to stay. Forever more. So, dear sister, it's my personal and humble belief that what begins as a simple heart skipping a beat, ends with that same heart exploding entirely into pieces, as it surrenders itself to its soul mate."

"Wow, Jennifer, I had no idea. Do you truly believe in all of this?" asked Kate, softly.

"Yes, I do," replied Jennifer, whole heartly.

"Was it the same process for Alex?" asked Kate, now equally curious, as to whether or not, the male counterpart felt the same intensity as the female.

"Not quite," replied Jennifer, "While he felt the same emotions as I did, he experienced them much differently than I did, in different stages."

"Really? How so?" asked Kate.

"While our love both ultimately came to the same conclusion, it grew differently," admitted Jennifer, "For example, while my heart first skipped a beat when I met him, his burned, before it skipped."

"Did it happen to him, in reverse order?" Kate inquired.

"Somewhat," answered Jennifer, "But I think the important lesson is that no two hearts are the same, just as no two loves are either. Each soul loves differently, and at different levels and stages."

For a moment, Kate pondered about Jennifer's words. Finally, she asked, "But if no two hearts are equal, then how can you be certain that one day, my heart will skip a beat, too?"

"Because you're my sister! My twin!" exclaimed Jennifer, as a matter of fact.

"Kate, I know your heart, just as much as I know my own. Even though you try so hard to conceal your feelings; one day, that brick wall you've built up is going to come crashing down. Mark my words."

"Why do you believe in this so much?" asked Kate, with a smile.

"Because this is all fate. Perhaps, even destiny. Everyone and I really do mean everyone, comes into our lives for a reason. Every soul has its own mate."

"How did you ever become such a hopeless romantic?" Kate teased.

"Because I've experienced it. And I know, in my heart, one day, you will too," Jennifer promised.

"Okay," said Kate, accepting her defeat, "Since I've never experienced such a notion, I suppose that I'll just have to take your word on it."

"Good, because I'm always right," said Jennifer, proudly and with a wink.

"I suppose so..." said Kate, as she rolled her eyes.

"They're so cute down there," observed Jennifer, who now shifted her attention back to Alex and Tom, who were standing outside in their driveway.

"Shall we go meet them now?" asked Kate.

"Yes, lets!" exclaimed Jennifer, who, like a bolt of lightning, quickly dashed right out of their bedroom.

Before Kate knew it, Jennifer was already halfway down the stairs, and only steps away from their front door.

"Hurry up, Kate! We need to go!" Jennifer screamed, from down the stairs.

"Alright, alright, I'm coming," Kate murmured to herself.

As she approached her bedroom door, Kate caught sight of herself on the mirror that hung nearby.

"Next time," she said to herself, "You'll have better hair, a fitted dress and those eyebrows are going to be tweezed. But most importantly, you're going to be more confident."

Walking past her the threshold of her childhood bedroom, Kate closed the door shut behind her. As she proceeded to walk down the stairs to meet with Jennifer, Alex and Tom, she laughed to herself. While she loved her sister dearly and often listened to her advice, somehow, this time, she felt that Jennifer was not entirely correct. Although Kate agreed with Jennifer, with regards to her confidence levels; she did however, think that Jennifer might have been wrong, with the matter concerning her heart. Kate, the practical and sensible sister, just couldn't imagine her own heart— the same calm, sturdy heart that sat buried deep within her chest— ever skipping a beat for anything, let alone for anyone. Not today, not tomorrow, not even in a million years. And since this was her heart and her heart alone, didn't she after all, know it best?

Present Day in Istanbul, Türkiye …

At a quarter to three o'clock, Kate suddenly heard a knock at her bedroom door. Curious as to who it was, she arose from her reading chair, walked over to her door and opened it. There, standing in front of her was her new assistant, Sally. As expected, Sally announced that her hairdresser and his crew, had just arrived and that they were now waiting for her downstairs.

"Isn't it a bit early?" asked Kate, pointing to the clock, which hung on her bedroom wall.

"Yes, Dr. Stanley, that's true," replied Sally, "If you prefer, I can have them wait for you down in the salon, until you're ready to meet them. That's where they'll set up shop for your session."

"No, that's quite alright," said Kate, "Maybe if I go down there early, then I'll be done sooner."

Following Sally's lead, Kate exited her bedroom, and she closed the door shut behind her. Once Kate arrived to the top of the staircase, Sally went about on her separate ways. Upon descended down the staircase, Kate was met by a man in his early fifties, with streaked black and blonde hair that pulled tightly into a straight ponytail. Dressed in all black, he was waiting for her, along with two other assistants. Once Kate took her last step on the staircase, she heard an outburst of a gasp, then a scream.

"Oh my God!" exclaimed Aslan, the hairdresser, "Alp, Ali, clear my entire afternoon schedule, immediately! We have work to do!"

Attempting to ignore his rather rude outburst, Kate politely proceeded to introduce herself.

"Hello, you must be Aslan," she began, "I'm Dr. Kate Stanley."

As she extended her hand to welcome him, her greeting was swiftly rejected and dismissed by the new visitor.

"Yes," huffed Aslan, folding his arms around his chest, with his nose held high. "I know exactly who you are," he said, "Now, if you don't mind, I need to concentrate."

"I beg your pardon?" replied Kate, feeling a bit appalled and wounded by Aslan's rejection and rudeness.

However, Aslan paid no attention to her and instead, he began inspecting Kate, from head to toe.

"Your hair is a mess," he began, "The color is all wrong…and those split ends, dear God, those split ends!"

Disturbed by the condition of Kate's hair, Aslan was ready to faint, right there and then, on the marble floor. However, his assistant, Alp, came to his rescue and quickly began fanning him. Once Aslan cooled down and returned back to his senses, Alp finally asked, "Shall I prepare the room?"

"Yes, immediately," commanded Aslan, now calmly composed.

"Surely, my hair cannot be that bad?" interrupted Kate, feeling a bit dismayed about her appearance.

"Oh, but it is!" exclaimed Aslan, as he looked directly at Kate disapprovingly, "And your eyebrows, my God, those eyebrows! When's the last time you plucked them?"

"Oh," replied Kate, now starting to feel a little embarrassed. "I cannot really say, but it's been a while."

"Of course, it's been a while!" shouted Aslan, "These eyebrows are so bushy, they resemble the amazon forest! Ali, sharpen those tweezers, immediately! We've got work to do!"

"Aslan, surely my eyebrows are not as bad?" asked Kate, hesitantly.

However, Aslan completely ignored her question and instead, he asked, "Are you even wearing makeup?"

"Actually, yes, I am," replied Kate. She further clarified, "But very little."

"Little?" huffed Aslan, "It's nonexistent!"

"I've cleared your schedule for the rest of the day," spoke Alp, after getting off the phone.

"Fabolous," agreed Aslan, "Now gentlemen, we must focus. We've got our afternoon cut out for us. Is the room ready?"

"Yes, Aslan," replied Ali.

"What time is her fitting with the dress maker?" asked Aslan.

"In exactly one hour," replied Alp, as he glanced at his watch.

"We don't have that much time to do all this work. Can we push her later appointment further out?" asked Aslan, hoping for a miracle.

"I don't think we can," replied Alp, "She's scheduled for a dinner with the ambassador at five o'clock, so we must have her ready within the next two hours."

"Ah," uttered Aslan, under his breath, "I wasn't anticipating this at all! Very well, it is what it is. We'll all need to work together to have her ready on time. Gentlemen, it's time to transform this ugly duckling into a swan!"

"I beg your pardon!" exclaimed Kate.

Although Kate was aware that, perhaps, her appearance might have been rather plain, but she certainly wasn't ugly! Like many other women, Kate experienced her highs and lows, regarding her appearance; starting from her teenage years and up. While Kate might have been critical of herself throughout the years; she was, however, unaccustomed to others, particularly mere strangers, criticizing her own physical appearance.

"Dr. Stanley," whispered Ali into Kate's ear, "Please, just trust the process. Aslan might be difficult, but he truly is the best."

"Thank you, I appreciate that," Kate whispered back to Ali.

"Yes, Dr. Stanley, please just go with it," also whispered Alp into Kate's ear.

"Fine," Kate whispered back to both Alp and Ali.

Although she had no other choice but to quietly sit and undergo this transformation, she wasn't too happy about it, either.

Closing his eyes to meditate, Aslan suddenly began performing spontaneous yoga moves with his arms.

"Is this part of the process?" asked Kate, confused by the sight before her.

"He's just getting into his mode," replied Alp.

"The man is a genius," added Ali, "He must channel his inner wolf spirit, in order to begin your session."

"Are you sure my session is for just hair and makeup?" asked Kate, with a raised brow.

"Quiet," screamed Aslan, maintaining his same yoga pose with his eyes shut, "I need total silence."

Following his direction, Kate and his two assistants remained in complete and utter silence. Finally, a few minutes later, Aslan reopened his eyes and appeared calmer.

"Alright. I'm ready. To the salon," he said, as he clapped his hands, signaling for all three companions to vacate the area and relocate into the proper venue.

Upon Aslan's command, Kate was escorted into the salon by Alp and Ali. Once she arrived into the room, she was quickly seated onto a large, oversized green leather chair. As Kate sat down, Aslan clapped his hands once more, and Alp and Ali immediately got to work. While Alp focused on her hair, Ali was in charge of her eyebrows. After sharpening the tweezer's blade, Ali went straight over to Kate's eyebrows and began plucking them. One by one, Ali plucked away several ingrown hairs from Kate's forehead and face, while Alp combed away her overgrown and unkept hair. However, Kate's hair, which was much thicker and darker than Jennifer's, was greatly in need of further assistance.

"She's going to need a thicker comb," remarked Aslan, who was supervising both Alp and Ali, from across the room.

"I thought the medium sized white comb with the feathered bristles would do the trick," replied Alp to Aslan.

"Utter nonsense," Aslan huffed, "You're going to need the large metal one, with the thick horses' bristles."

"I'm not certain that's necessary," interrupted Kate, whose face was now entirely covered by a web of her own hair.

"Dr. Stanley," replied Aslan, "Your hair is covered with some of the thickest knots that I've ever seen. If Alp doesn't use the stronger brush, then trust me, you will feel more excruciating pain with this current brush."

Out of fear, Kate gulped.

"Err…all right…please go on," she said, as she closed her eyes.

Aslan clapped his hands once more, and Alp, following orders, returned back with the desired hairbrush. As Alp began brushing her hair, Ali pulled a pesty piece of hair right above her left eye. The act was so painful, that Kate let out a large scream.

"Ouch!!" Kate yelled, as she squeezed her fingers tightly against the arms of her chair.

"I'm sorry, Dr. Stanley," admitted Ali, "I tried to be as careful as I could, but some of your facial hair just grew so incredibly deep."

"Ali" interrupted Aslan, "It's time to activate Plan B."

"Plan B?" gasped both Ali and Alp at the same time, with their mouths dropped open, in shock.

"Do we even have enough time to do that?" asked Ali, with a look of concern.

"We must," replied Aslan, confidently.

Kate's ears caught their surprise reaction. This, in return, sent butterflies down into her stomach.

"What exactly is Plan B?" asked Kate, hesitantly.

"Plan B is laser treatment," replied Aslan.

"Laser treatment?" asked Kate, with a look of terror.

"Yes, but don't worry, it won't hurt," replied Ali. Then he added, "Much."

"Wait, this can hurt?" cried Kate, who was very worried by this prospect.

"It depends, but some people might feel a burning sensation," admitted Ali.

"Ali," interjected Aslan, "Enough chatting. It's time to get to work."

As Ali briefly stepped out of the room, he soon returned with a large white robotic device, that resembled a laundry machine.

"Is that the laser treatment machine?" asked a nervous Kate.

"Yes," replied Ali, "Now, Dr. Stanley, I'll need you to keep still and quiet now."

Following his command, Kate sat still and closed her eyes, tightly.

"Plug it up and let's start the treatment," Aslan commanded.

Upon Aslan's orders, Ali followed his command and turned on the machine. The machine took a few seconds to warm up, before exerting a slight beep. Once it fully turned on, a green light displayed on its central command unit.

"It's ready," said Ali, looking directly at Aslan.

Pleased with the update, Aslan smiled and said, "Begin the treatment."

With permission, Ali began applying the laser treatment onto Kate. While the first application stung a bit, afterwards, the second and third application, Kate started to feel a burning sensation around her face.

"Ouch!" she exclaimed.

"Not to worry Dr. Stanley, we're done," Ali reassured.

"We are?" asked Kate, as she began to rise up from her chair.

"Not so fast," spoke Aslan, "Ali might be done for now, but Alp still has to cut and color your hair."

For the next hour or so, Kate remained seated, while the team worked their magic on her. It wasn't until half past four o'clock in the afternoon when she finally returned back to her bedroom, to prepare for dinner with the ambassador. As Kate sat down on her sister's vanity stool and dresser, she stared straight into the mirror and hardly recognized herself, at all. The image staring back at her wasn't the same Kate from this morning. Her hair was now shorter and blonde. Her face and eyebrows, once covered in hair, were now trimmed and bare. The simple black dress that she wore from this morning, was now replaced with a blue colored silk dress. And her face, that once wore minimal coverage, was now covered with a full set of makeup.

Reaching for the hairbrush she began stroking her new hair. Since her makeup was still fresh, Kate wanted to do one last comb through to remove any last-minute knots, before dinner. After brushing her hair, she looked back into the mirror and gave a half smile. It was bittersweet. Although Kate liked the new image that she saw in the mirror, she also felt guilty. Although she wished she could have attended these beauty events with the company of her sister; sadly, she had to do them in her absence. As Kate's eyes wandered across to the hairbrush, she noticed that the hairbrush still had traces of blonde hair within the comb's teeth.

"I thought I removed these all this morning," she said to herself, aloud.

Pulling the strands of blonde hair from the comb's teeth, one by one, Kate rolled them up into a ball, and then walked over to the garbage bin to throw it away. However, once she threw the hair into the bin, she noticed the hair land on top of another batch of hair. Noticing that the two batches of hair were slightly different from each other, Kate suddenly became aware that the hair that she just threw away wasn't Jennifer's, but of her own.

"I'm already becoming her," Kate reflected.

Suddenly, her heart began to race. To comfort herself, she gently placed her hand over her chest.

"Calm down," she told herself. "You need to do this for Jennifer, you must be brave!"

Walking over to the mirror, she stared at her reflection and reminded herself, "You are brave, beautiful, confident and most importantly, you're going to bring Jennifer back home."

Exiting her room, Kate walked over to the staircase, after closing her door shut behind her. As she descended down the staircase, she held tightly onto the railing, along her journey. Suddenly the light from the chandelier shined against the pearl on her ring. Although Kate's appearance was transformed, the one thing that remained constant right now in her life was her ring. The ring was the one link that connected her back to her old life in New York and her current one, here in Istanbul. Kate smiled to herself. Apart from everything, her ring was also a reminder of her sister. It, ultimately, was her lucky charm.

Once Kate reached the bottom of the staircase, she walked across the grand hall and slowly made her way into the direction of the dining room. It was there that she was greeted by the butler, George, a very tall man, in his late sixties, dressed in a black suit, a white shirt and a black bow tie.

Following George's lead, Kate was led into the dining room and once she stepped into that room, she was left stunned by the extravagant and glamourous sight before her. Shining and sparkling all around, the room was like a white pearl brightly glowing all across, from the marbled floor to the white painted walls and ceilings. The room was grand in size and could easily host a party of at least a thousand or more. White fire light candles surrounded the space, and in the middle of the room hung an enormous Victorian crystal chandelier that was placed directly above the dinner table.

Once they approached the table, George immediately pulled out a red velvet chair and gestured for Kate to take a seat. Gracious for his gesture, Kate thanked him, as she took a seat. Once seated, she caught sight of a very tall, wooden and white colored grandfather clock, located directly across from her in the room. Its dials were gold in color, and the time read five minutes to five o'clock. Kate was still early for dinner.

Staring across the table, Kate admired the fine and delicate embroidered tablecloth, which was simple yet elegantly refined. Above the table, sat cream colored china dishes, which were adorned with gold lining along with edges. They were accompanied by folded white napkins, polished silverware and crystal wine glasses. In the middle of the table, stood a golden vase with a bouquet of pink roses, which were similar to the roses found throughout the estate's garden. On the opposite side of the golden vase, were two pairs of white candles, each held within a matching brass holder. Due to the various colors displayed above on the table, the candles' light created a pinkish hue glow that was so incredibly beautiful, that Kate was transfixed by its beauty.

As Kate stared on, she noticed that everyone on the table came in two. A perfect pair. Two crystal wine glasses. Two pairs of napkins. Two pairs of plates. It clearly was a dinner for two. Suddenly, Kate began to grow nervous. The ambassador was due to arrive at any moment. After all this time, she was finally going to meet him; her phantom. Over the years, she had heard so much about him, and yet, she never, not once, caught a glimpse of his face. With her nerves continuing to escalate, Kate played with her ring, in an effort, to calm down. In times of uncertainty, Kate always gravitated back to the ring as a form of comfort.

Suddenly, a loud chime rang and Kate nearly jumped from off her seat. Catching hold of her nerves, Kate realized that the sound was only that of the white grandfather clock, signaling the change of hour. It was now exactly five o'clock and the ambassador was due to arrive. Consumed within her thoughts, her attention abruptly returned by the sound of a rather loud ahem.

"Ahem, Mrs. Barrett," interrupted George, the butler.

It took a long moment for Kate to acknowledge George, for this was the first time ever since her arrival to the mansion, that she was formally addressed as Mrs. Barrett. Since George wasn't a part of Gloria and her immediate team, as far as he, the butler, was concerned, Kate was indeed, Mrs. Barrett.

"Yes?" asked Kate hesitantly and not once looking up, as she continued to play with the pearl ring around her finger.

"The ambassador has arrived," George boldly announced.

Kate, whose eyes were cast down and transfixed upon the candlelight flame, flickering back and forth against the table, slowly lifted her head up and looked straight across. And there, he was. Standing tall and glorious, wearing a dark navy-blue suit. He proudly entered the room, confidently strolling in, with his shiny black leather shoes, tapping against the white marbled stone, as he made his way over to the table. It was there from across the table, where her eyes met his. And, for the very first time in her life, Kate's heart, the very same heart that always remained steady, calm and predictable, finally skipped a beat…

Chapter 15

John entered the room and Kate was entirely surprised by his appearance. He looked nothing at all from what she originally imaged, nor expected. Having never laid eyes upon him before, she naturally presumed that he was far older than his actual age. Previously, her sister described him as an only son, who came from a wealthy family from San Francisco. Not only was he well educated, accomplished and successful, but he was also the sole heir to the vast fortune to his family's business and estates. Hailing across the wineries and vineyards of Napa Valley, located north of San Francisco, John was the heir apparent to a multimillion-dollar inheritance.

Given that John was already an accomplished and successful ambassador, who managed the entire Istanbul embassy, consisting of a large staff, well over one hundred, Kate assumed that Jennifer married a much older and established man. A man, whom she imaged, was in his prime and even, perhaps, well into his late fifties. Furthermore, not only did she assume that he was older, but, due to his overwhelming duties and responsibilities, she speculated that he was aged, balding, obese and relatively shorter in stature. However, Kate couldn't have been more wrong.

Instead, in front of her was a young man, no more than thirty. Much to her surprise, he certainly didn't appear aged, balding, nor overweight, either. Rather, he was quite the opposite. He was tall, standing well over six feet, physically fit, with fair complexion, along with a full set of dark black and thick hair. Staring straight into his eyes, Kate noticed that they were piercing and icy blue. And his facial features were well defined, masculine structured, with not a single trace of a wrinkle. Apart from the realization that he was far younger than what she previously anticipated, Kate also had to admit to herself, that he was equally much more handsome and attractive than what she previously accredited him to be. But sadly, this revelation came at the most unexpected of times, for suddenly, Kate's heart, once more, skipped yet another beat.

Walking straight pass Kate, without a formal greeting nor introduction, John quickly took his seat, as he motioned to George to begin their meal service. Now, seated comfortable in his chair, which Kate observed resembled a throne, he proceeded to pour himself a glass of water. As she watched on, he pulled the napkin from off the table and gently placed it on his lap. With the utmost suave and debonair, he once again, waved in George's direction, further signaling the advancement of their evening. All the while, he hadn't yet acknowledged, nor looked at Kate's direction, which she found peculiar, especially, given that she was seated right next to him at the table.

Wanting to break away from the frosty atmosphere, Kate opened her mouth and was about to utter her first words in his company as a 'hello,' when she was abruptly caught short; for at that very moment, George arrived with their main course. Served on two separate plates, the main course consisted of grilled lamb, sauteed vegetables, including carrots, potatoes and onions, along with a side of wild rice and shepherd's salad. Upon arrival, George placed each plate down on the table and in front of them.

"As you requested, Sir," began George, "We've skipped the appetizer round and brought the main course only."

"Excellent," said John, as he finally spoke, breaking his long period of silence.

Noticing that his voice was deep, masculine and authoritative, Kate listened on as he spoke, with her keen and impressionable ears.

"And please," he added, "Proceed with the wine."

"Yes, Sir," replied George.

As George was about to exit the room to retrieve the wine, he suddenly turned around and asked, "Sir, after the main course, do you still want the dessert to be served?"

John, who already held his utensils within his hands in preparation for his meal, simply replied, "No, dessert tonight. Sweets are unnecessary for this occasion. The main course and wine shall suffice."

"As you wish, Sir. I will bring out the wine, immediately," said George, following John's command.

Meanwhile, Kate silently studied John from afar, half in astonishment and the other half in fear. Ever since his arrival to dinner, he not once greeted, nor acknowledge her presence. And now, it was becoming abundantly clear that he was intentionally cutting their evening short, in an effort to avoid her altogether. But why? That remained a mystery. Although he might not have been thrilled at the prospect with conversing and interacting with her, it appeared, that John also shared no desire to be on friendly or cordial terms with her, either. Currently, his tactic was to simply ignore her existence, through and through. However, Kate wasn't a ghost. Nay, she was very much a woman and his equal, made from the same flesh and bones, as he! However, rather than confronting his rude behavior, Kate reluctantly held her tongue. She reminded herself of her true mission and that was to find her missing sister. Therefore, if Kate needed to swallow her pride and force herself to become the peacemaker, while searching for common ground with this proudful man, who sat before her, then so be it! Ultimately, Kate was willing to cast aside her personal feelings and to offer an olive branch, in return for his cooperation.

"Ambassador Barrett, it's a pleasure to meet you after all this time," she began, while mustering up all of her inner courage to converse with him directly.

However, as soon as she uttered those very words, George returned back to the table, holding their bottles of wine.

"George, please proceed to pour the wine," said John, ignoring Kate's greeting.

"As you wish, Sir," replied George.

Following his orders, George proceeded to pour out the wine, as John picked up his utensils and began to devour his meal. As John carved and swallowed his lamb, Kate listened on to hear his knife and fork stroke across, back and forth, against his fine porcelain plate. The sounds of the utensils were similar to that of musical chimes, in which each scratch was equivalent to a musical tune. But apart from these 'sounds,' the evening, itself, was rather uneventful, somber and dull.

As the fire from the candlelight continued to burn and its flames flicker, Kate watched John, as he devoured every morsel of his meal and wine, for he was a hungry man, indeed. With each passing bite, it was growing clearer to Kate just how little he took notice of her company. Refusing to allow his neglectful mannerism to get the best of her, Kate reached over, picked up her utensils and took her first bite. While John ate and devoured his meal like a beast, Kate quietly sat on and ate her meal like a lady; never once scratching her plate with her utensils, in the process.

For a good while, neither of them spoke to one another. Not a single word or sound was uttered at the table. However, this was soon about to change. After finishing their first bottle of wine, John decided to pop open their second bottle. However, the second bottle was located at the far edge of the table, closest to Kate. Due to his bitter pride and arrogance, rather than politely asking Kate to pass the bottle over to him, John stretched over and attempted to grab the bottle for himself. Seeing him struggle to reach over, Kate, still wanting and trying to capture his attention, quickly grabbed it, before he even had a chance to touch it.

"Ambassador," she said with a smile, "Can I pour you a glass of wine?"

Without waiting for his response, Kate swiftly walked over to his side of the table and popped opened the bottle. Once the cork was removed, she poured the wine into his empty glass. Finally, for the very first time, he looked at her and his blue eyes acknowledged her presence. After capturing his attention at long last, Kate beamed with pride and smiled to herself. But instead of receiving a positive reception, his reaction and choice of words, were not at all what she expected.

"What is the meaning of this?!" he exclaimed, angrily.

"It's only wine," replied Kate, softly, surprised by his outburst.

"No," he scolded coldly, as he pointed his finger towards her and said, "That ring on your finger."

"My ring?" she asked, entirely surprised by his question. "It's my pearl ring. I've had this for years."

"Where did you get it?" he asked, with a crackle in his voice and a sense of desperation.

"It was a gift from my sister, Jennifer," replied Kate, directly.

Having remained silent for the entirety of their evening, the last thing Kate ever expected was for their first conversation to revolve around her beloved pearl ring, of all things. But rather than conversing with her, John remained still, motionless and scarily quiet. Feeling a bit uncomfortable, Kate hurried back to her seat. After a brief period of prolonged silence, John abruptly rose up from chair, exited the room and slammed the door shut behind him; all the while, leaving his newly poured drink still full. Having failed to bid her a goodnight, Kate was gravely disappointed from the outcome of their evening together.

"My God," Kate uttered to herself, after much reflection, "If he can't even sit and finish a proper dinner with me, then how's anyone going to actually believe that we're a happily married couple? Let alone, that we're in love?"

One Hour Later...

Across the estate, on the opposite side of the mansion, John sat down in his office on his black leather chair, drinking away his troubles, through another glass of whisky. By now, his hair was a mess, his vision already a bit blurred from the excess alcohol, and he was one step away from being borderline drunk, if he wasn't already. His evening with Jennifer's sister proved to be an unexpected disaster, and he, himself, knew that he had been a total ass to her. Although it wasn't his initial intention to have treated her sister in that manner; however, once he entered the room and saw her face for the first time, he also saw the same face of his enemy and once again, he was reminded of all the betrayal, hate and resentment he felt towards Jennifer.

Jennifer, his soon-to-be-former wife for the past five years, grew into both a stranger and an enemy to him. Oh, how he hated and resented her! While the world perceived them to be the happily married super-power golden couple, nothing could have been further from the truth. For years, John lived in a miserable and loveless marriage. Every time he saw Jennifer, he was confronted and reminded of all her lies, deceit and unfaithfulness. He always knew about her numerous extramarital affairs, but yet, he kept the truth hidden away from her. He discovered her unfaithfulness during his first trip to Croatia, just a month into their marriage. As part of ongoing security measures, he granted the U.S. Marshals' access to monitor and guard her, while he was away for training. It was there, during his first training mission, that he was informed by the U.S. Marshals that Jennifer had traveled to a private hotel, with an unidentified man. Later on, it was further revealed that the identity to the unidentified man was her chess instructor, after they were spotted kissing, outside of the hotel. To make matters worse, John received the news just one day shy of their first Valentine's Day together, as a married couple.

Rather than confronting her, John kept the news hidden. He decided not to reveal her indiscretions to anyone; with the exception to security, whom, after that day forward, John granted security the authorization to routinely monitor her whereabouts indefinitely, but most importantly, in secret. Ultimately, John didn't want her aware that he knew the truth about her lies, as well as her string of lovers. Although there were many times when John could have spoken up, where he could have confronted her privately and tried to make amends; but instead, he simply just didn't. The reality was that whenever he thought or considered confronting her, he became frozen, mute and numb. Why that was? Well, for the man who succeeded in every aspect of his life, his marriage was the one area in which he failed. And failure wasn't something he was proud of. Therefore, he remained ever silent upon the matter. Having chosen silence and ignoring the truth, over the years, he slowly buried himself deeper within his work, pushing Jennifer further and further away from him. What gradually began as arriving a few minutes late to dinner, eventually, became an hour late and soon enough, none at all. Within time, he ignored her entirely; arriving late after work, and leaving early in the morning. Within a few months into their marriage, John already moved out of their shared bedroom and into his own private wing. He rarely saw her anymore; let alone, maintained any ongoing intimate marital relations with her.

As John dedicated himself entirely to his career, he also partially self-acknowledged, that he shared some ounce of responsibility towards pushing his wife into the arms of other men. But at the same time, he expected so much more from her. When they married, he made it perfectly clear, as to what was expected from her. As the ambassador's wife, he needed a partner who was willing to support him with his mission. Having promised him that she ready for the challenge, during his first classified and confidential training in Croatia, she already betrayed him, before the ink even dried on their marriage license. And so, over the years, while John was away on various undisclosed and confidential missions, which he was prohibited from revealing to her, he knew, and expected, that for each and every one of those trips, he knew deep within his heart, that she was away on yet another rendezvous, with one of her many lovers.

But the real truth was that John ultimately, did not love her. Although, in the beginning, he was initially contempt and pleased with their union; in the end, their marriage operated more like a business transaction and nothing more. She needed a husband to acquire wealth and status, while he needed a wife for the further advancement of his career. He knew that a young and upcoming ambassador would not be taken seriously on the world stage had he simply been a bachelor without a wife; therefore, a wife was both necessary and a key requirement for his mission. While he genuinely admired and cared for her, he had hoped that eventually, with time, they would grow to love one another. Even become dear friends. Jennifer was attractive, social and came from a decent family. She was everything that one ought to seek for in a wife. On paper she was perfect; however, in reality, it wasn't so simple. After their marriage, John soon came to the bitter realization that what he imagined for their marriage to blossom into, never really came to be.

He couldn't force Jennifer to love him, nor he, in return, love her. However, he still wished, that at the very least, she would have respected their union and remained faithful to him, as he was always faithful to her. Even in the middle of her passionate affairs, John never once looked at another woman. Deep down inside, he always remained hopeful that one day, she would change her scandalous ways, and become the wife that she pretended to be so publicly well. Meanwhile, as they smiled away at the flashing lights and cameras, and danced away well into the late evenings at their various public gatherings and state dinners, it was all for pretend and nothing more.

Over the years, he got use to her frequent vase throwing at his office, and her standard foot stepping antics, during their dances at state dinners. While they promoted themselves as the happy couple, arriving together united, hand and hand, ascending down the grand staircase as a power couple, it was all a lie. For as soon as they climbed back up those very same steps to retire for their evening, the false fantasy that they created, instantly faded and reality soon settled in. After the cameras stopped rolling and the crowds dispersed, they parted and went about their separate ways, as mere strangers. Once upstairs, he remained on his side of the estate, and she, on the other; and it was as if, their shared evening downstairs entertaining guests, never even happened, in the first place.

Love it seemed, as John came to understand the hard way, was something that couldn't be forced. As much as he wanted to grow to love Jennifer, and she to grow to love him in return, it never quite reached fruition. It always failed along the way, and he knew, deep within his own heart, that neither one of them ever felt that spark; not that he ever believed in such silly romantic notions. Slowly, as the years progressed, they each grew further apart from one another. While his career soared to superior heights, his private life fell further down the scale into oblivion. But with newfound success, also came the pressure to protect his image, and to shield and conceal his wife's indiscretions. Therefore, years ago, when Jennifer approached him about marriage counseling, he was initially opened to the prospect. In fact, he was secretly delighted that she cared enough to even consider salvaging whatever broken pieces were left, in their already crumbling marriage. However, once the matter was brought to the attention of his political advisors, they swiftly advised against it. Concerned about the potential negative publicity associated with the prospect if, by somehow, their private sessions were inadvertently leaked to the press, they advised against it, as they believed that the end result, would affect public perception on them, in their capacity to fulfill their public roles. Ultimately, he was inclined to decline her request; however, that single decision, which, he, himself, privately acknowledged, helped served as one of the primary catalysts, for the ultimate decay and disintegration of their marriage.

As time passed, he felt Jennifer's unhappiness, just as he felt his own, within their union. John knew that his marriage to Jennifer wasn't going to last. Sooner or later, she was going to seriously fall head-over-heels in love with one of her lovers, and decide to finally divorce him, once and for all, and to start a brand new-life of her own, free from the pressures associated, with their political world. Eventually, when that day finally came, which he always predicted would happen, he accepted her request for a divorce, without protest. By now, he was already established in his career and well respected by his peers, on a world stage. Although John preferred to part ways with his soon-to-be-former wife as quickly as possible, for both of their sakes and sanities; they were advised to wait. With an upcoming presidential election looming in near sight, it was feared by his advisors that their divorce announcement could foster and generate bad publicity and thus, adversely negatively affect the outcome of the election. After they mutually agreed to temporarily wait, John expected them to remain silent and to keep a low profile. However, when she suddenly went missing, John came to the unfortunate conclusion, that she once again, lied and tricked him, yet again.

John wasn't entirely convinced that Jennifer had truly gone missing. Given her past history, John believed, whole heartly, that she voluntarily disappeared and ran away again, so that she could discretely sneak away to attend another one of her holiday rendezvous abroad, with a secret lover. However, this time, she went too far. She made the mistake of escaping to a romantic getaway, during a critical moment for them both. Since they agreed to the divorce, John wasn't entirely sure that this time, she would ever return back. And he was angry with her. This was the ultimate betrayal.

Having promised to stay until after the election, she lied to him, yet again. If the news of their divorce leaked prematurely, due to her blatant public display of her adultery, then it was sure to be a scandal of infamous proportions, which could ultimately, negatively affect their reputations, his upcoming project and the presidential election. When this news reached his staff regarding this crisis, they actively sought to seek a remedy to this potential scandal. It was during their research, that it was discovered by his security staff that his wife had a sister; a twin, to be precise. This was certainly a surprise. He recalled many years ago, before his marriage, that he did hear about her having a sister, but he was unaware that they were twins. Over the years, due to their frequent travels and high security clearance requirements, rarely anyone of Jennifer's relatives came to visit; and so, as a result, he never met her sister before. Much to his relief, when he received confirmation that the twin sister agreed to pose as Jennifer, on an interim basis, he was grateful and appreciative of her assistance.

While John intended to arrive to tonight's dinner as the host, in a professional, hospitable and dignified manner, the opposite occurred. Although he planned to have a short, yet productive evening with her sister, to both introduce himself and to thank her for her service; however, once he saw her, face-to-face, everything changed. Much to his surprise, she was the spitting image of Jennifer. Naturally, that shouldn't have come as a surprise to him, since they were identical twins; however, once he actually saw her in person, he was caught off guard and was yet again, reminded of all of the hurt and resentment he felt, arising from her sister's lies and betrayal.

Sadly, rather than striving to make a positive first impression upon her, John reverted back to his old ways and tried his very best not to make any eye contact with her, and to avoid her, at all costs. However, it wasn't until he caught sight of her ring, that his emotions got the best of him. From first glance, John had no doubt within his mind, that the shiny pearl ring around her finger was the identical pearl gifted to him in India, all those years ago. They were one in the same. Even the blue sapphire diamonds matched the same family stones that he customed styled onto the ring. A ring, that he gave whole heartly to his wife on their wedding day. Now, after all these years, the long-lost pearl, whom he always cherished and admired so dearly ever since his childhood, returned back to him. However, this time, it was worn on the hands of another woman, a total stranger. Although Jennifer previously claimed that she lost the ring due to her negligence, tonight, her sister confirmed the opposite. What he once thought lost, was actually gifted away as a present to her sister. Confronted with yet another one of her many lies, this time, John reflected that Jennifer went too far. At long last, he finally had enough!

However, as John sat down at his desk, drinking another glass of his whisky, he realized that although he was justified with his anger towards his soon-to-be-former wife, at the same time, it was unfair to have been so incredibly rude to her sister. After all, her sister was innocent in all of this mess. It wasn't her fault that Jennifer gave her the ring. In fact, the more he thought about it, the more he determined that it was a rather sweet and endearing gesture, that her sister cared enough to wear it out publicly, in the first place.

When exactly did Jennifer give her the ring? He asked himself. Five years ago, on their wedding day, Jennifer supposedly lost the ring. Did her sister have possession of the ring, this entire time? Did she wear it often, every day, ever since? John smiled at the thought. For some odd and peculiar reason, it was nice to know that someone, somewhere out there in this world, appreciated the ring, just as much as he did, and at the same time, they were willing to not only wear it, but to wear it out, proudly. Recalling Aasha's warning all those years ago, that the ring chooses its owners, John concluded that the ring ultimately chose Jennifer's sister. That somehow, destiny intervened. But the irony of it all, as he thought to himself, was that the pearl ring that he assumed was lost to him forever, finally found its way back to him, five years later, on the hand of the other sister, whom, he never before met, but was, at this very moment, going to be his new decoy wife. The ultimate twist of fate.

But what exactly was her name? The twin sister? Having been previously informed of her name, suddenly, he couldn't quite recall what it was. He knew that it started with the letter K, and that her last name was with an S. She was a doctor…a professor, as he vaguely recalled. Although she had the same face as Jennifer's, somehow, she was still slightly different. Her eyes appeared much kinder and gentler. Having caught a brief glimpse of her eyes when she attempted to explain to him about her ring, he noticed how sweet and innocent they looked, as they sparkled across the candlelight. Those were not the eyes of someone who frequently lied and cheated. And she smelled different too. Her scent was fresh and light, and not overpowering and floral, as Jennifer's had been. Although they were very subtle changes, they were still enough to capture his attention. Even to her credit, she went as so far, as to attempt to greet him at the table, while pouring him a glass of wine.

Taking another sip of his whisky, John glanced over to stare at the large portrait that hung above on his wall. Painted onto a large canvas and enclosed by a thick brass golden frame, the portrait was that of the planet, Earth. The portrait was painted with bright majestic blue, emerald green and white colors, along with a pure black background, representing the universe's solid darkness. Up close, while Earth appears to have everything desirable on its planet's surface, but as one steps further away to see the greater view of the portrait, it's also a lonesome tiny planet, within the larger scale of the unhabitable and ever-expanding universe. Ironically, the portrait was a bit symbolic too, because it also represented his own similar experiences, within his private life. While John, the man, might have everything that this world has to offer: from wealth beyond measure, education from the best universities, world renown fame, a prestigious career, talented advisors and every other possible materialistic possession one could ever wish or hope for; in the end, he was still very much alone.

Thus, as John sat down in his trusty black leather chair— a seat he grew so familiar with— while he continued to drink away his sorrows late into the night, all alone and in complete solitude. His office became his private sanctuary, and his own gilded cage. No one came in, and no one came out; and he remained, as he had always been, ever alone. There was much truth, in the famous proverb, that with great power, also comes great responsibilities— for John was an example of this. And for the man, who had the world at his disposal, he was also, very much at the same time, perhaps, the world's loneliest man.

Finishing his last sip of whisky, he slammed the empty glass on top of his table. No matter how dreadful tonight was, he decided that tomorrow was another day and he was going to make amends with her sister. As John stood up from his chair, he walked over towards his window and stared out to view the moon. Shining and sparkling across the midnight sky, the moon was full, bright and beaming with a white light. While the sky remained in pure darkness, John stared directly at the moon and admired its light and beauty; which was the only source of light, in an otherwise, dark night. As the moonlight shined across his face, he finally remembered her name.

"Kate," he whispered to himself. "Her name is Kate," he repeated, as he unexpectedly smiled to himself.

Slowly, he exited his office and retired off to bed, where he peacefully slept for the remainder of his evening.

Chapter 16

With the sun shining across her face, Kate awoke the following morning in her bed. As she lay down inside her white linen sheets, she was left to ponder about the night before and about her current circumstances. Last night, her dinner with the ambassador turned out to be a failure. Having hardly uttered a single word to one another, he abruptly ended their evening prematurely, after catching sight of her ring. How odd and peculiar was his reaction to her ring, she thought to herself. Already, she found him rather strange and unpredictable. In the past, she already presumed that Jennifer was happily married and content with her fairytale life, but now, she wondered as to what sort of marriage did her sister actually have with him, in the first place. Never once, did Kate ever suspect that the opposite might have been true. But given these circumstances, where exactly was her sister, now?

Glancing across the room, Kate stared at all of her sister's possessions, still left intact, as if she'd never been gone. This certainly wasn't the room of a person, who intended to abruptly leave, or even, disappear, willingly. Had Jennifer intended to intentionally leave on her own, then surely, she would have packed some of her precious belongings? Wouldn't she? Wouldn't she have left, with taking some of her precious jewels, or perfumes with her? Or, was Kate, entirely wrong? Even though it was years since they last saw each other, was it possible that Jennifer changed so much, that she was now a complete stranger to her own twin sister?

"Somehow, I've got to get to the bottom of this," Kate said to herself, determined to find answers to this mystery.

Hopping out of bed, Kate got up and left Tabitha behind, as she slept underneath her blankets, nearby. After quickly changing into her morning clothes, Kate began searching the bedroom, looking for any clues or hints that she could find. If Jennifer planned on escaping the mansion, then surely, she must have left some sort of clue? A note or letter? Perhaps, even some form of correspondence? Suddenly, like a light bulb switched on, Kate recalled that Jennifer always kept a diary. Ever since they were children, Jennifer always wrote inside of a diary. That tradition carried over into their teenage years, and eventually, into their college years. Surely, Jennifer's recording keeping habits still continued well into her adult years, too. Assuming that Kate's assumptions were correct, and that Jennifer still, indeed, kept a diary, then the better question now was, where exactly did she keep it?

Opening all of the drawers and pulling out all of the clothes, Kate began her search. When the diary failed to appear, she changed direction, and checked the closets, instead. But still, no diary. Turning her attention over towards Jennifer's shoe collections, Kate searched through each and every one of her shoe boxes; but still, no diary. She was almost ready to give up, when she saw Jennifer's purse collection in front of her. Determined to persevere, Kate inspected the contents of each purse, hoping and praying to find her diary, inside one of them. But, alas, no such luck. Suddenly, Kate heard an unexpected knock at the door. Who could it be? Curious as to who was there, Kate walked over to the front of her bedroom and opened the door.

"Good morning, Kate," said Lucas, with a smile. "May I come in?"

"Lucas?" replied a surprised Kate. "Certainly, please, do come in. I must say, I wasn't expecting you at all…"

"That's how I roll, Kate. But not to worry, I also brought breakfast," added

Lucas, as he lifted up a brown paper bag, with a tray of coffee.

Walking over to her balcony, he quickly unpacked the food and beverages.

 "Are you coming, or am I going to have to eat this all, by myself?" he asked, sarcastically.

"Oh, yes, I'm on my way," replied Kate, as she hurried over to join him. Once at the table, she pulled herself a seat and sat down next to him.

"So, Kate," he began, as he grabbed a plain white bagel and proceeded to spread cream cheese over the top layer of the bagel, with a knife. "I can call you, Kate, right?"

"Yes, of course. After all, I do call you Lucas," she replied, as she reached over to grab a cup of coffee for herself.

Having successfully established their relationship by an ongoing first name basis, Lucas took a bite of his bagel. Using his butter knife, he pointed in the general direction of her bedroom, which at the moment, was a complete and utter mess.

"What happened here? Are you trying to redecorate your room, already?" he asked, with a raised brow.

Distracted by his unexpected arrival, Kate completely forgot about the condition of the bedroom. Ultimately, she had been responsible for its massive mess. Her quest to locate Jennifer's diary, subsequently, left the room in a disastrous condition, with piles of clothing, shoes and purses, all scattered about and thrown across the floor.

"Somewhat redecorating," she lied.

"You weren't looking for something in particular, were you?" he asked, while taking another massive bite of his bagel and gulping down his warm coffee.

"Looking? What's there to find?" she asked sarcastically, while trying to divert his question. As it currently stood, Kate didn't really know anyone well enough here to trust, and if Jennifer truly did run away, then the less anyone knew about what Kate did behind closed doors, the better.

"I mean," she continued, "I just wanted to reorganize the clothes, since I can't seem to find anything here, that's all. As a professor, I'm generally used to things being systematic and organized. In contrast, this room is a bit unorganized, so I thought I might as well reorganize it and make my myself more comfortable, while I'm here.

"Relax," he abruptly interrupted. "It's your bedroom, do whatever you'd like. It's none of my business. Just take a bite of the bagel. Coffee alone, won't fill you up."

Passing over a bagel, along with a pack of cream cheese to her, Kate graciously accepted it. As she began to spread the cream cheese over her bagel, Lucas decided to ask her a few questions.

"That's more like it," he began. "So, tell me now, how's everything going, so far? Do you feel more settled in?"

"Things are going alright," she admitted. "Not much to really say or report, since I've only just arrived here, a couple of days ago. But today, I'm starting on my training."

"Ah, yes, your training," he repeated, "In that case, you will need this."

Reaching into his pocket, he pulled out a black mobile phone and handed it over to her.

"Here," he said. "This is your new official business mobile phone. You're authorized to use it for the remainder of your stay. Should you ever need to contact me, security, or anyone else from the estate or embassy, then please limit yourself to using this phone only. The network on this government phone is well secured and protected. But if you encounter any issues with it, then please report it to me, directly."

"Thank you, Lucas," replied Kate, as she grabbed hold of the mobile phone. "Will I also be receiving a laptop or computer, as well?"

"Ah, I'm glad that you asked this, as I do need to talk to you about this matter, too," he began, "As a matter of fact, I originally was going to give you one, but then, as I came to learn, your sister never kept one."

"Really?" asked Kate, surprised by that revelation. "Didn't she ever send or check on her e-mails? I'll admit, I find that rather surprising, that she didn't keep one for herself."

"I, too, was surprised," replied Lucas, "But after further investigation, as it turns out, she never did have a laptop. It was her assistant, Sally, who took care of all her correspondences and paperwork. All your sister had was just a mobile phone."

"I see," began Kate, "Let me guess, because of this reason, I'll only be assigned a mobile phone, too, won't I?"

"Exactly," answered Lucas, "Like I said before, back in New York, you catch on quickly."

While he took another bite of his bagel, Kate, wanting to take advantage of the detective being alone with her inside her bedroom, decided to press him about the current status of her sister's case.

"Lucas, are there any new updates in Jennifer's case?" she asked, as she took a sip of her coffee.

Suddenly, the color on Lucas' face changed. His pale white face turned red, and he stopped eating his bagel, altogether. Apparently, Kate's inquiry caught him off guard, and he was not at all pleased by her question.

"There aren't any new updates, Kate. I have everything under control. If, and when, I have any news or updates, that are approved and deemed appropriate to share, then I'll be the first to let you know. Until then, please don't ask any more questions, and just let me handle it."

"I'm sorry," spoke Kate. "I didn't mean to upset you, it's just that I'm concerned about my sister, having been missing for this extended period of time."

Slowly, the color of Lucas's face returned back to his normal shade of white. As soon as he calmed back down, he reached over to his bagel and took another bite, as if everything had returned back to normal.

"I get it," he said. "But if I were you," he began, with a piece of bagel still lingering inside of his opened mouth, "I'd focus on your adjustment to this place."

"I'm trying," Kate confessed. "I realize that it won't be easy, but I'm still going to give it, my very best."

"I have no doubt that you will," said Lucas, as he now, took a sip of his coffee to wash the bagel, he just devoured, down his throat. "But just a word of advice, if I may?"

"Of course, any advice is much appreciated," she said, as she too, finally took a bite of her bagel.

"Since I was the one, who brought you here in the first place, I do harbor some sort of responsibility towards you," he said. "Listen, I like you, Kate, and I can already tell that you're not like the rest of them. Not one bit. You're different."

"I am?" she asked, surprised by his honest admission. "How so?" she further inquired.

"You're very innocent," Lucas professed, as he took a sip of his coffee.

"I've been here long enough to know, that it's best that you just keep a low profile, do your assignment, and avoid making any new friends."

"Yes, and I do intend on being professional, at all times," added Kate.

"You do that," agreed Lucas. "Because the people here, trust me, they aren't your friends and they never will be. One day, they might smile to you, but the next day, those same friends will stab a knife down your back."

"Are they really like that? All of them?" asked an astonished Kate.

"Most, if not all," he replied. "Especially, Gloria. Watch out for her."

"What's wrong with Gloria?" she asked, now intrigued by his warning.

"Gloria, is the biggest pain in the ass out of all of them," he shouted, then gulped another sip of his coffee. "That woman thinks she owns this entire place, which I find annoying as hell!"

Suddenly, both Lucas and Kate broke into laughter. They equally agreed, that Gloria, for all her worth, was quite an overbearing and aggressive personality.

"Apart from Gloria, is there anyone else, whom I should watch out for? What about the ambassador?" asked Kate.

"Have you met him yet?" asked Lucas, his green eyes, now staring directly at her.

"Yes, last night," she replied.

"And your thoughts?" he asked, curious about her feelings.

"There's not much to say. Our dinner was very brief, and we hardly spoke a word to one another," she reluctantly admitted.

"Well, then," he said, smilingly. "That's the ambassador for you. He comes and goes as he pleases. But as I said before, you should just keep a low profile and focus on doing your job, that's all. If you need a friend or someone to talk to, then I'm around. Just use that new phone of yours to give me a call, anytime."

"A friend?" she asked, with a raised brow.

"Well, I'm the exception, of course," he replied, with a devious smile.

"Then, as my friend, is it fair to say that, I can trust you?" she asked, jokingly.

"Oh, you definitely shouldn't trust me, for I'm the worse one, of all," he replied, with a devil of a grin.

Then, both Lucas and Kate laughed, once more.

"Kate, you're a breath of fresh air here. I hope you don't change," he said.

"I doubt, that I ever will. I may be Mrs. Barrett for now, but deep down inside, I'm still Dr. Stanley from New York," she reflected.

"You'd be surprised to know, just how much this world can change a person. I, myself, speak from experience. Take this bagel, for example.

Fresh out of the kitchen oven. It's fluffy, moist and tasty. Everything that a person ought to wish for in a bagel, is here on our table. Now, in comparison, look at this bagel," then he reached over, into the brown paper bag and pulled out a second bagel, but this time, the bagel was burnt, black and ashy.

"As you can see," he continued, "This bagel is burnt. It's damaged, uneatable and in a minute, I will throw this pitiful thing, into the garbage bin. You see, Kate, this is what happens to those who come here. They arrive as a freshly baked bread, and leave as burnt toast."

"Lucas," whispered Kate, with sadness, "I had no idea…"

"Kate," he interrupted, "Even the purest, innocent and delicate of roses, can easily turn to black and whitter away, if left here long enough."

His message was delivered in such a very serious tone, that it certainly, caught Kate's attention. Ever since she met him, he always spoke and carried himself in a mischievous and light-hearted manner, that anything else that differed, seemed out of his character.

"But," he said, "I won't take any more of your precious time. We've got busy schedules, and I, myself, need to head out, now. But please, do enjoy the rest of breakfast."

Grabbing his coffee, he walked over to her door, and right before he exited her room, he turned around and said, "Goodbye, friend."

"Goodbye, Lucas," she said, in return.

An hour later, Kate arrived downstairs to meet Gloria to start her first day of training. However, instead of finding Gloria there, she met with Sally instead. According to Sally, Gloria summoned an unscheduled emergency meeting, and that her presence was needed, immediately. Following Sally's lead, the two women walked over into the executive conference room, where they saw Gloria, Bes, Carol, Tyler and Chef Homura already seated at the conference table. Not wanting to further delay this urgent meeting, Kate and Sally quickly took their seats, while Gloria, on cue, began the meeting's commencement.

"Dr. Stanley," Gloria began, "Thank you, for arriving on time. Now, that you're here, let's get down to business."

"Is this gathering pertaining to my impending training?" asked Kate, wanting to seek more clarification, before the meeting started.

"I'll get to that momentarily, Dr. Stanley," replied Gloria, as she shuffled her stack of papers on the desk, while appearing frustrated and stressed.

"I have called this emergency meeting," said Gloria. "Because this morning, I received news that in exactly two weeks from today, we're going to host our first diplomatic state dinner for this upcoming calendar year. As this will be Dr. Stanley's first state dinner with us, not only will we need to prepare for our standardized event planning and coordination, but we must also strive to accelerate Dr. Stanley's training and help her to get better acclimated with her new role, as soon as possible."

Immediate chatter began brewing in the room amongst the staff. However, with one single stare and a raised brow from Gloria, the staff grew silent and once again, Gloria took back rein of the situation.

"To prepare," Gloria continued, "I have a schedule for us all to abide by. Is this understood?" she asked.

Once again, the room fell silent. Gloria, content with their silence, continued on.

"First, Carol and Tyler, please start drafting our invitations and announcements. As we will need to hire a photographer, please ensure that they will be able to produce the official photographs in time for our press release. Afterwards, please work with Sally to coordinate and schedule a photo shoot with Ambassador Barrett and Dr. Stanley."

"We're on it," replied Tyler, Carol and Sally, and within seconds, they all grabbed their belongings, and exited the meeting to begin working on their assignments.

"Next, Chef Homura," Gloria continued, with her eyes laid upon him.

"Chef," she began, "Your task is to design an evening menu. In addition, please prepare the flower arrangement, centerpieces and seating arrangements for our guests. Apart from all of this, I also ask that you allocate some of your spare time, to thoroughly train and instruct Dr. Stanley on table etiquettes, specifically relating to our local customs and manners."

"Dr. Stanley, please don't take any offense with this matter," spoke Gloria, as she turned her attention towards Kate. "However, all new staff are required to undergo our formal table etiquettes training. While you may already have sufficient table manners of your own, within your private live as a civilian; however, now that you're a government employee, like the rest of us, you'll need to elevate yourself up to our golden standards."

"I understand and that's perfectly fine. I look forward to working with Chef Homura," said Kate.

"Splendid, absolutely splendid!" Gloria exclaimed, happily. "In that case, I'll just cross that one, off my list."

Just as Carol, Tyler and Sally before him, Chef Homura quickly excused himself and exited the meeting to start his assignment.

"Next, up, Bes," said Gloria, "Bes, you, perhaps, have one of the most, if not, the most important task, above all else. Apart from the procurement for the rental properties for the event, we also need you to start Dr. Stanley's dancing lessons."

"Dancing?" asked Kate, shocked by her revelation. "I wasn't previously informed about dancing, before. Am I to dance? In public?"

"Yes, dancing and yes, in public, too" replied Gloria, sternly. "Dancing is a huge element and activity for all of our formal state dinners and events. Even the previous, Madame Barrett, was always keen and active with her dancing skills. Therefore, the same will be expected from you. Also, since we don't want to draw any suspicion that you're impersonating her, you'll need to learn how to dance."

"But I've never danced before! Not a single day in my entire life! Never, not once!" exclaimed Kate, who was by now, extremely vexed and worried about this new and surprising prospect.

"Dr. Stanley, we all begin as amateurs," Gloria reminded her, "But, unlike most, you have an entire team supporting you. Why, Bes is one of the finest dance instructors that I know. As for myself, I'm a classically trained ballerina. I promise, he and I, will have you prepared and ready, in time for the state dinner."

"Yes, I do understand, but is two weeks ample time? I mean, can't we just invent some story, or even, use the excuse that I'm feeling ill or something…" Kate suggested.

"Dr. Stanley, we're all professionals. I promise, we shall get you up to speed and quickly. Although, granted, you might be unable to perform the tango right away, especially with the limited amount of time that we have, but we'll save that one for the very end."

"Tango? Wait, am I honestly expected to learn the tango, at one point or another?" asked Kate, who secretly began to panic.

"Why, of course, you are. Especially, during our upcoming NATO state dinner. It's simply tradition," replied Gloria, as she waved her hands carefree in the air, as a matter of fact.

"When exactly, is the next NATO state dinner?" asked Kate, concerned about this new and alarming prospect.

"It's still yet to be announced," admitted Gloria, "But in the meantime, we'll focus on getting you accustomed to the Viennese waltz."

"The Viennese waltz?" asked Kate, whose heart sunk down to the bottom of her stomach.

"Yes, the Viennese waltz. Perhaps, we should add the foxtrot, too, while we're at it. Bes, what do you think?"

"I say, let's see how she does with the waltz, first," replied Bes.

"Very well, we'll just have to wait and see," said Gloria. "In that case, Dr. Stanley, effective tomorrow, we'll start your first dance lesson. Although this might be your first training session with us, I thoroughly believe that as long as you can properly learn how to dance and successfully execute a dance step on your own, then everything else, is secondary, and will be far easier for you to learn and overcome."

Dancing, with one's two feet and whole body, was something that Kate never, ever, imagined herself doing in her life. Never. Not once. Not even in her wildest of dreams, or fantasies. But now, this was happening, and Kate needed to go along with it. Really, what other choice did she have? None, at all. Ever since they were children, Jennifer caught the dancing bug at an early age; whereas, Kate simply didn't. But now, the tables had turned, and Kate needed to step-up to meet the task. In the end, one way or another, Dr. Kate Stanley from New York was going to have to learn how to dance.

"Alright, if I must do this, then shouldn't we start earlier, rather than tomorrow? I have absolutely and I do mean, absolutely no experience with dancing. None, at all. I'm afraid that two weeks is simply not enough," Kate admitted.

"Ah, I'm very glad that you mentioned this," replied Gloria, "But, Dr. Stanley, I'm already one step ahead of you."

Reaching into her purse, Gloria pulled out a thick and heavy encyclopedia. To Kate's astonishment, Gloria placed the encyclopedia right next to her, on the table.

"Dr. Stanley, this is for you. Consider this as today's homework," Gloria directed.

"Homework? You mean, you actually want me to read this entire encyclopedia, from beginning to end?" asked Kate, who was surprised by this particular request.

"No, I don't want you to read it. You're a history professor, Dr. Stanley, I'm sure you've read this already or at the very least, something close to it. No, what I want you to do is to practice your walking, while at the same time, balancing this book above your head."

"What?!!!" exclaimed Kate, who nearly fell from out of her chair. "But why in the world, would you have me do this? What's there to accomplish, by having me do this?"

"Why, to practice your balance and posture," replied Gloria. "Besides, if you're to dance, then you need to develop good posture and become more balanced. And, as it currently stands, you're lacking these essential qualities."

"I am?" asked Kate, with a frown.

"Yes," replied Gloria and Bes, simultaneously.

"Therefore, because of this matter that I've now brought to your attention, you've got from now, until tomorrow morning to master your walk, posture and balance. So, Dr. Stanley, please do make use of that encyclopedia. If you can master this by tomorrow, then you'll be ready for your first dance lesson. Now, if there's no further questions, this meeting is adjourned," Gloria announced.

With the clap of her hands, Gloria concluded the meeting. Once everyone dispersed, Kate found herself alone in the room. Laying right across from her, was the dreaded encyclopedia. Much to her dismay, Gloria left it right there for her, located above the table. Not wanting to further challenge or protest Gloria's instructions, Kate reluctantly gave it and picked up the book, as she walked away.

For the next hour or so, Kate practiced walking up and down the hallway, as she attempted to simultaneously balance the heavy book above her head. Although the encyclopedia fell down several times onto the marbled floor, making a loud thumping sound in the process; Kate, nevertheless, retrieved the book each time, from up the floor, and continued to practice, once more.

When the second hour eventually came, Kate began to grow tired. She was almost ready to call it quits and retire back into her bedroom, when she suddenly noticed a light emit from down the hallway. Curious, as to who was there, Kate decided to follow the light. As Kate slowly walked further down the hallway, she soon discovered that the light was coming from inside one of the offices.

Walking closer to the room, she saw that the door was slightly cracked open. Her curiosity got the better of her, and she boldly decided, right there and then, to peek inside and to take a look. As she approached the door, she saw the ambassador, seated at his desk. With his head bent down, he appeared to be reading some sort of a document or book.

For a brief split second, Kate almost contemplated turning around and walking away; however, her conscience got the better hold of her. Running away wasn't going to solve any of her problems. Having made such a poor impression on him the night before, Kate knew that she needed to remedy the situation. Casting away their differences, she was going to try her best to make it right with him. If not for her or him, then at the very least, for Jennifer's sake.

Taking a deep breath, Kate knocked on his door and asked, "May I come in?"

John, who was deep in concentration, was surprised to hear someone at his door. No one ever came before. This was certainly, a first.

"Yes, you may come in," he said, curious and intrigued, as to who was there.

Suddenly, she walked into the room, standing brave and tall, while holding a large book, safely tucked away carefully, within her arms. Instantly, John was memorized by her appearance. For a moment, he simply stared at her with admiration, from across the room. Elegantly dressed, wearing a modest white dress with embroidered lace, she looked innocent and pure. Although she might have shared the same face as Jennifer's, her aura and spirit were uniquely her own. Even though John couldn't quite articulate and explain this observation, he could just simply feel and sense it, from within. And for some reason, her arrival brought an unexpected new sense of peace and serenity— an emotion, that was foreign to him.

"I hope you don't mind me coming here, unannounced," said Kate, politely.

Rising up from his chair, John promptly welcomed her in and gestured for her take a seat on the brown leather vacant chair, positioned directly across from him.

"Won't you please take a seat…" he began; however, midway into his sentence, it suddenly occurred to him, that he was unaware, as to how to properly address her. Should he call her by her formal given name and title, Dr. Stanley? Or, was it more appropriate to address her, using her new alias, Mrs. Barrett?

Sensing his hesitation, Kate interrupted and to his relief, she said, "You may call me Kate, Ambassador."

"Kate," he repeated, saying her name aloud for the first time in her company, and with an unexpected smile.

"Ambassador," she began, using in a serious tone, "I do realize, that we've, unfortunately, got off to a rather bad start last night; however, in light of this, I'd like to first begin by apologizing—"

"Please, don't apologize," he interrupted her. "I'm the guilty one. It is I, who owes you, an apology."

"You do?" asked Kate, as her eyes widened, due to her surprise by his honest admission.

She didn't expect this, at all. He was the last person in the mansion, whom she ever thought, who would voluntarily and freely admit their mistake openly, without fear, nor hesitation. But most surprising of all, apart from his own recognition of his error in behavior, was that he actually apologized for it, too. Let alone, to her.

Clearing his throat, he admitted, "Last night, I was most unwelcoming and cruel to you, and that was unbecoming of myself. You're a guest in my home and I, along with everyone else here, are especially grateful to you. Without your participation in all of this, we'd be in a complete mess. You're the candlelight to an otherwise, dark room. Please accept my sincerest apologies."

"Oh," replied Kate, who was completely caught off guard by his sincere apology.

"Why, yes, I gladly accept your apology," she added, "Thank you for saying all of this, too."

"Great, now, since that's settled," remarked John, after much relief. He continued, "May I call truce? Shall we now shake hands, as new friends and partners?"

"Yes, of course," she replied, as she graciously extended her hands over to his.

Following her lead, he did the same. Within seconds, they locked hands with one another. Together, their new friendship and alliance were sealed and bounded, through the simple gesture of a handshake. However, perhaps, simple wasn't such an accurate description; for when her soft and delicate fingers interlocked with his rough and muscular hands for the first time, John suddenly, yet unexpectedly, felt a jolt of electricity ignite, along the lower tips of his fingers. But before he could truly comprehend this new sensation, which felt strange and peculiar, she quickly pulled her hand away from his.

"Then, we are friends?" asked Kate, sincerely, as she stared at him, with caring eyes.

"Yes, I believe we are," replied John, still feeling the lingering sensation of that unexpected electricity, running through his fingers.

Closing his hand, he took a deep breath, then he added, "And I think that, perhaps, friendship is a good starting point for us, as we'll be working closely together, from here on out."

"I do, agree," replied Kate.

Recalling Lucas's warning earlier about not making friends with anyone at the mansion, Kate briefly contemplated, as to whether or not she could trust him. But, as she looked at him from across his desk, he seemed so incredibly sincere. For the first time, Kate gazed upon his face and noticed, that his eyes were a soft shade of blue. As she stared deeper into his eyes, somehow, she just knew and felt that the ambassador was an exception to this rule.

"So, if we're friends, can we trust one another?" she asked, feeling hesitant to hear his answer to her question.

Although initially surprised by her unorthodox question, given his past behavior the night before, John also understood and sympathized with her uneasiness.

"As new friends, I dare say that we're just going to have to take the leap and trust one another, if we're going to succeed here," he said, attempting to reassure her.

"Even though I, myself, don't yet know you," he continued, "I'm still willing to take a gamble and trust you. I might be a stranger to you, and you, in return, a stranger to me; but either way, I'm still willing to blindly place my faith in you. I hope that you're willing to do the same, with me. Are you up for the challenge?"

His words were convincing and proved to be successful, for Kate instantly approved and smiled. Her previously doubts and fears about him, were safely put to rest. But to his own surprise, as he watched her smile at him, he strangely felt this odd and strange sensation, growing from deep within his belly, that felt similar to butterflies, fluttering about, inside of him. Was he nervous? Or, was this joy? After living in solitude for far too long, he no longer knew the difference. Perhaps, a new friend is what he needed, all along. A companion to his own and lonely existence.

"Ambassador, I accept your challenge. Shall we shake once more, to seal the deal?" she asked, happily.

"As you wish," he replied, touched by her sense of enthusiasm.

Extending their hands over to one another, they again, locked hands and shook, once more, to seal their deal. And for a second time in a row, John once again, felt that same spark of electricity, ignite from the tips of his fingers. However, unlike before, this time, the electricity force expanded, spreading all the way up to the inner corner of his wrist. But, before he could truly understand what had just happened, she, once more, pulled away from him; leaving his hand empty and alone.

Gazing below at his hands, John pondered as to what might have served as the root cause for such an unexplainable spark of electricity. However, his thoughts were soon interrupted by her inquiry.

"What's this?" she asked, with her attention, now fully engaged upon the portrait hanging in his office.

Following her gaze, John watched, as Kate, using her index finger, pointed at his portrait of the planet, Earth.

"It's Earth, taken above from space. It just happens to be one of my favorite paintings," he replied, while at the same time, clasping his hand into a fist, attempting to capture the electricity she left behind, which he could still feel lingering about within his palm.

"What a lovely portrait. The colors are so vivid and it looks so incredibly real," she observed, never once, looking away, nor leaving her attention from the portrait.

"Believe it or not, it was gifted to me by an Islamic scholar," he added, as he opened his hand back again, and releasing the electrical energy back into the air.

"Really? I would never have guessed," she said, surprised by such a revelation.

"There's also a story behind this painting, too. Do you care to hear the tale?" he asked, as he sat back down in his chair.

Seeing him seated, Kate decided to join him. Having returned to her seat, she replied, "I would love to hear your story."

John unexpectedly smiled. No one else had ever commented nor questioned him about this particular painting. But, alas, after all these years, for the first time since he acquired this portrait, he finally had an audience to tell this tale to. Luckily for him, his audience of one, was most curious and eagerly waiting.

"This is the story of Adam and Havva; or as better known in the western world, as Adam and Eve, as told by Turkish religious scholars, with roots, stemming from Islamic history and tradition," he began.

"Once upon a time," he continued, "There was a blue planet, known as Earth, that was in great need of a caretaker. And so, God created

Adam, molded and sculpted from clay. For forty years, Adam remained lifeless; existing only as a silent inanimate object. But, then one day, God decided to breathe life into him; thereupon, appointing him to the vacant position as Earth's official caretaker. For centuries, Adam served God and carried out his important role, always remaining steadfast, patient and meticulous, with all of his various duties. Never once, did Adam fall short with his successful execution. Indeed, Adam was a very busy man and with each passing day, his responsibilities grew progressively more and more. But with great responsibilities, also came the rewards to his labor. As the planet's sole caretaker, Adam was blessed with the unlimited access to Earth's resources, in exchange for his loyalty and services. With an eternal supply of food, water, shelter, land, plants, fauna and animals, he also maintained ownership over the planet's gold, silver, minerals, emeralds, rubies, sapphires, diamonds and everything else, under Earth's domain. But yet, with all of these rewards, Adam still felt unsatisfied. While he was grateful to God for granting him all of these blessings; Adam, the man, and not the caretaker, also felt incomplete. Somehow, he sensed that although he was so incredibly fortunate; at the same time, there was also a dearth of humanly affection and companionship, absent from his own existence. After frequently watching and observing the Earthly animals frolic together in pairs, Adam soon became aware that his own life was also lacking a similar ally, to call his own. A partner. A mate. A friend. And so, at the end of each passing day, as the sun set and the moon rose up into the sky, it signaled the end of his shift and the start of his retirement for the evening. But with each passing night, Adam grew more lonelier, than ever before. Although Adam might have been the King of Earth, with the entire world and all of its glory solely within his transgression and possession; he was also, at the same time, Earth's loneliest man. But God, the creator, was not ignorant of his creation's internal struggles. As a compassionate God, God was well aware that his caretaker needed motivation, in order to continue on with his job. And so, God created a woman; a mate, for Adam, as a reward for his services and a promise, that never again, would he be alone. And alas, when Adam first saw the woman, his heart almost stopped beating altogether and suddenly, he gasped for air; for she was the most stunning and beautiful creature that his eyes had ever laid upon, before. Shining and glimmering before him, her hair was long and golden, like the sun. Her skin as white as snow. Her eyes green like the plants and fauna.

Her lips as red as the pomegranate fruit, which grew on the trees throughout the land. She was the essence of Earth's beauty, all wrapped up into one singular being. And as Adam gasped for air, he soon realized that she was the missing life source to his being and with this knowledge, also came the understanding that never again, would he be lonely. Feeling tremendously joyful and happy, Adam's heart was now complete. And so, Adam named the woman Havva, which means air; for she was the direct source to the very air, in which he breathed, from that moment onwards. And without air, one cannot live and survive on Earth."

Having spoken directly from his own heart, Kate was incredibly moved by his tale. As she attentively listened on, Kate was thoroughly impressed by his detailed account, as well as his passion for storytelling. Pulling from the parallels between his protagonist and himself, Kate silently understood as to why he had chosen to hang this particular painting in his office. She concluded that the ambassador, for all his worth, was, like Adam, in great need of a friend. Having blindly accepted his friendship for her sister's sake, Kate was now, glad that she had done so. Maybe, Lucas was wrong and that, not everyone here wanted to be an enemy. Perhaps, the ambassador was actually, in a greater need of a true friend and companion, rather than that of another enemy. For Kate believed, wholeheartedly, that kindness and compassion were far more desirable traits, than that, in comparison to lies and scheming. That in the end, good shall always triumph over evil.

"Your story, it's quite remarkably beautiful. And I dear say, I'm glad that we, too, are friends, ambassador," she said, at last.

John simply smiled. It was refreshing to have someone else actually interested in these matters, apart from just himself.

"This painting was the first gift that I received, when I initially arrived here, to Türkiye," he continued, "I like to keep it in my office, as a constant reminder to myself, that with great power, also comes great responsibility."

"In a way, I think you're rather much like Adam," Kate admitted, "You certainly seem to have many responsibilities here."

"In some ways, yes," he agreed. "But at the same time, whenever I feel overwhelmed or disappointed, with whatever obstacle that I might face, I simply glance back at this portrait, and somehow, it just motivates me. I suppose that, whenever I stare at it, I'm reminded that I, too, am just one man, living on a single planet, part of a universe, that's far greater, than I. And if God can help Adam, then I have faith that he can also help me, too."

Kate smiled at him, and her smile brought an unexpected peace to his heart. Strangely enough, he didn't yet understand, just as to why this was. Having met her only the night before, she already brought him great comfort. Suddenly, she accidentally brushed a lose strand of her hair across her face, with her finger, and to John's surprise, he once again, caught sight of the shine and sparkle from the pearl ring, which still wore around her finger.

"By the way, that's a beautiful ring," he said, as he looked directly into her eyes.

"Oh, yes, thank you," she replied, hesitantly. Recalling his odd reaction to the ring the night before, Kate realized this matter still remained the white elephant, in the room.

"It must be very special to you, as you wore it last night, as well," he said, while fishing for more information.

"It is. I never take it off. It is with me, always," she revealed.

"Do you mind me asking, as to why that is? Was it a gift?" he inquired.

"Yes. It was gifted to me years ago, by my sister," she admitted. "Actually, it was a graduation gift to commemorate my acceptance into my doctorate program. I guess you can say, that the ring reminds me of my twin. But apart from that, it's not the only reason as to why I choose to wear it. Honestly, I just love it for what it is. It's so rare and unique; it's truly one of a kind. And, I've never seen anything quite like it, before. Although I know that there are a million other finely shaped pearls out there in the world; but this particular one, is the only one that's so uniquely obscure and oddly formed, that the flaw, itself, is what makes it so incredibly beautiful and precious. I also find that the supporting blue stones, around it, just adds another layer of mystery to it as well, which is why I love it so much. It simply reminds me of the night sky: the pearl is the moon, and the blue stones are the stars. And truth be told, whenever I look at this ring, it makes me believe that even on the darkest of nights, there's always light. And where there is light, there is hope."

Her words touched his soul. Never before, had anyone ever describe the pearl to him, like she just did. Not even, Aasha. Kate, was the first person whom he had met, who saw the pearl for what it truly was and meant to be seen. How was it that this woman, from halfway around the world, whom he had only just met, understood the pearl better than most? Let alone, anyone from his immediate acquaintances.

"You know," he began, "A long time ago, I once saw a pearl just like yours."

"Really?" replied an astonished Kate, who was surprised that such a pearl, other than her own, even existed.

"Yes," confirmed John, affirmatively, "It was in India. A friend of mine had a pearl, exactly as yours."

"India? I simply had no idea that another pair even existed, especially from so far away. How did your friend come into possession of it?" she inquired, most curiously.

"It was a gift," he said, with a smile.

"Just like mine?" she innocently asked.

"Yes, exactly as yours. The same silhouette, bents, dips and flawed shape. It's baroque, you know," he added.

"Baroque? As in baroque style art?" she asked, most intrigued.

"Precisely. The pearl is baroque in style. From the Portuguese word, barroco, meaning flawed pearl. And, do you know, as to why the early Europeans decided to borrow the word, barroco, to name an entire art movement, in its honor?"

"I'll admit, even as a history professor, I'm not as familiar, with this time period in art history. But, please do enlighten me," she encouraged him.

"Ironically, it was due to a pearl, just like yours. The obscurity and peculiarity are what makes the pearl, so incredibly special and attractive to the naked eye. Seventeenth century early European artists were the first to recognize and acknowledge this concept, within their profession. They understood that in life, true beauty often arises from the irregularity and complexity in objects; which they themselves, in return, sought to transfer that very same philosophy into their art and craft; eventually, leading the way towards a revolutionary movement in art, within its own right. In the end, sometimes, what we presume to be ugly to one person, is actually, a treasure to another. It's just a matter of who's looking at the art, and who appreciates it, the most."

"Wow, that's so true," agreed Kate, now, staring down and admiring her own ring. "Beauty truly is in the eyes of the beholder."

"I couldn't agree anymore," said John, "And as for my friend's pearl, well, she always believed that the pearl chooses its owner, in order to bless them. A bit of ancient folklore, I know; but I, myself, do occasionally believe in a bit of magic, from time to time. The world is just so mysterious filled with wonder and enchantment."

"I agree. I too, believe in that sort of thing, sometimes. Even my own grandmother used to perform tasseography. But a blessing? That's a new perspective. Never thought of it like that, before. Now, I wonder, do you think that the same can also be said, with regards to my pearl ring, too?" she asked.

"Oh, I have no doubt, that your pearl is an identical pair to the one I saw back in India. Kate, that pearl ring is your lucky charm. I recommend keeping it nearby, always," he encouraged.

"I had no idea about this story. Thank you for sharing it with me," she graciously said, as she stared at him, with her eyes beaming with joy.

Catching sight of her happy emotion, John couldn't help but join her with a smile.

"Well, we're friends, after all, aren't we?" he asked, with a raised brow.

"Of course, we are," she replied.

"Well, then, friends share these sorts of stories amongst one another," he concluded.

"I suppose you're right," she agreed. A moment later, she caught sight of the stack of books laying on top of his desk. Curious, she asked, "Are you reading, all of these?"

Looking down at his desk, John saw that he did, in fact, have a large stack of books there; ranging from Niccolo Machiavelli's *The Prince* to *The Essays of Michel de Montaigne* by Michel de Montaigne.

"Yes, I am," he revealed, "I'm doing some research for an upcoming project that I'm currently working on. If you're interested, we do have a library here at the estate. You're more than welcome to use it, anytime."

"Really? I can?" she asked, excited by the prospect.

"If you prefer, I can take you there myself. I'll even give you, a personal tour," he offered.

"That would be lovely," she admitted. However, Kate realized that time wasn't on her side. For as much as she desired to visit the library, much to her dismay, she still had Gloria's assignment to work on.

"But, I'm afraid," she added, "That I might have to temporarily postpone our library tour, as I've got some homework to do."

"Homework?" he asked, most surprised by her admission.

"Yes, it's a request by Gloria," she further clarified.

"Ah," he said, as he finally understood. "Well, if it's coming from Gloria, then it must be important," he added, jokingly.

"Yes, I think it is," she said, as she sighed. "I suppose," she added, "I might as well be on my way now…"

"Wait, Kate, just a second," he interrupted.

"Yes?" she asked.

"As to your assignment, it wouldn't happen to involve practicing on balancing that heavy encyclopedia, would it?" he asked, with concern.

Kate's mouth dropped open. How did he know? Of course, he was right! Lost for words, she simply nodded in agreement, while, he, in returned, released a small chuckle of laughter.

"In that case, let's trade books," he proposed, as he quickly grabbed a copy of Machiavelli's *The Prince*, which happened, to be a rather thin and light-weight book, that was written with less than seventy pages, or so.

"Here, you take this one, and I'll take your encyclopedia. And don't worry, I'll return your heavy book back into the library later, and Gloria will never know. It'll be our secret," he promised, as he smiled and gave her a wink.

Naturally, Kate happily accepted the trade off, and she thanked him for his thoughtfulness and help in the matter. Having been rescued from this dreaded task, Kate got up from her seat and joyfully grabbed her new book with her hands. She was about to exit the room, but before she did, she turned around and told him, "Ambassador, I'm glad that we decided to be friends. Although I do realize that our circumstances are a bit complicated, I still hope that we can work together to find my sister."

"I hope so too, Kate. And I'm equally glad, as well. Also, please, call me John. It's only appropriate, since I do refer to you by your first name, after all."

"Very well, thank you," she said.

And then, following his permission, she slowly attempted to utter his name aloud. With his name emphasized at the tip of her tongue, she softly spoke "John," as her mouth and tongue grew accustomed to the sound of his mere name, spoken directly from her own lips. After saying her farewell, she gave him one last smile, before exiting his office completely and went about, on her own merry way down the hall.

After she left, John, now, alone again, in his office and back to his solitude, remained smiling. Her cheerful disposition, left him in a generally good mood. Having heard her refer to his given name, for the first time, he couldn't help but smile. For whatever reason, hearing her say his name aloud, and not his formal title, made him feel tremendously happy. And just why was that? He, himself, could not comprehend, as to why that was, precisely. But even more surprising, was that her unexpected and unplanned visit went so incredibly well, and to his further amazement, he rather enjoyed her company. Although Kate might have physically resembled Jennifer, but as he was coming to discover, firsthand, they were two entirely different people, with Kate having her own separate, yet unique personality, disposition and temperament. But even more intriguing to John, was just how refreshing those traits and qualities were, and just how curious, he now felt about learning more about her.

Years ago, John once read, from within *The Essays of Michel de Montaigne* by Michel de Montaigne, that the best of marriages blossoms out of friendship. It was one of the primary reasons as to why, he always remained optimistic, that he and Jennifer could, at the very least, become friends one day; but unfortunately, that never happened. Yet, he always remained hopeful, that their circumstances would, eventually change. But now, with Kate, he had a second chance. Although she might have just been his interim wife at the moment, having a good friend, even in the form of a pretend wife, was something still worth having. And for John, a man, who often spent his evenings alone at his office and in complete solitude, having someone to share his company with, a companion and an ally, even on a temporary basis, was something he knew that he was going to cherish and look forward to, from here on out.

Glancing over towards the front entrance to his office, John stared at the large crystal glass vase, located right next to his door. Suddenly, John laughed to himself. Had Jennifer, instead, visited him here today at his office, then that crystal glass vase would cease to exist. Why, he guaranteed that she would have used it as a weapon against him, and that she would have thrown it directly at him! He could even go so far, as to image, that broken vase, shattering into a thousand pieces onto the floor, with John sustaining some sort of injury, along the way. But with Kate, that vase remained untouched and intact. Having met her, he was now certain that, even with the passage of time, that same vase was going to still remain as a decorative object, within his office. John already calculated that Kate wasn't the sort of person to ever destroy such things, period. She, like him, was an admirer of art. But more than that, John could sense that she was kind and compassionate. She was already a blessing in more ways than one, and he himself, was the first to secretly acknowledge and appreciate this fact already, even if she, herself, remained unaware and ignorant on her part.

Chapter 17

"One, two, three and one, two, three," said Gloria, as she tapped her foot against the hard wood floor, with her heels.

"Back straight, chin up and arms wide," she added.

"And don't forget to smile," said Bes, who was now holding Kate, within an embrace.

"Are all these steps even necessary?" asked Kate, whose feet were still adjusting from wearing her standard flat shoes to now, sporting rather uncomfortably high heels.

"Dr. Stanley, mastering the box steps are crucial, as they are part of the fundamental foundation to the waltz. Without properly practicing it firsthand, then you will never be able to execute it, correctly. And may I add, if you are the succeed here, then it's imperative that you do," replied Gloria, firmly.

"Gloria, I do understand; but at the same time, if I have to do just one more twirl, then I don't think that my feet will ever be able to recover. Is there any way that I can at least practice wearing my flats?" asked a hopeful Kate.

"Absolutely not!" exclaimed Gloria. "Dr. Stanley, you need to start getting accustomed to wearing proper dancing shoes. A lady, especially a dancer, must always wear heels. Flats are simply out of the question."

Kate frowned. The prospect of permanently wearing high heels was an adjustment that she wasn't looking forward to, not in the very least. Furthermore, at that precise moment, her feet were already in so much exertional pain.

"Cheer up, Dr. Stanley," said Bes, who was still standing nearby to Kate, on the dancefloor. "Your new shoes will help to shape and improve your posture. Besides, your new pair of golden heels looks so lovely."

"I suppose," remarked Kate, still unconvinced about the value of her new pair of shoes.

Suddenly, Bes reached into his pocket and pulled out his handkerchief. Slowly and carefully, he began cleaning and wiping the streams of sweat, that were flowing down his face.

"Bes," began Kate, "I hope you don't take any offense by my inquiring this, but is there a specific reason as to why you seem to…err…"

"Sweat so much?" replied Bes, who took the liberty to say what Kate had thought, but was too shy to actually articulate.

"Yes, that's it. Again, I apologize in advance for suggesting this, but perhaps, this is a medical issue and…"

Bes simply laughed. And hard. He laughed until tears ran down his face, and his large belly began to shake from his own giggles.

"No, Dr. Stanley, it's not a medical condition. It's just my nerves. If you've had as many surprise audits as I have over the years, then you'd understand why I'm always so anxious and sweating."

"You sweat because of audits?" asked Kate, most curious about his reasoning.

"Constant surprise audits. I'll be the first to admit, I'm just not very good with unknown anticipation; and because of this, my fear of another surprise audit, often puts me over the edge and this results in my excess sweating. It's also ironic too, because I'm a classically trained Flamenco dancer, and dancers really shouldn't be sweating or perspiring, this much."

"Bes, I'm so sorry to hear this. Perhaps, there's some form of meditation that you can do, to help reduce your stress?" asked Kate.

"What Bes needs is a glass of water," interrupted Gloria, who was still in the room.

However, before Gloria could say anymore, there was a knock at the door and Sally swiftly entered the room.

"I'm sorry to interrupt the dance lesson, but the photographer has just arrived. Dr. Stanley is needed in the garden for her scheduled photo shoot with the ambassador," Sally announced.

"Is this photo shoot for the upcoming state dinner invitations?" asked Bes.

"Yes, it's for both the private invitations and the press release," replied Sally.

"Very well," huffed Gloria, "In that case, this concludes today's dance lesson. But, as a reminder, Dr. Stanley, please do continue to practice your box steps."

And just like that, Kate quickly exited the room with Sally. Now barefoot, Kate was practically hopping in the direction of the rose garden, dragging her swollen feet, still sore from her recent dancing lessons, behind her. Once she finally arrived to the rose garden, Sally quickly seated Kate down onto a white bench, underneath a willow tree. Since the photographer was still busy setting up his equipment, Sally left Kate behind to help assist the photographer and his staff with the set.

Meanwhile, as Kate sat down on the bench, she stretched her bare feet across the green mossy grass and began flexing her toes and heels back and forth, against the grass to help relieve the tension that she felt on her sore feet. Today's dancing lessons certainly took a toll on her, and the moist grass helped to serve as an unexpected comfort. As she rubbed her feet against the soft and moist grass, a gust of wind suddenly blew across her face, moving her lose strands of hair, along the edges her face. Wanting to set aside a private moment for herself, she closed her eyes and took a deep breath. With her eyes still closed, she listened to the birds humming above the sky, while she felt the sun shining across her face. When she finally opened her eyes, she immediately saw that directly across from her in the garden, was John, approaching her from afar. Dressed in a crisp white shirt, with black trousers, he was carrying his black blazer within his hands. It was the first time that she had ever seen him outside of the mansion and inside the garden. As he glided across the field, his black hair sparkled against the beaming sunlight and even Kate, had to privately acknowledge to herself, that he looked incredibly handsome. Then, unexpectedly, at that very moment, Kate's heart once again, skipped a beat.

What was this new, strange and foreign feeling tugging against her heart? Her heart never before behaved in this manner, so why was it acting like this now? Kate couldn't comprehend, nor rationalize as to why exactly this was. But she certainly felt something and whatever it was, it was entirely brand new and unexpected. Attempting to calm her nerves, Kate quickly placed her hand across her chest. However, this gesture failed, for her nerves continued to flicker. As John proceeded to approach her, the closer he came towards her, her heart started to beat faster and faster, and then suddenly, she felt warm and flushed. Her palms unexpectedly began to tingle. To help aid her uncalming nerves, she decided to cast her gaze down onto the floor, secretly hoping and praying that the greenery would relieve her tense nerves. But sadly, this too did not help. Rather, she soon began to feel butterflies stirring and floating about within her stomach and then, suddenly, at last, she heard a male voice address her by her given name.

"Kate, how are you today, my friend?" he asked her.

Lifting up her head up, Kate saw John right before her. Standing straight and tall, Kate noticed as to just how broad his shoulders were. Upon further inspection, she also observed that his chest was muscular and fit, and traces of his abs could be seen through the thin and sheer white fabric of his shirt. Such view, made Kate feel more nervous and anxious.

"I'm…I'm…just a bit tired…" she began to stutter, out of shyness.

"From the training?" asked John, with a raised brow.

"Yes, from the training," replied Kate, whose nerves, finally started to slowly level down, the longer she remained within his company. Feeling a bit more confident, she added, "Today's dance lessons were a bit intense. However, I must find a way to pace myself, for I fear that it will only get more complicated, with each passing day that I'm here."

"But it will get easier, that I do promise," said a concerned John.

With his gaze slowly moving from the direction of Kate's face to her below, John saw, most unexpectedly, two very exposed and bare feet, toes and all. Surprised by such an unexpected sight, he smiled and let out a small giggle.

Realizing that he had been giggling at her feet, Kate said, "I've never bothered before to wear such high heel shoes, that today was a first for me. And truth be told, dancing in such high heels for the first time, really proved to be a true challenge for my uncustomed feet."

"Wait, you've never worn high heels, before?" asked John, surprised by her admission.

Recalling as to just how much Jennifer prided herself with her vast collection of heels, John was astonished as to how much her twin sister had little regard, if any, for them. She was certainly the opposite of her sister. In fact, John, even on his first day on the job, had to practically bribe Jennifer with new pairs of Christian Louboutin shoes, in order to convince her to accompany him to the Cairo embassy. Yet, her twin sister never once wore them. In fact, she maintained a great dislike for them. This was certainly hard to image. How different they truly were.

"I've always gotten around wearing just flats. As a university professor, it's just more practical to wear flats, especially when walking around campus and giving lectures on stage, at the podium," she admitted.

"I do understand, but I still find this quite surprising, since your sister wore them regularly. In fact, I don't seem to recall ever a time, when I didn't see her wear anything else," reflected John.

"I know," sighed Kate, "We may be twins, but we are so very different."

"Yes, you are," quickly replied John. He then added, "But that isn't a bad thing, Kate."

"But isn't though?" asked Kate, in return. "If I am supposed to pose as her," she continued, "Then wouldn't it have been much easier, if I was more like her?"

"Kate, you just need to learn how to act the part, that's all. In one way or another, all of us, including myself, are pretending to be, or act as something apart from who we really are or feel. It's called politics," said John, who was now speaking in a more serious tone.

"But don't you find it a bit difficult to do, each day in and day out?" asked Kate.

John simply shrugged.

"It's how our world operates. It's what being a diplomat is all about. Convincing people and allies to believe in something, in order to accomplish a private goal for the greater good," he said. However, seeing the disappointment in her face, he added, "But over time, it does get easier and I know that eventually, it will for you, too."

"I don't think that it will ever get easier for me," Kate reflected, "However, easy or difficult, I'm still determined to do it for Jennifer. I just hope that…"

"What do you hope, Kate?" asked John, most attentive, with his blues eyes never once leaving her face.

As he stared deep into her eyes, Kate noticed that his own eyes were so strikingly bold and transparent that they resembled that of a clear blue lake. At that moment, she could simply feel the power of his gaze, piercing down upon herself and for a third time since their meeting, her heart skipped another beat, yet again. However, unlike the first time, it felt much different. This time, she felt a spark light up deep within her chest, which quickly penetrated across her entire body. Just what was this new feeling growing inside of her? Out of nervousness, Kate turned and looked away from John.

"I just hope that by pretending to be her, I also don't forget who I am too, along the way," she finally admitted, with John still standing behind her.

Her sincere words struck John's conscience hard. They were entirely unexpected and caught him off guard. Had John, himself, been pretending to be someone that he wasn't, for far too long? Had he, himself, lost his true self, along the way? Over the years, while he might have easily and routinely carried on with his charade with Jennifer, he had inadvertently gotten so accustomed to projecting the image of what others had wanted him to be, that he had scarcely remembered as to who he really was, behind the iron curtain. But if he stripped away all of these factors, including his own career and the embassy, then what exactly did John Barrett, the man, truly want for himself? Who was he, when he wasn't associated with this political arena? But, however, before John could even think and ponder any further, Sally soon appeared before them.

"Ambassador Barrett and Dr. Stanley," interrupted Sally, "The photographer is now ready. Please follow me and come this way."

Following Sally's lead, John and Kate were escorted over to the photography station, where they were met by both their assigned stylists and photographer. Since today's photographs were going to be released to the public, John and Kate were provided with their own personal trailers to prepare for a change of wardrobe, hair and makeup.

A few minutes later, John and Kate exited their trailers and returned back on set, as they waited for their photographer to help instruct them with their official pose. For years, John was accustomed to taking these annual photographs with Jennifer, but under entirely different circumstances. Normally, in the past, he would have silently stood, alongside Jennifer, in dead silence, with her giving him the cold shoulder in the process. To avoid her hostility, John generally arrived on set much later than scheduled. Often times, he arrived right on cue, just as Jennifer was well settled into her pose. Ultimately, John sought has much minimal contact as he possibly could with his estranged wife. Meanwhile, as they both displayed their smiles on camera with forced expressions, he counted the very seconds until the photographer gave them the signal that they were finally done; and boy, what a guaranteed relief it always was!

But today, it was entirely different. Unlike before, he actually arrived much earlier to the set than he previously did. In fact, if truth be spoken, it was the first time that he had arrived early to any photography shoot ever, period. And this time, he actually met with his partner, Kate, out in the garden and personally walked and escorted her to the set, together. This was a first for him, for he had never engaged with Jennifer in this same manner before. John was genuinely growing found of Kate, and he, himself, privately acknowledged that he thoroughly enjoyed her company. Kate, he thought, was sweet and sincere. She was the most unexpected surprise, who had literally tumbled straight into his life. And while he was going to be working, along by her side for the unforeseeable future, or at the very least, for the next few weeks, he already felt confident that his time with her was going to be well spent. For Kate, as he believed, was a breath of fresh air and her innocent gestures, such as her simple stroll across the garden with her bare feet, provided a form of comic relief to his life, that was otherwise, very serious and a bit too humorless.

Upon seeing Kate on set, he was in awe as to just how lovely she looked. Wearing a lavender colored silk slip on dress, her blonde hair pulled up into a bun and her makeup was very light and simple, yet classy. Overall, she was dressed very elegantly and resembled that of a true lady. For a long silent moment, John just stared at her. He observed as she gracefully walked onto the set, smiling and greeting all the staff, along the way. She was cheerful, friendly and glided with the utmost class and sophistication. As he watched her from afar, he studied the small strands of blonde hair that fell across her face. Suddenly, John began to feel a slight tingle develop, along the outer corner of his chest. Bewildered by such physical emotion, John quickly placed his hand across the source of this tingling sensation. What exactly was this new feeling? Having realized that his hand was lying directly across on his chest, he quickly grabbed hold of his hand. Was this his heart? Is this what liking and admiring someone felt like? He had never known.

"What do you think of my new shoes? Do you approve?" she asked, as she batted her eyelashes together.

Looking down at her feet, John saw that she was wearing a pair of lavender flats to match her new gown. As she lifted up her dress just slightly above her ankles to showcase to him her new shoes, he suddenly realized that she had purposely sought and chosen flats, in lieu of another pair of high heels. When he finally understood her motives for wearing her new shoes, he once again, let out a small laugh.

"Based upon your reaction, I assume that you must approve," said Kate, smilingly.

"Very clever, Kate," he quickly replied, "But I thought, that perhaps for this particular occasion, you might have at least opted for the fancier pair of shoes?"

"Well, the photographs will only capture the upper half of our bodies, and not our bottoms. Naturally, I figured that since my dress is long enough, no one else will know, nor notice my less than perfect, simple and flat pair of shoes."

"But I'll know," he said smilingly.

"That's because I already told you," she said, in return.

"Touché, Kate. Well then, it'll just have to be our own personal secret," he said teasingly. "But," he added, "What about me?"

"What about you?" she asked, with a raised brow.

"You get to wear comfortable shoes, while I, on the other hand, do not," he concluded.

"Your shoes are not comfortable? But you're a man! Your shoes are already flat!" she exclaimed.

"Ah, but there's a slight platform located on the heels of these pair of leather shoes," he said. He continued, "Why, wearing these shoes all day, every day, with an incline can be rather uncomfortable, too. Not to also mention, this tight belt that I wear across my waist each day, along with my suits, is rather of an annoyance as well. It seems that we all must make sacrifices in our own way, dear Kate."

"John, I had no idea," spoke Kate, with the utmost astonishment.

"Yes," he replied. He had of course, been teasing her, but she didn't quite comprehend that. He realized that she was so incredibly innocent, but he, nonetheless, was rather enjoying it.

"Yes, these are the sacrifices that I must make. Therefore, the next time you decide to wear your flats, think about what I said. Shall we walk over to the photographer now?" he said, while extending his arm towards her.

She, in return, agreed and together, they walked, hand in hand, over to the photographer.

When they finally approached the photographer, he instructed them to stand together underneath a white jasmine tree, which was located within the center of the garden. As they stood near one another, John quietly admired her. The whiteness of the jasmine flower brought out the soft and light purple hues from her lavender dress. Both the flower and Kate, as he noted, were elegant, sweet and pure. Although he stood only an arm's length away from her, and yet, even from this short distance, he could still smell her sweet fragrance and aroma. In fact, he was so incredibly close to her, that he could also sense her, and as it was, she appeared a bit tense. Catching sight of her trembling hands, rapidly twitching back and forth, he watched as her pale complexion grew pinker, with each passing minute. He realized that she was nervous.

"Don't be nervous," he gently whispered into her ear, hoping to calm her nerves.

Upon hearing his voice, Kate looked directly at John, and when her eyes locked into his, he immediately felt another spark light up deep within his chest. What exactly was happening to him?

"I'll be alright," she replied, calmly. "It's just that I don't do well with taking pictures, that's all. I'm just not that photogenic."

"You? Not photogenic? A pretty and elegant lady, such as yourself? I certainly find that hard to believe," he said, with all astonishment.

Kate simply smiled and let out a small laugh. And by her doing so, John, suddenly, once again, felt that spark light up within his chest. However, this time, it left a burning sensation.

"Alright," began the photographer, "I need the two of you to move closer to one another."

Following his instructions, John made the first move and took the liberty to move closer to Kate; while she, in return, soon followed after his lead. They continued to move closer with one another, until finally, they came into contact with one another directly, skin to skin and cheek to cheek.

"Perfect!" exclaimed the photographer. "Now, Mr. Barrett, please put your hands around Mrs. Barrett's waist."

John followed the photographer's request and proceeded to place his hands around Kate's waist. As his hands touched her fragile body for the very first time, he saw her flitch and then heard her take a small deep breath. Meanwhile, he, himself, took in a private second for himself to capture the moment, all the while, realizing that for whatever reason, having his hands around her waist felt so incredibly good and exciting. It was intoxicating.

"Wonderful," continued the photographer, "Now, Mrs. Barrett, move your head to face Mr. Barrett and then, look directly into his eyes."

Kate followed his directions and found herself staring right into John's eyes. To her surprise, she found his eyes to be kind, sincere and thoughtful. In that moment, she realized that not only was he handsome, but at the same time, he was also sweet and considerate. Furthermore, she knew, deep within her heart, that if she had to be standing here, at this exact and precise moment in time, posing in such intimate scenes with another male counterpart, then she couldn't imagine posing with anyone else, but John. She just didn't think it was possible, at all. Kate was naturally shy and conservative, and being so close to a man, any man, even in the form of a pose for an upcoming portrait, was so beyond her comfort zone. But somehow, John made her feel safe and secure. She knew that she was lucky to be here with him, and just him alone, and not with another.

"I seem to have run out of film, hold just a moment, while I gather a new roll," said the photographer. "In the meantime, try to look like you two are in love."

As the photographer stepped away, the couple just stood there, in silence, maintaining their pose and gazing into each other's eyes, never once, looking away. Kate could still feel his arms wrapped around her. But slowly, ever slowly, she could swear that his grip around her waist slightly tightened, one inch at a time, with each passing minute. The close proximately of John made her feel extra nervous, and so to break their silence, she decided to speak.

"What's your favorite color?" she asked, finally breaking the extended period of silence between them.

"I beg your pardon?" asked a surprised John, who appeared immerse within his thoughts.

"Your favorite color. What is it?" she asked again.

"Hmm…blue. It's blue. Why do you ask?" replied John, intrigued as to why she inquired.

"Then what you need is a pair of blue slippers," she revealed.

"A pair of blue slippers? But why?" he asked.

"To resolve your problem," she replied.

"To resolve what problem?" he asked, uncertain as to what matter she was referring to.

"Don't you recall telling me about your dilemma, relating to your uncomfortable work shoes? I mean, I certainly remember. I just thought that if you had a pair of your own comfy blue slippers, then you can secretly slip into them, back and forth, when no one's looking," she said, enthusiastically.

Surprised and astonished by her sweet and thoughtful suggestion, John unexpectedly smiled and let out a small laugh.

"Why are you laughing?" she asked, "I'm quite serious, you know."

"I know, that's why I'm laughing. It's rather cute of you to suggest it, too," he admitted.

"Cute? That wasn't my intention," she said, with a smile of her own.

"Perfect!" exclaimed the photographer, who had just returned with his new roll of film. "Don't move and whatever you, please don't stop smiling! You two look absolutely perfect and stunning in this embrace!"

For the next few minutes, John and Kate remained within their embrace. Once the photographer was finally done taking their pictures, he exclaimed, "Mr. and Mrs. Barrett, today's photo shoot will not disappoint! And if I'm being honest, I think these are going to be the best photographs that I've taken of the two of you, in years. In fact, these might be the best, ever!"

"Well, we have Mrs. Barrett to thank, of course. Out of the two of us, she's the photogenic one," said John, smiling and looking directly at Kate.

"Actually, you're right. She's very photogenic," agreed the photographer.

"I am?" asked Kate, surprised by their complement.

"Yes, you are," replied John, never once, leaving her gaze.

"Now," continued the photographer, "Let's get another photograph of you and Mrs. Barrett, but this time, in a kiss."

"A kiss!" exclaimed Kate. "Is a kiss even necessary? Aren't the previous photographs sufficient enough?"

John, not wanting to push Kate's boundaries and nerves any further for today, promptly came to her rescue.

"Unfortunately," he interrupted, "I have an important meeting to attend to right now; therefore, I'm inclined to agree with Mrs. Barrett, with regards to this particular matter. Our current photographs will just have to suffice."

He then added, while looking directly and straight into Kate's eyes, "The kiss," he emphasized, "Will have to wait for another time."

Having heard John's statement, Kate gulped. While she was relieved that she just narrowly escaped their kiss, she also knew that this was only for the time being. For some reason or another, she had the inclination that sooner or later, that kiss was eventually going to become a reality. Therefore, she predicted that the next time such a similar request or inquiry arose again, then she was most certainly, not going to be as so lucky enough, to escape his kiss for a second time around.

"Yes, Mr. Barrett, is quite correct," agreed Kate, "Now, if either of you don't mind, I, too, have another engagement of my own."

Within seconds, Kate immediately and swiftly dashed off, leaving John far behind her. As John remained standing there, he gently placed his hands across his lips. While he might have been the perfect gentleman by helping her to derail their kiss, he also had some regrets of his own. For had he truly been honest with himself, John, the man, and not the ambassador, had very much wanted to kiss her, even if it was staged. Whether it was real or pretend, permanent or temporary, it really didn't matter. For right there and then, all he wanted to do was kiss her. Just her. To taste and explore her lips, to feel her tongue against his. And the more he pondered about her, the more his desire and curiosity progressively grew. Alas, that unknown kiss, lingered across in the far corners of his mind, where it remained, within his constant thoughts.

Later That Afternoon...

"**D**r. Stanley, these are truly fabulous photographs of you and the ambassador, together!" exclaimed Carol.

"Yes, I concur. Today, was a success," agreed Tyler.

"Honestly, these are probably the best pictures that we've taken on record, for any of our previous press releases," added Sally.

"That's for certain," Carol remarked.

"However, did you manage to strike such a convincing pose? Have you modeled before?" asked Sally.

"Me a model?" asked Kate, surprised by her question. "No, I've certainly never modeled before. Why do you ask?"

"It's in your eyes and smile," Carol interrupted, "Your eyes are sparkling and your smile, it looks almost…what's the word…natural…organic…unforced."

"Natural, organic and unforced, nice choice of words Carol," interjected Tyler, sarcastically.

"You'll know what I mean," Carol rebutted, "Dr. Stanley, please don't take offense, but we're just not use to seeing this here. How did you manage to look so genuinely happy in these pictures?"

"Yes, how?" joined in Sally, who was most attentive.

"I'm not sure what you all mean. I was just being myself, that's all," answered Kate, in all honesty.

"Well, he looks happy here too," Tyler added, with a raised brow.

"Ah, you're right!" exclaimed Carol.

"That's also a first," said Sally.

Suddenly, Carol, Sally and Tyler, all looked directly at Kate's direction, with each of their expressions reflecting astonishment and utter amazement. Surprised by all of their unexpected attention, Kate quickly sought to thwart any further inquiry by drawing the conversation over to favorite photograph.

"I think we should go with this one," said Kate, as she handed her chosen photograph over to Sally.

"Good choice," agreed Sally.

"Ah, yes, this is a nice one," added Carol.

"Indeed," voiced Tyler.

"Great, so do you all agree, that I should go with this picture?" asked Kate.

"Yes," replied Carol, Tyler and Sally unanimously.

"Very well, I approve. Let's go with this one," said Kate, affirmatively.

"Dr. Stanley, we'll proceed to move forward with the invitations now, and start working on drafting our press release this afternoon," Tyler announced.

Gathering the remaining photographs, Carol and Tyler exited the meeting, leaving behind Kate with Sally, alone in her office. For the past several days, Kate's bedroom was in a state of complete mess and chaos. She had been searching and hunting for Jennifer's diary and so far, had no such luck. Although Kate successfully managed to avoid any cleaning services for her bedroom, so that she could continue to secretly search for the diary in private; she also knew, that eventually, she wasn't going to be able to deny housekeeping from accessing her bedroom forever, without drawing any suspicion. Eventually, she needed to tidy up the bedroom and allow the cleaning crew to resume access into her bedroom again. Therefore, the sooner she found the diary, the better off they all would be.

Recalling her previous conversation with Lucas a few days ago, Kate was privy to the knowledge that Sally was Jennifer's primary leading liaison, who managed all of her correspondences and administrative tasks. Perhaps, Sally had the information that Kate needed? Now, that Kate was alone with Sally, she decided to take advantage of this opportunity to privately converse with her.

"Sally," Kate began, "I understand that you were the primary transcriber for my sister's correspondences. Is this correct?"

"Yes, that's correct. As Mrs. Barrett's assistant, I wrote most, if not, all of Mrs. Barrett's formal letters and various correspondences," replied Sally, and then she added, "But now, that you're operating on Mrs. Barrett's behalf, I can also begin writing your correspondences, too, if you'd like."

"Oh, that's sweet of you Sally," replied Kate, gracious for her offer. "But since I really don't have many correspondences of my own right now, I think I'm alright. But thank you for your thoughtful consideration."

"Very well, Dr. Stanley, as you wish. If you change your mind, please let me know," said Sally.

"Umm, Sally," spoke Kate.

"Yes?" asked Sally.

"Are there any outstanding correspondences still remaining for my sister?" asked Kate.

"No, I don't believe so. Prior to your arrival, I completed everything that she asked me to do," answered Sally.

"I see," said Kate, "Please do forgive me in advance for asking, but did she ever happen to keep a journal or perhaps, even a diary? If so, that would be most useful for me to study, as a reference to help better understand my sister's role here. Also, what were the types of correspondences did you transcribe, on behalf of my sister?"

"Actually, I did purchase a diary for her a few years ago, but I'm unaware as to whether or not she actually wrote in it," said Sally.

"Wait, so she did in fact, have a diary?" asked Kate.

"Yes, she did. A gold one. But again, I'm not certain as to whether or not she used it, as she didn't share much private information with me. As for her correspondence, I transcribed mainly e-mails and paper letters addressed to the wives of the other diplomats. Typically, they related to formal invitations to various ladies' luncheons and other fundraising events," explained Sally.

"I see. Did she ever write to anyone else?" Kate further inquired.

"No," replied Sally, nervously. She further clarified, "Just to the ladies, that's all."

Her reaction was rather peculiar and suspicious, but rather than pursuing more answers, Kate decided not to press her any further about the subject. At least, not for now.

"Very well, then. Thank you, Sally," said Kate.

"You're welcome, Dr. Stanley. Is there anything else, that I can further help assist you with?" asked Sally.

"Actually, yes there is," answered Kate, "I'm a bit exhausted from my training today. Do you mind apologizing to Chef Homura and the ambassador on my behalf, that I'm unable to attend tonight's dinner? I think I need a night in to rest."

"But of course, Dr. Stanley, I will let them know. Do you prefer that I prearrange for a private meal to be delivered to your bedroom, later on this evening?" asked Sally.

"No, that's alright. I think I might just sleep in, altogether. But thank you Sally, for the suggestion," said Kate.

Afterwards, Sally excused herself and exited the room. Now, alone in the office, Kate proceeded to search through each and every drawer, cupboard and cabinet. But after opening each item, she alas, found absolutely nothing. Disappointed by her lack of findings, Kate reluctantly abandoned her office search and retired off to her bedroom. However, once in her bedroom, Kate continued her search for the diary, but this time, within the privacy of her own room. But, as such, she again, still had no such luck.

Hours later, by the time the clock stroke 11:00 pm, Kate was almost ready to give up on all hope, when suddenly a new idea came to mind. As she sat down on her bed, pondering about her dilemma and staring across at the messy bedroom, she remembered John mentioning that the mansion also had a library. Was it possible that Jennifer hid her diary in that library? In a room full of other books? It was certainly possible. Although the office and bedroom search both proved to be unsuccessful, all hope wasn't entirely lost. After all, today Sally confirmed that a diary did exist. Furthermore, it was specifically in the color gold. This was a helpful clue, for at least this way, Kate knew which colored book to search for.

With this new leading prospect, Kate was now, more than ever, determined to relocate her search into the library as soon as possible. Looking at her clock, Kate presumed that now was the ideal time to proceed with her search, especially, given that the library was most likely to be empty, as it was already so late into the night. And so, with Tabitha sound asleep on her bedroom floor, Kate, wearing her white silk nightgown, covered in her robe, with matching slippers, slowly snuck and crept out of her bedroom door, and gently tiptoed across the long, dark and narrow hallway, heading towards into the direction of the library.

By the time Kate reached the library's threshold, she pushed open the doors and was about to turn the light's switch on, when, to her surprise, she saw from afar, a bright light, blazing across in the form of an open fire, burning inside of the fireplace. Who lit this fire? Was someone already here? This late into the night? Curiously, Kate walked further into the room, and there seated across on the red sofa chair, adjacent from the fireplace and near the window, was John. Dressed within the same black suit and shoes from earlier in the day, John was seated and wearing a pair of reading glasses, with his feet leaning up against a nearby ottoman stool. From what Kate could see, he seemed to be surrounded by a large stack of documents and books, located right next to him, on the floor. His head was leaned down, and he appeared to be in full concentration, silently reading something against the moonlight.

Kate standing still, simply observed just how handsome he looked, seated there on his chair. His posture was proper and stern. His facial expression was rather serious, and he appeared to be in deep concentration. Overall, Kate noted that he displayed a mature, sophisticated, and intellectual demeanor. Furthermore, he seemed relaxed, calm and enjoying his solitude. Not wanting to disturb him, Kate was about to turn around and leave, when suddenly, without him even looking at her, nor lifting up his head from his reading, he spoke directly to her.

"Kate, please take a seat," said John, never once, leaving sight of his documents.

He knew that she was here? But how? She was as quiet as a mouse.

"How did you know I was here?" asked Kate, surprised by her

acknowledged presence.

Finally closing his file shut, he dropped his documents onto the floor, kicked his feet off the ottoman stool, removed his reading glasses and looked at her with an unexpected smile. Now, staring directly at her, he revealed, "I saw your shadow."

"You did?" asked Kate, surprised by his admission.

"Yes," he confidently replied, and with a grin on the corner of his mouth, he further clarified, "Against the wall."

"Oh, I see," said Kate, feeling a bit embarrassed for having been caught. Not wanting him to think that she was prying on him, she told him, "I wasn't spying or anything, just so you know."

"No, I didn't think you were," he concluded, "But now that you're here, why don't you go ahead and take a seat?" he asked, while pointing at the twin red sofa chair that conveniently sat directly across him, near the fire.

Accepting his offer, Kate proceeded to sit down on the empty chair that laid beside him.

"But how did you know that it was my shadow? It could have been someone else?" she asked, curious as to his reasoning.

"Lucky guess," he shrugged. "But the more important question is what brings you here into the library, so late at night?" he asked, with his gaze directly affixed on her.

"I just couldn't sleep and I thought that perhaps—" she began, but he soon interrupted her.

"Perhaps, that you could read a book and fall asleep?" he asked, with a raised brow.

"Yes, that's exactly what I thought…or at least, what I had hoped to do," she said, not wanting to reveal her true motives about secretly searching for Jennifer's diary.

"Well, Kate, you are more than welcome to read anything that you want here, anytime, day or night," he said, while emphasizing the word "night." He then asked, "Is there anything in particular, that you prefer to read, or are looking to find?"

"Nothing in particular," she quickly replied, "I just wanted to take a look and read anything that caught my interest."

Suddenly, Kate's own curiosity as to the purpose of his presence at the library intrigued her, so she, in return, asked him, "And what about yourself? Are you reading anything interesting, or important, so late into the night?"

"Oh, it's just related to work, that's all," he said, almost embarrassed, as he pushed his files further away, onto the floor and into a corner.

However, Kate caught a glimpse of his top file, and she could swear that she saw her name written on it. Was he actually reading her profile and studying about her? And if so, then why?

"Kate," he began, while changing the subject. "Now, that we finally have a private moment to ourselves, I understand that you're not only a graduate from NYU, but that you also teach there. An ivy league school. That's quite impressive," he said, while looking straight into her eyes, with respect and admiration.

He had been reading her profile! Her presumption was correct! Those documents were about her! But why the sudden interest in her? Kate wasn't accustomed to such attention.

"Thank you," she replied, taken aback by his unexpected complement and surprise interest. She further added, "I've been teaching at the history department for more than two years or so."

"Is there any reason in particular, as to why you chose to study history?" he further inquired. From the looks of it, he seemed most interested and keen to learn and know.

"It's a subject that I'm very passionate about. I actually specialize in Ottoman history," she clarified, still wondering as to why exactly he was so curious to learn more about her.

"How convenient, as we are in Türkiye, after all," he said, with a smile.

"Well, our ancestors, that is, Jennifer and I, our family is from here. At least from our mother's side," she said.

"Yes, that's right. Do you know much Turkish?" he asked.

"Yes, I do and so does Jennifer," she added.

"Really? I never heard her speak it," he said.

"She's just shy sometimes, especially, when it comes to speaking, that's all," she clarified.

"But you, on the other hand, are not?" he asked, most attentively.

"No, I'm not fearful of public speaking, or of speaking, in general. As a professor, it's my profession to speak, so that's why I'm seldom shy about these matters," she explained.

"Kate, that's an excellent quality. I think that's what I admire most about you, thus far," he revealed.

"Really?" asked Kate, surprised by yet another complement from him. As it was, she didn't understand as to why he already came to admire anything about her so soon, let alone, publicly share it with her.

"Yes," he said, "And since I've come to have had the pleasure of your company these past few days, I've already witnessed directly, just how lovely of a speaker you are. Kate, you've got impeccable speech. You carry-on your conversations with such pristine eloquence, and already get along with the staff here so very well. And now, I'm left to wonder, who is the real diplomat, Dr. Stanley or myself?" he said with a sincere smile, and then gave her a playful wink.

Kate immediately blushed. She hadn't expected him to complement her so highly, so when he actually did, she turned a bit red out of embarrassment. Kate just wasn't accustomed to such flattery.

"Is there a specific reason, as to why you chose to become a professor? As a history major, you could have also joined the state department, just like myself?" he further inquired.

Collecting her composure, Kate, in all seriousness, replied, "While I do realize that individuals with history degrees can pursue a variety of other career avenues, in my own case, I genuinely enjoy teaching."

"And why is that? Why do you enjoy teaching so much?" he asked, most intrigued by her statement.

"But why do you care to know?" she finally asked him, in return. In truth, she was equally curious, if not more, as to why he was suddenly interested on learning so much about her.

"Oh, I hope I did not offend you in any way—" he quickly said, in defense.

"No, you didn't," she interrupted, hoping to reassure him. "I was just curious to know, that's all…"

"Well," he said, now feeling more confident than ever, as she appeared more receptive and open to his questioning. Deeping his voice, he leaned in closer towards her and he said, "As we are new friends, I just wanted to better understand you, that's all. Especially, as the woman posing as my wife, I thought that, at that very least, I should have a better understanding as to what makes you…well…you."

"Ah, I see. I understand now," she said. Wanting to indulge him further about what makes her tick, she finally revealed, "Well, if you must know, teaching, in my opinion, is similar to being that of a storyteller. As for myself, I teach, because I thoroughly enjoy sculping young and impressionable minds. I, personally, take pleasure in educating, cultivating and persuading young people into learning the proper truth about history, while debunking mistruths. Often times, people acquire misinformation about history, especially, with social media, where the truth is generally obscured and everyone who claims to be a historian, actually isn't. As a result, people acquire the wrong facts about history. And in my case, I'm very proud of my Turkish and Ottoman roots. Sadly, the western world can at times, exhibit the wrong recollections about Turkish history, and as an Ottoman historian, it's my job to showcase the truth and dispel any negative and historical discrepancies. This why I teach history, and why I'm both a professor and a historian. I, ultimately, do what I do, in order to help my people. My life goals and pursuits are to help make a difference in this world, by cultivating young minds to start thinking and seeing the world, under a different pair of lenses."

For a long moment, John just stared at her, with pure astonishment and admiration. The more he learned about her, the more he began to feel a burning flame, flickering deeper across within his chest. But now, however, he was also aware that the flame's boundary was no longer limited to just his chest. Somehow, it crept further down, where it now, laid at the center of his heart. Alas, his heart was ever slowly, starting to beat and burn for this woman!

But before he could utter and speak another word, she beat him to the punch.

"Since I've told you my story, can I ask you as to why you chose to be an ambassador?" she asked, with her lips curved up, along the side of her soft and delicate cheeks.

Those lips. Her lips. He stared at them. It was intoxicating. He was transfixed. It was mesmerizing. They were soft, pink, moist and delicious. Upon gazing at them, he recalled just how much he wanted to kiss them, earlier in the day. Suddenly, as if he had previously been asleep within a dream, he finally awoke and was now fully aware, that she was seated across from him, wearing only a white silk nightgown. Although she'd been covered up inside of a matching robe, which was wrapped all around her, he could still see the shape of her hourglass body, along with her legs and thighs peeping through, from the sides of her robe. And to make matters worse, right above, along her chest, he could also see traces of her nipples and breast, resting against the sheer fabric of her nightgown...

Immediately, John looked away and stared down below to the floor, trying his best to avoid making any further eye contact with her. For if, dear reader, had he not done so and looked at her, even just for a minute longer, then he was certainly going to get an arousal. It really was just too much for him to bear! Luckily for him, she presumed that he was just busy pondering about a response to her question, when in reality, he was desperately trying to suppress his growing desire to unclothe her right then and there, and to make love to her on the spot! But, alas, after a minute to cool down, he once again, gained his composure. Mustering up all of his inner strength, he once again, looked her straight in the eye and proceeded to answer her lingering question.

"Like you, I, too, chose my profession, in order to help my people and community, while making a positive difference, in this world," he revealed, with a smile that melted her heart.

Pleased by his answer, she smiled back, in return. Although he was glad that she approved of his explanation, the reality was, it really was the honest truth. Like her, he selected his career for almost the same identical reasons, as to why she did. They were more alike, than either of them cared to admit.

"And that you do," she agreed, "Even though I haven't been here that long, I can already tell that you're good at what you do. Running and managing such a large embassy, with all of these staff, while still engaging at the same time, with your fellow diplomats can't be an easy task. Not everyone is capable of doing it. But yet, you still do. Every day, come rain or shine. And from what I've observed thus far, you certainly seem to help a lot of people, along the way. I know that I'm not alone, when I say that everyone here, including myself, thinks highly and respects you."

"Thank you, Kate, I really do appreciate that," he said, touched by her sincerity and kind words, "Sometimes, I feel so caught up with my work, and at certain moments, I can feel overwhelmed by it all, so hearing you say that, really means a lot."

Reaching over towards him, she gently placed her hands over his. Looking straight into his eyes, she said, "Good deeds never go unnoticed. Even if no one says it aloud, trust me, someone is always watching and admiring, even if it's quietly done so, from afar."

Upon hearing her thoughtful words, John looked at her and saw her blue eyes sparkling against the moonlight. With her eyes as blue as the moon and her hair as bright as the sun, she was the most beautiful woman he had ever laid eyes on. And as her hands touched his, his heart began to rapidly beat. In that moment, he was ready to leap across his chair, scoop her up into his arms, and carry her off to his bed. Alas, the lonely hermit, was no longer content with being alone. He had finally met his match!

But before John could respond to her complement, they heard the door crack open. It was soon followed by tiny footsteps creeping against the hardwood floor. Slowly, it was approaching closer and closer to them, until finally, they heard a very distinctive meow….

"Tabitha!" exclaimed Kate, who quickly jumped off from her chair and ran directly into the direction of her beloved cat.

When she touched down onto the floor, Kate quickly scooped Tabitha straight into her arms, snuggled her, and then began affectionately kissing and stroking her. And for the first time in his life, John actually felt jealous of a cat, wishing that he could switch places with it and be the one solely within Kate's arms instead…

"Ahem…" he said, trying to steal Kate's attention away from the cat.

"Tabitha, how on earth did you get in here?" asked Kate, still cradling Tabitha within her arms, not once noticing nor listening to John, in the background.

"Ahem…" repeated John, once more.

"Tabitha, you were supposed to be sleeping," Kate remarked.

"Ahem..." he repeated for a third time. Luckily for John, Kate finally heard him, this time around. Capitalizing on this unexpected opportunity, Kate quickly sought to introduce him to her beloved cat.

"John," she began, "Please meet Tabitha. She's my tabby cat." Then, returning her attention back to her cat, she said, "And Tabitha, this is John. He's an ambassador."

"Tabitha, it's a pleasure. Kate, may I?" asked John, as he reached over and began gently stroking and petting the yellow and orange tabby with his palm.

"Do you really want to pet her?" asked Kate, who hadn't expected John to take an interest in her pet cat.

"Actually, yes, I do," replied John, who by now, had completely captured and stolen Tabitha's immediate attention.

Soon enough, Tabitha swiftly trotted off away from Kate's arms, and slowly walked over towards John. Once she arrived to his side, she quickly rolled on her back, and waited for him to pet and rub her belly. And of course, being the gentleman that he was, did his very best to humor the cat.

"I can't believe it. She absolutely adores you!" exclaimed Kate, in sheer astonishment.

"Are you really so surprised?" asked John, who continued to rub Tabitha's belly, as she begun to purr.

"Actually, yes, I am. Tabitha doesn't like many people. Especially, strangers," Kate revealed.

"Well, I think that we can both agree, that I'm not exactly a stranger, anymore," he said, with the most seductive smile.

However, Kate completely missed his subtle attempts to seduce her and was instead, in full concentration, studying her cat. After a long pause, Kate finally said, "You certainly have a talent with animals. You must have had your own pets before. You must have."

"Well, that is true. I did have a pet once, but that was many years ago," he said.

"Really? What sort of pet did you have before?" she asked.

"It was a dog. A Lakeland terrier, to be precise. His name was Jeremy," he said, while still petting Tabitha.

"Jeremy, that's such a cute and lovely name for a dog! Do you still have him?" she inquired.

Her question caught him off guard, and for a brief moment, he remained silent. Afterwards, to her surprise, she saw a tear form on the outer corner of his eyes.

"I don't anymore," he softly sad, with a heavy voice. "He died a long time ago."

Detecting the pain and sadness within his voice when he uttered those very words, Kate truly felt sorry for him. Feeling the sudden urge and need to provide some form of physical comfort to him, she decided to lean closer to him. Having done so, she proceeded to reach over to grab hold of his hand. Once she did, she then placed hers against his, for a second time this evening. Finally, with his hands joined with hers, she said, "John, I'm so sorry."

Appreciating her kind and thoughtful gesture, he smiled at her and squeezed her hands.

"Thank you, Kate," he gently whispered to her.

With her attention focused directly at him, she looked at him with her bright blue eyes, which at that very moment, couldn't have been more sincere and loving. And then, to his unexpected surprise, she said, "By the way, you really do need slippers."

"I beg your pardon?" he asked, having been caught off guard by her usual suggestion.

"It's almost midnight, and here I am, wearing my comfortable pajamas, while your still dressed in your work suit. At the very least, you should be relaxing now, in a pair of your own comfy slippers, and not within your formal working shoes," she pointed out, as a matter of fact.

Having caught sight of his own reflection at the window, he realized that she was indeed, correct. It was so late into the evening, and he was still dressed in his formal and uncomfortable work clothes. Curious as to why she decided to bring up this matter now, he suddenly understood her motive: by changing the subject, it was her way of cheering him up after discussing about his late pet. And the truth was, it really worked too, for John's spirits were immediately lifted up.

Wiping away his tears, he released a little cheerful laugh. Kate, for all of her worth, certainly knew how to put him in a good mood.

"Very well, Kate, the next time you come visit me here, in the library," he said, "Please bring me a pair of slippers. Any pair of your choosing."

"What makes you think that I'll be back here again, to visit you?" she asked, teasingly.

"Oh, I've got a feeling," he began, "And if not you, then, perhaps, Tabitha might sneak back in…"

"Oh, yes, Tabitha," she said, with her attention now returning back to her cat.

But by now, Tabitha had long fallen asleep within John's arms. And so, Kate, slowly pulled Tabitha away and out from John's grip. Once she succeeded and took back ownership of the cat, Kate rose up from the floor, and she said, "It's been a long night. I think it's best that we all head off and go to bed."

Much to his dismay, his smile quickly turned into a frown. Not wanting, nor willing to let her go away so soon, John reminded her, "But you never did find that book to read."

"It will have to wait until next time. After all, tomorrow is but another day," she said, "Besides, Tabitha really ought to be in bed right now."

But as Kate began to walk towards the door to exit the room, she swiftly turned around, and she said, "John…"

"Yes, Kate?" he said, hoping that she had changed her mind about leaving.

"I just wanted to say to you, that it's far better to have loved and lost, than to have never loved before. I know that this saying can be a bit cliché, but there's still much truth to it. That's all," she said, before she exited the library completely, leaving him behind and alone in the room.

For a moment, her words echoed within his ear. He repeated to himself, "It's far better to have loved and lost, than to have never loved before."

And for the first time in John's life, he agreed with this statement. For the man, who had spent much of his lonely nights here alone in this library, he was beginning to finally understand that loving something or someone, was far greater, than never having to experience love, at all.

Looking outside of his window and staring at the midnight moon, with the moonlight shining across his face, he whispered aloud, with such longing, "Oh Kate, where have you been all this time?"

Chapter 18

"**S**he's finally here!" they all exclaimed.

"Who's finally here?" asked Kate, who sat at the dinner table, busy practicing her table etiquettes with Chef Homura.

"It's Mrs. Barrett," Sally interrupted.

"But I'm Mrs. Barrett. Well, at least, for the time being," Kate noted, as she returned her dinner fork back onto the table.

"Mrs. Barbara Barrett, the ambassador's mother," Gloria corrected.

"But she wasn't expected to arrive, until next week," spoke Sally.

"Well, that's Mrs. Barrett for you," remarked Chef Homura.

"Is there anything in particular, that I should know about, prior to Mrs. Barrett's arrival? Before today, I've never once heard about her until now," said Kate.

"Madame Barrett," began Gloria, "Is what one would call a free and vibrant spirit…"

"To say the least," Sally interrupted.

"Sally, please control yourself," scolded Gloria.

"Yes, my apologizes, Gloria," said an embarrassed Sally.

"Madame Barrett, can be an over-the-top type of personality. Naturally, Dr. Stanley, she will recognize you as your sister, so please, be ready to be referred to her as such; and whatever you do, only refer to her, in return, as Barbara. She will be expecting that much from you," warned Gloria.

"Okay, call her Barbara, got it," confirmed Kate. "Is there anything else that I should know?"

"My best suggestion is to just go with the flow," advised Chef Homura.

Hoping for a definitive confirmation, Kate immediately looked straight at Gloria. But for once, Gloria was completely speechless. As a result of Gloria's lack of direction, Kate's curiosity grew more. Just who exactly was Barbara Barrett?

Suddenly, out of nowhere, a fresh draft of air blew through the open window, making the white linen curtains flow and bend against the wind. As the curtains fluttered about in the air, the doors to the dining room immediately burst opened and a tall, curvaceous woman entered the premise. Elegantly dressed within a purple chiffon dress, she wore a matching purple and green silk floral roses that were stitched along her sleeves, and on her chest area, laid a bright ruby red jeweled oval brooch. Her hair was brown, short and styled in a pixie cut. She wore large diamond studded earrings, and carried with her a black Hermes Birkin purse. Aged in her sixties, Kate noted that she was glamorous, stylish and full of life. Furthermore, as she entered the room, a tiny small blonde and wheat colored dog, with large pointy ears and fluffy hair, trotted not far behind her.

"My darlings!" she happily exclaimed.

"Mrs. Barrett, it's so good to see you again!" exclaimed Chef Homura, who by now, had swiftly rose up from his chair, and within the blink of an eye, he was right there, kissing Barbara's hands.

"Oh, Chef Homura! You certainly, always know how to properly greet a lady!" exclaimed Barbara, who was tickled by the chef's friendly, yet intimate, and rather, unorthodox affectionate greeting.

"Welcome back Mrs. Barrett. We're most delighted to see you and little Jewel, again," said Sally, who took the liberty to bend down, and approach and pet the small Cairn Terrier on the floor.

"Sally, my dear girl! You're looking more lovelier, than ever before! And that gorgeous red hair of yours is just simply divine," complemented Barbara, while at the same time, directing her driver and other staff to move her excessively heavy, large and bulky luggage into her upstairs guest bedroom.

"Are you planning to stay long, Madame Barrett?" asked Gloria, who, already appeared rather annoyed by the entire ordeal.

Kate observed that although Gloria remained emotionless on the outside, she also suspected that on the inside, Gloria was really greatly displeased by both Barbara's excessive display of close intimacy with the staff, along with her outrageous amount of unnecessary luggage, for a relatively planned short-term stay.

"Gloria," huffed Barbara, "It's good to see you too. And no, I don't plan on staying too long. Just until after next week's state dinner."

Pleased by her statement, Gloria discretely smiled. Meanwhile, Kate, who was observing her from afar, soon realized that Gloria appeared rather happy and thrilled that Barbara wasn't going to stay here for an extended period of time. Was Barbara, actually Gloria's secret frienemy? This was intriguing! Kate secretly wished that she had a bucket of popcorn right now.

"And my darling, Jennifer!" exclaimed Barbara, at long last. "Please stand up and let me have a look at you, my dear girl!"

Following her request, Kate rose up from her chair and walked over to Barbara. Wearing an emerald green dress, Kate gave a small twirl around the room, leaving Barbara delighted by her gesture.

"Jennifer," spoke Barbara, "You look absolutely stunning. Simply beautiful.

Why, you're even prettier from when I last saw you. Did you lose more weight? You're much smaller than before. I say, you look much happier, too."

"Oh…why, thank you, Barbara," replied Kate. Wanting to deflect the attention away from her, Kate inquired, "And how are you, Barbara?"

"Well," smiled Barbara, "We've got plenty to catch up on, that's for sure. But now is not the time for chit chat, we'll save that for today's brunch at the country club. Chef Homura, your services will be needed this afternoon at the club."

"Mrs. Barrett, it will be my pleasure," replied Chef Homura.

"But Madame Barrett," interrupted Gloria, "Madame Jennifer might not have enough time to attend such brunch at the country club this afternoon, as she is already too busy and preoccupied with preparing for next week's upcoming state dinner."

However, Barbara simply laughed at such a notion.

"Gloria, the dinner is next week," Barbara reminded her, "Might I also add, that it is hardly an excuse. Jennifer certainly has more than enough time to dine with me today at the country club, especially, as it's been ages, since I've last seen my favorite daughter-in-law."

Spinning around and making eye contact with Kate, Barbara asked, "Jennifer, I'll see you at the country club for brunch, won't I? Because if you don't, then you'll be leaving your poor mother-in-law simply heartbroken. And you won't want me there all sad and alone, now do you? Especially, as it's my first day here, right?"

Not wanting to upset, nor offend her new mother-in-law, Kate nodded in agreement and thereby, promised Barbara to attend the bruncheon, no matter the circumstances.

"Wonderful!" exclaimed Barbara, happily. "In that case," she added, "I'll see you there at two o'clock this afternoon."

Immediately switching her attention over to Sally, Barbara said, "And this invitation also extends to my son, too. Sally, please ensure that John attends this afternoon's brunch, as well."

"But—" pleaded Sally.

"No buts, Sally," Barbara cautioned, "Please convey to him that we'll be expecting him for brunch, and if he should dare be late, then I'll call him directly and personally drag him in there, myself! Is that understood?"

"Yes, perfectly," replied Sally, as she gulped, "I'll inform Ambassador Barrett, immediately, to let him know."

"Fabulous!" exclaimed Barbara, joyfully.

Last, but certainly not least, Barbara focused her attention towards Gloria, and with the battering of her eyelashes, she boldly asked, "Gloria, my dear, I'm in need of a dire favor. Would you please help oblige me, as your dear old friend?"

Gloria, who had been standing there all this time, tried her very best to attempt to force an insincere smile. However, somehow, within the process, her attempts backfired, and instead, a small wrinkle managed to form in between her eyebrows and forehead, leaving Kate staring on, in astonishment and pure fascination. Meanwhile, Gloria, being the absolute professional that she was, replied, while also clenching her hands tight into a fist and grinding her own teeth, "But of course, Madame Barrett. Anything you wish."

"Fantastic!" exclaimed Barbara, "In that case, please see to it that Jewel is bathed using her special therapeutic shampoos and oils; her hair deep conditioned, brushed, styled and blow dried; and her nails trimmed and colored. Once she's bathed, please prepare and serve her special order of French filet mignon, along with a side of fresh crystal drinking water. Afterwards, please escort her outside for her evening stroll, then help her to retire into my bedroom. Oh, and if she's not too tired, then please read my darling Jewel a good bedtime story—but be sure not to read anything including cat characters within the tale, as Jewel is not a fan of them. Lastly, but most importantly, please see to it that her pink velvet bed is prepared and ready, by the time she's put to bed. Furthermore, please make sure that she's at the very least, tucked away into bed before nightfall, as Jewel's afraid of the dark. Finally, before I forget, please leave a small nightlight on for her. Hmm…let me think…is there anything else, that I might have forgotten?" asked Barbara to herself.

"Perhaps, her pink blanket and pillow?" asked Sally, innocently.

Immediately, Gloria shot Sally the most dreadful, scary and chilling look, that made Sally soon regret and wish that she had never, ever, suggested such a thing.

"Why yes! Thank you, Sally!" exclaimed Barbara.

Barbara, returning her attention back to Gloria, added, "Yes, please make sure Jewel's pink blanket and pillow is ready, in time for Jewel's bedtime. Of course, please remember to wash, steam, starch, iron and press the blanket. Afterwards, please have her pillow fluffed and dusted. As you may recall, Jewel's head is rather sensitive, so it's imperative that she always have access to a comfortable and fluffy pillow, at all times."

Finally, Barbara waved farewell to the remaining staff and then exited out of the room. Once she was finally gone, Gloria, whose pale complexion had now transformed into a bright crimson red shade, promptly grabbed Jewel out from Sally's arms, and then proceeded to angrily stomp out of the room, slamming the door shut loudly behind her.

To everyone's surprise, Gloria slammed the door so hard and with such force, that the walls and floor shook and vibrated, and the small landscape portrait, which hung above the table, actually tilted and moved sideways. Meanwhile, Kate, who had watched on in utter amazement, was now officially a huge admirer and fan of her new mother-in-law, whom she had only just met. Kate concluded, that anyone who had both the courage and stamina to stand up to the likes of Gloria, was most certainly, a person well worth knowing. What a breath of fresh air Barbara had been!

Later That Afternoon...

At a quarter until two o'clock, Kate arrived at the country club and walked down the hallway, looking for the entrance into the banquet room. She was nervous. During the entire car ride, spanning from the mansion and all the way to the country club, she pondered about, as to which sorts of conversations that she could safely engage upon with Barbara. Ever since Kate's arrival, her immediate staff already knew the truth about her, apart from George, the butler, and a few other minor staff. Luckily, for Kate, her interactions with them were limited, and all of them, refrained from asking her any personal questions, that only Jennifer, alone, would know the answer to.

However, that wasn't necessarily going to be the same case with Barbara. After all, she was John's mother and Jennifer's mother-in-law. And given Barbara's blunt personality, she was surely going to ask a specific question that was going to leave Kate's tongued tied, sooner or later. And for this reason, Kate ultimately decided that for today's brunch, she would purposely speak at a bare minimum. Hopefully, Barbara would be busy talking with Kate listening on, and eventually, once John arrived, he would carry on with most of their table conversations.

After reaching the end of the hallway, Kate finally arrived to the entrance to the banquet room. Once there, she gently pushed open the gold brass doors and entered into the room. Hoping that John arrived early and was already seated at the table, she instead saw only Barbara, seated and sipping a cup of tea, from a porcelain blue and white teacup.

"My darling Jennifer, please have a seat," said Barbara, as she welcomed Kate inside and motioned for her to take a seat beside her.

Following Barbara's lead, Kate promptly sat down. Once seated, Kate noticed that before her, laid an entire feast of goodies at the table. Elegantly placed above a lace pink linen tablecloth, where stacks of trays, each displaying a variety of tea sandwiches, scones, biscuits, sugar cookies and cakes, along with various jam, butter and other spreads. There were two large pots of tea, along with several matching teacups and saucers. And in the middle of the table, was the main dessert, consisting of an enormous, scrumptious, tasty and deliciously looking and smelling blueberry pie.

"Don't worry, this is just for our starters," said Barbara, as she pointed to the food at the table. "Later, we'll order real food. Breakfast style."

Surprised by her remark, the food already prepared and served at the table was for Kate, a regular and full meal, entirely by itself.

"I already spoke to John," began Barbara, "He'll be here in a few minutes."

"Oh, I'm glad," said Kate, who took the liberty to pour herself a cup of tea.

"Me too," said Barbara. "And that buys us some time for some girl chat."

Surprised by her suggestion, Kate almost choked on her tea. Barbara noticed.

"Jennifer, are you alright my dear?" asked a concerned Barbara.

"I'm quite alright," replied Kate. "The tea was a bit too hot for me, that's all."

"Oh, yes, it's still warm, isn't?" asked Barbara. "Next time, just try to drink it more slowly."

"Thank you, I will," said Kate, who then proceeded to drink a glass of water, to calm her nerves.

"How long has it been since we've last seen each other?" asked Barbara.

"Hmm…why yes, I believe that was last saw each other at that dinner, with that those dreadful French and Brazilian Ambassadors. What a total disaster that had been!"

Kate simply nodded and immediately, took a sip of her tea and then, slammed a small tea sandwich straight into her mouth.

"Yes, it has been a while. Perhaps, too long," sighed Barbara and then looking at Kate, she added, "And you're thinner, than what I expected. I'll admit, I secretly hoped to see more meat on you, by now."

"Really?" asked Kate, now holding her teacup and saucer within her hands. "But why?"

"Well, my dear Jennifer, this shouldn't come as such a surprise to you," answered Barbara, in all honestly, "Surely, you must have known that I expected, or at the very least, hoped to see you finally pregnant, after all these years."

Surprised by her unexpected statement, Kate almost dropped her teacup onto the table, but luckily, she managed to catch it in time, mid-air. Although Kate had speculated about a million different scenarios, as to which types of conversations she would discuss and engage upon with Barbara, this particular topic of motherhood, never once came to mind. Her pregnant? Or, more accurately, Jennifer pregnant? Did her sister actually want children? Or, John, for that matter? This was all, certainly a surprise.

"As you're already well aware, John is my only son. The sole heir to the Barrett fortune. And, might I remind you, that you've been married to my son now, for these past five years and counting. I think it's high time that you, two, finally have a child of your own. As for myself, I can't wait to finally be a grandparent!" exclaimed Barbara, happily and enthusiastically.

"I…I…understand…how you must feel," began Kate, nervously, "But…right now…it's just been rather difficult for us…especially, given John's career…he's just so busy all of the time…"

"That's no excuse," interrupted Barbara. "Listen to me very carefully, Jennifer. As you're elder, I'm speaking to you, having gone through it all. I speak to you now, with a lifetime of experience. When it comes to children, no timing is ever perfect. You just have to do it. It's really just that simple. Career isn't everything. Jobs come and go. If you base everything solely on your career, then you will be gravely disappointed, in the end. To live a life purely based upon the ambitions of a career is a very lonely, purposeless and meaningless life. In the end, family is everything. Love and children are what's most important in this world. The root of it all. To have descendants. One day, we'll be gone and buried, and all that will be left, here in this world, are our children and grandchildren to carry on our name. Our legacy. Since John already has you and his career is well established, it's time to move onto the next stage of life. Now, it's time to have children of your own, to carry on the Barrett name and legacy, for the next generation. This should be your goal for the next stage of your lives."

"Yes, but... it's just that…" began Kate, but with all honesty, she was truly lost for words.

"Are you two still sleeping in separate bedrooms?" asked Barbara, bluntly.

Alas, Kate was now officially tongue tied. Just what exactly did or didn't Barbara know about them? Not wanting to give herself, or Jennifer, away, Kate quietly nodded in agreement, all the while, secretly hoping that she didn't already betray her sister, in the process.

"We'll have to work on that one. For now, carry on as usual. Once this party of yours is done, then we'll work on getting you two back together and sleeping again in the same bedroom. I vow, if it takes me another month or so to get this all done and taken cared off, then so be it! As it is, I already anticipated as much, so to prepare, I've packed enough suitcases to last me an extra six months, if need be!" she exclaimed.

"But I thought you told Gloria that you planned on staying, only until next week?" asked Kate.

Tickled by her innocent question, Barbara simply laughed and took another sip of her tea.

"Oh, my dear Jennifer, surely by now, you, of all people, must know that we never reveal the absolute truth about everything to Gloria. Why, can you imagine, if she actually knew my plans to stay here, for the next foreseeable six months? Good God, she would have already sent a swarm of bees by now, to chase me out the house! Remember, there's a reason why I brought ten pieces of luggage with me for this trip," said Barbara, with a mischievous smile.

Suddenly, Barbara and Kate both burst into laughter. The truth was, Kate knew that Barbara was indeed, right. Gloria really would have sent a swarm of bees after her! Kate was glad that the mansion finally had someone to counterbalance the wrath of Gloria. Now, feeling more comfortable around Barbara's company, John soon arrived to join them at the table.

"Mother," he said, as he leaned in and gave Barbara a small peck on the cheek.

Walking over to Kate, this time, he bent down and said, "Wife," as he gave her a brief kiss on the cheek.

It was their first time having ever engaged upon any form of a kiss, even though it was merely limited to only their cheeks. Suddenly, at that moment, out of sheer nervousness and embarrassment, Kate's complexion quickly grew pink. John immediately saw and secretly smiled to himself. Even though he knew that she was nervous, somehow, he found her innocent nature sweet, refreshing and endearing.

"Have a seat John," said Barbara, who then reached over to grab a cranberry scone.

"Thank you, Mother," he said, as he pulled a seat right next to Kate.

George, the butler soon appeared. It seemed that both the mansion's butler and chef were specifically brought to the country club to cater to today's brunch. Once they were all seated, Barbara announced, "As I previously mentioned to Jennifer earlier, John, the tea and sandwiches are just starters. We'll be having a full standard breakfast, as brunch for today. I've already prearranged it, in advance, with Chef Homura."

Turning her attention over towards George, she directed him, "George, now that John's arrived, please proceed with the service for breakfast now."

"As you wish," replied George, who then, went back into the kitchen to gather their meal.

Five minutes later, George returned back to their table. He brought with him a cart, containing several plates of omelets, fruit, veggies, sausages, meat, cereal, milk, juice, toast, pancakes and oatmeal.

"Pancakes! Yippie!" exclaimed Barbara, who quickly grabbed a slice for herself, and began drizzling maple syrup all over them.

Looking over towards the couple, Barbara noticed each of them grabbing a separate bowl of oatmeal for themselves.

"Are you two really only going to eat just oatmeal? Especially, given that we have all these other more delicious and scrumptious food at the table?" she asked, with the most astonishing expression.

Neither John, nor Kate, each of whom, were each equally focused on their own bowls, took notice that the other party had grabbed the same meal choice at the very same time.

"But it's my favorite," they both claimed.

Surprised by the other's response, they looked at each other with complete astonishment. Did they really share the same favorite breakfast meal?

"Well, I suppose it's only natural for a married couple, such as yourselves, who've been married for so long, to eventually like and eat the same types of food," concluded Barbara. Furthermore, she added, "Although, I must admit, I'm a bit disappointed. With all of this delicious food, it's such a shame that it'll all go to waste, if neither of you intends to eat it."

"But it doesn't have to be a waste," Kate interjected, "We can always donate it to the local food bank."

"What a grand idea!" exclaimed Barbara, "I wish I had thought of that myself! Why, Jennifer, since when did you become such a humanitarian? John, your wife is simply too generous."

"Yes, she is," he said boldly, while taking a bite of his oatmeal.

Slowly, he began to lick the back of his spoon in the most seductive way, and then he proceeded to scoot his chair two inches closer over towards Kate. Ever so gently, his knee lightly brushed against hers, and Kate could actually feel him breathe against her neck. Suddenly, she felt a tingle shoot right down her spine, and her heart began to rapidly beat. Much to her surprise, she was growing more nervous; and yet at the same, she was actually starting to enjoy this unexpected thrill of him being so close and near to her.

"Why Jennifer, are you alright? I say, you're quite pink," observed Barbara, as she took another bite of her pancake.

"I am?" Kate innocently asked, all the while, turning a darker shade of pink, almost magenta, within the process.

"Yes, I agree. You certainly are. I wonder why?" asked John, as he devilishly joined in to cast his own remark. But in truth, he very well knew exactly as to why she was indeed the color pink.

However, Kate simply ignored him. She simply had to. She had no other choice. For if she didn't, then her nerves and complexion would have betrayed her, and she would have transformed from dark pink to scarlet red, within an instant.

"The room is just a bit warm," replied Kate, hoping that they would change the subject.

"Well, outside is sunny and lovely," Barbara admitted, "I say, why don't you and John enjoy some alone time together out in the park? You two should take advantage of this lovely weather and take a walk outside. Perhaps, even visit the horses!"

Kate immediately gulped. Right now, she felt extremely attractive to John, and if she was going to be all alone with him, then it was most certainly, going to be dangerous. With all honesty, just by staring right at him, Kate couldn't help but notice that his charcoal gray suit, that he just happened to wear today, had perfectly shaped his muscular hourglass figure. Furthermore, he even smelled lovely. It was the most intoxicating of scents. Was it cinnamon and spice? It certainly did smell nice.

"Are you certain? We don't want to leave you here all alone, especially since you've only just arrived to town today," Kate suggested, all the while, secretly hoping and praying for a miracle of her own, in order to escape her impending doom.

"None sense," replied Barbara, carefree, as she waved her hands in the air. "As we're all well aware, my son is always so busy. Therefore, having said so, this might be the one and only chance that we have for you two to getaway, and finally be together, *alone.*"

Emphasizing the word alone, Barbara immediately winked directly at Kate. Much to her dismay, Kate knew exactly as to what Barbara had meant by that. Alone time meant baby making time. Barbara was certainly determined to finally have that long lost grandchild of hers, wrapped around and safely tucked away within her arms, in no time.

"Mother, that's a grand idea. A stroll around in the sunshine might do us some good," interrupted John, this time.

"Wonderful!" exclaimed Barbara, joyfully. "Now, you two just get going. In the meantime, I'll invite Chef Homura to join me at the table for some company. Besides, he and I have much catching up to do, too."

But before Kate even had a chance to object, John immediately rose up from his chair and extended his hand over to her.

"Shall we?" he asked, with the utmost suave and the most charming of smiles.

Reluctantly grabbing hold of his hand, within an instant, he quickly pulled her up from her seat and soon enough, he proceeded to escort her out of the room and over to the porch.

"Have fun you two!" shouted Barbara, from behind.

"Oh, we will," he said, with a grin.

Leading her out from the back doors, they walked pass the patio, through the yard and finally, down a dirt road. Once there, John guided her down the path, which was the direct route to the horse stable. Meanwhile, back at the country club, Barbara continued to watch on and stare at them from her window. To amuse her, the couple smiled and waved to her, in return. Soon enough, once they eventually reached a safe enough distance away from Barbara's vicinity and prying eyes, Kate presumed that John would let go of her hand. However, much to her surprise, he didn't. This was peculiar. No one was around them, so there was no need to continue on with their charade. So why didn't he let go? Why did he continue to hold on?

Kate was about to remind him that Barbara was no longer spying on them, but she caught herself short and ultimately, decided not to say anything, at all. In truth, Kate rather secretly enjoyed it. It felt nice to have his strong hands intertwined and locked with hers. After all, they were friends and as friends, weren't they allowed to hold hands? Surely, that's what good friends do, don't they?

Meanwhile, John smiled. He, in return, knew exactly what she was thinking, because he had secretly thought much of the same, too. Rather than letting go, he spontaneously decided to hold onto her hand, with an even tighter grip. After all, he had waited a lifetime to meet someone like her, and now that he found her, he wasn't going to let her slip away from him, so easily.

John didn't quite understand just yet, as to what he felt for her, but he knew that he was beginning to feel something. What exactly that was, he wasn't quite sure. But this much he knew: every time she's around, he feels an unexplainable gravitation pull towards her. Every time she passes by, she catches his attention. Every time she smiles, his insides burn with fire. Every time that one single strand of blonde hair falls down upon her delicate porcelain face, he's mesmerized. And every time she speaks, he's captivated by her every word, speech, thoughts and ideas. Was this all lust or attraction? Or even, shall we dare say, the beginning embers of love?

As they continued walking down the road, they came across a field of white daisies. Captivated by their beauty, Kate suddenly stopped in the middle of the road. Distracted by the scenic view, Kate finally let go of his hand, which left John, extremely disappointed. Then, Kate did something completely unexpected and out of her character. Trotting off from the straight path, she climbed over the country fence and walk herself over to the open field of daisies. It was there, out in the field, where she picked a single white daisy for herself, from the newly trimmed mossy green grass. After frolicking through the field for a brief minute, she eventually returned back to their path to meet John, where she held onto her newly acquired flower within the palm her hand. The same hand, which had recently been previously linked to his.

"Just one daisy?" asked John, curious as to why she had picked only a single flower, and not a bouquet, like most other young ladies of her age would have done.

"Yes, just one. It's for memories," replied Kate, with a tinkle in her eye.

And then she added, "The truth is that I don't really believe in picking flowers, in the first place, as I find it rather selfish. I, generally, believe that flowers are meant to be shared, admired and loved by everyone. But this time, I, honestly, just couldn't help myself. They are so incredibly pretty. For once, I decided to make an exception to my own rule. This time, I chose to follow my heart, and not my head."

John smiled. It was rather sweet and innocent of her. However, at the same time, he realized that she was also, ever so slowly, crawling out of her oyster shell, like the hidden pearl that she was and leaving her rigid ways behind her. At long last, she was finally beginning to let loose. Much to his pleasure, he understood that she was growing more comfortable, while in his company. The very thought tugged deeper away, straight into his heart.

"Ah, memories," he sighed, and then, he teasingly smiled at her and said, "Well, it would be such a shame, if you only kept that pretty daisy hidden away, within the palm of your hands. Pretty things are not meant to be hidden. They should be shared and shown to the world. Here, please allow me to…"

Grabbing the daisy away from her hand, he gently tucked it away behind her ear, right next to her flowing blonde hair. As his bare hand graced upon her face, she shivered by his touch. For a moment, their eyes caught sight of each other, and they both locked eyes with one another. Each of them was beginning to feel some sort of sentimental emotion for one another; but yet, neither one of them, was quite ready to acknowledge and accept it, full heartily. Not yet.

"There," he said, as he pulled his hand away from her delicate face, "You look beautiful."

She smiled, and in return, his entire heart burned and beamed with delight.

"Thank you, John," she replied, with the biggest and brightest of smiles that he had ever seen, before.

Not wanting to allow his emotions to get carried away, he decided to quickly change the subject.

"If we continue down this road for another five minutes or so, we'll be at that horse stable," he said, while pointing towards the end of the road with his index finger.

"Sounds like an ideal plan," she cheerfully said, with a grin that felt as if cupid, himself, shot an arrow right above into the sky and landing straight into his heart.

Following his lead, they quietly walked together down the path, side by side. As he watched her from the corner of his eyes, his curiosity about her life and experiences, continued to perplex him. After a few long minutes of prolonged silence, John decided to use this rare opportunity to learn more about her.

"Kate," he began, "So that's your name."

"Yes, Kate is my name," she replied, almost mockingly and with a raised brow.

"Is it short for anything? Katherine? Katrina? Or perhaps, even Kathleen?" he inquired.

"No," she boldly responded, "It's simply Kate."

"That's rather unique," he observed, while still pondering about her name, within his mind. "Most people don't have usually have a nickname for a given first name."

"I know," she sighed, "But at least this way, it's easy to remember. Simple and straightforward."

"What you see is what you get?" John asked, most intrigued.

"Yes," she said, "Not too exciting, but that's my name. Although Anastasia would have been a lot nicer, don't you think? But maybe, Anastasia is just too exotic for me. At the same time, Kate is a bit of a plain Jane, too."

"I couldn't further disagree," he promptly interjected, in a rather serious manner and tone. "I've known quite a few Anastasias in my time, and I would trade all of them for a single Kate."

"Do you really mean that?" she asked. If he truly meant what he just said, then Kate was honestly and truly touched by his kind and thoughtful words.

"Yes, I really do," he said, most sincerely, "I can't tell you how refreshing it is to have someone like you in my life. In my world— excuse me, correction— our world, since you're now a part of it. Over the years, I've grown accustomed to being surrounded by so many insincere, immoral and dishonest people, that knowing at least one single, straight forward, and honest Kate is more valuable to me, than all the rest."

Upon hearing his heartful words, tears began to stream down from Kate's eyes. Never had anyone in her life describe her in that way. Not once, ever. Not her parents. Not her sister. Not even her own friends and colleagues. John was truly a gentleman, at best.

"Thank you, John," she whispered.

"You're welcome, Kate," he said, "And please, whatever you do, don't ever change. You are perfect, as you are. Exquisite and rare, just like that pearl ring, which you frequently adorn around your finger."

Looking down at her ring, Kate smiled to herself. It was the first time that anyone had ever equated her, as equal to her precious and beautiful pearl. His complements to her, were well received.

"By the way," he suddenly, interrupted, "We're here now."

Surprised by his announcement, Kate blinked twice at the sight before her. There, in front of her, stood a large brown wooden barn structure. It was most certainly a horse stable, for as soon as John pushed opened the doors, Kate immediately smelled a strong and distinctive animal odor, followed by various cries from the horses nearby. Finally, as she walked through the barn's entrance threshold, she was astonished by view.

There, inside, were several rows of stables, each sheltering numerous horses, all ranging in a diversity of breeds, colors and sizes. Each stable included a sign, posted right outside its door, with its listing written in all capital letters, naming each one of the horses located inside. All of the horses were fine, tall, muscular and appeared very much well-groomed.

Kate presumed it was their lunchtime, for each horse was busy chewing away on oats and hay. As she continued to walk further down on the middle aisle in the barn, which was made from hay and straw, she could hear John shouting for her from afar.

"Kate, come this way," he shouted to her, from down at the very last stable.

"How did you get down there so far, so fast?" she shouted back at him.

However, he failed to hear her, and she decided right there and then, not to shout any further, for fear that her loud voice would echo across the barn, and distract and provoke the eating horses. Either way, somehow, while Kate was occupied admiring the horses, John managed to find a shortcut to reach the back.

Following his voice, Kate proceeded to walk down towards his direction. When she finally arrived to his stable, she saw a giant, muscular, and brown colored velvet horse standing nearby him. The horse was simply magnificent. He was well groomed. Its hair was midnight black and was finely trimmed. But the most astonishing of all, right in the middle of its forehead was a very peculiar birthmark. It was colored white, and the shape of it resembled that of a star.

"Her name's Starlight," said John. "She's an English Thoroughbred. A champion of horses. Please, do come and pet her."

Amazed by its stunning stature, Kate slowly walked over and began petting Starlight. Ironically, Kate thought to herself, her name was most fitting, for Starlight was just as spectacular and as pretty, as a star. Furthermore, she also looked and felt just like pure velvet.

"She's absolutely beautiful," Kate remarked, who was simply memorized and transfixed by the horse's rare and exquisite beauty, reminding her of Pegasus, himself.

"Here, let me help you," said John, who by now, for a second time today, reached for her hands once more, and together, they both began stroking the horse together, with a large wooden brush.

However, somehow in the process, Kate unexpectedly tripped over Starlight's bucket of water on the floor, falling face forward into John. Luckily, John managed to catch her mid-air within his arms, and for a single and brief moment, they were inches away from a kiss.

For days, John yearned and dreamt of this very moment. Fantasizing about her numerous times within his mind, he secretly wondered as to how it felt to kiss her. For her lips to press against his. For her tongue to intertwine with his. He desired her, and privately, he secretly wished and hoped for his fantasy to come true. And now, much to his surprise, it was here. In this very second. But just when John thought that the impossible was about to happen, Kate quickly regained her balance and pulled away, leaving him utterly disappointed.

"I'm sorry," she said, wryly.

"Sorry?" he asked, so confused. What exactly was she sorry about?

"For falling," she said, almost ashamed for lack of composure.

"It's not your fault," he reassured her.

"I should have paid more attention," she added.

"It's okay, it happens," he shrugged.

"Is Starlight going to be, okay?" she said, while reverting her attention back to the horse.

Tickled by her innocent concern, John laughed.

"Starlight will be just fine," he said, with a smile.

"Are you sure?" she asked again, with a concerned look on her face.

"Starlight is made from thick skin. She can handle anything," replied John and then, suddenly, he had an idea.

"I say, Kate," he began.

"Yes?" she asked.

"Have you ever ridden a horse before?" he asked.

"No, never," she replied.

"Well, would you care to take a ride, along with Starlight and me? I know that she's been couped up here in this stable for a while now, so I'm sure she'd appreciate a ride around the park," said John.

"Really? Are you serious?" she asked, with a sparkle in her eye.

"Yes, I'm quite serious," he assured her.

"John, I would love to!" she happily and cheerfully exclaimed.

"Perfect! Let me grab her rein and saddle. Just give me a minute," he said.

After retrieving the equipment, John returned back to the stable with Starlight's rein and saddle, in hand. He quickly secured them onto Starlight, then afterwards, he led them down towards the back exit. Once they finally exited the barn, John climbed up on top of the horse, and then extend his hand over to Kate, motioning her to do the same.

"Don't we need to wear any special clothing or helmets?" she asked, after she climbed up and joined him on top of the saddle.

"Kate, we'll be fine," he said, "Besides, I'm a professional rider. I'll take care of you. I promise."

"Wait, do you have experience riding horses?" she asked, while trying to comfortably adjust herself above the saddle.

"I grew up riding horses," he replied, and then, with one tap of Starlight's reins, they were off.

"Hold on tight," he warned, while motioning for her to grab hold of him.

As Kate held onto John's waist, for once, she enjoyed the thrill and excitement of it all. Riding a horse was both free and liberating. It was new and unknown territory. A year ago, she never would have predicted being here, not in a million years. Back then, she was Dr. Kate Stanley, a professor specializing in Ottoman history at NYU. But now, she was posing as her twin sister, in a life that was the complete opposite of her own. Here, she was at the mercy of this majestic creature, which she had only just met, along with a man, who, no more than an hour ago, was in her eyes, a mere ambassador; but in truth, he was both an ambassador, as well as a classically trained and professional horseman. For a long moment, Kate sat there, allowing her free hair, which she had recently released from her bun, to fly across with the wind, as she watched and admired both the horse and its rider, from behind.

Although riding Starlight was an experience that went above and beyond any of her wildest dreams and expectations; she was now, equally interested, if not more, on learning about the rider, than she previously had been about his horse. It then occurred to Kate that while John had known much about her, she in return, really didn't know much about him.

"John," she began, while still holding onto him from behind, "Where did you grow up?"

Once again, he smiled. She had been interested on learning more about him. Suddenly, the urge for him to tease her increased.

"Why the sudden interest?" he teased.

Kate blushed. She hadn't expected him to put her on the spot. Luckily for her, she was behind him and he couldn't see her reaction. But somehow, she sensed that he knew that she was turning pink out of embarrassment, yet again.

But, without her speaking another word, he replied, "In Napa Valley, located in Northern California. An hour away from San Francisco."

"Is that where you learned to ride horses?" she inquired, most curiously.

"Yes," he replied, "My family owns a vineyard there, along with horses. During my childhood, I use to practice riding them every weekend, until I finally left for college."

"Does this mean, that you have several years of experience riding horses?" she asked.

"Yes," he answered, "Several."

"I can tell. You really do ride smoothly too and—" she said.

 "We're here," he interrupted.

"Where?" she asked.

"Just look straight ahead," he said, pointing directly across from them.

Looking straight ahead, Kate saw that they arrived to a hidden botanical garden. Much to her delight, there were hundreds of flowers scattered about, ranging in various colors and species, from pink and yellow tulips to white lilies, as well as several red rose bushes planted throughout. They were, quite honestly, some of the most beautiful flowers that she'd seen. The garden was most certainly, a spectacular view.

"Is this land still part of the country club?" she asked, surprised that she was standing right in the center of a real-life secret garden.

"Yes," he said, as he hopped off from Starlight, and then, reached over to help pull her down from the horse.

Once safely on the ground, Kate followed besides John, as he grabbed Starlight's reins by his hands, pulling the animal behind him. After tying and securing Starlight's reins to a nearby tree, his attention reverted back to Kate.

Reaching over, once they locked hands again, he pulled her towards him and said, "Follow me, this way."

Walking straight head, they moved a few paces over, until finally, they came across a pair of magnolia trees, which stood side by side to each other, in full bloom. And right behind those trees, was a small waterfall, with a tiny streaming creek, nearby. Staring at the creek, Kate noticed several small pink and purple lily pads, floating about above the water. She was absolutely mesmerized. Stolen from the pages of a storybook fairy tale, the waterfall and garden were a sight that one could only dream about!

"John, this place is absolute stunning!" Kate exclaimed.

"Do you like it?" he asked, wanting her to share her thoughts.

"Of course, I do," she replied and then, she turned around and asked him, in return, "But, where exactly are we?"

"It's a bit of a secret spot of mine," he admitted, "It's still a part of the country club, but since the land is so vast and mostly unexplored, not everyone at the club is aware that this place even exists."

"It's so beautiful," she whispered aloud, and then, she told him, "John, thank you so much, for sharing your special place with me."

Touched by her sincere words, John smiled.

"No, thank you for keeping me company," he said, and then, looking straight ahead, he added, "But, if I'm being honest, you're actually the first person that I've ever brought here, too."

"I am?" she asked, surprised by his revelation.

"Yes, it's true," he admitted.

"But why?" she inquired, most intrigued.

"It's my fault, really," he admitted, "I've spent too many countless days and lonely nights alone, at my office, always buried away at my work. Dedicating myself solely to my career was ultimately the downfall to my personal life. The real tragedy is that I failed to find a balance between my career and my private life. It was always work and nothing else. I realize that now. Somehow, one way or another, I allowed my life to simply pass on by, without me. And because of my own selfish ambitions, I missed out on having more special private moments like this."

"I understand completely," she promptly said, "I'm guilty of it too."

"You are?" he asked, most surprised by her admission. Not once, did he expect Kate, of all people, to sympathize with him. Not ever.

"Up until now, I, too, buried myself in my work. There's always just one last lesson to plan, or just one last paper to grade. It never ends. But, if I'm being truly honest, these are only excuses that I make to myself, and no one else. After graduation, I started my tenure at the university and thereafter, I just worked all day, all night, every day, winters and summers, all to no end in sight. I never once took a vacation. Not even a sick day. I never visited any of my friends or family. If there was a scheduled family event, I always rescheduled; or worse, I always pushed and extended our meeting dates out so far in advance, that when the eventual date actually came into fruition, I was a consistent no-show. Honestly, I can't even begin to tell you, as to just how many times over the years that Jennifer personally asked me to come and visit her. I, being the career obsessed woman, always skipped out on her. All I've ever cared about was my aspirations, ambitions and career. But now, being here with you, in this magical and surreal place, I've realized that I, too, have missed out on having more private moments like this. I, too, have inadvertently allowed my life to simply pass on by, without me, as well. Sadly, now, in Jennifer's absence, I've got so much overwhelming regret buried deep down inside of me. With each passing day, I grow more anxious and fearful that I'm really losing her. I'm just so terribly afraid that my sister might be gone for good, and that I may never see her again…" her voice trailed off, and she began to hysterically cry.

At that very moment, John's instincts took over. Without any fear, nor hesitation, he immediately grabbed hold of her entire body and pulled her towards him, embracing her in a warm and passionate hug. Her tears felt like knives pricking away at his heart, and at that very second, all he wanted to do was to comfort her. It was as simple and as natural as that.

"Shush," he said, as he attempted to calm her nerves down, by gently stroking her hair with his hands. He reassured her, "Everything will be okay. We will find her. Whatever it takes, we'll bring her back home to you. I promise."

Lifting her head up, she stared directly at him. Although her eyes had been covered in tears, his comforting words helped her tears to stop. With her safely tucked aways within his embrace, he, ever so gently, reached over and began wiping away all of her tears, one by one, with the stroke of his own bare hands.

"You promise?" she asked, while sniffing her runny nose.

"Yes, I promise," he vowed.

Deep down inside, John always knew that eventually, one day, Jennifer would return, sooner or later. He never doubted that. In fact, he was certain of it. He always presumed that she was far away, off at one of her many rendezvous, enjoying the sunshine at a private island with her lover, with the expectation that eventually, she'd return in time for their divorce proceedings. But what he hadn't expected was to fall for her sister, in the process. This part wasn't planned, nor calculated, at all.

Alas, that's what all of this was really, wasn't it? He was falling in love with Kate. Slowly, but surely. Kate had unexpectedly entered into his life like a gust of fresh wind blowing pass an open window, and just like the wind, it was only a matter of time, before that very air floated away and left him for good. While he promised Kate that he would do everything in his power to bring her sister back home, at the same time, he also realized that the sooner Jennifer returned, the sooner Kate would exit from his life for good. The very thought pained him, immensely.

Staring at the woman, whom he silently cherished, but yet, also knew that he could never have, John tried his best to keep her calm within his strong and caring arms. Once her temperament appeared to be more peaceful, John decided that it was best to return her back to the country club, so that she could rest more comfortably inside.

"We should probably get back, now," he finally said, "I'm sure Chef Homura could use a break from my mother."

Suddenly, Kate just giggled. She forgot that Chef Homura had taken their place at the table, as Barbara's form of entertainment.

"You're right," she said, "Is it a far walk back?"

"We'll ride Starlight," he said, "I'll drop you off with Mother, then I'll return Starlight back to the stables, myself."

"Are you sure?" she asked, not wanted to leave him alone.

"I'm sure," he replied, confidently.

Together, they slowly made their way back to Starlight. Once John was in close vicinity to the horse, he untied her reins, hopped onto its saddle, and then proceeded to help lift Kate back onto the horse. After securely seating her behind him, John gently tapped Starlight's rein, and within seconds, they were off riding back to the country club.

A few minutes later, they arrived to the club's front entrance. Following John's command, Starlight stopped and stood in place, as Kate slowly climbed back down to the ground. Once Kate's feet touched the ground, John, who was still seated on top of Starlight, waited for Kate to safely enter back into the building. However, as she was about to approach the door, there was a sudden and large scream, followed by a cry from afar, that caught both of their attention.

Immediately, Kate turned around. Looking straight ahead about a hundred meters away, Kate saw a young girl, dangling off from a tree branch. As Kate squinted her eyes to capture a better view, she saw that the branch, in which the child was nested upon, was breaking! If they failed to act fast, that child was surely going to fall!

"Help!" scream and cried the young girl, who couldn't be more than seven years old.

By this time, everyone from the country club, including Barbara, was outside standing, looking to inspect all of the commotion. But before anyone had the time to react, or call for help, John swiftly took command of the situation. Just like the Kentucky Derby, with one tap against Starlight's reins, John and his horse were off in an instant.

In no time, John rushed with Starlight at lightning speed across the park. Within mere seconds, they arrived over to the tree, just in time, as the branch broke in half. John's swift speed couldn't have been more perfect, for the moment he swooned in, he managed to catch the young girl safely within his arms.

His heroic deed, certainly did not go unnoticed. Upon releasing the child from his arms, the crowd immediately cheered and clapped in his support. The young girl's parents quickly rushed over towards them, and began hugging and kissing their daughter, whose life had just been spared thanks to John's swift actions. Meanwhile, Kate proudly watched on, as the crowd went wild with joy. They clapped, they cheered, they whistled. John was a town hero.

At that exact moment, that very singular moment, frozen and captured in time, Kate realized just how much she cared for him. And for the very first time, Kate felt another new yet foreign emotion growing, within the outer corners of her heart, but this time, it wasn't related to John, but towards her twin sister, Jennifer, her own flesh and blood…and that emotion was envy. Alas, Kate was green with envy, and she was jealous of Jennifer. But this was very much unlike her. She had never been the jealous type. Not once. Not ever.

Kate was always loyal and supportive to Jennifer. She had always respected Jennifer's belonging and never once dared to take anything away from her that wasn't hers. It was one of the primary reasons, as to why it was so difficult for Kate to initially agree to pose as her twin in the first place, because Kate always respected Jennifer's belongings and she didn't want to tamper with any of her things. But circumstances had been different and this time, Jennifer needed her, and Kate, the ever-supporting sister, put aside her teaching career and blindly flew halfway around the world to help her. And that, was typical of Kate. She was always the sister willing to sacrifice her own wants and needs, in exchange for her twin's desires, even though, that very same twin rarely did the same for her, in return. Although Kate knew and acknowledged this one weakness of her twin sister, she still stood by her. She was always loyal to her. But for the first time, she finally wanted something that didn't belong to her and that, was unlike her and it made her feel so terribly guilty. It was just so incredibly painful, that Kate, the professor, whose primary occupation is to speak, couldn't even find the words to articulate the amount of agony and despair that she felt buried deep, within her chest.

"Jennifer's so lucky to have him. He's wonderful," she whispered to herself, with such yearning and pain, within her voice.

However, she was not alone, for when she uttered those very words, Barbara, who was standing nearby, heard everything.

"Why Jennifer," spoke Barbara, with sheer surprise and astonishment, "Why do you refer to yourself, as a third person? You are Jennifer and my dear, you are lucky to have him, you are, you are," she said, in effort to help serve as a reminder to her.

Not wanting to protest, Kate silently nodded, in agreement. However, as she silently watched on from afar, with tearful eyes, she finally realized, at long last, that she was falling in love with the one man in the world, whom she could never have; and the immeasurable pain, that she now secretly harbored within her own fragile heart, was simply put: dreadfully and heartbreakingly unbearable to bear.

Chapter 19

Ten Years Ago in Balikesir, Türkiye …

"**G**o ahead and pick one," said Shakire, as she held up an exquisite turquoise blue and golden box, decorated with white pearls on the top and outer corners, within her hands. However, it wasn't any ordinary box, for it was a box of lokum, or better known in the western world, as simply Turkish delight.

"Are you sure that we shouldn't wait for Jennifer, to return?" asked Kate, hesitantly.

Shakire, Jennifer and Kate had all recently finished drinking their afternoon Turkish coffee. After reading the girls fortunes, Jennifer was most eager to record their grandmother's predictions into her diary. However, the ink to her pen had dried out, so Jennifer had briefly stepped away from the house to visit the market to purchase a new pen.

"Nonsense," replied Shakire. "You can't always wait around for Jennifer. Kate, it's high time that you start making your own decisions, by yourself."

Kate nodded in agreement to her grandmother. She then proceeded to inspect the candy box that lay open, within Shakire's hands. Similar to a candy shop, the candy box contained a vast variety of lokum, ranging in various flavors. Each candy was cut into separate, but equal rectangular squares, and were nicely arranged and lined up across, into five equal rows. Among the flavors, there were pink rose water, creamy caramel toffies, powdered sugar vanilla with walnuts, lemon and mint, burnt passionfruit, orange glazed, and almond, with a small hint of chestnut. And each of these flavors had at least two or three versions of it, within the candy box. However, the one that captured Kate's attention was the one, located right in the center of the candy box. It was a bright emerald green shade, which was decorated with tiny pieces of a diced nuts, generously sprinkled across on its top layer. It was the only one of its entire kind, in this particular candy box.

"Go ahead and choose," Shakire encouraged. "But you can only pick one, so choose wisely," she reminder her.

Kate continued to stare at that emerald green lokum. Unlike the rest, it appeared to be the only of its kind in the entire box.

"Green one caught your eye?" asked Shakire, who had followed her granddaughter's wandering gaze.

"How'd you know?" asked Kate, surprised that her grandmother knew, as to which candy, she liked best of all.

Shakire just laughed to herself and said, "It's pistachio. Go ahead, go on, take it."

Kate smiled and just as she began to reach over to grab it, Jennifer returned back from the market and abruptly pushed open the kitchen door's and entered the room.

"I'm back!" Jennifer announced, as she quickly slammed the kitchen door shut behind her.

"What's this?" asked Jennifer.

Quickly, Kate refrained from retrieving the candy, and instead, she answered "It's lokum."

"Yummy!" exclaimed Jennifer, happily.

Without even a second thought, nor consideration, Jennifer swiftly pushed Kate aside and within an instant, grabbed the emerald green lokum from out of the box, all for herself. Meanwhile, Kate watched on, as Jennifer forcefully shoved her desired candy straight into her hungry mouth. To her horror, Jennifer managed to lick and suck on all of the top sprinkled layers of the pistachio, before she eventually, attacked it's soft and chewy exterior, with a single bite. Sadly, Kate simply watched and stared as her sister devoured the emerald green colored pistachio lokum, right in front of her. The very same candy, in which, only mere moments ago, Kate was just about to claim for herself, as her first and special choice.

Meanwhile, their grandmother, unhappy with this outcome, was about to interject, when Kate gently tapped on her grandmother's hand, silently giving her a private signal, pleading that she not interfere. Although Shakire understood Kate's resistance, she didn't agree with her. However, in the end, she reluctantly remained silent, as she didn't want to get in-between the relationship with the twin sisters. And so, much to their dismay, both grandmother and granddaughter quietly watched on, as Jennifer proceeded to eat Kate's favorite emerald green pistachio lokum.

However, to their surprise, with just one single bite, Jennifer promptly threw the emerald green lokum back into the box and screamed, "Yuck! This taste absolutely disgusting! What in the world, is this horrid thing?"

"It's pistachio," replied Kate, astonished by her sister's outburst.

"Pistachio?!" exclaimed Jennifer, "Yuck, I hate nuts! Why didn't anyone say something to warn me? This is terrible!"

Immediately, Jennifer reached back into the candy box and for a second time, she grabbed another lokum, as a replacement. However, this time, she chose a safer and more commonly suitable flavor, the pink rose water lokum, which was one of the more frequent flavors found in every candy box.

"Serves me right for trying something so…so…so…" spoke Jennifer, but she couldn't find the correct word to convey or describe it.

"So unusual?" asked Kate, trying her best to finish her sister's thoughts.

"Yes! Unusual," replied Jennifer, "Besides, I hate green. Honestly, I've got no idea, as to what possessed me to pick it, in the first place. Anyways, pink is my favorite color and roses are my favorite flower."

Once in her hands, Jennifer threw the pink rose water lokum straight into her mouth, and she ate the entire piece of candy, without a single fuss. Afterwards, she exited the kitchen to return back into her bedroom, most eager to record and update her diary using her new pen, leaving Kate and Shakire behind and alone in the kitchen.

"Why did you allow her to take it?" Shakire finally asked Kate, directly.

Kate, whose eyes had been glaring down at the partially eaten emerald green lokum, simply replied, "Because I wanted to make her happy."

Her response did not please Shakire in the very least, and so, she replied back, by posing another question, "And did it make her happy?"

"No, it didn't," Kate admitted, with an uneasy and disappointed tone in her voice.

Shakire, whose expression remained stern but calm, asked another follow-up question, "Tell me, Kate, in the end, which did she choose?"

"The pink one," Kate answered.

"Exactly," said Shakire. "And so, all of your efforts to make her happy failed. In the end, she ate two pieces of candy; whereas, you had none. Oh, I had wanted you girls to eat only one, so that you both still had an appetite for dinner!"

Out of frustration, Shakire just sighed to herself.

"I'm sorry grandmother," Kate pleaded.

Although Kate had the best of intentions, she also realized that Shakire was indeed, right.

"Don't be sorry, Kate," Shakire responded and she further stated, "Don't ever be sorry. Always stand by your decisions, whatever they maybe."

"Grandmother," Kate began, "Are you mad at me?"

"No, Kate, I'm not mad at you," replied Shakire. "Not at all. On the contrary. In fact, I rather admire you for your sincere efforts."

"You do? But why?" asked Kate, surprised by Shakire's kind words. Not at all, did she ever expect Shakire to relay to her such an admirable complement.

"Kate, I'm afraid that you, unlike your twin sister, were born with a very generous heart," admitted Shakire, "But, at the same time, people, such as yourself, with big hearts, also must be extra careful."

"Careful about what?" asked Kate, most concerned at this potential prospect.

"Of the world," Shakire revealed.

Suddenly, Shakire directly turned her full attention over to Kate, and she forewarned her, "Kate, as you blossom into a young lady, many people, along the way, will attempt to take advantage of your kindness, both strangers and people of familiarities, alike. However, at the same time, you, in return, must learn how to find a balance, in between. As I always say, there's a time to laugh, and a time to cry. A time to offer help, and a time to ask for it. A time to love, and a time to hate. For you see, my dearest Kate, everything in life functions within a balancing system. Good and evil. Positive and negative. Yin and yang. The secret to life is all about finding a balance, regarding when to say yes and when to say no. But most importantly, learning and knowing the precise moment, as to when the proper time comes to fight back."

"But how do you do that? Especially, when it comes to fighting back?" asked Kate, as she intuitively listened on to her grandmother's wise advice.

"When you want something for yourself," replied Shakire, "It's okay to be selfish, once in a while, especially, when it comes to something that you really want. Do you understand, what I mean?"

"Are you referring to what happened today, with the emerald green lokum?" asked Kate.

"Yes, precisely," Shakire answered and she further added, "Kate, when you want something, when you really want something, then that's the appropriate time to speak up. Don't be afraid to fight for it. To say no, if you have to. Even to your own twin sister. Do you follow me?"

"Yes, I think, I do," admitted Kate, who now, suddenly began to feel a bit embarrassed and ashamed for not having the courage to speak up to her twin sister much earlier.

"Also, I think that by saying 'no' to your sister, every once in a while, isn't a bad thing, either. In fact, I think it might do her some good, as she's becoming a bit too spoiled, as of lately," remarked Shakire.

Looking straight into Kate's eyes, Shakire further explained, "Furthermore, by saying 'no' to her, that doesn't change, nor alter, the love that you two share for one another. Jennifer knows very well, that you love her. And, I, also know that she, too, loves you, just as much, in return. After all, you're twins. Two spitting mirror images of one another. A real-life Yin and Yang. You, my dear Kate, must simply learn how to stand up for yourself, that's all."

Kate nodded in agreement. She then promised Shakire that one day, in the future, she would do just that. Later on, as Shakire exited the kitchen, leaving the candy box behind, Kate pulled the remaining partially eaten pistachio emerald green lokum from out of the box. Taking a clean knife from out of the kitchen's drawer, she cut off the bitten end, where Jennifer's mouth had touched it. Once cut, Kate threw away the old eaten part into the garbage can, and she proceeded to dust off the remaining crumbs. Finally, at long last, Kate threw the remaining piece of the emerald green lokum into her mouth, savoring each and every last bit and morsel…and what almost never was, actually, miraculously came to be and the long wait, certainly, did not disappoint…

Present Day in Istanbul, Türkiye …

The state dinner was only a day away and ever since they returned back to the mansion from the country club, John was immediately summoned that same day to an unscheduled conference in Ankara. He was expected to meet with the Turkish Ambassador at the main office, to further discuss their upcoming pipeline project. Although Kate was unaware as to the specific details surrounding this classified project, as far as she knew, John was required to travel in person. As a result, John was to remain in Ankara until tomorrow night, and return back to Istanbul right in time to make a formal appearance at their upcoming state dinner.

With John away, Kate was blessed with a few extra days to herself, to try and help clear her mind of him. Ever since John saved that little girl and proclaimed a hero, her feelings about him left her so utterly confused and conflicted. She cared for him, that much she knew. Furthermore, whenever she saw him in person, her heart always reacts, in such an unfamiliar way, that she herself, is bewildered. As far as she understood, she admired and felt kindly towards him. After all, they were friends. But most of all, Kate also knew that deep within her heart, it was only a matter of time before she completely fell head over heels and madly in love with him, if she hadn't done so already.

Out of hopelessness, Kate just sighed to herself. Her situation was simply impossible. Falling in love with a man, who could never be hers, felt like a constant knife, pricking away at her very core. She was only here for a temporary basis and eventually, when, God willing, Jennifer returned, then Kate was destined to go back to New York City to the old life that she left behind. However, somehow, Kate had an inkling that her life, from here on out, was never going to be quite the same again. In fact, she was already changing. Transforming. Evolving. Her life at the mansion had shown her a new perspective of the world. Knowing John and possibly loving him, proved to her that one's career isn't everything. Living life and experiencing love were just as equally, if not, more important, than just having a career, alone.

For the past few days, Kate spent her evenings alone, in solitude, sitting upstairs and locked away, within the confinements of her bedroom. While her mornings and afternoons were often spent exclusively, with Gloria and Bes, practicing her dance steps, or with Chef Homura, working to help prepare the arrangements for the upcoming state dinner, her nights were spent alone in her bedroom, where she continued her secret search for Jennifer's diary. Up to now, Kate still hadn't located the diary and with each passing day, she was beginning to lose hope of ever finding it. However, Sally's confirmation about the existence of the diary helped to serve as a comfort for her; but yet, Kate still felt frustrated that she hadn't yet found it by now. If only she had the diary, she thought, then she would have all the answers that she needed. And what exactly were those answers? She, herself, wasn't entirely sure; but either way, she just knew that she needed to read it. Point simple and blank. Furthermore, perhaps, by locating the missing diary, then maybe, she would have some sort of a clue, as to the whereabouts of her missing sister, as well as a much better and thorough explanation, as to what precisely happened to her.

Meanwhile, as Kate was lying down in her bed and pondering about her troubled circumstances, she unexpectedly, heard a knock at her door. Immediately, she climbed out of her bed, walked over to the door, and she opened it. To her surprise, standing right in front of her bedroom door, was Lucas.

"Hello Kate," he announced. "Do you have a free moment?"

"Sure, yes," replied Kate. "Please, come on in."

"No, that's alright. We can discuss all that I need to say right here, outside of your door. Anyways, this will be brief," he said, with his tone already sounding a bit annoyed, in advance.

"Very well, what is it?" she asked.

"I recently had an unexpected and surprise conference call with the ambassador. He requested a status on my ongoing investigation, regarding your sister. As per our conversation, he directly asked that I share with you the latest update on her case," he coldly said, with a sense of bitterness within his voice.

Secretly, Kate was overjoyed. John was a man of his words. Just like he promised back at the country club, he stayed true to his vow to her, to return her sister back home, safely. As it was, he was already eagerly pushing and pressuring Lucas to move the investigation, along. However, at the same time, she also didn't want Lucas to see her obvious joy. For whatever reasons, clearly, he was gravely annoyed.

Therefore, Kate, in her most professional, serious and poker face, kindly asked him, "And do you have any updates?"

"Unfortunately, no, I do not. But this is perfectly normal, in these types of cases. It takes time. And like I said before, if and when, I do have an update, and if it's deemed appropriate, then I'll let you know," he proudly said.

"But if the ambassador has already asked that you update me with her case today, then isn't also safe to presume that any new and future updates have already been deemed appropriate? In particular, to me, her next of kin?" she asked, with a raised brow.

However, her rhetorical and challenging questions, didn't sit too well with Lucas. Certainly, not at all. In fact, his fair and pale complexion soon began to turn stark red.

"Please," he said angrily, while grinding his teeth, "Just leave the investigation to me! It's what I do best!"

"Lucas, I'm sorry, I didn't mean to offend," said Kate, cautiously, "I do trust you, with my sister's case. I just want to remain in the loop, that's all."

"Fine," huffed Lucas, sarcastically, as his pale complexion slowly returned and then, within an instant, he forced himself to showcase the most fakest and insincere of smiles.

"If there's nothing else," he said, "Then I'll be on my way."

Suddenly, out of the blue, as soon as Lucas turned his back and was ready to walk away, Tabitha darted out from Kate's bedroom. Once the cat passed through her threshold, she ran straight into Lucas, scratching and clawing him, along the way.

"Ouch!" he screamed in horror, as Tabitha violently attacked him.

But before Kate even had the opportunity to react, Tabitha ran fast ahead and dashed straight across down the hallway. To make matters worse, following her nearby, was none other than Jewel! It seemed that Tabitha was being chased and pursued by Barbara's pesky little dog.

As Jewel ran pass them, the little cairn terrier managed to push Lucas' legs apart in the process, where he immediately, came tumbling down onto the floor. Had Lucas been just one inch closer to Jewel, then Barbara's little dog was sure to have bitten him, right there and then, on the spot, and on his leg. However, once all the commotion finally settled down, Tabitha and Jewel, were nowhere to be found. Meanwhile, Lucas, lying on the floor, rolling around and shouting from extreme and excruciating pain. To Kate's amazement, he resembled that of a large and oversized lump of burning hay.

"Lucas!" exclaimed Kate, who quickly rushed over to his side and tried her best to help lift him back up.

However, Lucas was a hefty man, and his weight was a bit too heavy for Kate to lift, all by herself. Nevertheless, she still continued to try to push him back up, from off the ground. Finally, after much effort, she was able to somewhat help lift him up, but only partially. He, himself, struggled to push the rest of his remaining self, from his stomach and upwards. Leaning against the wall, he used all of his physical inner strength to eventually, rise back again, standing on his own two feet.

"I just hate animals!" he screamed loudly, at the top of his lungs. "Pain in the ass, cats and dogs! Good for nothing!"

"Lucas, I'm so sorry," Kate apologized, "Tabitha has never behaved like this before. I just don't understand what got into her. Maybe, she sensed Jewel coming and was trying to run away from her adversary, and unfortunately, you just somehow, got caught in the middle of their rift raft…"

"Wait, so it's my fault for standing here? Is that what you're trying to imply and say?" asked Lucas, harshly.

"No, not all. It's just that…" began Kate, who, at that very moment, really didn't know what else to say to him.

"Forget I asked!" barked Lucas. "Listen, Kate. I'm busy, you're busy. Let's just agree to go our separate ways, for now."

"Alright, Lucas, if that's what you want…" she said, but before she could say anything else, Lucas was long gone.

Rather than waiting for his return, which was very unlikely, Kate decided to go back into her bedroom. At least, in her bedroom, she was safe from the terrors of Tabitha and Jewel. Safe, at least, for the time being.

An hour later, Kate was getting ready to meet with her new dressmaker. As of yesterday, Sally informed her that the alterations to her new dress for their upcoming state dinner was complete. Protocol dictated that Kate perform at least one final dress fitting to determine, if any last moment alterations, were necessary.

Seated in front of her vanity mirror, Kate decided to pull her hair away, from off her face, and to pin her hair back up. However, when she attempted to retrieve her hair pin from the vanity's counter, it somehow, managed to slip away from her clutches, and inadvertently, accidentally landed above the hard wooden floor. Hoping that it didn't break, Kate proceeded to bend down to retrieve it, when to her sheer surprise, she saw that underneath the vanity's main drawer was another hidden drawer. A secret drawer.

This was most certainly, a surprise. Kate had never noticed this hidden compartment, ever before. Determined to find answers, Kate, whose entire body was now completely tucked underneath the vanity dresser, reached over and pulled open the newly discovered drawer. With much anticipation, as the drawer opened before her, a shiny golden book laid flat against its surface. Immediately, Kate quickly pulled the book from out of the drawer. And there, safely tucked away within her arms, was the long-awaited book that she had been searching weeks for. At long last, Kate finally discovered the location to Jennifer's secret diary.

Staring right at her clock, with a few hours to go until her appointment with the dressmaker, Kate decided right then and there, to open the mysterious golden book. Having done so, Kate proceeded to read the contents to Jennifer's diary, starting at page one…

A Few Hours Later…

Kate closed the book shut. She finally read the diary, in its entirety, word for word, line by line, page by page, and front to back. And now she knew. She knew everything. Everything about her sister. All her secrets, desires and lies. Even, her own scandals.

Having read her diary, as written directly from her own personal account, Kate realized that Jennifer lived in a modern-day gilded cage of her very own. While the world might have perceived that she had lived a privileged life from the outside, behind the mansion's interior walls, nothing was as it seemed. Even her own twin sister, Kate, was completely unaware as to Jennifer's actually reality.

The truth was that Jennifer was absolutely miserable living at the mansion. She hated being here. She was utterly unhappy. She disliked most of the staff, especially, Gloria. And, sadly, she was in a loveless marriage. She didn't love John. She never did. In fact, she was even unfaithful to him. She had many lovers. Meanwhile, all this time, Kate foolishly felt guilty about her true feelings for John; when in truth, Jennifer, not only didn't care for him, but that she cheated on him on numerous occasions, and was even, on the brink of divorcing him, once and for all.

But what about John? Was he also unfaithful to her? Was he even aware about all of Jennifer's extramarital affairs? For a long while, Kate pondered about these lingering questions. However, after much thought, she concluded, that no, John wasn't the unfaithful type. After spending these past several weeks within his company, she had personally gotten to know John. Having had the pleasure of knowing him, Kate knew, deep down inside her own heart, that he was genuinely, a decent, good hearted, loyal, respectful and honorable man. Even Jennifer had admitted much of the same, within the contents of her own diary.

And did John love Jennifer? At some point, he must have; otherwise, then why did he marry her, in the first place? But then again, Kate wasn't entirely certain. After all, John, too, recently agreed to a divorce; as Jennifer, herself, stated within her diary. Surely, he no longer had feelings for her, if they mutually agreed to separate?

However, at that very moment, Kate caught a glimpse of herself in the mirror, and she saw that the face staring back her, was indeed Jennifer's. Slowly, but surely, after spending all these past weeks at mansion, she was gradually and physically transforming into her twin sister. Mission accomplished, wasn't it? It certainly didn't feel that way. However, Kate couldn't help but wonder, the following: if every time John sees her, did he truly see Kate, as herself, or as the idealized version of Jennifer? And by some odd miracle, if John could eventually grow to care for Kate, just as much as she was growing to care for him, in return; then was it possible for him to one day love her, as her true self, and not as an alternative version to her twin sister? Kate sighed to herself. Only time would tell.

But what about Jennifer's own disappearance? Was it possible that she simply ran away? Away with one of her many lovers? To start a brand-new life? Or, had someone tried to do away with her? To kill her? And if so, whom? Someone from the mansion? One of the embassy staff? Sally? After all, she did threaten Sally's career, in the past, for discovering her secret affair with Badi. Sally was her personal assistant, so she knew most of her secrets, better than most. But, at the same time, Sally didn't seem like the type. From what Kate personally observed, Sally was a hard worker, whose primary focus was just simply to do her job. That's it. Surely, she had nothing to do with it? Right?

How about Gloria? Gloria, the infamous embassy coordinator, who ran the mansion and embassy, with a sheer and dominating force, using her iron fist approach. She was a difficult woman, to be sure. Furthermore, she and Jennifer seemed to have a rather dysfunctional and rocky relationship. Could Gloria have been responsible for Jennifer's disappearance? That was certainly, a real possibility.

Or better yet, had one of Jennifer's romances turned fatal? Was it possible that one of her lovers killed her? Could Badi, Demitri or another unknown lover, not disclosed or mentioned within the pages of the diary, have reemerged into her life and sought revenge? Anything was possible. But the worst possible scenario, the worst thought of all, to have ever crossed Kate's mind: Did John play a part in her disappearance?

Kate shivered at the very idea. No, thought Kate, not John. He would never hurt anyone. Never. Not ever. He was a hero, after all. Saving lives and lending Kate moral support. Why, just this morning, he was already pressuring Lucas to expedite the investigation, further along. Surely, he was innocent? Wasn't he?

As for Lucas, why did he act so strangely today? For whichever reasons, he always seems to take offense, whenever Kate questions him about the investigation. Could it be that he just doesn't like people stepping over his toes? After all, he did ask that she leave the case alone, in his personal care. But was that a mere suggestion, or an ominous warning? Or was it simply, detective talk? It was hard to tell.

How about the other remaining employees? Was Bes, Carol or Tyler somehow involved? Were they aware of her adulterous affairs and nature? Did they harbor some hidden knowledge, as to Jennifer's disappearance and whereabouts? And if so, why conceal it? Certainly, they must know something? After all, they were a part of her immediate circle, were they not? Her most trusted and sought-out advisors?

However, if not them, then perhaps, someone else from the other extended staff? The Butler? Or maid? Or dress maker? Hair stylist? Maybe, even the gardener? But, with a collective combined staff, ranging in the mere hundreds, all scattered about between the estate and embassy grounds, it's honestly impossible to keep track of all of them. At this rate, as Kate deduced, it's virtually inconceivable to pinpoint any specific employee, with direct ties to Jennifer, because in these past five years or so, she's interacted with just about everyone.

Alas, but certainly not least, there's still the matter concerning the ring, dare we not forget! Much to Kate's surprise, the revelation that her own beloved pearl ring was in fact, originally bestowed upon Jennifer, on her wedding day, as her marriage ring from John. No wonder he was so upset and angry at their first dinner! He must have seen the lost ring on her finger! But why on earth, would her sister give her this ring? Out of all other rings? Sadly, the diary failed to provide any insight into this topic. This vexed her. Jennifer's silence on this matter, left Kate so puzzled as to understand her sister's true intentions and motives for bestowing such an unorthodox gift to her. However, regardless as to how she obtained the ring, it was still, nevertheless, a much-loved gift from her sister. Therefore, as a sentimental keepsake, Kate decided to keep and cherish it, as a constant reminder of her much-loved twin sister.

In the end, after much reflection, Kate concluded that the most logical explanation for her sister's disappearance was that she simply ran away. After all, Jennifer disliked her restricted life here. Most likely, as Kate believed, she must have decided to take a holiday and ran off, with one of her lovers. Eventually, and hopefully, Jennifer was going to return back home, in time for her divorce. It was as simple as that. It had to be. What other logical explanation was there? And in truth, this explanation brought the most comfort to Kate, for at the very least, if Jennifer had truly runaway, then it also meant that Jennifer was out there somewhere, happy and comfortable, too. Eventually, within a matter of time, she was going to return back home to her. Safe and sound.

In the meantime, Kate needed to remain strong and to carry on with her normal duties, as usual. Until Jennifer returned, Kate needed to continue on with her charade, posing as her twin sister and playing the part of the ambassador's loving wife; all the while, maintaining peace with the staff, in the process. However, this time, it was going to be different. Much different. This time around, she was much more knowledgeable now, than ever before.

Having gained direct insight into Jennifer's life through her diary, Kate knew what needed to be done. And that started by first maintaining order, within the household. After witnessing all of the brutal behavior, hostility and corruption, firsthand, Kate could no longer allow Gloria to rule the mansion with her fierce and iron fist, while trampling all over everyone, in the process, just as she had been doing, all this time. For a change, she was going to now speak up and challenge her. Ultimately, Kate decided to do all of the things that Jennifer desired to do, as expressed within her diary, but unfortunately, lacked the courage to actually go through with it. As a second chance around for her sister, this time, Kate was going to properly play the role as the ambassador's wife, the correct way, in which her sister originally sought to be, but simply couldn't.

With regards to John and all matters concerning him…well, as far as he was related, Kate no longer felt guilty about her feelings for him; because in truth, John was a free man. However, moving forward, her only hope was that if John did have feelings for her, then she secretly wished, with all her heart, that he cared for her as herself, and not, as her twin sister, Jennifer.

As for the diary, she wasn't going to surrender it over to Lucas. Kate decided right then and there, that since her sister's diary had been private all this time, then it was going to remain private, so long as she had possession of it. Also, Kate was beginning to have her own real doubts and concerns about Lucas. Thus far, his personality was too unpredictable. Furthermore, his anger over Tabitha and Jewel this morning surprised her, and ultimately, his poor actions left her with a negative impression of him. For if a man fails to properly care for the general welfare of animals, then is he truly trustworthy, in the first place? At the very least, his character is rather, questionable.

Suddenly, Kate heard another knock at her bedroom door. It was sure to be Sally. Having been so preoccupied with the diary, Kate realized that she lost track of time. Looking at her clock, she was exactly, one hour late to her scheduled dress fitting appointment!

"Dr. Stanley," said Sally, in panic, "The dressmaker is about to leave. She's been waiting over an hour for you…"

"Oh, my goodness!" exclaimed Kate, as she stepped outside of her door.

"Sally, I'm so sorry. Please do apologize to the dress maker on my behalf, and let her know that I'm on my way. I just need a few extra minutes to collect myself."

"Very well, I'll relay your message to her, right now," replied Sally, who then, immediately, skipped down the hall and back into the dressing room.

A few minutes later, Kate stepped outside of her bedroom and began walking down the hallway, making her way to her appointment. However, as she passed by the long corridor, she heard someone crying, from afar. For a brief moment, Kate stopped to listen. It was the sound of a female. Someone was here, alone and crying. But why? For a split second, Kate contemplated, as to whether or not, she should simply ignore the unknown person's cries, or to carry on with her already late appointment and to ignore the mystery person's sorrowful pleas. However, Kate's conscience got the better of her, and she refused to turn a blind eye on a person, in desperate need of immediate attention. Someone was clearly in pain, and Kate simply couldn't turn her back on them. Alas, the dress fitting would have to wait. As it currently stood, Kate had far more important matters to deal with, at hand.

Following the weeping echoes, Kate proceeded to walk down the corridor and there in the far corner of the room, she saw the culprit, seated down on a bench, with her hands covering her face. To Kate's surprise, the young female crying was none other, than Carol. But, why was such a generally cheerful, warm, and confident young woman crying here, all alone, in the far remote corners and shadows of the estate? Something was clearly amidst, and Kate intended to get to the bottom of it, once and for all.

"Carol," said Kate slowly, as she approached her. "Are you alright?"

"Dr. Stanley!" exclaimed Carol, as she quickly attempted to wipe away her tears, "What are you doing here? You're supposed to be at your dressing fitting! You shouldn't be here! Nobody is supposed to be here. That's why I'm here. I thought I was alone."

"Carol, why are you crying?" asked Kate, who now, joined her on the bench and sat beside her.

"I'm so embarrassed, Dr. Stanley," cried Carol. "I didn't want anyone, especially you, to see me, in such a distressful state."

"But you're human, Carol," Kate reminded her. "Sometimes, it's okay to cry. We all do, from time to time."

"But it's not like me to do so, at all," admitted Carol, out of frustration. "I'm a professional. I'm not supposed to cry. My parents didn't raise me to cry like this. This is so unlike me."

"What happened? Did someone hurt you?" asked Kate, who was now, more than ever, concerned about Carol's general welfare.

"I'm not sure I'm at liberty to say," replied Carol, fearfully.

"Go ahead, please tell me," Kate began, speaking very soothingly, "I promise that whatever you reveal to me, it will remain confidential. You need not be afraid. It will all be alright. Whatever it is, I can help you."

"Are you sure?" asked Carol, "I mean, I'm supposed to be the one counseling and advising you, not the other way around."

"Carol, you know, back in my real life, I'm a university professor," Kate reminded her.

"Oh yes, that's right. I forget that sometimes. I mean, it's why we all call you Dr. Stanley, after all," said Carol, whose tears, finally began to stop.

"Well, as a university professor, I do have several students, around your same age, who, often seek my guidance and advice, on a variety of matters, from time to time. And just as I've managed to help my students in the past, I can also help you, too, if you'd like?" asked Kate.

For a brief moment, Carol hesitated. But after listening to Kate's reassuring words, Carol decided to take a deep breath and reveal the truth. Having earned her trust, Carol finally admitted to Kate, "It's Gloria."

"Gloria, made you cry?" asked Kate, who was now deeply concerned by Carol's honest admission.

Remaining silent, Carol just nodded in agreement to Kate's question.

"But why? How?" Kate pressed on, with great urgency.

"It's everything, really," admitted Carol, reluctantly. "Gloria's supposed to be my mentor. She's retiring within the next few months, so she's trying to groom me into her current position. However, recently she's made my job and life here, so incredibly difficult. Sometimes, I honestly believe that she's actually trying to sabotage me at my own job, so that she doesn't have to retire at all!"

"My goodness, sabotage? Do you really believe that's what she's trying to accomplish?" asked Kate, surprised by Gloria devious ways. Although Kate knew that Gloria wasn't one to be trifled with, picking on Carol was a new low, even for her.

"Yes, I do. She's always finding meaningless and petty errors in my work, and I'm a known perfectionist! But, to me, they're more like excuses, than anything else. But, Dr. Stanley, the thing is that I don't believe that she even wants to retire, in the first place. I, personally, think that she's being forced to retire, and because of this fact, she's desperately trying to find ways to cling on. The reality is that if I'm gone, then she'll have the opportunity to stay on and continue with her job, as if nothing ever happened to me! Dr. Stanley, mark my words, if anyone else after me comes along, as my replacement, then she'll do the same to them, too!" Carol loudly proclaimed.

"Hmm, I see. It's clear to me that she's using you as her scapegoat, isn't she?" asked Kate, with a raised brow.

"Exactly! Dr. Stanley, you nailed it! I'm her scapegoat. For as long as I need grooming, then she has an excuse to stay on board, for as long as she wishes. There's no one around to challenge or hold her accountable. She's absolutely milking it; but, I, on the other hand, simply can't stand this toxic environment any longer. The truth is that I'm ready to quit and return back home to California," sighed Carol, frustrated by her impending predicament.

"Carol, please don't do that. Don't ever give up on your dreams, not even for Gloria. If you quit now, then she wins and that's not fair. Carol, I promise you, I will find a way to help you," Kate desperately pleaded.

Suddenly, a brilliant idea came to Kate's mind, and so, she asked, "I say, Carol, what about Bes?"

"Bes? What about Bes?" asked Carol, confused by Kate's suggestion of him. Never once, had Carol ever equated Gloria with Bes, in the same sentence.

"Well, from my understanding," Kate began, "Bes has also worked for this agency for a long time. As I recall, he's served just about the same number of years, as Gloria has. In fact, I've often seen him covering her various duties, in her absence. Surely, he's more than capable of serving as your new mentor. Besides, Bes is a great teacher. I, for one, can attest since he, too, has been training me with dancing. He's positive, patient and kind. Traits more suitable for a mentor. If you permit, I'd like to speak with him, on your behalf. I just know that he'll make the perfect mentor for you. And eventually, in due time, with his guidance, you'll transition into your new role, the proper and healthy way."

"Wow, I just never considered Bes, as a possible mentor for me," reflected Carol to herself.

"Do you agree with my proposal?" asked Kate.

"Yes, of course. Anyone is better than Gloria, especially, Bes. But, how can we make it happen?" asked Carol, curious as to Kate's plans.

"Just leave everything to me," replied Kate, confidently. "Besides, what's the point of being the ambassador's wife, if I can't use some of my temporary influence to help others?"

And before Kate knew it, Carol immediately jumped up and gave her a huge hug.

"You're so wonderful Dr. Stanley!" Carol exclaimed, happily. "Thank you so much, for everything!"

"You're welcome!" exclaimed Kate, joyfully, in return. "Now, as I said before, just leave everything to me. In the meantime, I really must attend to my dress fitting appointment. That is, assuming that my dressmaker is still there."

"Oh!" exclaimed Carol. "Please don't let me keep you."

Finally, Kate waved farewell to Carol, and then she proceeded to walk the remainder down the hallway. When she eventually reached the dressing room, she saw Sally seated across with her new dressmaker, Ipek. Sadly, just as Kate had anticipated, they naturally appeared displeased by her tardy arrival.

"The dress is a new Calvin Klein, recently shipped over from New York. Using your last measurements, Ipek made some recent alterations to tailor to your shape," Sally announced.

"Thank you, Sally and Ipek. I apologize for being so late," said Kate, as she walked into the room.

Ipek, the dressmaker, did not respond but rather, her face remained expressionless. Ipek's peculiar behavior, left Kate confused as to whether or not, Ipek was truly angry, annoyed, or simply didn't care altogether. In either case, Kate tried her best to simply smile and approach Ipek with as much politeness and diplomacy, as she possibly could.

After Kate approached her, Ipek, still silent, quietly handed over the newly tailored black silk dress over to Kate's possession. Once in her arms, Kate walked over to a private corner in the room, which was covered with thick drapery, and she quickly changed into her new clothes. After slipping into her new dress, Kate stepped out from behind the curtains and once Sally caught sight of her, she beamed with delight.

"Mrs. Barrett, you look absolutely lovely!" exclaimed Sally, smilingly.

"Thank you, Sally," replied Kate, who, by now, standing right in the center of the room.

Suddenly, Ipek stood up from her seat and walked over to Kate's direction. Once she arrived, standing face to face with Kate, Ipek immediately began inspecting the trail of her dress. From all accounts, it appeared that the dress fit Kate as expected, with little to no alterations, necessary.

"The dress fits perfectly. No alterations are needed," spoke Ipek, at long last.

"Now, if you don't mind," Ipek added, "I have another appointment, which I am already *late* to."

Much to Kate's dismay, Ipek made certain that she emphasized the word "late" aloud, in her reply to publicly showcase her displeasure.

Immediately, Kate turned red out of embarrassment. Clearly, Ipek was angry at her due to her tardiness. However, before Kate even had a chance to apologize to her again, Ipek was long gone.

"It's alright, Dr. Stanley," spoke Sally. "I doubt that we'll ever see Ipek again. The agency usually hires new dressmakers for each new event."

"I see," said Kate. "Perhaps, it's for the best; as I'm sure that Ipek will never want to work with me, ever again."

"Don't trouble yourself about it," Sally remarked, "It's her lost, not yours."

Sally's kind words brought comfort to Kate, as the two women silently stood in front of the dressing mirror, and together, admired Kate's new dress. Although the dress was decent and fit Kate well, it was also at the same time, rather plain, at best. It was a standard evening dress that had shaped her figure nicely; however, it also appeared a bit too casual to serve as Kate's first official state dinner evening gown.

Unfortunately, time was limited and they were running out of options. As Kate started to silently ponder about her dress, she suddenly heard a large commotion from outside their door. The sounds were growing louder by the minute, too. Quietly, Kate just stood there listening. What exactly were those sounds?

After a long pause, Kate soon heard a very distinctive meow, followed by a loud bark. Immediately, afterwards, before Kate even realized what was happening, Tabitha ran straight into the dressing room and jumped up on Kate's dress. The pesty cat was followed by Jewel, who had been chasing after her. Within mere seconds, both Tabitha and Jewel managed to tear across Kate's new silk dress, leaving the edges all tattered and scratched.

"My God!" Sally exclaimed, in complete horror.

The entire time, Kate kept her eyes closed throughout the fiasco. By the time Tabitha and Jewel finally ran out of the room, Kate eventually reopened her eyes and saw that her once beautiful silk dress was now left in tattered pieces.

"My dress!" gasped Kate. "It's ruined! On Sally, what am I going to do? The state dinner is tomorrow and Ipek will never return back here…I just don't have enough time," sighed Kate, who was now extremely worried about her wry prospect.

"Not to worry, Dr. Stanley," Sally interjected quickly. "I can fix this."

"You can?" asked Kate, surprised by her admission.

"Please take off your dress, now," Sally commanded.

Following her instructions, Kate removed her dress and handed it over to Sally. Once Sally received the dress, she proceeded to walk over to the dressing table and pulled out a sewing machine from behind the storage closet. To Kate's surprise, Sally promptly began stitching the torn sections of the dress with her needle and thread, in hand. Within a few seconds, Sally had already nicely stitched closed several open holes by the stroke of her needle.

"Please take a seat, Dr. Stanley," said Sally, as she continued with her sewing. "This might take me a few minutes," she further clarified.

Once again, Kate followed her instructions and sat down on the chair. As Sally stitched and sewed, Kate looked on, in amazement. Clearly, Sally was not an amateur. Sally knew exactly what she was doing. She was a true professional. In fact, she stitched better, than Ipek, herself. Was sewing just another past time hobby for Sally? Or was Sally really a professional dressmaker, in disguise as an administrative assistant?

"Sally, where did you learn to sew like this?" asked Kate, who could no longer contain her curiosity.

"Wait, I'm almost done, Dr. Stanley," replied Sally, who was still in full concentration. "Just a few more stitches and there! All finished!"

Pulling the dress from out of the sewing machine, Sally handed it over back to Kate.

"Good as new!" she proudly exclaimed.

Upon receipt of the dress, Kate quickly changed back into it. As she stared into the mirror, Kate was shocked to see that her dress appeared practically brand new, without any trace of a previous tear, hole or even, a blemish. It was as if, Tabitha and Jewel, had never ruined her dress, in the first place.

"Sally, how on earth, did you fix this?" asked Kate, astonished by Sally's pristine work.

"Sewing is just one of my secret talents," replied Sally, smilingly.

"Do you sew, regularly?" asked Kate, whose curiosity was growing by the minute.

"Actually, yes, I do," Sally admitted, "Believe it or not, but I have an entire collection of dresses in my closet, that I've personally designed and stitched, myself."

"You do? Can I see them?" asked Kate, who was now more determined than ever, to discover firsthand, as to whether or not, Sally was indeed an aspiring fashion designer, in secret.

"Do you really wish to see them?" asked Sally, who was surprised and thrilled that Kate had taken an interest on her personal designs.

"Yes, I really do," Kate remarked and she further added, "If you design as well as you sew, then I might even be compelled to try on one of your dresses."

"Okay!" exclaimed Sally, joyfully. "In that case, please follow me to my room."

Upon Kate's agreement, Sally escorted Kate downstairs and into her private chambers. Once Kate entered Sally's bedroom, she was astonished to see that her personal space was covered from wall to wall, with various fabrics, textiles, designs, threads and even, a sewing machine of her very own, right smack in the center of the room. Suddenly, it became abundantly clear to Kate, that Sally was indeed a dressmaker, or better yet, a designer of some sort.

Passing through the threshold, Sally brought Kate to her personal closet, located in the far back corners of the room. When Sally finally opened her closet's door, Kate was amazed to see the rows of dresses hanging above, showcasing a variety of shapes, colors, textiles, fabrics and designs. Each dress was just as equally stunning as the one before. They were all like hidden gems, gently tucked away in an unknown, yet private collection that only Kate knew about and was the first to preview it.

"Sally, did you really make all of these on your own?" asked Kate, thoroughly impressed by Sally's secret talents.

"Every single last one of them," admitted Sally, proudly, "Not only did I make them, but I also designed, stitched and colored all of them, with my own two bare hands."

"Sally, you are so incredibly talented!" exclaimed Kate.

Glancing over, Kate saw one particular dress that caught her eye. It was a golden sequenced gown. It was hanging right next to her, on the rack.

"May I?" asked Kate, as she pointed towards the golden gown, with her finger.

"Of course!" exclaimed Sally, who was more than happy to showcase one of her private designs to her.

Gently pulling the golden gown from off her clothes rack, Sally handed the gown over to Kate to try on. Once in her hands, Kate took a brief moment to admire the exquisite beauty of the gown. Although the dress was a bit heavy from all the sparkling beads; it was nonetheless, spectacularly beautiful and breathtaking. The beads were all carefully crafted and stitched, with matching beaded straps that served as sleeves. Overall, the dress sparkled against the light and Kate immediately knew, that whoever was fortune enough to wear this dress, was going to be a modern-day Cinderella. Furthermore, the dress was a perfect hourglass silhouette and appeared to match Kate's exact measurements.

"May I try this gown on?" asked Kate, once more, seeking Sally's blessing to try on such a delicate and lovely gown.

"Oh my gosh, yes! Of course, you can!" exclaimed Sally, as she quickly helped Kate to peel off her clothes and switch over into the new gown.

Once Kate stepped into the golden dress, she immediately felt transformed. The dress simply fit like a glove. It was the perfect size to her figure and even the golden color from the gown, matched her skin's own complexion's undertone hues. Simply put, the dress was Kate's ultimate dream gown. Wearing it, she felt just like a princess attending a ball. This was it, thought Kate. This was the dress that she was searching for. Dreaming for. This dress was meant for her.

"Sally, may I wear this gown tomorrow evening?" asked Kate, hopeful that Sally would agree to her request.

"But what about Ipek's dress? It's still good to wear," replied Sally, hesitantly.

"No, I don't care for Ipek's dress. This is it. This is the right gown for me. I can feel it," said Kate, with much pride.

Sally wryly smiled, and then she asked, "But what about Gloria?"

"What about Gloria?" asked Kate, surprised that Gloria's name was even mentioned, within the same sentence as her dress choice.

"Gloria will be upset if you make such a sudden change, with your assigned dress. Especially, since she was the one who approved of your other dress, too. Also, you would technically, be wearing one of my unknown designs," admitted Sally, reluctantly.

"Wait," cried Kate. "Gloria chose my black Calvin Klein dress? The same dress from Ipek?"

"Yes," replied Sally. "She always makes all of the final decisions, regarding the specific gowns that Mrs. Barrett wears to these sorts of events."

"Was my sister aware of this?" asked Kate, in disbelief.

"Honestly, I'm not certain, but if I had to guess, I would say that more likely, she probably didn't. One way or another, Gloria always gets her way," said Sally, with great disappointment.

"Don't worry about Gloria," replied Kate, boldly. "Just leave her to me. Now, with your permission, I'd like to wear your dress to the state dinner. Please have this prepared and ready for me by tomorrow evening."

"Oh!" exclaimed Sally, in disbelief. The thought of anyone challenging Gloria's commands came as a total surprise. Suddenly, Sally smiled and said, "Dr. Stanley, of course you can! I'll have the gown pressed and prepped by tomorrow night."

"Perfect, thank you, Sally," said Kate, who was now beaming with delight.

"Is there anything else I can help you with, Dr. Stanley?" asked a very happy and grateful Sally.

"Actually, yes," replied Kate, with a raised brow. "Can you please tell me how someone as talented as yourself, end up working here? You belong in Paris, not Istanbul!"

"Oh, it's a long story," replied Sally, laughingly.

"That's fine. I'll wait," said Kate, as she sat herself down on Sally's sofa, nearby.

"Do you really care to know?" asked Sally.

"Yes, I do," Kate confirmed.

"Well, I never planned on being here, that's for sure. I'm originally from Boston. A little redheaded Irish-Catholic good girl, who innocently followed her then-boyfriend, Danny, all the way across the Atlantic Ocean and into Europe. For you see, Dr. Stanley, Danny was my childhood sweetheart. While he was an aspiring soccer player, I was an aspiring fashion designer. Much to our surprise, one day, Danny got recruited to play professionally for a European soccer team based in Milan, Italy, and I, a young teenager, barley eighteen years old, was crazy enough to join him. Sadly, I assumed, that since Milan is the capital of the fashion world, that I was going to meet my idol, Donatella Versace, in-person and somehow magically, I was going to be a world-famous fashion designer. Imagine that!"

"But that didn't happen, did it?" Kate interrupted.

"No, it didn't," sighed Sally. "After I moved to Italy, that's when my relationship with Danny started to go down-hill. A few months later, Danny eventually broke up with me and left me for another woman. It was just terrible! One of the worse times, in my entire life!"

Suddenly, Sally, began to tear up. Clearly, she was still not over Danny. Kate felt the immediate urge to comfort Sally.

"Sally, I'm so sorry," said Kate, as she extended her hands over to Sally's, in an attempt to comfort her.

"It's okay, it's not your fault," Sally reassured her, as she wiped away her own tears.

"So, what happened next?" asked Kate.

"Afterwards, I was all alone and penniless in a foreign country. I was practically homeless, if it wasn't for my old landlord taking pity on me, and offering me free shelter for a few additional weeks, in order to help me get back on my feet. But the reality was that I didn't want to return back home to Boston. Whether or not I was still with Danny, was irrelevant. By then, I had already decided that since I had traveled all the way to Europe, that one way or another, I was just going to make my dreams come true. But, in the meantime, dreams cost money; and so, I needed a job. And fast. Dr. Stanley, do you know as to which sorts of jobs are readily available to young single American females, who are all alone in Europe?" asked Sally to Kate.

Kate assumed that her choices couldn't have been good. But rather than speaking them aloud, she instead, asked Sally to tell her directly. And that, she did.

"Well, most single American women either become nannies and au pairs, or, they turn to illegal activities. Neither or which, were options for me. First of all, I don't speak a word of Italian, plus, I cannot stand children. Therefore, being a nanny or an au pair wasn't even an option for me. Second, I also couldn't get a regular job, on account of my lack of Italian. Lastly, as I said before, I'm a good Irish-American Catholic girl from Boston. My parents would have killed me if I tried to do anything remotely illegal, so that was that…" admitted Sally.

"But how did you end up here at the embassy? Here at the mansion?" asked Kate, who was still waiting to hear an answer to this lingering question.

"Yes, so when I finally realized that I didn't have much work options, I became rather desperate and depressed. Then, one day, out of the blue, as I was sitting down at a café, near my apartment, drinking my sorrows away over an extra-large cup of cappuccino and worried as to how I was even going to pay for my over expensive cappuccino, when suddenly, at the corner of my eyes, I saw a flyer at the window. It was an advertisement for an English-speaking secretary in need, for a working member of the U.S. Embassy in Rome, Italy. Immediately, I grabbed the flyer from off the window and contacted the embassy. A day or two later, I got an interview and was hired on the spot. Afterwards, I relocated from Milan to Rome, and worked for the then-U.S. Ambassador to Italy for about a year. Then, once he retired, an opening for a new secretary at the Cairo, Egypt embassy opened, which I applied to, as a transferee," explained Sally.

"And the position that opened up in Cairo, that was for my sister?" asked Kate.

"Yes, it was for Mrs. Barrett. And I've been working for your sister ever since. The rest is history. Now, by day, I work as Mrs. Barrett's personal assistant, but at night, I still work on my designs. Eventually, one day, I still want to become a world-famous fashion designer. It's just taking me some time to do it," said Sally, at long last.

"That you will," said Kate, happily. "And I'm going to help you. I promise."

"Dr. Stanley, you are too amazing, but how can you possibly help me?" asked Sally.

"Well, for starters, I'm going to wear your lovely gown tomorrow night. And once everyone discovers that you're the designer, then trust me, your phone line is going to be busy. Be ready," said Kate, with a smile.

"Oh my God, this feels like a dream! Thank you so much!" exclaimed Sally, as she began to tear up and in return, gave Kate a hug.

Afterwards, Kate exited Sally's bedroom, feeling content with today's outcomes. In fact, she had accomplished so much already. First, she discovered Jennifer's diary, read it and finally, she had comfort and a better understanding about her sister's past and whereabouts. Second, she ran into Carol, and she was unexpectedly able to help her with her work sorrows. Third, she completed her dress fitting and although things didn't quite go according to her plans; she did however, discover Sally's wonderful, yet secret talent. And now, because of it, she had a beautiful new gown to wear tomorrow night. However, there was one last task left to do for today. Luckily, for Kate, the person, whom she needed to speak to, somehow and miraculous, just passed by her down in the hallway.

"Oh Gloria, just the person that I needed to speak to," said Kate, as she attempted to stop Gloria, midway down in the hallway.

"Yes, Dr. Stanley?" answered Gloria, who also appeared to be in a bit of a rush.

"Three things," Kate began, "First, I decided that it's probably best that you hear this directly from me, and not someone else. Tomorrow night, I plan on wearing an alternative dress to the state dinner. I might also add, that this new gown is different from the selection of gowns that you had originally approved of, without my consent."

"What?!" exclaimed Gloria. "But you simply cannot do that! It's against protocols! Besides, how can you ever find such a suitable dress this last minute? As per our procedures, I must remind you, that you can only wear gowns made by American designers and not by any other foreign designers."

"Ah, but that's just that, Gloria," said Kate, with a smile. "It is an American designer. In fact, she's an upcoming designer. You might even already know of her. Why, her name is Sally Timmons, and come tomorrow evening, I plan on wearing one of her exclusive gowns from her new Fall collection."

"What?! Sally?" exclaimed Gloria, in confusion.

"Yes, that's right, our very own Sally. She's American and she's a designer. Therefore, it is appropriate that I wear one of her designs," said Kate, confidently.

Technically, Kate was absolutely correct. Sally was an American, and she was also a designer. Therefore, by wearing one of Sally's designs, Kate was in fact, in compliance to all protocols. Gloria was simply lost for words and left speechless.

"Second," continued Kate. "Effective Monday morning, Carol will now be reporting to Bes and he will serve as her new mentor, moving forward."

"Bes! But he's hardly qualified! Why, he's never trained anyone before!" yelled Gloria, whose face was beginning to turn red.

"Actually, that isn't true. He does have training experience. In fact, he's been training me, these past few weeks on how to dance. Also, given the fact, that he has just as many years of service just as you do here, I think it's fair to assume that he's more than enough qualified to groom Carol. Furthermore, he is both patient and kind, which I might add, are traits that Carol desperately needs right now, in order to successfully flourish here," said Kate, with full confidence.

"But you can't do that!" exclaimed Gloria, as she stomped her feet against the hard wood floor, while folding her arms together.

"Oh, but I can and I just did," said Kate, with full force and command.

"Then, I'll just have to tell the ambassador myself," huffed Gloria, who, was ready to personally call up John herself, as soon as she reached her office.

But Kate, being as clever as she was, beat Gloria right to the punch.

"Gloria," she calmly began, "You go ahead and do that, but please be aware, that I've already spoke to the ambassador this morning, and he agrees with me. In fact, he's already preapproved all of my requests."

Although this was technically a little white lie, as John was away and unreachable in Ankara, Kate also knew that had she really asked John, in-person, then he would have agreed with her, no questions asked.

"Why, I never have…" trailed off Gloria, who for the first time in her career, had someone challenge her on the spot.

"Finally," said Kate, with a victory smile, "Please send a copy of the embassy's official policies and procedures handbook over to my office, as soon as possible. Since you do tend to reference our protocols quite often, I've decided that I should like to take the time and read them thoroughly, myself."

At long last, Kate happily turned around and whistled as she confidently walked away, moving in the direction of her bedroom to retire for the remainder of the evening, leaving Gloria standing still, tongue tied and blue in the face.

Chapter 20

As John entered the grand foyer, he saw the Nigerian Ambassador from afar and greeted him with a wave. After his week-long stay in Ankara, he managed to arrive promptly on time for tonight's grand event. Overall, his trip was productive and everything else surrounding his pipeline project was going according to plan. However, his meetings with the Turkish Ambassador were rather long and exhausting. Although John would have preferred to have had an extra day or two to rest after his long journey back home, that simply wasn't possible due to his busy schedule. And now, the diplomatic state dinner was in session and from the looks of it, it already appeared to be a full house.

The estate was decorated all around, from each and every room, starting from the grand foyer to the balconies, and everywhere else in-between. Freshly cut from the garden, pink rose garlands were carefully placed all around, encircling the archways, entry thresholds and staircases. Each rose reflected a unique variation of the color pink, in which, no two shades were quite equally the same. Furthermore, the pink rose garlands projected a soft rosy glow against the dimmed candlelights, that in return, sparkled and glimmered throughout the property. In addition, all of the chandeliers were so extensively polished that the crystals shined like the stars up above in the midnight sky. Meanwhile, the marbled floors were scrubbed and mopped with such detail, that it was left as white and shiny like the first trace of snowfall in winter. Even the red carpets that were rolled out in honor for tonight's guests were pristine in color and hue, and were as crisp and red, just like a juicy and forbidden apple.

Throughout the room, John saw the many faces to all the usual diplomats and their wives in attendance. The very same groups of people, whom he had the repeated obligation to mingle and dine with over the years. The same crowd, the same dinners, the same conversations and the same laughter. It was always the same. Never anything new. And sadly, never anything truly authentic, genuine, or even real.

Unfortunately, John knew that in his world, everyone, in one way or another, was pretending to be someone, whom they weren't. Often times, the role in which they assumed were the complete polar opposite of their own personalities. It was a real-life political theater; in which, a smile was never truly a smile, for it seldom stemmed from the heart. A laugh was never truly a laugh, for its intention usually helped to serve, as a tool to impress the opposing party and not one's true self. Furthermore, a conversation amongst diplomats were never natural, nor authentic, for it was almost always strategically planned and carefully crafted by each nation state's vast team of advisors.

By habit, John usually arrived to these events, following either a lengthy meeting or an overnight trip. Furthermore, these state dinners were the seldom and rare occasions, in which he would see, converse and interact with Jennifer, as he assumed and played the role of her adoring husband and she, his ever-loving wife. But alas, once the night concluded and the guests exited the premise, he never again thought twice about it the next morning, other than crossing it off his busy work schedule to-do list.

But tonight, it was different. For the very first time in a rather long time, John searched for a new face from amongst the crowd. It was the one face that stood apart from all of the rest. In fact, at this very moment, it was missing from the vast sea of people, who stood before him. It was the face of someone; whom, unlike most of tonight's attendees, was honest, true and sincere. She was the exception to the rule. In a world rooted in political theater, she was the one source of fresh air that John had long waited for. That one particular face, was the face of someone that he had desperately tried to forget during his trip to Ankara, but failed to do. Her face was everywhere in his mind. And that face belonged to none other than our heroine, Kate.

Oh, how he thought of her! How he dreamt of her! How he fantasized about her! The woman who was posing as his interim wife. She was always on his mind. Constantly in his thoughts. Even during his meetings with the Turkish Ambassador discussing their project, she was all that he could think about. Wonder about. Ponder about. Dream about. Where she was, or what she was doing? Did she think about him, as much as he thought about her? Did she desire him, as much as he lusted for her? And dare he consider the most forbidden of all his inner and deep thoughts: did she have a crumble or better yet, even a tiny morsel or spec of feelings for him, like he had for her? For God only knew just how much of an avalanche of sentimental feelings and attachment that he already felt for her, all secretly buried deep within the vault of his own reluctant and stubborn heart.

John still didn't quite understand, as to what he felt for her exactly. He still couldn't properly define it. Nor could he verbally articulate it. But he could feel it. Just burning and penetrating inside of his heart. After spending these past few weeks with Kate, he not only genuinely enjoyed her company, but he had actually looked forward to seeing her. Her smile made him smile. And for once, his smiles with her were authentic and not forced. Their conversations were so surprisingly natural that every time she spoke, he was enchanted by her vocabulary and choice of words; for he knew, that whenever she spoke, she spoke from both her heart, and her mind. However, as intelligent as she was, she was also kind and thoughtful. Furthermore, her love for her cat, Tabitha, was a trait he found sweet, innocent and endearing. But this much John knew to be true: whatever he felt for Kate, it was something brand new, authentic and most importantly, it was real. Somehow, John's friendship with her was blossoming into a new level of attachment, along with a growing attraction to her that made him yearn with endless desire. But was it only on his part? Was it possible that Kate might also reciprocate his desires? And if she did, was she willing to surrender to them, once and for all?

Suddenly, he saw her. The face to the woman, whom he had long waited for. Ascending down the staircase, John watched her from afar and was immediately, enchanted by her radiant beauty. She was a real-life angel.

An enchantress. A goddess. A queen. Floating down from the very steps of heaven, she was walking directly towards him and he, in return, was left breathless. She was, by far, the most beautiful creature that he had ever laid his eyes upon. Dressed in all gold, with her sun kissed hair gently pulled aside from her delicate and porcelain face, she was gorgeous beyond measure. Equal to none. Then, without any expectation and for the very first time in his life, John's heart skipped a beat.

Out of fear, John quickly placed his hand across his chest. What was this new feeling growing inside this region of his body? Why was his heart reacting in this way? His own heart was starting to behave in a such a profoundly strange and foreign manner, that he, himself, was left utterly confused and bewildered. However, before he had the opportunity to further analyze this new occurrence within his own thoughts, Kate arrived and was standing right there in front of him.

"Hello, John," she greeted him, with the sweetest of smiles.

"Kate," he managed to whisper, as he gasped for air. After a brief moment, which felt like an eternity, he managed to collect himself and admitted, "You look absolutely stunning."

"You really think so?" she asked, innocently, "I made a last-minute decision to wear a new dress. Hopefully, the color isn't too bold and flashy for this event, as everyone else here seems to be styled in more muted and neutral tones."

"Pay no attention to any of the others here tonight," he promptly said.

"Please don't equate yourself with them. They aren't you and never will be. They're all the same; whereas, you are the belle of the ball."

Kate blushed. She didn't expect him to complement her.

"John, thank you, but surely," she began, "In a room full of famous diplomats and politicians, they cannot all be the same. Besides, I'm not that special."

"Kate, you don't give yourself enough credit," he abruptly said, in a harsh and scolding tone, that made Kate feel embarrassed for having uttered such a thing.

Suddenly, John looked directly into her eyes, with such fire and intensity, that Kate was ready to melt into his arms, right there and then.

"You are special and don't ever forget it," he firmly said, with determination. Moving two inches closer to her and now, standing right beside her, he added "And, you are beautiful too, inside and out."

For a moment, Kate thought he might actually want to kiss her. He was close enough. In fact, he was so close to her, it was as if they were breathing the same air. Meanwhile, his gaze was so intense that if she closed her eyes, she could swear that he was ready to lean in and seal the deal. But in a room full of other guests, it just wasn't possible…or was it? No, she thought, it was all in her mind. It had to be.

And just as she expected, rather than a kiss, John offered his hand to her, instead.

"Shall we?" he confidently asked, fully ready and prepared to escort her down into the ballroom.

While she was disappointed that their kiss failed to be, she still gladly accepted his offer and quickly grabbed hold of his hand. As they proceeded to walk down into the hallway, hand in hand, Kate decided to use this opportunity to engage in some lighthearted conversations with John, along their journey.

"My gown is actually one of Sally's designs," she admitted to him, as a conversation starter.

"Our Sally?" asked John, with a raised brow.

"Yes, our very own Sally," replied Kate, proudly.

"Well, then," laughed John, to himself. "I guess I'm just going to have to exclusively enlist in Sally's design services to the rest of the embassy, moving forward."

"Really?" asked Kate, surprised by his suggestion.

"I'm quite serious. Maybe she can share some of her magic with my own wardrobe, too," he said, in the most charming of manners.

"John, you don't need any magic. You're already lovely, as it is," said Kate, who then, immediately, grew embarrassed after she realized that she had just unintentionally commented on his appearance. To help clear the awkward mood, she further clarified, "What I meant, is that you dress lovely for a man."

John simply laughed.

"For a man? Why Kate, dare I ask, but are you trying to grant me a complement?" he asked, in a rather joking manner, which in return, made her blush.

Pulling her arm closer to him and with a deep and seductive voice, he asked, "So does this mean that you find me ravishingly handsome?"

Upon hearing his words, Kate immediately turned red. She was nervous. Having witnessed her reaction, John simply laughed to himself, once more.

"I'll take that as a 'yes'," he finally said, with a smile.

In an effort to calm her nerves, Kate just looked away from him. After a brief moment, she regained her confidence again and returned her gaze back to him. Finally, in a more serious tone, she bluntly asked, "Do you really want to contract Sally?"

For Sally's sake, Kate secretly wished and hoped that what he suggested was indeed true.

"I do," he replied, in all seriousness. "My philosophy is that any employee with such a superior skill, should have the opportunity to showcase their talent publicly."

"John, I couldn't agree any more. I know that Sally will be most appreciative and grateful for this rare opportunity," she said and then, she further added, "I know that I, personally, am already grateful to you for this."

"Well, then it's all settled. If it matters this much to you, then we'll finalize this matter, in the next coming weeks. Consider it as good as done," he said, affirmatively.

In that moment, Kate realized that John just wanted to make her happy. Even in the form of helping her assistant. He valued her, and her opinion. Surely, a man willing to help another person from the opposite sex, must harbor some sort of sentimental feelings for them? But if he did have feelings for her, then what exactly were they? Perhaps, if anything, at the very least, she thought, if what he felt for her wasn't at all romantic, then maybe, just having their friendship, in the meantime, was going to be the alternative and safe consolation that she needed, right now.

Suddenly, she smiled and then, he, in return, smiled too. Then, unexpectedly, his heart skipped another beat; twice, within the same span of the evening. However, unlike before, he wasn't afraid of his heart's condition or behavior; because, for whatever reason, it made him feel happy. Strangely, he felt genuinely happy to be around her. Eventually, when his heart skipped yet another beat thrice more, this time around, he reacted by squeezing Kate's hand. And hard. This, in return, made Kate squeal a little cry aloud. Feeling embarrassed for actions, he quickly sought to distract her by attempting the change the subject.

"While I escort you down into the ballroom," he stated, as in a matter of fact and business, "I think I should take this liberty to help better enlighten you about the backstories to some of our guests, who are here tonight in attendance."

"Ah, yes, that's a rather grand idea. After these past few weeks, I must admit that as much as I studied the official guests' list, I'm still not entirely certain as to who's actually who," she bashfully admitted.

"Don't trouble yourself with those particularities, for I'm here," he said, in the most reassuringly manner. He further vowed, "I will not leave you alone. I promise. Just remain by my side."

Kate felt tremendously comforted by his promise. For at this moment, she nervously felt like one of her own students attending their first day of class. In fact, she already felt the jittering butterflies, flying and floating about within her stomach. But somehow, with John by her side, she felt a little better. Furthermore, she was also comforted by his reassurance that no matter what happened here tonight, he wasn't going to leave her side.

"You see there, across in that bleak corner," he gently whispered to her, as he discretely pointed in the far-right direction of the hallway, "That's the French Ambassador."

"The tall one, with the dark hair and mustache?" asked Kate, as her gaze followed his description.

"Yes, that's him. That's Jacques. He's a rather nice fellow. Likes to tell several jokes. He frequently attends our state dinners and will go out of his way to chat with me, from time to time," he said.

"What about the woman, who's standing right next to him?" asked Kate, curious as to her identity.

"That's his wife, Claire," replied John, then leaning closer into Kate's ear, he said, "She's not too popular with the other wives here. However, please still be polite and cordial with her; but at the same time, try to also keep a safe distance away from her. Keep your conversations with her at a bare minimum and if you can, talk mainly about the weather or dinner. She has a reputation for being troublesome."

"Troublesome? What sort of trouble?" asked Kate, wondering as to what John had meant by his warning to her.

"Generally, she's notorious for spreading false gossip and rumors about people. Particularly, about our wives. Nothing is off limits with her. In the past, she's even gone so far as to threaten to publicly humiliate and complain about our embassy. So please, whatever you do, just promise me that you'll be careful around her," John forewarned.

After agreeing to John's request, Kate observed the French Ambassador's wife, Claire, from afar. She was a woman in her late-forties to early fifties, with curly brown hair that was styled with a yellow polka dot and floral headband; an unusual choice that Kate found rather unorthodox to wear, given that this was a more traditional and formal black-tie event.

To add more insult to injury, Claire was dressed in a gown that was not only an unflattering shade of orange, but it was also two sizes too large for her small petite figure. But if her outfit was unappealing, her facial expression spoke a thousand words of its own; for at that very moment, Claire had the most bored and depressed expression plastered across her face. As Kate further glanced at her, she realized that Claire's face was a bit too puffy and red. Furthermore, her lips were purple and swollen, and they appeared to be unnaturally too large for her small shaped face. Did she recently undergo a session of plastic surgery? Recalling Jennifer's diary entry about an unfaithful French Ambassador's wife, Kate presumed that this must be her. But where was the Brazilian Ambassador and his wife? The couple, in which, Claire was previously caught entangled within a rather messy and compromising position with?

"What about the Brazilian Ambassador and his wife?" asked Kate, abruptly.

"The Brazilian Ambassador and his wife?" echoed John. He obviously was curious as to why Kate had asked for them.

However, Kate didn't want to draw any suspicion. She still didn't want anyone to know that she had Jennifer's diary in her possession, not even John. To conceal any further inquiry into the matter, Kate decided to simply play innocent.

"I was just curious that's all. Nothing more. A few years ago, I read an article in the news that there was a trade dispute between France and Brazil. Some sort of an embargo between the two countries. Must be rather uncomfortable to be in the same room again, after such a public dispute," Kate calmly stated.

"Ah, I see, so you do follow current events, in addition to your history books," replied John, jokingly. "Yes, that's true. There was a trade dispute; but it eventually, came to an end, with both sides giving in. But it's now in the past and behind us all. Nothing for either party to still remain uncomfortable with each other."

"Does that mean that they're here tonight? The Brazilian Ambassador and his wife?" asked Kate.

"Actually, yes, they are. If you look to the opposite side of the hall, that's them. The chubby bald man is Alberto and the redhaired woman is his wife, Maria," explained John.

Following John's directions, Kate saw the couple from across the room. Just as John had described, the man was indeed, chubby and bald, with a large nose that sat right smack in the middle of his aging face. He was dressed in a plain grey suit and was drinking a glass of champagne. Next to him, was the redhaired woman. However, unlike Claire, Maria was dressed much more elegant and refined. Wearing a black velvet gown, the dress fit her figure like a glove. Her fiery red hair was long and flowing down her back, while her neck and face sparkled and shined from the white diamonds that hung from her necklace and earrings. Even Kate, herself, had to admit that Maria was a stunning and rare beauty.

"Maria's quite beautiful," Kate remarked to John.

"That's not surprising, as she's a former beauty queen. Back in the day, she was even crowned Miss Universe. Actually, that's how they met. Alberto was a former judge on the contest and she was a contestant. Afterwards, they married shortly thereafter."

"Really? A former Miss Universe as an ambassador's wife. Now, that's intriguing," said Kate.

"I suppose, if that sort of thing interests you. But Jennifer and Maria got along rather well. In fact, I believe that she even invited her to high tea; however, due to my transfer to Türkiye, I'm not certain as to whether or not their tea date ever formalized. More likely, Maria will seek to converse and mingle with you. But whatever you do, please stay clear away from her husband, Alberto. You just leave him to me," he forewarned.

Kate simply nodded in agreement to John's request. She recalled from the diary the unwanted advancements Alberto once made to her sister. John must have secretly known about Alberto's reputation, and she did not wish to upset nor offend his warning to her. Kate decided to stay clear from Alberto's path, no matter the circumstances.

"Wait, they are approaching us right now," John interrupted, as he straightened up his posture, pulled Kate closer to his side and smiled.

Meanwhile, Kate stared at him with pure fascination and amazement. Within the instant snap of his finger, John suddenly transformed from a normal civilian bystander who, along with Kate, were previously watching and admiring the crowd, as they descending down the halls, into a roman gladiator ready to enter the colosseum for battle. Alas, she realized that after all these weeks of training and preparing, the time had finally come to meet the world, firsthand. At long last, it was now showtime.

"John!" exclaimed Alberto, cheerfully.

Ever-so politely, John extended his hands to greet Alberto with a friendly handshake, but to his surprise, that gesture didn't quite go as he planned. Instead, Alberto pushed his hands aside, leaned in, and gave him a grand bear hug. It appeared that simple hand-shakes were not the ideal welcoming greeting for the emotional Brazilian Ambassador.

"It's good to see you, too. And thank you for coming," said John, as he tried his best to pull away from Alberto's grasp, to breathe some air.

Once Alberto's attention from John eventually faded, he then turned his direction to Kate. Within an instant, Alberto quickly grabbed hold of her hand, which she was reluctant to freely give; mostly, due to John's earlier warnings.

"Always a pleasure, Mrs. Barrett," said Alberto, as he leaned down and gave her a light kiss on the soft and delicate surface of her hand.

Lifting his head back up, he directly made eye contact with her. Once their eyes met, he gave her an unwelcomed wink. Instantly, Kate felt extremely uncomfortable within his company. Clearly, Alberto was a flirt; and she wasn't in the mood to humor him, right now. However, Kate also knew that as a consolation, John was by her side tonight; and as long as she remained besides him, then she was safe. Pulling her hand away from out of his tight grip, Kate, for the first time since her arrival to the mansion, forced herself to exert a pretend smile. Luckily, at that very moment, Alberto's wife, Maria, soon joined them; thus, rescuing Kate from having to engage upon a rather an awkward and unwanted conversation with him.

"The party is absolute wonderful! Fabolous job my dear, Jennifer!"

exclaimed Maria, happily, as she quickly joined arms with her husband.

Soon after, she walked over to Kate and gave her a kiss on the cheeks.

"Thank you, Maria," replied Kate, "I'm so glad that you were able to join us, here tonight."

"An excuse to visit Istanbul? You better believe that I was going to take advantage of your invitation," said Maria, with a smile.

Catching sight of Kate's beautiful gown, Maria remarked, "Jennifer, you look absolutely beautiful! I must know your secret! Who exactly are you wearing? Which collection is this? Why, I haven't seen this particular design on any of the recent runaways as of lately, and I was recently in Milan, too."

"Oh!" exclaimed Kate, who wasn't expecting Maria's complement on her gown.

"Why this dress? It's from a young and talented American designer. Her name is Sally Timmons," Kate revealed, and she further added, "In fact, Ms. Timmons personally custom designed this specific gown for me. It's a preview to her new upcoming collection that she's planning to launch sometime, in the near future."

"Well, now I know your beauty secret!" squealed Maria, "Jennifer, darling, you simply must get me in contact with this new young designer of yours! Since we have a few state dinners to plan soon, I can use a few new exquisite gowns to add to my collection."

"Maria, but of course," replied Kate, happily; but then, suddenly, Kate recalled her country's own internal policy about wearing homegrown designers, and so, she naturally wondered if Brazil also abided by similar protocols.

"Maria, I'm more than happy to recommend Sally to you. However, I must ask, are you even allowed to wear and showcase non-Brazilian designers?" asked Kate.

"Ha! I know as to which unofficial etiquette rule that you are referring to my dear; but unlike you Americans, we don't enforce these sorts of rules so strictly in our country. Besides, my husband is the civil servant in our family, not I," replied Maria, with a carefree wave of her hand. She furthered stated, "Everyone already understands that I'm a former beauty queen and as the Brazilian Ambassador's wife, my country expects me to represent them proudly abroad, and to look and dress in my best attires, at all times. This includes our state dinners and official ceremonies—regardless of who designs them. Also, given that your young designer appears to have mastered the intricate art of precious beading, which is something currently missing from my wardrobe, I'd be a fool not to use her services."

"Very well, Maria," smiled Kate happily, "I'll have Sally get in touch with your team first thing tomorrow morning."

"Wonderful!" exclaimed Maria, with joy, "And Jennifer, we really must schedule high tea sometime. I know that with our busy schedules, we just never had the chance, but I promise, we will have it soon."

"Yes, that will be lovely," said Kate.

"Fabolous! When are you planning your next trip to London?" asked Maria.

"London?" asked Kate, surprised by Maria's question. Did she really expect to have high tea with her in London?

"Yes, London, of course. Naturally, the best tea houses in Europe are at the Savoy. But don't worry right now, if you're uncertain about your schedule. I'll have our assistants coordinate it. Now, if you don't mind, Alberto and I really need catch up with Spain. Jennifer, we'll see you later in the ballroom," said Maria, as she hurly rushed to her husband's side.

Grabbing Alberto's arms, she aggressively pulled and dragged him towards the Spanish Ambassador and his wife, who were currently making their ways over to the ballroom. After Maria and Alberto left the scene, John sighed a breath of relief. He was glad that they were gone.

"I'm so happy that you're not like her," John muttered aloud.

"Like whom? Maria?" asked Kate, with a raised brow.

"Yes. Exactly. Just look at how she drags him. I'm glad that you're not like that," he admitted.

"And just how am I exactly?" asked Kate, with a smile.

"Perfect, in every possible way," replied John, as he quickly grabbed hold of her hand.

Kate simply blushed, as she turned a shade of red. Tickled by her reaction, John smiled at her, in return. As far as he was concerned, Kate was the sweetest and most charming debutante in the entire party.

"And I'm sure, Sally will be very pleased to learn tomorrow that Maria is interested in her services," he said, as he gently tucked away a lose strand of blonde hair from behind her ears.

Kate blushed once more. But before Kate had the chance to react and speak another word to him, John saw the Indian Ambassador and his wife arrive to the mansion. They entered the estate through the side door and were now standing in front of the ballroom's entrance.

"Kate," he interrupted, "Look straight across."

Kate followed John's direction, and there, she saw the Indian couple standing in between the threshold, with one foot in the hallway and the other foot in the ballroom. While the husband was moderately dress in a black suit with a red tie; his wife, like Maria before, was exquisitely dressed, and perhaps, even more beautiful than Maria. The Indian Ambassador's wife was wearing a traditional magenta colored sari, with silver beads, hemmed along the edges of her dress. She was adorned with bright green emerald jewelry, worn in the form of a necklace with matching earrings. On her wrists, were two sets of identical gold bracelets. Her long black hair was tightly braided, and she wore a bright pair of velvet green heel shoes.

"Is that the Indian Ambassador and his wife?" asked Kate, never losing sight of the couple.

"Yes, that's them. That's Raj and his wife, Riya," replied John. "Come, let's walk over and greet them."

Kate agreed and proceeded to follow his lead. In a matter of minutes, they quicky caught up to the couple; whom by now, had already long entered into the ballroom.

"Raj!" exclaimed John, "It's good to see you! Thanks for coming here tonight."

"John, just the man I needed to speak to," said Raj, as he walked over to greet John and Kate, in return. "And Mrs. Barrett, thank you for inviting Riya and myself here tonight."

"Yes, thank you, Mrs. Barrett for the invitation," Riya agreed. "Tonight's décor is simply enchanting."

"Why, thank you Riya. I know that John and I are equally pleased to have you both here tonight," replied Kate.

"John, would it be possible, if we could discuss the matter concerning India's aid in the pipeline project?" Raj interrupted. "I know that the night's still young, but I've recently obtained new testing results from our pilot testers. So far, the results to the new system are positive, but it's still rather urgent that we speak now."

"Raj, but of course, we can," replied John.

Immediately, turning his direction to both Kate and Riya, John personally asked them, "Ladies, do you mind, if we briefly step away to discuss these matters, in private?"

"Not at all," Riya quickly responded, "Jennifer and I have some of our own matters to discuss, as well. You two go on ahead. I'll escort Jennifer to our table."

"Great, thank you," said John happily, "Jennifer, I'll meet you later on. I promise that Raj and I will be away for only a few minutes or so."

Kate reluctantly agreed and upon her permission, John joined Raj, as the two men exited the ballroom and made their way over into his private office.

"Well, they left much sooner, than I expected," Riya remarked, as she reached over and grabbed hold of Kate's elbow and locked it in within hers.

"But better that they did. Let the men discuss their business, while we discuss ours."

Kate gulped. What sort of business was Riya referring to? Kate had absolutely no idea. In fact, she wasn't previously prepped for any unforeseeable political or business discussions with the other wives. But obviously, Jennifer must have discussed certain business matters with Riya, which Kate neglected to be privy to. Just how on earth was Kate going to pull this one off? Surely, she was going to make an error. Her initial plans relied solely on John remaining by her side, in order to help thwart and rescue her from these types of discussions. But now, with him gone, she was left all alone to face the music. And as a result, she was officially nervous.

"Which sort of business are you referring to, Riya?" asked Kate hesitantly and almost regretful that she had even bothered to ask this very question, in the first place.

"Why the matter concerning your gorgeous outfit, of course," replied Riya, with a devious smile.

Kate released a sigh of relief. Discussing her gown was something that Kate was perfectly capable of handling. Kate certainly dodged a bullet with this one.

"Jennifer," spoke Riya, "I really must have the business card to your designer. Since I have an upcoming appearance on the set of a new Bollywood movie, if I can somehow have something similar designed for me just like your dress…"

"Wait," Kate interrupted, "You have an appearance on an upcoming Bollywood movie?"

Secretly, Kate was a huge admirer and fan of Bollywood movies. While studying at university, her one escape from her studies was to stream and watch Bollywood movies. Kate had spent countless weekends watching marathons of various romantic films, staring her favorite lead film actor, Raj Shah Kumar. And in between writing her dissertation, Kate was often daydreaming that she was one of the lead heroines in the films, opposite Raj Shah Kumar.

"Yes, it's the latest Raj Shah Kumar film. Perhaps, you've heard of him? He's a very famous film star back in my home country," said Riya.

"Raj Shah Kumar…" repeated Kate, in disbelief. By now, her mouth dropped open, and she could barely exert the strength to hide and contain her overwhelming excitement.

And to Riya's credit, she caught sight of Kate's joyful reaction and smiled.

"I take it that you've heard of Raj Shah Kumar before?" asked Riya, with a raised brow. "I tell you what," she continued, "If you can give me the name and contact number to your designer, then I promise you that the next time you're in India, I'll personally introduce you to Raj Shah Kumar, myself. And if your designer is as good as I think she is, then perhaps, I can recommend her to other Bollywood film stars, too. Does this sound like a good deal?"

"Deal!" shouted Kate, joyfully and without a second guess.

"Fabolous!" exclaimed Riya, equally excited, in return.

"Her name is Sally Timmons. She's an American designer," said Kate, proudly.

"Sally Timmons…Sally Timmons…why have I never heard of her before…" Riya pondered aloud.

"Well, she's new," Kate interrupted.

"New? Is she still an amateur? An unknown?" asked Riya, who was a bit surprised and perplexed.

For a moment, Kate grew wry. Was Riya concerned that Sally was an unknown designer? Furthermore, if Riya knew that truth about Sally's previous work history, then would she still be interested in her designs?

"Riya, perhaps, you haven't yet heard about my designer, because she's so exclusive and highly sought after, right now," replied Kate, hoping to alleviate any concerns that Riya might have had.

"Highly exclusive and sought after?" repeated Riya, in complete fascination.

Although it wasn't Kate's original intentions to stretch the truth to Riya, meeting Raj Shah Kumar in-person was a dream come true. Up until recently, Sally was an unknown designer, whom Kate had only discovered, by pure accident. However, if stretching the truth, even just a tiny bit, meant that Sally could benefit from Riya's influence in Bollywood and potentially dress hundreds of other Bollywood stars, then Kate was willing to take the chance to promote her friend.

"Yes, it's precisely just that," Kate promptly responded, "In fact, she's so in demand, that she's been very selective on choosing her clients. As of now, many are currently still waitlisted to even schedule a dress fitting with her. Some are waiting months, if not, years on end. However, if you'd like, I can still put in a good word for you and ask that she personally take you on as one of her new special clients, as a personal favor to me."

"Oh, Jennifer, can you please!" cried Riya, desperately, "It's just so incredibly hard to find great designers these days! Sadly, practically everyone dresses in the same exact outfits, using the same similar silhouettes. Furthermore, with the added pressure of being an ambassador's wife, everyone back in my home country expects that I dress in a certain type of way, while maintaining a high degree of positivity. Why, Jennifer, you, of all people, should understand me. You must know how I feel!"

"That I do," replied Kate, soothingly, "But don't worry Riya, I'll have my assistant contact your assistant with all the details first thing, tomorrow morning."

"Thank you, Jennifer, you're such a dear! I'm looking forward to it!" exclaimed Riya, happily.

By now, the two women arrived inside into the ballroom. Upon entering, Riya immediately saw her assistant already seated at her table. Once again, she thanked Kate for her offer and soon excused herself, to join her party. Meanwhile, Kate caught sight of her own table and from there, she saw Barbara, comfortably seated and currently waving at her. She was, of course, gesturing Kate to come and join her for dinner. Kate smiled back at her and quickly, she scanned Barbara's table and noticed that seated beside her, were two other people, whom Kate hadn't previous met before. From what Kate observed, the person seated right next to Barbara's left-hand side was an elderly man, who was elegantly dressed in a dark blue suit. He appeared to have a sweet disposition, along with a friendly expression on his face. Nearby him, was a young female, who was also dressed in dark blue and ironically, greatly resembled him. Kate presumed that the pair must be a father and daughter duo.

Putting on a brave face, Kate decided to join Barbara's table and meet the unknown pair. At least with Barbara by her side, she thought, she didn't need to worry about saying the wrong things. Kate would just allow Barbara to be her normal bold, talkative self and consume most of their dinner conversations; whereas, Kate, in return, would simply engage in lighthearted table talk discussions.

Upon arriving to their table, Barbara cheerfully pulled out a chair and asked Kate to take a seat.

"Sit down, my dear Jennifer," said Barbara, "I've already poured you a glass of red wine."

"Thank you, Barbara," replied Kate, as she sat down on the chair and reached for her glass of wine.

"Barbara, this wouldn't be one of your wines?" asked the elderly man, laughingly.

"David, why of course it is! You don't think I'd come all the way here from California, dragging ten sets of luggage, without bringing some of my home-grown Napa wine!" exclaimed Barbara, with her carefree hands waving up in the air.

"Wait," interrupted the young woman, "Isn't there some sort of a government regulation against a civil servant promoting their own personal brand at a government sponsored event?"

"Yes," Kate interjected, "I did read something about that too recently, on the policies and procedures handbook…"

"Amy and Kate, you're both too serious! You all must learn to loosen up! Besides, I'm not the civil servant here, John is. Plus, might I add, these wines are from my own private collection that I personally dragged all the way from Napa, to serve as party gifts to our guests, free of charge!" exclaimed Barbara, who, herself, took another sip of her own wine.

"Don't worry, nothing will happen. Everyone comes to these parties expecting to try one of Barbara's wines," interrupted David, "So which year is it? 1970 or 1980?"

"Very funny, David. You're very much aware that I wasn't involved in the wine making business during those particular years, or even, decades," said Barbara.

"Yes, but the late Mr. Barrett was," David reminded her.

"As I'm fully aware. No, David, this is from a brand-new collection that I've been recently brewing this season. Recently, I've been experimenting on some new active ingredients. Hopefully, I'll be able to launch this new line sometime, within the next couple of years. Perhaps, you all can guess, as to what these new ingredients are?" asked Barbara, as she reverted her attention over towards Amy and Kate, with the hopes that they could correctly guess the mystery ingredients.

"Ladies, care to guess?" Barbara asked again, with a playful smile.

However, David, was the first to answer. He quickly gulped the remainder of his wine, and then he slammed the glass back down on the table. Ready for action, he bluntly stated his answer.

"Peaches," he said, as he released a small burp from out of his mouth.

"David!" exclaimed Barbara, horrified by his poor table manners, "I was asking the girls, not you!"

"But I'm right, aren't I?" asked David, jokingly.

"Girls, never mind him," huffed Barbara, out of frustration, as she appeared rather annoyed. "Go on, tell me what you think is in there. Take another sip, if you must."

"Raspberries?" asked Amy, as she gently placed her wine glass back onto the table.

"Nope," replied Barbara, with a giggle, as she, herself, took yet another sip of her wine.

"Hmm, strawberries, then?" asked Amy, again.

"Nope. Try again," said Barbara, who by now, had asked the waiter to bring over a second bottle of wine to the table.

"Well, if it's not raspberries or strawberries, then I certainly have no idea," concluded Amy, whose facial expression was now sour by defeat.

"Why not pour yourself another glass and try to guess again?" Barbara suggested, while she attempted to drink her second glass of wine.

"No, that's quite alright," responded Amy, "Jennifer, why don't you try to take a guess? Perhaps, you'll be luckier, than I."

Although Kate held onto her first wine glass still full within the clutches of her hands, she hadn't yet tasted it. Upon Amy's suggestion, Kate finally took her first sip. Although the initial taste of the drink was sour at first, after a brief moment or two, the sour taste soon turned sweet. Smelling the wine up-close, the overall aroma was gentle yet bold, elegant yet wild, and fresh yet woodsy. It was a combination of several elements, all rolled up into one unified concoction.

"I can taste a bit of mint," said Kate, at long last.

"Yes, there's a bit of mint in there! Great job Jennifer!" exclaimed Barbara, happily. "What else do you taste?"

"Well, I can also taste some traces of… watermelon?" asked Kate, who, herself, wasn't entirely certain as to whether or not, her own taste buds betrayed her.

"Yes, there's watermelon! Go on, keep guessing the rest! You're on a roll!" Barbara shouted aloud.

Taking another sip and after much thought, Kate finally said, "I know that you previously said that David was wrong for guessing this; but honestly, the only thing else that I can taste are peaches."

"That's it!" exclaimed Barbara.

"What?" David quickly asked, "But Barbara, I already guessed that, and you stated that I was wrong."

"David, I didn't say that you were wrong," Barbara reminded him, "I simply stated that the girls should be guessing, not you."

Then, Barbara and David both had a good laugh together at the table.

Turning her attention over to Kate, Amy whispered, "These two are just too much. But great job guessing all the ingredients, by the way."

"Thank you, Amy," Kate whispered back to her.

"Well, Barbara, I'm thoroughly impressed. This is one hell of a drink! When exactly do you plan on releasing this into the market?" asked David, who then proceeded to pour himself another glass.

"It's still at the testing stage, but I'm thinking more likely sometime next year or so," replied Barbara.

"Next year is too far out," said David, as he gulped the remaining liquid from his glass.

"Why is that too far out? Are you planning to reserve my new drink?" asked Barbara, jokingly.

"Well Barbara, if that's the case, then can I reserve a few bottles, in advance? At least, for this weekend? As it's for a special occasion," said David, who then smiled and winked at his daughter, Amy.

"That depends. What's the special occasion for?" asked Barbara, with a raised brow.

"Why, Amy's engagement party. Of course, you're all naturally invited and expected to attend. It's going to be held at my private cabin. Although I know that it's short notice, but I promise, it will only be for just for this weekend. Besides, this way, you all can finally meet Peter," David announced.

"Oh, my goodness!" exclaimed Barbara, excitingly, "It's been ages since we last visited your cabin in the Swiss Alps! Congratulations Amy, my dear!"

"Congratulations to you both," added Kate, happily.

"Amy, why didn't you tell me your happy news sooner?" asked Barbara, who was now, rather offended that her dear friends had previously withheld such important news from her.

"Father wanted it to be a surprise," replied Amy, who shyly blushed out of embarrassment.

"Why, this is such wonderful news! Naturally, we'll come, as I certainly want to meet this Peter fellow. Just who is he, exactly?" asked Barbara, now more curious, than ever.

"His name is Dr. Peter Murphy, and he's a dentist. They met back in New York, while they were both studying at college…" David explained.

"Which university did they study at?" Kate interrupted, as she was now, most intrigued as to which university the pair attended.

"I believe it was NYU," replied David, as he attempted to recall. He then turned his attention over to Amy and asked, "Amy, is that correct?"

"Yes, that's correct," Amy confirmed.

Kate secretly smiled to herself. Even being so far away from home, it was nice to still have some form of a reminder to the old world that she left behind. Furthermore, if Amy and Peter were indeed former NYU students, then it was very possible that once upon a time, they might have once sat inside her classroom as her former students. However, now, today, at this very moment, seated across from them, as Jennifer, Kate knew that they wouldn't recognize her. In fact, even she didn't quiet recognize herself, anymore. In truth, her old life in New York honestly felt like another lifetime ago.

"He recently completed his dental training and internship in Switzerland," continued David, "He plans on opening his own private practice in Connecticut, within the next month or. Amy and Peter plan to marry, before he returns back to live in the U.S. permanently."

"Yes, that's why I've been staying here in Europe, these past few months," added Amy.

"That's so romantic!" sighed Barbara, "David, please count us all in."

"Does this mean that you'll bring a few extra bottles of your new wine with you?" asked David, with a big smile.

"David, I'll bring all of my wines, if it means that we get to stay in your Swiss cabin for this weekend's celebration!" said Barbara, with conviction.

"Perfect!" exclaimed David, "However, now, I should probably mention that our weekend celebration will actually be held in another cabin, as my Swiss cabin is currently under renovation."

"Another cabin? Why David, are you actually suggesting that we stay at a hotel, instead? With such short notice, I'm not sure that we even have enough time to book..."

"Not to worry," interrupted Amy, "Peter will take care of everything. Luckily, we already have a private cabin reserved for us here in Türkiye."

"In Türkiye? Not in Switzerland? Why, are there even cabins and ski resorts here, in this country?" asked Barbara, surprised by the mere suggestion.

"Actually, yes," replied David, "In fact, you'd be surprised. Some of the world's greatest ski resorts are located here, in this great country of Türkiye. Besides, since we're already all here, we won't even need to fly. Isn't that wonderfully convenient? In fact, we'll all be catching a train, first thing tomorrow morning to head towards Kars."

"Kars?" asked Barbara, having uttered this city's name for the first time from her own two lips in confusion, as if it were a foreign planet that she had only recently discovered.

"Yes, Kars. It's a major metropolitan city located in northeastern Türkiye. We'll catch the early train tomorrow morning from Istanbul to Ankara.

Then, at Ankara, we'll transfer and travel directly onwards to Kars. I promise, you will all enjoy the ride. The landscapes and view of the Anatolian countryside are absolutely breathtaking. Truly, a fantastic scenery in action."

"Yes, it's really a sight to behold," added Amy.

"Really? A train that travels from Istanbul to Kars? I've only ever heard of the Orient Express," Barbara huffed.

"Actually, it's called the Doğu Express to be precise," interrupted David, "The Turkish letter 'ğ' is silent and elongates the surrounding vowels. Therefore, the Doğu Express is properly pronounced as the Doouu Express. Just think of it as the Orient Express in continuation."

"The Doğu Express? I've never heard of such a thing! Whose idea was this anyways?" asked Barbara, as she took another sip of her wine.

"It was Peter's idea. He figured that since we're already here in Türkiye, then it would just be more convenient for everyone if we just remained and vacationed here. He's just so incredibly thoughtful," sighed Amy.

"Plus, it will be a nice experience for all of us to enjoy the train ride. Like I always say, travel by train is much more ideal, than travels by plane," added David.

"You've never once said that before! This is the first time that I've ever heard you say such a thing," contradicted Barbara.

"Well, now I'm saying it; so, Barbara, feel free to record me. But most importantly, can I count you all in?" asked David.

"David, I'll admit, while I'm a bit disappointed that we're not going to stay in your Swiss cabin; however, with that said, I'd travel to Mars in a heartbeat, if that meant that I'll meet Amy's fiancé," said Barbara, happily.

"Barbara, you're too kind!" exclaimed Amy.

"Perfect," replied David, "I'm glad that our three additional train tickets won't be a waste, after all."

"David!" exclaimed Barbara, as she tapped on David's shoulder, to scold him for his joke.

However, Kate, who remained quiet all this time, finally decided that now was opportune time to remind Barbara that John and her had other plans this weekend.

"But Barbara," interrupted Kate, at long last, "Doesn't John have his meetings with…."

"Jennifer, darling, John can always reschedule," Barbara quickly huffed, "Besides, David and Amy are practically family, and we must be there for Amy's special day."

Suddenly, to Kate's surprise, Barbara leaned over into Kate's ear and whispered, "Besides, this will be the perfect excuse for you and John to spend some alone time together. Why, what can be possibly more romantic, than a weekend getaway? Imagine, traveling by train during the day, then spending the night in a remote cabin, where it's just you and him, alone together, all night long?"

Barbara's bold suggestion almost compelled Kate to spill her drink all over the table. Luckily, for Kate, she managed to miraculously catch it within seconds, with her shaking and nervous hands. Alone with John in a private cabin? All the way in Kars? In the snow? Just him and her? From sunrise to sunset?

All this time, somehow, she successfully managed to keep up with her charade by maintaining her own private quarters at the estate, far away from John. But now, having to actually spend the entire late night directly by his side and pretending to be his wife, that wasn't something that Kate wasn't anticipating for. What was she going to do? How was she going to get out of this one? Suddenly, the room began to grow smaller and Kate grew flushed. Desperately in need for some air to breathe, she promptly arose from her seat.

"Is everything alright?" asked Amy, with concern, as she quickly noticed Kate's uneasiness.

"It's the wine," Kate muttered, "I think I might have drunk too much of it…"

"But you hardly finished your first glass," observed Amy, who clearly paid close attention to Kate's habits this evening.

Barbara also caught word of Amy's observation too; however, she greatly mistook Kate's uneasiness to wine, as the means of a possible pregnancy. Therefore, with much premature excitement, she joyfully asked her, "Jennifer, my dear, could this possibly mean that you're—"

"Barbara," interrupted Kate, as she excused herself. She further explained, "David and Amy, if you all don't mind, I think that I might need to briefly step away for a moment to fetch a glass of water."

"My dear, you should sit back down. If you'd prefer, I can go and fetch some water for you, myself," replied a concerned David.

"No, that's quite alright. I think I also need to walk a little, too. A turn about the room might help revive my lingering energy," said Kate.

"Very well then. In the event that our paths don't cross again this evening, I can expect to see you and John this weekend at my cabin, correct? Amy, Peter and I will be waiting," David reminded her.

"Yes," replied Kate reluctantly, as a single word response. Afterwards, she quickly excused herself again from the table and walked over across to the opposite side of the room.

After narrowly escaping away from Barbara's prying company, Kate found herself standing alone, in front of the refreshment table and pouring herself a much-needed glass of water. While she sipped her refreshing cold water, her nerves slowly began to calm back down, as she peacefully listened to the classical music that played in the background. Due to the state dinner's budget, Kate was able to hire a professional band for tonight's event. Briefly, she closed her eyes to concentrate on enjoying the music; however, suddenly, she heard someone call out her name from behind her.

"Hello Jennifer," said the man.

Kate turned around and saw that standing before her was none other than, Lucas. Elegantly dressed in a crisp satin black suit, he accompanied it with a silk emerald green tie, which just so happened, to be identical to his own eye color. Like Kate, he too, was pouring himself a glass of water; however, he added a slice of a fresh green lime to his version of the drink.

"Hello Lucas," replied Kate, as she took another sip of her water. "Are you also taking a break?"

"Actually, yes, I am," he said. "I've situated all the men here tonight, and I'm confident that the premise is currently safe and secure. And now, I think I'm entitled to enjoy my well-earned and deserved drink."

"Oh, but we're only drinking just plain water. I can't say that there's anything particularly special about it, really," she remarked, surprised that Lucas even considered drinking water as a special treat.

"Ah, but that's where you're wrong, Jennifer," he said, with a devilish smile.

Surprisingly, this was the first time that he had ever addressed her formally as Jennifer; and for some reason, Kate got the impression that he was secretly enjoying it, in a rather sinister and devious way.

"Mine has a lime in it," he reminded her, and then he gave her a wink.

"Oh, well I suppose if…" she trailed off.

"I'm a recovering alcoholic," admitted Lucas bluntly, "And I haven't had a single drop of any alcohol in years. Water with lime is as far as I can go."

"Lucas, I'm so sorry. I just had no idea," replied Kate, shamefully.

"It's alright, it's not your fault. You don't know my past," he said.

"As you don't know mine, either," she added.

"But don't I? I mean, I'm the head of security. After all, I was the one, who personally ran your background check," he said, with a sarcastic laugh.

"I suppose you are right," Kate reluctantly admitted.

Suddenly, the band started to play a new song, and Lucas quickly gulped the remainder of his water, and then slammed the empty glass back down onto the table.

"Shall we dance?" he asked, as he reached over to offer his hand to her.

"Dance? As in us dancing on the ballroom floor?" she asked, in complete surprise.

"Why not? Don't you want to showcase your new dancing skills? After all, you've only been practicing your dance lessons every day for weeks now," he reminded her.

"Yes, I know, but studying is one thing and executing is another," she replied.

"Come now, Jennifer; I've been a gentleman, and I've politely asked for your hand. Now, if you choose to deny me this request, then everyone here will be left wondering as to why you were so coldly rude and dismissive towards me," Lucas warned.

Was that a threat? If she honestly refused to dance with him, then would that have truly sparked such gossip amongst the guests? Kate simply couldn't take that chance. Unfortunately, for her, she was going to have to accept Lucas' offer.

"Alright, but just one dance only," agreed Kate, reluctantly, as she reached over and gave him her hand.

After securing Kate's hands within his grasp, Lucas quickly escorted them down onto the dancefloor. Upon their arrival, Kate noticed that there were already several couples already busy and dancing about on the stage. For some reason, this brought some comfort to her ailing nerves; for that meant, that at least, she wasn't entirely alone. When the next song started to play, Kate realized that the music playing was one of the Viennese Waltz songs that she had previously practiced with Bes. Ironically, it seemed that Lucas might have chosen the most ideal time to dance, in order to publicly test and showcase Kate's new dancing skills.

"The time has finally come to dance the waltz now, Jennifer," he whispered into her ear, while he placed his right hand around the bottom half of her waist, that just so happened to border her behind. Unfortunately, this position made Kate feel extremely uncomfortable.

"You know Lucas, you don't have to continue to refer to me as Jennifer while we're dancing, here," she replied, pulling his hand higher above and closer to her precise waistline. "It's just you and me now, so you can call me Kate."

"Why risk taking a chance?" he asked cautiously; while at the same time, he proceeded to raise their arms into the air, in preparation for the waltz.

"Lucas are you left-handed?" asked Kate, who, up until now, was unaware of this fact.

Since Bes and her were naturally right-handed, Kate had practiced all of her dance steps, under the assumption that any of her future dance partners were going to also be right-handed partners, as well. However, if Lucas was indeed left-handed, then Kate needed to quickly retrace and calculate her own dance steps within her mind, in order to follow his new and opposite lead.

"I'm both actually," he said, while he quickly changed positions, using his right arm as his primary lead. "Sorry, sometimes, I naturally revert back to my left hand. I was born left-handed; but over the years, I had to learn to adapt to make use my right hand."

Just then, the lights dimmed low, and the surrounding couples on stage started to dance. As Lucas took his first steps forward, Kate gulped. At long last, the time to dance had finally arrived. Holding on tightly to Lucas as he glided across the dancefloor, Kate simply followed his lead. To her surprise, Lucas wasn't an amateur dancer. In fact, he seemed to know precisely as to what exactly he was doing. Luckily, by him knowing the proper execution of each of the dance steps correctly, the entire routine went about almost seamlessly. Thus, making her first dance, as smooth as a whistle.

"Lucas, if I didn't know any better, I'd say that you seem to have quite a bit of experience in this arena," Kate remarked.

"Are you that surprised?" he asked, as he twirled her around.

"Actually, yes, I am," she admitted, as she circled back to face him, once again.

"Well, there's a lot that you still don't know about me. You know, I do have a personal life apart from security," he reminded her.

"That's true. Sometimes, I forget that," she said.

"Too wrapped up in the charade, aren't you? You're starting to be more like her each and every day," he said, as he pulled her closer to him.

"What do you mean?" she asked, entirely confused by his statement.

"It's just that you fit in nicely here…perhaps, a bit too nicely, that's all," he clarified. He then warned, "But remember, this world is only temporary. Don't get too attached here. Nothing lasts forever."

Why was he reminding her of this? Why now? He already well knew that she understood that all of this was temporary. They all did. From the very beginning. In fact, they all knew that her sole mission here was to help relocate her sister and to prevent a scandal. After everything, why was he suddenly once again reminding her of all of this? Of what, they all already knew? And here, in the middle of the dancefloor, out of all places?

"Lucas, I'm very well aware that nothing last forever. As we both already know," she coldly replied, strictly emphasizing the word "both," as she swirled around in the opposite direction away from him.

"Good," he said confidently, "Remember, it's just a job. Nothing more."

His choice of words bothered her immensely. Yes, it was just a job. A mission intended to serve a purpose. However, Kate also felt a bit uneasy, because deep down inside, pushed aside into the far reaches of her mind, she knew that once Jennifer eventually returned, then she, just as Lucas reminded her, was meant to also return back to her old life in New York again. Back to being Dr. Stanley in the history department…and away from John. John, the man, whom she wasn't meant, nor supposed to care for…but did anyways. The very thought of leaving him, already felt like an open and bleeding wound that Kate wasn't yet ready to fully acknowledge, nor face.

"Yes, I understand," she finally said quietly, as he pulled her back to face him.

"I knew you would," he replied, happily. "As I said before, none of these people are your true friends. And now that we've cleared that up, I just wanted to let you know ahead of time that I've got some urgent business in New York to attend to. As such, I'll be away for the next few days. As my replacement, my deputy, Miles Ford, will serve as my backup, while I'm away. Have you met Miles yet?"

Although she found it rather peculiar and odd that Lucas had some urgent and last-minute business away from the embassy, none of that really pertained to her. All that mattered was as to whether or not, someone from his team planned on staying behind, to remain active on reviewing and investigating her sister's ongoing case.

"What about my sister's case? Will Miles be overseeing it, in your absence?" she asked, concerningly.

Surprisingly, Lucas laughed at her inquiry, and Kate, in return, found his reaction a bit strangely odd and rude. Almost like mockery. Apart from everything, her inquiry was a reasonable and logical question. Surely, it didn't merit, nor justify a laugh?

Without saying another word, he moved and twirled her back towards him. When they came face to face again, he smiled once more and held her even tighter, bringing her waist closer to his.

"I," he began, "Intend to remain active as the lead investigator in this case, even while I'm away. However, Miles will oversee certain things here locally, what I myself cannot do remotely," he said with a devious smirk across his face.

"I see," began Kate cautiously, "As long as my sister's case has not been forgotten—"

"Oh, her case has definitely not been forgotten," he interrupted her, "Not for a moment. Why, just looking at you, how could anyone forget about her?"

Kate remained silent. She really didn't know what else to say to him. Meanwhile, he, on the other hand, knew precisely what to say to her.

"Her case is always on my mind. No need for you to worry," he added.

"But you still haven't answered my last question," he continued, while shaking his right index finger at her, in a scolding manner. "Have you met Miles?" he asked again, with his tone being rather mocking and obnoxious, this time.

"No, I have not," she replied coldly and feeling yet again, uncomfortable near her close proximately to him.

For a split second, Kate contemplated as to whether or not, she should "accidentally" stomp upon Lucas' foot and then blame it as an innocent amateur's mistake; thus, creating the perfect diversion and distraction to help enable her to make a clean escape. As of now, Kate was growing to greatly dislike Lucas. His personality was becoming more obnoxious and condescending by the minute; which in contrast, was the complete opposite of John's. While John was kind, respectful and polite; Lucas lacked all of these essential traits. Had John been dancing with her and not Lucas, then she would have enjoyed her first dance; because as of right now, she was already counting the minutes until the music ended, so that she could exit the stage, as soon as possible. Unfortunately, Kate had no other choice but to bite her own tongue, and to force a bitter smile across her face.

"Well, Jennifer, today's your lucky day. Looking straight ahead, you'll spot a short man, with curly brown hair, standing near the entrance. That's Miles," explained Lucas.

Following Lucas' directions, Kate looked straight ahead and immediately spotted Miles. Just as Lucas described, he was indeed a short man, barely standing above five foot and three inches tall. However, Miles also appeared rather young. Perhaps, a bit too young? Was Lucas leaving her sister's case, within capable and experienced hands?

"Does he have much experience?" she bluntly asked Lucas.

Once again, he laughed and said, "Miles might be a rookie, but he's one of my best. He's very dedicated, hard-working and pays close attention to the smallest of details."

Meanwhile, as Kate remained locked within Lucas's tight embrace, John finally arrived to the ballroom. As he desperately searched through the crowd, looking for any signs and traces of her, he eventually saw her from across the room, dancing within the arms of Lucas. The mere sight of seeing her dancing with another, left him surprised. Although he had briefly stepped away from the party, he didn't expect to return and see her dancing and conversing with another man. However, it was a party after all and this was to be expected, wasn't it? But for some odd reason, it still bothered him. It bothered him that she was standing in such close proximity to someone else. It bothered him that she was talking and smiling to another. It bothered him that she was dancing so intimately in public with another partner. But most of all, what bother him the greatest above all else, was that she actually seemed happy and enjoying the company of another man, other than himself. All of this bothered him, immensely. But why? He, himself, just didn't quite understand the answer to that very question.

In the past, John had previously witness Jennifer dance and flirt with countless of other men during their many parties together; but none of them, not a single one, ever bothered him. Never, ever. John always remained calm, poised and collective. No matter the circumstances, he always smiled, looked the other way and continued about with his own private affairs; business as usual. But now, for whatever reason, it was entirely different. And this was most unexpected.

What exactly did John feel? At this very moment, he wasn't entirely sure. What was this foreign sensation, that made him feel…so…well, angry? Yes, that was the correct adjective! He was angry! But why? And he must have felt angry, too; for there weren't any other words to best describe this fierce emotion. However, with that being said, anger was only but a prefix to what he felt internally, for he had other emotions stirring, as well. Apart from 'angry,' John also felt another tingling sensation that reluctantly clutched itself around the core of his own heart, without invitation. A sensation that managed to cause his blue eyes to turn green with envy. It was an emotion that made him feel…well…jealous. Ah, yes, John was jealous of Lucas! Alas, he was jealous at the fact, that it was Lucas who was there, dancing away and holding onto Kate, and not him! What a surprising twist of fate! Oh, how he envied him right now!

The madness, in which he felt, was growing and spreading across his entire body, like a blazing wildfire set aflame. As far as he was concerned, he desperately needed to walk…no, run across the dancefloor! Right now, he was determined to interrupt their dance, and interject and impose himself there in between them, and thus, claiming himself, as her one and true partner; all the while, pushing aside his opponent, Lucas, to the furthest, darkest and most dreary remote corners of the estate.

But this was so unlike John's character; for as far as anyone else knew, he was often regarded to be a highly sensible, amiable and reasonable man. Although logically, it made better sense to simply allow the current dance number to run and to end on its own due course, as he waited for his next turn to dance with her; however, this is where all of his human and bodily senses, pertaining to logic and reason ended. As it was, he no longer cared about the proper rules and etiquettes deemed appropriate for polite society; rules, in which, he was expected to abide and comply with. Unlike before, this time around, he was willing to break all of the rules, if it meant being with her.

Honestly, there wasn't truly a rational explanation, nor justified reason for all of this, either. For in truth, John was solely compelled and dictated by his own pure inner emotions; strange and foreign feelings that he still struggled to understand, but at the same time, was learning to cope with. Currently, as it was, at this particular and exact moment, captured and frozen in time, John desired desperately to trade places with Lucas, in order to be the primary man by her side. That was the absolute truth; for nothing else in his world mattered to him. Not the party. Not the guests. Not the staff. Not his project. Not even his own family. Nothing. All that mattered to him right now, was her and only her. Just Kate. That was all. Plain and simple.

Furthermore, John concluded that although he failed to fully comprehend these new and mysterious feelings for her, as of right now; in the meantime, while he attempted to unravel these intense and plaguing emotions, he was just going to have to grow accustomed to them. However, with that having been acknowledged, after years of quietly standing behind in the background and watching others dance freely about, John decided to finally walk across the stage and claim his leading lady mid-dance for himself; an absolute first, for him. As impolite as this was, he didn't care. Ah, yes, John was most eager!

Stomping across the floor, with his hands tightly clutched down into a fist, John forced himself to smile the most uncomfortable and awkward expression across his youthful face, that by having done so, an ever-so-slight wrinkle suddenly appeared across his forehead. After hastily rushing across the stage, he finally made it to her side. Surprised by his unexpected arrival, Kate and Lucas both stared at him in utter confusion. However, their astonished reaction failed to thwart him from his determination.

"May I interrupt this dance?" he asked her directly.

"Right now?" she asked, still shocked that he was here.

"Yes, *now*," he replied boldly, in a rather commanding tone, as he emphasized the word 'now' in the process.

Now, Lucas, for all his worth, was a very intelligent man; and he clearly understood John's direct order, even if Kate, failed to do. After all, she was still innocent and naïve about their world. But, as much as he enjoyed her company, Lucas was willing to bow down for now and to wait for another opportune time in the near future to interact with her once again. Ultimately, at the end of the day, John was still his superior.

Without saying a word, Lucas pulled himself away, took a bow and walked off stage, leaving Kate in John's care. Promptly, John swiftly reached for Kate's hand and led her into their waltz. Much to Kate's astonishment, John was a far better dancer, than Lucas. While Lucas might have known all of the required dance steps correctly; he lacked any grace and charisma. Furthermore, he was way too aggressive as a dance partner and overall, he unfortunately exhibited a severe dearth of charm.

However, this wasn't the case for John. In fact, he was the complete opposite. Gracefully gliding across the stage with his two feet barley touching the floor, John guided and led Kate, with complete suave, comfort and ease. And for the first time since arriving on stage, Kate finally started to enjoy her dance.

"Did your meeting go well with the Indian Ambassador?" she asked, as he twirled her about.

"Hmm…what meeting?" John asked, in return.

Distracted by her enchanting beauty, John had long forgotten about his recent meeting with the Indian Ambassador. It was all in the past and it no longer matter. Right now, his attention was focused here, in this very moment. As far as he was concerned, he was simply enjoying himself, by dancing with the most beautiful woman in the entire ballroom; for Kate truly was, the belle of the ball. However, Kate wasn't someone who could so easily forget.

"Remember, the meeting? The one that you just held tonight, right inside of your office?" she asked, again.

However, Kate, having recently read from the embassy's policies and procedures handbook, recalled that John might not be at liberty to discuss these private business and confidential governmental matters with her directly. Therefore, in order to respect his privacy, she decided not the press him any further.

"Never mind, that I asked. I'm sure it's private business," she firmly admitted.

"Ah, yes, private business," he echoed her; unaffected by her observation, for he was too preoccupied enjoying his unexpected, yet blissful state besides her.

"Listen, John, since we're alone," Kate began, deciding that now was the perfect and ideal time to discuss Barbara's proposed trip to Kars with him, "There's something rather urgent that I need to tell you. It's about your mother."

"What about mother?" asked John, who was still lost within a dream-like daze.

"Your mother wants us to travel to Kars, via the Doğu Express to attend Amy's engagement party," Kate revealed.

"Amy's engaged? To whom?" asked John, reverting his attention back to her, while departing from his dream state and returning back to earth.

"Yes, she's engaged to a young dentist named Dr. Peter Murphy," replied Kate.

"Where will the engagement party be held?" asked John, now highly interested in this new and upcoming prospective trip.

"It's in Kars. David suggested that we embark on a train ride together, and then spend the weekend at a private cabin in the snow. Naturally, I tried my best to convince Barbara that this was a bad idea for us, but—"

"Actually, a weekend trip might do us all good," John bluntly interrupted.

"Do you really mean that? But that would ultimately mean that we'd be forced to share a bedroom together…" suggested Kate, nervously.

"You can have the bed. I'll take the couch," he replied confidently, as he twirled her about.

"Seriously?" asked Kate, once she twirled back and came directly, face to face with him.

"I am. Besides, I could use a break from all of this. Don't you?" he asked, with a devilish smile.

"A break?" she asked, with a raised brow.

"Yes, a break," he asserted, "Honestly, Kate, I think that we could all use a break from all of these damn parties and projects. I know that I certainly can. Why, wouldn't you prefer to spend a few extra days alone, away from the prying eyes of Gloria and the rest of the staff?"

"Kate," she repeated, happily, "You actually said my name. Here, out in the public."

"Why not? It's your name? Besides, it's safe to say that no one, other than us, can hear me. It's just you and me; alone together, here on the dancefloor. We're all that matters, not them," he whispered into her ear, with a twinkle in his eye.

Without Kate having had the chance to react to him, John quickly pulled her closer to him. While his left hand remained tightly wrapped around her waist, his right hand was intertwined within her own delicate and soft hands. Meanwhile, his piercing blue eyes stared straight into her own fragile blue eyes. Acknowledging the strong intensity of his stare, which was both passionate and demanding, Kate suddenly felt weak in the knee.

"So, you'll go?" he finally asked.

Without further reasoning and against her own better judgment, Kate, simply nodded in agreement to him. Naturally, John was delighted. As the music began to fade, he gave her one last twirl around the ballroom. When the music finally came to a conclusion, Kate, once more, came face to face with John. However, this time, it was different; for they were standing so close to each other, that their own lips were practically touching one another. Kate stared straight into John's eyes, and there, she saw the face of an angel. In his eyes and smile, she saw a decent man. A man who cared about his family. A man who cared about his employees. A man who cared about the embassy and the mansion. A man who cared about his fellow diplomats. A man who cared about his country. A man who even, cared about Tabitha. John was truly a genuinely good person, inside and out. Alas, as Kate looked into his eyes, she somehow managed to forget about all of the other guests. For in this moment, all that mattered to her, was him. The moment felt so incredibly magical.

Suddenly, what seemed to be the most impossible thing imaginable, magically came to be; for in that exact moment, John, from out of nowhere, actually bent down, leaned forward and kissed her, directly on her lips! As their lips came into contact with one another, Kate closed her eyes and surrendered to him. However, this kiss wasn't just a normal and simple peck on the lips. No, it certainly wasn't. For as soon as John's lips pressed against hers, his lips refused to leave hers. When his lips landed above the outer corner of her mouth, his tongue darted out and forced her mouth open wide.

Obeying his command, she opened her mouth, allowing John's tongue to swiftly invade, as he French kissed her, with such longing and desire, that Kate lost all form of her balance. Growing weak in the knee, John was forced to catch her mid-air, as he scooped her up into his arms, right there on stage. Finally, as she stood up, with her feet returning back to the floor, she once again, reopened her eyes. However, rather than seeing John staring right back at her; she instead, sadly witnessed John's attention revert and redirect to another fellow diplomat. Apparently, the two diplomats were now fully engaged and conversing about a rather serious discussion. Sadly, for Kate, it seemed that their unexpected kiss was now long over, but certainly, not forgotten; at least, not for her. Eventually, when Kate's senses returned back to her, she wondered as to why he chose to kiss her. Was it all for show? To impress their guests? Or, was it, because he secretly had feelings for her? Did he actually care for her? More than just friends? It was a mystery that was simply too vexing!

Later on, that evening, after all of the guests departed and the party was long finished, Kate sat alone in her bedroom, still pondering and daydreaming about their kiss. She replayed that exact moment, over and over again, inside of her head. Never for a second, did she ever consider, nor think that he was going to actually kiss her! But, worst of all, she actually enjoyed it! This was the biggest surprise of them all!

However, Kate also recalled Lucas' warning not to get too attached here; because everything in this world, including John, were all temporary. Kate already felt like she was living in a dream-like state; however, she also still knew that eventually, one day, she was going to be forced to awaken and return to her old world, back in New York. Back to her teaching days at the university and far removed from John. But for now, in the present time, her remaining days at the estate were still meant to be shared with John. And come tomorrow morning at the crack of dawn, Kate was about to embark on a train ride to Kars with him. But now that they kissed, how would things be between them? How was she to face him, without feeling a bit shy and nervous, on her part? And alone? Just he and her, together in a private cabin, out in the snow; with Barbara, right next door, rooting them on? The temptation was far too great!

As Kate touched her lips— the very same lips, which only but an hour ago, were locked away in a wonderous kiss with the man, whom she, up until this point, considered to be just her dear friend— she understood within her own fragile heart, that if he tried to kiss her again, just once more, then she wasn't going to be able to resist him. Kate just sighed. Her situation was simply impossible; for she very well knew, that she too, secretly wanted much more, than just one single kiss from him. It was all just too much to contain!

Meanwhile, John sat in his office, happily staring at the big and bright shining moon, humming and whistling a joyous tune to himself. For the first time in years, John was truly happy. Although it was never his intent to kiss Kate, but now that he had, he didn't regret it, not at all. Not for one second. For weeks, he had dreamed of kissing her and now, at long last, he finally did and it felt unreal and dreamlike. Furthermore, the kiss certainly didn't disappoint. In fact, it was truly wonderful and spectacular. Better than any of his previous expectations. Kissing Kate was the most adventurous, joyous and heartfelt events, within his entire lonesome existence. He knew that it was wrong of him having done so; but that still didn't change the fact that he enjoyed it. However, with that said, John also reluctantly knew what he needed to do, as a result of his actions. First thing, come tomorrow morning, he would speak directly to her and blame the whole incident, as nothing more than his compliance to the pressures of their charade. After all, they were hosting a public state dinner, posing as a happily married couple. Weren't happily married couples meant to kiss outside, in public? Surely, she, of all people, would understand him? Kate was a reasonable and rationale woman.

Taking a sip of his whisky, as his hands brushed against his own lips, John remembered their kiss once more. But now that he had finally experienced the sensation of her lips pressed against his, he strangely felt a bit unsatisfied. Having kissed her and experiencing firsthand, the sweetness and tenderness of her delicate and soft lips; he now, also grew curious about everything else. How would it feel, if he actually held her, just once? How would it feel, if he pressed her soft and delicate body against his, while he kissed every inch of her? How would it feel, if he stripped off all of her clothes, exposing her gentle and bare figure before him? What then? Would he then be fully satisfied?

John sighed. His situation was simply impossible. Then, at that very moment, John glanced across the room and stared at the portrait that hung above his office wall. As he looked and admired the painting, he thought about Adam. What did Adam feel after he ate that forbidden fruit? After tasting it, did Adam want more of it? Was he satisfied with just one bite? One single bite? Furthermore, even if Adam was well aware of the consequences associated with eating the forbidden fruit, if given a second chance, would Adam still make the same choice? Was it all worth the risk?

John pondered about these complex questions privately to himself. But after much reflection, John concluded that no, Adam wouldn't have been satisfied with just one single bite; for man's curiosity about the unknown, by far exceeds man's own private fears. As for himself, John already knew within his own heart, that their kiss wasn't going to be enough for him. No, it was certainly not enough to sustain him. Having recently discovered as to just how tasty and delicious her lips were— which were as sweet and as juicy, as the fairest and golden of apples— he was never going to be satisfied, with just the sole memory of their kiss. No, it was absolutely out of the question! After all, John was a hungry man, with an appetite for knowledge. Therefore, from this moment onwards, John was never going to be completely satisfied— not until he experienced all of her now; mind, body and soul.

Chapter 21

As promised, the very day, as soon as the sun rose up into the morning sky, George personally hand delivered three iron crisp sealed white envelopments to John, Kate and Barbara. Of course, the letters were Amy's official engagement invitations, along with their respective train tickets to Kars. By ten o'clock, Kate and Barbara arrived separately to the train station. Luckily, for Kate, John hadn't yet arrived and by divine intervention, she miraculously managed to avoid John completely altogether. However, Kate knew that eventually, she was going to have to come face to face with him again, and soon. Indeed, the clock was ticking away, and not at all, in her favor.

Oh, how she dreaded that anticipated moment! How was she going to act around him now? Was she supposed to pretend that their kiss never happened? That it meant absolutely nothing to her? That it was all for show and nothing else more? That it was intended purely for publicity? But if their kiss was really staged, then why did she feel the way she did? For in truth, their kiss actually meant something to her. In fact, it meant a whole lot to her. Ever since last night, their kiss was all that she could think about. It was constantly lingering inside of her mind and within her own private and inner thoughts. Not only had she secretly enjoyed it; but her own heart wanted to burst out into happiness, like a star erupting from a nuclear fusion. Kate was blissfully happy, yet at the very same time, she was also so incredible fearful and afraid about the mysterious and unknown road that lay ahead of her.

Heavens, what was to become of her? Surely, John didn't feel the same way like she did, didn't he? For if he did, he would have said something to her by now, shouldn't he? He would have stormed into her bedroom in the middle of the night and demanded to speak with her, right there and then, wouldn't he? For God only knew that Kate failed to sleep, not a single peep last night. All night long, she tossed and turned inside of her oversized, but sleepless bed. Back and forth, and side to side; even Tabitha seemed annoyed by Kate's restlessness. Come the midnight hour, while Kate still lay awake and alone inside of her bed, anticipating their upcoming trip, she stared up at the moonlight. It was shining brightly against her dark bedroom ceiling, as she counted the hours until daylight. She counted and counted; and once she thought that she was done counting away, she continued counting some more. She counted the hours, the minutes and even, the very seconds to when she would see him again, face to face. Oh, how she dreaded that upcoming encounter! Of seeing John again! Better yet, of this entire trip, all put together!

However, what Kate feared the most, above all else, was that when she finally faced him, then what exactly was she going to say to him? Was she honestly expected to simply laugh it off and pretend that their kiss meant nothing to her? That she forgave him and that she didn't want it to happen again? No repeats? Which, of course, was a huge lie, because Kate did want to kiss again! She really did, too. Kate wanted to kiss John for a second, and a third, and a fourth and a fifth time…and so on and so forth. The point being, that Kate simply wasn't satisfied with just one single kiss. No, she certainly was not! Now, that she'd previewed the sweet aroma stemming from his soft and passionate lips, she wanted more. Much more. In fact, she wanted to experience all of him, inside of her. Desperately, she wanted to give into her own secret desires and surrender herself over to him, while permitting him to devour and consume her, with the mutual expectation that he never, ever let her go.

Furthermore, his unexpected, yet wonderous kiss, awoke several hidden and unspeakable desires that she now acknowledged, but needed to confront. And now that she finally recognized her intense attraction to him, how was she going to be able to tell him all of this? How was she going to admit to him, that she actually cared about him? That, not only was she attracted to him, but that she also harbored feelings for him? And most importantly, that she was no longer satisfied with just 'pretending' to be his lover; but instead, this time around, she actually wanted to become his lover, for real?

Somehow, that art of pretending slowly…started to feel…well…sort of…real. Yes, real. Kate was beginning to possess real feelings for him…and attraction. But was it also mutual on his part? Did he share the same identical feelings, as her? Did he suppress her similar yearnings and desires, that she secretly felt for him? And now, having realized all of this, how was she going to carry-on around him? What sort of small talk might she need to engage upon with him, in order to help deflect her crippling nerves and repressed sexual desires? Because here on out, she already knew far in advance, that each time she saw him, she was going to look at him with hungry eyes. Moving forward, how was she ever to maintain her calm composure around him? How was she ever going to publicly hold his hand again, without secretly wishing and hoping for him to never let her go? And if by any chance, he somehow happened to kiss her just once more, then she knew, without a shadow of a doubt, that his kiss was going to be the end of her.

Ultimately, Kate came to the conclusion, that what she really needed was time apart from him. Time apart, in order for her to mentally process all of these new feelings and emotions, privately. But alas, time just wasn't on her side; for any moment, John was expected to arrive here at the train station, any second now. And then, Kate was going to have to face him again, and soon. Furthermore, there was still the train ride, the private cabin and their shared bedroom. Kate sighed to herself. Fate, it seemed, had been cruel to her. Yes, very cruel to her, indeed.

Upon boarding the train, Kate glanced at her wristwatch and saw that it was ten minutes past ten o'clock. At precisely half past ten, the train was scheduled to depart the station. Meanwhile, John still hadn't yet arrived. Secretly, Kate wished that by some odd miracle, he would miss this train. Although she knew that eventually, their paths would cross again; that still didn't prevent her from hoping. At least time way, she'd have some alone time with herself, and remain as far as she possibly come from him.

What if John was too preoccupied in an unannounced, unscheduled and last-minute meeting? Maybe, he would skip the train ride and just meet them later on in Kars? Perhaps, he would opt to fly instead, and arrive to the cabin much later this evening? Or better yet, come tomorrow morning? Or, dare she assume the worse, and not even at all? After all, he was in the middle of a busy project, was he not? Regardless, his delay and potential absence was going to inadvertently buy her extended alone time; something that she so desperately needed right now.

As the clock slowly neared the departure time, John was still nowhere in sight; therefore, Kate released a sighed of relief. Upon boarding the train, Kate quickly joined Barbara to enjoy a warm pot of black tea, as the two ladies sat together inside of their private carriage, which was located up front, in the first compartment. Although Kate was happily content with their party of two; Barbara, on the other hand, was not.

"Wherever could he be?" cried Barbara, "This is so unlike him!"

Unlike Barbara, Kate remained secretly thrilled by the lack of John's appearance; and so, she relished and savored her warm tea in peace, as she happily sipped it from her porcelain teacup. As she gently placed the teacup back onto its saucer, Kate suggested to that perhaps, John was too preoccupied and busy with the general affairs of the embassy.

"He better not have canceled! That much, I can say!" exclaimed Barbara, angrily, "I vow, if he doesn't come, then I'll never forgive him!"

Suddenly, the bells whistled and the doors started to close. It was now, half past ten o'clock and the train was ready to depart from the station. With the train's engine running and in full operation, Barbara frantically searched for her son from outside of their window. Although it appeared that this upcoming trip was going to be limited to only the two women, fate, it seems, had other plans; for as soon as the train's doors were just about to completely close, a black leather briefcase jolted, like lightning, from out of nowhere. Somehow, the briefcase managed to wedge itself, in-between two opposing doors, preventing them from fully closing. As the conductor gasped at such a sight, two male hands soon followed after the black briefcase, pulling the doors wide open. With the entrance doors reopened, the man with the black briefcase causally walked in…

"Just in time," he confidently announced, with a huge smile shining across his cheerful face.

"John?" gasped Kate. Out of shock, she managed to drop her teacup onto the floor, making both a dreadful stain on her dress, as well as a small puddle, nearby.

"My dear Mrs. Barrett!" exclaimed John, as he strolled over towards Kate, and then, without any reason, nor explanation, he gently gave her a small kiss along her forehead.

Afterwards, he slowly bent down and collected all of the broken pieces to her empty teacup and saucer, and then he rang the bell for the train hostess to come and fetch a new replacement. Once that was all settled, John made his way over to Barbara and, in an effort to humor his mother, he also bestowed a small kiss along her forehead, as he exclaimed, "Mother!"

However, Barbara wasn't so easily amused; so, she huffed and reminded him that he was, in fact, late.

"Really?" replied John, amusingly. Referencing his watch, he said with a big smile, "According to my calculations, it appears that I've arrived precisely on time."

"Just in the nick of time," interrupted the train hostess, who now, stood at their entrance corridor and holding their replacement dishes within her arms. "If you'd arrive just a second longer, then those doors would have certainly crushed you into pieces."

"Well, then it's a good thing that I travel by briefcase, isn't it, Mrs. Barrett?" teased John, as he gave Kate a wink.

For a brief split second, Kate failed to recognize that she was indeed *the* Mrs. Barrett, in which he was referring to. In fact, this was the very first time that he'd ever publicly referred to her as such. After the hostess delivered their new tea set and placed it onto their table, Kate remembered that at least for now, she was Mrs. Barrett; and so, she smiled and carried on with their charade.

As the train prepared for departure, its wheels began to run in motion. Ready to embark upon their long journey, John comfortably sat himself down on an empty seat, which was located in-between Kate and Barbara. Due to his close proximity, Kate gulped. She was nervous. To help conceal her nerves, Kate decided to revert her focus on pouring herself a fresh cup of warm tea. Reaching over to grab an empty teacup and saucer, she noticed from the corner of her eyes, that a second pair of teacup and saucer slid down from across the table and landed right next to her, nearby.

"If you don't mind, I'll take a cup, too," said John, as he handed the empty second pair of dishes over to Kate.

Meanwhile, Kate just simply stared down at the empty teacup in front of her. To her dismay, the outer rim of the teacup was completely covered by John's imposing hands, with the exception to its handle. It seemed that John's gesture purposely intended for their hands to cross paths with one another. However, Kate, being far too nervous to engage in any physical contact with him, instead, opted to reach over and grab the handle directly herself; which luckily, proved to be successful, for it was completely free from his tight grip.

"How do you take your tea?" she asked, after having captured the teacup away from him.

"Same as you," he answered, never once leaving sight of her.

"Very well," she said, trying her best not to make direct eye contact with him. "Black tea, no sugar, with a dash of milk. That's way I like to drink it these days."

"I know," he boldly admitted.

Instantly, she was taken aback from his response; for it genuinely surprised her. Was this true? Did he really know, as to how she drank her tea? How did he learn? And if so, why was he even interested to have learned this, in the first place? Neither of her own friends and family back home, knew as to how she took her tea. Sadly, not even her own twin sister knew her drinking style, either.

Thus, his reply made Kate grow even more anxious and nervous; for she truly believed that he was indeed, telling the absolute truth. It appeared that John really did seem to know almost everything about her—even down to the tiniest of details, such as her tea preferences. But again, how did he know? Somehow, one way or another, he must have noticed and observed by now, her specific drinking habits during their many dinners and engagements. Furthermore, she did catch him early on, reading her personal profile back in the library. Maybe, that's how he knew? But even then, why did he still care to remember?

As Kate nervously begun to pour the tea into the teacups, her hands started to fidget and shake. John immediately took notice and within lightning speed, his hands quickly moved over to covered hers with his. Together, he and her, held the heavy teapot safely within the grip of their united hands.

"Please, allow me," he said to her, as he gently pulled the teapot away from her tight grip.

Without saying another word, John proceeded to pour the tea into two separate teacups: one for her and one for him. After pouring the tea, he reached over for the pitcher of milk and then, he added a small dash of milk into each respective teacup. Finally, he gently placed the teacup before her, allowing her the chance to freely retrieve the teacup for herself, once she was calm and ready.

"It's still a bit hot," he warned. "Just wait a few minutes to cool off, first."

Kate agreed, and John reverted his attention over to his mother.

"Mother, would you care for a cup of tea?" asked John to Barbara.

However, Barbara simply laughed and said, "Tea? My darling, I had other plans in mind…"

Reaching deep into her purse, Barbara pulled out a bottle of wine.

"Wine? So early in the morning?" asked John, in sheer surprise.

"Correction, it's almost the afternoon," Barbara responded, affirmatively.

"Is that one of your test wines?" asked Kate, most curious as to why Barbara was carrying a random spare wine bottle inside of her purse.

"Why yes! You remembered! Now, if you two don't mind," continued Barbara, as she abruptly stood up from her seat, "I intend to share my new wine, with the other guests and crew members aboard this lovely train."

"Wait, you're leaving us here, all alone?" cried Kate aloud.

"Yes," John interjected. "You're honestly trying to attempt to advertise and sell your new wine aboard this moving train? Honestly, Mother…"

"Now, you two don't look at me like that," Barbara swiftly forewarned. "I've managed to bring three separate suitcases for this trip, for a particular reason."

"Mother!" shouted John, in disbelief.

"Are you planning to sell all of these bottles, here, on this train?" asked Kate.

"Perhaps," replied Barbara, with a smile. "But for now, I've got this one bottle in my hand, so samples it is."

"But what about Amy's party? David did pre-reserve a few bottles of your new wine," Kate reminded her; all the while, realizing that Barbara was the one other person, that prevented her from remaining alone, with John's sole company.

"Jennifer, my love, don't worry. That's why I have the third suitcase," replied Barbara, with a wink.

"Dear God, Mother! Are you honestly telling us that you packed three suitcases, consisting of wine bottles? What about your clothes?" asked John, annoyingly.

"That's what shopping is for," Barbara remarked. "My darlings, I'll simply buy new clothes there, along with a fourth suitcase."

"There should be a limit!" exclaimed John, while shaking his head, in disapproval.

"Oh John, do lighten up! Now, if you don't mind, I've got some work to do," said Barbara, with conviction.

Taking her bottle of wine, Barbara happily exited their private carriage, as she joyfully hummed a tune and joined the rest of the remaining passengers and crew, seated inside of the other carriages, nearby. With Barbara long gone, Kate realized that right now, she was completely alone, with John. Naturally, with just the two of them here, they were, one way or another, going to have to confront and discuss about their kiss last night. Weren't they? After all, that was still the white elephant in the room. But somehow, Kate just wasn't ready to face that particular discussion. At least, not yet.

For a long few minutes, silence consumed their private carriage. Neither he, nor she said anything, at all. They both equally and quietly sat down, as they independently sipped their tea and peacefully stared across at the scenic view from outside of their window. So, this was how it was going to be, she thought to herself. Silence. Blissful and complete silence; the absence of sound. However, Kate couldn't have been more wrong; for as soon as she thought that silence had become her dear sweet friend, John, at long last, was the first person to suddenly break it.

"About last night," he said directly. "We need to talk about last night."

Kate gulped. She wasn't exactly sure, as to what he was about to say. Was he going to admit that he actually enjoyed it? After all, ever since he arrived, he seemed to be in a rather jolly and good mood. Or was he going blame the kiss on the party? Truly, that was the logical and reasonable explanation. While the latter appeared the be the most likely answer; somehow, it still bothered her. On the one hand, admitting that their kiss was simply part of their charade, brought a sense of relief on her part; but at the same time, she also felt…well…a bit disappointed.

But this was absolutely ridiculous! Why ever, should she be disappointed by all of this? Well, sadly, Kate already knew the answer her own question. Much to her dismay, Kate secretly wished, with all of her heart, that John would admit that he, too, enjoyed their kiss. For if John enjoyed their kiss, then it meant that he also harbored romantic feelings for her; and those feelings exceeded well above, then just friendship. However, if he admitted the latter, then it also meant that he failed to mutually share the same romantic feelings, that she felt for him. Either way, both outcomes were going to disappoint her; one way or another.

"Kate, you don't ever have to worry about us. I'm your friend, no matter what. Please forgive me…I just got a bit carried away…with our charade…that's all," he finally admitted.

Alas, maybe, that was just the problem. The origins to her dilemma. Perhaps, just being 'friends' was the root of her internal struggle. For in truth, Kate wanted to be more than friends. Looking across the table and staring directly into his piercing blue eyes, Kate just knew, inside of her own fragile heart, that she desperately wanted more, than mere friendship. She had grown past that. Although having John as her dear friend was wonderful; somehow, now, it just wasn't enough. Kate craved more. She wanted love. Love, in all of its forms and glory!

"The charade…yes, of course. I understand," she softly spoke, while feeling gravely disappointed, in the process.

Out of distress, Kate tugged tightly against her dress, using her bare hands. While she forced a wry smile across her sad face, underneath the table, her hands desperately searched for an outlet to release her disappointing anguish and despair; for tugging away at her dress simply wasn't enough anymore. Even though she expected him to admit as such; it still failed to lessen any of her pain. But, dear reader, if only she had known the truth! For, if John had truthfully spoken directly from his own heart, then his true intentions and motivations for kissing her would not have disappointed her. Not in the very least! Unbeknownst to both parties, John also felt the same heart ache and pain, such as she. Furthermore, while it was the proper protocol for him to conceal his true feelings for her; the reality was that he secretly wished to just once, speak the truth freely and to admit his affections for her.

Sensing her uneasiness, John quickly sought to change the subject; which Kate, in return, was most grateful for. First, he spoke about the weather, then he switched their conversation over to how lovely their tea was; and then, finally, he commented on how nice the train's interior designs were. However, all of John's attempted conversations proved to be a bit strange and awkward; because the reality was, that both he and Kate, were still thinking about their kiss and no matter as to how hard he tried to redirect their attention over to something else, the memory of their kiss still lingered about, within the far reaches of their minds.

As a last resort, John finally suggested that they spend the remainder of their train ride engaged in more productive matters, independently. Kate, of course, agreed. While he opted to catch up on his reading; she, on the other hand, took the liberty to admire the beautiful scenic view, from right outside of their window. However, John's attempts to refocus on his reading failed miserably; for as soon as he opened his book to chapter one, he simply couldn't concentrate. Instead, John found himself peeking away, through the rough edges of his book and secretly spying on Kate, who sat directly across from him.

"What are you thinking about?' he asked, feeling rather curious, yet impatient to know, as to what precisely was currently preoccupying her mind.

"Oh, I was just admiring the snow and wondering if today was going to be my lucky day to finally spot a snowflake. I've never actually seen one before," she replied, with a sigh.

"Wait, you've never seen a snowflake before? But don't you live in New York? Surely, you've witnessed and experienced plenty of snow seasons on the east coast? Why, at some point or another, you must have seen a snowflake, over there?" he asked, with a raised brow.

"Actually, no, I haven't. While I've spent many winters in both New York and Türkiye, I've not once seen a snowflake. In fact, I've never actually even stopped to admire the snow. Not since my childhood. Over the years, I've only glanced at the snow from afar, while quickly rushing by to get to work, or looking through my apartment's window. However, I've never took the initiative to really stare and admire it. But looking at it now, it really is so incredibly beautiful," she revealed.

"Ah, I see. Similar to stopping to smell the roses?" he asked, in an effort to better understand her.

"Exactly. Now, after all these years, I'm hoping to catch a glimpse of it. I've been most patient," she said.

"Well, generally, snowflakes have a greater tendency to form, when there's thicker snowfall. Unfortunately, it seems that we only have light patches of snowfall, as of right now," he explained; however, John quickly sensed her disappointment, and so, he added, "But perhaps, you might still see a snowflake in Kars. It tends to snow more heavily, over there."

"I hope so," she wishfully stated.

Reverting her attention away from their window and back to their carriage, Kate noticed John's book, now closed shut and laying on the table.

"What are you reading?" she asked, now curious about his activities.

"Oh, this is just some reading material for my project. It's called Banker to the Poor—"

"By Muhammad Yunus?" she quickly interrupted.

"Why, yes, it is? Have you read it before?" he asked, most surprised.

"Actually, yes, I have. It's a fantastic read. I thoroughly enjoyed the author's advocation for micro-lending loans. It's no wonder why he won the noble prize for it," said Kate, as she reached over and poured herself another cup of tea.

John was truly impressed. Not only had she read the same novel, but she was also well informed about the author's accomplishments and subsequent awards. Intrigued, John wondered as to what her thoughts were, regarding the author's underlining message.

"Would you care for another cup of tea?" she asked, as she reached over and grabbed his empty teacup.

"Er, yes, that would be nice," said John, as he reached over and handed the pitcher of milk to her for their tea.

"So, what did you think about the book? About his theory on micro-lending?" he asked.

"Well, as I said before, it's really a fantastic read and I, myself, do agree with Yunus' promotion for micro-lending. Having spent my early childhood here in Türkiye, I know that for some people, the fine line separating poverty from comfort, often lies in-between a few dollars and in some extreme cases, mere pennies," she explained.

"Have you experienced poverty like that before?" he asked, fascinated by her previous response.

"Myself, no. But I've met people who have before. Family acquittances. Farmers in rural villages, from the eastern provinces. Often times, some of them only needs just a few extra dollars to purchase their seeds to grow their crops and get back on their feet. Needless to say, without these programs, some of these family would fall into further debt and eventually, bankruptcy; ultimately leading to starvation and in some worse cases, death," she said.

"I agree. It's true. Many years ago in India, I once knew a young woman, whose entire livelihood depended on such a loan. She was a basket maker; a widow, with small children. Without these loans, she would never have been able to step foot into the marketplace to sell her baskets. Actually, she's one of the primary reasons, as to why I even became a diplomat, in the first place," he said, recalling his time spent abroad in India as a youth.

"Really? You decided to become a diplomat, after meeting a basket maker in India? I thought that you chose your profession, in order to better help your community? At least, that's what I recall from our conversation back in the library," said Kate, surprised and fascinated by his admission.

"Technically, I never lied to you. As a child, I always knew that I wanted to help my community; to make a difference in the world. However, the key is in the method; for it's the choice of method that determines the impact of our aid to the world. And on that fateful day when I first met Aasha—that's her name—that's when I was ultimately, inspired to pursue a career in politics," he revealed, in a serious tone and manner.

"And why was that?" she asked, as a follow-up.

"Because I, too, directly saw how such a similar program helps families. Like you said before, to save a family from bankruptcy and starvation. After realizing as to just how much a specific targeted policy and program can alter a person's entire life and course of destiny, that's when I finally decided to become an ambassador."

"Destiny; it's a funny concept, isn't? I mean, exactly a year ago, I was in New York, sitting alone in my office and grading papers; all the while, desperately wishing that I could instead, be outside enjoying the snow, rather than, remaining inside of my tiny and stuffy office. Now, one year later, I'm on the Doğu Express, watching and enjoying the snow from outside of our train's window, with the strong possibility of seeing a snowflake on the opposite side of the world," she said, with the happiest of smiles.

Her happiness was contagious. Looking at her and seeing as to just how happy and thrilled she was at the prospect of catching a glimpse of a snowflake, it brought John a tremendous sense of joy and an appreciation for the future. Seeing the excitement in her eyes, his own eyes light up as well.

"Destiny is a funny thing," he agreed. "Exactly one year ago, I, too, was inside of my own stuffy office—"

"Your office is not stuffy, at all," Kate interrupted. "I've been there, so I know. On the contrary, it's quite lovely."

"But that's not fair. Technically, I've never gotten the opportunity to see your office, firsthand," he jokingly reminded her.

"That's true," she admitted. "Perhaps, one day."

"One day, it is. I'll have to take you up, on that offer," he boldly claimed.

"But what's in it for me? If I let you see my office, then what do I get in return?" she asked, teasing him in return.

"I'll appoint you as my official consultant," he promptly stated. However, this time, he sounded very serious.

"A consultant? Really? Me?" she asked, completely taken back by his proposal.

"Why not? You're extremely knowledgeable about various subject matters, and an experienced and talented professor. Sadly, most people within the agency have never even heard of the name Mohammad Yunus; and yet, you have. You're already one step ahead of most candidates. Plus, I value your opinion. But most importantly, Kate, I trust you. After all my years spent at our agency, I say safely say that trust and honesty are rare qualities in this line of work; they seldom come hand-in-hand," he reluctantly admitted.

Kate was truly touched by his praise and admiration of her. Just by being herself, she managed to earn his respect and capture his undivided attention.

"Alright, it's a deal. The next time you're in New York, I'll personally give you a tour of my office, as well as the university's campus, while we're at it," she playfully said.

He smiled in agreement and together, they drank the reminder of their tea. Silently, they sat and admired the snow, which by now, had covered the nearby land and mountains with a thick white blanket, leaving no inch of green pastures left behind. Still curious, John wondered as to why Kate cared so much about seeing that snowflake.

"Can I ask you a question?" he asked, after sipping his last drop of tea.

"Yes, of course," she replied, while placing her teacup back down onto the table.

"Why do you care to see a snowflake, so much? Is it for their beauty?" he asked, wondering her reason.

"Well, I suppose, that's part of it," she began, "After all, they are lovely objects, and I'm sure that I'll eventually admire them, when I finally see them. But that's not the real reason."

"Then, what's the real reason?" he pressed on.

"Well, I suppose it's because I've always been fascinated by the fact, that no two snowflakes are alike. None of them are identical. Really, they're like thumbprints, with each snowflake being unique and unlike the previous one before. And coming from someone who's one half of an identical pair of twins, being special and unique is rather important to me," she admitted.

"But Kate, you're already special," he interrupted, "And you don't need anything to prove this, either. You and Jennifer are two very different people."

"I know, but we still have the same face, eyes, family history and background…" she began to trot off.

"That doesn't matter," he said, as he reached over to grab her hand, as he held it with his. With his hands gently caressing her hands, he said, "You are Kate; lovely and sweet, but most importantly, one of a kind. There's no one else in this world, that's quite like you."

"But I'm living her life," she softly whispered, as she turned her head to the side to look away from him.

"In order to help find her," he reminded her, "Listen, I realize that this charade has been rather difficult for all of us; but most especially, for you. However, I promise that you can safely rest assure that I certainly know and remember who you are and while it's just the two of us here, alone, then you can always just be yourself around me. Plus, I rather enjoy your company. I must admit, I've grown rather accustomed to you, my dear Kate," he said, with a twinkle in his eye.

His kind and thoughtful words brought great comfort to her. Turning around, she looked straight into his eyes and said, "But that's not the only reason, as to why I'm waiting to see a snowflake."

"Then tell me. What's your other reason?" he asked, desperately wanting her to reveal the truth.

"I do realize ahead of time, that this might sound a bit crazy; but I've always had this premonition that if I can catch a glimpse of a snowflake, then something magical will happen."

"Magical? In what way?" he asked, puzzled by her statement.

"Magical, in the notion, that if a person can wish for something that's so preciously beautiful and rare, and if that same person is willing enough to patiently wait for it, even if it takes a million years, then something magical and wonderful is bound to happen, once they finally see it, don't you think? As for myself, I've been waiting my entire life to see a snowflake in-person. I suppose that you can say, that it's just me wishing to see the impossible. Me, hoping to witness something that I've only read about in books, but never actually saw. I know that this all might sound silly and childish, especially coming from a serious history professor, such as myself; but in my heart, I know that once I see it, then something wonderful is going to happen for me. I mean, haven't you ever wished upon a shooting star? Hoping and wishing for something that you never thought imaginable? Yet, still willing to patiently wait for it?"

Meanwhile, John just stared on and admired her, as she spoke; for he was simply enchanted by her choice of words. Fascinated that such a person; nay, a soul, existed in this world. Even in his wildest of dreams, he couldn't have imagined her. She was beyond his own comprehension. Kate was smart, kind, generous and beautiful. Inside and out. Over the years, he read many books written by several authors, with each author crediting their written work to a particular muse. In the past, John never understood such a concept; for how could a man cherish and credit their life work to the inspiration, arising from one single woman? John failed to understand this. At least, not until today. For at this moment, John suddenly came to the realization that Kate was his real-life muse. His ideal woman, in personification and in the flesh.

"It's not silly or childish at all," he replied.

Suddenly, John looked straight into her eyes and without a second thought, he admitted, "Kate, I understand you. I, too, know what it's like to patiently wish and wait for the impossible. Even I'm guilty of searching for shooting stars."

"And did you ever find it? Your shooting star?" she asked, hoping that he did.

As he locked eyes into hers, he smiled and replied, "No, but along the way, I found something far greater."

Innocently, she smiled back, in return, and for the next few hours, they quietly sat together, admiring the scenic view from aboard the train. As Kate patiently watched the snowfall from outside of their window, still eagerly hoping to catch sight of her snowflake, John peacefully watched her from across the table. As he patiently observed her every move, from the flickering movement of her hair to the twinkle in her blue eyes, he privately thought to himself, that after years of waiting for a shooting star, he had finally stumbled upon a star of his very own in her; all the while, learning what his version of heaven looked like, here on earth.

447

Chapter 22

By midnight, the train arrived to the Kars station. An hour later, the party eventually reached their final destination at the cabin. Due to the snowy weather, they arrived much later than originally anticipated. Given their late arrival, they were greeted by the hotel bellman, since by then, their hosts were long fast asleep in their bedrooms—much to Barbara's disappointment. While the bellman led the way and helped to escort them upstairs into their chambers, Kate's anticipated fears about sharing a private bedroom with John were quickly put to ease. Luckily, for her, as soon as they entered into their bedroom, John immediately fell asleep on the sofa, which was located on the far opposite side of the room. Given their long journey, John was very tired and exhausted from their travels.

While John was busy sleeping, Kate took her time to unpack her suitcase. Once she finished unpacking and was ready to retire for the evening, she hopped onto her bed, curled up inside of her bed sheets and released a huge sigh of relief. Much to her surprise, everything so far had gone rather exceptional well. Earlier in the day, they tackled the very important, yet extremely awkward discussion surrounding their "kiss." Although Kate was a tad bit disappointed with the outcome, their discussion concerning the matter was still nevertheless, all settled and put to rest; never again to ever be revisited and forever forgotten. It was long behind them. And now, here she was in the city of Kars, inside of a cabin and relaxing in her bed; which, just so happened to also be located in the very same room as John. Although this living arrangement wasn't preferably ideal; but now that it happened, Kate no longer felt as fearful or as scared, as she previously had been. In fact, she felt quite the opposite. In truth, Kate actually felt rather comfortable and relax with him sleeping so closely nearby. Regardless of her affections for him, Kate also knew that John was a man of his word and that no matter what, he would never, ever, comprise her honor, without her permission. Furthermore, by visiting such an unfamiliar, secluded and remote region, Kate felt more safe and secure simply be being around him.

As she lay in bed with her body completely covered up by the hotel's white linen sheets, starting from up her neck and down to her feet; Kate was more than ready to doze off into her dreamworld. However, when she attempted to close her eyes to sleep, she just couldn't keep them close. Much to her displeasure, her eyes kept reopening and they just simply refused to remain shut. Again, she tried once more; but yet, her eyes constantly rolled back open. Furthermore, each times her eyes reopened, they always, without fail, constantly gravitated to stare directly towards John! This was simply too irritable and too much!

Out of respect for his privacy, Kate tried her best to look away; but sadly, she just couldn't. The temptation was far too great. Much to her dismay, her curiosity about him, ultimately, got the best of her. While he slept, she wondered as to how looked asleep. Was he equally as handsome in the night, as he was during the daylight? Was he a deep or gentle sleeper? Did he toss and turn in his sleep, just like she did?

Unfortunately, Kate had so many questions lingering inside of her mind, without a definite answer. Suddenly, it occurred to Kate, that if she didn't take advantage and look in his direction, then she'd never have another chance again. Alas, Kate desperately needed answers to these plaguing questions! For her own sanity, she needed to regain the peaceful clarity and serenity of her mind by extinguishing her rather intense, yet insufferable curiosity! And so, out of her better judgment, she gave herself permission to stare straight ahead, with her curious eyes; the same eyes, in which only few moments ago, refused to remain shut.

Meanwhile, John, peacefully slept on the sofa, with his back turned away and his face facing towards the wall. As Kate stared at him, she admired his dark black hair, which shined against the moonlight. Lying quietly still and motionless, Kate admired his fine muscular body, through the snippets of skin that she saw peeking through the edges of his shirt. Kate sighed to herself. He certainly was handsome, she thought. However, the longer that Kate stared at him, she realized that he didn't have a proper blanket. Instead, the upper half of his body was covered with only his jacket, which left his bottom half open and exposed to the frosty cold air. Surely, with this snowy weather, he'd freeze tonight? Why, he was most certainly going to catch a cold by sleeping in this poor condition!

Without further delay, Kate immediately climbed out of her bed and retrieved a spare blanket from the linen closet. Walking over to his side, she slowly moved to cover his body with the blanket, while her own body slightly leaned against the soft edges of the sofa. However, as soon as Kate placed the blanket over John's body, he unexpectedly, turned around. Before Kate had a chance to escape, John's arm suddenly caught hold of her body! Unconsciously, in his deep sleep, John managed to pull her forward down onto the sofa and inside of his blanket! Luckily, a nearby cushion prevented Kate from falling down completely, leaving her standing frozen-stiff in mid-air, with her the upper half of her body wrapped up inside of his blanket, and her bottom half of her body outside of the blanket and standing up. Somehow, Kate found herself sandwiched in between John, the blanket and the cushion!

What was she to do? How was she going to escape? To make matters worse, she was in the most compromising and embarrassing position, of all! Suddenly, Kate began to panic. Attempting to regain her nerves, Kate looked down upon his face and once she understood that he was still sleeping, her fears slowly began to dissipate. As she continued to stare at him, she noted that this was the very first time that she'd ever seen him in such a vulnerable position. For a brief moment, she just stared away and admired his beauty. Up-close, his features appeared more structured and refined. His eyelashes were darker and thicker, than what she originally imagined; his nose strong and clearly defined, similar to that of Zeus; and his curly dark hair, that ever-so-slightly hung right above his forehead, left an unexpected shape of an open-heart right in the middle. Overall, he simply looked angelic and peaceful, she thought.

"He's beautiful," she finally whispered aloud to herself.

However, as soon as she uttered those very words, John's arm abruptly pushed through the cushion, which had previously served as the sole divider separating her from between the blanket and him. As a result, John somehow managed to grab her from the behind. Once more, he pulled her towards him, and further down back onto the sofa. Again, Kate froze. By now, the cushion had completely fallen onto the floor, and Kate's entire upper half of her body, including her chest, were subsequently leaning down and pressed against his warm body. To make matters more complicated, John's hands were now firmly rested upon her delicate and soft buttock. Any further movement, then Kate was surely to fall completely and land right above John.

Kate gulped. What was she going to do? If she tried to pull herself away from his grip or better yet screamed, then he was surely going to awaken only to discover them in this rather embarrassing, yet entangled predicament! And in this position, of all things! God forbid, if that should happen, then how was she ever going to explain to him with a straight face, as to why she ended up alone, inside of his bed? She'd never have the courage to face him ever again! Why, she was ready to die right here, right now, from mere fright!

Although she came to his bedside tonight with pure and good intentions, would he actually believe her? That she honestly came to his side, for the general welfare of his health, on a dark and gloomy evening? Alone, in the middle of the night? In a romantic getaway, inside this cozy cabin? Even after their kiss? The reality was that had the roles been in reverse, Kate wouldn't have believed him; so why would she expect the same from him, in return?

Searching for an escape plan, Kate accidentally caught sight of her own reflection against the mirror, that was located right beside the sofa. With the bright moonlight shining against the mirror through the window, Kate saw herself from the corner of her eye. To her own horror, she saw that she wasn't wearing her standard white pajamas, as she had previously assumed; but instead, she was actually wearing one of her special white negligees! Having arrived to the cabin so late into the evening, Kate was so tired when she changed out of her day clothes, that she must have thrown on the first pair of eveningwear that Sally had packed for her inside of her suitcase. To her great disadvantage, it was an extremely revealing night gown, too! Suddenly, Kate grew more anxious, for in the mirror this time, she saw her full figure projected in the image and to her shock, she realized that her white negligee was much more revealing that she had previously anticipated! To her surprise, she saw that she was wearing a sheer white lace lingerie, that not only tightly tugged against her figure, but it also generously exposed the traces of her bare body, including the silhouettes of her breast, hips, legs and buttock. If, God forbid, John awoke right now, then he would see everything!

Kate shivered with that very thought! Suddenly, John groaned and before Kate knew it, his hands quickly wandered across her body, leaving her behind and moving upwards towards her breasts; where his hands ultimately, relocated and remained, firmly planted against her right bare breast! Kate was horrified! One of her actual breasts were right now, tightly held within John's clutches! Each second was proving to become worse and worse for her! And then, when Kate presumed that the worse was over, she was once again, proven wrong; for this time, when his hands reached further to squeeze her breast, his fingers gently slid underneath her padded lace strap and reached as far as her nipples!

Instinctively, Kate let out a little squeal. Meanwhile, John, still busy asleep, must have subconsciously heard Kate's reaction, for he somehow managed to smile in his sleep. Immediately, Kate caught sight of his unexpected facial expression, but before she had the chance to react, he squeezed her nipples once more. And then, his restless hands continued to travel along her breast and eventually, his hands managed to cup her entire breast within his palms, and with one giant and swift movement, he squeezed her.

This was *the ultimate* tipping point for Kate! Now feeling incredibly weak in her knees, Kate fell completely forward and landed right on top of John. As she fell onto him, his hands caught her on her buttocks, and he managed to bring her closer to him. By now, Kate was not only face to face with a sleeping John, but their bodies were firmly joined together, as one.

As Kate desperately tried to pull herself back up, her knee glided across his leg, and she unexpectedly felt his private parts brush up against her. Lifting her head up to see how it happened, to her surprise, she saw that John was having an erection! Somehow, she managed to excite him, even in his sleep!

"Dear God!" she whispered to herself. How was she going to survive this? John was sure to wake up by now! He had to, right?

At this point, Kate really didn't know what else to do. However, one way or another, she knew that she had to do something. Somehow, she needed to act and quickly discover a way to escape from John's embrace and return back to her own bed. Far across on the opposite side of the room, safe and sound.

Acting upon her instincts, Kate slowly peeled his arms off her buttock and for a brief moment, it seemed to be working. Kate even managed to stick her right leg out of the sofa and onto the floor again. With one slight hop, she was actually going to successfully make it out of his bed completely! However, as she was about to do this, John suddenly called out her name.

"Kate," he spoke aloud, with his eyes still closed.

Was John awake? Did he know that she was here? Inside of his bed? However, when Kate stared down upon his face, she realized that he was only speaking to her through his sleep.

"Kate," he called again, while remaining in his sleep.

"Yes," she replied, in soft whisper.

Although she didn't want to fully wake him, Kate decided that if she could perhaps, humor a half-asleep John, then maybe, just maybe, she could convince him to subconsciously let her go. At least this way, all of tonight's fiasco would be forgotten, and this entire experience would be nothing more, than just one bad dream.

"Kiss me," he pleaded.

"What?" she choked, in surprise.

"Kiss me, Kate," he repeated again, as he regained and retightened his grip around her.

For a long moment, Kate just stared at him in bewilderment. Was he honestly asking her to kiss him? Her, Kate? Why, it was only just a few hours ago, when he professed to her that their last kiss meant nothing more, than his compliance to their charade. A public and staged kiss meant to showcase and prove their affection for one another. But now, here they were, all alone, with no one else to prove otherwise. And yet, John still wanted to kiss her. Freely and wholeheartedly. Although he was still sleeping, he was probably and more likely, dreaming about her. He must have, right? After all, he did call out her name. Her name and only her name: Kate.

Unexpectedly, Kate smiled to herself. Having realized that if John could dream about kissing her, then maybe, it also meant that deep down inside, he also cared about her, too. Perhaps, even desire her.

Not willing to deny his request, she suddenly leaned down and actually kissed him! As their lips met each other for a second time, John passionately locked his tongue into hers, and the pair embraced in a wholehearted kiss. Once John's needs were fulfilled, he finally released her and Kate quickly hopped out of his bed.

By the time, John rolled again and turned his back against the wall, Kate was already back into her bed, covered up inside of her blankets and pretending that none of this had just happened. That, all of this, was only a part of her imagination. Better yet, a dream! However, as Kate reflected and gently touched her lips, she couldn't deny that this wasn't a dream and that they did indeed kiss; for the traces of his intoxicating scent was still lingering on her. Furthermore, as much as he claimed that their first kiss was nothing more than for show, their second kiss seemed to prove, otherwise.

Kate sighed to herself. Today was a roller coaster of emotions. But what did it all mean? Their second kiss obviously established his attraction to her, but why exactly did he call out her name in his sleep? Did he subconsciously know that she was there? Or was he, in fact, as she suspected, dreaming about her? Did he always dream of her? Come tomorrow morning, would he wake up and recall what had just recently transpired between them here, tonight? Unfortunately, Kate now had more questions floating about inside of her mind, with little to no answers in sight. What had started as simply looking for snowflakes back in Istanbul, ended with the urgency to discover the truth about their latest kiss in Kars. While she failed to see the snowflake on her train ride, she also knew, that one day, when the time was right, she was going to see it, eventually. However, with regards to their current kiss, she wasn't sure, if she was ever going to receive a truthful answer from John. But after tonight, she had, at the very least, one of her questions answered: John was indeed, a very deep sleeper!

Chapter 23

The next morning, Kate awoke to find an empty room. Gazing over to John's side of the room, she noticed that he, along with his shoes, were long gone. It seemed that John had already exited the premise, while Kate was still asleep. However, after last night, it was far better off this way. At least, with John away, Kate had the privacy to get ready, in peace and comfort. Nerve free.

An hour later, Kate arrived down to the lobby. In the waiting room, she searched about looking for John, Barbara, David and Amy; but to no avail, she couldn't locate them. When she saw no sight of them, Kate walked over to the front desk to inquire about their whereabouts. As she waited in line to speak to the front desk agent, she noticed a peculiar looking man ahead of her. He was tall, olive complexion, with thick curly dark brown hair, dressed in all black and wearing a thick green leather jacket. For some odd reason or another, he appeared to be screaming and yelling at the hotel agent.

"I demand that you rent me a room! It's imperative that I stay here at this cabin tonight!" yelled the man.

"But sir, unfortunately, you didn't schedule a prior reservation and currently, we're completely booked," replied the hotel agent.

"This is a matter of life and death!" screamed the man far louder than before, and at the top of his lungs.

Springing across the desk, the angry man viciously grabbed the hotel agent by his collars, and thereby, knocking over the desk telephone onto the floor, nearby. As the man aggressively held his neck by his bare hands, the hotel agent urgently pleaded for help. Meanwhile, Kate, who was standing behind, witnessed the entire incident. Immediately, she took a step back and yelled loudly for security. Upon hearing Kate's screams, the angry man quickly released the hotel agent from his grip and soon ran off towards the exit. However, along the way, he managed to bump directly into Kate.

"Durny!" he exclaimed, as he slammed and pushed Kate aside, while he quickly darted out through the cabin's front entrance doors.

"Durny?" echoed Kate, wondering to herself, as what precisely did that particular word actually mean.

"It's Belarusian. However, I highly advise that you not repeat it, as it's a derogative word," replied the hotel agent, as he gasped for air.

"Are you alright?" asked a concerned Kate, who then, proceeded to walk back over to the front desk.

"I'm alright. Thank you for asking," replied the hotel agent, as he soon caught his breath and took a sip of his water.

"Would you like for me to call for help? I know that my scream might not have caught anyone's attention here, but I also have the number to a private security firm. Perhaps, we can launch a formal complaint," suggested Kate.

"No, it's not necessary," replied the hotel agent. "Mafia thugs like him try to stay at this hotel all the time. Luckily, whether or not we're available, my employer refuses to rent out any of our rooms to them, no matter the circumstances."

"The mafia?" asked Kate, in complete surprise.

"Yes, the mafia. Sometimes, it's Belarusian, Russian, Armenian, Georgian or even Arab; but they're all one in the same. They all come here to pose as wealthy oligarchs, but the reality is that they're all really mafia thugs in disguise; wearing nothing more, than an expensive pair of suits," explained the hotel agent.

"But why here? Is Kars not a safe area?" Kate inquired, intrigued by his revelation.

"Kars is perfectly safe; but like most of the Black Sea region and our northeastern providences, these mafia thugs migrate over here for their businesses and eventually, they integrate and unfortunately, become a part of our daily lives," answered the hotel agent. However, sensing that he, perhaps, spoke too much of the truth, he further clarified, "But don't worry. As long as you're our guest, then you can rest assure that here at our hotel, you're in a safe environment. Besides, men like him stay away from the tourist sections. As long as you don't venture away from your tour group, then you have absolutely nothing to fear in Kars," the hotel agent attempted his best to reassure her.

"I see," spoke Kate, not wanting to press the hotel agent any further. Now, feeling glad that Miles was accompanying them on this trip, Kate said, "Thank you for your advice. I'll certainly take note of it."

"Excellent. In that case Madame, is there any way that I can be of service to you?" inquired the hotel agent; who by now, returned back to his desk, continuing on with his work, as if the previous altercation never occurred in the first place.

"Err, yes," replied Kate, "I actually originally came here to inquire about the whereabouts of my group. I seemed to have arrived late and…"

"The name of your party?" promptly asked the hotel agent.

"Barrett or Lawrence," replied Kate, "It's one or the other."

"Ah, yes, I do have a note here," said the hotel agent, "It appears that they're already eating breakfast at the restaurant. Mrs. Barrett, please allow me to escort you over to your table."

Following his lead, the hotel agent escorted Kate into the restaurant, where she saw her party seated at the back of the restaurant, facing the window. At the table, she saw Barbara, John, David, Amy and a young man, with light blonde hair, brown eyes and fair complexion, whom Kate naturally assumed to be Peter, all there seated. As soon as Kate approached the table, John immediately stood up and pulled out a chair for her to sit in.

"Thank you, John," said Kate, as she sat down in the chair, that John had graciously provided for her.

"You're most welcome, my dear," replied John, who then, promptly returned back to his seat.

"Kate! You're here! My darling, you really must try a stack of these delicious blueberry pancakes! They're simply heaven!" exclaimed Barbara enthusiastically as she, herself, started pouring a heavy dose of maple syrup, all over her own personal stack of blueberry pancakes.

"Mother, I'm one step ahead of you. I've already prepared my wife with her plate," announced John, with a smile.

"You have?" asked a happily surprised Kate, as she stared at John in disbelief.

As John placed Kate's breakfast platter before her, which consisted of a stack of blueberry pancakes, along with scrambled eggs, potatoes and fruit, he also brought a small vase of red roses to accompany her meal on the table. By sheer amazement, Kate was simply lost for words. In truth, John's kindness and generosity truly resembled that of a sincere gentleman at heart.

"Last and most importantly, here's your morning tea," he said, as he placed a white ceramic mug next to her plate.

"Tea?" she echoed.

"Yes, black tea; along with a dash of milk. Just the way you like it," said John, with a smile and a wink.

"You remembered," Kate whispered to herself.

However, John heard her and so, he added, "I always do."

His choice of words, immediately sent chills down Kate's spine. Truly, his impactable attention to details were strikingly remarkable; especially when it came down to her.

"Ah, that's so romantic!" sighed Amy from across the table. Moved by John's romantic gesture, Amy elbowed Peter in the stomach and warned, "Once we're married Peter, you better do the same for me, too!"

"Peter, I dare say that you've certainly got some competition. As it stands, our John has now set a rather high standard as to how the gentlemen in our family treats our special ladies," joined David, as he took a bite of his cereal.

"Well, technically, I did ask the waiter to bring Amy some water," Peter reminded them. "That's got to count for something."

"That certainly doesn't count for anything!" exclaimed Barbara, as she stuffed a large slice of her pancakes straight into her mouth. "Anyone can ask for water; but it takes a true gentleman to prepare breakfast! Especially, these divine pancakes!"

"Barbara, for the record, I also helped to assist Chef Homura's Sous Chef to prepare this meal, as Chef Homura is still in Istanbul," David revealed.

"You, make pancakes? David, my dear old friend, I've known you for many years and not once have you ever made such a dish! You certainly must be lying!" cried Barbara.

"Alright, you've got me. Although I might not have, for say, made the pancakes; but I did bring out the maple syrup. Certainly, that's got to count for something, right?" asked David, teasingly.

"Yes, it does; for pancakes without maple syrup is a crime," replied Barbara, as she took another bite of her pancakes. "But I daresay, why did Chef Homura not come with security? The chef always travels with us."

"He's actually back in Istanbul working on creating a new menu for our upcoming NATO state dinner, which is scheduled to take place within the next two weeks. As a result, his Sous Chef is here in his place instead," John announced.

"We're scheduled to have another state dinner at the mansion?" asked Kate, surprised at the prospect of having yet another political event, so soon after their last one. The one, in which, they last kissed— excluding the accidental kiss from the night before.

"Yes, we've got one more. However, I've already spoken to Gloria and the rest of the embassy staff this morning, and the preparations are already on the way, as we speak. Unlike before, this time you won't need to trouble yourself, with all of the redundant work. The staff will take care of it all," replied John.

"Oh, but last time, it honestly wasn't any trouble," Kate admitted.

"My dear Jennifer, please have the staff do the work. Especially, Gloria. After all, it's their civic duty. In the meantime, you just sit down here, and enjoy the lovely breakfast that my son's prepared for you," Barbara suggested, as she grabbed yet another stack of pancakes from the table.

"Another party at the mansion; why, that sounds so wonderful!" cried Amy. "Jennifer, which gown are you planning to wear? Or better yet, what dance shall you perform, this time around?"

"The gown? Well, I'm afraid that I haven't even thought that far ahead," Kate admitted, "But with regards to the dance, I believe it's the tango…"

"The tango?" John interrupted, this time and in complete surprise. "You're planning to dance the tango?"

"Well, the tango's been the latest dance that I've been practicing. Naturally, I presume that Gloria and Bes will be expecting me to dance it at our next event," said Kate, as she took a sip of her tea.

"The tango! Why, that's so romantic! I only wish that Peter and I were there, to see it!" exclaimed Amy.

"Then, why don't you?" interrupted Barbara. "I'm certain that John and Jennifer wouldn't mind, wouldn't you?"

"Well, that all depends. Mrs. Barrett, as you will be the one dancing the tango, do you mind?" asked John, with a devious smile.

"Actually, I don't mind. It would be lovely, if Amy and Peter came," replied Kate.

"Fabulous! It's settled; we're coming!" agreed Amy, while she joyfully clapped her hands from excitement.

"Well since that's all settled; can we all head out to the ski lodge, now? We've already reserved our appointment and we shouldn't be tardy," Peter reminded them.

"Wait," interrupted David, "Before anyone leaves this table, I'd like to make a toast."

"Here, here," John joined in, as he tapped his glass of orange juice with his knife. He was soon followed by Kate, then Barbara, then Amy and finally Peter, who all copied suit and tapped away at their respective drinks, as well.

"Amy," David began, "You've been the light of my life. My darling daughter. Perfect, in every possible way. A father couldn't have wished for a better daughter."

"Aww, Dad…" Amy interrupted, as she began to form tears inside of her eyes.

"My dear, please let me continue," replied David, smilingly and beaming with pride.

Redirecting his attention over to Peter, he continued, "And to Peter, my future son-in-law. Never in a million years, have I ever considered giving my daughter away to anyone less worthy, than perfection. However, you come pretty close. That's why I know that when I'm long gone and buried, I can take comfort, in the fact, that I know firsthand, that you'll take good care of her, in my absence."

"David, you're hardly into your golden years. You've still got plenty of years ahead of you. The best is yet to come," John interrupted.

"Yes, I agree; the best is yet to come," David repeated; and then, he further clarified, "But none of us, lives forever."

"Maybe, if you drank more of my fine wine, then you all might live an extra twenty or thirty more years, or so. At the very least, you'd all be more rejuvenated, refreshed and far more relaxed," said Barbara.

"How's that even scientifically possible?" asked Peter, a doctor, who was most skeptical by such an unscientific and bold statement.

"My dear Peter, sometimes, it's best to just savor and enjoy," replied Barbara, as she reached into her purse and pulled out a miniature travel sized wine bottle.

To his astonishment, Barbara handed the miniature travel sized wine bottle over to Peter.

"Mother!" cried John, "You actually carry such things inside of your purse?"

"Why not?" replied Barbara, nonchalant, "Why, I intend to promote my latest flavor, in every possible way. After all, I'm an entrepreneur."

Meanwhile, David simply laughed at Barbara's honest, yet humorous confession.

"Barbara, please don't ever change," laughed David, cheerfully.

Shifting his attention over to John and Kate, he added, "As for John and Jennifer, may Amy and Peter both follow in your example and footsteps. May they, too, have the similar long, loving and lasting marriage, just as you, two, share. That's my honest and sincerest wish."

"Here, here," agreed Peter, as he, along with Amy, raised up their glasses, in honor to David's message.

Barbara, Kate and John soon followed in suit. Afterwards, Peter stood up from the table and was about to make a public speech of his own.

"First of all, thank you David, for all of your kind words," Peter began, "Second, thank you everyone, for coming to Kars to celebrate our engagement. To be honest, I'm still surprised that Amy even agreed to marry me, in the first place."

Suddenly, everyone at the table started to laugh at Peter's joke, and with a smile, he continued, "While it might have taken a few extra meetings to help persuade and convince Amy to date me, in the first place; I, on the other hand, always knew that she was the one for me."

"How romantic!" exclaimed Barbara, "And how was that? How did you know?"

"Because she always had faith in me. Regardless of my own self-doubts, Amy remained steadfast and confident, in my ability to succeed with my dental license examination. Even when I, myself, wasn't too sure. After all, I was an exchange student, living abroad in a foreign country, with a scholarship, feeling homesick, missing my family and questioning myself. But no matter how I felt, she still chose to stand by me. Even when we were just friends," replied Peter.

"Wait, so you were friends, before you became lovers?" asked Kate, who was now, most intrigued.

"Yes, we were," answered Amy. "And then, gradually, after a period of time, we grew closer with another; and then, eventually, as we got to know each other better, we blossomed into something much more romantic."

"But for me, it was much more different," Peter interrupted, "I didn't need to wait. I always loved her. At first sight."

"That's lovely and all; but now that you're together, what are your plans, moving forward?" asked Barbara, as she continued to pour more maple syrup over her pancakes.

"Well, first, we first plan to marry in Europe, as soon as possible. Since I still have my residency in Switzerland, we're planning to marry and honeymoon there, before we eventually, return back to the United States," replied Peter, as he smiled in Amy's direction.

"Have you opened your new practice, yet?" asked John, this time. "Previously, David casually mentioned to me, that your intentions are to run and operate a private dental business in that state of Connecticut. Is this true?"

"Yes, that's correct. I plan on practicing in Connecticut, as that's where I'm originally from. But first, I'll have to take and pass one more medical examination, once I arrive there," said Peter.

"Peter, are you referring to passing the National Board Dental Examinations? Are you anticipating your results on that examination, prior to launching your private practice?" asked Kate, as she took a bite of meal.

"Yes, that's the examination. I'll need to pass that, in order to practice in the United States. Currently, I'm studying for that exam, as I also wait for my savings account to mature, with interest, in the process," replied Peter.

"Peter, do you have enough funds to open your own private practice, in the foreseeable future?" asked Barbara, now curious about Peter's financial funding.

"I'll answer this one," interjected Amy, this time, "Peter's late Aunt Gertrude left him a generous inheritance that's been in escrow, ever since he was a teenager. According to our lawyers, once Peter acquires his medical license, then he will become eligible to start collecting his inheritance, thereafter. Otherwise, he must wait until age thirty to collect."

"How very interesting," replied Barbara, "That's so unlike Amy's and John's fortunes. Although, David and I, long ago finalized our wills establishing their inheritances, never once, did I ever consider creating specific limitations to my own son. As it stands, there are no conditions in mine."

"Nor mine," David interjected, "Both Amy and John will equally inherit, all of my vast estates and properties, once I'm gone. No conditions, or questions asked. Fortunately, for them, they have consistently proven themselves worthy to me, time and time, again. As a result, they are both extremely precious to me; which is why, I entrust their happiness in the hands of Peter and Jennifer, to look after and care for my beloved children, in my absence."

Upon hearing David's praises, both Peter and Kate smiled at him, in return.

"David, you can peacefully rest assure, that your daughter will be carefully looked after, with my capable hands," vowed Peter, confidently.

"Peter, I'm very pleased to hear that," replied David. "And now, that we've established this, you all should probably start heading outside to the ski lodge and check us in, before it starts getting crowded with the other tourists."

"That's a grand idea. Peter, I'll join you," said Amy, as she too, stood up from her seat.

"Count me in, as well. I, too, need to briefly step out to make a phone call. But in the meantime, Jennifer, there's no need to rush. I'm going to leave Miles here to monitor you and mother. Once you're ready, he'll escort you directly to the ski lodge, okay?" asked John, in a serious manner.

"Miles? Where is he exactly?" asked Kate, as she scanned the room, in search of their bodyguard.

"He's right there, behind you," John whispered, "If you slowly turn around, you'll see him over there at the next table over, reading a newspaper and drinking a cup of coffee."

Following John's instructions, Kate slowly turned around and saw that behind her, was indeed, Miles. Just as John described, Miles was there quietly seated and reading his newspaper. Immediately, Kate agreed with John's request; and upon her approval, the party exited the premise, leaving Barbara, David and Kate behind to enjoy the remainder of their breakfast. Once the coast was clear, Barbara immediately turned her attention over to Kate to discuss their latest gossip.

"Well? How did it go last night?" asked a very enthusiastic Barbara.

"How did what go?" asked Kate, as she took a bite of her fruit.

"You know, *last night?*" repeated Barbara.

"What about last night?" asked Kate again, as she felt rather puzzled by her inquiry.

"You know…It was your first time alone with John, after so long…" Barbara hinted.

"Oh!" exclaimed Kate, "You mean, if we…"

"Well, did you? I must know!" Barbara shouted.

Instantly, Kate turned as red as the very strawberries that laid across her breakfast plater. Although Kate couldn't straight out admit to Barbara what she had hoped to hear; at the same time, the truth was that something *did* happen between. After all, last night they kissed. And for the second time too, mind you. Even though John might not have even been aware that such a kiss occurred— not once, but twice— Kate certainly remembered. In fact, his scent and imprint still lingered across her lips. Furthermore, he cried out her name in his sleep and even went as so far, as to ask her to kiss him. "Kiss me Kate," she recalled his soft whispers, as she tumbled right onto him inside of his bed last night.

"Barbara, must I remind you, that some of us here, are still eating our breakfast? Besides, leave the poor girl alone," said David, as he took another bite of his cereal.

"Oh, hush David! I'm speaking to my daughter-in-law, and I'll ask her whatever I so choose to," replied Barbara, boldly.

Returning her attention back to Kate, Barbara asked, with a twinkle in her eye, "Well, did anything happen last night?"

"It was late; we both just slept," replied Kate, not wanting to admit the truth about their kiss to Barbara; all the while, leaving Barbara gravely disappointed with her answer.

"Not to worry my dear, there's always tonight," Barbara concluded. Then, looking straight into Kate's eyes, she added, "But I trust that our luck will be far better."

Kate was left speechless. What was she going to say to Barbara? How could she make a promise for something, that she had no control over? Although Kate secretly harbored feelings for John, how could she be sure that he also felt the same way? How could Kate lure John in, if his heart wasn't hers, to begin with?

Luckily, for Kate, Barbara soon excused herself from the table. While Barbara was away fetching her warm winter coat back inside of her hotel room, Kate found herself alone at the table in David's company. As Kate looked across the table, she noticed that David's fair complexion soon grew pale. Unexpectedly, sweat drops started to form around his forehead, and his thin and balding grey hair above his head, suddenly stood up from static. To make matters worse, underneath his glasses, his eyes appeared glossy and glazed. Overall, David looked unwell.

Concerned over his welfare, Kate asked, "David, are you feeling alright?"

"I'm fine," replied David, hesitantly. "I'm probably just late taking my medicine, that's all."

Reaching into his pocket, David pulled out a large shaped brown medicine bottle. As he attempted to open the medicine bottle's tightly sealed cap, his hands started to shake and tremble. Eventually, when David pulled open the lid, the medicine bottle inadvertently flew out from his frail hands, and landed right onto the floor. Rolling down the carpet, the medicine bottle bypassed Kate's direction and stopped right near her feet. Seeking to help aid David, Kate promptly bent down to retrieve it. As she grabbed the medicine bottle, she noticed the words "Docetaxel" written on the front label.

"Doceta…" Kate repeated aloud, as she grabbed the medicine bottle in her hands.

"No need to even attempt to say or sound it out aloud, my dear. All of these medicine names and medical terminology, all sounds like Latin or Greek to me," said David to Kate.

"That maybe, but either way, here you go," said Kate, as she returned the medicine bottle back to David's possession, by gently placing it back onto the table, near his glass of water.

"Jennifer, can you please do me a favor? Do you mind taking two pills out for me? I'm afraid with my jittering hands, I'm not entirely confident that I won't have any more repeats with this darn thing," David admitted.

Following David's request, Kate proceed to take the pills from out of the medicine bottle, when she noticed that David appeared more paler, than before. To her surprise, his coloring had vastly changed. From sweety to clammy, David was now bordering the color yellow.

"David are you sure that you're, alright?" asked Kate, as she handed the pills over to David.

"I'll be fine, after I take this medicine. Serves me right for taking this so late, in the morning too," replied David, as he quickly tossed the pills straight into his mouth.

After swallowing the pills, David appeared much more relieved. Within a minute or so, his coloring slowly returned, gradually shifting from yellow to white to pink. He almost looked like his old self, again.

"We should probably start heading out now, to meet the rest of them," David advised, after he finished drinking his entire glass of water.

"David, are you sure that you want to come, along? If you prefer to stay behind to rest, I can let the others know," Kate suggested.

"Nonsense! This weekend is for my daughter, Amy. Why, I promised her that I'd be there, no matter what! Even if this will be the last time…" spoke David softly, with tears forming inside of his eyes.

"David? Is everything alright?" asked Kate again, as she glanced across the table and this time, specifically zoomed in to review David's medicine bottle from afar.

Wiping away his tears, David stared directly into Kate's eyes and at the very moment, she understood that David was truly ill. Furthermore, not only was David ill, but for whatever reasons, he didn't want the status of his health publicly known as of yet, not even to his own daughter. However, as sad and as tragic all of this truly was, David desperately pleaded for Kate not to speak another word of what she had just seen transpire, here inside of this very room.

"Jennifer, I trust that this stays between us. I don't want anyone else to worry, especially, Amy," David pleaded.

"Is it serious?" asked Kate, softly.

"It's still too early to tell," replied David, truthfully and unwilling to lie to her. "For the past few weeks, I've been visiting a cancer specialist back in Washington, D.C."

"David," Kate interrupted, "Is there anything that I can do to help you?"

"Nothing more, than what a regular doctor can do," replied David, "But I have faith in God that no matter what, I'm going to be okay. That's really all that I can do. That anyone in my condition, can do. But in the meantime, I intend to have my affairs straighten up and in order; which includes seeing Amy married off and John remaining happily married to you."

"Your secret is safe with me," Kate promised.

"Your secret is safe with me," David repeated, with a smile. "You know, those are the very same words that my late wife, Elizabeth, use to say to me, all the time. 'Your secret is safe with me.' But I suppose that's what all good wives say to their husbands, as a method of reassurance. And it works, too; for God only knows that, we diplomats, are difficult men to love. Why, even Elizabeth, had a difficult time loving me. I don't deny it; that's why I loved her, so damn much. She was the ideal wife. The perfect ambassador's wife. Just as you are to John."

"I'm far from perfection," Kate admitted. "And I'm not ashamed to admit it, too. To be honest, half of the time, I'm not entirely certain, as to what I'm doing exactly, either. Right or wrong, or wrong or right; sometimes, I just can't tell the difference. And some days, I'm just lost beyond words. But truthfully, I've just been taking it all, just one constant small step, at a time."

"But my dear, that's the best way to do it, too. The fact that you try or care; the very fact that you've remained by John's side, all this time, it means something. More than you know. If you can survive being married to John for as long as you have in this political arena, while maintaining the ability and stamina to still look at each other with loving eyes and even to go so far, as to still behave like newlyweds, especially, after all these years, it's truly remarkable," David concluded.

"You really believe that?" asked Kate, in disbelief. Was it possible that apart from themselves, other people truly saw them as a genuine true couple, who actually cared for one another?

"I do. That's why you're perfect in your role, as his supportive wife. It's not easy for family members to take on that very important, yet supportive role, too. Believe me, I know. It causes friction and isolation. I was lucky enough with Elizabeth and Amy, but that wasn't the same case, with everyone else inside of my immediate family. Sometimes, as a civil servant, you're forced to make certain difficult decisions, for the sake of your country and career. Decisions and choices that I, personally, have come to regret, over the years. Decisions that can force a person to go so far, as to turn your own back against your own flesh and blood. Sadly, I've experienced it all the hard way; and as the years have passed by, I've learned that somethings just can't be undone," David reflected, with a heavy heart.

David's words struck an eerie chord with Kate, especially his choice of word concerning 'career.' Sadly, it was her own career, that in large part, served to alienate her apart, from her own twin sister. Something that Kate still regretted to this very day and as a result, she was still desperately seeking to make amends to.

"Career is a funny thing. You know, I turned my back on my own son; all for a stupid mistake that he made years ago, way back in his youth. All for the sake of my career! And now, because of it, all these years later, I still have no idea where he is, or what he's doing. Or even, whether he's alive or dead," cried David, as tears began to stream down across his cheeks.

"Have you ever tried to reach out and find him?" asked Kate, as she handed over to him a tissue, which he graciously accepted.

"Too much pride for an old man," replied David, as he quickly wiped away his tears. "Besides, if he cared, then he'd have sought my forgiveness too, years ago."

"Maybe, he just couldn't find you. Perhaps, he changed so much over the years, that he's afraid that you won't recognize him, anymore," said Kate, who couldn't help, but to also reflect upon her own situation with her estranged sister.

"I will always recognize my children. All of them. Always. No matter how much they change, or grow. Time and distance know no boundaries to a parent. One day Jennifer, you'll better understand this, once you have a family of your own. But thank God for John. Ever since he came into my life, he's helped to serve as that missing void in my heart."

"John is a good man," Kate admitted.

"He is. Both a good man and son," said David, proudly.

"He's truly perfect in every possible way," said Kate, with a beaming smile, as she admired and stared at the red roses that John previously gifted her for breakfast.

"He loves you very much, you know. Truth be told, I, myself, didn't realize, as to just how much he actually loves you, too. At least, not until this trip."

"Really? Why do you say that?" asked Kate, as her own heart suddenly began to race. Was it possible that John not only cared for her, but that, he actually loved her?

"Since we're having a heart-to-heart conversation, I'll be perfectly honest with you. When you two first got married, I'll admit, I had my own self-doubts and reservations. Naturally, as John's father figure, I want the absolute best for him. Both he and Amy are my world. Even though it's been years since we last saw each other in-person, with him traveling the world and I living back in the United States; somehow, I always sensed that John wasn't entirely happy in his marriage. Now, I know that I'm not his biological father; but at the same time, I've always considered him to be one of my own. Furthermore, as his surrogate father, I just felt like something was always a bit off. Honestly, right now, I feel a bit guilty and ashamed for admitting all of this to you. I know that it's rather unfair," said David, embarrassed for having spoken so truthfully, without reservation.

Although Kate couldn't freely admit to David that his inkling about them was actually true; for John's marriage to her sister was certainly, less than ideal, behind the scenes. However, as such, Kate chose to remain silent. Quietly, she reached over and lightly touched David's hand, and then, she smiled. Her kind gesture caught David's attention, and he, in return, approvingly smiled right back at her.

"But," he added, "I don't think this way anymore and this trip, in particular, helped to convince me, otherwise. Why, you should have seen in-person, just how much effort John put into preparing your breakfast this morning. He really went out of his way to make everything perfect for you. In fact, he cooked everything on your plate, himself," David revealed.

"He did?" asked Kate, surprised by John's kind gesture. She had no idea that John, even knew how to cook, in the first place.

"Yes, he did. He really wanted very much to impress you," said David.

"And it worked too," admitted Kate, with a huge smile.

"All he wanted to do was to make you smile. That's all. Nothing more. In my book, if someone is willing to do whatever it takes to make another person happy and expects nothing more than a smile in return, then that's true love, in its simplest and purists of forms," said David, convincingly. Rising up from his chair, he stated, "I'm feeling much better now. I think my medicine is starting to kick in. Let's not keep them waiting."

Just then, Barbara returned back to the restaurant, and the remaining party, along with Miles, exited the cabin and made their way over to the ski lodge. By noon, they arrived to their destination. Situated above a snowy hill, the ski lodge was surrounded by several tall and luscious pine trees. It was covered by several feet of white snow, all encircling around the premise. The sky was free and clear of clouds; with the except of the burning bright yellow sun that shined all throughout, leaving a blinding and glaring overcast across the snowy floor. Furthermore, it was clearly the winter season, for the area was surrounded by several other tourists, all dispersed throughout the resort, wearing their heavy winter suits and attire, and most ready to participate in their skiing sports and activities.

Taking a seat on a vacant bench located at the bottom of the hill, Kate quickly scanned the area in search for John. From a distance, she saw him, slowly approaching them. He, along with the others, were carrying various ski equipment with them. Once they reached them, Kate noticed that an additional person had accompanied their party.

"Everyone, may I introduce you all to Mr. Volkan Kaya. He's going to be our ski instructor and tour guide for today's activities," John announced.

"It's a pleasure to meet you all," said Volkan.

"It's our pleasure to meet you, too," added Barbara, who for some reasons, didn't appear too keen and happy at the prospect of skiing. Without making any eye contact with Volkan, Barbara swiftly turned her attention directly over to John to express her concerns. "Now John, while I appreciate your efforts for coordinating all of this," she began, "And Mr. Kaya, I'm sure that you're a lovely instructor; however, with that said, there's absolutely no way, that I'm going to climb all the way up that snowy hill, only to ski back down, as an amateur! Especially, not after eating three stacks of pancakes!"

"But why not?" Amy interrupted. "There's a lift that we can take to go up the hill. Plus, Volkan is a fantastic ski instructor. He can coach us, as to how to properly ski downhill."

"My dear, dear Amy," replied Barbara, who by now, grew extremely annoyed and gravely upset. "For the past sixty-five years and counting, I've not once skied a day in my entire life! Not ever! I, above all else, value my life and comfort, which is why I must kindly decline your offer to participate in this upcoming activity."

"I'm sorry to interrupt; but I too, agree with Barbara," said Kate, who, along with Barbara, was absolutely nervous about the prospect of skiing; for she, like Barbara, had never skied before.

"Ladies, neither one of you needs to do anything, that doesn't agree with yourselves. You have my permission to stay behind and watch us," John encouraged.

"Wonderful! In that case, we'll sit right here and watch you all from afar," spoke a very relieved Barbara. "David," she said, "Will you join us?"

"Given that this might be the last time that I travel to Kars in the foreseeable future, I think I'm going to take advantage of this rare opportunity and enjoy myself out in the fresh snow," replied David.

"Alright, since that's all settled, are we now ready to depart?" asked Volkan.

"I think so," replied John.

"Okay, let me take a head count…" said Volkan, as he started to count aloud the number of attendees in the party.

"It's just going to be four of us," added Amy.

"Four is a good number. Alright, if you all can grab your equipment, please come follow me up into the lift. We'll take the garden route," Volkan instructed.

"Actually," Peter interrupted, "Can we go the scenic route, instead? I heard that the scenic route has a much nicer sky view of the mountains."

"Well, that depends," replied Volkan, "The scenic route might have a nicer view, but it's a bit more challenging, as it's up higher in elevation and in a more isolated area."

"What's the difference between that and the garden route?" asked John.

"The garden route is a more popular destination, plus, there's more skiers on that route. It's designed more for amateurs, and is much lower in elevation. But the choice is really yours. It doesn't matter to me, either way," Volkan explained.

"Oh, I do hate crowds! If the scenic route has a nicer view with less people, then I'm game with Peter's suggestion," said Amy, enthusiastically.

"Given that we're all here to celebrate and commemorate Amy's and Peter's engagement, then I vote that we go with Amy's preferred route. What do you say John?" asked David.

"Since Mother and Jennifer will be sitting down for this round, I'm perfectly content with skiing this scenic route, as the four of us are already experienced skiers," replied John.

"Alright, the scenic route it is," announced Volkan, "Please, come follow me this way."

As the party departed and traveled up the hill via the ski lift, Barbara and Kate remained seated on the bench, with Miles standing guard, nearby. Meanwhile, the weather was growing colder, and Barbara and Kate were doing their very best to stay warm. As Kate tightened up her scarf, Barbara was left with no other choice but to complain.

"It is so cold and dreary out here!" exclaimed Barbara, miserably. "Why did they pick such a depressing place to celebrate Amy's engagement? Honestly, we should have traveled to a warmer climate like the beach and not the freezing snow!"

"If you'd like, I can lend you an extra pair of my scarf," Kate suggested, in an attempt to divert Barbara's ranting; which apparently, started to annoy even the quiet and reserved Miles.

"A scarf will not do," Barbara huffed, "What we need is a warm drink, like hot chocolate, or something. I say, Miles, can you please be a dear and fetch us some hot chocolate?"

"Honestly, Barbara, I'm perfectly fine," replied an embarrassed Kate, who didn't want to trouble Miles, with any inconveniences.

"Mr. Barrett specifically requested that I not leave either one of your sides, while he's away," replied Miles, sternly.

"Well, I'm Mr. Barrett's mother, and I'm ordering you to make an exception. Later on, if he makes a fuss about this, then you can tell him directly that I asked you to do so, on account of my freezing nerves!" Barbara pleaded.

Having listened to Barbara's pleas, Miles contemplated on what to do. For a brief moment, he appeared torn and nervous. Although it was certainly a risky decision for anyone in his position to go against the order of his superior; however, Barbara was another force to be reckoned with, altogether.

"Miles, it's alright," said Kate, reassuringly, "I'll stay here with Barbara. We'll be perfectly fine and safe. Please just go ahead and grab Mrs. Barrett a cup of her hot chocolate."

"Alright, if it's okay with you, Mrs. Jennifer Barrett," replied Miles, purposely using the name *Jennifer*, in order to distinguish between the two ladies.

While Miles stepped away, Barbara was finally content at the prospect of drinking her long-awaited hot chocolate drink; therefore, at long last, she quietly sat and began to scroll through the various pictures of her wine bottles inside her mobile phone. With Barbara quietly preoccupied and Miles away, Kate now, focused her attention on watching John and the rest of their party arrive safely to the top of the hill.

As Kate squinted her eyes, she noticed that the hill was indeed isolated, just as Volkan predicted; for she could easily spot the five of them, including Volkan, standing on the side of the hill, absent of a crowd, with her naked eye. However, the longer Kate stared at their direction, she also noticed something odd and peculiar. Hidden on the outer corner of a tall tree nearby, was a green figure, standing from behind. Initially, Kate couldn't tell as to what that figure was; however, it was moving, that much she could tell.

Compelled by her sudden curiosity, as well as an unusual eerie feeling forming within the lower pits of her stomach, Kate decided at last minute to pull out her mobile phone. Having grabbed her mobile phone, she quickly opened it and launched the camera feature. With her camera feature turned on, Kate zoomed directly into the scene to gain a better close up. To her surprise, she saw that the green figure was an actual man. Zooming up even closer, Kate realized that the man wasn't just any ordinary man, but it resembled the identical angry customer, who previously attacked the hotel agent this morning. But why was he there, of all places? Was he following them? If so, then why? Did he know someone from their party? And if he knew one of them, then why was he suspiciously hiding in the bushes and secretly watching them from afar? Something didn't feel quite right.

As Kate continued to observe the unknown man from her camera, she studied him in great detail. Upon further review, her suspicions about his spying were confirmed; for he was indeed, keenly watching John and the rest of their party, as they departed down from the slopes. One by one, the skiers began to ski downhill. First, came Amy, then Peter. Meanwhile, as David, John and Volkan waited for their turn, the unknown man continued to spy on them from behind. However, unbeknownst to all, while the man was busy spying on them, Kate, in return, was busy spying on him! Eventually, when John's turn to ski downhill finally arrived, Kate noticed that the man suddenly pulled out a gun from inside of his pocket! To make matters worse, his gun was now directly aimed in the direction of John!

"Oh my God!" screamed Kate, in horror. Out of fear, she immediately dropped her mobile phone straight onto the floor.

"What is it my dear?" asked Barbara, most surprised by Kate's sudden and unexpected outburst.

"Where's Miles? Is he back?" asked Kate, with a great sense of urgency.

"No, he's still at the café, waiting for my hot chocolate. I say, Jennifer, are you alright?" Barbara inquired.

"John! John! John!" yelled Kate, at the top of her lungs; all the while, desperately hoping and praying that he could miraculously hear her warnings. But sadly, he failed to hear her voice; for Kate was simply too far away from him.

Acting upon her instincts, Kate quickly jumped off the bench and ran over to the bottom of the hill. Hoping to capture his attention, Kate began waiving her arms up and down. Amazingly, it miraculously seemed to work. John appeared to have seen her signal. For a brief moment, Kate was relieved. He could see her; and if he could see her, then she could warn him. With his attention still directed at her, Kate yelled to 'look out from behind,' and she even went as far, as to make hand gestures resembling that of a gun, with her own fingers. However, her attempts to warn him about the gunman proved to be a failure; for John completely misunderstood Kate's warning. Thinking that Kate was instead waiving 'hello' to him, John stepped forward and waved right back to her. From the looks of it, it seemed that John was now getting ready to go downhill; ignorant of the fact, that an armed and dangerous man was standing right behind him, with a gun.

"If he skies downhill with his back turned, then that gunman will surely shoot him!" cried Kate. "Once John approaches the foot of the ski slope, he'll be vulnerable! The gunman is just waiting for his chance to shoot. At that point, John will be a clear and open target! I've got to do something to stop this!"

With Miles still away, Kate decided to take action into her own hands. Instantly, she ran as fast as she could over to the lift and in one swift swoop, she hopped onto an open seat. As the lift slowly climbed up the hill, she once again, tried to wave over to John. To her relief, he appeared to be waiting for her at the top of the ski slope. As long as John waited there for her; as long as he didn't ski downhill; then Kate had a chance to save him.

She just needed to stall him, to buy more time.

Meanwhile, as the lift continued to climb up, Kate prayed and she prayed, until she eventually, reached the top of the hill. Once she arrived, she quickly ran over to John's direction, while she screamed for John, David and Volkan to all move aside. When Kate's warning finally registered to them, all three men turned around and upon doing so, the unknown man quickly shot fire into their direction. While the gunshot missed John completely, it managed to hit Volkan, instead. With a gunshot wound to his right arm, Volkan immediately collapsed onto the floor, while his upper body was now covered with blood.

By now, the entire ski resort heard the gunshot and a commotion began to grow amongst the crowd from down below. As the gunman repositioned himself to attempt a second try, Kate quickly ran as fast as she could to try to divert and thwart his efforts. With the second bullet having been released from his gun and making its way towards John's direction, Kate arrived just in the nick of time to stop it. Pushing John aside and onto the ground by the sheer force and strength of her entire body, the couple came tumbling down upon one another, as they both fell straight down onto the pile of snow.

Meanwhile, as the second gunshot missed John as its target, the bullet, somehow, managed to ricochet across the metal rooftop of a small outhouse, where it then bounced back and hit a nearby tree, which was covered in snow. As the snow fell down from the tree, it landed right on top of both David and gunman, trapping the pair within the thick layers of snow, in the process.

With Kate lying directly above John, with his arms tightly wrapped around hers, and hers around his, they both held onto each other for their joint welfare and safety. Both covered in snow and equally rapidly breathing in and out for the fresh air to enter their lungs, they were in complete shock, as to what had just happened.

"Kate…" John whispered, as he stared directly into her eyes.

"Yes?" replied Kate, as she looked right back into his eyes, while she struggled to catch her breath.

"I think you just saved my life…" John finally admitted, in disbelief.

"As long as you're safe; that's all that matters to me," replied a relieved Kate, as she buried her head onto John's chest.

Her words struck deep into John's heart. His safety mattered to her. To his amazement, Kate had run like a mad woman, all the way up the snowy hill, in order to save him. But more than anything, she had risked her own life to push him away from that gunshot. However, before John had the opportunity to say anything else to her, a man started to scream at the top of his lungs for help.

"Help! Help! Help! I've been shot!" yelled Volkan, who remained lying down on the ground and experiencing excessive pain.

After hearing Volkan's cries, Kate immediately rolled off from John's chest. Upon standing up, Kate reached over and helped to lift John back up. Once the pair were back on their feet, they ran over to Volkan's aid. Upon seeing his condition, John immediately removed his scarf and tied it over Volkan's bleeding arm.

"Where's David?" asked Kate, now growing concerned about David's lack of appearance.

"I think here's still over there, under that pile of snow," replied Volkan, as he used his unharmed arm to point in David's direction.

"There's two piles of snow," Kate observed. "Which pile is David trapped under?"

"The pile nearest to me is David. The furthest pile is the gunman. When I was shot and fell onto the snow, I also saw David collapse, along with the gunman, too," replied Volkan.

"Wait, Kate, don't go!" cried John, as he watched Kate immediately dash over to David's location.

However, it was far too late; for Kate had already arrived to the scene and without a second thought or hesitation, she began to dig through the snow. Luckily, David's pile wasn't that heavily deep and after a few pushes, Kate managed to shove the first top layer of snow and located David's head and upper body.

"David?" cried Kate, hoping to get a response from him.

However, David remained still and motionless, as he lay there, half-buried in the snow. Was he hurt and unconscious? Was he in too much pain? Or, worst of all, was he dead?

"David?" asked Kate, once more; but as before, he gave no answer.

By now, Kate was ready to give up hope. However, suddenly, David, with his eyes still closed, miraculously managed to crack open his mouth, just ever-so-slightly. Once David's mouth pierced opened, he began to repetitively chant the following the words:

"Owen, Owen, Owen…"

Chapter 24

"Will he survive this?" asked a very distressed and emotional Amy, who was submerged in her sorrow, with gushing tears streaming down her face; similar to a flooded river, during a violent and turbulent storm.

"As of now, I honestly cannot accurately assess his condition. However, it's best that we act immediately and airlift him soon to the nearest hospital, which is located right in the next town over for treatment," replied the first responder.

"Do we have enough time to get him to the hospital? I mean…I mean…will he make it in there, still conscious?" asked Amy, with her voice cracking in the process.

"Ms. Lawrence, nothing is for certain; however, I still do recommend that we at least still try," replied the first responder.

"Oh Peter! We might lose him!" Amy shouted aloud, as she collapsed right into Peter's arms, and then, she began to shake and sob uncontrollably.

"There, there my love, please don't cry. Everything will be okay, I promise," said Peter reassuringly, as he gently tried with all his might to comfort Amy.

Taking command of the situation, Peter took it upon himself to ask the first responder, "If we agree to the airlift, then how long will it take to transport him to the nearest hospital?"

"Ten minutes or so; fifteen minutes at maximum. Otherwise, it's almost impossible to travel down on this icy road by car, within all these piles of snow. It will be far too dangerous," replied the first responder.

"Alright, I agree; let's airlift him to the nearest hospital and now," replied Amy promptly, as she fought back her tears and attempted to regain her composure.

"Okay, we're on it," replied the first responder, "But first, I just have a few questions, before we proceed any further."

"Is this even necessary? As long as David remains lying down here unconscious, every second of his rescue is precious! Can't you see that my fiancé is gravely upset!" exclaimed Peter, who was rather upset and frustrated by the entire situation.

"Sir, I understand. I promise that we will move the patient, as soon as we can. But as medical responders, we also need to be aware, as to whether or not the patient has any known allergies that we should be aware of?" asked the first responder.

"No, he doesn't have any," replied Amy, as she wiped her eyes away and onto Peter's shoulders.

"Okay, that's good," replied the first responder, "Now, is he currently on any medication?"

"Apart from his daily vitamins, I don't think so," Amy answered; and turning her attention over to Peter, she asked him, "Peter, do you recall Father taking any medicine, other than his vitamins?"

"No, not that I can recall," Peter reflected.

"Okay, no allergies and no medications," repeated the first responder, as he jotted down this information into his notepad.

Meanwhile, Kate was standing nearby and heard the entire conversation. Although Kate didn't want to intrude in their private discussion with the first responder; however, she did catch David this morning, in the act of taking his cancer medication. Even though Kate previously vowed not to reveal David's secret to anyone, their circumstances since breakfast had vastly changed from then to now. As a result, David's livelihood literally depended upon on her sole decision to speak up. Therefore, Kate decided to do the right thing and come clean.

"Wait," cried Kate, as she anxiously looked at Amy and the first responder.

"Kate?" spoke John, thinking that she was in fact, referring to him.

"Amy and Peter," she clarified, "Today, at breakfast, I saw your father taking pills. I didn't mean to see it, but I did. The bottle just managed to roll passed me and…"

"Pills?" repeated Amy, in disbelief.

"What sort of pills?" asked Peter, who was also surprised by Kate's unexpected revelation.

"It was called…," Kate began. However, she knew that once she revealed the medicine's name, then the truth about David's health would be known. But at the same time, David's life was hanging by the thread and time was ticking. No matter the circumstances, Kate knew that she needed to reveal the medicine's name. And so, finally, at long last, she said, "It's Docetaxel."

"Docetaxel? What an odd name for medicine. Peter, have you heard of such a thing? Do you even know what's this prescribed for?" asked Amy, wanting further clarification, as to what this strange and foreign sounding medicine was used for.

"Generally, it's prescribed for…" Peter began, but then, suddenly, he stopped himself short, as if he finally managed to put two and two together.

"Well? What's it used for?" Amy repeated.

"Well…" Peter continued, "I'm not really sure how to say this lightly, my dear. But Docetaxel is used to help treat cancer."

"Cancer?" spoke Amy, in disbelief.

"Yes," confirmed Peter.

"Peter, why would Father be taking pills for cancer?" asked Amy, still failing to recognize nor suspect, that her own father was secretly battling the disease, in private.

"Amy, do you recall your father attending any recent doctor appointments, before this trip?" asked Peter, hoping to gain more insight.

"No, not to my knowledge. But Peter, this is absolutely silly. Why on earth would Father be taking that Do..Doce…oh whatever you call it!," huffed Amy.

Reverting her attention over the Kate, Amy said, "Jennifer, I know that you mean well, but you must be mistaken. You have to. My father doesn't have any cancer, and he would never take such a pill. I mean, if he did, then surely, he'd have told me, wouldn't he?" she asked, now looking directly at John.

However, John knew very well that Kate would never in a million years, mistake a bottle of Docetaxel for anything else, other than its true face value. After all, Kate was far too clever for that; but most importantly, she was also honest and truthful. Furthermore, John also knew David, as well. Indeed, if David did have cancer, then John was most certain that David would have fought heaven and hell to conceal it. In fact, John was now convinced more than ever, that David must have purposely hidden his health problems from both he and Amy, in his effort to lessen the burden of any consequential grief and pain that his own children might have experienced, having been privy to such calamity.

Not wanting to delay David's medical care, John reframed from answering Amy's question and instead, he directed his attention over to the first responder.

"Please take note of this for the doctor," said John, "How soon can we transport him?

"Already, got it down on my notes," replied the first responder, "We're now ready to airlift him over to the next town. But unfortunately, we only have room for three family members to join us aboard the helicopter."

"Amy and I will be there," replied Peter, hastily.

"I'll take the third seat," said Barbara, having spoken for the first time, since David's accident.

"Mother, the helicopter might not be the safest way for you to travel right now," John suggested.

"Oh nonsense! David needs me and I intend to go. Honestly, you can't stop me!" exclaimed Barbara. "Besides, it's far better that you stay put. With such a crazy man still out on the loose, it's safer that you stay behind and protect your wife!"

"I'm afraid, that I, too, must also agree," said Miles, having recently arrived to the crime scene, with two additional police officers besides him.

"John," spoke Kate slowly, as she looked straight into his eyes, "Maybe, it's best that we listen to them. At least this way, we can help work with Miles to catch, whomever is responsible for this."

"Sadly, I think that you're probably right," replied John, reluctantly.

Having agreed to their suggestion, John and Kate remained on the ground, as the rest of their party flew off. Once the helicopter lifted off the ground and ascended up into the air, Miles handed John and Kate a copy to the police report. With the document safely secured within the grasp of their hands, Miles quickly proceeded to debrief them.

"His name is Ivan Koval," Miles began, "He's a member of a wealthy Belarussian mafia, operating here in Türkiye. Based on our intelligence, we believe that today, you were his specific target out here. Luckily, due to Mrs. Barrett's quick response and the unexpected snowfall, we've managed to capture him. As of now, he's been arrested and is in custody with the local Turkish police."

"Miles, I recognize this man from our hotel," Kate interrupted him, as she skimmed through the report and saw a picture of the man. "This morning, before breakfast, I saw him arguing with the hotel agent in the lobby. He was trying to get a room, and when he was denied lodging, he became violent. He even went as so far, as to attack the hotel agent."

"Koval does have a history of violence," replied Miles, "But I'm not at all surprised. Most thugs like him usually exert this type of barbaric behavior out in public."

"But why would he be after me?" asked John, naturally concerned, having recently discovered the identity of his assassin.

"We're still investigating that. Over the years, Koval has been involved in a string of shady and illegal activities, partnered up with the mafia. Mostly, they've been related to drugs and the illegal smuggling of various goods across the black market. But oddly enough, this is the first time that he's ever been arrested for attempted murder. A first; even for a petty criminal like him," Miles explained.

"That might be; but then, why suddenly go after John, as his first attempted assassination target? How does hurting John, benefit him or the mafia, in any justified and meaningful way?" asked Kate, worried and distressed by this new revelation.

"I honestly can't say," Miles admitted, "At this time, we really can't narrow down a specific motive, other than perhaps, Koval must have known about your diplomatic status as the American Ambassador and someone paid him off to do a hit job."

"Paid him off?" Kate repeated. "You mean that he wasn't acting alone?"

"Possibly. Koval owed a lot of money to several international creditors. Apparently, his black-market smuggling schemes and deals caused him to incur a lot of debt. I highly doubt that someone like him went out of his own way to attempt such a bold and risky attack against the ambassador's life, without gaining any monetary reward from it. No, I believe that someone else, aside from Koval, is behind this. Koval is only but a pawn to a much larger threat," said Miles.

"But how does operating within the black market, cause someone to fall into so much debt?" Kate inquired.

"Easily," replied Miles, "It means that he took in, more than he could sell. Often times, these thugs smuggle in luxury goods worth thousands of dollars, but can only sell it back using the local, yet lower currency for far less than the original purchasing price. And in Koval's case, that's exactly what happened to him."

"My goodness," said Kate.

"And Mr. Barrett," spoke Miles, as he turned his attention over to John. "Even though we tried our best to disguise and present you as a regular civilian for this family trip, someone still sought to find and take you out."

"But who would do that?" asked Kate.

"That depends, Mrs. Barrett. Mr. Barrett, do you have any known enemies?" asked Miles, in return.

"No, not that I'm aware of," answered John.

"But couldn't it be just anyone," Kate interjected, "I mean, as a public figure, John is well known by all, around the world. It could be anyone, even a foreign enemy government."

"That's very true," Miles agreed, "Being a public figure makes any person more vulnerable and susceptible to these sorts of unfortunate threats."

"Sadly, you can never take a day off from being a public figure," Kate reflected.

"I agree; once you're in the public eye, then you're in there for life," said Miles, and then he added, "But until we have more answers, it's best that you and Mrs. Barrett continue to keep a low profile, until we can relocate both of you into a new private location."

For a long moment, John remained perfectly quiet and still. He was in full focus and trying his best to absorb all of this new and overwhelming information. No more than an hour ago, here at this very spot, he was enjoying a happy afternoon and sporting fun-filled activities with his family. But now, an hour later, so much had transpired and changed. By one fatal act, David currently resided in a hospital bed, with life threatening injuries, as he secretly and privately fought cancer alone, unbeknownst to John previously.

Sadly, John's life had, quite literally, flashed before his eyes. Having survived an attempted assassination, John lived to tell the tale. But now, at this very moment, John's primary concern was not of himself, but for Kate. While John knew the risks associated with his line of duty after joining the agency; Kate, on the other hand, did not. She, unlike him, didn't sign up for this sort of risky life; therefore, she didn't deserve to be put into harm's way, to serve as collateral damage. What if Koval succeeded and had actually killed one of them today? What if the bullet missed him and hit her, instead? God forbid, if Kate had been injured or even killed, then John would have been absolutely devastated. Devastated beyond repair. Kate, the sweetest and dearest person in all of his acquaintance, was innocent in all of this mess. Her safety was his number one priority and if truth be told, it was his only priority.

"Should we just return back to Istanbul?" John asked Miles, directly.

"Unfortunately, due to the upcoming storm, all flights have been cancelled. As a result, the same also applies to the train tracks and roads. For the most part, we're snowed in," Miles replied.

"We can't leave Kars?" asked Kate, in panic. After this hectic day, the stress was starting to get to her.

"Not at least for the next two days; which is why it's especially important that we immediately move to relocate you both into a new and safe location. As we speak, Ivan Koval might be in jail for now, but he's still working for someone. Until we discover who that someone or entity is, then you and Mr. Barrett are still in grave danger," Miles warned.

"Do you have a recommended lodging for us?" asked John, calmly.

"I do. It's a small lodge nearby, just straight down the hill and located within the city center. Furthermore, I've also taken the liberty to speak directly with the local Turkish police. Fortunately, they've already agreed to supply us with an extra pair of their officers. Therefore, I, along with the local police, will be able to remain in your service, as your official bodyguards for the remainder of your stay in Kars," replied Miles, confidently.

"Great work Miles. Please proceed with coordinating all of these necessary arrangements. Mrs. Barrett and I would like to relocate and retire there, immediately," John ordered.

Upon John's commands, Miles moved forward with arranging their transportation to their new location. An hour later, they were escorted into their new lodge, accompanied by two other police officers, including Miles. The lodge was a humble two-story cabin, which included two large balconies, two private bedrooms, a tiny kitchen, bathroom and a small cozy living room that included a fireplace. Once they all settled in, John and Kate quietly sat peacefully together in the living room, while Miles and the other officers remained outside on-duty and monitoring the premise.

Since the weather was quite cold and dreary, John decided to that a nice heated and cozy fire would warm them up. Using the spare logs located right near the fireplace, John slowly gathered them up, one by one. While John was busy moving the logs into the fireplace, Kate was seated down on a red velvet sofa, located right across from him.

"It's too bad that we don't have any chestnuts with us to roast," said John, jokingly, in an effort to help cheer them up a bit.

However, ever since they arrived to the lodge, they both remained silent for the most part. After today's unforeseeable events, Kate's mind was still preoccupied with the entire calamity. Over and over again, she replayed that accident back in her mind. Although there were still many questions left unanswered, the one question that still lingered about was as to why did David repeatedly chanted the name "Owen," while he lay unconscious in the snow? Was there something significant about that particular name? Whom, in fact, was Owen?

"John, may I ask you a question?" Kate asked, in a rather serious tone and manner.

"Of course, you can always ask me anything," John replied, as he reached into his shirt pocket to search for a match for their fire.

"Who's Owen? After the accident, David called out his name. And I don't recall meeting such a person on this trip," she said.

"Owen is David's son," replied John, as he continued to search for a match, but this time looking inside of his jacket pocket.

"His estranged son?" inquired Kate.

"You knew about that?" asked John, in return, with a raised brow.

"Oh…well…he did mention something over breakfast about an estranged son, but other than that, that's as far as I'm aware," Kate clarified.

"Hmm…interesting that he would discuss that with you; especially, since he never speaks of him, ever. I, myself, have never once met him," John reflected.

"Why utter his name, then? I just find it so oddly strange and peculiar, for one to cry out the name to a person one's estranged from," noted Kate.

"Maybe, he feels guilty for his past fall out with his biological son. Especially, given his current health condition…" John trailed off, as he finally professed and accepted the truth about David's cancer diagnosis.

"Do you think that he subconsciously called out for his son, as a result of this accident?" asked Kate.

"That's very possible. Maybe, that's why David was so insistent upon all of us coming up here together, in the first place. Perhaps, to celebrate one last family gathering, before his health further deteriorates. Even though David and I share a very close foster family relationship, I can still never replace his son. Blood is thicker than water; and Owen is his own flesh and blood. In the end, I suppose that David truly misses him and secretly longs to make peace with him. I personally believe that if David assumed that he was dying, then it seems to me that his dying words and last wish would be to reunite and see his son for one last time. Sadly, it only took a near fatal accident, for him to admit, as such," John concluded.

"I suppose, when one's faced with the brink of death, they will call out to their beloved, no matter the circumstances. Time and distance know no boundaries to the heart," said Kate.

And then, without him even asking, Kate reached into her purse, pulled out a match box, and then handed it over to John.

"You carry a match box? But I thought that you don't smoke," said John, surprised that Kate carried such items inside of her purse.

"I don't smoke. Actually, it's from my first aid kit. I always carry a small version of it in my purse. You know, just in case there's an emergency. Like the need to light a random fire in a secluded cabin," Kate teasingly admitted.

"Kate, you never cease to amaze me. You're certainly full of surprises," John chuckled, with a joyful laugh.

Holding the matchbox inside of his palm, John couldn't help but wonder as to why earlier today, Kate risked her own life to save his. She wasn't obligated to save him. She didn't owe anything to him. No debt at all. Rather than putting herself in harm's way, she could have easily alerted Miles and let the police handle it, instead. But no, she didn't do that. Rather, without any fear nor hesitation, she courageously ran up the hill and blindly pushed John aside to safety; all the while, risking her own precious life, in the process. But again, why did she do it? Why did she save him? And why, in that particular manner? Kate owed nothing to him; therefore, why on earth did she do it? Was it possible that maybe, just maybe, she cared for him? The very thought excited him and brought a shiver down his spine.

After lighting the match and releasing the fire onto the logs, John stood still and watched the tiny spark of fire quickly grow and transform into a large and burning flame. A flame, so strong and so fierce, that it immediately altered the temperature of the room; changing it from an icy and cold space into a warm and heated cabin. As John stared deep into the flames of the dancing fire, a sudden urge of passion began to grow and dance within him. Enticed and encouraged by the flickering embers of the fire, John decided right there and then, that tonight, he needed answers. Answers, as to why she sought to save him and from her own lips, directly. Her soft and luscious lips. Lips, that as of now, he desperately wanted to devour and conquer, once and for all.

Turning away from the fire to face her, he suddenly asked her, with his voice deep and serious, "Why did you save me?"

"You would have done the same for me," she quickly replied; however, his facial expression was so intense and passionate, that Kate started to feel a bit nervous and hot; both, at the same time.

"Yes, that's true. In a heartbeat and without a second thought. But that still doesn't answer my question. Why did *you* risk *your life* to save mine?" he asked again, now staring directly into her eyes.

Suddenly, Kate felt a strange yet unusual sensation emerge, from within her own body. A peculiar sensation, that for some reason, made her want to rush over to his side, throw her arms around him and kiss him again, for a third time. And as the fire continued to grow and expand, Kate fantasized about removing all of her clothes, one by one, right in front of him and then surrendering herself over to their passion…but no…she thought…she simply couldn't. Surely, he didn't feel the same way, as her. Did he? They were just friends, after all. Weren't they?

"Think nothing of it," she quickly dismissed it, as her senses miraculously returned back to her. "Anyone would have done—"

"No, they wouldn't," he interrupted. "What you did to today, no one else would have done similar for me. Kate, you're quite a remarkable woman."

"Why, why…" uttered Kate, who really at this moment, couldn't find any other words to say.

"I'm glad that you're in my life," he admitted, with a huge smile across his face, which made Kate's heart melt into pieces.

"I'm glad that you're in my life, too," she also admitted, with a smile of her own, that in return, tugged against his own heart, as well.

"And I'm glad that we are…that we are…" he began, but then he stopped himself short; for in truth, he, himself, wasn't sure as to how to properly finish this sentence.

For what exactly were they? They were pretending to be married in public and in private, they were supposed to be friends; but was friends still the proper word? Did friends long to kiss each other? To daydream, as to how the other partner would taste like, if they happened to kiss them? Or, to fantasize as to how their bodies would feel like, pressed against one another? Were these inner feelings and desires, that he secretly harbored, still constitute as merely friendship? Or, was it now, so much more? And if so, was this feeling also mutual on her part?

"Friends?" she asked, almost hesitant, having said so. But her choice of words felt like a knife stabbed directly into his heart.

Yes, it was technically true; they were indeed, good friends. But was that all? Nothing more? Somehow, John was gravely disappointed with her answer; because being limited to just only as a 'friend' was far too simple now. Deep down inside, John longed for more. He yearned for her to admit that they were more than just friends. Beyond the mere confinement of friendship. An admission; nay, a confession, that their mutual relationship had evolved into something much more. He longed for her to confess that she had sentimental and romantic feelings for him; just as he, had for her, in return. But more than anything, he secretly wished, that now, being alone together here inside of this secluded cabin, she was finally ready to explore these newfound feelings together with him. But, sadly, for now, this simply, wasn't to be.

"It has been a long day," said Kate, as she finally, rose up from her chair, "I think it's best that we retire for the evening."

"Err...yes, perhaps, you are right," replied John, now gravely disappointed by her impending departure.

"I'll go ahead and take the room at the far end of the hall. You can take the front room, with the larger balcony," she said.

And then, just like that, she was gone in an instant; while John remained in his solitude, alone in the room with the blazing fire. A fire, that was now, ironically, burning full blast, with such ignited flames, that it truly was a shame that it was only going to be in the presence of a solo party of one. As John deduced, it seemed that his feelings of passion, was only on his lonesome part; because had Kate shared the same mutual passions and desires as him, then she would have stayed there with him, right?

An hour later, John retired into his bedroom and from the edge of his private balcony, he stared out into the night sky. As he watched the white stars float about within a circular motion amongst the dark sky, with the cotton white snow covering the floor below, it was a beautiful contrast, between white and black or light and dark. Curious, he wondered if Kate, who was on the opposite side of the cabin, was also watching the same night sky from outside of her own bedroom. Furthermore, he wondered if she was still awake and if she so, then was she still searching for her fallen snowflake; even now, so late into the night? And when she eventually saw it, he wondered as to how she would finally feel having seen it. The truth was, that he wondered about so many things regarding her. But more than anything else, he wondered as to how she truly felt about him. These very thoughts were simply maddening!

Suddenly, out of the darkest corner of the night sky, John unexpectedly saw a bright yellow light shoot straight across the open field. As the star traveled across the dark sky, it left a bright white and dusty trail behind it. After years of waiting for a shooting star, John finally saw one; here, in Kars, of all places. As the star descended down towards earth, John held his breath and with all of his heart, he made a single wish.

"If only it could be…" he whispered aloud to the stars, knowing very well, that what he just wished for was truly the impossible.

However, dear reader, believe me when I say, that sometimes, unbeknownst to mankind, fate, herself, has a funny way of answering our prayers, in the most unexpected of ways. And with that being said, it just so happened, that the stars, on this particular and ominous of nights, were indeed, listening to him, with keen and impressionable ears.

Chapter 25

ate took her last dance step, as she finally tumbled down, landing straight onto her bed. Her attempts to practice her late-night tango choreography, within the privacy and comfort of her bedroom, was proving to be rather difficult and exhausting. Much to her dismay, the tango was far more complicated to dance to, in comparison to the waltz. Furthermore, without a partner to practice with, the tango was proving to be almost impossible to master and execute. As it was, Kate was quite ready to quit her dance practice tonight, altogether.

However, dancing was her cure. It helped to clear her mind; and clearing her mind is exactly what she needed to do. Because right now, all that she could think about was John. Here she was, alone with him, in a private cabin, tucked away in the country, far away from the city and literally, snowed in. It truly was, in every sense, a romantic getaway. But John wasn't her lover. He was only her friend, and he was just down to hall. Probably, sleeping by now, as he was an early sleeper.

If circumstances had been different and leaned in her favor, then she wouldn't be here dancing alone in her bedroom, so late into the night. Instead, she would be across the hallway, dancing within the arms of the man, whom she was secretly harboring feelings for. Romantic feelings. Secret passions. Yearning desires. Furthermore, whenever she closed her eyes shut, all she saw was him. His face. His eyes. His smile. His lips. Even when she dreamed of his lips, she remembered what it felt like when he kissed her. How truly magically and wonderful it all felt! And if truth be told, she wanted more. Much more. More than just a kiss.

While she had prematurely excused herself from the living room earlier tonight, she did that to be away from him. With the fire blazing intensely in front of them, Kate desperately needed to suppress her sudden urge to rush straight into his arms and make love to him. Therefore, she found solace and comfort on practicing her dance steps, in preparation for the next upcoming state dinner that was scheduled to take place soon after they returned back to Istanbul.

By now, Kate was too exhausted to continue on with her dancing. Besides, it was now, rather late and almost nearing to midnight. Honestly, Kate should have been sleeping by now; however, she was afraid that once she closed her eyes and went to sleep, then she was destined to dream about John, again. Sadly, the truth was, that she was always dreaming of him now, as of lately.

Just then, Kate heard a ringing sound that began to play. Following the sound echoing inside of her room, Kate eventually discovered that the origin of the ring was coming from her own purse. As she opened up her purse, she reached in and pulled out a mobile phone. But this wasn't her mobile phone, it was John's. Immediately, Kate recalled that after the accident, John temporary gave his phone to her to hold onto for safe keeping, during all of the commotion. However, Kate must have forgotten to return the mobile phone back to John; hence it was still here, in her possession.

Looking at the mobile phone, Kate saw that he had a missed call from the embassy.

"What if it's important? What if it's about David? What if this message, can't wait until tomorrow?" she asked herself, aloud.

As much as Kate preferred not to walk down the hallway and enter into John's bedroom— especially, given this late hour in the night— she knew that ultimately, she had to. John was a busy man, with several duties and responsibilities, and if someone was calling his mobile work phone this late into the night, then it certainly had to be important. Unfortunately, Kate knew that she had no other choice, but to return his phone right now.

And so, out of her better judgment, Kate grabbed John's mobile phone and walked out of her bedroom, making her way toward John's bedroom; all the while, failing to realize that she probably should have looked in the mirror first, beforehand, prior to leaving her bedroom. For if she had, then Kate would have realized that she was still wearing her silk lingerie! And if given a chance, she probably would have opted for a change of wardrobe; for what she was currently wearing was rather quite revealing, indeed!

Chapter 26

John heard a knock at his door. This was unexpected. Miles and the other officers were supposed to be camped outside of their cabin. If this was an emergency, then they should have called him as he requested, instead of physically knocking at his door this late into the night. Apart from Kate and himself, there wasn't supposed to be anyone else inside the cabin. Also, it was almost midnight. Surely, Kate was sleeping by now? But if it wasn't Kate, then who could it possibly be knocking at his door, at this late hour?

Once more, the knock came again at the door; so, John walked back into his bedroom through the balcony and rapidly made his way over to his bedroom door. Upon opening his door, to his sheer surprise, he saw Kate standing there. She was still awake. But to his even greater surprise, she was wearing practically nothing at all; with the exception of an extremely revealing white silken nightgown, that just so happened to perfectly emphasize the intimate shape of her glorious body, revealing her bare chest, stemming from her neck and all the way down to her nipples…

"Kate?" John chocked, out of both surprise and excitement. "What are you doing here?"

"I'm sorry to wake you…umm…did I wake you up?" she asked, hesitantly.

"No, not at all. I was up. But I thought you were sleeping," he replied, as his eyes remained hypnotized at her sexy outfit that practically screamed seductress.

"No, I didn't. I couldn't. I was actually practicing my dance steps," she admitted.

"Dancing at midnight?" he asked, with a raised brow.

"I just needed to clear my mind," she confessed, "But then, I heard a ring and realized that I still had your phone in my possession."

Reaching over, Kate suddenly grabbed hold of his hand and place his phone back into his grip. However, as her hands met his, something entirely unpredictable yet magical, all at the same time, finally happened. Before either one of them had ample enough time to logically process as to what was occurring right now, their bodies soon took over with full force and each of them found themselves surrendering over to their hidden desires and suppressed passions. One minute ago, Kate was delivering John his phone and the following minute, she was already locked into another passionate and enticing kiss with him. But unlike before, this time, their kiss lingered on…and on…and on…and neither one of them, was willing to pull away.

By that one single kiss, a new and passionate love affair came into being. With each passing minute, their lovemaking continued to progress. A kiss turned into two kisses, then three and four…and before they knew it, they were lying on top of John's bed, ready to take their newfound romance to the next level.

Slowly, John began to tenderly peel off Kate's clothes. First, her silk stockings and garter belt were removed…and then, her corset…and then her bra. John swiftly threw them aside, until all that was left on her was nothing more than her underwear. Slowly, he placed his hands inside her underwear, and as his hands began to touch and explore her most intimates of parts, Kate suddenly released a moan from pleasure. Impressed by her sudden arousal, John acted promptly and carefully peeled off her remaining garment, leaving her stark naked and ready for his attention. For a brief moment, John simply stared at her naked body in fascination; for she was most beautiful creature that he had ever laid eyes upon before. Lying naked there inside of his bed, it was as if Venus was there staring right back at him. The curves to her hourglass body, along with her voluminous breast, brought excitement throughout his own being. Suddenly, John lost himself and the immediate urge to possession her overcame him.

By the mere touch of his hands, she shivered from excitement. After years of waiting to lay with another man so intimately, and he, waiting for another woman, like her, in return; they both equally welcomed each other's advances full heartily. Upon removing all of her clothes, John began to suck on her bare breast. Slowly, he licked across her soft and tender bosom, until he eventually reached her nipples. And once his tongue glided across her hard and perky nipples, he squeezed them and this left her screaming and yearning for more. Delighted by her positive reaction, John moved onto her other breast and continued to lick and suck her some more.

Blushing red from pure enticement, John briefly pulled away; leaving Kate feeling a bit disappointed by their momentary pause. However, she didn't have to wait long; for as soon as John moved away, he began to remove all of his clothes. First, he removed his shirt, exposing his muscular abs and physic, that left Kate licking her own wet lips and wanting more of him. Afterwards, he removed his trousers, leaving him left with nothing else but his underwear garments. Looking right at him, Kate could see that not only was his strong, muscular and wet body ready for her, but that his manly package was extremely large, heavy and protruding! As it was, John was most ready to enter and explore her! Soon enough, he was going to make her his!

Stunned by his enormous male package, Kate stared in awe, as John tenderly removed his last remaining article of clothing. With one pull, he was left standing there bare naked, right in front of her. Although for weeks, Kate fantasized on numerous occasions, as to how he would look like with his clothes off; and now, seeing him so up-close in all of his glory, she certainly wasn't left disappointed. In fact, he was almost perfect. From his tall and muscular body, to his angelic face; John was truly a real-life god in the flesh. A Warrior. A King. A man, whom, she was most ready to surrender to wholeheartedly and without any hesitation. If this had been a war, then she was desperately eager to freely surrender herself over to him, as his personal slave; for at this moment, she was his.

Excited by the stunning sight before, Kate squealed with joy, as she licked her lips and began touching herself, uncontrollably. Staring right at his thick and hard package, that was expanding by the minute, Kate grew more anxious by each passing second. John immediately caught sight of her, and her excitement made him even more determined to claim her, as his own.

Returning back to his bed, he continued their lovemaking by introducing himself to the rest of her body. First, he kissed and caressed her full and swollen breasts, then her stomach, then her legs, then her outer thighs, then her inner thighs and then eventually, her most intimate part of her body…which left, Kate screaming from sheer pleasure! Oh, how wonderous it felt! How breathtaking and magical, it all was!

Her screams brought a smile across John's face. Making Kate yell from pleasure, brough him great satisfaction in his ability to fulfill her sexual needs. Slowly, John pulled away and upon doing so, he moved his hands over to her inner thighs. With her thighs in his hands, he gently began to push them apart, as he positioned himself even closer to her.

Feeling John so incredibly near to her, Kate rolled her head back and pulled her hair from all of the anticipation and excitement. At long last, their lovemaking was graduating to the next level. Within a few seconds, they were finally going to be united as one!

Upon opening her thighs as wide as he possibly could, John bent down to position himself right above her. Once he felt confident that she was safe and comfortable underneath him, he decided to move forward in his pursuit of claiming her as his lover. Pulling her hips another inch closer to him, his hands traveled down from her hips to her inner thighs and then…he felt her. She was wet, wide and eager for his welcoming. And John, most certainly, wasn't going to let her down. As their bodies met together, skin to skin, John knew that the time to unite with her was now. She was ready…and so was he.

With one swift thrust, John entered straight into her petite body and soon, he lost himself completely. After making his first thrust, Kate immediately yelled so loud, that for a split second, John was afraid that he came in too strong, and that his tall and muscular frame might have been too large and overwhelming for her small and petite figure. However, he couldn't have been more wrong; for not only was Kate's body perfectly designed for his, but she already loved every second of his movements. In fact, she was growing even more addicted to him, by the minute!

After screaming and moaning from the newfound pleasure that he brought to her, Kate wanted more. Quickly, she grabbed him from behind and pulled him even closer to her, as she opened up her legs even further apart. Then, in an effort to help him, she began to move her body up and down to follow his rhythm. With her hands gently massaging his buttocks, as he moved, she moved, too. Unlike her failed attempt earlier this evening on practicing her dance steps alone in her bedroom; this time around, Kate now had the perfect partner, as they danced together inside of his bed. Ah, yes, Kate thought. Indeed, they were dancing in bed! How lovely and romantic, this was!

As Kate followed his lead, John continued to move into her, as she followed him up and down in his bed, with her large breasts bouncing and jiggling up in the air, in front of him. Between her voluminous breasts and her rising movements, John simply couldn't contain his ever-growing excitement. As she grabbed hold of his behind again, she gave a slight squeeze, that brough John into full ecstasy. As her body was moving further and further inside of him, he continued to thrust and penetrate himself, more and more into hers.

As they continued to move up and down, Kate yelled and screamed from pure pleasure and nirvana, as his bed continued to violently shake and vibrate from their lovemaking. As delighted as Kate was; John, too, was also equally delighted and happy, well beyond words. As she screamed; he screamed. After years of celibacy and weeks of repressed sexual frustration that he had built up inside due to his attraction and desire of her, John's fantasizes were finally becoming a reality. At long last, he was finally united with the woman, whom he had dreamed about for so long.

John continued to move and thrust into her, until finally, they eventually reached their climax, as they both screamed at the top of their lungs due to their great mutual satisfaction in their long lovemaking session. For a brief moment, John actually thought they were done; however, to his surprise, Kate quickly rolled over and before he knew it, she had climbed up on top of him. Round two was about to begin! This was certainly most unexpected! A marathon in the making!

As she lay on top of him, like the queen that she was, she began to mimic all of his prior moves by kissing him on all of the same places that he had previously kissed her, right before. First, she kissed his chest, then his stomach, then his legs, then his outer thighs, then his inner thighs and finally, she reached his manhood, where she began to passionately kiss and suck it with such force, intensity and vibration, that he moaned with desire! With each suck, John rolled his head and closed his eyes, as he waited for more. And she certainly didn't disappoint; for the more she continued to please him, the more he screamed for more! Ah, yes, Kate, was everything that he had imagined that she would be and so much more!

To his surprise, just when he thought that nothing further could ever beat the physical and blissful sensation that he was already currently experiencing, he was once again, proven wrong. After Kate had kissed each and every inch of his body, she slowly made her way on top of him again, where she remained seated right above his very own manhood. As John rolled his head back, Kate lowered herself even closer down to him, until finally, she entered him directly and they were once again, united together as one.

As their hot and wet bodies met together, skin to skin, Kate gradually rocked her body back and forth, up and down, and side to side. At first, she moved slowly; however, once her body got more comfortable, her rhythm progressively increased, more and more, until finally, she was riding him faster and faster and faster…. like a champion horseman at the Kentucky derby! He was hers to conquer; and conquer she intended to do!

Out of sheer pleasure, John screamed with desire and she in return, did the same. As she rocked and rode him from above; he, in return, lifted up his hips and pushed himself to enter her even deeper. She screamed. He smiled. And then, with his bare hands, he grabbed her thighs and sought to pull them further and further apart. Having done so, he then reached for her hips, and with one swift move, he pulled her even closer down to him; where, they immediately, both moaned and screamed by their mutual orgasm, as they each climaxed together, at the exact same time.

Hours later, after several lovemaking sessions, Kate exhaustingly, yet peacefully, slept soundly within John's warm and caring arms inside of his bed. While John stared down at her, as the two of them remained comfortably wrapped up together inside of his blanket, he simply watched and admired her. He admired her for her beauty, her body, her mind, her soul, but most of all, he admired her just for her. She was one of a kind. A secret treasure that he had discovered, all for himself. She was everything that he had ever dreamed and wished for, all wrapped up into one person. And to top it all off, Kate was the best lover that he had ever had. His heart, mind and body had never felt this way before. Never in his lifetime, had he ever had a partner, that fulfilled both his physical and emotional needs, such as she.

Looking out his window from across his bed, John noticed that it was still snowing. Unexpectedly, he smiled to himself. For the first time ever, he was content and satisfied with his life. And surprisingly, it had nothing to do with either his career, his family, the embassy, the mansion or anything else. Here he was, alone in a secluded cabin, away from civilization, in a remote part of Türkiye, having just survived an assassination attempt, and yet, he was still happy.

Suddenly, it was right there at that very moment, that he finally realized that his happiness didn't depend upon any tangible materialistic, financial or even superficial things. All that matter was being with the one woman, whom he loved dearly. The same woman, whom he had admired from afar, for so long. The very same woman, whom he even gone so far, as to make a wish upon a shooting star for.

With Kate still sleeping tenderly within his arms, he leaned down and slowly whispered into her ear, "Kate, I love you."

Even though he was well aware that she was still sleeping and probably didn't even hear his confession, he still said it anyways and with a huge smile, which stemmed directly from his heart.

Chapter 27

One Week Later in Istanbul, Türkiye …

"Tabitha? Oh Tabitha? Here, kitty, kitty…" Kate shouted, as she walked down the hallway.

"I think I just saw her downstairs, chasing Jewel," replied Sally, who had happened to just walk pass Kate.

"Really? I was just there a moment ago and didn't spot her. I suppose that I should return down there and try again," Kate pondered aloud, as she scratched her head.

"Wait, Dr. Stanley," Sally pleaded, "Before you do that, I really need to run the itinerary for the upcoming NATO state dinner with you."

"Sally, can't this wait until later? Perhaps, even tomorrow?" asked Kate, as she was still focused on trying to relocate her missing cat.

"But the party is next week, and we still haven't selected your new gown, as of yet," Sally reminded her.

"Sally, you're my personal stylist and designer now," replied Kate, "Besides, I trust your instincts and style. Not to mention, that you already have my measurements. I have the utmost faith that you'll design or select something decent for me. Speaking on this subject, have the other wives contacted you as of yet, about your designs and dresses?"

"Oh Dr. Stanley!" replied Sally, with a huge smile. "If only you knew! Ever since you wore my dress at the last state dinner, my phone line has been ringing nonstop! It seems that everyone in your inner circle, now wants to wear one of my dresses!"

"There, you see, I was right! You're a world-famous designer now, who's more than capable enough to select my next gown. As I said before, I trust your instincts," Kate reaffirmed.

"But, Dr. Stanley, we really still need to…" Sally started to trail off; but it was far too late, for Kate was long gone and already half-way down the staircase.

Upon descending down the stairs, Kate saw Bes quietly seated on the sofa, located in the reception room. He appeared to be reading some form of documents, while sipping a warm cup of tea.

"Oh Bes," Kate shouted, as soon as she arrived by his side, "Have you seen Tabitha?"

"Actually, yes. I just saw her in the kitchen, playing with Chef Homura. The chef was so busy and preoccupied with her, that he completely forgot to make my afternoon tea! Imagine, that! Why, I had to prepare this cup all by myself!" cried Bes, distressed by this unraveling turn of events.

"Thank you, Bes," said Kate, "I'll go into the kitchen and check, then."

Walking by the grand dining room, Kate pushed through the swinging front doors to enter into the kitchen. Upon entering the room, she saw Chef Homura by the counter, chopping raw onions. To her surprise, his eyes were full of tears. Somehow, it seemed that Chef Homura wasn't immune to the powerful strength of an odor produced by the overpowering onion.

"Chef Homura, have you seen Tabitha?" asked Kate, "Bes, recently mentioned to me a few minutes ago, that he last saw her here in the kitchen and playing with you."

"That was before Tyler showed up!" exclaimed Chef Homura, "Here I was, enjoying my time in your kitty's company, and then, that awful brute of a man showed up and took her away from me!"

Much to Kate's surprise, Chef Homura began to cry hysterically. Suddenly, it occurred to Kate, that perhaps, Chef Homura wasn't tearing up as a result of the onion; but rather, he was actually crying tears of sorrow, over the rejection of her cat. Furthermore, it also appeared that Tabitha might have preferred Tyler's company over Chef Homura's, and because of this, Chef Homura wasn't at all too keen nor happy with this disappointing revelation.

"Chef Homura, do you happen to know, as to where I might find Tyler?" asked Kate, with a raised brow.

"I think he took her outside, after I refused service to him and Bes, regarding their afternoon tea. The nerve of them asking for tea, after stealing Tabitha's attention away from me! Why, I've never been so offended, in my entire life!" yelled Chef Homura, as he slammed his oversized butcher's knife onto his chopping board—leaving Kate shaken by surprise.

"Err…alright, thank you, Chef Homura. I'll just go and check outside, then," Kate quickly murmured, as she promptly exited the kitchen and ran outside into the garden.

Entering into the garden, Kate immediately saw Carol nearby, seated on a bench nearby and holding a stack of letters in her hands. She appeared to be alone, stressed and dare we say, a bit agitated. Given the busy and concentrated nature of Carol's attention to her letters, Kate briefly contemplated as to whether or not she should ask Carol about Tabitha's whereabouts. However, since Carol was the only other person in the garden, other than Kate, she decided to take her chance and ask away.

"Carol," Kate began, "Have you seen Tabitha? Chef Homura mentioned to me that she came outside here with Tyler; but I can't seem to find them."

"It's true; she was here earlier with Tyler. But then, he was unexpectedly called for a last-minute meeting, so he asked me to watch her. But that was before…" replied Carol, as she stopped mid-sentence and nervously looked down onto the floor.

"Before what?" asked Kate, who suddenly, began to grow worried that something foul might have happened to Tabitha. Why else would Carol act so nervous?

"Well…that was before…Barbara showed up here…with Jewel. After Jewel arrived, Tabitha and her began to play…or at least, I thought they were playing, but I guess, they weren't," Carol admitted.

"Playing?" asked Kate, most curious as to where this particular story was heading to.

"Well…it was more like…chasing…yes…that's it…it was chasing. Like I said, Jewel started chasing Tabitha, then Tabitha started running down the garden. Then, before I knew it, the most disturbing and horrible thing happened!" exclaimed Carol.

"Carol, what exactly happened?" asked Kate, whose heart immediately sunk down to the pits of her stomach.

"Dr. Stanley, I don't know how to put this any lightly," Carol began, "But in the blink of an eye, Tabitha and Jewel ran through Barbara, like the speed of light! Honestly, it just happened so fast, too! Before I had time to react, Barbara abruptly came tumbling down and falling on top of Gloria, who just happened to be standing nearby her. Suddenly, there was a large thumping sound, as the two of them fell directly onto the floor, where they both landed right on top of that very rose bed!" exclaimed Carol, as she immediately pointed to the crime scene.

Following Carol's direction, Kate saw a large pile of decimated rose petals, all scattered across a nearby dirt path. Much to her dismay, all of the previous newly bloomed roses in that bed, where sadly, now reduced to nothing more than mere particles and dust. Somehow, the fall must have been ugly and messy, she thought. Then, it suddenly occurred to Kate, that those very roses had thorns too, and that unfortunately, those prickly thorns must have pricked both ladies upon their fall.

"Dr. Stanley, it was such an incredibly ugly scene! Barbara and Gloria were both covered in full dirt, from head to toe, and also pricked by the roses' painful thorns, too! But to make matters worse, after falling, they actually began fighting with another! Just like Tabitha and Jewel before them, it was a real cat fight!" yelled Carol, as she attempted to reenact for Kate, as to what she had previously witnessed, firsthand.

"My God, what happened next?" asked Kate, who was now, very concerned by this latest revelation.

"Honestly, Dr. Stanley, I'll admit; I, too, began to panic. In the middle of all that chaos, I actually considered running away from the scene, in order to avoid them at their worse, altogether. But before I could escape, Barbara asked for my assistance to help lift her back up. And so, I ended up staying and helping to pull her back up; and then, followed by Gloria. Afterwards, to my surprise, they started fighting, once again! But, Dr. Stanley, as truth be told, I'm not entirely sure, as to which catfight was worse; the initial fight fought between Tabitha and Jewel, or the preceding fight fought by Barbara against Gloria! Really, it was just too much!"

"Well, I suppose that after all these years of informal jabs at one another, Barbara and Gloria finally reached their boiling points and ultimately, each unleashed their mutual frustrations out against one another," Kate somberly concluded.

"Dr. Stanley, I totally agree. Anyways, to still answer your question from earlier, during the fight, I also saw from the corner of my eye, Jewel and Tabitha running down the garden lawn, leading straight into the gazebo. And if I were to bet my money on it, I'm certain they're probably still there right now," explained Carol as she pointed in the direction of the gazebo, located further down the garden's walking path.

"Thank you, Carol, for all your help. I'll go ahead and check it out," said Kate, as she stood up and began walking down the garden's path, in the direction of the gazebo. However, before she completely walked away, Carol called out to her.

"Wait, Dr. Stanley," shouted Carol, "I really do need to discuss these NATO invitations with you, regarding next week's upcoming state dinner."

"Don't worry, I'm sure they are fine, as is, Carol. Please just move forward and proceed with what you have," Kate yelled from behind, as she continued to make her way down the garden's paths; and now steps away from the gazebo.

After a few minutes of walking, Kate soon arrived to the front entrance of the gazebo. As she approached it, she suddenly heard a dog's bark. It must be Jewel! This was certainly a good sign! Surely, Tabitha was inside the gazebo with Jewel. At long last, Kate had finally found her beloved cat.

"Tabitha, I've found you at last!" Kate exclaimed, as she happily hopped inside into the gazebo.

However, much to her dismay, Kate's presumptions about Tabitha's whereabouts were soon proven wrong. Although Jewel was indeed, inside the gazebo, as suggested by Carol; Tabitha, on the other hand, was not. Upon entering the gazebo, Kate saw Jewel seated above Barbara's lap. But the most surprising of all, was that Barbara looked almost unrecognizable! In contrast to her usually highly styled and polished self, Barbara was now, covered completely in dirt, with her hair a total mess, and her purple dress tattered into shreds!

"Barbara?" asked Kate, in a state of complete and utter shock, as to Barbara's baffling and untidy appearance.

"Jennifer, my dear, you've come to help calm my nerves, haven't you? Why, can you imagine the audacity of that woman!" cried Barbara, as she continued to stroke Jewel's coat with her hands, in an effort to calm her unsettling nerves.

"Ah, yes; Carol just recently told me what happened. It's most unfortunate. I'm truly sorry to hear about your fall. Are you alright?" asked Kate, who took a seat nearby Barbara, inside of the gazebo.

"Thank heaven for Jewel being here, to help calm my raging nerves! Imagine, that woman actually blamed me for falling onto her! Why, she even went, as so far as to accuse Jewel for orchestrating this entire accident! Imagine, such a ridiculous accusation! As if my precious Jewel would commit such a hideous crime! Why, my darling girl is a lady, not a tramp!"

huffed Barbara, angrily.

"Perhaps, it's best that we return back into the house?" Kate suggested.

"To see that woman again? Absolutely not! At least, not until, I first, calm back down, again," replied Barbara, as she shook her head in disagreement.

"Very well. In the meantime, I can just sit here with you, until you're ready to go back inside," said Kate.

"Ah, this week really hasn't been ideal, for our family, has it?" sighed Barbara. She, of course, was referring to their unfortunate accident in Kars.

"How's David doing, by the way?" Kate inquired, in a more serious tone.

"His condition remains stable. Apart from a broken leg and a few minor bruises, he'll survive the skiing accident. But the cancer, unfortunately, is another story entirely," Barbara sadly admitted.

"Barbara, I'm so sorry," apologized Kate.

"Don't be; it's not your fault. These unfortunate things do happen. However, I remain hopeful that with the proper medicine and therapy, David will pull through this. He must," concluded Barbara.

"How's Amy and Peter holding up?" asked Kate.

"Naturally, Amy's a complete mess; which is expected. However, thank goodness for Peter. That boy is her rock!" exclaimed Barbara.

"I'm so happy for her that she has a good and supportive partner to help her navigate through these hard and difficult times," Kate proclaimed, with a smile.

Smiling in return, Barbara said, "Well, enough about them. I'm more interested on hearing about you and my son. After today's unfortunate turn of events, I absolutely long to hear good news! Please tell me that things went exceptionally well between you and John, while alone in Kars."

As Barbara jabbed away directly at Kate's stomach with her elbow, she couldn't help but smile; because the truth was, that everything that Barbara had hoped for, actually really did happen, too. As it turned out, John did have feelings for her, and the pair of them, finally gave into their passions and desires. For the remainder of their stay in Kars, they made love the entire time. In fact, Kate never once left his bedroom, nor his bed. They kissed and made love, and when they weren't making love, they were either sleeping or eating— all in preparation for their next round of lovemaking. Even when they showered, they were always together and never once separated. In fact, he never once left her side, and because of that, she never felt more happier before, in her entire life.

Eventually, once the snow settled back down and the roads cleared up again, they left Kars and returned back to Istanbul, by private plane. However, upon their arrival to Istanbul, John was immediately summoned to return to Ankara, to attend another round of meetings. And ever since then, he's been gone. In fact, today was Kate's first day back at the mansion since her trip; which is why, she was so eager to find and reunite with Tabitha.

"Oh, my dearest Jennifer, your reaction says everything!" exclaimed Barbara, joyfully. "I just knew that you two loved each other!"

"Love?" asked Kate.

Somehow, it never once occurred to her that John might actually love her. In fact, she, herself, wasn't entirely sure if she loved him too, in return. Although she knew that she cared for him, and that, she was attracted to him; but did she actually love him? Had their newfound romance blossom into something much more? Was it truly love? And if so, then how would she know? At which point, in time, does any person come to the realization that they're in love with another person? Another equal soul? A soul mate?

"Yes, my dear. Love," Barbara reaffirmed.

"But how can you tell? That is; that we're in love, with each other?" asked Kate, who was most eager to learn about Barbara's thoughts on this matter.

"My dearest Jennifer, a mother can always sense about these sorts of things," replied Barbara, "However, I, too must make a confession. Please forgive me in advance, but in the past, I, myself, wasn't too sure if you two truly loved each other. Sadly, I wasn't entirely certain as to whether or not your marriage was indeed, a love match or a marriage of convenience. But after spending these past few days in-person with you both, I'm now convinced that you two are a perfect match for one another."

"Really? You thought that we didn't love each other, before?" asked Kate. If Barbara really believed this, then she must have assumed this with regards to her twin sister's relationship with John, and not with her.

"Yes, I did consider it. Sadly, I'm ashamed to admit that when you first got married, I did have my own doubts and reservations. Initially, I suspected that your hasty marriage was more of a matter of convenience; which naturally, might explain why I still don't have my grandchildren, as of yet," Barbara remarked, as she patted Kate's stomach; which in return, made Kate blush in the fiery shade of hot red.

"Needless to say, I had my doubts. But, like I said before, all my previous presumptions and reservations have all been recently put to rest. Rest assured, I'm fully confident that you all love one another. Although, I suspect that he might love you the most," she said, with a beaming smile that glowed across her face.

"Really? You honestly believe that he loves me, more than I do?" asked Kate, most intrigued by this unexpected and bold statement.

"I do," replied Barbara, confidently. "My dear Jennifer, I say this wholeheartedly, because I've seen the way he looks at you. Why, every time I've caught him staring at you, whether it's at dinner or casually walking down the hallway, he always seems to have this rather particular shimmering sparkle shining inside of his blue eyes. It's a very unique sparkle, too. Honestly, it's more like a twinkle; in which I swear, his blue eyes almost appear as emerald green…a color, that even I, as his own mother, never saw in his eyes before. It's almost as if he's just so incredibly happy by simply being around you, that even his own blue eyes— a color that he was born with— magically transform to a new shade of green, born out of pure happiness and bliss. It's truly spectacular. But apart from this, he also carries that particular look of love. I know this for a fact, for I have seen it once before in my lifetime and that was with his father, my own dear late husband, Mr. Barrett."

"Wow, I didn't realize that he looked at me in that way," Kate whispered to herself, practically forgetting that Barbara was seated nearby her.

"And," added Barbara, with a raised brow, "I've also seen the way that you look at him, too."

"You have? How do I look at him?" asked Kate, who wasn't entirely certain as to how she appeared to others, whenever she was around John.

"Like a woman whose heart has been recently struck by the arrow of love," replied Barbara, enthusiastically. "And might I say, that if a couple, such as yourselves, who've been married for so long; but yet, can stare at each other, as if they're still newlyweds with those same hungry eyes, then that's something truly quite remarkable. Yes, quite remarkable, indeed. Furthermore, as his mother, I couldn't be any happier," she said, with a tear forming at the corner of her eye.

Touched by Barbara's kind words, Kate reached over, grabbed her by her hands and said, "Thank you, Barbara."

"No, thank you," replied Barbara, "For being there for my son. I know that he appreciates you more, than you can ever know. Even though he can't ever find the proper words to say aloud; but as his mother, I know the truth."

Slowly, Barbara stood up from the bench and with Jewel still in her arms, she said to Kate, "I should probably return back to the mansion; for heavens knows, that I'm in desperate need of a warm bath. But you, on the other hand, need to retrieve that cat of yours, before she continues to suffer at the clutches of *that dreadful woman.*"

"If only I can find her," admitted Kate, reluctantly.

"Well, when I grabbed Jewel, she took Tabitha. As we speak, they're probably still with the gardener inside of his office right now, discussing as to how to replant those darn roses! Personally, if you ask me, I recommend doing away with all of these insufferable roses altogether; for their thorns are far too dangerous! Honestly, it's much safer to plant tulips instead, rather than those prickly and pesty roses. Why, one day, when my grandchildren are grown and playing right outside this very garden, they might get hurt. After today, I'm now convinced that they'll be far safer playing in a field of tulips, than a bed of roses; for unlike roses, tulips don't have any thorns!"

"Barbara, that's a great suggestion. Perhaps, a variety of more diverse flora and fauna should be incorporated into this garden, as it might do us some good here. After all, not everyone prefers a rose," Kate reflected.

"My dear, that's a very wise statement. A wise statement, indeed. It's true; not everyone likes roses, because we're not meant to admire solely roses, alone. Why, if God loved only roses, then the earth wouldn't have all these endless varieties of plants and flowers. Personally, I've always preferred a nice bouquet of lavenders. Speaking of which, were you aware that lavender is one the best ingredients for wine? It adds a higher degree of sophistication to the mouth's palate."

"Interesting, I had no idea," Kate admitted.

"Yes, lavender is the key ingredient. In fact, lavender is the cure for many other ailments too, such as headaches, high blood pressure and asthma. It can also treat various skin blemishes, and is a true stress reliever. I suppose that's why I tend to wear the color purple so much, because lavender is my favorite flower. But you know, my dearest Jennifer, a long time ago, when I first met Mr. Barrett as a young girl, I use to love roses, especially red ones," Barbara revealed.

"What changed your mind?" asked Kate, who was most intrigued by Barbara's statement.

"Roses might be beautiful and attractive at first; but after a long while, their excitement dwindles down. Eventually, like us humans, they naturally grow old and their enchanting beauty and fascination soon fades away. Therefore, there must always be something more substantial, than mere beauty alone. At least with lavender, not only is it a pretty flower, but you can also use their extracts for various things, including wine making. But the same cannot also be said about roses; for they are a flower limited to primarily beauty. And so, in the end, I believe that the longer you remain in the company of roses, the more likely you'll be pricked by the needle of their infamous thorns!" shouted Barbara, as she pulled a random rose thorn from off of her dress.

"Here, please let me help you," said Kate, as she quickly rushed over to Barbara's side and helped her to remove the remaining rose thorns from off on her dress.

After all of the remaining rose thorns were completely removed, Barbara told Kate, "Eventually, these thorns do get old. That's why, contrary to popular belief, not everyone in society likes them. Furthermore, if you live as long as me my dear, then you'll realize that in the long term, people tend to choose faithfulness and stability, over something that's beautiful and unpredictable, like a rose. Do you understand what I mean, my dear?"

"Yes, I think I do," replied Kate, as she slowly realized that sometimes beautiful things are meaningless, if they aren't rooted in something that's more substantial, authentic and real. Even commonly flawed objects are more useful, than pretty and shiny museum artifacts that are untouchable and unattainable.

"Great!" exclaimed Barbara, joyfully, "Which is why, come next spring, we must revisit this garden's landscape and seek to plant safer and child-friendlier plants, in time for the arrival of my first grandchild."

Not wanting to break Barbara's hopeful heart, Kate smiled and promised, "Very well, come next spring, we'll grow some lavender, in your honor."

"Fabolous!" Barbara happily shouted, "Now, you better on hurry and speak to that gardener of yours directly. Otherwise, in your absence, that woman will persuade him to plant more roses, instead!"

"I suppose you're right, Barbara. Again, I'm truly sorry about your unfortunate accident this afternoon. And if Tabitha might have been the cause for any of your troubles, I greatly apologize in advance," said Kate.

"Not to worry, my dear. It's neither of you, nor Tabitha's fault. Unfortunately, it's because of that dreadful woman. But not to worry, I'll get my revenge. I always do. Speaking of which, after this untimely incident, I do believe that Jewel will need another bath to clean up. Naturally, I shall personally request that Gloria bathe her, once again," proclaimed Barbara, with the most devious of smiles.

After excusing herself from Barbara, Kate continued to walk straight down the garden's path and eventually, she arrived to the far end of the estate. Upon her arrival, she noticed a small white colored bungalow situated right behind a willow tree. Given that this was the only architectural building structure located around, Kate presumed that this had to be the gardener's office. However, as Kate soon approached the office, she saw that the door was wide open and neither the gardener, nor Gloria, were there.

"Gloria? Tabitha?" cried Kate. However, no one answered.

Disappointed, Kate was ready to give up on her search, when suddenly, she heard footsteps from right behind her. Quickly, she turned around and ran over to the door. As she reached the front door to the office, she noticed a gust of wind brush against a bush, located nearby. Looking out into that direction, Kate swore that she saw a shadowy figure pass right by and jump over the fence. But this was crazy, wasn't it? How could there be a shadowy figure, in the middle of the afternoon? Were her eyes playing tricks on her?

"I probably just need to eat something," Kate uttered to herself aloud.

Suddenly, out of the blue, Kate saw another shadowy figure emerge from that very same bush. However, this time around, the figure was much smaller in size and stature, and it even managed to release a very distinctive meow. As the sunlight shined across the figure, transforming it from a shadow into a being, Kate saw a little orange and yellow tabby cat emerge right in front of her. At long last, it was none other, than Tabita herself!

"Tabitha!" shouted Kate, as she quickly ran over and embraced her kitty with a huge hug; and as Kate cuddled and kissed Tabitha, the cat, in return, began to lick her owner's face.

"I've missed you so much! I'm so glad that I've finally found you!" exclaimed Kate, as she held Tabitha tightly in her arms. However, something from Tabitha's collar managed to get caught inside of Kate's hair.

"Wait, what's this?" cried Kate, as she attempted to pull the foreign object from out of her hair.

With one strong tug, Kate removed the foreign object from out from her hair. Afterwards, Kate looked at it for inspection. To her surprise, it was a small piece of paper. A note. How peculiar, she thought to herself. Out of curiosity, she opened the note and to her surprise, it was an actual letter specifically addressed to her. It read as the following:

Dear Kate,

If you want to hear the truth about your sister, then come to the side entrance of the grand bazaar, near the gold shops. Be there tonight at 6 o'clock. Come alone and tell no one. I'll reveal myself then.

Signed,

Anonymous.

Immediately, Kate dropped the letter onto the floor. She was in pure and utter shock. Someone knew the truth about her sister's disappearance and whereabouts. At long last, Kate was finally going to learn the truth. But at the same time, she needed to go alone. What was she going to do? If she told John or anyone else from the mansion, then they would stop her. She was certain of it.

As it currently stood, neither Lucas nor his security team, had any potential leads in her sister's case. What if Lucas never found her? What if this was Kate's one and only chance to save her sister? Given the circumstances, the benefits of reuniting with her twin sister again, greatly outweighed any of her looming risks. Furthermore, Kate also knew that deep down inside that if she was ever going to see and speak to sister again, then she needed to follow Anonymous' instructions to heart. Besides, the grand bazaar was a public and crowded place. Surely, she was going to safe, right?

Later That Evening…

It was almost six o'clock in the evening, and Kate was standing precisely where Anonymous had previously instructed her to be. Although there weren't any security cameras nearby, there were at least hundreds of other people surrounding her. At least this way, she wasn't entirely alone. And if she wasn't alone, then she was safe. Furthermore, if Anonymous even attempted to do anything foul to her, then there were hundreds of potential witnesses surrounding them. No matter what, Kate knew that she was going to survive this. She was going to be okay. One way or another, she was going to once again, return to the mansion and back into John's loving arms. Her beloved John. Suddenly, Kate released her breath and took a brief sigh of relief.

However, it then suddenly occurred to Kate, that she had absolutely no idea as to whom she was waiting for. Unfortunately, the letter provided no such details, nor any instructions, as to whom she was going to meet with. No description whatsoever. Just that they would find her. Based on this limited information, Kate concluded that whomever she was going to meet here tonight, they already knew who she was and how she looked like. The very thought brought shivers down Kate's spine.

Suddenly, Kate heard footsteps from the opposite side of the alley. It was directly across from where she was currently standing. Immediately, Kate looked straight ahead. However, the alley was dark, and she couldn't really see as to whether or not, someone was standing there. But then, as her eyes slowly adjusted to the darkness, she noticed a dark figure emerge from out of the shadows. As the streetlight shined across the figure, transforming it from a shadow into a being, Kate finally came face to face with Anonymous…and she was left standing in complete shock. It was as if a closed curtain had finally just been pulled wide open to expose the hidden truth.

For a long moment— a moment which felt almost like an eternity here on earth— Kate was completely lost for words. Silent and frozen, there she quietly stood. Slowly, as her mind fought against her muscles to her own body, she fought with all of her inner strength to regain her senses back again. It was an internal war, fought between her mind and her body; but luckily, Kate's mind ultimately won and so, she mustered up all of her inner and physical strength to force her mind to signal to her lips to once again, speak. As she pressed her lips down together, she used her tongue to force her words to exit through her mouth, which by now, had grown numb by pure fear.

Finally, with her hands still shaking and trembling from disbelief, she gasped aloud, "Jennifer?"

Chapter 28

Four Years Ago in Athens, Greece…

"You know Jennifer, you don't have to be the ambassador's wife anymore. We can just run away together. Leave everything behind and start over again," said Demitri, who was seated at the edge of their shared bed and staring right outside of their hotel window, with a breathtaking view overlooking the Aegean Sea.

"It's just not possible and you already knew that Demitri," replied Jennifer, as she remained lying inside of their bed, with her bare and naked body covered up with their messy white linen bedsheets.

"From the very beginning, you knew that at some point, this relationship was going to come to an end, once we started it. After all, I'm still married," she reminded him.

"But you don't love him! And you never did!" he strongly proclaimed.

"My feelings are irrelevant here. It still doesn't change the facts; and now, this needs to end. We can't meet anymore," she stated sternly.

"But why? Why does this have to end? You're happy and I'm happy; so why should we abruptly end this liaison that mutually satisfies the both of us?" he asked, desperately hoping that somehow, he could help convince her to find the means to change her mind.

"Because someone knows," she reluctantly admitted.

"And, so what!" he exclaimed. "Just come clean and tell them all the truth! Be done with it, already. Maybe then, we can freely runaway together. Just you and me."

"I just…I can't…" Jennifer softly whispered, as she turned her back towards the wall and away from him— all in an effort to help conceal her tears that she desperately sought to hide from him.

"And why not?" he pleaded, once more.

"Demitri, please don't ask me anymore! No matter how many times you try, I'm still going to give you the same exact answer," she boldly said, with a hint of anger in her voice.

"But you don't love him! Plus, you hate the mansion and the people there! They're all fake and deceitful! Jennifer, as you lay trapped inside that golden cage of yours, our lives are just passing us by, as we speak. Now is the time to cease the moment, and alter our fates. Come, let's run away together, while we still can. It's still not too late," he said, as he attempted to reach over to grab her hands.

However, Jennifer wasn't in agreement; and so, she pulled her hands away from him.

"Demitri, please stop it!" she cried. "I just can't okay, I just can't…"

"But he doesn't love you," he reminded her.

"And what, you do?" asked Jennifer, in a sarcastic and mocking manner.

However, Demitri wasn't in the mood for any sarcasm; for his intentions for her were very much sincere and true.

"Actually, yes. Jennifer, I do love you," he finally admitted.

For a few long minutes, they both remained in complete silence. By now, Demitri returned back inside of their bed and lay right behind her. However, Jennifer still remained in her same position, with her back turned away from him and facing the wall. She was still, more than ever, eager to maintain a safe distance away from him. The less she saw of him, the better off she was.

"Are you afraid?" he finally asked, as he placed his arms back around her waist, pulling her closer towards him from behind.

"Yes," she quietly admitted.

"Of what?" he asked, hoping that this might be the possible breakthrough that he so desperately had been waiting for.

However, she remained silent and unfortunately, Demitri took her silence as the ultimate deal breaker. It was truly over between them. There was no turning back, after this point. Suddenly, he abruptly got out of bed and walked over to the far corner of their room.

"It's because I'm poor, isn't it? If I had been rich and famous like him, like the ambassador…" he finally said angrily.

"That's not true," she interrupted him, ending her long period of silence.

"Yes, it is," he insisted, "Otherwise, you wouldn't have hesitated to leave him."

As he walked over towards the door, Jennifer closed her eyes shut. She knew that this was the end. In a few moments from now, he was going to exit her life for good and never to return. The reality of him leaving, suddenly hit her hard. But before he completely walked out of the door, he turned around, one last and final time.

"Jennifer, you'll come to regret this day in the future. Mark my word. Even a poor man knows that choosing money over love, will never buy your happiness. You go ahead, go ahead and live in that luxurious mansion of yours! Go ahead and live in that superficial gilded cage! Be the ambassador's wife, and watch yourself perish miserably away and eventually, die heartless and loveless!" he shouted, as he violently slammed the door shut behind him, and exiting her life forever.

After he was gone, Jennifer just lay there and cried. She cried for losing Demitri. She cried for their lost love. She cried for the future that was robbed from her. Eventually, once her tears finally dried out, she pondered as to why she didn't agree to run away with him, in the first place? She really could have. Apart from Gloria's threats, which would have ceased to have any merits had Jennifer simply told the truth; nothing else was stopping her. By now, if she wanted to divorce John, she really could have. He was already well established in his career and up until now, she played the dutiful role of the perfect wife, as she had promised him. Furthermore, they never signed a prenuptial agreement, and as a result, she could have walked away from the marriage with more than enough money. Therefore, money really wasn't a factor that prevented her from leaving. Hence, what exactly was stopping her?

Sadly, the truth was that Demitri was only partially correct. Jennifer was afraid. But she wasn't fearful about the possibility of losing her wealth or status. No, it wasn't that at all. Demitri couldn't have been more wrong. In truth, she was afraid of spreading her sleeping wings and flying off into unknown and unpredictable territory, where she would have to start all over again from scratch. Where would she go? What would she do? How would she live? What was her identity outside of the mansion? Independent from John? Beyond being the ambassador's wife? A role that she had grown into and became so accustomed to.

As much as she hated her life at the mansion, it was also the only life that she had known ever since her marriage. Although she deeply resented the gilded cage in which she resided in; she was also still, at the same time, fearful to leave it entirely all behind. For as much as she wished to live a new life, she was also equally terrified. Petrified of the unknown. What if the grass wasn't greener on the other side? What then? She still didn't yet have the full courage to entirely leave the darkness for the light, and to further venture out into the unknown to discover that answer for herself.

Meanwhile, as she remained fearful today to move forward in her life, she also knew that this fearful emotion was only temporary. One day this was going to change. One day, she was going to be strong and courageous. One day, she was going to have the strength to finally move on. One day she was going to run away from it all. Eventually, when this day came, as she predicted, she was going to be ready to finally run away and never look back, ever again.

Present Time in Istanbul, Türkiye …

"Jennifer, is that really you?" asked Kate, as she blinked her eyes a few times, in order to make sure that the image standing before her wasn't just an apparition, or her tired imagination playing tricks on her. She needed to be certain that the image standing in front of her was truly Jennifer, her twin sister, in the flesh.

"Yes, it's me," Jennifer admitted, as she fully stepped out from the dark shadows and walked directly into the bright light.

"But how's this possible? Where have you been? What happened to you?" cried Kate.

At this very moment, Kate had millions of questions racing right inside of her mind. However, before Jennifer even had the opportunity to speak, Kate quickly ran over to her sister, threw her arms around her and embraced her with an enormous hug. A hug that she thought was never going to happen, but did. It was just too good to be true!

"I've missed you so much!" Kate happily cried, with her arms tightly tugged around her beloved twin sister. "I actually thought that I was never going to see you again!"

"I've missed you too," said Jennifer, as she too, began to cry.

"There's just so much that I want to tell you, but where do I even begin?" Kate admitted.

"Perhaps, I should be the first to start," Jennifer interrupted. "But first, let's have a seat, as we really do need to talk."

Luckily, there was an empty bench nearby, so the two sisters quickly took a seat. Upon sitting, Jennifer took a brief moment to take a deep breath and collect herself. Once she was finally ready, she began to speak.

"Kate, as you might have already gathered," Jennifer began, "Tabitha's note is from me."

"Yes, I gathered, as much. But why did you do that? Why didn't you come and speak to me directly?" asked Kate, most curious as to why her sister sought her out in such a secretive manner.

"It's because I needed to meet with you alone, and as far away as possible from the mansion," replied Jennifer, cautiously.

"Jennifer, what happened to you? Did you leave on purpose? Did you plan all of this, on your own?" asked Kate, who was now gravely concerned about her sister's motives and reasons for leaving.

"Plan all of this?" remarked Jennifer, who was astonished and appalled by Kate's accusations. Her sister's assumptions about her already felt like a knife stabbing right into her heart.

"Kate, I didn't plan anything. I promise you that everything that I've done thus far, has all been reactionary. Kate, someone actually tried to kill me," Jennifer revealed.

"Kill you?" Kate gasped, in complete horror.

"Yes, kill me," Jennifer confirmed.

"But who? Who would want to kill you?" asked Kate, horrified by her sister's revelation.

Jennifer took another deep breath. She knew that the information that she was about to reveal might come as a complete shock to her sister. Regardless of her impending reaction, Jennifer knew that she still needed to tell Kate the truth, once and for all. After a long pause, Jennifer finally opened her mouth and proceeded to reveal the culprit's true identity to her sister.

"It's Lucas," she finally admitted his name aloud, underneath her breath. In fact, the mere utterance of his very name against her tongue, felt like a huge weight had already been lifted off her shoulders. At long last, the truth was now out in the open.

"Lucas?!" exclaimed Kate, whom, as Jennifer anticipated, was left shocked and appalled by this surprising news.

"But I just don't understand… he's supposed to be protecting us… he's the head of security! How…how… how did this happen? And why?" asked Kate, still frantically disturbed by this new information.

"Yes, it was him. Lucas," Jennifer confirmed, boldly. "It happened just a few weeks ago. I'm embarrassed to admit this, but he texted me…compromising pictures…of me on my private phone. Afterwards, he even went so far, as to threaten me with blackmail."

"Blackmail?" echoed Kate.

"Yes, blackmail," Jennifer repeated.

"But what information did he use to blackmail you with?" asked Kate, most concerned.

Slowly, taking another deep breath, Jennifer knew that she needed to confess the absolute truth to Kate. However, at the same time, she still felt ashamed to openly admit it. Although Jennifer might not have lived the perfect and sinless life, she still didn't want her sister to judge her for her past indiscretions. Regardless of her mistakes, Jennifer ultimately didn't want to lose her sister's love, admiration, but most importantly, her respect.

"Now, Kate, I'm not proud of my past. These past few years, I've lived a rather complicated life at the mansion…" Jennifer admitted, uneasily.

However, unbeknownst to her, Kate was already well versed about Jennifer's secrets and as a result, she acquired a more direct insight and thorough understanding into the psyche of her twin sister, more than she had ever known before; including from their own childhoods. Apart from her own personal trials, tribulations and experiences at the mansion, Kate had recently discovered and read her secret diary and by doing so, she was already well aware about her sister's private affairs. As a result, Kate sympathized with her sister's unhappy and private struggles; therefore, she didn't judge her for any of her past mistakes. Therefore, without any negative judgment, Kate generously extended her steady hands over and grabbed hold of Jennifer's trembling hands. This mere simple act of kindness touched Jennifer's heart tremendously, down to her very core.

"I know Jennifer," said Kate, as she sought to comfort her sister by maintaining her firm hold of her sister's hands, that were now gaining strength and becoming more stable.

"You do?" asked Jennifer, completely surprised by Kate's positive reaction.

Capturing this breakthrough moment, Kate decided that she, too, needed to confess everything. In addition to Jennifer's confession, Kate also needed to reveal her truth about her discovery of Jennifer's diary, and the fact, that Kate had already read and learned about everything. Everything about Jennifer's past. Her discovery of her sister's loveless marriage to John and their impending divorce. Her adversarial relationship with Gloria. Her past lovers. Her unhappiness at the mansion. And everything else in between. But above all else, Kate wanted Jennifer to understand that none of her past mistakes mattered to her. They were all buried in the past; irrelevant now, in the present. In this very moment, all that mattered to Kate was that Jennifer was still alive; safe and sound. Furthermore, Kate even grew to love and cherish her twin sister even more, for she finally understood at long last that what Jennifer desperately needed as of right now, was that of a friend. And just as Kate had offered her right hand to befriend to John, she now extended her left hand over to Jennifer.

"Jennifer," Kate began, "Before you say anything else further; I too, have something to confess to you, in return."

"You do? But why? What could you possibly have to confess to me?" asked Jennifer, confused and perplexed by Kate's statements.

Similar to her sister right before her, Kate slowly took a deep breath of her own. Once she released her breath into the air, she gently admitted,

"Jennifer, I read your diary. I know everything about your past. However, I just want you to know, that you don't have to worry about or be ashamed over anything in your past. Please just know, that as your twin sister, I love you unconditionally. I also don't judge you, either. Rather, I think I better understand you now. Having walked in your shoes these past few weeks, I think that I can understand and relate, as to how everything must have all been difficult for you these past few years."

Upon hearing Kate's confession, Jennifer's eyes immediately grew watery. Her sister's surprisingly sympathetic words comforted her tremendously. By her acceptance, Jennifer now had the courage to finally reveal the rest of her truth. After a brief and long pause, Jennifer wiped away her tears and began to tell her tale.

"Having read my diary, you must already be well aware that John and I are in the process of a divorce," she finally spoke.

Kate simply nodded in agreement; and so, Jennifer continued on with her story.

"And as such; given our impending divorce, I was seeing another man at the time. To avoid a scandal, I tried my best to keep our relationship secret and discrete. But somehow, Lucas learned about my affair and to this day, I still don't know as to how he knew. Either way, upon discovering my affair, he sent me compromising pictures of Ivan and I," she said.

"Do you still have those photographs and text messages?" asked Kate.

"Actually, yes, I still do. After that night, I just threw my phone straight into my purse and never looked at it again. I just simply couldn't. Honestly Kate, after my accident, I just left everything as it was; including my mobile phone," said Jennifer.

"Accident? What accident?" asked Kate, concerned about this new revelation.

"Well, after Lucas sent me those text messages, he threatened to release those photographs, if I didn't meet him at the grand bazaar that evening," replied Jennifer.

"Wait, did you actually go to meet him at the grand bazaar? Alone?" asked Kate, surprised that her sister went to face Lucas all by herself.

"Yes, I did. Somehow, I stupidly thought that I could just pay him off and to simply be done with it. But boy, was I wrong! Instead, not only did he *not* want any money, but he also came with a gun and even chased me down with it! He honestly pointed his gun directly at me, and then, he tried to shoot and kill me!" cried Jennifer.

"My God! That bastard!" exclaimed Kate. "How did you escape?"

"I just ran away," replied Jennifer, "Honestly, I was just so incredibly scared and frightful. But somehow in the midst of our confrontation, one way or another, I miraculously found the courage to bolt out and run. After escaping, I just continued to run and run and run and run. As fast as I could. I just kept running. Without turning my back, I ran as fast as I possibly could, down the halls of the grand bazaar. To my advantage, I had gotten pretty far away from him, too. Then, suddenly, without seeing, I managed to run to the edge of a darkened staircase, where I fell down four flights of stairs, landing straight into a dark pit. After my fall, I was surrounded by nothing but pure darkness."

"Oh my God!" Kate gasped. "Jennifer, how did you survive?"

"Believe it or not, but it was the darkness that saved me," replied Jennifer. "Since I was lying down in the bottom of that dark pit, Lucas couldn't see me; therefore, he couldn't find me. Eventually, out of frustration, he must have left the bazaar."

"What do you mean that he must have left? Are you not certain?" asked Kate.

"I can only presume, as I was unconscious at the time," Jennifer revealed. "Unfortunately, due to my injuries, I didn't awake from my fall, until the following morning. One moment, I saw nothing but darkness and the next moment, there was light. Eventually, when I finally awoke, I found myself lying face down on the bottom of a dusty cold floor, with the bright and beaming sun shining across my bruised face, while the rest of my body was adjusting to the excruciating pain that was piercing throughout my muscles and across my entire being. From head to toe, I was covered in blood, along with black and blue bruises. Considering how badly I fell, I still managed to survive my fall with minimal injuries. Apart from a few major bruises and scratches here and there, I made it out with only a twist to my right ankle, that has since healed."

"Did someone eventually find you?" asked Kate, anticipating her sister's response.

"Sort of," replied Jennifer; she continued, "Right before I went to the grand bazaar to confront Lucas, I bumped into Selim Yildiz, the hotel owner of Istanbul's Four Seasons Sultanahmet, in the hotel lobby. Upon bumping into him, Selim personally gave me his business card. Since I discreetly traveled that day with my private mobile phone, I didn't have any other telephone numbers saved inside of my phone to call. In a twist of fate, the only telephone number that I had in my possession was Selim's number that was listed on the front of his business card. And so, I took a chance and dialed his number. And to my even greater surprise, he actually came to my rescue."

"But you could have also called the police, too," Kate reminded her.

"Kate, that wasn't a likely option. If I had contacted the police, who would have believed me? Lucas is the owner and CEO of a major international security firm. He's adored by many in our community, including high ranking officials and other important people at the embassy and mansion. And they in return, are loyal to him. Meanwhile, I was the unpopular and soon-to-be former wife of an ambassador, who had disappeared that afternoon to meet with her secret lover. No, it was his word against mine. I know for a fact, without a shadow of doubt, that Lucas would have denied everything. If I had returned, then one way or another, he would have still leaked my pictures out into the public domain; thereby, destroying my good name and reputation. And eventually, it would only be just a matter of time, before he killed me, once and for all. After all, I saw his face, and I know what he's really capable of," Jennifer explained.

"What happened after Selim came?" asked Kate, wanting to learn more about Jennifer's rescue and recovery efforts.

"Without any questions, Selim came to my rescue. Within minutes of me calling him, he arrived to the scene in no time and got me out of the darkness. Then, slowly, he nursed me back to health, while I remained safely hidden inside the comfort of his luxury hotel. Ever since he rescued me, I've been staying there; hidden away, all this time," she said.

"Wait, you've been in Istanbul this whole time?" asked Kate, surprised by this shocking revelation.

"Yes," replied Jennifer, "I've been here in Istanbul, but under Selim's protection. Honestly Kate, he's simply wonderful! A real-life hero! A gentleman. He knows everything about my past and yet he, just like you, doesn't judge me for it. He's a good man and…" she began to trail off.

"And?" asked Kate.

Taking a brief pause, Jennifer slowly admitted, "Kate, I love him. With all of my heart. Truly and madly! But most importantly, he loves me, too. Selim loves me for me and asks for nothing, in return. He's everything that I could have ever wished or hoped for. But most importantly, I know that one day, Selim will make an excellent father to my future children."

Upon hearing Jennifer's joyful admission, Kate just lovingly smiled at her sister. After everything that Jennifer suffered these past few years, she deserved her happy ending. If Selim was the source of Jennifer's blissful happiness, then Kate was absolutely thrilled for her sister's new future.

"Jennifer, I'm happy for you," said Kate, as she reached over and gave her sister another emotional and heartful hug. Slowly, Kate pulled herself away and asked, "What happens next?"

"We intend to marry. Honestly Kate, the truth is that if it wasn't for you, then I wasn't going to ever come out from hiding," Jennifer reluctantly admitted.

"Wait, just like that, you were just going to run away and not tell anyone the truth? Why would you even do that?" asked Kate, who was disappointed by her sister's neglectful admission.

"Sadly, yes," replied Jennifer, truthfully. "Kate, I know that at first, this might sound rather difficult for you to fully comprehend. However, after years of dreaming about and yearning to run away, I finally found the opportunity to do so, and I didn't even have to try. I didn't even have to take the first steps. All I had to do was fall down a flight of stairs, in order to escape and run away from it all."

"Jennifer, you can't honestly mean that, can you?" asked Kate, with a concerned expression painted across her face.

"But I do," said Jennifer, boldly. "But before I say anything else, there's one more thing that I must admit to you."

"What's that?" asked Kate, most curious as to what exactly Jennifer wanted to admit to her.

"While I was missing, I convinced Selim's chauffer to secretly drive by the mansion. I just needed to see it in-person one last time, before I completely disappeared for good. But then to my surprise, I saw you there, standing outside in the garden from afar," Jennifer shyly admitted.

"You saw me?" Kate gasped.

"Yes, I saw you. From outside of Selim's limousine window, I saw you there outside, from the behind. You were in the rose garden, along with John and the others. Without even seeing your face, I already knew that it was you, too. I could just feel it. For only you, my twin sister, could resemble me so much— even from the behind. For a brief minute, I watched and saw how you interacted with them, and they with you. And to my surprise, I even saw John actually smiling and it appeared genuine, too. After all these turbulent years, this was the first time that I ever saw him truly look happy. Without even trying, you just seem to get along with them all so well, and they with you, in return. You just simply fit into their complicated world, better than I ever could. It's as if you were born for this part. A missing piece to their jigsaw puzzle. Playing the part of the ambassador's wife, just comes so natural to you. And somehow in that moment, I realized that my twin sister not only switched lives with me, but that she was far better at being me, than I was of being myself," Jennifer admitted.

"That's not true," Kate interrupted, in a harsh tone and manner. "I'm not better at being you. You're Jennifer and I'm Kate. Always have and always will. We're two peas in the same pod. I've only been posing as you as a diversion, in order to save you from a public scandal!"

"Kate, I know. You don't need to explain anything else. I'm well aware as to your reasons for doing what you did, and I thank you for it. From the bottom of my heart. You've always been such a wonderful sister to me. Always selfless, loyal and brave. And because of this, I ultimately decided that somehow, one way or another, I needed to come and see you, one last time," Jennifer revealed.

"But Jennifer, you don't have to leave abruptly like this," cried Kate.

Refusing to bid her sister a final farewell, an idea suddenly came to Kate's mind.

"Wait, Jennifer, can I take a look at Lucas' previous text messages to you?" asked Kate.

Suddenly, Jennifer grew red from embarrassment. She hadn't expected Kate to ever ask to see them. Given the private and personal nature of the photographs, Jennifer shivered at the very thought of sharing them with another person, let alone her sister.

"Jennifer, please, you don't need to feel shy or nervous about sharing this with me. I'm here to help you, that's all," Kate gently reassured her.

Comforted by her words, Jennifer decided to accept her sister's assistance. Reaching into her purse, she pulled out her mobile phone. Immediately, Jennifer navigated to her previous received text messages, opened them and then handed her phone over to Kate. Upon receiving the mobile phone, Kate took one look at the photographs and gasped.

"Jennifer!" she exclaimed, "I recognize this man!"

"What?" asked a stunned Jennifer, who suddenly grew extremely confused and bewildered, as to why her sister apparently recognized the same man in her photograph: Ivan, her former lover.

"Are you certain?" asked Jennifer, again.

"Yes, I do. I recognize this man. I've seen him twice, before," Kate confidently confirmed.

"You recognize Ivan? My former lover?" asked Jennifer, with a raised brow.

"Yes, he's the same man, whom I saw in Kars! He's the person, who attempted to kill John at the slopes! He's part of the Belarusian mafia!" exclaimed Kate.

"My God, Kate; this is really shocking news! I had absolutely no idea," Jennifer gasped.

Unfortunately, for Jennifer, she mistakenly presumed that she was going to be the deliverer to reveal all of tonight's shocking secrets; but in an alternative twist of fate, as it turns out, she was the unexpected receiver for an even far greater surprise, in return.

For a brief moment, Kate pondered about their troubling circumstances. As it currently stood, Lucas, their Chief Security Officer at the embassy, was not only a confirmed criminal who blackmailed her sister, but he also tried to kill her, too. Meanwhile, Ivan, her sister's lover, was also the very same man, who recently attempted to assassinate John back in Kars. Furthermore, Miles and the local Turkish police also confirmed that Ivan was an active member of the Belarusian mafia. Suddenly, Kate self-questioned Lucas' true reason for his absence on attending their Kars trip. Although he claimed that he was away attending a new business venture in New York, was this in fact, true? Did Lucas really send a substitute escort in his place, as a scapegoat? And if this was all true, then what was Lucas' motives? Why did he seek to hurt Jennifer, in the first place? If his motives didn't involve money, then what was he after? And apart from Lucas, there was also the mystery concerning Ivan. Why did Ivan want to kill John? Was Ivan jealous that John was the soon-to-be-ex-husband to his former lover? Did Ivan and Lucas know each other? Where these two presumed isolated events, actually all interconnected?

After a long period of silence, Kate finally asked, "Jennifer, did Lucas ever say to you, as to his reasons for blackmailing you with these pictures?"

"No," she quickly replied, "He never did reveal his motive. But like I said before, on that night, he did confirm that it had nothing to do with the money."

"This just doesn't make any sense," said Kate, out of frustration. "Why would a man, like Lucas, aim to blackmail you, if it wasn't for the money?"

"Kate, I honestly have no idea. But now, there's the other issue concerning Ivan. I honestly had no idea that he was even capable of committing murder. If I had known before, then I would never have gotten involved with him, in the first place," reflected Jennifer.

"Jennifer, I realize that this might be a long shot, but do you think that it's possible that perhaps, Lucas and Ivan have been working together as partners, all of this time? I mean, in order for Lucas to obtain these photographs, someone had to tell him your location at the time. Given how secretive and careful you were that day, Ivan was the only other person who knew about your precise location that day, as he was there personally with you," Kate proposed.

"That's very true. However, at the same time, Lucas is also in charge of our technology unit at the embassy, so it's possible that he might have hacked into my private mobile phone and tracked me down. But apart from this, we also have this whole added mafia factor now, and I have absolutely no idea as to how this all plays out for us all, in the end. But whatever it is, we're in serious danger," Jennifer concluded.

"Well, for starters, we need to force Lucas to confess about his crimes, and thereby, use his confession as the means to set the records straight," Kate finally deduced. "He simply can't get away with what he's done. I refuse to accept this. Even though Ivan might already be rotting away in jail, Lucas still roams outside as a free man; while you remain in hiding and I continue to masquerade as you."

"Kate, I just can't face him again!" yelled Jennifer, "Honestly, all I wanted to do tonight was to just come and say my final farewells to you, before I run away to start my brand-new life with Selim. I don't want any trouble; I just want my happy ending!"

"Jennifer, are you honestly serious about running away in a time like this?" asked Kate, who was, at this very moment, greatly disappointed in her sister's selfish act of abandoning her in their mutual moment of crisis.

Without saying another word, Kate took Jennifer's silence as an admission of guilt.

Suddenly, Kate, succumbed by her emotions, said, "After knowing all of what Lucas is capable of, are you really going to leave me behind? To remain alone, inside the same mansion as him, while I continue this charade as acting as you? To carry on as before, as if tonight never happened? Are you truly this selfish? What about me? I'm I suppose to give up my life permanently to pretend to live yours? For what, the next month? Or two? Or a year? Or twenty years? Or forever? And what about John? Or Sally, Carol, Bes, Tyler and even, Gloria? What about everyone else at the embassy and the mansion? What about our safety? Jennifer, we're dealing with a mad man! And now, more than ever, we're in extreme danger! You confirmed this much, here tonight. And it's only a matter of time, before Lucas puts two and two together, and figures out that we met each other and that now, I know the truth. Do you really not care about us? I mean, John came so close to dying. I…I…I…almost lost him that night…."

Out of extreme frustration, Kate finally broke down into violent tears. As she collapsed down onto the bench, she just cried her heart out. Alas, she was now scared and worried. But most of all, she was disappointed in her sister. Disappointed in the reality that unlike Kate's sacrifice to her; Jennifer, in return, preferred saving her own skin, rather than staying behind and helping Kate in her time of need.

With a guilty conscience, Jennifer reached over to grab hold of Kate's hand; but she was too late, for Kate abruptly pulled it away, as she turned her back away from her. Although Jennifer knew that she was in the wrong, she also just didn't know how to face it all, again. After years of waiting, at long last, she had finally escaped away from her gilded cage; but now, her twin sister, her own flesh and blood, wanted her to actually return back to it. But, having finally tasted the sweet flavor of freedom, how could she ever return again and this time, willingly, too?

"Kate, you must know that I love you very much," she began, "But how can I ever return back there? How can I face it all, once more? After being so unhappy for so long, I just don't want to relive it all, for a second time. How can I face them all alone, again?"

"But this time, you won't be alone! It won't be like how it was the last time.

Unlike before, now you've got me to help fight your battles, by your side. Jennifer, I promise you, we'll defeat him, together," Kate vowed, as she now ceased crying and returned back to her old courageous and strong self.

"Together?" asked Jennifer, with a smile. It had been so long, since she had someone on her side. But more than that, she was proud that her sister was ready to stand up and kick Lucas, straight from the behind!

"Listen, Jennifer, these past few years, I know that I've neglected you. Unfortunately, I focused too much on my career, that sadly, I ignored fostering our relationship together. Honestly, I shouldn't have waited this long to see you. I should have visited you much sooner. Maybe, even attended one of your state dinners and parties. This way, you could have shared some of your burdens with me; instead of solely relaying and confiding into your diary, alone," Kate admitted.

"Kate, it's not your fault," Jennifer promptly interrupted, "One way or another, I chose this life. My life. Just as you chose yours. Don't ever apologize to me or anyone else for it, too. You have a right to live your life, however you so choose to live it. Regret free. Judgment free. If having your successful career is what you desired, then my dear sister, you've earned it. Rightfully so, too. You've worked so hard. Please, don't ever apologize to me for anything; because the truth is, it is I, that should be apologizing to you. It was never my intention to inadvertently pull you into my mess. Can you please forgive me?"

Touched by her sister's sincere apology, Kate replied, with a smile, "That all depends. Can you forgive me too, in return?"

"Of course," replied Jennifer, as the two sisters leaned in and gave each other another warm hug.

"My goodness Kate, you really do care about him, don't you?" asked Jennifer, as she finally pulled away from Kate.

"Care for whom?" asked Kate, innocently; not in all the least, aware as to precisely 'whom' her sister was referring to.

"Oh, I think you very well know, as to 'whom' I'm referring, too. Did your heart skip a beat for him?" asked Jennifer, who then elbowed her sister on her side.

Suddenly, Kate's heart plummeted to the floor; for she realized that her sister was referencing John.

"Jennifer!" exclaimed Kate, nervously. "Now's not the time to discuss this…"

"Actually, now's the perfect time to discuss this. If Lucas somehow manages to kill us all tomorrow, then I want to know today as to whether or not you truly found love, before either one of us dies next!" exclaimed Jennifer.

"Jennifer! What a terrible thing to say! Plus, I just don't know how to even begin to discuss my relationship with John to you…" replied Kate, who suddenly felt extremely shy about discussing her newfound romance with her sister.

"Listen Kate, you're my sister and no matter what, I love you. Besides, John and I are practically divorced. In truth, our marriage functioned more as a paper marriage of convivence, rather than anything else romantically. Come to think of it, we've been living separate lives, all the way back from the very beginning. Either way, I've always said that he's a good man. I still stand by that. But most importantly, if he's good to you, then I'm equally happy for you both," Jennifer happily admitted.

"He is and I do love him," replied Kate and then, she further admitted, "I love him very much. But can I ask you a question? Something that has been bothering me, for quite some time now."

"Yes, of course you can ask. What is it?" asked Jennifer, curiously.

"Why did you give me the pearl ring? I understand that it was originally gifted to you from John on your wedding day. Why did you decide to give it to me?" asked Kate.

"Well, this is a hard one. After coming here and meeting with John in-person, I can understand as to why you'd ask me this question, too. Well, I suppose from the very beginning, I just knew in my heart that somehow, this ring belonged to you. Pearls for Kate, as I always said, ever since we were children. Anyways, the pearl ring never fit me properly, not even on my wedding day. No matter how much I tried, that ring just didn't work out for me. It simply couldn't work out. Since day one, that ring just never felt right to me. It was as if the pearl ring and I were a complete mismatch. Looking back at it all, it probably was an omen that foreshadowed my marriage. That John and I were a misfit; but you and him aren't. I know that this all might sound silly to you, but I just knew that the ring was yours. I can't really explain it; but somewhere in the back of my mind, I just knew that only you, and you alone, would know how to care for it best. Better than I, ever could. One way or another, the ring just found its way to you, as if it was always meant for you; using me as a vessel for its safe passage to get to you. But now, as I stare and admire it around your lovely finger, I'm confident that I've made the correct decision to gift it to you all those years ago, because that ring never once sparkled on me, as much as it does on you," Jennifer explained.

For a brief moment, Kate also stared and admired her beloved pearl ring. Indeed, Jennifer was correct. Even in the darkest of nights, the opal color from the pearl, along with the sapphire blue diamonds, still found a way to sparkle and shine against the moonlight. The ring's glow and brightness knew no boundaries. At long last, Kate finally acknowledged to herself that she and the ring were really meant to be; just as Jennifer had said before. Somehow, fate found its way to intervene in her life, and because of it, she now appreciated her ring even more, than she had ever done so, before.

Watching her sister, Jennifer smiled and said, "You know, I've always wondered, as to whom he was ultimately going to end up with one day. But now, I've realized that I've should have known that you two were the perfect match for each other, all along. You're both just so similar. If only you had gone to my wedding reception, all those years ago. Maybe, if he had met you first back then, then he'd have married you instead, all the way from the very beginning. In either case…"

"My heart did skip a beat, just so you know," Kate suddenly interrupted. "And many times, too," she added.

"Well! Then, he's truly the one for you!" exclaimed Jennifer, happily. "Wasn't I right, when I told you all those years ago on our prom night, that it was going to happen for you too, one day?"

"Yes, you were right," admitted Kate.

As the sisters sat on the bench, they both reflected about tonight's turn of events. After all, this evening was filled with various unexpected revelations, truths, emotions and challenges. But no matter the circumstances, after tonight, Kate and Jennifer both knew that they now had each other to rely on, moving forward.

"What are we going to do about Lucas?" asked Jennifer, finally.

"Does this mean that you're planning to stay?" asked Kate, in return, and with a raised brow.

"Yes, for the time being," Jennifer reluctantly admitted. "But what are we going to do? How can we defeat him?"

In all seriousness, Kate pondered about Jennifer's question. How were they going to defeat him? Suddenly, the most brilliant of ideas came to her mind.

"Well Jennifer," began Kate, with a devious smile, "Since I've been posing as you all this time, I think that it's only fair that you start to do the same now too, don't you think?"

Intrigued by her suggestion, Jennifer grinned a devious smile of her own in return, as she happily agreed to Kate's proposal. After all that they had witnessed and experienced together, Jennifer already well knew that whatever plan Kate had concocted within her own brilliant mind, then it most certainly was going to be a page turner and now, Lucas wasn't going to stand a chance against the likes of them!

Chapter 29

With one single touch, Kate tumbled right into John's trusting and sturdy arms. As she gently collided against his bare skin, she closed her eyes to fully embrace and enjoy this blissful moment. He, of course, had recently returned home to the mansion, after a long period of absence. After his travels to the capital, John was most eager to reconvene their passionate love affair, that first began with a lingering kiss back in Kars. Ah, yes, their first time together was a memorable and passionate night of lovemaking, that neither one of them could cease to forget. Ever since that fateful and momentous night, he longed for more. He yearned for their reunion.

It had only been an hour since John's arrival to the mansion, when he soon found himself again in the company of Kate's presence. Had it been a spontaneous coincidence, that he just-so-happened to bump into her, while visiting the library at this particular hour? A mere coincidence; nay, a pure happenstance, that he magically appeared in the very same room as her? At that exact same moment, which coincided with her arrival? Precisely at three o'clock in the afternoon, sharp on the dot? Not a second sooner, nor a second later? This identical time of the day, in which Kate was known to have regularly visited the library, at this particular hour?

Ever since her initial arrival to the mansion, John watched and observed her, as she retreated into the library at precisely three o'clock in the afternoon daily, without fail. Out of curiosity, he often pondered as to why she routinely wandered off into the library, at this particular hour of the day. It wasn't until he finally asked her directly as to why she did that, that she confided in him that her three o'clock tea and book read routine was one of her regular pastimes and habits from her previous life as a history professor that she simply couldn't give up—not even while undercover. It was that mere sense of her honesty, that kept him ever intrigued by her. Unlike everyone else in his life, Kate was truly the only real genuine and honest person in all of his entire acquaintances. Even his own mother was guilty with her occasional tall tales and white lies, from time to time. And so, he continued to study her from afar, while remaining ever fascinated by her every breath and movement.

In truth, he was always watching her. Observing her. Studying her. Learning about her. All the while, growing more and more fascinated by her, with each passing minute. Whether it was an accidental glance of her from across the room, or a glimpse of her reflection projected into the mirror or cast upon a moving object, even for a brief fraction of a mere second, he never ceased to miss it for his eyes constantly remained affixed upon her. John, himself, failed to understand how this was even possible to begin with. How was it, that somehow, he always knew when she was around him? It was almost as if, he could sense her. Feel her around his vicinity. But most surprising of all, the more he watched her, the more he came to adore her. Ah, yes, the more he stared directly at her, the more he desired her. And when he managed to close his eyes to think about her, the more he yearned for her. Now, after weeks of longing and dreaming about her, she was finally standing before him, in-person and in the flesh. For a split second, he actually blinked; feeling fearful this image of her was nothing more than a false mirage and that he was still asleep in his bed and dreaming of her. But atlas, thankfully, he was wrong. Indeed, she was real. Standing across from him in the library, John wanted nothing more than to completely consume and devour her, right there and then.

Much to his surprise, it seemed like that she too, felt the same desire and lust, just as him. With one prolonged stare, absent of the battering of an eyelash nor the utterance of a single word, she immediately ran directly towards him and threw herself straight into his arms— all the while, in the process, abandoning her half-sipped cup of tea and opened book back at the reading table. Grabbing hold of her waist, he tightly pulled her towards him, as he bent down and gave her a kiss. With one kiss, it soon blossomed into more. He kissed her with such intensity, it was similar to that of a blazing fire that burned straight across from the source of his own lips.

Over these past few weeks and counting, his feelings for her had progressively grown and evolved with such accelerated intensity, that even he, failed to recognize his own reclusive and lonesome self. Ever since their first encounter, it felt as if an unknown spark hidden deep away inside of him, spontaneously ignited into a flickering flame. As John came to imagine, his feelings for her were equivalent to that of a newly lit candle, whose burning wick progressively grew within the fire; a fire, that eventually would come to consume and destroy both itself and its own source, leaving the candle to nothing more than melted traces of wax scattered about. And just like the candle, John's passions for her were born from that same flame; with a fire that had since spread across his whole being, engulfing his entire heart in the process, and leaving him destined to perish, following the same destiny as the candle before him.

Meanwhile, Kate, in return, reciprocated his kisses, with an equal amount of pleasure and desire on her part. After their lips sealed their combined fates together, John carefully lifted her body off the floor and straight into his hungry arms, while he carried her across the other side of room. Upon arriving to a strong and sturdy oak wood library desk, located right in the center of the room and directly across the bookshelves, John eagerly pushed through the various collections and volumes of old library books stacked above the table onto the floor. As the pages of Plato, Homer, Aristotle, Shakespeare and Darwin all came crashing loudly down onto the hardwood floor, John gently placed Kate above the table and began to undress himself in front of her.

To his sheer delight, while he undressed, she also moved to remove her clothes, as well. Her act of uniformity brought an unexpected smile across his face. Kate's mere excitement and eagerness to join him in their upcoming lovemaking session, was the proof that he needed, in both his mind and heart, that even without any spoken words, he knew that she cared for him, too.

After removing his last remaining article of clothing, John was now standing there in front of her, stark naked and ready to claim her. Without waiting for her to even finish, he abruptly moved over to her side and quickly helped her pull off the rest of her clothes. After removing her bra and underwear completely, he gently leaned her down across the table, as he climbed above to join her. Once she was comfortably positioned near him, he slowly placed his warm body over hers, as he covered her small, fragile and soft body, underneath his strong, hard and muscular figure.

As she lay there underneath him, John passionately kissed her, while he stroked and smelled her thick and luscious hair. Oh, how lovely she smelled, he thought! To his amazement, Kate smelled of the sweetest and most intoxicating of scents! Oh, how he adored her scent! She smelled just like a freshly cut bouquet of roses, with a hint of honey and lavender, along with a dash of freshly picked grapes— a similar scent, that brought him back to his very own childhood in Napa Valley. By far, Kate was the sweetest and tastiest of all the world's perfumes and wines, all put together in one. But best of all, at this very moment, she was his. All of her. Every single last inch.

Moving his lips across her lips and down towards her neck, Kate gently pushed her head aside, giving her neck freely to him to explore. Slowly, his hands moved along her soft, shiny and silky hair, and towards the center of her breasts, where he began to softly caress them within the palm of his hands. Ever-so-slowly, he moved to lick and suck her breast, one nipple at a time. At first, he was gentle; and then, the more he sucked, the more he wanted her. While his lips focused on her breasts, his hands moved down to explore and play with her tiny waist; eventually, making its way down to her buttocks, as he pulled her further towards him. As his hands glided across into the inner corners of her wet and moist thighs, she released an unexpected and innocent squeal. Her sudden reaction excited him so much that he too, in return, moaned and groaned like a wild beast! With his entire body now fully engulfed above her, he pulled her another inch closer to him.

Unexpectedly, as his hands caressed with hers, he suddenly felt something tug against him. Looking down, he saw that it was the pearl ring. The very same pearl ring that he had mistakenly thought was once lost, but somehow, miraculous found its way back to him. Staring directly at her beautiful face, he smiled. Kate's face was the sweetest, kindest and most angelic face that he had ever laid his eyes upon before. She was everything that was good and wonderful in this world; all warped into one singular being. As he continued to stare at her, much to his dismay, he noticed that her eyes were shut closed.

"Please open your eyes," he commanded, with a sense of desperation and agony within his voice.

"What?" she asked, surprised by his request.

"Open them. I want you to see me. The real me," he desperately pleaded.

Upon his command, she opened her eyes and saw that before her was a man, in desperate need of her immediate attention and approval. How lonely he must have been all these years living in solitude, she thought to herself. After years of being in the spotlight, where he was forced to act and play a part that wasn't him at all, inside the ruthless environment of the political arena, Kate realized that now, in the comfort of his own private life, John wanted her to see him as he really was. She understood that after everything they went through, he wanted them to bond over their lovemaking experience together, in their truest and most authentic form. Somehow, the need for her to see him, the real him, mattered and became important to him. As it was, he was extremely vulnerable and needy. But now, unlike before, she was here for him and wasn't about to leave; she had no intention of it. Suddenly, at that exact moment, Kate felt a desperate urge to convey that very message to him, too.

"John, I'm not going anywhere. I'm here to stay," she said.

"You promise?" he asked, with a look of desperation within his watery eyes.

For a long moment, she stared at him. Looking straight into those deep blue-green eyes of his. For all his worth, he was the sweetest and kindest of lovers. He was everything that she had ever dreamt about in a man. Even in her wildest of dreams, she couldn't have imagined him. He was perfect in every possible way. A modern Prince Charming. Even though Kate was already well aware that she loved him; it was here, at this very moment in time, that she understood that her feelings for him exceeded far above love. It was beyond that. Suddenly, Kate realized that

John was her everything. Her friend. Her mate. Her soul. He was, in every right, her entire world wrapped up into one singular being. He was her very own breath of life.

"Yes, I promise," she replied, with a twinkle in her eye.

Her heartfelt promise brought tremendous joy to his heart. Upon uttering those very words, he smiled, as he quickly parted her thighs further apart and slowly brought himself closer to her. With her legs tightly wrapped around him, Kate grabbed hold of his chest and pulled him closer to her. Now, at last, she was ready to surrender to him, once and for all. And he noticed it, too. Therefore, with one swift swoosh, he accepted her offering, as he entered inside of her completely. As he pushed his way in and penetrated back and forth with her, Kate released a large moan of pleasure. This was ecstasy, in its finest form!

Hours later, after their extended lovemaking marathon concluded, John fell fast asleep above a warm woolen carpet, located right above the floor. As he soundlessly lay and slept besides her, Kate held him tightly within her arms, as she slowly stroked and caressed his dark and luscious hair with her fingers. Once his hair was parted aside, she bent down and gently placed a small kiss across his forehead. As he peacefully slept, she quietly pondered about what lied ahead of them. Could they really have a future together? Was this prospect really possible? Was Kate going to be able to keep her promise to him? Her promise of never leaving his side?

Just a day ago, this prospect seemed likely. However, ever since Jennifer's reappearance, Kate began to experience her own self-doubts and as a result, was now uncertain about the statuses of everything. Was this going to be the last time that she was ever going to be intimate with John? The last time that she would lay together with him, inside of his loving and caring arms? After tomorrow night, were things ever going to remain the same, just as they were before? Or, were they all going to part ways, with each of them returning back to their old and normal lives? But after everything, what exactly was normal, now? Did normal mean having Kate living back in New York alone, or remaining here in Istanbul with him? Were they destined to finally have their happy ending by remaining happily together, in their current blissful state?

Suddenly, Kate began to weep. After tomorrow night, Kate knew that she was going to finally have an answer to her questions. However, the reality of what was about to come next simply terrified her; for if it was going to be a negative outcome, then Kate simply wasn't yet ready to face it. She couldn't. She didn't have the strength. After all these years of waiting, Kate had finally found the love of her life. But now, as she lay within his arms, she realized that he was ever-so-slowly, slipping away from her very fingers. What was she to do? How could she prevent the inevitable?

Quietly, she continued to lay there and silently weep, as she desperately held onto him as tightly as she possibly could; as if she were holding onto dear life. Deep down inside her own fragile heart, Kate knew that this was most likely, going to be the very last time that they were going to be together. Therefore, as John quietly and peaceful slept in her arms, unbeknown to him as to what was about to happen next, Kate leaned down and quietly whispered into his ear:

"John, I love you."

Even though he failed to hear her confession, she still said it anyways; for she desperately wanted her heart's desires spoken into existence. In Kate's mind, she believed whole heartly that if she proclaimed her silent wish out into the universe, then perhaps, there remained the slight possibility that it could still come true. Wiping her last batch of tears away from her eyes, she turned and rolled away from him. As she moved over to her side, her dry eyes quickly noticed the peculiar title to one of the fallen books on the floor. It was Sun Tzu's *The Art of War*. How ironic that out of all of the various books within this vast collection of this library, that the one book to have fallen right beside her was none other than *The Art of War*. It was both an inspiration and a forecast, as to what was about to happen next.

"It's time," she said, with conviction.

Chapter 30

"Dr. Kate Stanley?" asked the guard, as he reviewed and read the name, as listed on the photo identification card, which he currently held in his hand.

"Yes, that's correct. That's my name. Dr. Kate Stanley, just as it's written down," replied Jennifer, confidently.

"Dr. Kate Stanley," repeated the guard, twice more, "I thought that only diplomats were invited to these formal events?"

"Sir," began Jennifer, "If you review the list again, you will clearly see that my name is listed there, as one of the invited attendees. And to answer your question, yes, non-diplomats can be invited to these formal state dinner events, too."

Once more, the guard reviewed his guests' list again and sure enough, the name listed as Dr. Kate Stanley was indeed published there, listed in plain sight.

"Your name is here," replied the guard, in amazement. "But how does a doctor get invited to a NATO summit? Shouldn't you be at a medical conference, instead?"

Alas, Jennifer was growing impatient. Tonight, time was of the essence; and as of now, her precious time was being wasted right outside here, debating with this extremely talkative, yet insufferably annoying guard. Oh, why couldn't she have conversed with another lame and mute guard, instead?

"I'm not a medical doctor," she replied coldly. "I'm a history professor, and I've been personally selected and invited to this summit, as an honored and registered guest."

"A professor? Really?" asked the guard, most curious about her background.

By now, Jennifer was simply lost for words. According to Kate's precise instructions, she should have been long ago admitted inside and already seated at her table. But instead, Jennifer was far behind in their plans and unfortunately, she was still attempting to execute phase one of their secret operation. Really, this was too much!

"My sister is the American Ambassador's wife, and I've been invited as their special guest," said Jennifer, in an effort to change the subject.

However, her desperate attempts on changing the subject, only created more questions.

"A sister? I didn't know that there was a sister," remarked the guard.

But his remarks only further frustrated Jennifer. And so, rather than continuing on with her charade as being nice and polite; Jennifer decided that now, she needed to revert to her regular old sassy and bold self, and to be more direct and firmer with him.

"Just so you know, I'm always invited to these special events through an open invitation. Although I seldom and rarely attend these parties, this time around, I finally took the liberty to come. As you can see from my identification card, I've traveled all the way from New York City just to come here. Now, may I please proceed to enter?" Jennifer finally asked, in a rather assertive and demanding tone.

"I see, how very interesting," replied the guard, with a raised brow.

Taking one last glance at her photograph on her identification card, he said, "A sister to the ambassador's wife. A professor. Not a medical doctor."

Suddenly, he laughed and finally remarked, "It's not every day that a New Yorker—"

"Sir," interrupted Jennifer, at long last. "As I said before, my name is Dr. Kate Stanley. I'm the sister to the ambassador's wife and a guest to this party. As I've said before, since my name, as listed on my identification card matches your guests' list, I ask that I be let in, now."

"Very well, hold your horses," replied the guard, "There's no need to get angry. You can come in, now."

At long last, the guard finally opened the entrance gate. Within seconds, Jennifer hastily walked right through it and returned back to the old world that she previously left behind. At first glance, Jennifer was immediately enchanted by the beautiful scenery before her and was simply lost for words. With one glimpse into the mansion, her breath was taken away by the spectacular glitz and glamour that shined and sparkled in front of her. Even though over the years, Jennifer had hosted countless amounts of parties here at this very same mansion; somehow, this time around, as a new guest, it was as if she had briefly stepped away, only to return to a brand new and hidden world that she had never once seen or even knew existed before her time. Truly, this particular party was different. It was by far, remarkable. Unlike previous events, this year's state dinner really went well above and beyond, and Jennifer couldn't help but notice this. By far, this party had exceeded all of Jennifer's previous expectations and standards.

Glancing at the room, Jennifer admired the shining gold décor that sparkled across the entire estate. From the silk curtains to the linen tablecloths, to the ladies own evening gowns, everything in near sight sparkled and glimmered against the bright crystal chandeliers. But if that wasn't enough to capture one's attention, then the mansion's endless supplies of floral garlands of rose bouquets were certainly eye catching. Adorned with every possible shade, ranging from lilac to blush, and coral to crimson, roses surrounded the party from each and every corner. Furthermore, as Jennifer leaned against the entrance balcony, overlooking the ballroom, she was left standing amazed at the magical and fairytale-like-environment taking place in front of her. Plucked right out of a storybook, the ballroom was decorated fit for a queen. All the walls were pristine white, the carpets sparkling in red and even the silverware across the table sparkled and shined. In all of her years, this truly was the first party that had ever left such an impressionable and positive opinion upon her.

"The staff truly outdid themselves this year," she quietly whispered aloud to herself, in amazement.

Searching across the ballroom once more, Jennifer attempted to capture a rare glimpse at all the current attendees inside of the room. As she glanced directly across from her, she recognized a few familiar faces. Of course, they were none other than the infamous French and Brazilian Ambassadors and their wives. Although this was technically a NATO summit, the party's generous invitations also extended over to other countries, who were not necessarily all NATO members, but were at the very least, on friendly terms with the United States. Thus, countries like Brazil and India, were amongst those nations in attendance.

As was the similar case just like before, the French and Brazilian Ambassadors, along with their wives, appeared to be mingling about and conversing with their respective peers in the busy crowd down below and over inside of the ballroom. Naturally, Jennifer presumed that they were all probably engaged in yet another lame and boring discussion about the weather— a conversation that she most certainly didn't miss. Not at all, in the very least. Slowly, as Jennifer continued to watch from afar, a faint but genuine smile formed on the outer corners of her mouth. Never in a million years, did she ever think that she would return back here again… and yet, here she was; but under very different circumstances. This time around, she returned as a guest and not as the hostess; and as a result, it was rather refreshing and dare she even admit, actually bearable.

However, while so much had changed and transpired ever since she left, the only thing that sadly, remained constant and predictable: both the French and Brazilian Ambassadors' wives were still poorly styled! Ah, tragically for them, how little had changed in that arena for those unfortunate women! Although their styles were still ill and utterly dreadful; at the same time, Jennifer had to also admit that at the very least, their dresses seemed much better improved from the last time she saw them.

Alas, had these ladies finally hired a new and decent dress maker? While this year, the wives might have worn better tailored dresses to match their figures and complexions; they sadly, still lacked the required confidence, sophistication, charm and charisma that Jennifer had previously mastered during her tenure, as one of the other wives. With much conviction, Jennifer believed wholeheartedly that had she attended this event as her true self, then she was most certainly guaranteed to have been crowned as the best dressed. Funnily, this very thought brought an unexpected sense of accomplishment and satisfaction from within her.

Suddenly, Jennifer caught a rare glimpse of herself in the mirror. Standing right beside her was a giant hallway mirror. Staring at her reflection, Jennifer saw what was perhaps, the biggest transformation of all: herself. There, in front of her, was no longer her normal blonde-haired self; but rather, a brown colored brunette, with her new dark hair pulled back into a simple ponytail. Unlike before, her makeup was at a bare minimal, with her signature red lips having been replaced with a lighter shade of pale pink. Furthermore, her outfit was more posh, professional and conservative; with her now sporting a formal black dress, along with a matching blazer. The once glamorous ambassador's wife was now transformed into a serious and established history professor. Oh my, the tables had certainly turned!

However, before Jennifer had the opportunity to even entertain such notions as to dance away into the ballroom masquerading as her sister, the giant grandfather clock that stood in the middle of the hallway, suddenly struck nine o'clock sharp.

"Oh dear, I'm late!" Jennifer nervously exclaimed.

Alas, the time had finally come and Jennifer needed to hurry. Right now, Kate was still waiting for her and she was running late. From here on out, each and every one of her steps counted; otherwise, any further delay could result in their plans going estray. Therefore, Jennifer needed to ensure that nothing else further hindered upon the successful execution of their mission.

Jennifer sighed. Up until this point, she had done everything right. Ever since she reunited with her sister, Jennifer spent the remainder of her time preparing for this evening back at Selim's hotel. Following Kate's specific instructions, Jennifer purchased a matching black suit and leather briefcase from her nearest department store, and then, transformed her signature blonde hair to brown. And just like that, Jennifer was instantly transformed into her twin sister, Kate!

As fate would have it, arriving back into the mansion, as Kate, couldn't have been easier and more perfect. Luckily, after years of extending an ongoing annual invitation to her sister, who lived abroad, Kate's name was already automatically prelisted on the official guests' list— weeks in advance, too. Furthermore, since Kate had always declined her previous invitations, none of the other security guards or staff members couldn't neither deny nor confirm that Jennifer really wasn't Kate after all; because no one had actually met the real Dr. Stanley in-person before. Although Kate might have posed as her these past few weeks, it was only a select few high-ranking employees, who knew the truth about the switch. As far as everyone else was concerned, Jennifer might as well have been the real Dr. Stanley; for no one else knew the true face behind the professor, apart from a given name that was regularly prelisted on the official guests' list booklet.

Unfortunately, if it hadn't been for that dreadful security guard, Jennifer would have arrived here ten minutes earlier; which would have given her the proper head start that she so desperately needed. Given how exceptionally large the mansion was, plus the exceptionally enormous crowd of people here tonight, Jennifer knew well in-advance that she needed enough sufficient time to walk across the grand entrance foyer, down the hall and then eventually, sneak into her old office to meet with Kate. Carefully, Jennifer calculated and factored in the strong possibility that one of their guests might attempt to try to stop and chit-chat with her on the spot. But then, Jennifer recalled that unlike before, this time around, coming as her sister, she was going to be unrecognizable. Surprisingly, she, herself, had to admit that it was nice to blend in amongst the crowd for a change.

"It's time," she finally said, as she swiftly tiptoed down the hallway, lurking in-between the shadows.

Meanwhile, Kate impatiently sat down at her desk inside of her office, tapping away with her fingers and staring directly at the wall clock, right above her door. It was now five past nine o'clock, and Jennifer was still nowhere in sight. Where exactly was she? She was supposed to be here, several minutes ago! If their plan was going to succeed, then Jennifer needed to be in the same room as her!

"Damn it, where is she?" Kate cursed aloud to herself.

"Did I just hear you curse?" asked a male voice, who suddenly appeared from out-of-nowhere, and was now, standing right in front of her door.

"Lucas," Kate replied, hesitantly.

"I don't believe I've ever yet heard you curse before. I say, is something troubling you, Kate?" he asked, with a raised brow.

"No, no, nothing is wrong…I was just lost in my own thoughts, that's all," she replied nervously.

Sadly, the truth was that Kate was indeed nervous. After all, she was about to confront a man, who was not only dangerous but also a criminal. Although Kate was the true mastermind behind their plot to overthrow him tonight; at this very moment, she was also scared and fearful. To make matters worse, her strategy wholly depended upon her sister being here at her side…but right now…. she wasn't.

"May I come in?" asked Lucas, with a devious smirk across his face. Like the wolf that he was, he clearly had no intention of remaining standing outside her door for an extra minute longer than necessary.

"Of course, please come in and take a seat," replied Kate, as she gestured him to sit at the empty seat, directly across her.

As he sat down, Kate stared impatiently at the clock, while desperately hoping for Jennifer to soon arrive. If Kate was going to confront Lucas for his crimes, then she needed her twin sister here to serve as both their witness and her moral support. Where was she? Why was she so late? According to their plans, Jennifer should have been here ten minutes ago. Didn't she realize as to just how crucial and important this all was? Jennifer couldn't have abandoned her, in her greatest time of need, could she?

"Is something amidst?" Lucas asked, with a curious but taunting tone within his voice.

"No, nothing at all," replied Kate hastily, as she bravely looked at him straight in the eye.

"Very well," he calmly replied, in return. "In that case, should we just cut straight into business, or…"

Suddenly, a gust of wind floated across through her office door, and before Lucas could even complete his sentence, Jennifer was standing right there inside of Kate's office. Relieved, Kate immediately took at ease. However, to both sister's surprise, Lucas was smiling on and actually appeared to look…happy?

"Ah, Jennifer, you're finally here, right on time," he remarked joyfully; not once, having been deceived by her disguise.

Reverting his attention back to Kate, Lucas said, "I believe that's probably why you called for this meeting here tonight, correct?"

"Lucas, you owe us an explanation," Kate demanded, coldly.

"Yes," agreed Jennifer, as she sat down on the extra empty chair, near her sister. "We're all ears. Start speaking."

"At long last, the time has finally come," he said, with a gigantic smile plastered straight across his face. "I knew it would come, eventually…"

"Yes, and you better start speaking," Jennifer harshly interrupted.

"Yes," agreed Kate.

"Very well, you two," Lucas answered, now looking and sounding more serious.

"Kate," he began with a sigh; and then, looking directly at her, he said, "Isn't nice to hear your *real* name again? Spoken so freely aloud? In the open public? Why, you, especially of all people, should understand me best. After all, we both can relate to the power of a name…"

"The power of a name?" Kate repeated, in half confusion.

However, her reaction only made him mockingly laugh, in the one of the most sinister and evil laughers that either one of them had ever heard before, in their entire lives.

"Well," he annoyingly huffed, "Perhaps, it's time that we have this conversation. Are you all ready?"

"Stop stalling, speak already," Jennifer demanded, as Kate nodded in agreement.

"Alright, tell me," he began, "How does it feel to assume another person's identity? To live each and every day answering to a name that you very well know isn't your own natural birth name? To walk around town, parading as someone else; all the while, hiding who you truly are to the world. I mean, doesn't it get tiring? I'm sure that you do feel that way. Posing as Mrs. Jennifer Barrett, the ambassador's wife; when in reality, you're really the one and only Dr. Kate Stanley, the accomplished and prestigious history professor from NYU. I mean, don't you miss being, Dr. Kate Stanley? Doesn't it just get so incredibly tiring to constantly pretend to be someone else, other than true yourself? I know that I certainly do."

"What the hell are you taking about? Who are you?!" Jennifer passionately yelled.

"Who am I? Who am I?" laughed Lucas, obnoxiously. "I'll tell you who I am."

Turning his direction over to Kate, he looked directly into her eyes and said, "Kate, at least, when this is all over and done, you can return to being your old self again; while I, on the other hand, never can."

"Lucas," spoke Kate, softly this time, "What exactly are you trying to tell us?"

With a beaming smile, Lucas asked, "Does the name Owen Lawrence, ring a bell?"

"Owen?" Kate suddenly gasped, as if an unexpected light bulb finally switched on. "Your Owen Lawrence, aren't you?"

"In the flesh and bones," Lucas announced, with the utmost pride, as he pranced closer over to the edge of Kate's desk, moving his chair forward, and then, sitting himself down, while he kicked his legs upwards and rudely placed them right above her clean desk.

"Wait, I've heard of this name before. Your…your…David's son?" asked Jennifer, in disbelief.

"His one true son," replied Lucas, "Correction: His only son, to be precise. Plus, if it wasn't for your precious ambassador, then I'd probably still be included in my father's life, as his righteous heir."

"Wait, this is all about your anger and jealousy, over John's relationship with your father?" asked Kate, trying her best to make sense of his motives.

"Jealousy is not the correct term. It's about justice," he clarified.

"Justice over what? That your father preferred John over you? What gave you the right to blackmail and attempt to kill me!" Jennifer screamed, angrily.

"Ah, ah, ah, Jennifer, I'd watch your tone around me. Besides, you're already in enough trouble. Or should I say troubles? After all, you've had what one…two…three…four lovers in these past few years, at least? Or is it more than four? I mean, at this point, do you even still bother counting your share of lovers, or have you already lost count?" he asked laughingly, while he began to mockingly count aloud with his chubby fingers.

Unfortunately, Jennifer wasn't at all amused and was quite ready to kill him herself, right there and then.

"I mean," he continued, "God only knows as to just how many scandalous affairs you've had behind his back, ever since you married the ambassador. If I were you, I'd learn to be more careful and discrete, next time," he warned, as he tauntingly waved his index finger back and forth, right in front of Jennifer.

His insults were growing too unbearable for Jennifer; because at this very moment, she was all but ready to leap right across from her chair and choke the life right out of him. However, Kate shot her one look to beg to her calm down. If they were going to successfully get to the bottom of all of this, then they needed to do it rationally and most importantly, calmly.

"Why did you do all of this? Why did you try to blackmail and then attempt to kill my sister? Why do you continue to parade as Lucas Oliver, when you're really Owen Lawrence?" asked Kate, calmly.

"Ah, Kate, the rationale and logical one. You know, out of the two of you, I'd choose you, a respected lady, over your slutty sister any day, in an instant," Lucas remarked, with a smirk across his face.

"I might be rationale, but I can promise you that it won't last for long. At least, not until you start explaining yourself to us," Kate forewarned, this time.

"Very well," he replied, laughingly, "Since I'm in a rather jolly and good mood, I'll humor your request. But first, since we're already being honest with one another here, I no longer need to continue my charade as Lucas. With that being said, let start with our proper introductions."

Looking directly at Kate, he said, "Hello, Dr. Kate Stanley, my name is Owen Lawrence. It's a pleasure to meet you. Now, I believe that it's your turn to now introduce yourself to me."

Utterly appalled by his bizarre and delusional behavior, Jennifer stared at Lucas, as if he were a crazy mad man. But, Kate, on the other hand, decided to bite her tongue and to play it safe by humoring him.

"Hello, Owen. My name is Dr. Stanley and it's a pleasure to meet you, too," Kate carefully said.

Beaming with delight, Lucas exclaimed, "It's just so good to hear my name again, after all these years! Isn't good to hear your name spoken too, Kate?"

Kate simply nodded in agreement, while Jennifer annoyingly rolled her eyes.

"Now, Kate, ask me why I had to change my name to Lucas? Why I had to forgo my birth name and adopt a new name, as my identity?" Lucas attempted to asked; but instead, it came out sounding more like a command, than a question.

"Very well," Kate agreed, "Why did you change your name?"

"Excellent question!" he exclaimed. "And because you asked, I will tell you why. But first, let me begin by telling you a story."

"I'm sorry, but this is really too much," Jennifer finally interrupted, as her patience started to grow thin. "Unlike me, my sister might be able to put up with your bullshit, but this is ridiculous! Now, just tell us why you did what you did!"

"Mrs. Barrett, I suggest that you watch your tone around me. Your sister kindly asked me a question, and I intend to give her an answer," Lucas coldly replied, as he now reached over, grabbed a bottle of whisky and started to pour himself a drink.

"I thought that you don't drink?" asked Kate, who suddenly recalled from their last dinner party, that Lucas or Owen, or whichever name that he now went by, was a recovering alcoholic.

"You remembered?" Lucas asked, most impressed by Kate's keen memory and attention to detail. "Yes, it's true. I don't drink. However, I think that tonight, after all these years, I finally deserve a long-awaited treat. Do you care for a drink?"

"No, thank you," Kate politely declined.

Moving his gaze over to Jennifer, he said, "I'd offer you a glass too, but on second thought, I think I'm going to end up drinking this entire bottle myself, right now."

Unamused, Jennifer simply rolled her eyes again, but this time, in complete disgust.

"Not to get off topic, but you were saying," Kate reminded him.

"Ah, yes, my story," he repeated, as he was getting ready to take the first sip of his whisky. "Well, my story ironically, begins with alcohol."

Silently, Lucas quietly gazed at his glass, as he appeared distressed. It seemed that perhaps, even this mad man had a bit of a conscience, after all; because if he didn't, then he wouldn't have hesitated nor agonized to take the first sip of his drink. But soon enough, eventually, his own fears vanished and in one swift large gulp, he managed to drink the entire glass in a single sip. Afterwards, he violently slammed the empty glass onto the table, as he then proceeded to pour himself a second round.

"I almost forgot as to how good this feels," he admitted. "You know, most people might presume that I'm just a drunken fool, but the actual truth is that apart from tonight, I've only drank once before, in my entire life."

"That doesn't make any sense. You've already just admitted being a recovering alcoholic," Jennifer interrupted.

Rather than responding to her, Lucas just continued to laugh on and said, "Back to my story. Please bear patience with me, for it's a good one. I promise not to disappoint."

"Lucas, please tell us what happened to you," Kate pleaded.

"I will," he replied; and then, for the first time, Kate saw tears form within his watery eyes. Whatever his tale was, his past was clearly an extremely painful and sore subject to revisit.

"As I said before, I only drank once in my entire," Lucas admitted. "The truth is that I didn't even want to drink at all that night, but I was pressured to do it."

"If you're trying to get us to feel sorry for you, then it's failing miserably," huffed Jennifer.

However, Lucas just ignored her and smiled on, as he took another sip of drink and continued with his story.

"About fifteen years ago, it was my twenty first birthday. Back then, I was a young and enthusiastic officer in the military— the army, to be specific. After completing four years of service, I was promoted to oversee a secret operation in Afghanistan. At that time, I remember how happy and proud I was to serve my country. But sadly, I was young and foolish about the true and cruel nature of this world," he said, with a somber and melancholy tone within his voice.

As he took another sip of his drink, Kate observed as to just how incredibly sad he looked there. For a brief moment, she almost felt sorry for him. Well, almost, that is.

"Anyways, as I was saying, it was the night before my deployment. Since it was my birthday, the other officers wanted celebrate my birthday and new promotion at the local bar. Believe it or not, this was my first time at any bar, too. For you see, when you grow up as the son of an ambassador— especially, someone as strict and as honorable as my father— you tend to live a squeaky clean, quiet, and drama-free life; absent of any looming scandals or questionable behaviors and attributes. For if you did, then my father and his embassy staff would be right there on my ass, working to deescalate and deter any brewing crisis. Sadly, we embassy kids grow up living inside a fishbowl. Similar to a gilded cage. But either way, the truth was that I always wanted to make my father proud; which is why I always strived to do the right thing and aimed to stay away from any trouble."

"Really, so what the hell happened to you?" asked Jennifer, sarcastically.

Amused by her sudden outburst, Lucas just laughed, as he finished the remainder of his drink. Afterwards, he poured himself yet another glass. By now, he was on his third round of whisky, as he continued with his tale.

"On that night…that fateful night…what started out as one glass of whisky soon turned into a second glass…then a third…and then a fourth…and before I knew it, I was so incredibly drunk and intoxicated that I couldn't see anything standing before me clearly. Given that this was my very first-time drinking alcohol, I honestly had no clue nor concept, as to how little or how much I was supposed to drink. Sadly, no one from my group of so called "friends" cared to warn, nor stop me. Ironically, they all stupidly laughed and thought it was funny. Stiff Owen was finally letting loose! Eventually, once the celebration and party were all over, I needed to return back home, as I was scheduled for an early flight to Afghanistan in the morning. However, by then, everyone else had already left the bar a long time ago; leaving me behind stranded, all by myself and drunk. Sadly, on that one fateful moment…that one singular moment that's forever frozen inside of my mind for all eternity…a moment so memorable that I'm cursed to relive…over…and over…again…I made a terrible decision that has altered the entire course of my adult life…a regretful decision that I'm still paying the consequences for…even to the very day."

Briefly, Lucas stopped his tale, put his feet back down onto the floor and out of frustration, ran his fingers through his hair. Upon taking another sip of his whisky, he violently slammed his glass back onto the table; thereby, spilling the remaining liquid onto the desk, which managed to leak through a stack of documents, located nearby.

"As you see can already see, these inconvenient accidents are the direct effects of my drinking. Why, I've managed to get all of these documents soaking wet!" he shouted, and then laughed in a rather sad and pathetic way. "But the difference is, these papers can all be replaced; whereas, my life can't."

Concerned and curious about the origins to his bizarre psychological state, Kate calmly asked, "Owen, what happened to you on that night?"

Surprisingly, the mere mention of his real name shined an unexpected light and glow upon Lucas' face. It had been years since someone had finally acknowledged and addressed him by his given birth name; and for whatever reason, it brought an unexpected joy to his blackened heart. However, it is important to note and if truth be told, a name is never just a name. For in the end, is it not our names, in which history will remember us best by, long after we've departed from this earthly world?

"You said my name," he said, with a wry smile. "Kate, you do realize the significance and power of a name, don't you? Why, over time, people might come to forget our prior deeds and past indiscretions, as well as our physical appearances, occupations and family relations; but history always remembers a name. Yes, a name becomes one's cloak of identity. In fact, prior to coming here tonight, all of you heard of an Owen Lawrence, even if you merely recognized him as just the passing name of a long-estranged and forgotten son; however, all of you failed to connect that he and I, were one in the same, now did you? Your facial expressions prove my point, exactly."

However, Jennifer, was growing impatient and wanted to get down to the truth. "As you were saying," she reminded him.

"As I was saying," he continued, "One moment I was at the bar and the next moment, I had the car keys in my hands. Before I knew it, I was behind the wheel driving. The roads were empty that night, and it was supposed to be a short ride, between the bar and my apartment. Only five minutes. Imagine that!"

"But you didn't make it back to your apartment safely in those five minutes, did you?" asked Kate, in all seriousness.

With tearful eyes, Lucas answered, "No, I didn't."

Wiping away his tears, Lucas poured himself one round of whisky, gulped the entire cup down his throat and then finally revealed, "Along the way…. there was an accident…I… don't remember much about the accident…but all I know is…that we all…survived…including the bicyclist…whom I hit."

"You were thrown out of the military because of this accident, weren't you?" asked Jennifer, this time.

Lucas shook his head in agreement, and then he said, "That one mistake cost me everything. My career, my family, my inheritance, my livelihood, my future— everything. Not only was I kicked out from the military, but I was also released with the status of a dishonorable discharge.

I was so incredibly ashamed. By far, it was the single most devastating event in my existence. I was completely ruined. For the first time in my life, I did something wrong. I, who did everything correct up until that one fateful moment, made a mistake. I, who got the good grades, listened to his parents, stayed out of trouble, always strived to be the best son and brother— for the very first time in my entire life, I did the wrong thing. I made the wrong choice and it cost me, so dearly. If I could go back in time and redo it all, then I would have never gone to that bar that night. Tragically, in the end, I was involved in a scandal of my very own making; and sadly, it proved to be too much for my father. Rather than forgiving and helping me to navigate this accident through therapy, my father completely disowned me and turned his entire back on my life. But worst of all, after the incident, I realized that my so-called beloved father— the man, whom I spent most of my life admiring as my idol, turned out to care more about his career, as the world-famous American Ambassador, then he did, as simply being just my father. In the end, my father's primary and only concern was keeping his reputation intact and preventing his career from souring due to this scandal. Sadly, he didn't even care about me, his own child; his own flesh and blood. Of course, at that time, he also listened to his advisors, who were specifically recruited to help evaluate and deescalate this crisis. In the end, after much of their persistent persuasion, he ultimately chose to follow their recommendation and sought to distance himself away from me by disowning me. Not only did he cut me off financially and emotionally out of his life, but he also forbade my own mother and sister from having any direct contact with me, ever again. His selfish decision cost me my family, my inheritance, my identity and everything else in-between. His actions on that fateful day, sealed my fate; for that was the day Owen Lawrence died and Lucas Oliver was born."

"Basically, you're admitting that you made a mistake in the past, and because of it, your father disowned you. I'm sorry, but these sorts of disagreements happen almost every day to millions of other families around the world, but the difference is that they get over it! Why didn't you?" asked Jennifer, coldly.

Immediately, Lucas shot Jennifer the most chilling of looks that sent a shiver down Kate's spine. His face was blood red, and he appeared to be angry. Jennifer's attempts to jab his open wound seemed to work.

Perhaps, too well.

"The key difference is that your precious ambassador came into the picture," replied Lucas angrily, as he grinded his teeth. "Had he not entered into our lives, then things between my father and I could have turned out very different. Maybe, we might have managed to have worked things out."

"But you can still make amends with your father," Kate interrupted. "It's still not too late. You can still do the right thing, Owen."

"Kate, it's too late," he reluctantly admitted. "I've been Lucas Oliver for far too long now."

"But I still don't understand, as to why you changed your name?" asked Jennifer.

"Really? Is that *too* difficult to believe?" he retorted. He continued, "Can you imagine applying for a new job, under the name of Owen Lawrence? The name to a person, who's fresh off a sizzling hot scandal. Let's see…the media knows your name…as well as the public, who's watching the broadcast media…and then there's the private businesses reading the print media…and then…there's everyone else in between. To top it all off, your name is the same name as the disgraced son to one of the most famous, powerful and wealthiest American ambassadors—but yet, that very same ambassador wants absolutely nothing to do with you. Tell me Jennifer, what's one to do? What's one expected to do? Let me answer this one: you logically change your name. Personally, I already well knew that if I was ever going to one day make a comeback again, then I needed to accomplish this as a new man; under a new identity and most importantly, under a brand-new name— a name that was unrecognizable. As I said before, names are important and as such, in order to reinvent myself, I required a new identity. Hence, Lucas Oliver was born."

"Thus, OL becomes LO. A twist to the name of Owen Lawrence, but in reverse order," Jennifer smirked aloud.

"Exactly. Although I might have changed my name, I still found a way to retain some traces to my original and old self, all at the same time," he proudly remarked.

"How utterly creative of you," Jennifer huffed sarcastically.

"Owen, this still doesn't explain, as to why you committed these crimes," Kate reminded him.

"Ah, but I'm still getting to that," he happily replied. "After changing my name, things started to go in my favor. Soon afterwards, I got a job working in the security industry. As a former military operative, my military background and combat skills proved to be invaluable experience that carried directly over into the private security sector. After a few years working as an entry-level private security officer, I eventually ventured out and opened my own security business, under the company name of Orion Securities, headquartered in New York. By then, the rift between my father and I still hadn't improved. But, as the famous saying goes, when one area of your life is in decline, the other area succeeds. This proved to be the same case with me. While my family life was nonexistent; my business, on the other hand, was blooming. Life was starting to look up. Everything started coming up roses. But, unfortunately, for men like me, good things never last forever. Eventually, what goes up, soon comes back down."

"What happened next?" asked Kate, as she attentively listened to his story.

"One day," he continued, "Out of the blue, I unexpectedly received a letter in the mail addressed to Owen Lawrence, my former name. Immediately, I already knew that the contents to this particular letter was directly related to my estranged father, because no one else ever since, has referred to me by my birth name. Just as I suspected, as it turned out, the letter was indeed sent by my father's attorney. Apparently, his attorney was able to successfully track my current location through several inquiries made at the local postal office, with regards to my latest change of address filing. Although he failed to collect my new and proper name, he still managed to find my current mailing address. I suppose that my previous decision to keep a forwarding address to letters still sent under my old name, might have played a big part with my father's attorney's deduction as to my whereabouts. Either way, I received the letter and upon opening it, I came to discover that inside it was a formal legal notice, which stated that a revision was made to my father's most recent will. It seemed that even though my father previously cut me off financially, he still kept my inheritance intact. That was, until John entered into the picture."

"Wait, so you blame John for stealing your inheritance?" Kate inquired.

"Yes and no," he admitted, "It's much more complicated than that. It was never just about the money. I have money. Plenty of it. I'm actually a self-made millionaire, several times over. Orion Securities is an extremely successful entity that operates all across the globe. Surprisingly, I've become a wealthy man, on my own right."

"If it wasn't about the money, then what was it?" asked Jennifer.

"Principle," replied Lucas. "It's always been about the principle. You don't grow up as the ambassador's son, without clinging to certain values and ethical codes of honor and principles."

"And what was the principle?" asked Kate, this time.

"In summary, the letter indicated that I had been removed from all of my father's various assets and estates. As a consequence of this transaction, I was, and still am, no longer eligible to inherit anything from my father, if and when, he passes away. Nothing. Not a single penny. Initially, I was content with this decision, as I had already expected as much. Naturally, I presumed that my share had simply switched over to my younger sister, Amy, and if that had been the case, then I would have been perfectly fine by that," he explained.

"How did you come to discover that John was the one, who took over your share, instead?" asked Kate, who was intrigued and concerned, both at the same exact time.

"After reading that letter, I decided that perhaps, the time had finally come for me to reach out and attempt to make amends with my father. But the problem was that I had absolutely no clue, as to where he was precisely. For you see, being part of a diplomatic household, my family has always moved and bounced around, country to country. Ever since I can remember, we've always been more like traveling nomads, moving place to place, without a permanent base to call home. Given that it's been several years since I've last seen them, I had absolutely no idea, as to where my family now lived, nor how to even contact them, in the first place. All I had in my possession was that letter sent by my father's attorney, with a return address back to their law office. With nothing else in sight, I reverted back to that very same return address and one day, I actually got the courage and showed up in-person to my father's attorney's office in New York and got my answers. It was there inside of my father's attorney's office, belonging to a Mr. Clifford W. Marble, esq., that I learned that my father was a widower, who retired from the agency some time ago and was now employed as a tenured college professor, residing in the Washington, D.C. metropolitan area, with my younger sister. Luckily, for me, Mr. Marble was an enthusiastic talker, who revealed to me that not only had I been completely removed out of my father's amended will, but that my name was actually replaced with an entirely new person, who wasn't even my sister or blood relative. A surrogate son. A non-blood relation. A former student, who shared similar aspirations as my father. Another young man, in which my own father served as his personal mentor and in return, that same stranger was now acting on my behalf by serving as that replacement void to the missing son and brother that my father and sister so longed for. Sadly, it seemed that my father not only erased me from our family history, but he also sought to replace me, too. Hence, another example to the important significance of a name. Honestly, I can't even begin to tell you all the rage that I felt, once I learned the truth about all of this."

"Because of this revelation, you sought revenge, didn't you?" asked Jennifer.

"To be honest, yes, I did," Lucas admitted, truthfully. "But it's taken several years to strategically plan and execute all of this. After discovering his ultimate betrayal and deceit, I vowed on that day to claim justice through my revenge. This time around, my father wasn't going to get away so easily by eradicating my entire existence, nor was this so-called John character going to take over my life and steal my inheritance so easily, either. And so, in due course, I waited…I planned…and I plotted."

"But none of this is John's fault," Kate interrupted. "John only sought David's company to serve as his mentor. A fatherly figure to replace his own late father, whom he lost at such a young age."

"John's innocence in all of this is debatable. All I know for certain, is that he could have denied and withdrawn his inheritance rights with relation to my father's will and instead, give his share over to Amy, but he didn't do that, now did he," Lucas concluded.

"He tried," Jennifer interrupted, this time. "On our wedding day. Even I remember it. Initially, he refused, but David wouldn't hear it."

"Well, he could have tried harder," responded Lucas, "But alas, he didn't. And so, because of his shortcomings, I ultimately decided to seek my revenge. It took me some time, but I was most determined."

"I don't understand. You've been working for John for several years now. Are you honestly telling us, that you've been plotting against him, since the very beginning?" asked Jennifer.

"Yes, that's exactly what I'm saying," Lucas admitted, "From the very beginning, I knew that it was going to take me some time. While I might have lost everything to him, the one and only thing that I didn't lose and still managed to retain was time. Luckily for me, I've always been a rather patient person, too."

"And you used Orion Securities, as an excuse to gain direct access to John, didn't you?" asked Kate.

"All I had to do was charm his mother, Barbara, to get on her good side, which wasn't too difficult to do. By hiring the right "thief" and staging a phony robbery, I ensured that I, alone, saved the day and was crowned as the victor. Lastly, by implanting myself at her party, I made certain that I was standing at the right place at the right time, which ultimately, came to be," he admitted proudly.

"My God, I remember Barbara telling me about that day, too!" exclaimed Jennifer, in pure astonishment. "We all thought you were a hero! How wrong we were! You certainly did play us for fools!"

"I did what needed to be done, in order to gain access into the mansion. The end always justifies the mean. Needless to say, it worked," he said, with a devious smile.

"Afterwards, your company won the contract to work for the embassy, correct?" asked Kate.

"Yes. Barbara's recommendation sealed the deal. Also, that same year, I further expanded and relocated Orion Securities main operations to abroad," replied Lucas.

"But Orion Securities has been operating with the embassy for several years now. Why did you wait so long to execute your revenge plot?" asked Kate, who was most curious.

"Why Kate, does a rose suddenly appear, right after its seeds having just been planted? No, it doesn't. It's because all good seeds take time to mature and blossom," he laughingly said.

"You didn't plant roses! You planted Venus traps!" exclaimed Jennifer, angrily.

But her negative remarks failed to wound his pride, for Lucas simply laughed even more.

"Venus traps or roses, it doesn't matter," he replied coldly. "What matters is that I planted the seeds to my revenge. And now, I seek to harvest what I've sown. Kate, none of this should come as such a surprise to you. After all, you're a history professor. A specialist in Ottoman history. I mean, you do recall as to what the Sultan's sons did to one another, in order to ascend to the throne? Or must I remind you?" he asked, with a playful and wicked smirk upon his face.

"I'm sorry, but I'm not following," Kate admitted. "How does my knowledge about Ottoman history, have anything to do with this?"

"Everything," he quickly replied. "It has everything to do with it. I guess I will just have to enlighten you all. As you may recall, many of the Ottoman sultans had several sons. While the sultans almost always had legitimate sons born from their first and legal wives, they also, on occasion, had other sons, born from their concubines living inside their harem. While one could argue that the eldest first-born legitimate son, birthed from their first wife was the true heir apparent, that wasn't always the case. Rather, it required a battle, in which the winner became the victor. The new sultan. Do you recall, as to what happened to the other losing sons?"

"They died," replied Kate, with a frown.

"They were killed…eliminated," he emphasized. "By the new incoming sultan. Furthermore, if the newly crowned sultan had any other remaining full-blood brothers born from their own mothers, he killed them, too. He killed them all, in order to prevent any potential civil wars from occurring later on, in the future."

"I'm sorry, but how does this moment in history, have anything to do with John and you?" Jennifer interrupted.

"It's because I'm the rightful heir, while your precious ambassador is the illegitimate son. John stole my life and I intend to take it back!" he viciously exclaimed, as he threw his empty glass across the room; thereby, breaking into a hundred tiny pieces, all scattered about.

His violent nature and tenacities, startled Kate and Jennifer. As the glass came crashing down against the floor, they each prayed for this meeting to come to a safe end. Clearly, Lucas growing more upset by the minute.

"You personally hired Ivan Koval, as your hitman, didn't you?" asked Kate, trying to regain Lucas' attention. It worked.

Returning his attention back to Kate, he smiled and said, "Do you realize, that apart from myself, there are several other people, who also want the ambassador dead? Finding another mutual ally to kill him was fairly easy."

"You were our Chief Security Officer! You were supposed to be protecting us!" Jennifer angrily shouted.

"If that was the case and John had other enemies, then why did you specifically seek out Ivan?" asked Kate, as she continued to maintain her calm and unemotional poker face.

"It's because of the ambassador's little pipeline project," he replied. "There's a lot of Belarusian oligarchs and politicians, who don't want his new pipeline program to ever see the light of day. If his project proves successful, then the gas monopoly that's currently controlled and dictated by the Belarusian government, which connects the natural gas from Russian owned Siberia into Europe via Belarus, will finally have competition through a fair and open market. Furthermore, if the Europeans have an alternative option to obtain gas via the Turkish straits, then several Belarusian oligarchs, whose businesses are owned, operated, and controlled by the Belarusian mafia, won't be too pleased by this new prospect. Needless to say, there are several of them, who are most willing to do almost anything to stop the launch of his new program. Ivan just so happened to be one of them. All I needed to do was to reach out to the mafia, recruit Ivan, and then, assign him as your sister's new tennis instructor. The rest is history."

"You bastard! You set me up!" screamed Jennifer scornfully, at the top of her lungs. However, Lucas didn't flinch at all, not one single inch.

"Blame yourself, not me. You're the one, who slept with him and carried on with that scandalous affair. You openly committed adultery, based on your own free will," he remarked, with the utmost disgust.

"If that's the case, then why did you choose to blackmail my sister by sending her salacious pictures of her and Ivan, alone together?" asked Kate, still trying to connect the dots to his devious plans.

"Because alas, the time had finally come for me to enact my plot for revenge. After all, time was ticking away. For years, I stayed silently hidden in the furthest and darkest corner of any given room; patiently waiting for the ideal moment to unravel my revenge. However, part of the problem was that I ridiculously presumed that I always had sufficient time to do so; and then, suddenly, one day, I no longer did. Time, as it seemed, was beginning to slip away from my very own fingertips," he admitted.

Suddenly, Kate understood. Lucas had to act fast on his revenge plot, because of David's cancer. If David were to die in the foreseeable near future, then Lucas didn't have enough ample time to alter David's will and reclaim his inheritance.

"You learned about David's cancer," she said, softly.

"I did," he replied, with a heavy-heart. "Even though I haven't seen nor visited my father in several years, ever since I had that meeting with his attorney, I always assigned one of my men to follow and keep a close watch on him and Amy, at all times. Till this very day, they still continue to debrief me with the intelligence pertaining to their most recent whereabouts and activities."

"You've been spying on David, all this time?" asked Jennifer, in amazement.

"Yes, I have. Amy too," he admitted.

"But why did you bring Jennifer, into your revenge plot?" asked Kate.

"Because she's his wife!" he exclaimed, out of frustration. "As I expressed before, I intend to ruin him, in each and every possible way! If the world knew that the dashingly charming and perfect American Ambassador had an unfaithful wife, who cheated on him with a key member of the Belarusian mafia, then…well…that would certainly be a scandal, now wouldn't it?"

"Then why didn't you just expose my affair? Why did you threaten to kill me?!!" Jennifer shouted, angrily.

"Exposing your affair alone, wasn't enough to completely ruin him," he reluctantly admitted. "Eventually, in due time, the world would soon learn about your upcoming divorce and then, they'd be inclined to forgive him and turn the other cheek. Perhaps, even pity him; for it's far easier to forgive a soon-to-be ex-wife moving on with her new lover, than a so-called happily married wife who was previously unfaithful. Naturally, the public would lean with option one, as the narrative. Unfortunately, for men, like the ambassador, they have such luck; whereas, for men, like me, we're dealt with the worse bit. Furthermore, if the world came to forgive him, then he'd still be able to retain his successful career, my father's love and in the end, his life would continue to proceed as normal, just as it had so right before. No, I refuse to accept this. I couldn't take that chance."

"Owen, you still didn't answer the question. Why did you try to kill my sister? If your intentions were to ruin John, then wouldn't it have been far more effective to make his life miserable, rather than killing her? After all, killing Jennifer would be too easy," said Kate, directly.

"I attempted to kill your sister, in order to get to John. Ultimately, I realized that I could cause more damage to him with her dead, than if she was still alive," he finally revealed. "If I was successful on eliminating your sister, then he'd be the number one suspect in her death. Spouses always are. Plus, given Jennifer's unfaithful track record and the fact that it was your sister alone, who personally asked for the divorce, then the ambassador had a real and legitimate motive for killing her. Lastly, if the public perceived him to be the true killer…well…then…he'd really be done for and I would have successfully accomplished what I originally sought out to do from the very beginning."

"But you failed with that," Kate reminded him.

"Yes, I did and sadly, that was most unfortunate," he angrily replied, while he grinded his teeth and turned red in the face.

"You're a total asshole!" Jennifer shouted.

"Am I? Coming from you, I'll take that as a compliment," Lucas remarked, along with a wink.

Jennifer, on the other hand, wasn't at all amused. Meanwhile, Kate continued to press on. Regardless of his negative attitude, she still wanted answers.

"Why still go after John, then? Why have Ivan pursue an unsuccessful assassination attempt against him in Kars?" she asked him directly, point-blank.

"Well, something needed to be done," he replied. "Unfortunately, your sister managed to escape and the ambassador still continued on with his business, as usual. Meanwhile, you were already here; but yet, you failed to accomplish what I originally sought you out to do."

"What *I* failed to do?" asked Kate, astonished by his bold accusation.

"But I complied with all the requirements!" exclaimed Kate. "I did everything that was asked from me! My God, I took all those dance lessons and even learned to dance the waltz! I think I've been far more compliant, then expected! Besides, it was the agency, who requested for my help, not you!"

"Oh Kate, sadly, that's where you're gravely mistaken," Lucas revealed. "It was I, who recruited you. As you may recall, it was I, and I alone, who personally found and escorted you here, all the way from New York. This wasn't a mere coincidence. The truth is that it was always my idea for the agency to take you on, from the very beginning. If it weren't for my men gathering intelligence about you, no one else within the agency, nor the ambassador, would have ever known about your existence. In fact, prior to my reports, they'd never even heard of your name before. It seems that your so-called loving twin sister did a rather impeccable good job at concealing your identity."

"I thought that I was supposed to serve as a diversion to prevent a scandal? Is this not, correct?" asked an emotional Kate, who at this very moment, suddenly felt used and betrayed.

"Kate, you were always *my bait* and nothing more," he mockingly and cruelly admitted. "I might have fooled the others into believing your role as the safe decoy to divert a scandal, but you were always my bait. Always. The worm to my fishing pool. Like I said before, your sister got away and that wasn't supposed to happen. Now, Jennifer was out in the world, having seen my face and being a witness to my crime. I couldn't allow her to get away with that, now, could I? To make matters worse, when she failed to return back home after that night…well…I needed to find a way to lure her back in."

"Once I discovered that Kate was acting on my behalf, you knew that I would eventually return back home, didn't you?" asked Jennifer, in all seriousness.

"Precisely," Lucas replied, with a grin. "And," he added, "It seems that my plan worked, too."

"Okay," began Kate, as she wiped away her tears and feeling rather upset by the recent knowledge, that she too, had been yet another pawn in his sick and twisted game.

"Whatever your intentions were with me, it really doesn't matter," she said, "But why did you try to kill John?"

"My father's cancer diagnosis," replied Lucas, truthfully. "If my father dies today, as a result of this unfortunate illness, then his current will immediately goes into effect and after everything that's transpired, John will still be able to collect his inheritance through my father. Therefore, he needed to be eliminated. The sooner, the better."

"Is that why you decided to travel to New York and send Miles as your replacement officer, during our Kars trip? To serve as your alibi?" asked Kate, hoping to receive a confirmation from Lucas.

"Yes," he replied.

"Is Miles a part of all of this, too? I mean, someone close to us must have informed Koval of our whereabouts? Otherwise, how else could Koval have known about our specific location in Kars, on that particular day?" asked Kate.

"Miles is too much of an honest man to ever be pulled into my corrupt web of deceit and lies," Lucas replied. "No, it wasn't him. But apart from that, you're correct about your other assumption. Yes, there was another person helping us."

"It's probably another one of your wretched security guards, who were helping! Or better yet, another mafia thug!" exclaimed Jennifer.

"Wrong again," replied Lucas, with a smile. "Rather, think of someone much closer."

"Closer?" asked Kate, in sheer surprise. "Someone from Kars?"

"Yup," he said. "Care to take a guess?"

"We don't have time for guesses! Enough of these silly games!" yelled Jennifer, once more.

"Fine, I'll relieve you all from the anticipation," he said. "If you must know, it was Peter."

"Peter?" repeated Kate. "As in Dr. Peter Murphy?"

"The very one," Lucas confirmed, as he reached over and poured himself another drink.

"How? Why? He's engaged to your sister, whom you haven't spoken to, nor seen in years," Kate reminded him.

"That might be true. Needless to say, he's still been under my thumb these past few weeks. As you might recall, it was he, on that day, who suggested which path to ski on," said Lucas.

"Wait a minute, how did you know that it was Peter, who suggested that we take that path?" asked Kate.

Suddenly, Kate recalled David's peculiar and repetitive chanting of the name "Owen" over and over again, right after his accident. It wasn't because David felt some sort of near-death remorse, but that he actually saw Lucas, in-person and in the flesh, right out there on the ski slopes! Lucas wasn't in New York, at all. Instead, he secretly followed them directly to Kars. He was there, all along, watching them all this time!

"You…you were there, weren't you?" she asked, in horror.

"Yes, I was there…hiding in one of the trees," he replied, happily. "When Koval missed his target, I was right there behind him, ready to step in to fix his mistake. Unfortunately, my father saw and recognized me, so I quickly fled the scene. The only reason, as to why the ambassador's still alive today is due to my father. Had he not seen me, then our conversation right now, would be very much different."

"Regardless, John survived! No matter what, you still failed!" exclaimed Jennifer.

"Really, can she please just shut up, already?" Lucas asked Kate. "Honestly, I'm growing extremely annoyed by her constant outbursts."

Unfortunately, Kate was at a loss for words. Thus far, she wasn't sure, as to which of the many revelations that she was most surprised by: the fact that Lucas was secretly there with them in Kars, or that Peter betrayed them. However, the further Kate pondered about the situation, the more she grew convinced that it really shouldn't have been that surprising that Lucas had followed them, as he always seemed to have the habit of hiding within the shadows. However, Peter was the exception of the two. Overall, he appeared to be such a friendly and amiable fellow, who genuinely seemed to be so incredibly in love and devoted to Amy. How could he betray her and her family? Alas, Kate needed to learn the rest of the truth.

"Owen, why did Peter help you? Did you hire him to get close to Amy?" Kate finally asked, after much thought.

"Amy's innocent, in all of this," he quickly replied, in an effort to defend his sister. In the end, it seemed that for all his worth, Lucas still maintained some brotherly affection over his younger sibling.

"Then, why Peter?" she asked, once more.

"Kate, these days, do you realize how expensive medical school? Apart from the rising costs of tuition for most Americans to attend American universities, but can you imagine how much it costs an American student to attend a European college, as a foreigner? For starters, as a foreign student, they'll be forced to pay much higher student fees, along with housing and board, too," said Lucas.

"What the hell are you taking about?" Jennifer interrupted.

"Not to worry Jennifer, my questions are only directed to Dr. Stanley, at this time," he clarified.

"Universities might be more expensive in Europe; however, Peter attended with a full scholarship," Kate answered, confidently.

However, Lucas just laughed on and shook his head in disapproval.

"Is that what he told you all? Dr. Stanley, you couldn't be more wrong!" he exclaimed, while he continued to laugh and giggle, even more than before.

"Stop laughing! You can't ask us questions, then laugh at us when we answer them!" Jennifer shouted.

"Okay, okay," Lucas said, as he collected himself again, after such excessive laugher.

"Please allow me to help clarify that Peter," he emphasized, "Did *not* attend medical school on a scholarship. There were no scholarships."

"No scholarships? Then, how did he attend?" asked Kate, astonished by this new revelation.

"By taking out student loans. Several hundreds of thousands of dollars," replied Lucas.

"That he couldn't afford to pay back, and fell straight into debt," Jennifer interrupted.

"Exactly," he said. "Now tell me, Kate, how does a poor and recent college graduate, who owes several thousands of dollars in debt, magically finds the financial means to support and care for my sister? My sister, who comes from a wealthy family in her own right, and is already accustomed to living in such high standards? How does he afford to pay for my sister's lavish wedding, along with a new house and furniture for their new life, together? How will they travel together throughout Europe during their honeymoon? Plus, the costs associated with the new medical office, that he plans to open in Connecticut, what of that? Peter might have exaggerated his economic history to my family by lying to you all about his scholarship, but he couldn't fool me. I always knew the truth about him. Peter is nothing more, than a poor kid from the slums of New Jersey, who wanted nothing more, than to marry into my wealthy and established family for his own financial and social gain. That's all."

"Peter might be poor, but he genuinely loves and cares for your sister," Kate admitted.

"Love?" huffed Lucas, in disgust. "Love is just another lie that we tell ourselves. If he truly loved my sister, then he never would have agreed to work for me."

"What exactly did you have him do?" asked Kate.

"Intel," Lucas replied, with a devious smile. "After all, he was my mole. He kept me informed about your whereabouts, at all times. But alas, sadly, he and Koval both failed with our mission. If I had taken matters into my own hands much earlier, then Koval wouldn't be in jail. Furthermore, I'm certain that in due time, my father would have removed John from his will, reallocated those funds over to Peter and then, I would have gotten my revenge! If only you, Kate, didn't get in the way on those slopes, then I would have had a clear shot!"

"But you failed," said Jennifer, boldly.

"Not yet," he answered. "Perhaps, the time has finally come for me to take back my name. My birth name. Besides, you two have already acknowledged me as Owen. Given that I've already spent a good portion of tonight revealing all my secrets and truths to you all, I feel that I'm now left with no other choice, but to reclaim my birthright and to finish what Peter and Koval failed to do."

"What are you saying?" asked Kate, hesitantly.

"I'm done talking, now," he answered, with a sadistic smirk painted across his face. Finally, he said, "From here on out, I believe I will just show you."

With Kate and Jennifer eagerly seated at the edges of their seats, Lucas reached into his upper left-hand jacket pocket and slowly pulled out a shiny and silvery object. For a brief moment, Kate and Jennifer couldn't see what that object was. However, Lucas soon lifted the object up into air and right above his head. As he brought the object further down, leveled towards his face, the two sisters soon realized that what Lucas was holding was a gun! A long and silver gun, which, at this very moment, was now aimed at their direction!

Chapter 31

As Kate closed her eyes tightly shut, her life suddenly flashed before her. Only yesterday, was she in heaven, blissfully happy within the arms of her beloved John, the love of her life. But now, in contrast, today she was in hell and facing the very devil, himself. Although Kate knew that her time on this earth was limited; however, she wasn't yet ready to leave this world behind, either. There was still so much that she wanted to say and do. An endless list of unfinished business. After all, Kate still had her students back home to teach. Plus, her cat. What would happen to Tabitha, if she perished? And John? After everything, Kate still didn't yet have the opportunity to tell him that she loved him, face-to-face. Even though she previously whispered into his ear her confession after their last lovemaking, he was still sound asleep and probably didn't even hear her. What if she left this world, without him ever knowing how madly and dearly she cared for him? That John meant everything to her. That he was the true love of her life. The sum of all her existence. Was this truly the end?

"Are you sure that you really want to go through with this?" asked Jennifer, calmly.

"Why not? I've waited long enough," replied Lucas obnoxiously, while he continued to maintain his grip and control over the silver gun, tightly held within the grasp of his hands.

"We can make a deal," Jennifer pleaded.

"A deal? Why in the hell, should I ever make a deal with the likes of either one of you," Lucas huffed, sarcastically.

"A deal. Our lives, in exchange for our silence," stated Jennifer.

"I don't need to make a deal for that. I'll kill you both and then I'll have your silence," Lucas mockingly laughed. "There's really no point on negotiating this. You've already lost. Your fate is sealed. Now, just close your eyes and die in dignity."

Suddenly, without saying another word, Lucas lifted his gun straight ahead, released its safety lock and was about ready to pull the trigger. But before Lucas could release the trigger, the most unexpected of circumstances happened. Out-of-nowhere, Tabitha emerged and with one incredible and swift jump, she flew down from above the bookshelf that stood behind the desk, and landed directly on top of his shoulders. Meanwhile, Jewel followed from behind and miraculously, she bolted across the carpet, thereby knocking Lucas straight forward, headfirst, onto the ground, where he managed to slam his head against the hardwood floor. Upon falling, Lucas' gun accidentally released a bullet into the open air. Luckily, the bullet managed to strike only a vase, located in the far back corner of the office; leaving only a small pile of shattered glass on the carpet. Everything else within the office remained intact— safe and unharmed. It seemed that fate had unexpectedly intervened.

"Run!" Kate screamed, as soon as she caught a moment of her breath.

"Wait," Jennifer yelled, in return. "Not until I grab the recording first!"

"Recording? You recorded me?" Lucas yelped, as he struggled to regain his consciousness and the balance to once again, lift himself up from below the floor.

"Yes!" Jennifer screamed. "And now, you're done! Come on Kate, let's go!"

With one bold dash, the twin sisters quickly ran out of the room and entered into the hallway. As they swiftly ran down the hallway, they heard Lucas wailing and screaming from behind.

"What are we going to do?" asked Jennifer, as she continued to run, alongside her sister.

"Do you still have the recording?" asked Kate, as she continued to keep up with her sister's pace.

"Yes, it's still in my hands," replied Jennifer, with much relief.

"Where you able to record everything?' asked Kate, hoping to receive a positive confirmation.

"Yes, I think so. Once he began his confession, I started recording. I used both phones. But just in case anything happens to me, here's the second copy," said Jennifer, as she handed over the second recording over to Kate.

"Perfect," said Kate, as she grabbed hold of the device. "Now, we just need to safely make it back into the ballroom and hand these recordings over to the Turkish Authorities and the U.S. Marshals."

"The Turkish Authorities and the U.S. Marshals? You've contacted them, already?" asked a surprised Jennifer.

"Yes, I did; as of yesterday. As it turns out, Lucas didn't have a very good reputation, with either one of them. In particular, the U.S. Marshals are more than eager to see his government contract between the agency and Orion Securities completely disposed of. If his contract is terminated, then there's a strong possibility that they can be reinstated back to their old posts."

"But Kate, how are we going to hand these tapes over to them, before Lucas reaches us, first?" asked Jennifer.

"Miles is at the party. All we need to do is find him, give him the tapes, and then, he'll take care of all the rest," replied Kate, confidently.

"Miles? Why Miles? Doesn't he work for Lucas?" asked Jennifer, confused by Kate's instructions.

"He's a mole. A double agent. Miles is really a U.S. Marshal working undercover as an Orion Security Officer. His real name is Murat Firat, and he's an American of Turkish origin. He's been spying on Lucas for years now. According to Miles, he's always suspected Lucas for numerous crimes, but unfortunately, he never had enough solid proof to pursue and dispose of him. Apparently, Lucas is high up on the U.S. Marshals' agenda. Their agency wants their jobs returned back to them at the embassy, and they are willing to do whatever it takes to bring him and Orion Securities down, in order to accomplish their goal. Recently, I only came to discover the truth about Miles, after our last meeting. After you revealed to me your dangerous and deathly encounter with Lucas, I immediately contacted the local Turkish police."

"You did? Why did you do that?" asked Jennifer, in complete surprise; never once, suspecting her sister to do such a thing.

"Because we needed help," answered Kate. "If we couldn't trust the local embassy police, then who else could we turn to? If not the Americans, then we needed the Turks. Therefore, after our last meeting, I went straight to the Turkish police. Using my Turkish language skills, I demanded to speak directly to the Turkish commander, where I came to learn that they were already working alongside with Miles. Apparently, Lucas is already a suspect for a string of other black-market and drug smuggling crimes, here in this country."

"Somehow, I'm not surprised to hear that about him," Jennifer remarked, as she and Kate continued to chat and run down the grand, but rather long hallway.

"I've already spoken to Miles, and I believe that we can trust him. Miles also has contacts with the local Turkish police, and he's already recruited them, along with a few extra other U.S. Marshals to serve as undercover backups to the party. At this point, all that we need to do is just to make it into the ballroom safely, and then hand either one of the tapes over to him."

"Are you certain that Miles isn't somehow, covering up for Lucas? Can we really trust him?" asked a concerned Jennifer.

"I'm certain. Besides, he's all we got," Kate concluded.

"That's very true. But as of right now, we've got bigger fish to fry. Sooner or later, Lucas is sure to catch up with us. What if he gets to us, before we get to Miles?"

"Well, it'll be a lot harder to get to us, if he can't tell either one of us apart," replied Kate, with a smile.

"What do you mean?" asked Jennifer, with a raised brow.

"Jennifer, it's time to remove your wig," Kate commanded.

"The wig? Kate, I can easily remove my wig, but we're still wearing two different outfits. Obviously, Lucas is going to know it's me, on account of my black dress and your golden gown," Jennifer stated.

"That's why I asked Sally to design this special dress, just for this occasion," replied Kate, with a smile and a wink.

With one pull of her strap, Kate's golden dress completely fell down onto the floor, revealing a form fitted black gown hidden underneath her previous gown. Most importantly, it was a gown that was now completely identical to Jennifer's own dress.

"There," said Kate. "Now, no one can tell either one of us apart."

"Kate, you are brilliant!" exclaimed Jennifer, happily.

"Thank you. Now, it's show time," said Kate, as they finally reached the ballroom's entrance.

For the first time in their lives, Kate and Jennifer arrived together to a given venue, resembling each other identically, in both their appearances and attires. Upon entering the ballroom, they quickly split up: Kate gravitated towards the left side of the room, while Jennifer proceeded to walk along to the right. To their advantage, the ballroom was large and crowded enough, for no one to have easily noticed that there were two of them in the room. While Kate was busy mingling with the other guests on the left half of the ballroom, Jennifer concentrated on the right half— until at least one of them eventually reached Miles, first.

As Kate walked across the ballroom, she tried her best to keep an eye out for Jennifer; while at the same time, scanning the room and searching for Miles. According to their plans, Miles was supposed to be already here and waiting for their return, inside the ballroom. However, at this very moment, Kate failed to locate him through this busy crowd. Sadly, there were simply too many people, all around. But time was still ticking and sooner or later, Lucas was going to find them; therefore, Kate needed to act fast and find Miles, before Lucas got to them, first.

Suddenly, the lights dimmed down and the orchestra began to play music. Slowly, the guests migrated over to the dancefloor, with their respective partners. With a mass exodus of anxious people flocking to the stage, Kate gained a much better view of the ballroom's overall interior. Finally, there at the far end of the room, closest to the exit, Kate saw Miles standing near the back exit door, along with two other officers. At long last, Kate found him. Now, all that she needed to do was to simply cut straight across the stage and make it to the very end.

"Kate," said a voice, suddenly.

Immediately, Kate turned around and to her surprise, she saw John standing before her. Unfortunately, Kate never previously factored John, with part of her plans. Naturally, she presumed that he'd be away and far too busy mingling with the other ambassadors; that the possibility of them ever running into each other at the party was almost slim to nothing. However, Kate couldn't have been more mistaken.

"Shall we dance?" asked John, as he swiftly took hold of her hand.

"Right now?" asked Kate, anxiously.

"Why not?" asked John, laughingly. "Everyone else is here, dancing with their wives. Why not us?"

Had the circumstances been different, then Kate would have loved to have danced with John. Within a single heartbeat, Kate would have thrown and surrendered herself straight into his arms, while they wistfully floated away onto the dancefloor, without ever expressing an opposing thought. However, this wasn't the proper time. Kate couldn't afford to waste not a second more. One way or another, she needed to make it across the stage and over to Miles. However, there were several dancers currently blocking her walking path towards him. Suddenly, Kate realized that if she were to reach Miles successfully, then perhaps, dancing wasn't such a bad idea, after all; for if she danced with John, then she was almost guaranteed to make it straight ahead and reach the end of the ballroom.

"Very well, let's dance," Kate enthusiastically agreed, as she followed John over to the dancefloor.

Once they reached the stage, the previous waltz came to an abrupt end and the conductor signaled to his orchestra to start the next song. After a long and quiet pause, the music began to play. But the next song choice that came to play, left Kate standing still.

"The tango?" gasped Kate.

"Why Kate, do I detect a hint of fear within your voice?" asked John, teasingly.

"It's just that…the tango is so…so…so…" Kate started to trail off, finding it difficult to finish her thought.

"So passionate," added John, attempting to finish her sentence.

"Yes," Kate admitted.

"Come now, Kate, you've been practicing the tango for several weeks. Now, is your chance to finally showcase your hidden talent to the rest of the world. Besides, you've got me as your handsome partner; therefore, what could possibly go wrong?" he asked, ever-so charmingly.

But before Kate could utter another word in response to his statement, the music grew louder, forcing the pair to take their places and begin their dance. As John's grip on Kate's hand grew tighter, he gently pulled her onto the stage. When their eyes finally met each other, the room fell silent, as the music grew more intense, giving birth to the passion of their impending tango.

Meanwhile, on the opposite side of the ballroom, Jennifer was busy searching for Miles, as well. As she glanced around the room, looking for both the man-in-question and a safe and secure exit, she also couldn't help but wonder about the whereabouts of her sister. Did she beat her to Miles? Did he now have the tape, securely held within his possession? Was this nightmare now finally over? Then, suddenly, she saw Kate from the corner of her eye. To her surprise, Kate was standing right in front of none other, than John.

For a long moment, Jennifer silently stared at the couple from afar, as she watched the pair interact together, for the very first time. To her amazement, John seemed different from the last time she saw him. Unlike the man of a thousand tasks, tonight he seemed solely focused on one important task at hand: Kate. Curious, Jennifer keenly watched on, as John stared directly into Kate's eyes, while he remained completely focused and transfixed upon her and ignoring the long stray of his other fellow ambassadors standing nearby, most eager for his attention. Apart from being most attentive to her, John also looked fully engaged with his conversation with her— even going so far, as to hold her hand, ever-so tightly. But the most surprising of all, was that John had a peculiar twinkle in his eye…that seemed…as if…he was almost…well…happy?

Amused, Jennifer couldn't help but smile. In all of her years with him, she had never seen this happy, ever before. Why, the way he simply stared at Kate…why…he'd never…ever before…looked at her, in that very same way! No, concluded Jennifer, this was the first time that she'd ever seen John look at another person, with so much love and care within his eyes. Deep down, Jennifer knew that while the lips could easily tell a lie, the eyes told an entirely different story. It was one's eyes, that spoke the truth of one's own heart, no matter the circumstances. And at that very moment, Jennifer realized that somehow during her absence, John found his match.

As for her sister, Kate looked absolutely memorizing. With the low dimmed chandelier lights, Kate dazzled and shined across the stage, while she appeared to be blissfully happy with her partner. For the first time in Jennifer's life, she finally saw the look of true love in twin sister's eyes. If Jennifer had any previous self-doubts about her sister's true feelings and affections for John before, then they were now quickly put to rest; for it was with the utmost sincerest clarity that Jennifer knew that Kate was absolutely head-over-in-heels in love with John, and he the same with her, in return.

"They really do bring out the best versions of themselves through each other," Jennifer whispered to herself, with admiration.

Suddenly, a tear fell from Jennifer's eye. Truly, she was happy for them. Both. All these years, she had always prayed for her sister to find happiness, and the same for John, too. Although she and John failed in their relationship, Jennifer also knew that they were always a mismatch, even from the very start. But now, after discovering her own happiness with Selim, seeing John and Kate happily together, made her feel a little bit better. Unlike before, Jennifer no longer felt so guilty about leaving her old life behind and starting anew; because if the pair standing before her could, then why couldn't she, too?

But alas, time was still ticking away, and Jennifer soon remembered her urgent mission to locate Miles. Scanning across the room, Jennifer finally spotted Miles standing at the far corner, near the exit. Now, all Jennifer needed to do was to walk over to Miles, and inform him that they finally captured Lucas' confession on tape. But before Jennifer had the chance to even take one step forward, the ballroom suddenly multiplied. What began as a small handful of dancers standing on stage, was now covered with a sea of people, all dancing away to the music of the night. If Jennifer was ever going to successfully make it across to Miles, then she was going to have to dance her way to him! Although Jennifer was never shy of a good dance; but given such short notice, who could she possibly find, as a last-minute dance partner?

Searching throughout the ballroom, Jennifer quickly realized that she didn't have many options. Most attendees were either already dancing on the ballroom floor with their own dance partners, or were seated at their tables and eating dinner. Sadly, there simply weren't as many other remaining single by-standers left. Time was ticking and sooner or later, Lucas was going to catch up with them and she needed to beat him. She had to. Their lives depended upon it. But before all hope was lost, Jennifer spotted an opportunity. An available match. As the male silhouette turned around before her, she realized that her only available potential dance partner was a short man, who was a bit chubby, bald and appeared to have a bad case of the sweats; for at that very moment, he was sweating excessively from the top of his forehead, right down to his palms. As the man pulled a handkerchief from his pocket top dry his face, Jennifer realized that the man standing before her was none other than Bes, from the mansion! For a brief moment, Jennifer cringed at the very thought of dancing with him; especially, given his sweating condition. Why, his sweaty hands were sure to rub off on her delicate fingers! However, Jennifer quickly weighed her options carefully and ultimately, she knew that she simply had to dance with him. And so, Jennifer took a deep breath and took a step forward into Bes' direction.

Meanwhile, as the orchestra began to play, Kate found herself standing opposite from John on stage. Carefully, he positioned them for their upcoming tango, with their arms extended directly apart, and him ready to lead the way. While he remained proud and confident, Kate, in contrast, felt so incredibly uneasy, that even her own knees began to shake from such fright. On the one hand, there was the matter concerning dancing the tango in public— a dance that she had still yet to fully master, as she was absolutely fearful of performing it in front of a crowd— and second, there was the dreadful situation pertaining to Lucas, and the imminent threat he posed to Jennifer and her. However, before Kate could contemplate even further, the lights dimmed down and the audience fell into complete silence.

"Just follow my lead," said John, in his attempt to reassure and comfort her.

Sensing her agitation, John tried his best to help ease her fear by pulling her directly into his strong and dominant frame; all the while, making her well aware that no matter what happened next, he wasn't ever going to allow her to fail. Certainly, not on his watch.

Much to her credit, Kate did indeed, follow his lead. As he stepped forward, she stepped forward. As he moved over to the right; she too, moved over to the right. Furthermore, when he turned back and over to his side; she too, followed his exact steps. Slowly but surely, she was dancing the tango with him.

"You see, it's not that bad," he whispered into her ear.

"You're right," she agreed, in amazement.

"So far, so good?" he asked, with a raised brow.

"So far, so…" she begun to say, but before she could complete her sentence, she suddenly saw Lucas enter into the room.

Standing right at the ballroom's entrance, Lucas was as red as an apple. Clearly, he was angry and ready to attack. Time was running out. No more delays. One way or another, Kate needed to get to Miles and quickly!

Shifting gears, Kate promptly took charge of the situation. Without further warning, Kate swiftly changed their chorography and began to lead John. This unexpected shift in their dance steps certainly caught John's attention; however, rather than being distraught, he was instead, amused by Kate's sudden change of interest.

"A leading lady isn't quite traditional for the tango," he remarked, laughingly.

"I thought that I might shake it up a bit," she replied, with one eye looking at John and the other eye watching Lucas.

After taking control, Kate pushed their way through the crowd of other dancers, transporting them from the center of the stage, over to the far-right hand corner, towards Miles' direction. While Kate pushed forward, John marched right behind her. Surprisingly, when Kate pulled John into a close embrace, he silently understood her unspoken queue and in return, he added his own special moves in the process by twirling her into a full circular spin. Although Kate was only mere inches away from Miles, she also knew that her untimely decision to take the lead, might have likely caused an embarrassing entanglement for John's reputation, in front of his fellow peers, due to her poor execution and bad attempt to dance the tango. However, to Kate's sheer surprise, the audience suddenly began to roar and cheer for them. It seemed that Kate's unorthodox dance moves certainly caught the crowd's attention, and the entire room began clapping and whistling for the unpredictable dance duo!

For a brief moment, all seemed well. At long last, the nightmare was almost over. With only a few steps away from Miles, the crowd continued to cheer them on. It was almost time. Soon enough, Kate was going to turn the tape over to Miles, and then everything was going to be okay. Everyone, whom she cared deeply for, was going to be safe from any harm. As Kate approached the edge of the dancefloor, she caught Miles' attention and made direct eye contact with him. With John standing across from her, she briefly bent down and pulled out the recording tape from underneath her slip pocket, which was located inside of her dress. Finally, Kate extended her hand over to Miles, who by now, had already started to run towards her direction. And then, just as Kate was right about to transfer the tape over to him, a sudden and loud pop burst from the scene. It was a gunshot!

Immediately, the orchestra ceased playing the music, and the audience started to scream and run in panic. As the dancers continued to flee the scene, Kate looked at her hand and realized that in the midst of this unexpected chaos, her tape suddenly went missing! Looking across the stage, Kate saw that her tape was badly damaged and was now lying on the floor, broken into several pieces! It seemed that the gun shot managed to hit and destroy her tape! The very evidence that they so desperately needed, in order to incriminate Lucas for his crimes, once and for all!

"Looks like you won't be needing that, anymore," Lucas remarked laughingly, as he walked across the stage to join them.

Along the way, Lucas passed by the broken tape and with his eyes directly staring into hers, he lifted up his heavy leg and in one swift move, he stomped all over the remaining pieces of her tape—smashing them into further dust.

"What's the meaning of this!" John screamed, red with rage.

"Nothing of your concern, Ambassador," replied Lucas, with a sadistic smile.

"What do you mean, it's nothing of my concern? You've scared the hell out of everyone inside of this room!" exclaimed John, angrily.

However, unfortunately for John, Lucas was no longer interested with his dealings with him. This time around, his attention was directly aimed at Kate, only.

"Where's your sister?" asked Lucas, with a raised brow.

"Sister?" repeated John, in confusion.

"Yes, her sister," Lucas repeated, while he purposely placed a strong emphasis on the word 'sister.' Suddenly, with a devilish grin painted across his ugly face, Lucas said, "Ambassador, didn't she tell you…why, they've been partners, all along."

"That's a lie!" yelled Kate, in her immediate defense.

"A lie? Really? Well, where's that sister of yours? Have her come forward, so that she can confirm for us the truth about your games. We both know that she's here tonight, right in this very same room, don't we," said Lucas, while enjoying his new game of manipulation.

"Games?" repeated John. With a heavy heart, he asked, "Kate, did you lie to me? I…I… trusted you."

"No, I never lied to you, John!" exclaimed Kate. "John, he's the criminal! He's behind everything! Please I beg of you, don't believe him!"

"She's telling the truth," Miles interrupted, who was now, at long last, standing nearby them and helping to confirm Kate's version of the story.

"Why Miles, you too?" asked Lucas, with a sadistic grin.

"Yes," replied Miles.

"Well," huffed Lucas, "Either way, now, neither one of you have any proof!" he exclaimed, as he began to laugh hysterically and uncontrollable—just like the true and devious villain that he was.

"Wait," yelled a woman suddenly, from afar. As she approached them, Kate soon realized that it was Jennifer who called and came to their rescue.

"Jennifer?" gasped John aloud. "Where did you come from?"

"We'll catch up later," replied Jennifer, and then, she quickly yelled, "Bes, play it now!"

By the press of a single button, Bes played the tape recording via the audio speakers, while the entire audience listened to Lucas' confession play aloud throughout each and every room inside of the mansion. By his own admission, it was made perfectly clear on tape before all, that Lucas Oliver was indeed Owen Lawrence, the estranged son of retired Ambassador David Lawrence. Furthermore, the recording also confirmed his long quest for revenge, which resulted in a host of other various crimes, including the assault and attempted murder of both the ambassador and his wife. At long last, Lucas was going to be punished and held accountable for his crimes!

"Arrest him!" John ordered, while screaming at the top of his lungs.

Immediately, Miles signaled to the rest of the other officers to pursue their arrest; however, right before Miles could reach over and handcuff him, Lucas made one last and final surprise. Within the blink of an eye, Lucas managed to grab hold of Kate's arm, as he violently pulled her over towards him, with her back facing him. While he continued to hold her against her will, Lucas quickly pulled out his gun from his pocket and then, using that same gun, he directly aimed it right across the side of her head.

"Don't do anything, or else I'll shoot and kill her!" Lucas warned, as he aggressively held onto Kate, like a ragged doll.

"Please, don't hurt her! I'll give you whatever you want! Just please, don't harm her! Take me, instead!" John pleaded, in desperation.

In an instant, John's heart began violently pounding, as he witnessed his worst and most unimaginable fear come to life. Suddenly, his body grew gravely cold and tense. Standing still like an immobile zombie, John's entire being was covered with goosebumps, on every inch and ounce of his body.

"Anything?" replied Lucas, with a raised brow and smile; satisfied on how quickly the tables had turned in his favor.

"Yes, anything," John directly guaranteed, without any hesitation.

"Okay, I'll let her go, on the condition that I can walk away from here, as a free man and everyone says nothing about what just happened here. It will be as if tonight never happened, in the first place," Lucas firmly demanded.

"Alright, you have my word," John vowed. "Now, I beg of you," John desperately pleaded, as his face grew white with fear, "Please release her to me."

"You really do care about this one, don't you ambassador?" asked Lucas, in a rather sinister and mocking tone. "I don't blame you," he added. "Even, I, also took an interest in her, myself."

In an effort to further increase John's agony, Lucas pressed harder against Kate's tender arms; but before he could even attempt to make another move, John instantly rushed over and threw himself, right on top of Lucas. As the two men came tumbling down onto the floor, Lucas had no choice but to release his tight grip on Kate. Once he let go of her, she slammed right down onto the ground right beside them, falling like a used and disregarded old toy. While the two men besides her fought, Jennifer quickly rushed over to Kate's side, and immediately, she dragged her sister safely away from the heightened escalation.

"Wait," cried Kate, "We must get to John! We can't leave him behind!"

Suddenly, a gun shot fired. Immediately, Kate's heart sunk. Was someone shot? Did someone get hurt? Dear God, was it John? Luckily, Kate didn't have to wait long to get answers. Soon afterwards, Miles came rushing over to John's side. As it turned out, during the conflict between the two men, Lucas' gun managed to slide down onto the floor, where it landed nearby to Miles. In one swift move, Miles immediately retrieved the gun and proceeded to shoot a bullet nearby, in an attempt to stop the fight and regain Lucas' attention. However, in the process, Lucas, instead, pulled himself away from John's tight grip. After freeing himself, Lucas threw John aside and then, he bolted away, running straight out of the exit door, leading into the back garden.

"He's getting away!" cried Jennifer, in panic, as she saw Lucas fleeing the crime scene.

"Don't worry, I'll take it from here," replied Miles, confidently, as he quickly took command of the current crisis. "I have all of my men in place. We're ready. He won't make it far."

Meanwhile, Kate immediately ran over to John, who was currently still lying down on the floor.

"John, are you alright, my love?" said Kate, as she fell onto the floor, right beside him.

"I'm fine, but most important, are you alright? If anything happened to you, then I just don't know what I would have done…" John trailed off, as he swiftly threw his arms around Kate, and held her as tight as he possibly could, within his embrace.

"John, I'm okay," Kate reassured him, "But I think you just saved my life."

"Kate," John replied, as his coloring slowly returned back to him.

Then, in the most serious of tones, John said, "Kate, this shouldn't come as a surprise to you. I would risk my life a thousand times over, if it meant that you'll be safe from any harm. Never forget this. Not ever."

Instantly, Kate locked eyes with him, and at that very moment, she was just about ready to kiss him, when they were unexpectedly interrupted by Jennifer.

"Ahem," she announced herself.

"Yes?" asked Kate, in return.

"I don't mean to ruin this romantic moment, but Lucas is getting away, as we speak! Honestly, we must act fast to stop him, right now!" exclaimed Jennifer, as she passionately sought to remind them of Lucas' fugitive state.

"There's not much that we can do, right at this moment," John reluctantly admitted.

"Besides," John continued, "He's escaping outside onto Turkish soil. Legally, we don't have any jurisdiction to capture and arrest him, outside of this embassy. I would have to get in contact with—"

"Perhaps, not legally for the Americans, but not for the Turkish police. Luckily, for us, he's just crossed straight into my territory and now, finally, we've got him," Miles interrupted, as he reached into his pocket and pulled out his badge, identifying him as Murat Firat.

"You're with the Turkish police?" asked John, in amazement, as he was thoroughly surprised that one of his men had been working undercover.

"Wait," cried Jennifer, "I thought that you were with the U.S. Marshals?"

"Technically, I'm with both camps. As an officer in the Turkish police, I've also been collaborating with the Marshals, in our mutual efforts to arrest Lucas. Also, my name's Murat Firat, not Miles Ford," he said, with a smile and a wink.

Suddenly, an unexpected loud noise burst right outside of the mansion walls; which in return, vibrated the interiors inside of the ballroom. As the crowd quickly gathered and rushed outside onto the balcony to see all of the commotion, Kate and her companions, all followed behind the crowd. It was there at the balcony, from a bird eye's view, that they all witnessed a fiery orange and red brazing fire burn across the smoky sky. Amazingly, the source of the fire was so incredibly close, as it was located just outside the mansion's gates. Furthermore, the fire was so large and powerful, that pieces of broken debris floated across the sky and scattered ashes fell among the mass audience, who were all standing in attendance.

"What happened?" asked Jennifer.

"He got into his car to flee the scene; but he didn't go too far, before he crashed into that olive tree, right over there," replied one of the guests, as he used his index finger to point towards the blazing fire.

"Is that his car burning out there?" Jennifer, inquired, in complete shock.

"Yes, and he's most certainly dead."

Chapter 32

"You must forgive him," David pleaded, from his hospital bed. "No matter the circumstances, you have to forgive him."

"I can't," admitted Amy.

"But you have to try," David advised. "You have to be the better person, which I know that you are. Please, don't repeat the same mistakes, that I made in my past."

"Father, your situation with Owen was entirely different from mine," Amy reminded him.

"It doesn't matter," answered David, with tearful eyes. "It really doesn't matter. Forgiveness is required from all of us, as we're all equally sinners."

"Father, that's not true," Amy insisted.

"Yes, it's true. We're all sinners. We all make mistakes. We're all human," David concluded.

"But father…" spoke Amy.

"If I had forgiven your brother earlier all those years ago, then maybe he'd be here today. Alive. Maybe…just maybe…I could have saved him. Changed him. Prevented him from becoming the monster that he became in the end," David admitted, with much regret.

"Father, you can't blame yourself for Owen's evil deeds! He was a monster! His actions had nothing to do with us! Owen committed those evil deeds, all on his own. It had nothing to do with your upbringing. Everything that he did, he did out of his own free will," Amy boldly proclaimed.

"But Amy, I disowned him at a young and impressionable age. It's because of me…because of my own selfish regard to my reputation and career, that I turned him away. I turned by back and closed the door on my only son, due to a mistake he made as a young and foolish boy…not even yet a man. Due to my selfishness and ego, I lost him and your mother. Now, sadly, there's no turning back. No hope for redemption. He's finally gone…" said David, as he began to weep.

"Father, please don't cry," Amy begged, as she rushed over to console her grieving father.

"Amy, please just try to find it within your generous and loving heart to forgive Peter. I know that you can. You have to. Eventually, I'm not going to be around here forever. Now, especially, given that your brother is dead. As your father, it's my duty to ensure that you'll be looked after, once I'm gone. My only wish is to you see married and taken cared for," David pleaded.

"Father, you're going to survive this. Besides, no matter what happens, I'm going to be okay, too. I promise," Amy reassured him.

"Does this mean that you'll forgive Peter?" asked David, with a sparkle of hope in his watery eyes.

"Yes, I'll forgive him," replied Amy, reluctantly.

In the end, Amy didn't have the heart to disappoint her ill and grieving father. If lying to him gave him peace, then Amy was willing to say whatever it took to keep her father happy. Regardless, of her own personal feelings about the matter, Amy decided to bite her tongue and humor her beloved father.

Kissing her father's forehead, Amy briefly excused herself from her father's hospital bedroom and walked straight out into the hallway. After everything that had recently transpired, she was dreading this very moment. But alas, she needed to face her own demon: Peter.

The time had finally come for her to meet with Peter, her fiancé, who was currently waiting for her, right outside her father's room. Seated down on one of the many hospital chairs in the waiting room, with his head buried within his arms, Peter looked like a dreadful mess. His hair was all out of place and his clothes were wrinkly, along with several coffee stains scattered all over. Sadly, only twenty-four hours ago, Amy thought that Peter was the most wonderful and loving man in the entire world. A man, whom she wanted nothing more, than to wrap her loving arms tightly around him. However, now, she wanted nothing more, than to grab his neck by her own bare hands and kill him! Oh, how so much had transpired, just overnight!

Last night, everything changed for her. It was there at the NATO state dinner, where Amy discovered that her long lost brother, Owen, was not only still alive and well, but he was also a dangerous criminal, living under the alias of Lucas Oliver, the CEO and Chief Security Officer of Orion Securities. Not only had her estranged brother terrorize everyone in attendance, but he nearly got her friends killed, too. To make matters worse, Owen was also responsible for the skiing accident that almost claimed the lives of their father and their dearest friend, John. The same dear friend, who had stood by her side all these years, by serving as a foster brother to her. But if that wasn't enough, her own fiancé, Peter, was also his accomplice! Really, this was all way too much! No matter his excuse, Amy knew that she could never move forward to marry Peter. Not now, not ever.

"Amy!" exclaimed Peter joyfully, once he saw her enter into the waiting room.

Although Peter seemed happy to see her; Amy, in contrast, wasn't as equally amused to see him, at all. Instead, Amy only agreed to see him at the hospital, in order to gain some final clarity about what really happened. Alas, Amy was most eager to get this over and done with, so that she could finally close this difficult chapter in her young adult life and move on, for good.

"Amy, please give me a chance! I can fix everything!" he pleaded, as he fell down onto the floor, while desperately seeking for her forgiveness and mercy.

"Peter, get up from there," Amy commanded. "We need to talk."

"I'll tell you everything," Peter promised.

"Well, you better start talking. For starters, why did you betray me?" she asked angrily.

"Betray you? I didn't betray you! I did it for us!" exclaimed Peter, in desperation.

"For us? How was aiding my cruel and demented brother, helping us?" asked Amy, who was now gravely upset and confused by his admission.

"Your brother offered me a deal, that if I served as his secret informant, then in exchange, he was going to transfer his portion of your father's inheritance to me— leaving us with your family's entire fortune, without having to share it with anyone else. My love, with that sort of money, I'd be able to afford to open my new dental practice in Connecticut, while still having enough money left over in the bank to buy us a newly customed built private mansion of our very own. I figured that this way, I'd finally have the financial means to provide and keep up with the proper life-style that you were accustomed and born into," Peter explained.

"Oh, Peter, how could you! Did you really believe that I was this heartless and cruel? That I was this incredibly superficial? I mean, don't you know me by now? Or did you even truly know me, at all? Because if you did, then you'd already know that I've never carried about the money! Not ever!" exclaimed Amy, as she immediately began to cry out of sheer frustration.

Quickly, Peter dashed over to Amy's side, in his hopeful attempt to console her.

"Amy, I might have exaggerated about my past history and background," he began, "But the truth is that we're poor and we've always been poor. I only attended these elite universities solely based on student loans, alone. Unfortunately, as it stands, I'm in so much financial debt, that it will honestly take me several years, if not decades, to pay everything back to the banks. At first, I was content with living a simple and modest life, free from the burden of living excessively and keeping up with society. But then, I met you and everything changed. Amy, you grew up wealthy and privileged. You've never known what it's been like to struggle financially. To grow up living in the slums, and part of a family living off of welfare. No, Amy, I couldn't allow you to experience my same upbringing. I was determined to provide for you, by ensuring that you had the lavish and luxurious lifestyle that you deserved. That's why I did, what I did and I have no regrets."

"But Peter, your actions almost cost my father his life!" Amy angrily yelled.

"Yes, but I did it for the greater good. Listen Amy, you need to accept the truth that your father is dying. As a matter of fact, he's only got just a matter of a few months," Peter confessed.

"Don't say that!" Amy exclaimed.

"But it's the truth and sadly, you need to hear it. To face. You need to accept that your father is already dying, as we speak. Furthermore, as it currently stands, if we don't do anything to alter his will, then once he's dead and gone, his fortune…. your fortune…our fortune…it will not come to us, in full. Amy, you're his rightful her; especially, given your brother's untimely passing. Plus, John doesn't deserve not a penny from your father. If we're forced to share the inheritance, then that income, combined with my practice, will not be enough to sustain us, well into the future. At least with your brother, had Owen survived that unfortunate car accident, then I'm certain that he would have given us everything, including the additional royalties earned through his successful enterprise via Orion Securities. Plus, now that's he's deceased and without a family of his own, you're his next of kin, who stands to also inherit his company, too," Peter explained.

"Peter, are you even listening to yourself? How can you say such things?" asked Amy, with a heavy heart.

"Because I want you to know everything. I want us to start being on the same page. For us to stand together, as a united front. Amy, I love you.

Regardless of our pasts, it's still my intention to marry you and to claim you as my loving wife. And we can still have that perfect life, too. The life that we originally envisioned, together. A happily ever after, for us both. All you need to do is just forgive me, so that we can work past all of this," Peter insisted.

But alas, Amy wasn't in agreement with Peter's vision of their future… her future... at least.

"You know," Amy began, as she wiped her wet tears away from her eyes, "Before I came out here to meet with you, my father advised me that I should forgive you. He practically begged me, too."

"You see, your father is a very wise man. It's because he wants the best for you, and he knows that I'm still good for you, too," replied Peter, with a glimmer of hope still lingering about within his eyes.

"As I said before, my father begged me to find the courage to forgive you. He reminded me that all men are sinners; and so, he asked me to be the better person," Amy explained.

"Amy, you are. You are a wonderful person, which is why I love you so damn much," Peter admitted.

"Either way, I do forgive you Peter," Amy finally confessed, as she looked straight into his eyes.

"Oh, Amy! Thank you! I promise that you won't ever regret this decision! I will do whatever it takes to make you the happiest woman alive!" yelled a thrilled and excited Peter, as he immediately threw his arms around Amy and locked her in an embrace.

However, their embrace was short-lived; for soon afterwards, Amy quickly pushed Peter away and off from her, while she announced a rather shocking revelation of her very own.

"Peter, I do forgive you, but at the same time, I'll also never forget what you did, too; which is why, sadly, I can no longer marry you. Not now, not ever," she boldly proclaimed.

"Not marry me? But why? You just said that you forgave me!" yelled Peter, in shock and in horror.

"Forgiveness is one thing and stupid is another; and I've never been one to be stupid," replied Amy coldly.

"Amy, I don't understand. What exactly are you trying to tell me?" asked a devastated Peter.

"I forgive you, because I don't want to end up, just like the monster that my late brother became. It's because of his hatred and anger, that he wasted most of his adult life busy plotting revenge. Sadly, Owen never let go to the past, which is what he should have done years ago. He should have let go and moved on with his life. Maybe, this way, if he did, then he would still be here, right now, with us," Amy confessed.

"But that's your brother's fault. Not yours," Peter clarified.

"Precisely; which is why I'm doing myself this favor, right now. Peter, I'm willing to forgive you, so that I can forget you. Do you understand me?" asked Amy, with a heavy heart.

"Amy, is this it? We're just going to part ways, like nothing ever happened?" he asked.

"Well, that's just it. Something did happen. Peter, all actions have consequences and sadly, this is a consequence to your devious dealings with my brother. This is it. Goodbye Peter," said Amy, forcefully.

And before Peter could say another word to object to Amy's proclamation, she swiftly removed her engagement ring from her finger, and then, she reached over and aggressively grabbed hold of Peter's hand. Once she forcefully opened his palm, Amy placed her engagement ring back into his possession. Now, it was official. There was no turning back. Their engagement was over.

"Well, Amy, there's nothing else that I can say, at this point. Although I understand your views, but I'm still disappointed that you failed to see my side of the story, too. Sadly, I just wish that circumstances could have been different for us, that's all. But please just know, that no matter what happens next, I will always love you, unconditionally," Peter confessed, while feeling rather melancholy about their failed romance.

After having been rejected by the love of his life, Peter reluctantly walked down the hallway to finally exit the hospital, for good. Meanwhile, Amy failed to turn around to look back at him when he left; not once, did she even bother to wave a final goodbye to him, as he entered into the elevator. Once Peter was gone, Amy returned back into her father's bedroom and sat down on the empty chair besides his bed. While her father peacefully slept, Amy silently watched over him, with loving and caring eyes. After the numerous strings of shocking revelations that had recently came into light these past twenty-four hours; time still remained the greatest mystery, above all else.

Whether or not David survived this devastating ordeal, no really one knew. But this much Amy did know for certain: for however long David still had left to live on this earth, Amy planned to remain right by his side, for however long it took for David to heal. Surprisingly, Amy found comfort and solace in this. Although she might have lost her true love, Peter; at least, for now, Amy still had her father and that was plenty enough for her. In the end, Amy came to realize that sometimes in life, letting go and saying goodbye is what one must do for the sake of peace, regardless of how much it hurts and agonizes inside one's soul.

Meanwhile, back at the mansion, Kate was ready to say a few goodbyes of her own. With Jennifer's reemergence from hiding and Lucas' crimes brought into light, the case was finally closed. Alas, the time had finally come for this professor to leave Istanbul and return to her old life back in New York.

"Are you sure that you don't want me to help you pack?" asked Sally, who was standing next to Kate's bed, while Kate was busy gathering and packing away her belongings into a suitcase.

"There's really not much left," Kate admitted. "Honestly, I arrived here with literally nothing, at all. But unlike my arrival, this time I'll depart with a few extra pairs of these lovely gowns that you've recently gifted me."

"I promise to send you more, too. After all, you're my muse and number one client," Sally laughingly remarked.

"By the way," Sally added. "I also think that you made the right decision to revert back to your natural brown hair. It's much more sophisticated. Besides, blonde hair is so last season."

"Well, don't tell that to Jennifer, as she's still a blonde," replied Kate, laughingly. "But in truth, blonde hair will be rather difficult for me to maintain and style on my own. Although, I must admit, it was rather fun while it lasted. But for now, I'm keeping some of my blonde highlights to help serve, as a reminder of my time spent over here."

"A reminder of your time spent here, what a nice way of putting it," Sally remarked.

"I suppose that it's rather symbolic, isn't it? After all, you arrived as a brunette and now, you're leaving and keeping a few traces of your adventures here, in the form of your blonde highlights. In the end, I guess that once we leave home, we can never truly return back ever quite the same again. At least, I know that's true for me."

"That's very true," agreed Kate, "I suppose that's the same case with me, too."

"Either way, blonde, brunette or redhead, it really doesn't matter! Honestly, Dr. Stanley, I simply can't thank you enough! Because of you, my phone line has been ringing nonstop!" exclaimed Sally.

"Does this mean that you've already told them, that you're leaving to open your own fashion company? Remember Sally, you can always open up another studio in New York, near me," Kate playfully teased.

"I haven't yet, but I will. As for New York, maybe one day. But for now, it's going to be Milan," replied Sally, happily.

"Oh my, Sally, your dreams are finally coming true, after all! I'm so incredibly happy for you!" exclaimed Kate, as the two ladies embraced in a hug.

"Knock, knock, can we come in?" asked Carol at the door, who was also accompanied by Bes and Tyler.

"Of course, please do come in!" exclaimed Kate, who was happily surprised to see the trio together inside of her bedroom.

"Are we having some sort of unannounced meeting?" asked Sally, who was also equally surprised to see them unannounced.

"Not formally, but we still wanted to stop by to say our goodbyes to Dr. Stanley," Carol admitted.

"Is this really going to be goodbye? It seems like you've just arrived here, only but yesterday. Besides, we still have more dance lessons to practice and rehearse. Why, we never did finish our tango lessons," Bes reminded Kate.

"I think it safe to say that Dr. Stanley is already a pro at the tango. I mean, at the party, she was the total belle of the ball! The Ambassador and Dr. Stanley certainly caught everyone's attention last night with their version of the tango," Carol interrupted.

"Yes, I do believe that the Spanish Ambassador was most impressed by your unconventional dance moves," added Tyler.

"Not to go off subject, but did you hear the good news, yet? Our very own Carol has been promoted to be the next embassy coordinator. Once Gloria retires next month, Carol will be taking over her role. Furthermore, until Carol is completely comfortable in her new position, I've already agreed to stay on board, to help serve as her mentor," Bes proudly announced.

"Carol, that's such wonderful news! I'm so happy for you!" exclaimed Kate, as she quickly rushed over to Carol and gave her a congratulated hug.

"Dr. Stanley, thank you. If it wasn't for you, then I don't think that any of this could have happened, at all," Carol admitted.

"Nonsense," replied Kate, "You've earned this position, all by yourself. I had absolutely nothing to do with it. You got this position, because you worked hard for it."

"Thank you again, Dr. Stanley. After everything that I experienced, I promise that in this new role, I will strive to treat all of our staff with the dignity, kindness and the self-respect that they deserve," Carol vowed, with much conviction.

"I'm truly happy and proud to hear that, Carol," said Kate, smilingly.

"But I'm not the only one with good news. Tyler also got a promotion, too," said Carol, as she elbowed Tyler right in the stomach.

"Come now, Tyler, do tell them," Bes added.

"Very well," spoke Tyler, in a serious and professional tone. "Given that the election results are now in and we've elected a new President, I've been offered and accepted to become the next Assistant U.S. Attorney General, under the upcoming administration. Effective next month, I'll be leaving the embassy and traveling back to Washington, D.C."

"Impressive, isn't it? Imagine, our Tyler as the new Assistant U.S. Attorney General!" exclaimed Bes, enthusiastically, as he clapped for joy.

"Congratulations Tyler!" exclaimed Kate, proudly.

"Yes, congratulations!" Sally cheered on.

"Oh, Dr. Stanley, whatever happens, please do keep in touch!" Carol exclaimed.

"Yes, please do promise!" added Bes.

"Yes, I promise. Also, if either one of you decides to travel to New York, then please come and visit me, too," replied Kate, as she walked over and gave each of them a farewell hug.

Unexpectedly, a knock suddenly came at the door. Turning around, Kate saw that it was none other than Gloria, standing right there at the entrance to her bedroom door. Without uttering a single word, the staff silently excused themselves and cleared the room, leaving Kate alone with Gloria. Once everyone was gone, Gloria walked herself in and took a seat at the empty chair, near the foot of Kate's bed.

"Alone at last," sighed Gloria.

Ever since their last disagreement relating to her treatment of the staff and the dinner party, it had been several days since they last spoke. At this point, Kate wasn't entirely sure what to expect next. Regardless of their differences, given that Gloria was already here and seated before her, Kate was ready to face her, either way.

"Yes, Gloria?" Kate asked, with a raised brow.

"You know, Dr. Stanley, apart from our differences, I've always admired you. From day one, I said to myself, now that's a clever woman," Gloria admitted, as she reached into her pocket, pulled out a cigarette, lit it with a match, and then, proceeded to take her first puff of it, while leaving a ring of smoke right behind her.

"Gloria, do you smoke?" Kate asked, rather surprised that Gloria, having ran the mansion with an iron fist and was notorious for following the rules and avoiding any society taboos, would in return, be someone who secretly maintained the ill and unhealthy habit of smoking.

"That I do," replied Gloria, with a satisfactory smile. "What can I say, everyone's got a guilty secret; but please do me a favor and let's just keep this as our little secret. The others don't need to know."

Kate nodded in agreement. Her secret was safe with her.

"I knew that I could trust you," Gloria said, with much admiration. "Trust isn't something that comes off so easily for me. By now, I presume that you've already heard about my retirement next month. Naturally, Carol will be taking over, as can be expected."

"Yes, I did hear that," Kate admitted.

"Good. You know, it's honestly about time that I start to enjoy my retirement. For God only knows that I've been here far too long. Much longer than I, myself, ever expected," said Gloria, as she took another puff of her cigarette.

"My, my, where are my manners. Dr. Stanley, would you care for a cigarette of your own?" asked Gloria, as she reached over and offered her one.

"No, it's quite alright. I have a long flight ahead of me, so I rather not," Kate politely declined.

"Very well, suit yourself. Dr. Stanley, you know, now that I'm to retire, I'm not exactly sure as to what I'm supposed to do next, at this point. Amazingly enough, this is going to be the second time in my entire life, that I've honestly felt a bit lost. The fear of the unknown. Tragically, I suppose that you can say that my identity has been attached to this role for so long, that I've practically forgotten as to who I am outside of my profession," Gloria somberly reflected.

"Sadly, I, too, can relate. Before I came here, I, myself, have been guilty of the same," Kate admitted.

"I see. And do you know who you are, now?" Gloria asked, with a raised brow.

"I think I do; but like the rest of us, I'm still slowly piecing it all together," replied Kate.

"I'm glad to hear that. You know, once upon a time, before I joined the agency, I was a dancer," Gloria revealed.

"Really? Is that why you also taught dancing, here?" asked Kate, who was now, most intrigued by this surprising revelation.

"Yes, but I wasn't just any dancer. I was a professional ballerina. In fact, I toured all of Europe and America with my dance company. Back then, I was known by my stage name, Catherine Durac, which also happens to be my birth name, as well. Perhaps, you've heard of my name before?" asked Gloria, who by now, finished her first cigarette and was now lighting up her second one.

"Wait a minute, you're a Kate, too?" asked Kate, astonished that they also shared the similar first name.

"Out of everything, you managed to catch that," laughed Gloria. "Yes, I was. I still am. Why, do you think we got along so well together?" she asked, with a smile.

"I can't believe it," Kate remarked. "You know, come to think of it, I have heard of you before. My grandparents use to attend your concerts in New York. I remember them saying that you were one of their favorite dancers in the world. But then, suddenly, they said she, or err…you…just disappeared one day after a show in New York. They told me that you just danced one day, and then the next day you were gone, mid-season. Did you quit?" asked Kate, who was now practically star-struck that her own personal dancing instructor was none-other-than an actual world -famous prima ballerina!

"Yes and no," Gloria admitted. "One day I was a dancer, and then the next day, I was just someone else. But it wasn't exactly my choice."

"Do you mind me asking you what happened?" Kate asked hesitantly, while feeling uncertain as to how Gloria was going to react by her asking such a personal question.

"Two words: Viktor Petrov," answered Gloria, as she took another puff of her cigarette.

"Was he another dancer?" asked Kate, who was now very interested to learn more about Gloria's past.

"That he was. Based on your reaction, I take it that you've never heard of him, before?" asked Gloria, with a raised brow.

Silently, Kate simply nodded her head in agreement.

"I can't say that I'm so surprised by that, as we were all dancers so very long ago. But yes, he was another dancer too…as well as my lover. What can I say, I was young and foolish back then," Gloria shrugged.

"As we all are," Kate pointed out.

"True, but some of us, are more foolish than others. Either way, after our last show in New York, he abruptly ended our engagement. There was…of course…as usual…another woman. Another much younger…prettier ballerina from our dancing crew…who also just happened to be my understudy," Gloria sadly confessed.

"That's horrible," said Kate, who for the first time, was beginning to see a bit of emotion through the unexpected tears forming within Gloria's eyes, which were normally stonelike and emotionless.

"Yes, it was. But to make matters far worse, I was pregnant at that time, and he didn't even care about the baby. In fact, he went so far, as to ask me to abort the baby and that he was most willing to pay for the procedure, too," Gloria revealed.

"My God!" exclaimed Kate, as her jaw dropped open from such suspense.

"Naturally, as a respectable and proudful woman, I declined his offer. One day, I felt like I was on top of the world. On the one hand, I had my successful career and on the other hand, I had my new family through my fiancé and unborn child. And just like that…puff it was gone. Just like this cloud of smoke from my cigarette," Gloria explained.

"What did you do?" asked Kate, as she reached over and handed Gloria a box of tissue.

"Thank you, my dear," replied Gloria, as she graciously accepted Kate's offer.

"Well," she continued, "I certainly didn't wait around to watch Viktor and Elena dance on stage, as the new stars of our show— while I danced behind, as their backup dancer. Also, I should mention that because Viktor was the sole owner of our dance company, once he was done with me romantically, he was also done with me professionally, too."

"That's just awful," Kate remarked, with great distaste.

Touched by her sympathy, Gloria just laughed on, as she wiped her tears away with her tissue.

"Yes, it was," Gloria admitted. "But you know, Dr. Stanley, my name's Gloria Renaud after all and I simply refuse to give up so easily."

"That's very true," replied Kate, with a smile. After all this time, Kate was starting to admire and better understand Gloria, on a whole new level.

"As his former lover, I knew all of his secrets," Gloria revealed. "I paid attention. Every phone call that he made, the letters he received and the people that he visited— I watched, observed, listened and learned everything from behind his shadow. The truth was that Viktor was actually an undercover KGB agent for the Soviet Union, who was working in disguise as a dancer. It's how he was able to finance our dance company, while we experienced low peak sales during the Cold War. Whether or not our shows sold out on ticket sales was irrelevant, because Viktor always had enough money in the bank to fund our lavish productions, as well as extra money to spare. No matter the cash flow, Viktor always managed to maintain luxurious housing for our dancers, as well as upscale dance studios located in the most pristine of neighborhoods, and high-paying salaries for all of our crew. Sadly, the reality was that his dance company was really a front for the Soviet Union government. Using our show tours as an excuse, Viktor was able to freely travel across through various international territories, without any questions from other foreign governments nor the need of a visa, in order to report back his intelligence about our host nations to the Kremlin. And as his former lover, I had knowledge about all of his transactions and contacts."

"My God, Gloria! Where you endangered by knowing about these confidential matters and information? How did you end up working at the American embassy? What did you end up doing, next?" asked Kate, who was absolutely shocked by Gloria startling revelations.

"I went directly to the French and Americans," Gloria boldly replied. "The following morning after Viktor ended our engagement, I walked straight into the French embassy in New York and confessed about everything to them. As a French citizen by birth, the French were naturally, the first embassy I contacted. However, since this was during the peak conflict between the U.S. and the Soviet Union, the French government eventually decided to get me into direct contact with the Americans, where they in return, made a deal with me. In exchange for my testimony, the Americans granted me not only automatic American citizenship, but they also offered me a new job, along with permanent housing, security and even a new identity. As long as I worked for the Americans, I was safe. Therefore, from that day on, I've been Gloria Renaud ever since and I've never once looked back. Afterwards, I became a member of the embassy, traveled all over the world and even met my late husband, Boris, while I was working at our Kenya office. Overall, I've lived a very happy and comfortable life. But I think that's what's most important, above all else. Kate, when you find yourself at a crossroad in life, you just have to be selfish and make the best decision for yourself and keep going. You know what I mean?" Gloria hinted.

"I think I do," replied Kate, after much reflection. Just like Gloria, she, too, was also at a crossroad in her own life. At this point, all that Kate could do was to keep moving forward.

"Do you mind me asking what happened to your baby?" she asked.

"I ended up miscarrying the child," Gloria admitted. "But I can't say that it was such a bad thing. Truthfully, I was actually rather relieved when it happened, too. And I never did end up having any other children with my late husband, either. It just never happened for us. Although I do realize that many women greatly desire to be mothers, but in my own humble opinion, I don't think that every woman is meant to be a mother and I'm one of them. In all honesty, I loved my career and husband and truly, that was enough for me. Having grown up as an only child to a military officer, I've never known what it's been like to care for children. Although one might say that the staff here sometimes acts more like children than grown adults, and that they might as well have been my own surrogate and adopted children. But I suppose that due to my years of dancing and strict military upbringing by my father, it made me a perfectionist; which is why, I might have been a bit strict with the staff over the years. It's not that I ever meant to be mean to them, it's just that I come from an older generation, with exceptionally higher standards. Ultimately, I think that's also one of the primary reasons, as to why I was so harsh with your sister. It's because she reminded me so much of myself, when I was her age."

Kate was touched by Gloria's confession. Ever since Kate's arrival to the mansion, she was finally beginning to understand and relate to Gloria. Gloria, like many of us, wasn't a bad character, she was simply misunderstood. As for her sister, Kate was most intrigued as to how a young Gloria could be so similar to Jennifer, and so she inquired to Gloria as to how that was.

"Because I know what it's like to get carried away with a man," Gloria admitted. "Your sister came to us at such a young age. In my opinion, she married far too young, before she even had the chance to fully grow and learn more about herself. I just didn't want to see her end up like me: alone, unmarried, pregnant and penniless. Back in my day, that was the worst possible outcome for a woman, to be unmarried and pregnant; although nowadays, I must admit, society is much more forgiving, but in my time, it simply wasn't. I just didn't want to see her make the same foolish choices and end up like me."

"But that's where your wrong Gloria," Kate interrupted. "It's when you left, that you found yourself. I think the same can be said for my sister, too."

"You're probably right," Gloria sighed, in agreement. "You've got a good head on your shoulders, Dr. Stanley, that's why I like you. You've got brains and charm, which is something that even I cannot teach. You are simply born with it."

"What will you do after all of this?" asked Kate.

"Well, for the second time in my life, I'm going to have to reinvent myself, once again. Perhaps, this time, I'll move to New York and teach ballet to real civilians. People, who actually, want to learn dancing, and not those, who are forced too," replied Gloria, as she looked directly over to Kate, with a smile.

"That sounds like a lovely plan," said Kate, as she smiled back at her and added, "And since you'll be in New York, I'll be waiting for your visit."

"That's a promise that I'm willing to make," Gloria vowed.

And then, in the most unexpected of moves, Gloria walked over and gave Kate a huge hug. A hug with so much passion and force, that Kate could barely breathe.

"You know Gloria, after all this time, you can call me Kate, now," said Kate, as she slowly pulled herself away from Gloria's bear hug.

"Certainly not. Furthermore, from one Kate to another, you'll always be Dr. Stanley to me, just as I will always be Gloria to you," replied Gloria, with a wink. As she wiped away the remaining tears in her eyes, she said, "Goodbyes are always too difficult for me, so let's just bid adieu for now."

Afterwards, Gloria escorted herself out of the room, while Kate grabbed the rest of her belongings and headed down outside and into the hallway. However, once she reached the foot of the grand staircase, she managed to run into both Barbara and Chef Homura, at the same time. Ironically, each of them was carrying their respective pets: Jewel with Barbara, and Tabitha with Chef Homura.

"I see that Jewel and Tabitha are finally getting along," Kate happily observed.

"Yes, it seems that they finally grew accustomed to one another, after all," Barbara noted.

"Dr. Stanley," said Chef Homura, as he sniffed and appeared to be tearing up, "I'm just going to miss you and kitty, so much!"

Suddenly, Chef Homura immediately exploded into a bucket of tears, as Barbara gently sought to sooth and comfort him.

"Now…now…come Chef, she'll be back, again. And I do believe that it'll be a lot sooner, than we all think," Barbara boldly remarked, as she looked directly into Kate's eyes and winked at her in return.

"You know, you can all visit me at any time in New York, too. My doors are always welcomed to you both," Kate reassured them.

"Hmm, we shall see," replied Barbara, who for some odd reason, wasn't entirely convinced that Kate would be leaving at all.

"I tell you what, Kate…" Barbara began; but midsentence, she was soon interrupted by Kate.

"You said my real name," Kate surprisingly acknowledged, having heard Barbara refer to her own given name, for the very first-time.

For the past several weeks, Kate had been addressed under a variety of aliases, ranging from Jennifer to Mrs. Barrett, to Dr. Stanley and the ambassador's wife. But somehow, hearing her real name spoken straight from Barbara's own lips, brought an unexpected sense of satisfaction, where Kate couldn't help but smile. It was as if, Barbara had publicly approved of and recognized her, not as her sister, but as her true and authentic self.

"Of course, my dear. Why, that's your name, after all," replied Barbara, as a simple matter of fact.

"It's just that…" began Kate, but somehow, she just couldn't quite find the exact words to finish her thought.

However, Barbara sensed that the time had finally come for them to have a heart-to-heart conversation. And so, upon Barbara's request, Chef Homura took ownership of Jewel and Tabitha, and escorted the pets outside for some fresh air, leaving the two remaining ladies alone to partake in their much-needed chat.

"He's just so attached to your cat," Barbara admitted. "I'm afraid to say this, but I do believe that he will grieve the most over the departure of your pet, more than anyone else. In the meantime, I think it's best that he spends as much quality time as he can with the pets, until we leave."

"Barbara, are you also planning on leaving?" asked Kate.

"Eventually, I do. But for now, I've got a few words that I'd like to say to you right now, while I still have the chance to do so," replied Barbara, in a more serious tone.

"Yes, please do. I'd like to hear your thoughts," said Kate, politely.

"First and foremost, whether your name is Kate or Jennifer, Regina or Emma, I really don't care. To me, a name is only but a title we are given at birth, that's all. What matters most is the person's character behind the name, and not the other way around. And to me, whether you go by Kate or Jennifer or Emma, you're absolutely wonderful, just as you are," explained Barbara, with a huge smile painted right across her glowing face, that Kate, herself, swore lit up the entire room.

"Barbara, that's really too kind of you," said Kate, as she blushed from embarrassment. "I really don't know what to say, but…"

"No, Kate, you're the kind one," replied Barbara, as she reached over and grabbed hold of Kate's hands, as she placed them into hers.

"Thank you for everything that you've done for my son," Barbara continued. "For the longest time, he's been sheltered away and living his life like a closed-up oyster. But then suddenly, you came along and transformed him. And from what I've seen, it turns out that my oyster of a son actually had a hidden pearl within him all along…and that pearl was…you."

Touched by her sincere and kind words, Kate briefly pulled herself away from Barbara to wipe away her tears. Having done so, Barbara managed to catch sight of Kate's pearl ring on her finger.

"That ring is well suited for you," Barbara remarked, smilingly. "But whatever you decide to do, please know that you've got my blessing."

"Thank you, Barbara," Kate whispered, as she reached over and gave Barbara a hug.

"Well, you've got a long journey ahead of you, it's best we not waste any more time," Barbara added. "After all, you still need to say goodbye to him, too."

With those final words, Barbara said her farewell and soon departed, thereafter. Meanwhile, Kate continued on with her journey downstairs. When she finally arrived down at the bottom of the staircase, she saw her luggage was already there standing, near the front door. Alas, her time at the mansion had come to an end.

But before Kate could exit through those front doors, she had one last stop to make: John's office. As Kate proceeded to walk down in the direction of John's office, she suddenly heard her name called from behind her. Quickly, she turned around and saw that her twin sister, Jennifer, was there standing right in front of her.

"Kate," said Jennifer, as she called out for her sister.

"Jennifer? I thought that you already left last night," replied Kate, who was surprised to still see her sister at the mansion.

"I did, but I came back. I didn't want to leave this time, without saying a proper goodbye to you," she admitted.

Immediately, both sisters quickly embraced in a long and emotional hug.

"Please promise me that we won't wait another several years, before we see each other again," Jennifer pleaded.

"I promise, I won't allow it," Kate vowed, in return.

"Me too," added Jennifer, in agreement.

"Kate," Jennifer began, in a serious but reassuring tone, "I want you to know that John and I have already made our peace last night. We've both moved on with our lives, and as such, I genuinely want you all to be happy. You both deserve it. Please know that you have my blessing."

"Thank you, Jennifer," replied Kate, with tearful eyes.

"He might have been a difficult man for me to love, but I wasn't an angel to him, either. But things can be different for you and him," Jennifer insisted.

"I don't know, Jennifer. So much as happened, that I just feel overwhelmed," Kate admitted.

"Don't be overwhelmed," Jennifer instructed her. "Lucas is gone and all is well. It's time for you to finally live your own life and be happy. Please, whatever you do, don't give up on your one chance for true love."

"You truly believe that he loves me?" asked Kate, in amazement.

"I do," Jennifer confirmed. "Honestly Kate, any doubts that I might previously have had were quickly laid to rest last night. Why…I mean…just the way he looked at you when you two danced…in all of my years with him, not once did he ever look at another woman, let alone another person, like the way he looked at you! Mind you, I've known him for years, too! Plus, the way he seemed, when he saw Lucas take you as his hostage…why…I honestly thought that John was going to die, right there and then, from fright! I've never seen him look as terrified, as he did like that before. I mean, the man even risked his own life to save yours! He'd never do that for another person!"

"Please don't remind me," said Kate, as she closed her eyes, desperately trying not to relive that terrifying moment, again.

"Fair enough," said Jennifer, in agreement. "But you must know, that you've captured that man's heart. This much I know for a fact, is true."

"And now I'm leaving," Kate hopelessly admitted.

"It's never too late to change your mind," Jennifer reminded her.

With those final words, the two sisters gave each other one last hug, before they each went on their own separate paths. As Jennifer returned back to the grand foyer, Kate proceeded to walk down the first-floor main hallway. As she passed by all of the mansion's various paintings and décor, Kate took a moment to silently observe them, for she knew that they were going to be the last and final time that she would see them.

Eventually, Kate made it down to the end of the hallway and in front of John's office. This was going to be the first time she saw him, since the events from last night. Out of all her farewells today, Kate knew that this one was going to be the hardest of all. Taking a deep breath, Kate knocked at his door.

"Come in," replied John, as he was reclining down on his office chair and busy holding a stack of papers that he was currently reviewing.

"Are you busy?" asked Kate, as she entered the room.

"Kate," he replied, with his eyes beaming with joy. "I was just thinking about you."

"You were?" asked Kate, in surprise.

"Yes, and about our future. But first, please have a seat. Can I get you anything to drink? I see that you also changed your hair, too," he remarked.

"Water will be fine. And yes, I decided to return back to my natural hue," replied Kate, as she sat down on the empty seat, located right across from him.

"It's lovely," John complemented her with a smile, while he proceeded to pour her a glass of water and himself, a glass of whisky.

After delivering the glass of water over to Kate and returning back to his desk, he suddenly noticed a white rectangular box there, along with a baby blue ribbon tied all around it.

"What's this?" asked John, who was surprised to see such an unexpected item placed above on his desk.

"It's my gift to you," replied Kate, shyly, as she blushed and quickly looked away.

"For me? Well, can I open it?" he asked, with a twinkle in his eye and a curved smile from the outer corners of his lips.

"Of course, it's all yours. You can do whatever you'd like with it," Kate admitted.

Upon her permission, John immediately untied the blue ribbon and impatiently ripped through the outer wrapping. Once he removed the top cover to the box and pulled through the paper lining, he saw that before him were a pair of velvet blue slippers. Kate's gift was certainly an unorthodox gift and out of curiosity, he questioned her as to why she decided to gift him such an unusual item.

"A pair of slippers?" he asked her, as he pulled them from out of the shoe box.

"Well, it's for the next time you decide to spend another late evening in the library. Rather than wearing your formal dress shoes, this time, you can finally loosen up, relax and recline on your reading chair, with a more comfortable pair of shoes," she explained.

Suddenly, John recalled their first late night meeting at the library. That night, it was the first time, he realized as to just how truly special she was to him. And just like the rarest edition in his entire library collection, she was, by far, the most valuable of all.

"Kate, this is so sweet of you. You really didn't have to—" he began, but in the process of his speech, she managed to interrupt him.

"I wanted to," she quickly said.

"Kate…" he began.

And then, finally, without him further analyzing nor second guessing, the most important three words that one any could ever speak in their lifetime, came into being.

Without any further control, the words finally slipped through his very own lips:

"I love you."

"I love you, too," she gently whispered back to him, in return.

"Oh Kate, my darling!" he promptly exclaimed, with his heart burning from the joy, resulting from the confirmation of her mutual feelings. Quickly, his hands sought to reach for her hands from across the table.

As her hands entered into his, he said, "From here on out, I promise that things are going to be different for us, now. We no longer have to pretend. We can be together finally, as we are."

"As we are?" Kate asked.

"Yes, as we are," replied John, confidently.

But unbeknownst to John, 'as we are' was, at this very moment, part of the problem.

"John, before I came here, I had a life of my own," Kate began, as she swiftly pulled her hands out from his grip and away from him. Taking a deep breath, she told him, "Before I came here, I had my own identity. I was a history professor. I was Dr. Kate Stanley, who specialized in Ottoman history. I had a life of my own, outside of the embassy, outside of this mansion. I wrote several historical articles for publication, and I gave lectures to young minds, on a daily basis. I lived a simple life and for good or bad, the life I led was mine, and mine alone. And it's been an honest and simple life, too."

"Kate, what are you trying to say?" asked John, nervously.

Meanwhile, Kate could detect the sheer hesitation lingering within his voice, as he asked her that very question. And what she was about to say next, already felt like a knife plummeting straight through her very own dying heart.

"You know," she continued on, with her story, "Before I left home, I asked my students an important question. A question, that even I, at the time, didn't realize as to just how important it really was, until now. I asked them that if the Ottoman sultans had ventured outside of their cage system, then would history have turned out any different? And now, after living here at the mansion these past several weeks and experiencing all that I have come to experienced firsthand, I think I finally have an answer to my very own question. But unfortunately, it's far more complex, than what I originally thought possible."

"Please go on," he said.

"After much reflection," she said, "I think that had the sultans ventured outside, then they would have acquired a much different perspective about the world— just as I do, right now. But in the end, I think that changing an entire system by oneself alone, just isn't possible. However, at the same time, I believe that the experiences and lessons that I've learned here, have taught me how to become a better teacher. For the first time in my life, I've gained a real-life understanding as to how the world really operates, and not by presuming it be a certain way due to a book I read; but rather, from living through it, directly. In the end, I think that we were all trapped within our own cages, of our own making. From the outside world, my sister appeared to live the dream life, filled with wealth and glamour; but in reality, she was trapped living in a role that she was never designed for, in the first place. Meanwhile, you led the powerful role as the U.S. Ambassador in public; but behind closed doors, you, too, were trapped dealing with a vast array of the endless responsibilities associated with running the embassy, that it unfortunately, consumed all areas of your life. As for myself, I was trapped by the limitations due to my career, resulting in the very simple life that I led back in New York; and because of it, I was too afraid to venture outside of my comfort zone and to experience life directly, and not just dreaming about it through the pages of a textbook."

"But we can change all of that," John interrupted. "We can break free from these cages and rebuild our lives, together. With you by my side, we can live the life that we were always meant to live. This time around, we can both have a second chance."

"But John, that's just it. I would be living your life, not mine. To be with you, I'd have to give up on my career. A career that I've worked so hard for, too. John, I love you so very much, with all my heart. But, at the same time, I also can't forget who I am, too," said Kate, with a heavy heart.

"Kate, I love you, too. I promise that we will find a way," John reassured her.

"But what if love isn't enough?" asked Kate.

"Kate, I've spent my entire adult life focused on just one area of my life. For years, I, too— just like the Adam from my painting here— was buried away with my studies and career; and all the while, I forgot how to live my own life, in the process. But then, you came along and you changed all of that, for me. You, Dr. Kate Stanley from New York, changed my life. You, and you, alone. You changed me for the better. Today, I stand here before you as a better man, because of you. And now...all of this...the embassy...mansion...cars...money...prestige...all of this...it's all meaningless, if you're not a part of it."

Taking a deep breath, he admitted, "Kate, you're my entire world. You're the very air that I breathe. I think of you every second of the day, and when I'm sleeping, you're the only one I dream about. You're my Havva. And without you...I'm nothing...and I...cease being."

Silently, Kate just sat there in astonishment. She was both equally stunned and touched by his admission. He truly loved her, that much she knew. And she, in return, loved him endlessly, too. But tragically, their worlds were so very different. Even if she agreed to stay, how could they ever make it work?

Without waiting for her to utter not one single word, John took the liberty to further say: "Kate, you don't have to say anything. Not one word. All you have to do is just breathe, and I already love you. Your mere existence alone, is all I need. All that I will ever need, from now until eternity. Kate, I love you, unconditionally."

By now, tears started to fall from Kate's swollen eyes, that somehow, managed to sparkle and shine like crystal diamonds. If she had followed her heart, then she would have thrown herself straight into his loving arms, and forget about everything else. But Kate, following her mind, knew that she still had responsibilities on the other side of the world and in the end, she still needed to honor those commitments. And so, without looking at him, she slowly removed the pearl ring, the ring in which she wore daily for the past several years, and placed it right in front of him on his desk.

"You should have this back," she softly whispered, as she quickly turned away and ran as fast as she could out of his office.

For a long moment, John sat still, completely motionless at his desk. Only a moment ago, he was in heaven, but now, he was in hell. Within the split of a second, Kate was here with him; and now, she was gone and all that was left of her, before him was a pair of slippers, a pearl ring and the half drunken water that she left behind. In the end, sadly, this was all that he had left of her.

Suddenly, a cold draft of air floated out from his office and through the window. John, still feeling paralyzed from her rejection, somehow, found the inner strength to rise up from his chair and walked over to close his window. As he closed the window shut, he saw from the view afar, Kate entering into a black limousine and drive off into the sunset. Alas, she was now gone. Gone for good. Immediately, John gasped for air, for at that very moment, he could no longer breathe.

Chapter 33

A week had passed since Kate's departure and John sat in his lonesome office, feeling devastated, depressed, heartbroken and utterly and pathetically, alone. The love of his life had slipped away from his fingers and she was now, halfway around the world back in New York; while he remained behind in Istanbul, sitting in the same leather chair in his office, back to his old life, as if nothing had happened nor changed. But this wasn't entirely all true, for everything did change. He changed. He met Kate and they spent several weeks together, which had honestly been, one of the happiest times of his entire life. They were certainly memories that he planned on cherishing forever more.

John, the man, and not the ambassador, had, for the first time, learned to love and to be loved, equally in return. Now, he was forever changed by that very love, and as a result, he was never going to be the same ever again. Miraculously, Kate managed to turn his lonely, private and solitude existence upside down, and because of her, his world was altered. She had shown him love in the purest of forms and he in return, opened himself up to her in ways that he never knew possible. Kate proved to him the possibility of living life to the fullest, alongside a true ally: a friend, a lover and a life partner. Instead of just getting by in life by burying himself within his work, she exposed him to a new way of living; to a life that he never thought possible. Sadly, that hope was now all lost and gone, and all that remained of her was the small glass of water that she left behind on his desk, no more than a week ago.

Just as she left it, Kate's glass of water remained at the very same spot on his desk, unmoved and untouched. Remarkably, it still contained the same liquid of water that she previously drank, along with the traces of her pink lipstick still imprinted along the glasses' rim. For days, he just sat at his desk staring at the glass and thinking about her. She was constantly in his waking thoughts. Even when he closed his eyes, she was all that he could see and picture. And when he reopened his eyes, there always remained the impossible hope that somehow, she was going to magically reappear in front of him and that the misery he experienced in her absence, was nothing more than a bad dream. A nightmare. But once he reopened his eyes and saw that she wasn't there, he returned back to his sad reality, and thereupon, he continued to once again stare at her glass. The glass that she left behind. Along with the pearl ring, the glass was his last reminder of her.

And that damn pearl ring! Oh, how it haunted him! Ever since the day Jennifer lied to him about the disappearance of the ring, never did he ever image that it would one day return back to him with Kate. The very woman, who ended up being the love of his life!

Keeping true to his promise to Aasha, all those many years ago in India, he kept the ring for his future bride, Jennifer. However, she turned out to be the wrong choice of bride for him, from the very start. Reflecting back on his past, John wondered that if he had met Kate before Jennifer, then perhaps his life right now would have been much different. Without a shadow of a doubt, John knew that he would have married Kate and not her sister, and if he had, then Kate would still be here right now with him, and rightfully wearing the pearl ring as his wife. But now, sadly instead, he was all alone with the ring, but with no Kate. Damn it to hell! The ring was cursed!

However, before John could dwell on the past any further, he unexpectedly heard a knock at the door. It was Barbara. Without him even saying a word, Barbara entered the room and sat down in the empty chair across from him. It had been days since he last saw his mother. He had been avoiding her, but it wasn't intentional. Truly, John just needed his own space and time alone, to deal with the pain and agony that was silently squeezing the very life force stemming from his heart.

"John, you look absolutely terrible," said Barbara, who, not wanting to kill any more time, got straight to the point. No flattery nor sugar coating about the situation.

"Do I really look that terrible?" asked John, as he managed to catch a glimpse of himself in the window.

Unfortunately, for him, he looked far worse than he imagined. Staring at his reflection, John saw that his hair was tangled, his shirt unbuttoned, his facial hair was starting to grow hairy and to add further salt to his wound, he also had a bit of dried drool still lingering along the traces of his mouth. All in all, John was a complete and utter mess, to say the least.

"If I'm being honest, yes, you do. Actually, more than terrible. You look absolutely dreadful. When's the last time you bathed? Let alone changed into a clean pair of clothing. I dare say, you've been wearing the same pair of clothes since the last time I saw you last week," she said.

For a brief moment, John was in complete shock. Had it really been a week, since he last showered? Or better yet, changed into a clean pair of clothes? Since the moment Kate left him, he remained frozen in-time, and had not once stepped outside of his office, ever since. Tragically, John had lost count distinguishing between the days and the nights, as he remained inside of his office— frozen and paralyzed in his leather chair. Sadly, he neither ate nor drank; even though, George regularly delivered him a daily meal each night and left it at his desk, which John refused to touch and never ate. Although George made several previous attempts to collect the glass of water that Kate left behind, John constantly stopped him at every try, even going so far as to threaten to fire him on the spot, if George ever walked out of his office carrying that glass of water, which was now, so incredibly precious to him. But apart from that glass of water, John had lost tract of everything else, including his own hygiene.

"I take it from your silence that I'm correct," said Barbara with haste, not wanting to waste any more time. She continued, "And now that I've brought this matter to your attention, what are you going to do about it?"

"Nothing, absolutely, nothing," replied John, coldly. "Mother, I don't mean to be rude, but I very busy reviewing all of these files and documents, and I rather be alone right now, if you don't mind."

"But I do mind," replied Barbara, angrily. "You're not yourself, and I want you to tell me directly, as to just why this is."

"Mother, I beg of you, please leave," John pleaded, out of desperation.

"No, I want you to say it. Come on, let it out. Clear it, out of your chest. It's not healthy to keep everything all bottled up inside," said Barbara.

"Mother, just what exactly do you want me to say? Or even admit?" he asked.

"The truth," Barbara boldly stated.

"The truth? You want to hear the truth?" he asked, in a rather upset and mocking tone.

"Yes, the truth," replied Barbara, firmly. "And I'm not leaving, until you do."

Folding her arms against her chest, Barbara began tapping her feet against his wooden floor, waiting for him to finally speak.

"The truth," he repeated again, in an attempt to mock her; however, his tone didn't come out that way. Instead, it sounded like a man ready to confess his hidden secrets. Alas, his tongue was about ready to betray, even him!

"Go on," said Barbara. "Say it, I'm listening."

"The truth…the truth…well…" John began, and then suddenly, he closed his eyes, searching for the inner courage to say what he himself did not want to admit openly. But alas, his tongue betrayed him and without realizing it, he began to speak straight from his heart and leading out to his mouth.

"The truth is…I'm…devastated," he admitted in defeat, after a long sigh of resistance.

"Yes, I'm devastated," he continued, "Devastated beyond words. Right now, it feels as if my heart has been ripped straight out of my chest and I'm desperately gasping for air. But each time that I try to breathe, my body becomes paralyzed, and I no longer understand nor have any more control of myself. I'm lost and confused, and when I try remember as to why I feel this way, I'm once again, reminded of what I've lost and the pain only grows further deeper—to the point that every muscle, every blood vein, every tissue, every scar is further damaged, well beyond repair. Truly, I don't know how I'm supposed to cope with this despair. I long to see her…to touch her…to kiss her…to look at her once again in her blue eyes and tell her that without her, I am nothing but dust. And this ring, this damn pearl of a ring, is all that I have left of her….and damn this blessing to hell! For if I don't have her, then nothing else matters anymore. It's all meaningless. It's as if time stands still, while I'm left waiting and hoping for a miracle. Because the truth is…I never imagined that such a person in this universe even existed. And now that I've found her…now that I know firsthand that such a person…a soul…a human, even exists here in this world, how can I ever be the same, again? I can't! I'm forever changed just by speaking to her…by dancing with her…by listening to her…by hearing her…by touching her…by just knowing her and…by loving her. Just her. The madness I feel is pure agony and despair. She's in my constant thoughts. When I sleep…when I first awake…when I attempt to eat or drink…when I try to get fresh air or open my eyes to look outside, she's all I see…think…feel and I don't know what to do… it's pure madness and insanity! And this is the truth!"

Closing his eyes, John finally put his head down above his desk. Trying desperately to forget the truth, that his heart finally revealed to another. Meanwhile Barbara, having heard what she had so longed to hear, decided that now was the ideal time to advise her son about his pending future.

"John," began Barbara, slowly, "As your mother, I couldn't be any prouder of all of your achievements and accomplishments. Up until now, you've always done the right thing, and you've been extremely successful, in whatever you've set your mind to. Ever since you were a child, you were always busy with your studies, learning all those languages, traveling all over the world and graduating and starting your career at such an early age. And you did all of that, based on your own merits. Even with all our family name, wealth and fortune, you still managed to carve your own identity and make a name for yourself in this world, all by yourself. You're always thinking of others and putting their needs above your own, including mine. In truth, your generosity and easy-going nature, always made my job, as your mother, quite easy. It's why your father and I never wanted another child, because we were perfectly content with only you. Why, I never did need a nanny with you, as you were always perfect… perhaps, a little too perfect. Which is why now, I think it's time for you to maybe stop being so perfect, because being perfect all the time can eventually become a bit too exhausting. I also think that after all these years, you finally deserve a chance to enjoy your own time finally, for yourself. Now, my darling John, is the time to be selfish, for a change."

"Mother, what exactly are you trying to say?" he asked, as he looked directly into his Barbara's eyes.

"John, I think it's time that you took a little break from this place. From both the embassy and the mansion. Time away from here, will do you some good. You've worked too hard for so long, that I think it's high time that you finally took a real vacation," said Barbara.

"I can't…there's just too much to do…" he said, while staring down at the various files, which currently laid open above his desk.

"But John, that's where you are wrong," Barbara interrupted firmly. "You can. There's always a choice and now, it's time for you to choose; so, choose wisely."

"To choose what exactly?" he asked, with a sense of desperation within his voice.

"Love," replied Barbara happily, with a smile. "It's still not too late, my son."

"But what about the embassy? I'm still in the middle of the pipeline project," replied John, who was once again, stared at all the piles of files and documents on his desk.

"What about the embassy?" echoed Barbara. "It's existed long before your arrival and it will continue on, long after your retirement. Besides, there's no end date for this project of yours. Why, you can always reassign a new replacement to help serve, as your substitute for this project. There's always a way. John, my darling, there's a time and place for everything. The world operates and moves through a balancing system. A time to work and a time to rest. A time to fight and a time to love. A time to give and a time to take. Life is just too short, my dear. Also, from the looks of it, I think you've already made your decision, a long time ago. That's why you look so incredibly dreadful, as you continue to pine away in pure agony. My darling, you know what to do; now, please find the courage to make it happen. Just a bit of advice from your dear old mom."

Suddenly, Barbara rose up from her chair, walked over to John and placed a kiss above his forehead. Finally, before exiting out of his office, Barbara turned around and right before she closed the door behind her, she said, "John, remember, you deserve to be happy. Now go and fight for her. She does love you too, just so you know."

For a good while, John just sat there in his chair, reflecting about the wise words his mother shared with him. After all, she was right and he knew it. As John stared once again at the half empty glass of water that Kate left behind, he realized that this glass of water alone, wasn't sufficient to sustain him. Just having the memory of her, in the form of an inanimate object, simply wasn't enough for him. His appetite for her was far stronger. He craved her. He missed her. He needed her. But most importantly, he loved her. At long last, John understood with much clarity, that if having his career meant living apart and away from her, then he no longer wanted it. Something needed to change. He needed to change. Furthermore, he learned from his past mistakes with Jennifer, and he didn't want to repeat the same errors, again. Kate was far too precious and special for him to ever risk losing her for good. And now, at long last, he was ready to fight for her, and to return the pearl ring back to its rightful owner!

Glancing at the far corner of his office, John saw the new pair blue slippers that Kate recently gifted him, right before her untimely departure. They were still inside of their gift box. Still untouched, unworn and unused. Looking down below, John noticed that he was still wearing his formal black leather loafers. They were his standard working shoes, after all.

"Perhaps, the time has finally come for me to kick off these loafers and start wearing my new slippers," he said to himself, with a smile.

Ironically, it had been the first time in days, he had smiled, too.

With much courage, John stood up from his chair, walked over to the far corner of his office, and grabbed the box of slippers. However, before leaving his office completely, he took one last glance at his favorite painting of Earth, which currently still hung above on his office wall.

"If Adam could leave paradise for Havva, then I can do the same," he said to himself proudly and confidently, without a shadow of doubt.

Finally, at long last, he exited the room, closing his office door shut behind him for good.

Chapter 34

One Month Later in New York City…

Passing through the busy hallways of NYU's history department, Kate was about to conduct her first classroom session, since her arrival back to New York. As she walked down the main hallway, she noticed how little things had changed. Overall, in her absence, everything had mostly stayed the same. The same wooden stairs, the same glass windows, the same groups of students, and even her own office was still, very much the same. Everything remained the same. It was as if, time stood still while she was away, and her adventures overseas never happened; like as if she had never even left the university, in the first place. However, there was one noticeable change that Kate quickly observed: the unoccupied office, right next door to hers, was now occupied. It seemed that the university finally recruited a new history professor to the faculty, after all. Glancing over towards the new office door, Kate hoped to catch the name of her new colleague; however, no name was listed. It seemed that at this time, no official announcement had yet been published.

Turning the corner, Kate suddenly noticed a large crowd of students gathering right outside of her classroom. This was unexpected. Apart from Kate's upcoming prescheduled lecture, there weren't supposed to be any other activities scheduled during her same time slot. Searching through the mass crowd of students, Kate managed to recognize Jason, her favorite student, from amongst the crowd.

"Jason, why are all these students gathered outside, here? Is there some kind of rally?" asked Kate.

"Dr. Stanley!" exclaimed Jason, excitingly. "It's good to have you back!"

"Thank you, Jason. It's good to be back, too. But why are all these students lined up, right outside of my classroom?" asked Kate, again.

"You don't know?" asked an astonished Jason.

"Know what?" Kate echoed, who by now, was growing more confused by each passing minute.

"They're all here for you!" Jason exclaimed.

"What?!" exclaimed Kate, surprised by his revelation. "But why?"

"They're all here to see you. Why, everyone wants to sign up for your class this semester, to meet the real-life Dr. Stanley, aka the former ambassador's wife. We've all heard about your grand adventure! You're famous now! A celebrity!" cried Jason, enthusiastically.

Kate was lost for words. Never in a million years, did she ever imagine that her oversea mission would catch the attention of her own students. Apparently, Kate got it all wrong; not everything stayed the same, just as it was before she left— at least, not with regards to her students. Plus, just exactly, how many more students did she now have? From the looks of it, the crowd was more than doubled the size from when she last taught here, all those months ago.

"Make way, Dr. Stanley has arrived," Jason proudly announced to the crowd.

Immediately, the crowd split into two, creating a large open path for Kate to pass on by. As she walked down the path, the students began cheering, clapping and whistling. Truly, Kate was touched. In her wildest dreams, Kate never expected to receive such a warm welcoming. Passing by the crowd, Kate smiled on and thanked all of her students. When she finally approached her classroom door, the remaining students quickly opened it for her— giving Kate, a well-deserved grand entrance.

Once Kate entered into her classroom and walked over to her podium, she noticed that her classroom was now completely filled to the absolute maximum capacity. A sea of students sat in each and every chair possible available in the room. As for the remaining students, who weren't so lucky as to have a chair of their own…well… they were all left standing.

Taking a deep breath, Kate decided that now, it was officially time to return back to her reality. Back to her old life. Back to her world, before the embassy. Before the mansion. Before John. And so, as she had done so a million times before, she wrote the main subject of the day, the Ottoman Empire, on the chalkboard and began her opening classroom lecture, in the form of a question.

"Class, I thank you for attending today's lecture. Now, it's time that we get back to business," she began. "My question to you for today, is why was Sultan Suleiman, the Magnificent, rule known as the golden age during the Ottoman Empire?"

Scanning across the room, Kate immediately noticed that her student, Becky, quickly raised her hand.

"Yes, Becky," said Kate.

"Dr. Stanley, how was it like to pose as your twin sister?" asked Becky, who was also currently preoccupied jotting down her own notes, as if she was a future journalist on assignment.

"Ah, Becky, that has nothing to do with my original question," replied Kate. "Perhaps, I can answer your specific question another time," and then, she emphasized, "in private."

Moving on, Kate proceeded to scan the classroom once again and this time, she saw Jason raising his hand.

"Yes, Jason," said Kate, with the hope that good old Jason wouldn't let her down.

"What was it like to stand-up against and defeat a real criminal?" asked Jason.

"Jason, that's not an answer to my question. Remember, we are discussing about the Ottoman Empire, not about my personal life," Kate reminded Jason, as well as the rest of her other students.

Once more, Kate scanned the classroom and this time, she saw her student, Sarah, eagerly raising her hand.

"Yes, Sarah," said Kate, as she smiled over to Sarah, with the hope that this time, she was finally going to get a real and factual answer to her question.

"Dr. Stanley, will you write a tell all book? And if so, when is it expected to be released? Maybe, next fall?" asked Sarah, who at that same time, was also recording herself asking this very question with her mobile smart phone.

"Sarah, your comments are not related to today's topic. No, at this time, I will not be writing a book," Kate confirmed. "Also, as a general reminder, please, no live recordings of our classroom discussions. It's against the university's policies."

"But you still might write a tell all book, one day, right? Maybe, later on in the near future?" asked Sarah, once more, after she quickly turned off her mobile phone's recording at that precise time.

At this point, Kate simply ignored Sarah's comments and once again, searched through from amongst the crowd, looking for a new student to call upon. Suddenly, in the middle of the room, she saw a hand raised high, but unfortunately, she couldn't catch a glimpse of their face. Taking another chance, Kate asked the unknown student to reveal their answer.

"What would you say to the ambassador, if you had a second chance to see him, again?" asked the unknown student, in a deep sounding male voice.

For a brief moment, Kate's heart suddenly managed to skip a beat; because for whatever reason, the man's voice sounded so eerily close to John's. It was uncanny and entirely unexpected. However, it was virtually impossible for this unknown mystery person to be John, since he was currently half-way around the world, back in Istanbul, Türkiye, and busy working away with his never-ending assignments at the embassy.

Slowly, Kate took another deep breath. Realizing that her students were far more preoccupied on gaining the firsthand scoop on her recent real-life adventures than they were learning about the distance past, Kate decided to dismiss her class early today. In truth, it was far better to have her students restudy the classroom material for tomorrow, than to continue on with her lecture this afternoon and receive more intrusive questions about her personal life. But to make sure, Kate asked one last time.

"Does anyone else have an answer to my original question; specifically related to the subject pertaining to the Ottoman Empire and not a question directly associated with my personal life?" Kate boldly asked the crowd.

However, the crowd fell silent and so, Kate immediately had her answer.

"In that case, class is dismissed. But everyone, please do study the reading material tonight and be ready to discuss Sultan Suleiman, the Magnificent, at tomorrow's class session."

As the students hurried out of the classroom, Kate returned back to the chalkboard and began erasing the board. However, she was soon interrupted by a male voice, coming from behind her. Someone, it seemed, was still inside of the classroom with her.

"But I had an answer to your question," replied the man's voice from behind.

Surprisingly, it was the exact voice to the unknown student, whose voice remarkably resembled John's.

For a moment, Kate just stood there, still and frozen. Although she desperately wanted to turn right around, she didn't, because the truth was, she wasn't yet ready to see, as to who exactly was standing right there behind her. Naturally, if it wasn't John, as she suspected, then sadly, her heart was going to greatly be disappointed. However, on the other hand, if it was miraculously him, then how was she going to face him? After everything?

Regretfully, Kate had abandoned him so abruptly back in Istanbul. To make matters even worse, she hadn't even spoken to him, since that dreadful day. Unfortunately, due to her own neglect, John had never known, as to just how miserable she really was, ever since she last saw him. Sadly, by no fault of his own, John remained ignorant and unaware about all of the sleepless nights that she alone endured, ever since her arrival back to New York.

Although she desperately tried to be courageous and strong; at the same time, she very well knew that if he ever attempted to call her back again, then she was afraid that this time around, she was going to leave everything in her life behind and join him for good. But the ultimate truth was that she still missed him. So incredibly much. Their separation was immensely painful for her. She yearned for him. But mostly importantly, she loved him and wished with all her heart, that if and when she finally had the courage to turn around, that she would get another second chance and that the unknown mystery man standing right behind her was really and truly, John.

"What's your answer?" asked Kate, slowly, as she continued to stand still, with her back turned away from him.

"Aren't you going to turn around and face me?" he asked.

"No," replied Kate, with hesitation. "I'm sorry…I just…I just can't," she admitted, with great agony.

"Very well, as you wish," he said, as he took another step behind her.

If she wasn't going to turn and come to him, then he was going to come to her!

"I'll just have to say it, then," he began. "Sultan Suleiman's rule was prosperous because of a woman. One single woman. A woman, who was able to emerge from out of the harem's shadows and transform him, from the inside and out. She served as his inspiration. As his companion. As his friend. As his sole ally. She encouraged him. She advised him. She helped him. But most of all, she loved him. Just him, as a man, and not as a king. As for myself, it's been a once in a lifetime experience to have met my own real-life Hurrem…and Kate, that's you. It will always be you, and only you.

Kate, you're the love of my life."

As Kate silently listened to him, tears began to fall across her face. It was John. Her wish came true. He came back to her. Just her.

"Now, that I've answered your question. I want you to answer mine, in return," he said, as he slowly took another step behind her.

"And what's that?" she asked, while continuing to remain still.

"What I recently asked you during class," he reminded her.

Finally, at long last, she felt him standing, right near her. She could even see his shadow appear against the wall in front of her. With one more slight movement on her part, then they were most certainly going to collide with each other.

"My question was," he continued, "What would you say to the ambassador, if you had a second chance to see him, again?"

"I would tell him…" she began; however, her voice started to crack, due to the excessive tears that she was desperately trying to conceal, but was failing to do.

"You would tell him…" he echoed her.

"I would tell him that I miss him and that…" she chocked again, but finally, this time, she mustered up all her strength and finally said, "And that I love him, too. I love him so much and not a single day passes by, that I don't think about him….and…I regret, each and every day…that I left him behind back in Istanbul."

"Oh, Kate!" he happily exclaimed, as he immediately grabbed her from behind and forced her to come face him.

When she finally saw him at long last, she threw herself straight into his arms and began crying hysterically.

"Shush, Kate," he gently whispered to her, as he began to calm her down, by stroking her hair and squeezing her body tightly around his, with his bare arms.

"Don't cry anymore," he said. "I'm here and I'm not going to leave you. I'm not going anywhere. I'm here to stay."

Slowly, Kate calmed back down. After her senses returned, she just stared at him. And then, finally, she smiled right at him, which, in return, melted his heart.

"But how's it possible?" she asked, so confused by his grand proclamation.

"How do we make us work? You belong at the embassy, and I here at the university."

"It can work and it will work," he confidently urged.

"Besides, you're looking at the newest faculty member in your department. Why, as of yesterday, I've recently been appointed as the new joint professor in the history and international relations departments. My formal new job title is now diplomat-in-residence. In fact, my new office will be next doors to yours," he said, with a wink.

"What?!" she exclaimed. "It's you! You're the new professor!"

"Yes, it's me," he joyfully admitted. "I start this Monday. The official announcement is forthcoming."

"I can't believe it!" she exclaimed, in amazement. "But what about the embassy? The project you were working on? You can't leave those all behind?"

"But that's where your wrong Kate," he said. "I can leave them all behind and that's precisely what I did. If having my career means being apart from you, then I don't want it. A leave of absence and a sabbatical from the agency might do me some good. Besides, the new U.S. Ambassador to Türkiye can look after the Istanbul post now and oversee the remainder of the pipeline project. I'm looking forward to being with my Kate, and, as I might add, I'm actually, looking forward to teaching. Inspiring young minds with all my experience and adventures. I honestly think I'm going to enjoy it."

"You'll be a terrific teacher," said Kate, as she stared deep into his eyes.

And then, while still wrapped up within his arms, she said, "I've missed you."

Pleased by her admission, John further squeezed her body even tighter and gave her another big smile that warmed her heart.

As he lifted up her chin to face him, he wiped her remaining tears away and said, "Come now, Kate, did you honestly think that I was ever going to let my favorite professor get away from me, so easily? Plus, I did have this pearl ring to return. It belongs to you and only you."

For the first and final time, John placed the pearl ring back onto Kate's rightful finger, and then, he leaned down and was right about to kiss her, when she interrupted him midway and said with a big smile, "So does this make me officially and legitimately, the ambassador's wife?"

"I suppose," he shrugged, in return, while admiring the pearl ring, now safely secured back onto her finger, as its rightful owner.

"But you do realize what this makes me, in return?" he asked, as he pulled her closer back to him.

"What's that?" she asked, most curiously.

"The professor's husband," he whispered into her ear, and then, he moved forward and finally, he locked her into a long and passionate kiss.

As they stood there kissing, it suddenly, began to snow. And as the snowfall fell across and consumed the entire streets of New York City, a single snowflake, in the shape of a rose, which was so incredibly beautiful, that it resembled that of a winter rose, fell right outside of Kate's classroom window. The very same winter rose, that had appeared in Kate's coffee grounds, as foretold by her grandmother, all those many years ago…

Epilogue

One Year Later…

Kate signed off her zoom application and closed her laptop shut. After teaching for one semester in person at NYU since her return back to New York City, Kate finally accepted a new teaching position to work as a full-time online professor to teach her classes remotely. With all the publicity and media attention that she received from her time and adventures posing as the ambassador's wife, students from around the world were most eager to enroll in her virtual classes to meet the real-life Dr. Kate Stanley. Furthermore, by remotely teaching online, Kate now had the ability to interact with a more variety students from around the world, and not solely limited to just the New York metropolitan area.

As for John, he taught besides her for one semester at NYU. However, after the new U.S. President took office, John was later recalled back into the agency, and as a result, he and Kate both agreed for him to end his sabbatical and begin service as the newly appointed U.S. Ambassador to Spain. Apparently, it was the Spanish Prime Minister (and not the Argentine Prime Minister) that had been so impressed by his and Kate's tango dance at the NATO state dinner, that he personally requested for John to serve in his new role. With Kate's blessing, John accepted his new position, while Kate, herself, transitioned over to become a remote instructor.

With regards to John and Kate, they're now happily married and sailing away on a private yacht, located right in the middle of the Mediterranean Sea and traveling to their new Spanish destination, so that John can begin his new assignment. While waiting for the yacht to dock onto the Spanish port, Kate was reviewing some of the letters and postcards that she recently received from Jennifer, Barbara and the rest of her friends back at the embassy.

After Jennifer's divorce from John was finalized, Jennifer soon after remarried Selim and immediately, they started a new family of their very own. Currently, Jennifer and Selim are expecting their first child, who is due by the end of this year. In addition to her new family, Jennifer now freely wears all of her favorite Coco Chanel, Louis Vuitton and Gucci outfits on a daily basis. Plus, since Selim is an international hotel entrepreneur by trade, Jennifer has various properties and homes all over the world, in which, she herself also freely decorates, without anyone's pesky interference.

Upon Sally's resignation as Jennifer's former assistant at the embassy, she retained an ongoing contact with the agency to serve as a part-time wardrobe consultant. Since then, she's relocated to Milan, Italy to build her new fashion company. As of now, Sally's become a rather successful up-and-coming fashion designer. After Kate debuted her first design at the NATO state dinner, Sally's designs quickly caught on with the wives of various heads-of-states, diplomats and other socialites. Eventually, in due time, her designs caught the attention of none-other than Donatella Versace, herself! In fact, as we speak, Sally is busy away at the Versace fashion house and collaborating with Versace for an upcoming collection that's expected to launch sometime spring of next year.

After ending her engagement with Peter, Amy moved back to Washington, DC to dedicate herself fulltime to help nurse David, back to health. After many difficult and stressful months spent at the hospital, with David undergoing several extensive chemotherapy sessions, his health has greatly much improved. With much love, his cancer is currently in remission.

As for Lucas' security firm, Orion Securities, John terminated the agency's contract with the company. A few weeks later, John reinstated the previous Marshals back into service, with the provision that they recruit more highly skilled officers, in return, which they eventually, agreed to do. With regards to Orion Securities itself, it was later sieged in its entirety by the IRS. Apparently, Lucas also had other fraudulent crimes as well, which included a heavy dose of backed taxes that were never once paid for. Not wanting the deal with the financial woes of his disastrous company, Amy and David forfeited any potential inheritance that they might have acquired from Orion Securities over to the IRS. In the end, ironically, even Lucas' own inheritance to his family wasn't worth claiming.

As for the embassy's staff, Gloria kept her promise, retired and relocated to New York to open her new dance company, specializing in youth ballet. Upon her retirement, Carol took over her position and is now the new embassy coordinator. Shortly afterwards, an advertisement for Carol's old position was posted, but the last time Kate read from Carol's previous e-mail written a few weeks ago, the position has since been filed. As of now, Carol is currently in the process of training her new replacement, Melody, to the team. After the negative experience that she personally underwent while working under Gloria's direct supervision, Carol vows not to make the same mistake with Melody, as she intends to modernize the embassy into a more positive environment fit for the next generation.

After announcing his new role as the recently appointed Assistant U.S. Attorney General for the incoming newly elected U.S. President, Tyler quickly relocated over to Washington, DC. It was there in Washington, DC, that he ran into Amy, who, along with David, had also moved back into the area. Surprisingly, during one of their many political events, Tyler and Amy ran into each and they somehow, managed to hit it off. Apparently, the two of them are currently dating and are now, officially a new couple.

With regards to Bes, he's still happily working at the embassy, with no intention of retiring anytime soon. However, Carol has written that ever since he danced with Jennifer at the NATO state dinner, his sweating habits have since much improved. Apparently, whenever he's in the office, she can often smell a very distinctive scent of ginger every time he passes by.

As for Chef Homura, he's recently taken a break from the embassy. However, rumors are circulating that he's secretly on set filing another upcoming season of his smash hit television cooking competition series, *Flame*. But one thing that can be confirmed for certain is that Chef Homura now has a kitty of his very own. A small white Persian kitten named Cookie.

Meanwhile, Barbara is back to her travels and is currently staying in France, where she's visiting a new vineyard in the Champagne region. Being the entrepreneur that she is, Barbara's looking to expanding Barrett & Son's winery abroad into France. Since John and Kate will be moving to Spain, Barbara plans on visiting them soon in the near future, just as soon as her French tour concludes.

"Who's ready for some champagne?" asked John, as he popped open the cork from out of the champagne bottle.

"Is that the same champagne bottle that your mother recently mailed to us from France?" asked Kate, who was right now, lying down on a folded white chair, wearing a striped swimsuit, straw hat, black sunglasses and enjoying her time sunbathing.

"The very one," replied John, as he began pouring out the champagne into two separate crystal glasses.

"I thought that you were supposed to be busy studying and practicing your Spanish?" asked Kate, as she glanced over towards his chair and saw that his Spanish language lesson book was now closed.

"I am, but I can always use a break," he happily replied. "Besides, it'd be a shame to let this champagne go to waste here in the middle of the sea, with this beautiful sunny weather."

"I suppose if you must…" said Kate, as she finally pulled off her sunglasses from off her face.

Within the blink of an eye, John was soon right beside her, placing both glasses onto the nearby table.

"Let's have a toast," he said, as he raised his glass high up into the air.

However, Kate just smiled on and said, "I think that I'm going to have to pass on the drinks, for today."

"But why?" asked John, surprised by her rejection. "French champagne is your favorite."

Once again, Kate smiled on but this time, she motioned over to her belly and said, "We're expecting."

"Expecting?" asked John, who for a brief moment, was completely dumbfounded by her statement.

Slowly, he began to comprehend the happy news, until finally, he understood as to just what exactly "expecting" had meant. Afterwards, he yelled and laughed from pure delight.

"A baby!" he yelled out into the open blue sea.

"Yes, a baby," she confirmed happily.

"Oh, Kate, this is such wonderful news!" he joyfully exclaimed, as he ran directly towards her, gave her a huge hug, and then leaned down to kiss her.

"What do you think you're carrying?" he finally asked, as he placed his hands over her stomach.

Without any hesitation, she replied, "I feel that it's a girl."

Staring down at the pearl ring on her finger, which as of now, was her wedding ring, she said, "And if it is a girl, then I want to name her Pearl."

Touched, John simply smiled. The pearl ring had truly come full circle. In the end, the ring was now rightfully on the finger of his beloved wife and soon, in a matter of a few months, it was going to be the name of his unborn child.

"Very well," he said beamingly. "Pearl it is."

"You see, Pearl, your father already agrees with your new name," she said happily, while rubbing her belly.

"But under one condition…" he added.

"A condition?" Kate echoed, not expecting John to counter negotiate their unborn child's name choice.

"Yes, under one condition," he requested.

"Alright," she said. "What's the condition?"

"The condition is that if you are in fact, as I, myself, personally suspect, carrying twins, then I want our second daughter to be named Havva," he said, in all seriousness.

"Twins?!" exclaimed Kate. The very thought had never previously crossed her mind. Not for a second.

"Why not?" he asked, calmly. "After all, twins do run in your family and you very well could be carrying a set of two, as we speak."

For a moment, Kate just sat there thinking. What if John was right? What if she was carrying twins? And what if, they were twin girls? Would they be like her and Jennifer? What future adventures were in store for her unborn daughters, as they grew up? Kate thought long and hard about John's condition but eventually, she agreed that the name Havva was truly a lovely name. Pearl and Havva. Lovely names for her beautiful unborn twin girls.

"Very well," she said, "I agree with your condition. Pearl and Havva, it is."

Happy by her response, John smiled on, as he gave Kate another kiss on her lips.

"Thank you, Kate, for everything," he blissfully said, with all of his heart.

"John, I love you," said Kate, joyfully.

"Kate, I love you, too," replied John.

Staring down towards her belly, he further said, "And I love you too, my girls."

"But what if they turn out to be boys?" asked Kate, with a raised brow.

"They won't," John answered, in full confidence. "They're girls and they're twins. Please don't ask me how I know, I just do. I can even feel it in my bones."

Reaching over, John quickly grabbed the two glasses and champagne bottle, and then, he walked over towards the edge of the yacht.

"We won't be needed this, anymore," he yelled, as he threw all of the remaining champagne out into the sea.

"John, what are you doing?" asked Kate, who didn't expected John to throw away their very expensive bottle of French champagne out into the middle of the Mediterranean Sea.

Soon enough, John returned back to Kate's side; but this time, he had two new crystal glasses with him.

"Here you go, Mrs. Barrett," he said, as he handed over the new glass over to her.

"I think this drink is more appropriate for us, don't you think?" he asked, with a smile.

"What's this?" she asked, while smelling and inspecting the orange new drink in her hands.

"Why, it's orange juice, of course," he said, with a wink.

Happily, Kate smilingly approved. And then, at last, Kate and John both tapped their glasses together and made a toast.

"To new adventures," he said, as he raised his glass up and towards the sea.

"Yes, to new adventures and whatever, they may be," she added, as she took her first sip of her drink.

Finally, Kate moved over towards the far side of her chair, giving John enough room to join her, which he did. As they both lay together in each other's arms, staring straight into the sunset, with the wind blowing in their direction, sailing away in their yacht, along the beautiful blue sea and waiting to arrive to their next destination, they were both so incredibly blissfully happy and excited about their upcoming new, exciting but unknown future, which awaited them on the other side of the sea.

Two Years Later in Balikesir, Türkiye …

Slowly, Kate turned off the gas burner to her late grandmother's kitchen stove, as she grabbed the brass copper cezve to pour the boiling hot Turkish coffee into two separate but small golden expresso cups. Upon doing so, Kate then transported the coffee from the kitchen counter and onto the dining room table, where she handed one cup over to Jennifer, while saving the second cup for herself. Both sisters, who were recently vacationing in their grandmother's old house, quickly drank their coffee, turned their cups upside down onto their saucers and as tradition, each of them made a wish.

"Alright," began Jennifer, as she hurriedly swallowed her last drop of coffee. "You go first."

"Okay," said Kate, unreluctantly, as she reached over to grab Jennifer's cup. Lifting up Jennifer's cup from its saucer, Kate started inspecting the dried coffee grounds.

"Do you see anything?" asked Jennifer, impatiently.

"I see…I see…" Kate began to say.

"You see what?" Jennifer pressed on.

"I see…I see…" Kate continued.

"Yes…" asked Jennifer, in suspense. "Tell me what you see?"

"I see…lines…" said Kate, while remaining in full concentration.

"Lines?" Jennifer, repeated with a raised brow. Out of everything, she hadn't expected such a sighting to appear inside of her cup.

"Yes…and lots of them…" added Kate, while still examining the coffee grounds within in her hands.

"And?" asked Jennifer, in full anticipation.

"And…and…I see dots…" replied Kate, this time.

"Dots?" Jennifer echoed.

"Yes…dots…and lots of them…" replied Kate, as she continued to inspect the coffee grounds.

"Okay, lines and dots. So…what exactly does it mean?" asked Jennifer, who was starting to grow disappointed by the results to her sister's fortune reading.

"I think that…" Kate began to say.

"Yes, you think that…?" asked Jennifer, with excitement. Finally, Kate was going to reveal something interesting with her predictions.

"I think that…you…better…read this for yourself, because I simply don't see anything else nor do I fully understand this, either…" Kate finally and overwhelmingly admitted, after much defeat.

"Give me that," Jennifer demanded, as she forcefully grabbed the cup right from Kate's hands. However, for a few long minutes, Jennifer, too, just sat there in complete silence, as she attempted to read her own coffee grounds for herself.

"Anything?" asked Kate, hoping that unlike her, Jennifer had a much better talent and luck, than herself.

"Kate, you jinxed it! Now, I can't see anything!" exclaimed Jennifer, angrily.

"Here, why don't you try reading my cup now, instead. Maybe, you'll have better luck," Kate suggested, as she handed over her coffee cup and saucer over to Jennifer.

Disappointed, Jennifer grabbed the cup from Kate's hands. Just as

Kate had done so right before, Jennifer also lifted the cup from off the saucer and began inspecting her sister's coffee grounds. However, after a few long minutes of deep concentration and inspection, Kate finally decided to ask her sister for an update.

"Anything?" asked Kate, curiously.

"Well…" began Jennifer, "I see…I see…"

"You see…" echoed Kate.

"I see lots of…" Jennifer continued.

"Lots of…" Kate repeated.

"I see lots of…lumps. Yes…lots and lots of black lumps," Jennifer concluded, with full confidence.

However, Kate just laughed on.

"Those lumps are the coffee grounds. They don't mean anything," replied Kate, laughingly.

Humored by her own defeat, Jennifer joined Kate in her laughter.

"Honestly, Kate, that's all I see," Jennifer admitted. "At least you saw lines and dots, I can't even see that here, myself. All I see are just lumps. Lots of thick dark and black coffee lumps and that's it. I'm even worse than you!"

Then, both sisters began to laugh hysterically aloud.

"Face it," Kate concluded. "It's not for us. Neither, one of us have the talent. Somehow, the fortune telling gene skipped our generation."

"That's for sure," Jennifer agreed.

"The art of tasseography simply isn't our forte," said Kate, as she then proceeded to collect and wash the two remaining cups and saucers back at the kitchen sink.

Joining her, Jennifer walked into the kitchen and started to towel dry the newly washed dishes that Kate had recently just washed. Suddenly, a new thought crossed her mind.

"I say, Kate," Jennifer began.

"Yes, Jennifer?" replied Kate.

"Even though the talent of tasseography might have skipped us, but I was just wondering, do you think that maybe, just maybe, it didn't skip them?" asked Jennifer, as curious as ever.

And by "them," Jennifer was referring to their daughters. As it miraculously happened, by the grace of destiny, Jennifer and Kate both happened to each birthed their own sets of twin daughters. Jennifer was the mother to three-year old twin daughters, Rose and Daisy; while Kate had her own set of twin daughters, Pearl and Havva, now aged two years old. Both sets of twins were identical to each other. However, Kate's daughters were a mixture of blonde and brown haired, in which Pearl had brown hair, while Havva had blonde, but both of Kate's daughters had green eyes. In contrast, Jennifer's daughters were both red haired (in which, apparently the red hair gene ran strong on Selim's side of the family) and their eye colors were a mixture of blue and grey, in which Rose had blue eyes and Daisy had grey. Both sets of twins were currently busy playing in the living room, located right across from the kitchen. Together, Kate and Jennifer just silently stood by at the kitchen's threshold, as they watched their children play from afar.

"It's hard to say," Kate finally answered, after much thought. "It's still too early to tell. Besides, we're still learning about their own distinctive personalities. I mean, who knows who'll they'll take after?"

Afterwards, Kate returned back into the kitchen and proceeded to wash the remaining dirty dishes.

However, Jennifer stayed behind and secretly smiled privately to herself. For as Jennifer peeked right through the door to spy on the children, she observed that while Pearl and Daisy were busy playing dress-up with Jennifer's old shoes and handbags; Rose and Havva were quietly seated together on the floor, curled up inside of a woolen knitted blanket with Tabitha by their side, and attempting to read a small children's book aloud. In the end, it seemed that Kate spoke too soon; for it was quite clear to Jennifer on that bright and sunny summer day, that Rose and Havva took after Kate, while Pearl and Daisy took after her.

ABOUT THE AUTHOR

Kristina Stangl is an American author. She was born and raised in San Francisco, California, USA. She holds a Master's degree in Public Administration, MPA; a Bachelor of Arts in International Relations, with a minor in Middle East and Islamic Studies from San Francisco State University; along with Teaching English as a Foreign Language (TEFL) credentials from the University of Toronto, Ontario Institute for Studies in Education. Before writing her first novel, Kristina previously worked in both the public and private sectors, having served in the United States federal government for nine years. In addition to writing, Kristina enjoys traveling across the globe and visiting famous and historical sites, which she documents on her social media accounts. To date, she has traveled to over thirteen countries, three continents, and speaks three languages. When Kristina not traveling or writing, she's at home experimenting with baking new desserts, pies and other sweet treats.